GW00417892

OMNIBUS EDITION

VIETNAM: GROUND ZERO
VIETNAM: GROUND ZERO P.O.W.
VIETNAM: GROUND ZERO UNCONFIRMED KILL

CHAPTERS
65 £2.50

The Parrot's Beak

It was late afternoon when Master Sergeant Anthony B. Fetterman caught the first faint whiff of an odor he'd smelled many times before in war.

Tyme moved over to Fetterman and asked quietly, "You smell it?"

"I think we might have found the patrol," Fetterman answered.

Through the gaps in the trees they saw the remains of the ARVN ranger patrol they'd been sent to look for. There were about a dozen men lying on the trail. The man closest to them seemed to have a black face, and for an instant Fetterman wondered if there had been any Americans with the South Vietnamese patrol. But as they approached, he could see that the body was alive with flies, each fighting the other to get into the man's mouth or nose or eyes.

Another man had both hands locked on his abdomen, in a desperate and dying attempt to keep his intestines from snaking out the huge hole in his stomach. His eyelids were open, but again the eyes were obscured by flies.

Fetterman shrugged. This was Vietnam.

VIETNAM: GROUND ZERO

ERIC HELM

A GOLD EAGLE BOOK
London·Toronto·New York·Sydney

All the characters in this book have no existence outside the imagination of the Author, and have no relation whatsoever to anyone bearing the same name or names. They are not even distantly inspired by any individual known or unknown to the Author, and all the incidents are pure invention.

All Rights Reserved. The text of this publication or any part thereof may not be reproduced or transmitted in any form or by any means, electronic or mechanical, including photocopying, recording, storage in an information retrieval system, or otherwise, without the written permission of the publisher.

This book is sold subject to the condition that it shall not, by way of trade or otherwise, be lent, resold, hired out or otherwise circulated without the prior consent of the publisher in any form of binding or cover other than that in which it is published and without a similar condition including this condition being imposed on the subsequent purchaser.

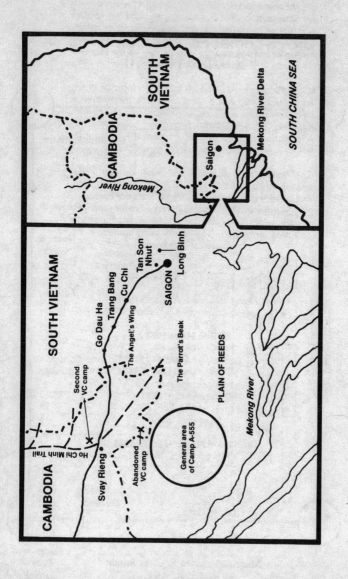

U.S. Special Forces Camp A-555
(Triple Nickel)

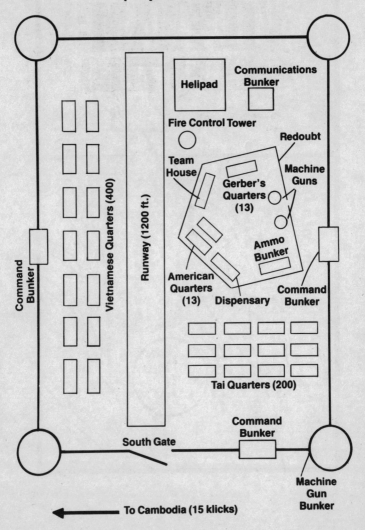

Helipad

Communications Bunker

Fire Control Tower

Redoubt

Team House

Gerber's Quarters (13)

Machine Guns

Vietnamese Quarters (400)

Runway (1200 ft.)

Command Bunker

Ammo Bunker

American Quarters (13)

Dispensary

Command Bunker

Tai Quarters (200)

South Gate

Command Bunker

Machine Gun Bunker

To Cambodia (15 klicks)

VIETNAM:
GROUND ZERO

PROLOGUE

**MEKONG RIVER REGION
SOUTH OF THE
PARROT'S BEAK,
REPUBLIC OF VIETNAM**

Lieutenant Chuyen Tri Lam had been in the Vietnamese army for all of his short adult life. His family was well connected so he had received favorable assignments, including the one to the rangers. That didn't mean that he wasn't a good soldier, only that he had some opportunities that weren't available to his colleagues.

The patrol into the former heart of VC territory was one such opportunity. The Americans at the Special Forces camp had driven most of the VC across the border into Cambodia. They only returned in small groups to lob a couple of mortar shells at the camp or to briefly terrorize the villagers.

The patrol should be routine and would look good on Lam's service record. As leader of the expedition, any glory would be reflected on him and would enhance his reputation with the men who never ventured from Saigon. And, if there were no glory to be found, he had still taken his men into the heart of VC territory.

Lam didn't expect trouble. Charlie was gone. Charlie was on the run. It was Charlie that was now afraid.

Lam had just completed these comforting reflections when there was a deafening explosion at the side of the trail. Lam's first thought was that one of his men, falling out into the jungle to answer a call of nature, had stepped on a booby trap. As he turned to stare, the world seemed to explode around him. To his right he saw the muzzle flashes as the enemy raked the trail with devastating fire from AK-47s and SKSs. Lam's elite rangers were dropping fast, trying to unsling their weapons, trying to load and return fire or trying just to get down out of the way. Trying to stay alive for a few more seconds.

As the intensity of the shooting increased, Lam tried to draw the handsome pistol his father had given him at his commissioning. As the pistol cleared his holster, he took a hit in the shoulder. The force of the impact spun him around, ripping the pistol from his nerveless fingers to fall among the wounded and dying ARVN on the trail.

Another round tore into his guts, blossoming out his back in a crimson jet of blood. Lam never felt the pain. He just fell, rolled to his side and was angry because his general had told him the VC were all gone. As his vision failed, his last sight was of his platoon lying shattered on the jungle floor while the VC ambushers pumped round after round into the bodies. They wanted no prisoners.

THE CHINESE OFFICER in tactical command of the VC stood up, carefully staying behind the firing line, and shouted, ''Cease fire! Cease fire!''

When it was finally quiet, he took a few minutes to study the massacre. The ARVN had walked into the ambush and never fired a shot. Their unit discipline was nonexistent, their noise discipline lax and their response under fire predictable. They had been bunched together, without a real point, no flankers and no rear guard. Obviously, these dead men were not from the Special Forces camp. They had been too poorly trained, and they wore the uniforms of the Saigon puppet soldiers.

The officer signaled his men out of their ambush positions to check the bodies, pick up the weapons, which included a couple of the new American M-16s, and look for documents. He didn't try to stop them from swarming onto the trail to strip the watches, rings, boots and equipment from the dead—the Vietnamese believed it was their right to these spoils.

As the Chinese stood over the body of the foolish young ARVN officer, he noticed the fancy pistol lying near the dead man's outstretched arm. It was a legal trophy. A legitimate spoil of war. And it wasn't beneath the dignity of the Chinese officer to take it. Such a fine weapon should belong to someone who would appreciate it. He picked it up, checked the magazine and the safety and tucked it into his pocket. He then signaled his men, sent the point out and started his indirect retreat to Cambodia. He knew that even if the Americans at the nearby Special Forces camp knew the patrol had been ambushed, they would not have had time to react. There would be no pursuit of his unit and no reason for haste. He would continue his mission, swinging more or less toward Cambodia, and hope that he would find more easy pickings.

1

U.S. SPECIAL FORCES CAMP A-555 IN THE PARROT'S BEAK REGION NEAR THE CAMBODIAN BORDER

Radio watch during the day wasn't a very important task if there were no patrols out, and for the first time in a month, there were none out. Army Special Forces Staff Sergeant Galvin Bocker didn't mind sitting in the fairly cool, dimly lighted communications bunker, his feet propped up on the scarred plywood of the makeshift counter, waiting for radio messages. It beat working in the sun, filling sandbags and stacking them around a newly constructed antimortar bunker.

A sudden burst of static drew Bocker's attention to the radio. He dropped his feet to the dusty plywood floor and reached over to turn the gain knob on the olive drab UHF radio. He picked up the mike, acknowledged and slid a pencil from the top pocket of his sweat-stained jungle fatigues. It might be cool in the commo bunker, but the humidity of the afternoon—the unseen enemy in Vietnam—seemed to invade everywhere, even the sandbagged, Z-shaped entrance of the bunker.

"Zulu Ops, this is Big Green Ops. Prepare to copy," said the voice over the radio.

"Roger, Big Green. Ready," Bocker replied.

"Advise Zulu Six that Big Green Six has received inquiries from higher-ups regarding the failure to report of an all-indigenous patrol in your AO. Please ask Zulu Six to investigate and report soonest."

Bocker stared at the message pad, reading over the light pencil scribbles to make sure he'd gotten it all. "Roger," he said, "investigate and advise."

"Roger. Out."

As the radio lapsed into silence and Bocker ripped the top page off his pad, he wondered briefly what the ARVN had gotten themselves into and how the Special Forces team was supposed to find them with no information to go on. He hoped the captain knew something that he hadn't told them. Bocker turned to make sure that his Vietnamese counterpart, Sergeant Xuyen, was handy. Xuyen had been recently elevated from the ranks to work with Bocker, and the young and eager Vietnamese had shown a real interest in radios and seemed to have a knack for working with them. "You stay and listen carefully," Bocker said. "Something important happens, you let me know. I'll be with Captain Gerber."

Outside the bunker Bocker blinked in the bright afternoon sun. If the humidity inside the commo center was bad, outside it was worse. The first jolt seemed to send the lungs into shock, making it hard to breathe. Just another June day in paradise, Bocker thought as he started for the team house over near the runway. He slid to a sudden stop. Off to the right near the helipad, which was marked by four dark-green rubberized sandbags that held down the large black mat painted with a bright-yellow H, he saw two other team members helping a helicopter crew unload a UH-1D slick, a Huey. Captain Mack Gerber was sifting through the boxes of C-rations, piles of web gear and new knapsacks, crates of ammo and bayonets for the M-14s, checking the contents of each before he signed for it.

"Say, Captain," said Bocker as he walked over. "Got a message here that you need to take a look at."

Gerber stood, wiped a sleeve across his forehead to soak up the sweat and then rubbed a grimy hand against the front of his stained jungle fatigues before he took the paper from Bocker. He scanned it quickly. "Well, shit," he muttered, shaking his head. "That's all we need. Anything else?"

"No, sir. That's it. You want me to take out a patrol? It's my turn."

For a moment Gerber didn't say anything. He just stared at the message, remembering what he had been told about the Vietnamese patrol. The information had come from Saigon, but had been sketchy because the Vietnamese had been afraid it would be compromised before the patrol could hit the field. Gerber had said nothing about it to his team; they didn't need to know. When Gerber had queried Lieutenant Colonel Alan Bates, his command officer at B-Team Headquarters, Bates had told him not to worry about it. It was an all-Vietnamese show.

Leaving Bocker's question unanswered, Gerber said, "Tell Sergeant Fetterman to meet me in my hootch in a couple of minutes. We'll decide what to do after we've had a chance to look over the maps."

Gerber watched his commo sergeant stride across the compound. A career officer who had just celebrated his thirtieth birthday, Gerber was six feet tall with brown hair, which was longer than regulations said it should be, and blue eyes. At two hundred pounds, he was carrying a little more weight than he had as a rookie, but he kept in good shape and the pounds were solid. He had been in the Special Forces for most of his Army career because he believed the Special Forces had the best soldiers in the world. But he was getting tired of having to fight everyone at American headquarters in Saigon for everything he needed, including food, weapons and uniforms. Saigon seemed to think that the masses of supplies being sent from the United States were to be stockpiled and counted, but not used by the men in the field. They seemed to get upset if anyone actually wanted to *use* the supplies.

It wasn't just the supplies, either. This new request from Big Green, which translated into Brigadier General Billy Joe Crinshaw, was just one more example of the haphazard way things were being done. Saigon felt the Vietnamese needed a more active role out here near Cambodia so they sent out a patrol that was probably made up of city boys and officers with commissions bought from the government. When they got into trouble, Gerber was tasked to find them, but had to operate in a vacuum. They were out here "somewhere near the Mekong River, south of the camp." That's all he knew. It was a typical Army bullshit assignment, but if he didn't find them quickly, Crinshaw could call him to Saigon for an ass chewing, never mentioning the fact that Gerber had had no concrete information.

Shaking his head as he thought the situation over, Gerber reached for a clipboard and scribbled his signature on the various forms, acknowledging receipt of the supplies. That done, he tossed it into the cargo compartment of the helicopter for the crew chief to store. Finally, without another word to anyone there, he turned and walked to his hootch.

Gerber's home in Vietnam was a small structure located next to the team house inside the redoubt. It was U.S. Army standard issue all the way. Sandbags were stacked about waist high around the walls, the belief being that in a mortar attack the occupant would either be on the floor trying to avoid flying shrapnel or in the fire control tower directing the counter-mortar fire. Inside, Gerber sat on a metal cot covered with a paper-thin mattress and leaned against the wall of plywood and bamboo matting. Beside the cot was a nightstand made from an old ammo box, and on it was a bottle of Beam's Choice. Gerber winked at his green-label "Pepsi" and resisted the temptation to reach for it.

He looked over at his desk, one that he had made himself from discarded wood torn from old ammo boxes and pieces of bamboo, and his eyes took in a pile of papers, most of them Army forms he was required to fill out that seemed to have no useful purpose. Reports on the number of hours of rifle instruction given to each of the strikers in the Vietnamese companies and how often they were able to hit the bull's-eye. Did the Vietnamese prefer the standard U.S. Army target of a rectangle with a notch cut out or did they want something else? Reports on how often the Vietnamese washed their uniforms and what kind of soap they used. Some of the reports demanded information that should have been classified, others were instructions on how to deal with the Vietnamese and the Tai, or advice on how to organize his companies and ordnance. The advice and the instructions always seemed to contradict each other and were usually written by staff officers who never got into the field or, even worse, by civilians who understood nothing about war.

The tap at his open door broke into Gerber's reflections. Looking up, he saw the small dark team sergeant standing in the rectangle of light. Master Sergeant Anthony B. Fetterman was the veteran of three wars and countless conflicts and was probably the toughest man Gerber had ever met. Yet Fetterman didn't look anything like a combat soldier. He looked as if he should be selling pots and pans door-to-door. He was someone you wouldn't notice if you walked past him on the street. Unless you saw his eyes. There was a hardness behind them that suggested Fetterman was a man who meant what he said and could back it up. He was friendly enough when you got to know him, but reserved until he learned whether you measured up or not.

"You wanted to see me, Captain."

"Yes, Master Sergeant. Come in and grab a chair. We've got a minor problem to solve." When Fetterman was sitting in one of the two lawn chairs that Gerber had imported from Saigon for conferences in his hootch, Gerber continued. "Seems some of our allies may have stepped into some shit. Saigon says they've lost a patrol out here somewhere."

"I see," said Fetterman, nodding. "And you want me to go out to find it."

"If it wouldn't be too much trouble."

"Know where they are?"

Gerber got up and moved to his desk, where he pulled a map from under the pile of papers. He turned to face Fetterman and pointed to an area nearly fifteen kilometers, or klicks, southsoutheast of the camp, in the maze of rivers that belonged to the Mekong and near the village of Ap An Minh. "From what I've been told, they were down here somewhere. Can't really tell you more. Saigon kept everything under wraps so that Charlie wouldn't learn about it and ambush them."

"Uh-huh," said Fetterman. "I'm just supposed to go wander around out there and find these guys."

"Shouldn't be that difficult."

Fetterman snorted. "Knowing the Vietnamese, and I assume from what you've said they are Vietnamese, we'll be able to hear them from a couple of miles away."

"Who do you want to take with you?"

"I suppose Sergeant Tyme and two squads of the Tai. Maybe Sergeant Krung as senior Tai NCO. That would give me about twenty-five people."

Gerber looked at his watch. "It's getting pretty late in the day to begin something like this."

"No problem, sir. Shouldn't take more than an hour to get ready. We could move out at dusk, walk a couple of klicks and settle in for an ambush. Or, I suppose I should say, set up an ambush for the practice it will give our people on how to do it. Tomorrow we can sweep through the trees south of the Song Vam Co Tay and see what we can find."

"Okay. Remember, we're going to send out Bocker and Washington tomorrow on that civic action mission to Moc Phong. They're going to provide a little medical aid to the villagers, but they shouldn't cross your path. Just be aware of them."

"Anything else, Captain?"

"That's it. I'll see you at the gate before you move out."

THE SOUTH GATE WAS NEAR the center of the south wall of the camp. The approach was controlled by large sandbagged bunkers flanking each side, along with .50-caliber machine guns backed up by four M-60s. Six rows of concertina wire protected the wall, and the path through them was irregular and concealed.

As Gerber approached, he saw Fetterman and his choice of second American on the patrol, Sergeant First Class and light weapons specialist Justin Tyme, a bright kid destined to spend the rest of his life living down his parents' sense of humor. Sergeant Krung and the Tai who would make up the two squads were off to the right of the gate getting their gear in order.

Gerber stood to one side, still sweating in the heat of the evening. The red ball of the sun had nearly disappeared behind the dark, distant hills across the border in Cambodia, and in the failing light he watched Fetterman and Tyme checking the packs carried by the Tai. Gerber knew the Tai tended to throw away things that were sometimes needed because they couldn't see the point in carrying them. Clean socks, a poncho liner and the like were things the Tai felt they could do without. Fetterman would want to make sure they had everything they would need, as well as extra food, which was little more than packets containing rice and fish heads, and extra ammo. The 7.62 rounds for the M-14s that some of them carried were heavier than the .30-caliber ammunition the rest had for their M-1 carbines. With the Tai done, Fetterman and Tyme checked one another's packs, and then Fetterman came over to speak to Gerber.

"Anything else I should know about this boondoggle, Captain?"

Gerber gave his shoulders a little shrug. "You know as much about it as I do. I don't even know the recognition codes the ARVN were using, or if they were given any. They should have had them, but Saigon didn't tell me about them, and now no one there seems to know a thing about it. I would hope that they will be careful before they start shooting, but I doubt that, too."

"Yes, sir," said Fetterman, "I guess that means I better spot them before they spot me."

Gerber grinned at the seasoned sergeant. "I guess that's exactly what it means."

"We'll try to get back in two days—by Thursday. If we don't find anything and we haven't had any problems, we might stay out another day. We'll call if we plan to do that."

Gerber glanced to the right and left and saw that the Vietnamese guards on the walls and in the bunkers were all at their stations, too far away to eavesdrop. He leaned closer to Fetterman and said, "Normal check-in times. Break squelch twice if everything is okay, once if you need help." It was a standard procedure that only the Americans on the camp knew about. At midnight and at noon Fetterman would key the mike button on his PRC-25 twice so that

Bocker or whoever was on radio watch would know that Fetterman and his patrol were safe. It was a way of passing information by radio without really transmitting it.

"Anything else, Captain?"

"Just good luck and good hunting."

"Thank you, sir." Fetterman turned, pointed at Tyme and then toward a clump of trees about five hundred meters away.

Tyme nodded his understanding, opened the flimsy wire gate and escorted two of the Tai out to set up a point, even though they hadn't yet cleared the perimeter wire. Then Sergeant Krung led the main body of the patrol out. Fetterman and two Tai brought up the rear.

From a position near the command bunker on the south wall, the largest and best armed of the bunkers and the one that had the field phone so that the officer in charge there could relay information to the fire control tower, Gerber watched the patrol disappear into the elephant grass several hundred meters from the south side of the camp. When he lost sight of them, he headed back to the commo bunker so he could study the maps tacked to a piece of plywood that hung there.

ONCE CLEAR OF THE CAMP, out of sight of the men in the bunkers and the twenty-five-foot-high fire control tower, Fetterman turned to the east. He was paralleling an old trail probably made by farmers on their way to the rice fields on the west side of the camp, figuring that the lost Vietnamese patrol would be east of camp near the river. The Mekong River, with its wide tributaries winding out of Cambodia, made it the best route of travel. In riverboats, the Vietnamese patrol would have had access to a large area. Much of it was open paddy, and since there were no reports of the patrol, they must have stuck to the swamps and jungles south and southeast of the camp. Fetterman decided that it was the most logical place to begin his search.

An hour out of camp Fetterman ordered his men to take up ambush positions. Then, when it was fully dark, he moved them quietly nearly a klick to the east in case someone had seen them deploying in the light. By moving, he hoped to break up any attempt to attack the ambush from the rear. He wasn't yet out of mortar range of the camp so if he were attacked from the rear, he could call for artillery support.

When they were settled again, he had the men take turns eating and then told half of them to try to get some sleep. At midnight the other half got a turn to sleep, and at two everyone went on full alert. Fetterman believed that most of the action, if they ran into trouble, would happen between two and three in the morning. It was the time of the day when everything was at the lowest ebb, and even if he had spent years working the graveyard shift, three o'clock in the morning would see him at his least prepared. It happened to everyone.

Two o'clock, then three, came and went and nothing happened. At four o'clock, an hour before sunup but with false dawn on the horizon, Fetterman reduced the alert, leaving only a couple of men awake while the others caught up on their sleep. At seven they all ate a breakfast from the C-rations menu. Today's special was cold scrambled eggs that tasted more like processed pulp from a paper-box plant. Adding salt made the eggs taste a little better. But not much. When the meal was finished, the men buried the remains of cans and wrappings. Tyme mumbled a few words, as if giving last rights at a grave site.

Fetterman hoped they could make good progress before the sun rose high enough in the sky to bake the ground and turn the jungle into a sauna. Without the sunlight beating on them, the humidity that never quite allowed the sweat to dry was at least bearable. With the sun, it drew the strength out of a man like a giant syringe, turning the strongest man into a weakling who staggered through the jungle and elephant grass praying for a chance to sit down, not caring whether the enemy was close or not. Within half an hour Fetterman had his team up and marching, paralleling the Mekong, but staying in the trees out of easy sight of anyone on the river.

Neither Fetterman nor Tyme had any real search plan. Without some guidance from Saigon, Fetterman could only guess what the Vietnamese leader would do, and knowing most of the Vietnamese in Saigon, Fetterman believed the man would take the path of least resistance. That meant he wouldn't get too far from the river and would stick to the trails and paths in the jungle. He was also searching for some clue of the ARVN passing. The ARVN would not concern themselves with trying to conceal their route. They would chop their way through the jungle and leave the remains of their meals on the ground. They might kick out their fires, but the burned wood would be left in plain sight for all to see. The VC, on the other hand, had learned how to move through the land without leaving a trace. Fetterman had learned a lot from them.

At noon they took a one-hour break. Again they ate a cold meal. Fetterman had the boned turkey. He used as much salt on it as he could stand because of the heat and humidity. Besides, the salt made the food edible if not palatable. When he finished the meal, he drained the last of his water from one of the three canteens he carried and then rested. Although they had been crossing fairly level terrain, Fetterman felt as if he had been running up and down hills all morning. Sweat had soaked his uniform so that it was dark green. There were rings of salt under his arms and down his back. The Tai, who had grown up in a similar environment, didn't seem to be holding up very well, either. Three of them lay sprawled on the ground, breathing rapidly as if they couldn't get enough air.

After an hour of rest, Fetterman changed the direction of the march and now headed his patrol due west toward the Cambodian border at a point where a tributary of the Mekong crossed into South Vietnam. By late afternoon Fetterman was convinced he wouldn't have any luck finding the patrol and decided he wouldn't be surprised to learn that the whole platoon of South Vietnamese rangers either had defected to the other side or had gone to Cambodia to find sanctuary. That sort of thing was not uncommon among ARVN troops.

It was about that time he caught the first faint whiff of an odor that he had smelled only a day and a half after he landed in France in 1944. Checking the wind, which was just a light breeze from the southwest, Fetterman altered his direction again so he was moving directly into it.

When Tyme finally smelled it, he moved over to Fetterman and asked quietly, "You smell it?"

"I think we might have found the patrol," Fetterman answered.

Staying off the trail, using the trees and bushes for cover, the unit moved forward. Fetterman took the point with Krung. They knew they were close to their destination when they heard the buzz-saw racket of a hundred thousand flies. Then, through a series of gaps in the trees and bushes, they saw the remains of the South Vietnamese patrol. There were ten or twelve men lying on the trail, their bodies shattered by the bullets that had been pumped into them. Fetterman knew what he would see when they got closer because he had seen similar things before. The man closest to them seemed to have a black face, and for an instant Fetterman wondered if there had been any Americans with the South Vietnamese patrol. But as they approached, Fetterman could see that the body was covered with flies, each fighting the other to get into the man's mouth or nose or eyes.

Fetterman tied a handkerchief around his head, covering his nose and mouth, before he stepped on to the trail. The stench from the dead seemed to rise from the trail in an almost visible fog. One of the Tai troopers turned away from the carnage and threw up violently, the remains of his lunch splattering the man standing next to him. Others stood at the edge of the trail, staring down at the broken, bloated bodies. There were severed limbs lying next to some of the dead. The ground was a strange rusty color, as were the uniforms of the dead men. Dried blood was everywhere, and sticky pools of it puddled near a couple of the bodies. Huge black flies sucked at the crimson pools.

Fetterman crouched near one of the bodies and saw that the man had taken seven or eight hits in the chest. He could see the neat, rounded bullet holes of the entrance wounds. He could also see the jagged wounds of the exit holes. These were nearly fist sized, with bits of bone and shriveled internal organs protruding. Another man had both hands locked on his abdomen in a dying and desperate attempt to keep his intestines from snaking out of the huge holes in his stomach. His eyelids were wide open, but his eyes were obscured by flies.

Slowly he moved from one body to the next. The number and type of wounds changed, but there was always the same fatal result. This man was missing his face, left hand and both his legs. The next had no head; there was a huge pool of blood where it should have been. Lying facedown a few feet away was another man. He was missing both arms and most of one leg. Still another had been cut nearly in two, the intestines piled almost on his thighs.

Tyme approached, having set up security. He had placed two men at opposite ends of the ambush site and then sent flankers into the trees to watch for enemy movements.

"How long ago did this happen?" Tyme asked.

"It's hard to tell in this environment. The heat and humidity accelerate the decay, but I wouldn't think it was much more than forty-eight hours ago," Fetterman replied.

"So what do we do now?"

Fetterman stood up and stepped over a couple of bodies to the side of the trail. He had noticed that there were no weapons, no watches, no rings and no boots on any of the dead. Some wore parts of uniforms, but those were the pieces that were so badly shot up or bloodstained that no one would want them.

He pulled out his map, which was covered by plastic so the humidity or rain wouldn't ruin the paper, and studied it quietly for a few minutes. It wasn't far to Cambodia, only a matter of ten or fifteen klicks. To the north were hundreds of paddies—open ground that would leave a VC raiding party vulnerable to air attack or artillery fire. To the south was the Mekong River—impossible to cross without help. To the east were more rice fields and swamp. The only open route to Cambodia with sufficient cover was a meandering course that would easily triple or quadruple the distance.

"Near as I can tell," said Fetterman, "the guys who did this should still be in South Vietnam."

"So what?" asked Tyme. "We've finished our mission."

Fetterman glanced at his second in command and then stepped past him to the bodies on the trail. Sure, the South Vietnamese were soldiers and they had walked into an ambush that had killed them, but it seemed somehow excessive to put fifteen or twenty rounds into each man. There was something indefinable about it, almost as if the VC had been shooting helpless men. Something cold and cruel about it. Fetterman wasn't sure what it was he felt. He knew he could easily pull the trigger in an ambush and kill the enemy trapped in it. He could sneak up behind a sentry and cut his throat, but he didn't think he could stand over an unconscious wounded soldier, put a pistol to the man's head and coldly pull the trigger. It seemed inhuman. More inhuman than fighting a war because you had reduced it to a level where you were murdering people.

He looked back at Tyme and asked, ''Wouldn't you like to get the guys who did this?''

Now it was Tyme's turn to look again at the ambush site. He had been sickened by what he had seen; it was hard to look at mutilated human bodies and not feel something. He nodded once and almost whispered, ''Yeah, I would. But they've got to be long gone by now.''

''Not necessarily,'' responded Fetterman. ''We've got two things going for us. One is the terrain. They can't move all that rapidly because they'll be spotted. Hell, we've got airplanes and helicopters all over the place, and they're always looking for the enemy. That has got to slow them down. Means they only travel at night.''

''But they've got a two-day head start,'' interrupted Tyme.

''May not matter because of point two. They'll think they're out of this free and clear. No survivors to point the way. No survivors to run to us for help. They move only at night because they feel no pressure to run. They follow the trees and the jungle and avoid the open ground. That gives us a chance to catch up because we don't have to do either. We only have to travel ten or twelve klicks to their fifty or sixty.''

''We've completed our mission,'' repeated Tyme.

''This was a very well-coordinated ambush,'' said Fetterman. ''Well executed. There is no evidence of any return fire or any enemy casualties. In the last year we've run into this kind of operation again and again. It might be the same guy running each of these shows. I think that we should try to get into a position so that we can ambush him.''

"Ambush who? You're guessing about something with no evidence at all. The captain's not going to like this. He'll want us to report back immediately to evaluate the data."

"But there's a chance we can catch them and eliminate them before they can get back to Cambodia!" Fetterman insisted.

Tyme shrugged and glanced at his watch. "We've only got a few hours of daylight left."

Fetterman folded his map and stuffed it into the pocket of his fatigues. "We have an opportunity here we may not get again. We can guess, with a fair degree of accuracy, where that VC patrol is going to be. And I think we can get them."

"It's your show," said Tyme reluctantly. "You can do what you want."

WITH THE EXACT COORDINATES of the ambush site noted so they could be given to the Vietnamese in Saigon, Fetterman and the rest of his men moved off to the west. Leaving the trees, they entered an area of paddies, where the men walked on the dikes, small walls of dirt only eighteen or twenty inches high that kept the muddy water in the paddy. He didn't like using the dikes—the VC might have booby-trapped them—but he didn't have time to avoid them. Besides, the accepted method for walking through a rice field was to step on the plants so you didn't sink in the mud and that angered the farmers. This way kept the farmers happy and allowed them to cover three or four klicks an hour.

Although Fetterman tried to keep the men moving rapidly, the heat and humidity of the late afternoon sucked their strength. Everyone was covered with sweat, their uniforms darkened by it. Fetterman found it necessary to take frequent breaks, scattering the men around the paddies to try for some sort of security. But the open ground made it difficult, and no one wanted to sit in the water. It might have been cooler to do that, but the method of fertilization made the idea repulsive. The human waste dumped in the paddies gave the water a stench that stuck with you like a second skin.

At dusk they were less than a klick from the Cambodian border, south of the Parrot's Beak and slightly north of the Mekong River.

Here the jungle tapered until it was only a couple of hundred meters wide, and although there were other places to cross the border, this seemed to offer the best protection. Fetterman stationed his men in the trees, separating them by fifty meters where the jungle was thin and fifteen meters where the underbrush and trees were thick. He had them eat another cold meal, and although they didn't complain about it, he knew they were getting sick of the cold C-rations. A little heat and a lot of salt helped. The franks and beans he had taken were fairly good even cold. When he buried the empty cans, he realized that his pack was now three or four pounds lighter for getting rid of the heavy C-rations.

They went to half alert after they ate, but at midnight they returned to full alert. Fetterman crept around the perimeter, checking on the Tai to make sure none of them slept.

It was just after four-thirty, with the sky beginning to lighten in the east, when Fetterman heard the splash of someone falling into water. At night, sound traveled a long way. Fetterman couldn't be sure where the noise originated, but he took it as a sign that the enemy was close. Quietly he passed the word for the unit to pull together and form an L-shaped ambush on one side of the tree line, facing into the jungle.

For ten minutes Fetterman crouched near a huge palm, his eyes on the horizon, trying to use the expanding light of the rising sun to see the enemy soldiers. He was sure it was too early for a farmer because the farmer would be afraid of being shot as an enemy in the night. Everyone knew only two types of people ventured into the dark in Vietnam: the Americans and the VC.

Finally, in the early light of the dawn as it filtered through the trees and the ground mist, Fetterman thought he saw movement. As he concentrated his vision, a shape darted around a tree and disappeared behind a bush. He waited patiently, hoping that Krung and his Tai would also be patient, ready for the enemy when they got closer.

Slowly, quietly, the enemy slipped through the trees, weaving in and out to avoid thorny bushes and fallen trunks. They were nearly in Cambodia, yet even with the safety of the close border, they maintained their unit integrity and noise discipline.

Fetterman let the single point man walk by, and as he disappeared into the undergrowth, Fetterman rose to his knees and tossed two hand grenades into the middle of the VC unit. They exploded with a crack and a roar in the stillness of the jungle, followed by an instant of absolute quiet, as if everyone and everything were trying to figure it out. Then the jungle erupted with noise. Fetterman and his men opened fire with small arms and a single M-60 machine gun. The ruby tracers of the American-made rifles laced through the jungle alone for a second, then were joined by the green tracers used by the enemy. In front of him Fetterman could see the flash of grenades as they detonated in fountains of sparks. The monkeys and birds, jolted awake by the sudden impact of the weapons, added their voices to the din, and the jungle was transformed.

Suddenly all the firing seemed to be outgoing. Only red tracers and the distinctive bangs of the American M-14s and M-1s could be seen and heard. Nothing came from the other side. Nothing from the AKs.

"Cease fire," ordered Fetterman. "Cease fire!"

For a moment Fetterman waited, trying to detect the sounds of men among the noise of a thousand birds and animals. Carefully he got to his feet and inched toward the enemy position.

He ordered Krung to take half the Tai force and sweep to the left, away from the ambush site. Tyme swept to the right with the rest of the patrol.

Fetterman soon stumbled on the bodies of two NVA soldiers. He stopped only long enough to claim their weapons and then hurried toward the edge of the tree line. When he was joined by a couple of Tai from Tyme's group, he handed them the AKs and raised his binoculars to his eyes. He thought he could see the enemy fleeing in the distance, less distinct now that the sun was rising and creating more ground mist.

The Tai soldiers dropped to their knees and opened fire, their red tracers lancing forward and then dancing skyward as they ricocheted off the ground.

Fetterman scanned the area, seeing some of the enemy as they dived for cover, then got up again and dodged toward Cambodia.

He kept searching until he saw a flash of khaki-colored uniform. He swept by it with his binoculars and came back, but it was gone. The growing light helped, but he couldn't locate the target again.

The enemy was four hundred meters away and spinning to return fire. They were nearly to the border, if not already across it, and they seemed to slow down, knowing that the Americans couldn't and wouldn't follow them.

Again Fetterman found the khaki uniform, but could only see the man's back. He kept his attention focused there, watching the enemy soldier as he ran for the protection of the border. Fetterman mentally begged him to turn around, to allow him a single glimpse of the face, but the rifle fire from the Tai and the proximity of Cambodia conspired to keep the man's face turned away.

Suddenly Fetterman realized he was letting the man escape. He had wanted to be sure, but there was no way to do it. He shoved the binoculars into their case and pulled his weapon, making sure that a round was chambered before sighting carefully on the enemy's back. With each second the distance increased. Fetterman began to slowly squeeze the trigger, telling himself not to rush the shot. To let the weapon fire itself. When he felt the satisfying recoil of the rifle, his target had disappeared. He could no longer see him, and Fetterman knew he had missed.

As Fetterman took in the situation, he realized most of the enemy had gotten away across the border into Cambodia. Not far away. Not more than a klick, if that much. But the border made it impossible to follow.

Tyme approached, his M-14 rifle in his hand, and said, "Let's get out of here."

At first it was as if Fetterman hadn't heard. He was going to tell Tyme that they had to get that guy, that he was too dangerous to leave alive. They had to kill him, no matter what the cost. Then he realized all the cards now belonged to the VC. Fetterman and his men were almost in Cambodia. They were out of useful range of the American artillery in the fire support bases. And they had already been in the field for the time allotted them. They would be out of food and supplies by nightfall. Reluctantly he agreed with Tyme. "Okay," he said, still staring into the distance where he had seen the khaki-clad officer disappear. He was sure, for no good reason, that his target was a Chinese. Fetterman hadn't seen the face, and the NVA did wear khaki uniforms, but Fetterman knew.

"I'll get you yet, you lucky bastard," he promised the empty jungle.

2

U.S. SPECIAL FORCE
CAMP A-555

While Master Sergeant Anthony B. Fetterman was searching for the lost Vietnamese patrol, his commanding officer, Mack Gerber, was in the commo bunker listening to Big Green demand his presence in Saigon. Although it was hard to get anyone upset about going to Saigon, Crinshaw had managed it because Crinshaw summoned a person to Saigon for one reason only—to rake him over the coals.

Gerber remembered the other times Brigadier General Billy Joe Crinshaw had made similar demands. None of the meetings had been pleasant. Crinshaw was a general of the old school who believed that wars were won by massed firepower and infantry support. He didn't believe the Special Forces had a place in a real army. He considered the Green Berets an elitist bunch of troublemakers who were good in barroom fights but who should be thrown out of the Army.

Crinshaw also believed in the old ways—if he gave an order, it should have been anticipated so that he could have the result immediately. He tolerated the enlisted men only because someone had to do the work that was beneath the dignity of the officers. Bates had once described General Crinshaw as ''a man of the century—the nineteenth century.''

Having received his instructions over the radio from Crinshaw himself, Gerber slowly walked from the commo bunker to his hootch so he could pack for an overnight stay in Saigon. He spied the nearly empty bottle of Beam's sitting on his nightstand, picked it up, pulled the cork and took a deep drink, trying hard to set his throat and stomach on fire. He drained the bottle, and then he carefully corked it.

A moment later Bocker knocked and stuck his head in. "Chopper radioed, Captain. Said he was about five minutes out."

"Okay," said Gerber, staring at the empty bottle. "Find Lieutenant Bromhead and have him report to me. What's Sully doing?"

"Think he's trying to place those new claymores we got in this morning."

"Find him and have him get over here, too. Make it snappy. I don't want to keep that chopper on the ground any longer than I have to."

"Yes, sir."

A minute later Bromhead knocked and stepped in. He saw Gerber stuffing a change of clothes into a knapsack and said, "You wanted to see me, Captain?"

"Yeah. Sit down. I'm off to Saigon to see General Crinshaw about something. You'll have the camp for tonight. Intel says there's nothing building around here just now, so it should be quiet. But you might want to check with Kepler anyway."

"Why do I suddenly have a feeling of déjà vu?" asked the young first lieutenant.

Gerber drew the straps tight on his knapsack. He grinned and said, "I give up. Why?"

"Seems that every time you're called to Saigon, the shit hits the fan here."

Gerber shrugged. "I don't think you've got anything to worry about, other than Fetterman's patrol."

Gerber dropped his pack on the makeshift desk and sat in the chair behind it. He studied the young officer standing in front of him. Johnny Bromhead was not yet twenty-four. In the past few months he had developed a knack for handling the men, both the American NCOs and the Vietnamese strikers. Everyone respected him now, and Gerber had come to rely on Bromhead, certain he would be able to take care of anything that happened.

There was another knock on the door, and Sully Smith, the senior demolitions sergeant, entered the room. "You wanted to see me, Captain?"

"Just to say that I'll be out of the camp tonight. His Royal Highness has called for an audience." Gerber immediately regretted his words. He might not respect Crinshaw, he might not like him personally, but he shouldn't say anything to communicate those feelings to the men under him.

"At any rate," he continued, "while I'm in Saigon and Fetterman is out with his patrol, I'll want you to fill in as the team sergeant, assisting Lieutenant Bromhead tonight.

"As I told Lieutenant Bromhead, your only problem is Fetterman's patrol. If he steps in some shit and you're required to lend support, remember that we now have fire bases around here for artillery support, fighters based at Tan Son Nhut and Bien Hoa, and we can even get some infantry help from Cu Chi. Just think things through."

Bromhead nodded and then said, "No problem, Captain."

From outside they could hear the rotor throb of an approaching helicopter. Gerber stood and reached for his knapsack and M-14. "That's my ride," he said. "See you tomorrow."

As THE AIRCRAFT TURNED to the north, Gerber looked out the open cargo-compartment door. Ten months ago the land spread out beneath him had been a sea of elephant grass broken only by the rice fields of a hundred local farmers. Now in the center of the large plain and on top of a slight hill stood Camp A-555, or Triple Nickel as the men called it. The camp was rectangular with a short runway on the western side. Just off the eastern edge of the runway was the redoubt, oval-shaped and not more than seventy-five meters across. The redoubt was just an earthen breastwork that was five feet tall and had only one tiny entrance on the east side, which was protected by three .30-caliber machine guns.

Six strands of concertina surrounded the whole camp. Scattered among the rows of wire were claymore antipersonnel mines, barrels of foogas, trip flares and booby traps. The nearest cover for an attacking force was a clump of trees almost five hundred meters away on the south side of the camp.

The helicopter broke away from the camp after climbing to altitude by the standard procedure of circling. In the event of an engine failure, they would then be in a position to autorotate back into the safety of the camp and wouldn't have to land in the paddies or elephant grass. Gerber kept searching the ground below him as if he were on a reconnaissance flight rather than a routine ride into Saigon. He couldn't talk to the flight crew because of the turbine roar and the ever-present popping of the rotor blades. All the crewmen wore helmets to allow them to communicate among themselves, and without one all Gerber could do was sit back and look out the doors as the wet green of the rice fields slipped beneath him. Breaking the monotony was an occasional village—just a few hootches with corrugated tin roofs that flashed in the sun to betray their location in the clusters of palm trees.

Highway 1 from Go Dau Ha to Trang Bang flashed by. It was a two-lane paved road with light traffic made up of Lambrettas, ox carts and military trucks and jeeps. The trees had been cut back so that there was open land for fifty meters on each side of the thoroughfare to prevent ambush. The only places where the trees came close to the road were near the tiny villages.

Gerber let his mind roam. If he didn't, he would think of Crinshaw, and there would be enough time for that when he got to Saigon. He had no idea what Crinshaw wanted. But he was tired of being pulled out of the field to take Crinshaw's all-too-frequent abuse. He knew that it was partially his fault; he had done things in the past that had made Crinshaw look bad. He and Bates had conspired to put Triple Nickel in the heart of VC territory when Crinshaw had wanted it closer to Tay Ninh. They had used General Hull's authority to get it done. Crinshaw had lost face when he lost the fight. That hadn't been the only thing, either. Both he and Bates had worked the supply system to foil Crinshaw, and that hadn't helped the situation. Gerber knew that Crinshaw was just looking for an excuse to nail him, and he didn't like walking a tightrope between Crinshaw and the enemy.

Gerber was momentarily surprised when the helicopter suddenly seemed to drop out from under him. Through the cargo-compartment door he could see they were now only three or four feet above the ground, racing toward a huge gap in a tree line half a klick in front of them. Helicopters were required to fly under the approach path to Tan Son Nhut airport. Once through the trees they would pop up to five or six hundred feet to be cleared into Hotel Three, the helipad at the airfield.

They turned left and Gerber could see the runways, hangars and sandbagged bunkers of the Air Force complex at Tan Son Nhut. They gained a little more altitude and then lost it all, coming to a hovering stop a couple of feet off the ground. A second later they touched down, and before the pilots had time to shut off the engines, Gerber, his knapsack and M-14 in hand, was running in a crouched position across the grass of the helipad.

He was almost to the terminal, an unpainted wooden structure under the tower, when a dark-haired NCO in freshly starched fatigues approached him. The man came to rigid attention in front of Gerber, saluted and asked, "Are you Captain Gerber?"

Gerber nodded in reply, and the NCO continued talking. "I have a jeep. General Crinshaw asked that I meet you here and escort you immediately to his new office complex." The sergeant reached out and tried to take Gerber's knapsack.

"That's all right," said Gerber. "I can manage. You been waiting long?"

"Not all that long. The pilot radioed the tower when he was twenty minutes out."

The jeep ride took Gerber past the world's largest PX, a post exchange that would rival any of the department stores in the States. Gerber had only been in it once, but that was enough for him to know he could buy anything he wanted there except a woman, and if he wanted that, he needed only to step through one of the many gates leading out of the air base.

The sergeant stopped his jeep in front of a new two-story building that had recently received a coat of light-blue paint. A board-walk led to double entrance doors directly in front of him. Off to his right a flagpole sprouted from a bed of brightly colored flowers, but there was no flag on it.

As Gerber retrieved his knapsack from the back of the jeep, the NCO said, "General Crinshaw's office is on the second floor. There's a sign on the door."

Gerber nodded his thanks and wondered how the sergeant kept his uniform looking so crisp in the humidity of Saigon. Gerber felt as if he had just stepped out of a sauna.

Upstairs in Crinshaw's outer office sat the same tight-lipped master sergeant that Gerber had seen on all his other trips to see Big Green. The office and the furniture—just a desk and chair for the sergeant and a couch for visitors—might be new, but Crinshaw's aide definitely was not.

When Gerber entered, the sergeant picked up a field phone, spun the crank and said quietly, "Captain Gerber is here."

As he placed the handset of the phone on the cradle, he said, "You may go in now, sir. I'll watch your weapon."

Stepping into Crinshaw's inner sanctum was like walking into a refrigerator. It couldn't have been more than sixty degrees in the room. The new office was large, paneled in rich mahogany, carpeted with thick broadloom and lined with bookcases. Captured weapons, mounted on plaques like game fish, hung on a wall near a single curtained window. It seemed as if General Crinshaw were trying to freeze everything in sight with a gigantic, brand-new air conditioner.

Inside were two other American officers, one of them Lieutenant Colonel Bates, Gerber's immediate superior, the other a major Gerber didn't know. Sitting in a large leather chair was a Vietnamese general. Standing behind him were three Vietnamese officers.

As Crinshaw impatiently waved him forward, he said in a voice that barely concealed his sarcasm, "What the hell is going on out there, boy?"

Shit, thought Gerber. Here we go again. Just what the hell was going on, and why were all these others standing around collecting dust? He thought of all the things he wanted to say, but settled for, "I'm afraid that I don't follow, sir."

Crinshaw seemed not to hear as he stormed on. "There's a Vietnamese ranger unit missing out there. What are you doing to find it?"

Suddenly Gerber understood. This had nothing to do with Gerber or his camp. It was being done to placate the Vietnamese general. "We've got a large patrol scouring the countryside for the missing men," Gerber said. "We're standing by, prepared to lend whatever support they may need."

"A single patrol?" Crinshaw asked, incredulous.

"I felt that deploying more men in that area would be counterproductive, General."

"You let *me* be the judge of that, Captain," Crinshaw said in a hard, sharp tone as he pushed a piece of paper across the highly polished surface of his mahogany desk. The Special Forces captain read the words ordering him to go to the field and to do anything and everything necessary to find the missing Vietnamese. "Do you understand that?"

"Yes, sir."

Crinshaw motioned to the Vietnamese officer and said, "General Vo, do you have any questions for this officer?"

General Nuyen Van Vo of the Army of the Republic of Vietnam stood, his hands behind his back. He took two steps forward and looked at Gerber with stern disapproval. "How long has your patrol been out?" he asked.

"Since late yesterday," replied Gerber.

Vo turned and translated the response for the others. There was a hurried conversation in Vietnamese, but Gerber, who had learned a lot of the language in the past few months, couldn't catch much of it. It was too fast for him.

Vo now ignored Gerber and looked at Crinshaw. "I think, General, that you should dispatch more men into the patrol zone. I also think you should find someone who is a little more capable to run your base there. I will be waiting for some word about my missing men."

Crinshaw got up and came around his large ornate desk, holding out his hand. "You may be assured, General, that we will resolve this matter to the satisfaction of everyone."

"I would hope so," Vo said as he shook Crinshaw's hand. Then he turned, nodded to Bates and the major and left. He was followed by the other Vietnamese officers.

Just before the door closed, Crinshaw shouted, "Damn it, Captain, how long am I going to have to cover for your stupid mistakes!"

Twenty minutes later Alan Bates escorted Gerber out of Crinshaw's office.

Downstairs, as they walked to the front door, Bates said, "Don't let all that crap get to you. Crinshaw has to keep our allies happy. That was mainly to let them know that we're as concerned about their men as we are about our own."

"Yeah, well, Crinshaw could have told me all that himself. I figured out what was happening, but it would be nice if the General would take the time to explain it. And the comments by the Vietnamese general were totally unwarranted."

"Of course they were," agreed Bates. "Crinshaw is playing a political game with our allies, and you got caught in the middle."

"I don't suppose that Crinshaw is about ready to DEROS," said Gerber.

"Generals don't have year-long tours like the rest of us, so I'm afraid that you can't hope for that."

Gerber stepped forward and pushed open the door so Bates could exit first. "Yeah, I know. But it would still be nice."

Outside, under the bright, starry night, Bates tried to change the subject. "How are things between you and that flight nurse?"

"You mean Karen Morrow?"

"That's the one."

"Not good. Besides, she rotated home two weeks ago and was mad that I couldn't get to Nha Trang to say goodbye."

Bates climbed into the driver's seat of the jeep he had checked out of the motor pool earlier in the day. He unlocked the steering wheel and dropped the padlock and chain to the floor. "We could have worked something out," he said.

"I know. But I think she was almost happier to have it that way. Now she can go home mad at me. Maybe she'll write, but somehow I doubt it."

Bates shot a glance at Gerber, who seemed to have taken a sudden interest in the surrounding territory. Gerber hid his emotions well, and if it hadn't been for a knot of muscles bunched at Gerber's jaw, Bates might have believed that Morrow meant next to nothing to Gerber.

"You want to eat at the club?" said Bates as he started the jeep. "I'll buy the steaks."

For a moment longer Gerber was quiet. Then he smiled and said, "I never turn down a free meal."

JUST INSIDE THE FRONT DOOR of the Tan Son Nhut officers' club was a sign instructing incoming personnel to deposit their weapons in one of the boxes provided. Gerber didn't like the idea, but while Bates stood by and watched, Gerber slid his M-14 into the box farthest from the door.

Bates pushed open the second door that led into the club proper. Inside, the large room was hazy with cigarette and cigar smoke and packed with two or three hundred people. One wall was dominated by a gigantic bar and to the left of it was a door with a sign over it that read, General Officers Only. Gerber couldn't figure out why anyone would *want* to enter a room that contained only generals.

"You want to eat in the main room or the bar?" asked Bates.

"The bar," said Gerber. "We'll be able to get a drink faster in there."

Bates turned to look at Gerber once again, wondering what was going on below the surface. Gerber seemed to be in control, but he also seemed about to explode. Something had to give, and in a combat environment it would give very soon. Bates couldn't have a man in the field who had his mind clouded with a lot of other problems.

They found a corner table away from the bandstand and the ring of huge speakers. Both men knew that the band, now in the process of setting up, would soon be blasting rock and roll at the crowd.

Almost as soon as they sat, they were approached by a Vietnamese waitress in a tiny black skirt and a tight red blouse that was open almost to her navel. Her jet-black hair hung to the middle of her back and was damp with sweat. The skin between her breasts glistened. It was goddamned hot in the bar.

Bates ordered the steaks for both of them, T-bones, medium rare, with baked potatoes, and a bottle of red wine. While they were waiting for the meal to arrive, they went through half the bottle without much conversation.

As they ate their meal, the band started playing at a level that drowned out even the sound of the jets taking off from the nearby airfield. By the time they finished eating, the band had quit for a break. Bates, holding the wine bottle—having just poured another glass for each of them—used it to point at the bar.

"Thought you said that your nurse friend had rotated home."

Gerber turned in his chair and looked back over his shoulder. He saw a blond woman, fairly tall, standing at the bar with her back to him. The hair looked lighter than it should have been, but there was no mistaking the pose, the shoulders and the shape, even through the loose-fitting fatigues.

Gerber turned back and shrugged. "I thought she had. I don't understand."

"You going to talk to her?"

Gerber smiled sheepishly. He pushed back his chair and stood. "Of course," he said. Then more quietly, almost as if he didn't believe Morrow was still in Vietnam, he said again, "Of course."

Slowly Gerber approached the bar. The blonde was talking to a young pilot, and Gerber waited until there was a break in the conversation before putting a hand on her shoulder.

"Karen," he began as the woman turned. He looked into her green eyes, saw the blond hair that hung in bangs to her eyebrows and stopped speaking. The woman was almost a dead ringer for Karen. Same size and build and looked enough like her to almost be a twin.

For a moment she met Gerber's incredulous stare and said, "You must be Mack Gerber."

"Yeah, that's right," Gerber said. "Have we met?"

"No," she replied, grinning.

Now Gerber was thoroughly confused. He took a step backward and looked at the woman in front of him for a moment. "You look enough like a woman I know to be her twin sister," he said.

The woman smiled again and laughed lightly. "You must mean Karen."

"Yeah," Gerber replied, nodding his head. "But how did you know?"

Finally she let out a deep, throaty laugh and then reached out, touching Gerber on the arm. "I'm sorry, I shouldn't do this to you. Karen is my sister. She told me all about you, showed me a picture and asked me to keep my eyes open for you."

"I didn't know Karen had a sister," Gerber said, still staring.

"I'll bet you didn't know she had a husband, either," the blonde said, her laugh subsiding to a wry smile.

Gerber felt a cold, clammy hand twist his stomach. "You're joking," he finally said.

"Hey, don't take it so hard. It's the same thing you guys do all the time. Lead some poor girl on and then run back home to the wife." The woman's tone was almost flip, taunting.

Gerber shook his head. He didn't know whether to laugh, get angry or get drunk. Maybe all three. He wanted to say something to the woman, but he didn't know what. Finally he turned and without a word headed back to the table where Bates was sitting, drinking wine and trying not to notice what had happened.

Gerber dropped into his chair, poured a healthy shot of the wine, downed it and then searched wildly for the waitress. "Damn it," he growled. "I want something with a little more kick."

"Everything okay, Mack?" asked Bates.

"Yeah, everything is fine. Just fucking wonderful."

"That wasn't Karen," said Bates, pushing slightly.

"No, that wasn't Karen. That was her sister. Karen is home with her husband."

A dozen responses ran through Bates's mind, but all he could come up with was, "Oh."

"Yeah. Oh. Now can we get something real to drink?"

Karen's sister walked up to the table and stared into Gerber's eyes.

"Look, Captain, I think that I may have misread the situation between you and my sister. If I have, I'm sorry about what I said."

Gerber didn't say a word, and as she turned to go, Bates stood and said, "Can we buy you a drink, ah . . ."

"Morrow. Robin Morrow. And yes, you can."

Bates flagged down the harried waitress and ordered Beam's Choice all around. When the drinks arrived, Morrow turned her attention to Gerber and said, "I didn't know how you felt about my sister. I'm sorry that I was so callous about it."

Gerber picked up his bourbon and stared at the dark liquid. "Don't worry about it," he said coldly. Gerber was brooding and he knew he was brooding. And to make it worse he was sure that Bates knew it, too.

As if from a great distance he heard Bates say, "So, Robin, what do you do here in Saigon?"

FOURTEEN HOURS LATER, after Gerber had made a C-123 flight to Dau Tieng, a Huey flight into his camp and had been briefed by Fetterman on his mission and the discovery of the remains of the Vietnamese patrol, he was on another Army helicopter heading back to Saigon. Isolated from the crew by the whine of the turbine and the popping of the rotor blades, Gerber had little to do other than reflect upon the massacre that Fetterman had described and the plan that he had evolved.

They had been sitting in Gerber's hootch, a bottle of Beam's between them, while Fetterman detailed his case of the enemy unit to the Cambodian border.

"I had to break contact at the border, Captain," said Fetterman. "It was getting late, and I couldn't follow him without jeopardizing the patrol. I'd still like to take a squad out to get him, though."

Gerber held up his hand as if to halt an infantry squad. "Get him?" he asked. "You've jumped over something here."

"I saw him. I had him in my sights and he got away. He got away again."

There was suddenly something else in the tiny room. Something other than the heat and humidity and red dust that tried to bury everything. Gerber, not fully understanding it, reached for the bottle of Beam's, jerked the cork free and took a healthy swig.

"You're not making sense, Tony."

"It was the Chinese officer. You know the one I mean. Kepler and his intelligence boys have heard rumors about him for months. We've seen him on a couple of operations. Always in the distance. Always in the background, advising the VC and the North Vietnamese."

"And you're sure it's the same guy," said Gerber. "How can you tell?"

Fetterman reached across the desk and took the bottle from Gerber's hand. Before drinking, he said, "It has to be. Every time we've run into him, it's with enemy units that understand what they're doing. Well trained, well disciplined. It's almost like his signature. His signature was all over that ambush. The man is a military wizard."

"Okay, Tony, suppose you're right. He's still a Chinese national, and he's in a neutral country as long as he's in Cambodia. There's not a lot we can do about him under those circumstances. For us to cross the border could cause an international incident—if we were caught. It's a move neither of us has the authority to make. I assume that you are suggesting that we cross the border."

"The CIA has been running cross-border ops for a couple of years, and there's been no international repercussions. Besides, everyone knows the VC and NVA have bases in Cambodia," said Fetterman.

"Don't be naive, Tony. You know that we can't do it. When we get close to Cambodia, we have to explain our every movement, and we have to report our position to Saigon almost every hour. Makes no difference that the VC can run across the border like they're stepping over a crack in a sidewalk. We don't have that luxury."

"But we have to do something to kill that man, Captain. He's too dangerous."

At that moment Bromhead stepped through the door and looked at Gerber.

The captain waved him forward. "Come in, Johnny. You might want to listen to this."

"Did I hear Tony suggest that we smoke someone?"

Fetterman hesitated before replying. He was wondering if he had said too much already.

"I want to go after that Chinese officer who has been causing us so much grief," he said abruptly.

"We didn't learn that tactic at the Point," said Bromhead, moving toward the cot so that he could sit down. He reached for the bottle of Beam's, hesitated and let his hand drop away without touching it.

"No, sir," said Fetterman. "But I didn't think you were one of those ringknocker types."

"But kill him? Just plan his death like plotting a murder?"

"Oh, come on, Lieutenant," Fetterman snapped. "Let's stop beating around the bush. That's what this is all about. We go out hunting the enemy, setting up ambushes to increase the body count. We talk about rules of engagement and land warfare, but it all comes down to one thing: killing the other guys. I'm merely suggesting that we, for this once, don't rely on random factors to determine the targets. I suggest that we go out and kill that Chinese officer."

Gerber stood up and walked to the door and shut it. As he sat down again, he said, "I don't know."

Fetterman shifted his attention to Gerber. "We plan missions to eliminate specific units. We learn that a VC hard-core regiment is working our AO, so we devise a mission to destroy it. All I'm saying is, we're doing the same thing on a much smaller scale."

"Tony, you don't have to convince me," said Gerber. "But I can understand Johnny's point of view, too. Somehow this just doesn't seem right. Targeting one man. It reduces this whole thing to a personal confrontation."

"So what, Captain? That's how war used to be fought. Each knight, wearing distinctive colors, fighting knights in other colors. Each man identifiable to the others. The Chinese officer is the same. Distinctive."

Gerber remained quiet, staring at Fetterman's boots, which had been recently shined. Gerber never ceased to be amazed at the master sergeant. He was always in a clean uniform with polished boots. Not necessarily spit shined, but polished. He went by the book most of the time. Why was he now advocating such a rogue action?

"This isn't right," said Bromhead. "What you're saying makes sense, but it still sounds like we're sanctioning an assassination."

"Think of it as going out to destroy a specific unit," Fetterman replied.

"It's still plotting a murder, no matter how we dress it up," said Bromhead.

And the hell of it was that Bromhead was right, Gerber thought. It was plotting a murder. A murder of a foreign national in a neutral country. Gerber couldn't just nod his head and tell his men to go out and do it. He had to tell someone that he was planning such an action, and that was why he was in the helicopter heading back to Saigon. While neither Bates nor Crinshaw would give approval for an assassination, Gerber had another contact that might see the value of such a mission. As many of the Special Forces officers in Vietnam, Gerber had a case officer who haunted the dark, cold, lower reaches of the MACV headquarters. Sometimes the CIA needed help with a mission, and they sent someone out to a Special Forces camp. Sometimes it was the other way around. This was one of the times it was the other way around.

At Hotel Three Gerber avoided the terminal building and walked to the gate. There he found a taxi, and as he got into the back, he told the driver to take him to the MACV compound on the other side of town. Upon arrival, he paid the driver with a handful of MPC, the military script issued for use in the local economy to prevent black-marketing, and headed inside. The American MPs at the gate didn't even blink as Gerber approached. He was obviously an American.

Gerber pushed open the first of the large glass doors, entered, went through another set of doors and into the nearly uncomfortable air-conditioning of the headquarters building. He walked along the tiled floors, avoiding speaking to the men and women he encountered until he reached a stairway. At the bottom he was stopped by a guard standing in front of a gate of iron bars that ran from ceiling to floor. He asked Gerber to produce an ID card, then used a field phone sitting on a small desk to verify that someone inside knew Gerber and would meet him.

Once through the iron gate Gerber turned down another corridor lined with cinder-block walls that were damp with condensation. Rust spots where metal chairs, tables or cabinets had been set and later removed stained the tiled floor. Gerber halted in front of a dark wooden door and knocked.

The man who opened the door was short. He had dark hair and dark eyes and a sunburned complexion. He wore a white suit that was wrinkled and stained. His thin black tie was pulled down and the collar was open. He held a big hand out, not so Gerber could shake it but so he could pull the Special Forces officer out of the hall.

Inside, one wall was lined with a series of gray four-drawer filing cabinets. The one in the corner was massive with a combination lock on the second drawer. A battleship-gray metal desk, the top littered with papers and manila file folders, was shoved into the far corner. Four empty Coke cans were lined up against the edge closest to the wall. A small chair was near the desk and a larger one sat next to it. A single picture, showing cavalrymen fighting Sioux Indians and labeled The Wagon Box Fight, was hanging on the wall. The office, because it was below ground and had no windows, was entirely artificially lit. The super-cooled air from upstairs did not reach down to this level, but it was still cooler than it was outside the building.

"Mack Gerber," said the man, "have a seat and tell me what you have on your mind."

"Just like that, Jerry," said Gerber. "No 'how are you?' No 'how are things at the camp?' Just 'have a seat and tell me what's on your mind'?"

"Okay." Jerry Maxwell smiled as he sat behind his desk. "How are you? How are things out at that camp of yours?"

"I'm fine, thank you. And things aren't all that great out at the camp. That's why I came down here." Now Gerber smiled. "See how nicely that works?"

"Don't get cute, Mack," said Jerry. "Just because you have a paper saying you're an officer and a gentleman, it doesn't mean you can give etiquette lessons."

"I believe that Congress only commissions us as officers now. That gentleman crap went out a long time ago."

"You win. You want a Coke or something?"

"No, thanks. I'd like to get straight to a problem I have and see what we can do about it."

"Okay," said Maxwell, pushing a stack of paper out of his way so that he could lean an elbow on his desk. Several reports with cover sheets stamped Secret were revealed.

For the next thirty minutes Gerber detailed the confrontations his patrols had had with the Chinese officer, concluding with the most recent attack on the ARVN rangers. He told the CIA man all that he knew and all that he suspected, explaining that the role of the Chinese soldier seemed to be as an adviser and tactical commander. Gerber also told the case officer that the Chinese had good military training, that he rarely missed opportunities to ambush ARVN and American patrols and that dozens had been killed by units led by him.

Maxwell finally held up a hand to stop Gerber and said, "So you want to go hunting, right? You want to target this guy?"

"We want to eliminate him, yes," said Gerber. "Gains us two things. First, we will kill the one man in our AO who seems capable. Without him, we'll be fighting the same kind of rabble operating in the rest of South Vietnam. This guy is very good. And second, we show the VC that we can go anywhere. They are not safe in their own camps if we decide to eliminate them."

"This guy's base is in South Vietnam?" asked Maxwell.

Gerber scratched his forehead and stared at the floor for a moment. Then he said, "We think he's operating from a base about twenty klicks inside Cambodia."

"Uh-huh. And you want to go chasing after him, across the border, even with a hundred military and Congressional directives prohibiting cross-border operations."

Now Gerber grinned as if he had just heard something funny. His only response was, "Yeah."

"Okay, Mack," said Maxwell, idly flipping through the papers on his desktop. "I'll let you in on the big picture. Something new has been added. The folks at home are not pleased with our involvement over here. So far, it's mainly college kids of draft age who aren't thrilled with the prospect of winning an all-expenses-paid vacation to the dream spot of Southeast Asia, but that dissatisfaction is spreading. The President wants us to do something to help get us out of here."

"That's interesting, Jerry, but what has it to do with my problem?"

"I'm coming to that. The DCI, along with some of the intelligence people here, have decided that a war of attrition is not the answer. Hell, MacArthur said that fifteen years ago. Stay out of a ground war in Asia, and here we are, right in the middle of one.

"Anyway," continued Maxwell, "the DCI and the others have decided that we should go directly after the enemy leader. Cut off the head and the snake dies. In the last month—and I warn you, this is all top secret—but in the last month we've sent out a half dozen sniper teams to eliminate a number of high-ranking enemy political and military leaders."

Gerber stared at his friend for a moment, wondering if he were being kidded, and then saw there was no humor in what he was being told. Assassination teams had been dispatched to kill enemy civilians. Assassination was being sanctioned by the highest levels of the American government. For some reason that surprised Gerber even though he, along with Fetterman and Bromhead, had discussed the same thing only hours earlier.

"This is sort of a pacification-by-assassination plan," said Maxwell quietly as if someone might overhear. "There's no written directive sanctioning it, and it doesn't even have an official code name, although someone has suggested we call it Phoenix. You know, the new government rising from the ashes of the old."

"I take it," said Gerber, choosing his words carefully, "that you are telling me to go ahead with the plan."

"Not in so many words. In fact, if you get into trouble, I will deny that this discussion ever took place. But if you think this

Chinese is a big problem and his death will shorten the war, then by all means go after him."

"Into Cambodia and smoke a foreign national?"

"Captain, I will not give you permission to violate the military instructions and regulations under which you operate, nor will I tell you to violate the neutrality of a foreign government. I will tell you that a successful mission will not be questioned."

"And by successful you mean . . . ?" Gerber asked.

"I mean that no one hears about it and your target is quietly eliminated."

3

HOTEL THREE, TAN SON
NHUT AIR FORCE BASE,
SAIGON

Gerber stood in the terminal building of Hotel Three near the corner window where he could watch the helicopters operating from the field. Six large cement squares marked the official landing pads, and a wide grass strip paralleled a chain-link fence on the far side, about a hundred meters away. The helicopters that were haphazardly scheduled, the ones that flew in from the outlying camps without distinguished visitors, were required to land on the grass. The one that Gerber waited for would have to land there.

While he waited, he considered the assignment he had been given. He smiled to himself, remembering that there really wasn't an assignment at all. Just a civilian who worked for the CIA telling him that no one would squawk if his men entered Cambodia secretly, found the Red Chinese officer and shot him. If they got in and out without anyone noticing them, it was a successful operation.

Outside a Huey came to a hover, turned toward the tower momentarily and then settled to the ground, its rotor still spinning and its engine running. A large white hornet was painted on the front, identifying it as a helicopter from the 116th Assault Helicopter Company. Without waiting for the clerk behind the thin plywood counter to call his name, Gerber grabbed his knapsack and weapon and ran out the door.

Dodging a couple of Army privates and one massive sergeant, Gerber hurried to the helicopter. He stepped up on the skid so that he could look in the aircraft commander's window and shouted over the turbine noise, "Catch a ride with you to Triple Nickel?"

The pilot, a young warrant officer who looked as if he belonged in high school, nodded and said, "I'm on my way to Tay Ninh. We can drop you off."

Gerber held a thumb up and grinned at the young pilot. "Thanks," he shouted.

When the helicopter took off again and they reached altitude, away from the staggering heat and crushing humidity of the ground, Gerber realized he was spending too much time in Saigon. He had been there two nights in a row. This time he had taken a room in the Bien Hoa BOQ so he would be away from Saigon. He had used the field phone system to route a call through Cu Chi, Dau Tieng, Song Be and Tay Ninh to the switchboard at his camp, if switchboard was the right word for it.

He told Bromhead he'd been summoned to Saigon for another briefing about the disposition of enemy troops in the AO and not to worry. It was a routine briefing and he'd be back by noon the following day.

Then he'd gone to one of the many officers' clubs around Bien Hoa, had another steak dinner and watched as a group of Vietnamese strippers took off their clothes while bored men sat around and drank heavily.

In the morning it had been easy to catch a ride back to Saigon and then discover who had aircraft coming in. He waited until he saw one with insignia he recognized. As many who had been in Vietnam for several months, he knew he could get anywhere in-country by waiting around the airfields.

At A-555 the helicopter landed in a billowing cloud of purple smoke from a marker grenade Bocker had thrown so that the aircraft would have a landing point and an idea about wind direction. The pilot had alerted the Special Forces sergeant that they were inbound, and he had decided to meet the aircraft at the pad himself. Gerber leaped out of the cargo compartment and waved his thanks as the aircraft lifted to a hover, sucking red dust up from the ground and blowing it into a fog that obscured everything until the chopper cleared the wires and was climbing out rapidly.

As the helicopter disappeared, Bocker, who had been standing at the edge of the pad, approached. He didn't salute—none of them ever did. It wasn't a good idea to salute in the field because it pinpointed the officers for the enemy, not that they expected any VC to be close enough at the moment to see them.

Shouldering his knapsack, his rifle in his left hand, Gerber said, "Morning, Galvin. Is Fetterman around?"

"When I last saw him, he was in the team house eating breakfast," Bocker replied.

After Gerber had dropped his knapsack in his hootch, he made his way next door to the team house. Fetterman sat at one of the tables, a cup of coffee in front of him, reading a week-old copy of *Stars and Stripes*.

Gerber poured himself a cup of coffee from a pot standing on a small table next to the door and then sat down opposite Fetterman. "Morning, Tony," he said.

Fetterman carefully folded his paper and set it down. He grinned and asked, "What's the good word?"

Gerber shot a glance at the Vietnamese woman who stood behind the counter that separated the tiny kitchen from the rest of the team house. He lowered his voice, keeping his eye on the woman, and said, "I want to meet with you, Lieutenant Bromhead and anyone else you want with you on this. Say my hootch in twenty minutes."

"Meaning?" asked Fetterman.

"Meaning your trip to the west," answered Gerber.

Gerber was sitting on his cot when the others arrived. Fetterman took one of the lawn chairs to the side of the desk. Bromhead grabbed the metal folding one behind it, letting Tyme have the third and last. Gerber watched the three men for a moment, wondering what was going on in their minds. None of them knew he had been to Saigon to meet with the CIA case officer. In fact, only Fetterman knew there was a CIA case officer.

"Gentlemen," said Gerber, "this is a general planning session for our mission to the west. Given the nature of this mission, I don't think it's a good idea to take notes. The fewer written documents we have, the fewer problems we'll have."

All three of the men looked confused. Gerber said, "Sergeant Fetterman has made a suggestion that we dust the Chinese officer. I think that the idea has some merit and want to discuss it."

"As I said before, Captain—" Bromhead began.

Gerber cut him off. "You misunderstand Johnny. We're not here to discuss whether or not to go on the mission, we're here to plan it."

"Yes, sir."

Now Fetterman spoke up. "I've been thinking about this for some time, Captain. We know the Chinese officer operates from a base in Cambodia, not more than thirty klicks from here. He's been running patrols and ambushes in our AO for a couple of months, and if he were farther away, we wouldn't have seen him so often. We also have an idea of the location of the enemy camps from the aerial recon the Air Force has flown for MACV and Army Intelligence."

"All right," nodded Gerber. "We've all had the same briefings about that in Nha Trang. What's your point?"

"I think we can limit the search area quite a bit by using that information. Maybe Sergeant Kepler can get us some more by going to Nha Trang personally. Hell, he's the intel specialist with the team, he should be able to get us something."

"Let's get to the logistics of this," ordered Gerber.

"Easy enough, sir," replied Fetterman. "Since this is a cross-border op, we'll want to take sterile equipment. There are enough weapons in our captured arms store to outfit a company if we want. Sergeant Tyme has checked most of them out and can pull enough for us."

"That's right," agreed Tyme. Tyme was a tall, sandy-haired man in his midtwenties. He seemed to have no real passions in life other than weapons. He lived, breathed and dreamed small arms. There were only a few light weapons made in the world that Tyme could not identify, break down, clean and repair. "Some of the rifles have suffered battle damage, shrapnel into the stock or bullets into the magazine, that sort of thing, but quite a few of them are in mint condition."

"I assume," said Gerber, "that you'll be using one of them to make the kill."

"Oh, no, sir," said Tyme. "I'll be taking a specially adapted M-14 with an automatic ranging sniperscope mounted on it. I'll file the numbers off so that it can't be traced directly to us, but I'm afraid that everyone will know that it was manufactured in the U.S., if it comes to that."

"That reminds me," said Fetterman. "We'll be wearing standard fatigues, but with no U.S. markings or patches. Again, if the enemy should get their hands on any of it, they'll know the source, but not the who."

"Except for the soldiers," said Gerber.

Fetterman smiled slyly. "Well, maybe not. I'll want to take Krung and five or six of the Tai. Their ethnic makeup is remarkably like that of the Cambodes. If they don't speak, I don't think anyone is going to be able to positively identify them."

Fetterman stood and gestured at himself. He was a small man with a dark complexion. Sometimes, when he had been drinking, he joked about an Aztec heritage, and his facial structure, with the long hooked nose, did suggest he had ancestors in Mexico.

"I can pass as a Hispanic if I'm not required to speak Spanish in front of anyone from South America or Mexico."

Wiping some sweat from his forehead, Gerber said, "You're obviously planning to take Tyme with you."

"Yes, sir I know that he stands out like a sore thumb, but he's our best marksman. I thought we could dye his hair and stain his skin to make him a little less identifiable. His Nordic features are a problem."

"You know," said Tyme, "you all make it sound as if we're not going to make it."

"Just covering the bases," said Gerber. "Have you thought about the rest of this, Tony? Mission specifics?"

"Yes, sir. The mission specifics," repeated Fetterman. "Providing Sergeant Kepler can get confirmation on the enemy base location, either through the intel network he has set up or from the classified sources available in Nha Trang, we'll leave the camp in about a day and a half at 1700 hours. We'll patrol to the south, then turn west to the border, crossing at one of three locations. Once inside Cambodia we'll halt for a day or so, set up an advance base before we move deeper to the NVA camp.

"Once we've located that, Sergeants Tyme, Krung and I will find concealment so that we can observe the enemy. Ideally, we will be able to identify our target and make the kill at about dusk. That will give us all night to evade back toward our advance base if possible, or provide an opportunity to lose anyone tracking us if we can't get back to our advance base."

Bromhead let out a low, quiet whistle. "Damn! I don't like the sound of this."

"You have a real problem with that, Johnny?" Gerber snapped.

"No, sir. Not at all. I just don't like the sound of it."

"With luck," continued Fetterman, "the enemy won't realize what has happened for a while and give us an even better head start."

"Why wouldn't they?" asked Bromhead.

"Well, sir, we're going to make the shot from about a klick if the conditions are right. That's why we need to take the M-14 instead of one of the weapons from our captured stock. The single report could be lost in the distance. If the man is alone, it might be several minutes, maybe twenty or thirty, before someone finds him. Long-range sniping produces some weird results because it's the last thing the enemy is going to suspect."

"And if your man is out on patrol?"

"We're prepared to stay put for a couple of days observing. Give us a chance to learn the routine of the camp, but if the target presents itself earlier, we won't pass up the opportunity," answered Fetterman.

Gerber stood up and moved toward the front of his hootch. "A couple of days after you've deployed, I'll mount a large patrol and move to the region of the border. Tony, I'll get together with you a little later and outline a specific route so that you'll be able to locate us. That way, if you're being pursued, we'll be in a better position to lend a hand.''

"So what's the code word?'' asked Bromhead.

"We wanted something that would be confusing to anyone who picked it up and that would not possibly be used by any one else. Something unique,'' Fetterman said.

"Fine,'' said Bromhead. ''The code?''

Fetterman smiled. "I will report that we have sighted Crinshaw's body.''

SIXTEEN HOURS LATER the project became more complicated. Gerber, who was eating a cold breakfast of Cheerios from a single-serving box—the cereal covered in cool milk he had made earlier with lukewarm water and powder—heard the noise of approaching helicopters and picked up his glass of reconstituted orange juice. Since the only scheduled flight had come and gone, he stepped to the team house door and saw that a formation of five Huey helicopters was obviously on approach to the camp. He glanced toward the commo bunker in time to see Bocker exit it and run for the helipad.

Bocker slid to a halt and tossed a smoke grenade onto the center of the pad. He retreated as soon as he saw it begin to burn, the purple smoke blowing leisurely toward the northeast. Gerber caught Bocker's attention, and the commo sergeant changed direction and headed for the team house.

As Bocker approached, Gerber asked, "Who the hell is that?''

"Don't know for sure. Call sign was Crusader One-Two. That's a unit from Tay Ninh according to the SOI, but the pilot refused to provide any more information.''

Gerber reached into the team house so that he could set his empty juice glass on the table that held the coffeepot. He grabbed his beret from the hook next to the door and said, "Okay, let's not fool around. I don't like this at all.''

"It's probably just some kind of search-and-destroy mission that wants to use our camp as a temporary base,'' Bocker said as the two men started forward.

"They should have coordinated it with me first," said Gerber, his eyes on the inbound chopper. "Let's get some people around the pads and have Lieutenant Bromhead swing one of the machine guns in the northeast corner of the camp so that it's aimed at the pad. We'll give them a welcome they don't expect."

As Bocker trotted off, Gerber ran to his hootch, grabbed his M-14 and two grenades and headed to the helipads. There he met Fetterman, who was holding an M-3. Fetterman pointed to the fire control tower, and Gerber turned to see Tyme scrambling up the ladder.

The helicopters crossed the outer wire, settling toward the ground. Gerber sent Fetterman to a stack of sandbags to cover the lead ship. Bocker had gone back to the commo bunker, picked up his weapon and was now crouched in the Z-shaped entrance. Bromhead and two of the Tai had lifted one of the .30-caliber machine guns and turned it and its tripod so that they had an unobstructed field of fire that could rake the entire helipad and a long section of the runway.

As soon as the helicopters were on the ground, men started piling out of them. The crew chief of the lead chopper leaped to the ground from his position in the gun well, a long cord from his helmet still connected to the radio jack and a small black button in his hand. He opened the copilot's door, and when the crew chief jumped back out of the way, the pilot stepped down, pulling the flight helmet from his head.

Brigadier General Billy Joe Crinshaw stood squinting in the morning sun. Gerber made no move to come forward. Crinshaw stood in the cloud of swirling red dust and handed his flight helmet to the crew chief. Then, ignoring the rotor blades, he stepped close to Gerber.

For an instant, as the whine of the Huey turbines quieted, Gerber considered what he was going to say. He didn't like people appearing on the horizon without announcing their plans, and although the VC and the NVA didn't have Huey helicopters, he thought it was a stupid move. Over the sound of the dying engines, Gerber shouted, "I could have shot your ass out of the sky."

Crinshaw momentarily stiffened at the hostility of the remark, let alone that it was a junior officer who had made it. He stood there silently, waiting for Gerber to say more.

"Next time you come in here, you tell us who you are. There's no need to drop out of the sky like some demented bird of prey."

"Watch what you're saying, Captain," Crinshaw cautioned him.

"General Crinshaw," said Gerber, "there are some very real military considerations here. I have to know who is approaching the camp and why they are coming in. An unidentified flight of helicopters cannot be tolerated. If the lead pilot had not made the request for smoke on the pad, we would have had no idea who you were."

"The pilot was acting on my orders. You do not question my orders, Captain. Never question them."

"The point here is—" started Gerber.

"The point is," interrupted Crinshaw, "that I wanted to look over your operation. And I see it's pretty weak. You make big talk about shooting us out of the sky, but you only have a single rifle."

Gerber was going to tell him about the machine gun crew covering them and point out Bocker, Fetterman and Tyme, but decided it would prove nothing. Rather than prolong the debate, he said, "What's going on here?"

He could see men who had arrived on the helicopters unloading supplies. Cardboard boxes of C-rations, crates of ammo, extra weapons, M-60 machine guns and even a couple of 60 mm mortars.

"Let's watch those smart-alecky tones, Captain," said Crinshaw. "I brought these boys out for some first-hand training and experience in the field."

A major who had arrived on one of the choppers approached from the rear and stood waiting. He looked like a regular Saigon commando. He wore a camouflaged uniform, but it had been starched so that it held a knifelike crease even in humidity high enough to wilt concrete. He had highly polished insignia on his collar that flashed in the sunlight and even wore spit shined boots. He was a stocky man, not more than five foot seven, with a bulky jaw and soft, pale eyes. His face was a pasty white, as if he didn't get out in the tropical sun very often.

Crinshaw stared at Gerber for a moment longer and then turned to the major. "Get your equipment together and prepare to move it out of here."

Although no one told the major where to take his equipment, he spun and began ordering his men to gather it so they could get it away from the helipad.

"The aircraft, General," Gerber reminded him. "We can't let them sit here all day."

Crinshaw looked irritated and then said, "Yes, of course." He held a thumb up, telling the lead pilot he was released and could take off.

Gerber waved Fetterman over and said to him, "Take the major and his men and find a place for them."

Two hours later Gerber was back at the helipad waiting on another flight of choppers, this group carrying a Vietnamese general who was bringing in men to recover the bodies of the dead rangers. As he and Bocker waited, he leaned close and asked, "Kepler get away?"

"Got the morning resupply chopper. He shouldn't have trouble with the connections to Nha Trang."

When they could see the helicopters clearly, Bocker tossed a yellow smoke grenade onto the center of the pad.

Just as the helicopters touched down, Crinshaw arrived to watch. He stood with one hand on his head, holding down his baseball-type fatigue cap as the rotor blades tried to lift everything into the swirling wind they created.

The Vietnamese general, obvious in his tailored uniform and rows of brightly colored ribbons, stepped down from the cargo compartment. He then turned and held his hand out so that the woman traveling with him could exit. As she entered the bright light from the shadows in the cargo compartment, Gerber recognized her immediately.

Crinshaw stared in disbelief and demanded, "Who in the hell authorized that woman to be out here?"

She pulled a folded piece of paper out of the top pocket of the khaki bush jacket she wore and handed it to Crinshaw. "You did, General. You signed it yourself a couple of days ago and General Vo was kind enough to give me a lift."

Crinshaw grabbed the paper from her, stared at it, saw his signature scrawled at the bottom and knew he had been had. It had been a request that Morrow, R., be allowed to report on the activities at Special Forces Camp A-555.

Crinshaw recovered nicely. He handed the paper back to Morrow and said to Gerber, "You see that she gets everything she wants. Everything."

Morrow turned and grinned at Gerber, acting as if she had never seen him before.

When Fetterman arrived moments later, Gerber said, "You'll have to find a place for Miss Morrow."

"That's the least of our problems, Captain," he said, motioning to the helipad.

Gerber took a moment to look at the new group of men, the two generals standing near each other, talking quietly, the seven helicopters sitting on the pad, their rotors spinning slowly, and the new piles of ammunition and explosives. He was thinking about the mission that Fetterman had planned for that night—providing Kepler could confirm enemy camp locations—and how they were going to operate with everyone falling all over everyone else. Finding quarters for Morrow was definitely the least of their problems.

He turned back to Fetterman and said, "Let's get these people out of here and get their equipment stored."

"Everything still on for tonight?"

"I don't know. Let's hang loose, wait to hear from Kepler and then see how the situation breaks."

4

FIFTH SPECIAL FORCES HEADQUARTERS, NHA TRANG, REPUBLIC OF VIETNAM

Sergeant First Class Derek Kepler sat in the anteroom of the Fifth Special Forces Intelligence Officer watching the ceiling fan revolve slowly as it fought a losing battle to stir up a breeze. Plywood paneling stained a dirty brown covered the office walls from the floor to the midpoint, where screen hidden behind louvered one by sixes climbed the rest of the way to the ceiling. That was to let in any breeze that might be blowing, in a futile effort to keep the inside comfortable. The canopy from a parachute flare was suspended under the rafters.

Kepler was the intel specialist for Mack Gerber's A-Team and had been with Gerber's group since they had deployed to Vietnam. His job was to learn all he could about the enemy's troop movements, locations, the local population, the climatic conditions they might face and anything else that could be helpful. He also had a network of agents spread through the villages and hamlets near the camp. They were supposed to tell him of anything unusual, such as VC recruiting trips or reprisals that took place. Most of the agents were people who wanted to do something to help the Americans or who hated the VC.

It was his own agents who had first alerted him to the VC-NVA base camp just over the Cambodian border, and they had given him a good idea about its location. Recon photos from the Air Force had helped him pinpoint it, although it was information that had done him little good until now. Since the captain had asked him to verify the site of the camp, he found his knowledge helpful. He hoped he could get more recent recon photos from the intelligence officer and possibly determine if the camp had been moved. The VC didn't like to stay in one place too long.

After nearly thirty minutes of sitting in the outer office on an old wrought-iron settee with gaudy green fabric and a dozen rips that had been patched with electrical tape, the clerk typist, who had been ignoring him, stood. He moved to the door that was closed, knocked once and looked inside. He turned, glanced at Kepler and said, "The major will see you now."

Kepler got to his feet and stepped past the clerk. The office he entered had an air conditioner humming in one corner, trying hard to keep up with the heat and humidity outside, but slowly losing the battle. It was cooler in the office, but not much.

The major stood and came around a scarred metal desk stuck in one corner. He was a tall, thin man with prematurely graying hair and bushy black eyebrows that were in stark contrast to his sharp, fine features. His brown eyes had laugh lines radiating from them, and his mouth carried an amused grin. He had his hand out, meaning he didn't expect a salute from Kepler. "Welcome to Nha Trang, Sergeant—or maybe I should say Derek," he said. "How have you been?"

Kepler shook the major's hand. "Just fine, lately. I trust that my reports have been getting here satisfactorily."

The major sat on the corner of his desk and pushed a nameplate with a major's oak leaf stuck into a blue field and the name Houston inscribed to one side of it. "Everything has been coming in just fine. I appreciate those updates on the VC movements. Helps us coordinate the activities for the other teams in your general AO."

"Yes, sir. Just trying to do my job. I do have a bit of a problem, though, and thought you might be able to help."

"Anything you need," said Houston.

"I wondered if you had any new aerial recon of the Parrot's Beak region. I need to look at things along the Cambodian border. Charlie seems to be building up there somewhere."

Houston scratched his chin and said, "I don't recall seeing anything about that in any of the new classified. You have anything more specific?"

"No, sir. That's why I thought looking up the latest recon photos might help. I can compare them with what I've seen before and spot the trend."

"All right," said Houston. "I'll pull the stuff out of the safe. Parrot's Beak region?"

"Yes, sir. About fifteen or twenty klicks on either side of the border."

Houston stood and moved to the door. "Wait here and I'll see what I can find."

When the major was gone, Kepler took the opportunity to examine the office closely. On the wall next to the door were the obligatory captured weapons. Houston had an RPG-7 mounted on an oak plaque and an AK-47 with a small brass plate attached to the stock claiming both weapons were captured on August 17, 1964, in the Plei Me area.

A scarred conference table surrounded by four chairs sat at one end of the office. The finish was dull and cracked, the varnish burned where lit cigarettes had fallen. The chairs weren't in any better shape.

Just as Kepler sat down in one of the chairs, the door opened and Houston reappeared carrying a folder that was stamped Secret top and bottom, front and back. Before Kepler could stand, Houston slipped into one of the other chairs and slid the file toward the Special Forces intel officer.

Kepler took the photos from the folder. Each one was also stamped Secret in red letters. He used the map that was enclosed in the file to orient the pictures so he could recognize some of the major terrain features, such as the point where the Mekong River crossed the border and the Moc Hoa canal. Once he had the pictures laid out in order, he began to study them. The black-and-white photos, shot from over thirty thousand feet, didn't contain much obvious detail for the untrained eye.

Using the magnifying glass that Houston took from the middle drawer of his desk, Kepler carefully examined the area where he believed the enemy camp to be. At first he saw nothing except the tops of the palms that formed the upper level of the triple-canopy jungle. Slowly he began to see things that didn't seem to belong— symmetrical shadows that betrayed the presence of a low building, and a point of light where the corrugated tin of a roof caught and reflected the sun. Kepler spread a piece of clear plastic on the photo and then traced the shadows and reflections with a grease pencil. By erasing and changing the lines, he had soon drawn the portrait of the enemy camp. It was an oval, containing fifteen or twenty buildings as well as a dozen small structures that could be sheds. He even found what he thought was the outline of a truck hidden under the trees, but the resolution of the photo wasn't quite good enough for him to be sure.

All this time Houston sat across from him, smoking cigarette after cigarette until the atmosphere in the room took on the hazy blue of a nightclub. He said nothing as he watched Kepler work through the photos.

Having confirmed the location of the VC base, Kepler went back over the photos looking for other evidence of VC activity. He found a place on one picture that might have been a snatch of the Ho Chi Minh Trail and an enlarged area near it that might have been one of the rumored rest stops along it. He located a number of single structures, little more than hootches, that probably belonged to rice farmers. He checked the coordinates of them all, memorizing them because he knew that Houston would not let him carry the information out in writing. To do that, he would need permission from nearly a dozen sources, including the Air Force and the CIA.

He was about to quit when something caught his eye. Studying it under the magnifying glass, he became convinced that he had found another base—smaller than the first and hidden better, but an enemy camp all the same. Then, as he searched through the blacks and whites of the trees in the photo, he felt his excitement grow. He sat back, stared at the ceiling in disbelief and then turned back to the picture.

"What is it?" asked Houston, puzzled.

"I don't think I believe it," said Kepler, unable to keep the surprise out of his voice.

Houston stood and came around the table so he could get a close look at the photo.

Kepler held the magnifying glass and pointed with his free hand. "Right here," he said, circling an area with his index finger. "If you look closely, you'll see what appear to be bleachers sitting in the shadow thrown by that large tree."

"Yes. So?"

"Look very carefully now." Kepler put a finger on the photo at the side of the bleachers. "This," he said, "is the instructor. Right here are the students. It's a picture of a damned VC class!"

For a moment Houston didn't say anything. Then he laughed out loud and said, "My God! I think you're right."

"Of course I'm right. The fucking VC sitting around in a fucking class."

After making a series of quick measurements to determine distances and directions from the first camp to the second, Kepler scooped up the photos, tapped the edges on the table to align them and stuffed them back into the file folder. He stood and said, "I guess that does it, sir. I've seen what I need to see."

"Anything else?" asked Houston.

"No, sir. That should do it."

Houston picked up the folder and said, "I'll get this back in the safe. You need anything else, let me know."

Kepler left the intel office and turned up the corridor, heading toward the radio room, where he could use the lima lima to make a call to the camp, providing they could get the routing to work. The phone system the Army was building in South Vietnam was not the efficient operation that Ma Bell had in the World. It was a haphazard conglomeration of switchboards and commo wire that was down more often than it was up. But Kepler wanted to stay away from using the radio if he could. Fewer people could listen in on the land line.

The switchboard operator, a Spec Four in sweat-stained fatigues who looked as if he were fifteen years old, said he didn't think he would have any luck because things were acting up all over. He could not define what things were acting up, but he sat in a folding metal chair and cranked the handle that rang phones on other switchboards anyway. He pulled wires from some slots and jammed them into others, asking operators to route him on farther to the west. Finally, with a jury-rigged line that ran from Nha Trang to Phan Rang to Phouc Binh to Dau Tieng to Saigon to Tay Ninh, he was able to ring the switchboard in the commo bunker at Camp A-555.

Bocker picked up the phone on the second ring, listened for a moment and then handed it to Fetterman, who was checking the radio equipment he'd take with him on the mission.

Fetterman took the receiver of the field phone and said simply, "Go."

"I have confirmed the location," said Kepler.

"Understood," said Fetterman.

"Be advised that I have also discovered a second prime location fourteen klicks to the southwest."

"Understand a second location fourteen klicks to the southwest."

"Roger that."

AS SOON AS HE HUNG UP Fetterman grabbed one of the maps from the chart table and plotted the information. He examined the terrain, looking for hills and valleys, rivers and ravines and swamps and jungle that could make the patrol impossible. There was nothing on the maps to indicate he couldn't get from one camp to the other if he had to.

That done, Fetterman left the commo bunker, stepping into the late-afternoon heat. He put a hand to his forehead to shade his eyes and went looking for Gerber.

He found Gerber in his hootch, working on a report that Crinshaw had determined. It was a listing of the supplies used in the past two weeks to establish a new antimortar bunker, and a description of the ammo requirements of the perimeter defense weapons—meaning the .50- and .30-caliber machine guns located in the bunkers on the four walls. The report was a make-work project that would be of no benefit to anyone.

Gerber stopped working when a shadow fell across the floor in front of his desk. He then waved Fetterman in, capped his pen and said, "What can I do for you?"

"Kepler reported in. He confirmed the location of the base camp and said he'd found another several klicks away."

"That cause you a problem, Tony?"

"Only if it turns out that the VC have moved."

"Then you're still planning to go tonight?"

"Well, sir, that's the real problem. Seems odd, doesn't it? We're about to embark on this mission and both the Vietnamese and the American high command decide to show up with a series of excuses about why they're here."

Gerber turned so that he could stare at the master sergeant. "Are you suggesting a leak somewhere?"

"I'm merely calling attention to an amazing coincidence."

"This whole thing was your idea, Tony. We're under no time constraints. We can postpone it if that would make you feel better." Gerber hadn't told Fetterman that the CIA was interested in the mission. The CIA wanted to see it accomplished, but had put no time restrictions on it.

Fetterman wiped a hand across his forehead. "No, sir. As I say, I'm merely pointing out a coincidence. Besides, we're supposed to be running patrols."

Gerber sat back and locked his fingers behind his head. "Crinshaw and his boys could cause us some real trouble if they learned where you are going."

"No reason they should, Captain," said Fetterman. He thought for a moment, his eyes on the dusty plywood floor. "Unless you think we should delay until the generals are out of camp, I would say that we go ahead."

"How soon do you want to jump off?"

"About an hour before dusk. Give us a chance to get away from here before we lose all the light."

FETTERMAN STOOD in the early evening light near the gate in the center of the south wall of the camp. He was looking at the crowd of men who loitered around it. Not only were Tyme, Krung and the five Tai of his patrol there, but there were also fifteen other Americans brought by Crinshaw and almost fifty Vietnamese brought by Vo. All were suddenly preparing to leave the camp on their various patrols. Crinshaw and a half dozen members of his staff were nearby, watching everything that was going on.

Leaning close to Gerber, Fetterman said, "How in the hell am I supposed to get out of here with nine-tenths of the American and Vietnamese population in the camp watching?"

"Just follow the normal patrol route. Once you're outside the wire, I doubt anyone will pay attention to you." Gerber then noticed the collection of American-made weapons carried by Fetterman's men. "I thought you said this was going to be a sterile mission?"

"I did, Captain. But with Crinshaw standing here to ask questions, I figured we'd better carry the American stuff. Besides, the M-1s are nearly as good as sterile. So many have been given to so many foreign countries, they shouldn't raise eyebrows. Hell, the VC carry them."

At that moment Tyme came over to report. "The Tai equipment checks out. I've been through their packs to make sure that they have everything they're supposed to."

"And you?" said Fetterman.

Tyme nodded. "The scope's in the bottom of my pack, protected by clean socks and a poncho liner. I've also cushioned it in mosquito netting."

"I take it you're all ready, then," Gerber said.

"Yes, sir," replied Fetterman.

Gerber held out his hand to his master sergeant. "Good luck and good hunting. We'll be listening for your first check-in. I'll go over to Crinshaw and see what I can do to hold up his people and give you a chance to fade into the night."

"Sounds great," said Fetterman as he pushed open the flimsy gate. Everyone figured that if the VC got to the gate, it would make no difference if it were sturdy or not. The enemy had to be stopped before it penetrated that deeply into the camp's defenses.

As Gerber engaged Crinshaw and his patrol leader—the major who hadn't been in the field—in conversation, Fetterman and his men worked their way through the perimeter. They entered the elephant grass, trying to avoid the pathways they had made on earlier trips. Fetterman was breaking the trail, being careful because, during the dry season, the grass could cut through cloth fatigues like a razor.

He looped to the south, toward the clump of trees they all too often used as a staging point once outside the camp. He halted under the trees and spread his men out in a circle so that they could guard all approaches. He watched the camp and soon saw the other patrol following the trail that Fetterman had made.

That in itself was not sinister. It might not mean anything other than that the patrol leader was inexperienced. Elephant grass was hard to walk through, and until you learned the trick of twisting the foot as you stepped on it, it was very tiring to break a trail. The major was following the path of least resistance.

Although Fetterman didn't think the other American patrol would be following him, he didn't trust Crinshaw. In the past the general had done things to hurt camp operations, like refusing to issue the new M-16s because the old M-14s were still serviceable, and ordering people to Saigon at critical moments. That hurt operations. It wasn't outside the realm of possibility that Crinshaw had told his men to follow Gerber's. Rather than heading to Cambodia, Fetterman turned farther to the south, keeping the clump of trees between him and the other American patrol. Just as they were leaving the trees, Fetterman turned back long enough to see that General Vo's patrol had now joined what was turning into a parade.

As the last of the light began to fade, Fetterman halted again. He set his men in an L-shaped ambush, pairing them up so that everyone had a buddy. Once that was done, he crawled along the rear of the ambush and found himself a place to hide. He picked a position where he could see the trail they had just followed.

He heard them long before he could see them. Their equipment rattled, they were talking and, unbelievably, two of the men in the rear were smoking. Fetterman crawled back to his ambush and told his men to fall back, away from the trail. He grouped them together, hiding under bushes and behind fallen palms. They lay there quietly and watched the other American patrol stumble by, oblivious to everything around them.

When Crinshaw's men were out of sight and Fetterman could no longer hear them, he silently moved among his men. He tapped each on the shoulder to alert him and then pointed west toward Cambodia. The point man, Sergeant Krung, took his compass out, checked the luminous dial and sighted on a light-colored palm trunk in the distance. He used a long stick to feel the ground in front of him so that he didn't fall into hidden holes or walk into trees he might not see in the dark.

They kept moving through the night, the pace slow but steady. They rested more often than usual because there was something about the night that made travel more difficult. A man had to use all his senses to the maximum. He had to stare into the inky black trying to see things that might be in the way. He had to listen so intently that it seemed the ears moved like radar antenna. Fetterman could actually feel his ears twitch as he heard the sounds of the nocturnal jungle animals in the distance. Although it wasn't nearly as hot as the daytime and he didn't have the sun baking his skin, Fetterman was covered with sweat. Sometimes he thought he preferred patrolling in the daylight.

About two o'clock, just as they stopped for a short break, the rain started. For a few seconds it was no more than a drizzle that didn't reach through the thick jungle growth to the ground. But then the clouds opened up and the rain poured down in sheets, rattling through the triple-canopy jungle, bouncing off the leaves until it reached Fetterman and his men.

For thirty minutes it rained hard, the sounds of the jungle drowned in the roar of the precipitation. Fetterman wanted to move, knowing the VC wouldn't be out in the lousy weather, but he was afraid his patrol would become separated. The only thing he could do was sit tight, wish he were dry and wait for the rain to end.

It was nearly three before the weather had cleared enough that Fetterman could resume the patrol. Again Krung took the point and slowly led them closer to Cambodia. As the sun came up, they were still fifteen klicks from the border, but all alone in the jungle. There was no sign of Crinshaw's men. Not far away, only a klick or so according to the map, was open ground where paddies bordered a swamp. It would be easier to travel over that type of terrain, but Fetterman wanted the protection of the jungle. He kept his patrol moving through the dense, wet jungle avoiding pathways, crawling around fallen trees and jungle undergrowth when they had to.

At nine in the morning, as the sun was beginning to heat the jungle and the steam was rising from the earth, Fetterman decided it was time to halt. The men had to get the wet socks off their feet, and they needed a chance to rest after marching all night. Besides, there was no point in getting too close to Cambodia in the daylight.

Fetterman rotated the duty so that everyone had a chance to sleep and eat a cold meal. By late afternoon they were ready to break camp.

Fetterman made sure each of the men drank a lot of water and took salt tablets, although the crushing heat of the day had passed. He also made sure each man drained the canteen he was drinking from because he didn't want the water of a partially filled one sloshing around. As always, each man carried three or four canteens to be sure the patrol had sufficient water. Given the territory, just north of the Mekong, there were plenty of places to fill canteens, and Fetterman had a large supply of halazone tablets to purify water.

As it started to get dark, they neared the Cambodian border. Fetterman took a number of final compass readings, plotted them on his map and then pointed it all out to Tyme and Krung.

"We'll cross the border about an hour from now, in total darkness," he said. "I want to travel about ten or twelve klicks after that. Give us some distance from the border and put us fairly close to the VC camp."

Tyme took the point, leading them nearly due west. The others in the tiny patrol followed closely, with only a meter separating each man from the soldier in front of him. Fetterman brought up the rear and could only see the man directly in front of him.

Fetterman wasn't sure of the exact moment they crossed into Cambodia. There was no change in the terrain; the jungle was as heavy as before. There was no physical obstacle they had to climb and no guard posts to avoid. Just the seemingly endless jungle filled with the sounds of the creatures of the night and the buzz of the mosquitoes as they searched for victims.

They continued moving slowly, feeling their way through the jungle with their walking sticks. Clouds moved in to obscure the moon, making travel even more difficult.

About four in the morning, Fetterman began searching for a campsite, but it was nearly nine before he found what he wanted. One with good cover and many ways in and out. There was low brush around it so he could see anyone approaching and, by staying down, escape. He established a rotating guard, keeping half the men awake and watching while the other half slept or ate. And then the patrol settled in to wait for nightfall.

MACK GERBER SAT in the team house drinking coffee spiked with Beam's and relaxing. He had spent most of the previous day trying to convince Crinshaw that nothing unusual was happening and that the patrol he was running was normal. In addition to that, General Vo was wandering around, talking to the Vietnamese in the strike companies, ignoring the Tai.

Gerber had just finished his coffee when Crinshaw entered. Without a word Crinshaw walked to the coffeepot, poured himself a cup and then sat down on the other side of the table.

"What's going on out there, boy?" he demanded.

"What's going on out where, General?" asked Gerber.

"Let's stop dancing around," said Crinshaw. "Where is your patrol? I've talked to my people, and they say that your people disappeared."

Taking his time, Gerber stood, moved to the coffeepot and refilled his cup. He turned, sipped and said, "You mean that your people were following mine?"

"I said to stop the dancing. My people say that they watched yours head into the jungle and disappear. Now where the hell did they go?"

"The itinerary was not rigidly established. Sergeant Fetterman was told to play it by ear. He had a general patrol zone, which I'll be happy to show you, but I don't know his exact location."

"I'm not buying that, Captain. You have to know his location. Otherwise, you couldn't give support if he needed it."

"You know that I can tell you a general location, but if the sergeant needs help, he'll have to call for it."

"Okay, boy, I'll let you get away with that. Now, why did he work so hard to lose my people?"

"Then you're saying that they were out there to follow my men?"

"Just answer the question."

Gerber moved to the table and sat down, wishing he could pour a couple of fingers of the Beam's into the coffee now, but he knew Crinshaw wouldn't approve. "They were not trying to lose your people. I would imagine that Sergeant Fetterman was following standard field procedures, and if your people couldn't keep up, or lost sight of them, then I would think it is their fault and not Fetterman's. Not to mention the fact that it isn't good policy to throw that many patrols into the field following each other. Gives the enemy too much notice of who's going where. Besides, my men weren't advised to maintain contact with yours, so they had no reason for doing so."

For a moment Crinshaw didn't say anything. He stared at Gerber, trying to force him into saying something more, but when Gerber didn't fall into that trap, he said, "I'm going to stay here for a couple of days and watch your operation. I think there are things happening here I should know about."

Gerber drained his coffee, set the cup down and stood. "That's fine, General. You stay as long as you want. Now, if you don't mind, I'm going to check our defenses."

FETTERMAN WAITED FOR DARK before he broke camp. It was nearly 2300 hours when they moved out again, heading for the large VC camp Kepler had identified for them. They moved through thinning jungle, crossed dozens of open rice fields, sometimes staying on the dikes to keep from making noise in the water, other times moving through them because the farmer had already drained them. They had to circle a couple of farm hootches, and once when they saw a light bobbing through the trees in front of them, they had to take cover, but the light never came close and soon disappeared. They heard no noise from the area and never did figure out what it was.

Overhead they heard a number of airplanes, most of them small propeller craft. Once or twice there were jets, but they never saw any lights from them. Fetterman thought they might be from bases in Thailand, heading to missions in South Vietnam.

The patrol kept up a steady pace, stopping for rest every hour. Fetterman let Tyme keep the point, sure that the young NCO would be able to handle the job. Leading a patrol through foreign territory at night was no easy task, especially when it was the enemy's territory. But Tyme didn't seem to have a problem. He avoided the pitfalls with what seemed to be a psychic ability. He kept them marching in as much of a straight line as the jungle would allow.

Tyme halted at about quarter to three, and Fetterman crawled forward, past the Tai who had dropped into hiding places as soon as Tyme had stopped moving.

He found the young sergeant lying prone, facing north. He put his mouth next to Tyme's ear and asked, "Why have you stopped?"

Tyme pointed ahead and said, "We're here!"

5

**VIETCONG BASE CAMP,
NORTH OF KOMPONG
RAU, CAMBODIA**

As the sun came up, Fetterman realized the camp was deserted. The camp was oval in shape, with short guard towers every fifty or sixty feet along the perimeter. Unlike the American bases in South Vietnam, there were no open killing fields outside the wire. The bush and jungle had been cut back so that the guards could see into the trees, but there was no open ground. But now the guard towers were deserted, and the fences were falling down. From his position, slightly above the VC camp, Fetterman could see a half dozen buildings that resembled barracks, long, low buildings with corrugated tin roofs and a row of small windows just under the eaves.

Near the center of the camp was a shed that might have housed a generator, and near it was a low, squat building that looked as if it were made of cement blocks and could have been the armory. There was a larger two-story stone building with steps leading up to it that might have been the headquarters, and a half dozen other small wooden structures.

Near the larger stone building were the remains of two trucks. One of them looked as if the back end had burned. Weeds and bushes had grown up around the vehicles and buildings, hiding some of the doorways, the ground and the walkways.

"Looks like they're gone," said Fetterman.

"Now what?" asked Tyme.

"I want Krung and the Tai to split into two squads of three men each and keep to the trees to cover us. Then you and I will enter the camp."

When the Tai were in place, Fetterman and Tyme began to work their way down the hillside, keeping to the cover of trees and bushes, dodging from hole to bush and back to hole as much as possible. While one of them moved, the other guarded, reversing their positions every thirty meters or so. When they were near the wire, they got down to crawl forward. Although he was worried about it, Fetterman had discovered no evidence of land mines or booby traps as they approached the fence. They found cover under a large flowering bush where they could study the inside of the base. There was still no sign of movement.

Finally sure there was no one left on the inside, Fetterman whispered, "We'll split up. We're looking for anything that might tell us about the VC, especially any documents that might be useful to Intel when we get back. If you find any useful military material, move it outside. We'll either take it back with us or destroy it before we move on."

They moved to the wire, found a large hole in it and avoided it. Fetterman figured that they could get through anywhere they wanted to, and if Charlie were going to booby-trap the camp, he would do it in the most likely spots. A hole in the wire, providing easy access, was a likely spot.

They separated, each moving along the wire for fifty meters. Fetterman cut the wire near one of the guard towers and entered underneath it. Once inside Fetterman carefully climbed the short wooden ladder so that he could search the guard tower, but there was nothing in it. When he looked back, he saw Tyme was already inside, heading toward the camp's center.

Tyme moved carefully through the compound, watching for trip wires, depressions in the ground and places where the leaves of the weeds were tied back, all things that indicated booby traps. He passed the generator shed, noting the oil stains on the hard packed ground.

Near the center of the compound, he came to the large stone headquarters building. The wood of the porch was partially burned away. The doors in the front were missing, and except for a few panes that showed evidence of bullet holes, all of the glass in the windows had been removed. Inside, the walls had been stripped of everything that might have been useful. There was no furniture left in it. No light fixtures. No wire. No papers. Nothing.

Tyme went out the back door toward the two trucks. One of them was an American Dodge and the other a Soviet ZIL. They looked almost the same, as if the builders of one had copied the other.

Neither had tires. Slowly Tyme opened the hood of the Dodge, being careful when he lifted it. Inside, he found almost nothing. Every piece that could be easily removed from the engine was gone. There was no battery, no wires, no spark plugs and no hoses.

He walked around the outside of the vehicle, opened one door of the cab and looked in. The seats had been taken out. The steering wheel, the gauges, even the door for the glove compartment, had been removed. The truck bed had been burned, but the gas tank had not exploded. He was looking at the skeleton of the truck.

The ZIL was in a little better shape. It hadn't caught fire. The only interesting thing in it was a plaque, inscribed in Russian, that probably detailed the operating instructions. For a moment Tyme thought about trying to pry it loose and then decided against it. It was that kind of trophy hunting that got people killed.

Across the camp Fetterman was having no better luck. He had found the officers' quarters in a small building near the long barracks. It had once been divided into individual rooms, but the partitioning walls were gone now, and only the stud marks remained on the floor. He searched carefully, knowing that things sometimes slipped from sight, and those in a hurry to leave an area sometimes overlooked those things in their haste.

All he found was a color photograph of an undressed blonde. Fetterman recognized the picture. He had seen it a couple of months earlier in a *Playboy* magazine. The magazine itself was over a year old so that alone didn't provide any clues about how recently the VC had been in the camp.

Back outside Fetterman worked his way to the long barracks. The first one contained nothing but stripped walls and empty space. The floor was worn in the center, and there were squares of fresher-looking wood where the cots or lockers had stood. The windows were small and let in only a little light. With no breeze it was hot and humid inside.

Fetterman walked slowly through the building, spotting nothing of value. Debris from outside, mostly palm leaves and dirt, littered the floor. In one corner he found an empty U.S. Army C-ration can. That and the picture of the naked blonde indicated the VC from the camp had raided an American outpost at some point.

As Fetterman left the building, he realized they would find nothing they could use in the camp. The VC were gone and had taken everything with them. To continue to search the camp would just waste time, time that could be used heading to the new base that Kepler had spotted on the aerial recon photos.

Tyme had just finished searching his sector of the camp when Fetterman approached. Without exchanging a word they worked their way back through the base to the wire, and then each exited, using the hole that Fetterman had cut.

AT CAMP A-555 Gerber was talking to his counterpart, Captain Minh, in the commo bunker. Gerber had briefed the Vietnamese officer about the mission because, technically, Minh was the camp commander. Besides, Gerber trusted him as much as he trusted any of the men on his team. Sergeant Bocker stood to one side, keeping a watch on both the doorway and the radio.

"You may have to take the company out tomorrow without me," warned Gerber. "I'm not sure exactly what Crinshaw has in mind. I don't know why he has picked now to make his visit, but he's going to make the patrol difficult. Make it hard to get a company out of here without having to answer a lot of awkward questions."

"I'm not sure that I can help you, old boy," responded Minh in his clipped British accent. "General Vo is causing as much trouble. It's almost as if someone has spilled the beans."

Gerber moved to the battle map that decorated one wall of the bunker. It showed the location of the camp, and a couple of sites that Intel suspected of being VC strongholds. Turning from it, Gerber said, "I could put Bromhead in operational control. He's quick enough to handle anything. I just don't want him leading the patrol that could blow up into an international incident."

"If either of us go out, we're liable to alert one of these rear-area louts," said Minh.

"Still, it's not fair to send Bromhead. He'd go happily and do a good job, but damn, he's so young."

"So what do you plan?"

"If I'm still having trouble with Crinshaw tomorrow, I'm going to send the company out under the control of either Sergeant Bocker or Sergeant Kepler. Then, first chance I get, I'll go out with another patrol and link up with them."

"What do you want me to do, old boy?"

"I want you to find out what the hell is going on. Why do we suddenly have brass running all over the place? Then find out where the hell the leak is, if there is a leak, so that we can eliminate it."

"You think Vo or Crinshaw know what's going on?"

"I don't think Vo knows much. He's here to recover the bodies of the dead rangers. I doubt that Crinshaw knows exactly what's happening. But he suspects something. That's what has me worried."

A little later Gerber found Robin Morrow sitting alone in one corner of the team house. She had spread her notebooks and reference materials over one table and had a steaming cup of coffee sitting in the middle of the litter. She seemed to be concentrating on the coffee and ignoring everything else.

After pouring himself a cup that contained most of the grounds, Gerber walked to the table and sat down opposite the reporter. "I didn't get a chance to tell you how much I enjoyed your first meeting with General Crinshaw," he said.

Morrow looked up and smiled. "I'm afraid I don't understand."

"You did a number on him. Tricked him into letting you come out here. And you had the documentation to make it stick. Anything you need, you let me know and I'll see what I can do. You deserve it."

Bromhead entered the team house and came over. "Miss Morrow," he said, "I hope you found your accommodations to be satisfactory."

"Why so formal, Lieutenant?" she asked, smiling. "The accommodations, as you call them, suck. It's hot and muggy. The floor is dirty, the roof leaks and there are insects running all over the place."

"And we've given you the best we have," responded Gerber, getting up. "We even moved the rats into the latrine so you'd have more room. If you two will excuse me, I've got a couple of things I've got to do."

When Gerber was gone, Bromhead said, "Are you enjoying yourself out here?"

Morrow drained her coffee and said, "Of course I'm not enjoying myself. I'm out here to do a job."

Bromhead suddenly felt like a teenage boy in the presence of an older woman. Anything he said was going to be wrong or misunderstood. He had known when he asked his question that no one really enjoyed being hot and miserable ten thousand miles from home, but some people enjoyed their work and that compensated for the misery. He wondered what he could say to Morrow because he wanted a chance to talk to her.

"Of course," she said, softening, "I do enjoy my work."

Trying to cover his embarrassment, Bromhead reached for her cup and asked, "Would you like some more coffee?"

"What I would really like," responded Morrow, "is an ice-cold beer. Or a Coke. Anything cold."

Bromhead put the cup down and headed for an old refrigerator. "I'm afraid there might not be much of anything in here, and if there is, it might not be too cold."

"That's okay, Lieutenant. I'll consider anything under a hundred to be cold."

"Call me Johnny. Everyone does." And as he said it, he realized how young it made him sound. Men were called John or Jack. Boys were called Johnny. But it was too late to take it back.

"Okay, Johnny. You can call me Robin. Now what's a nice guy like you doing in a hole like this?"

"Well, it's a long story," he said as he pulled a couple of beers out of the icebox. "You're in luck, Robin. We've got a couple of Millers." He opened them using his P-38 and handed one to Morrow.

"Thanks." She smiled at him staring into his eyes for a moment longer than necessary. "Now, I have all day. Why don't you tell me how you ended up here."

FETTERMAN HADN'T been too happy about the first camp being deserted. It meant he was going to have to move deeper into Cambodia. It meant he was farther from help if he needed it. It meant there could be more enemy soldiers between him and the border. But there was nothing that could be done. If he were going to complete the mission, he would have to accept the additional risks and move closer to Svay Rieng, where Kepler's information put the new camp.

The patrol spent the rest of the day chopping their way through jungle so thick with undergrowth that in places they were only making fifty meters an hour. They had to rotate point men every few minutes because the burden of cutting through the vines and bushes in the heat of the afternoon quickly sapped a man's energy. The men gulped their water at each rest break, downing it hastily. Fetterman was concerned about heatstroke, and he made sure that everyone took salt tablets.

An hour before dusk the point man stopped moving and Fetterman crawled forward through the clinging vines that grabbed at his uniform until he reached Krung kneeling near the split trunk of a palm. Before Krung said anything, Fetterman heard noise filtering through the trees. He listened, concentrating, and heard voices speaking Vietnamese and the rattling of metal equipment.

He looked back over his shoulder and waved the others to cover. Then, with Krung flanking him on one side and Tyme on the other, he crept slowly forward, carefully pushing the branches of the thorny bushes aside until they were closer to the source of the noise. Through gaps in the foliage, Fetterman could see soldiers moving. He caught glimpses of NVA uniforms and VC black pajamas. And he saw a couple of AK-47s slung on the shoulders of the soldiers. He looked right and left and then signaled for Krung and Tyme to back up so they could return to where the others waited.

With the Tai in a loose circle around Fetterman, Krung and Tyme for security, they held a hasty whispered conference. Fetterman started it, saying, "I think we're up against the Ho Chi Minh Trail. We're going to have to cross it."

"I don't like having a major enemy supply line behind us," commented Tyme.

"I don't, either, Boom-Boom, but to complete the mission there's no choice. The enemy camp is on the other side of it."

"So how do we get across the Trail without the VC knowing we're here?"

"That, my boy, is the problem. We'll have to cross in the dark, probably extremely early in the morning. Right now I suggest we take the opportunity to eat and get some sleep. I think we're going to have to put in some long hours during the next few days."

At 3:00 a.m., when there was little noise along the Trail, no sound from the jungle and everything was at a low ebb, Fetterman motioned Tyme, Krung and the Tai forward. They crawled carefully, quietly, edging their way toward the Ho Chi Minh Trail.

When they finally reached it, Fetterman was surprised. Although he'd heard about the Ho Chi Minh Trail since he'd arrived in Vietnam, he had thought it was something like a normal jungle trail. Maybe a little wider than most, better defined than most, but a trail nonetheless.

But what he was looking at was anything but a trail. From the edge of the jungle, where he now crouched, to the other side was nearly twenty meters. Looking up, he could see the jungle had been carved out under the triple canopy. The vegetation of the jungle came right to the edge of the Trail, but there it was cut back, as if the mowing machines used by the highway departments in the States had been used to retard the growth. There didn't seem to be a break in the cover, and everything on the ground must have been invisible from the air.

The surface of the Trail looked almost like concrete. He reached out and touched it and realized that it was compressed earth and pea gravel. And it was smooth. There were no potholes or roots sticking up through it. It was as well maintained and functional as some of the new interstate highways being built back in the World.

He sent Tyme to scout along the Trail to the north and Krung to the south. Then he inched forward so that he could survey more of the Trail. The section he could see was straight for a hundred meters in either direction. The only thing missing were the cars and the white lines down the center. This wasn't a trail. It was a goddamn highway.

Both Tyme and Krung returned quickly and reported that they had seen and heard nothing. That done, he had Krung and one of the Tai set up the light machine gun so that it could cover them as they ran across the Trail. Fetterman fell back and to the right to protect the machine gun's flank. When he was set, he signaled Tyme with a single short whistle.

Tyme stepped cautiously onto the Ho Chi Minh Trail. He heard the pea gravel crunch under his jungle boot. It sounded incredibly loud in the quiet of the night. He sprinted across the Trail, stopping short because he didn't want to dive into the jungle on the other side. He pushed the foliage out of the way, stepped over a rotting log and crouched, turning so he could watch as the Tai followed.

When they were in position, their light machine gun covering the Trail as Krung's had on the other side, Tyme whistled once, signaling Fetterman. Together with Krung and the remaining Tai, Fetterman crossed and then had them move into the jungle.

Fetterman kept them moving until it was nearly dawn. Then he began searching for a place to hole up. Again he tried to find a place that wasn't likely. He dismissed a cave that had a good source of water: if push came to shove, he didn't want to be trapped inside. He did, however, have each of the men fill their empty canteens from the cold, clear stream and add halazone tablets to purify the water.

A few minutes later he found a more suitable site. It lacked a source of water, but made up for it with a good view of the surrounding territory. Fetterman spread the men out so that they could get some rest and eat another cold meal. They rotated the security so that everyone had a chance for some uninterrupted sleep.

Fetterman, again tired of the cold meals that had no taste, opened the single flat tin of peanut butter and crackers that he had packed. The peanut butter was of the poorest quality. There was a layer of amber-colored oil on top of peanut butter that was so hard he couldn't stir it up. If they hadn't been in Cambodia, he would have tried to heat it. Instead, he just ate the crackers and buried the tin.

They passed the heat of the afternoon lying quietly in the shade of the bushes and palms of the jungle. Even though they weren't exerting themselves, they were uncomfortable, sweating heavily. Late in the day clouds blew in, blotting out the sun. The clouds brought a breeze, making things a little more bearable.

When it had been dark for over an hour, they moved out again, walking slowly, listening to the sounds of the jungle around them. The normal sounds of the jungle at night. Animals scrambling through the underbrush or up the trees to avoid predators. Insects announcing the temperature with chirps or their presence with buzzing.

Near midnight a new sound penetrated the jungle. At first it was no more than a quiet hum that sounded like a persistent insect, but as they moved toward it, it became louder and steadier until it changed to the rhythm of machinery. Then, through the thick jungle trees, Fetterman saw a point of light. An electrical beacon that led him and his patrol straight to the enemy compound. Fetterman hoped they weren't going in like moths, blinded by the light and careless of the dark. Men died that way.

They circled the base slowly, staying a klick or more away from it, looking for the best place to set up and observe the activity inside camp. By five they had found exactly what they wanted, a place on a rise that was shielded by thick undergrowth for their protection, but gave Fetterman and Tyme an unobstructed view. Krung and the Tai were now scattered around the jungle, protecting the position taken by Fetterman and Tyme.

As the sun broke through the low-hanging clouds, Fetterman and Tyme saw a huge, almost circular compound that boasted six long barracks at the northern edge. Ten or twelve smaller buildings, possibly officers' quarters, were near them. Nearby were the motor pool, a generator shed and the mess hall. What Fetterman took to be the headquarters stood in the center.

He glanced at Tyme as the younger man shrugged off his knapsack and began unwrapping the automatic ranging sniperscope, which he had almost lovingly packed. Tyme set it carefully on top of his M-14 and tightened the mounting screws. When he finished, he sighted on a number of objects, just to get the feel of the weapon again.

Then he checked the magazine he and Fetterman had prepared. They had loaded the rounds themselves using 43.2 grains of 4064 powder. That was a little hotter than desirable, but was needed because of the range from which they were operating. They had also used a 168-grain boattail hollowpoint slug. The magazine contained twelve of the special bullets.

Tyme would have preferred to take a practice shot or two, just to be on the safe side, but he would have one chance, possibly two if he could get the second shot off fast enough, and that would be it. He would have to trust his calculations made at the camp a week earlier and hope that nothing had jarred the scope sufficiently to throw off the precision of its rangings.

He looked back at Fetterman and said, "It's up to our Chinese guy now."

6

NORTH OF SVAY RIENG, SEVENTEEN KLICKS INSIDE CAMBODIA

Fetterman lay in the short grass of the rise, hidden among the bushes and trees, his binoculars to his eyes as he scanned the enemy base a klick away.

Tyme, who had been observing the camp through the ART scope, whispered to Fetterman, "This is no good. The range is too great in this light. We're going to have to get closer."

"Sun'll burn off the haze quickly," responded Fetterman.

Tyme shook his head. "We need to get closer."

Fetterman crawled backward and found Krung, who was watching the downslope side of the rise. He formed Krung and the Tai into a rear guard and told Krung they were to move closer to the enemy camp. Krung's job was to make sure the jungle directly behind them was clear of VC.

That done, Fetterman eased forward again to find Tyme, and the two of them began to slowly work their way through the thick jungle undergrowth, careful not to disturb the birds and monkeys overhead in the trees.

It took them nearly three hours to move to within seven hundred meters of the camp before halting again. Fetterman used his binoculars to watch the activities slightly below them. From one of the small hootches on the north side of the camp near the long barracks, two men exited. One of them wore the bright-green uniform of an NVA officer, and the other wore the khaki of a Chinese officer.

As the two men walked slowly toward the two-story headquarters, Fetterman scanned the camp looking for other Chinese. He turned his attention back to the NVA and Chinese, who had stopped while the NVA officer picked up something that had been lying on the ground. He examined it momentarily and then tossed it with an underhand motion toward the wire.

Three men and a woman, all wearing the deep green of NVA enlisted personnel, left one of the square buildings as the two men passed it. There was a flurry of saluting as the two groups passed one another.

"That our man?" asked Tyme, who had been tracking the two men through his scope.

"I'm not sure," said Fetterman. "I only saw him the one time, and that was from the rear as he was running for Cambodia. Build seems to be right."

Tyme pointed to the right and said, "There's a slight depression over there. Be good cover for us."

Fetterman nodded his agreement, and the two men crawled to the new position. Tyme pulled a rotting log around slightly so that it would provide support for his weapon. With his combat knife he dug out some of the wood to give his rifle a firm base. He checked the markings on the scope and the rifle a final time to make sure they were still properly aligned and then settled down to wait.

For several hours they watched the enemy camp. The only Chinese officer they saw had left the headquarters building and walked toward a square structure that sat in a cluster of radio antennae. Fetterman studied the man as well as he could, convincing himself this was the Chinese officer they had come after. From the rear he looked the same. Broad, square shoulders and a long torso.

An hour later the man left the radio shack and began to walk slowly across the compound toward the barracks. There was no one with him.

The conditions were almost perfect. It was late in the afternoon, and the target was alone. Tyme asked, ''Do we take him?''

Fetterman was staring through his binoculars, watching the man walk, trying to see something that he recognized from the brief glimpse he had had of the Chinese on the morning after they'd found the remains of the Vietnamese patrol. There was so much that he thought he recognized, but it was so little to go on.

''Yeah. Take him,'' said Fetterman finally.

Tyme slipped the safety on his weapon and worked the bolt, ejecting a good round. He wanted to make sure he had a round chambered properly. He set the cross hairs on the back of the Chinese officer, tracking him for a moment, trying to compute the speed the man was walking. He then shifted the weapon, leading the Chinese by nearly four feet because of the extreme range. He took a deep breath, let it out, took another and let it half out. He squeezed the trigger slowly, applying pressure until the weapon almost fired itself.

The crash of the shot was apparently unheard by anyone. For what seemed like several seconds the Chinese officer walked on toward his hootch. Tyme had already fired a second round and was now watching the scene below him although he knew he should be up and running.

The Chinese officer took the first shot in the shoulder. He staggered under the impact, but didn't fall. Stunned by the sudden pain, he reached back, as if trying to brush away an annoying insect.

Having seen the first round hit, Tyme should have gotten to his feet, but he stayed, mesmerized by what he saw. The second bullet hit the officer in the middle of his back. The 168-grain slug, slowed by the bone and tissue it hit, still had the power to pierce the man's chest and exit through one of his ribs. Blood and bone spattered the ground in front of him. With the muscle control suddenly gone from his legs, the Chinese crumpled to the ground, blood spreading under his shirt.

As soon as he saw the first round hit, Fetterman stored his binoculars and got to his knees. He waited for a moment, watching Tyme, and then said, ''Let's get the fuck out of here.''

They worked their way back up the hill toward the Tai, who were watching the VC base for signs of pursuit.

As soon as the patrol had put the hill between themselves and the camp, Fetterman grabbed the handset of the PRC-10 and keyed it long enough to announce, "We have sighted Crinshaw's body."

"Why aren't the VC responding? They should be after us by now," Tyme asked.

"They haven't figured it out yet," said Fetterman, pointing to the east so that Krung would take the point.

As they began their escape through the jungle, there was a wavering scream of a siren from the camp. Fetterman said, "Now they've figured it out!"

FOUR KLICKS FROM the Cambodian border, Gerber and one hundred and five men from the Tai strike company were moving north to south on a preplanned course. They had been out for just over twenty-four hours, and during that time they had seen two NVA soldiers who had escaped into the jungle and one VC who hadn't. They had buried the body in a shallow grave, keeping the weapon as proof of the KIA for Crinshaw.

The first night they had set up a perimeter without any real trouble. Around midnight two mortar rounds had landed in the center of the laager, doing no damage and causing no casualties.

Gerber immediately ordered out a counter-mortar patrol, but they found nothing in their two-hour search. There were no more incoming rounds, and the men, on a half alert, passed the night quietly.

The next day they were awake early and had a fairly substantial field breakfast. Gerber allowed the men to have fires to heat their rations. The Tai boiled water for their rice. The Special Forces NCOs cooked the scrambled eggs and ham from C-ration boxes. Sam Anderson, the newest member of the team, had a perverse taste for the ham and lima beans, which no one else liked. All the Americans shared the canned bread and jam, and topped off the breakfast with canned pears.

As the sun climbed higher, heating the jungle, they began their patrol. The line of march was generally to the south, but angling toward the border. Twice American aircraft flew overhead, and one made a close pass, as if to identify the men in the column as friend or foe.

It was late afternoon when Gerber reached the first of the rendezvous points. He spread two platoons of the strike company along a trail through the trees in an L-shaped ambush. The third platoon was scattered behind it as perimeter security that could be quickly organized into a relief force. Then all he could do was wait for Fetterman and his patrol.

FOR MORE THAN TWO HOURS Fetterman and his men had been rushing through the jungle. They hadn't heard any VC or NVA behind them, but they would certainly be there. Now they were approaching the Ho Chi Minh Trail, and if they couldn't cross it quickly, the enemy would have a chance to close the gap between them.

Fetterman came up to Krung, who was lying on the ground at the edge of the trees looking out across the expanse of compressed earth and pea gravel. Crouching, Fetterman could see they were in trouble. The traffic was heavy for so late in the day.

Most of it was bicycles, but no one was riding them. They were all being pushed. The handlebars had a long pole tied to them so that the VC walking beside the bike could steer. Another pole stuck up where the seat should have been so the porter would have a way to balance the load. The frame supported huge sacks of supplies or equipment. Some of it was rice and some was mortar rounds; some of it couldn't be easily identified.

Surprisingly, there were two trucks. One of them was barely keeping up with the foot traffic. The other was weaving in and out of the bicycles.

There were also soldiers, both male and female, moving along the Trail. Each carried a personal weapon. Most of them had SKSs, but some carried the AK-47 assault rifle.

Fetterman eased forward so that he could look farther to the north. He couldn't see a break in the formation, and he cursed quietly to himself. There wasn't going to be an easy, quick way to cross, and he didn't like the idea of his patrol being trapped between the Trail and their pursuers.

Fetterman crawled away from Krung to where Tyme waited. He put his lips close to Tyme's ear and said, "We'll have to move to the south, paralleling the Trail, and hope that the traffic breaks soon."

"Is that likely?"

"Hell, I don't know. But right now it's all we have, and we don't have time to debate it."

Tyme nodded and turned so that he could alert the others. Once again Krung was sent out as the point. They moved quickly and quietly. Behind them there was no sign of their pursuit.

As the daylight faded, the traffic began to thin. Some of the men and women halted in the rest areas scattered along the Trail. Others dropped off to sit on the side, resting and eating their evening meal. Fetterman and his patrol kept edging along, looking for a place where they could cross without alerting Charlie. He knew the enemy from the camp had to be close, and now there was more enemy in front of him. Running to the south was gaining him almost nothing.

Fetterman scattered his men through the jungle, three of the Tai watching their rear in case the VC managed to catch up, while he, Tyme and Krung spread out to watch the Trail. For ten minutes no one new appeared. All he could see was three NVA soldiers who had stopped by the side to eat supper. If it hadn't been for them, crossing would have been almost simple.

Fetterman decided he couldn't wait any longer. He crawled to where Tyme was hiding under a large bush, watching a small green snake trying to sneak up on a rodent that was already dead.

Fetterman pointed at the ground in front of him, telling Tyme to stay still, then moved off to bring Krung over. When he had them together, he said, "We're going to have to take out those three guys."

Krung grinned at the American master sergeant.

"We're fortunate," said Fetterman, "that all of them have taken up positions on our side of the Trail. We'll take ten minutes to get ready, then we'll hit the targets at the same time, using our knives.

That done, we'll cross immediately, taking our rear guard with us. We'll do it in one mass gaggle. Questions?"

"Shouldn't we cross one at a time as the manual says?" asked Tyme.

"Shit, Justin. Forget the fucking manual. It's more important to get us across," said Fetterman. "Krung, you take the guy farthest from us. Tyme, you take the one closest, and I'll take the other. When you've killed your man, fall back to here. Anything else?" When no one said anything, Fetterman added, "Then we go ten minutes from right . . . now."

Tyme was in position in less than seven. He had worked his way silently through the jungle behind his target, taking each step carefully, rolling his foot from heel to toe slowly so that he didn't snap a twig or rustle the decaying vegetation. He took each breath slowly, rhythmically, forcing himself to be calm. As he lowered himself to the jungle floor and crept closer to his target, he kept his mind on his task. All of his senses were working overtime watching the jungle so that he didn't disturb the animals that might be near.

When he was less than a yard away, he stopped and rocked back so that he was on the balls of his feet, ready to spring. He slowly pulled his Randall combat knife from its sheath, gently wiping the blade on the sleeve of his sweat-soaked jungle fatigues as he waited, his eyes shifting back and forth from his watch to his target.

When the second hand reached the twelve, Tyme leaned forward, reaching for the enemy soldier, who was hunched over his last meal. He stole a glance right and left, but saw neither Krung nor Fetterman.

Without waiting for any kind of sign, Tyme sprang ahead, grabbed the enemy's chin, lifted and sliced neatly through the throat. He heard the whisper of razor-sharp steel on the tender flesh of the neck and felt the warm blood gush over his hand.

As he pulled the head back, the soldier's helmet fell off, revealing long, jet-black hair. Tyme looked into the soldier's eyes with growing horror. He had just slit the throat of a young woman. His knife paused in midair before he delivered the thrust up under the breastbone so that he could pierce the woman's heart, finishing the job.

Her dark-brown eyes held his for just an instant, then clouded over. She kicked her legs out spasmodically, drumming her heels on the packed earth of the Ho Chi Minh Trail. She died a second later, Tyme's knife still hovering over her chest.

Tyme moved slowly, as if he had to think out each step before he took it. He dragged the body into the bush, picked up her pith helmet and tossed it in after her and then stood staring at the blood that stained the front of her uniform. He kept his eyes away from the gaping wound in her throat.

Fetterman touched his shoulder and asked, "You okay?"

"It was a woman," Tyme said, shaking his head.

Fetterman thought for a moment before replying. Tyme was obviously upset, but there was no opportunity to worry about it now. "So what?" said Fetterman, shrugging his shoulders. "She was an enemy soldier."

Before either man could say anything more, Krung ran up and said, "VC!"

Fetterman turned and saw a single enemy soldier approaching from the north. The VC saw them and grabbed for the stock of his weapon, trying to swing it around so that he could fire. Fetterman reacted quickly: he dropped to one knee, raised his M-1 carbine and squeezed off a single shot before the VC could fire. The round hit the enemy in the face, exploding out the back of his head, and he collapsed to the Trail.

"That tears it," said Fetterman, "we have got to move now!"

7

NEAR THE CAMBODIAN BORDER, SOUTH OF THE PARROT'S BEAK

It was almost dusk when Gerber reached the last of the rendezvous points. He deployed the strikers in three platoons, each watching a section of the border. Gerber was in command of the center section so that he could take charge of either the right or left flank if he had to. Kepler headed up the unit closest to Cambodia. It was spread on-line just inside the trees and facing a series of rice fields that spread out into Cambodia, giving him a clear view for three or four klicks. Behind him, deeper in the trees, Sam Anderson commanded the third platoon. He guarded the left flank and the rear. The remainder of the force formed a circle inside the tree line that could be used as a reserve or blocking force, whatever the situation demanded.

All they had to do was wait until morning, hoping that Fetterman and his tiny group made it to them by then. If not, Gerber would begin to move back along his original line of march, holding at each of the previous rendezvous points. He would keep circling until Fetterman arrived, or until it became obvious that he wasn't going to make it.

When the evening meal had been eaten and the remains of the food and cans had been buried under three feet of jungle dirt and rotted vegetation, Gerber moved among the men quietly, advising them of their jobs for the night. He would leave one man in three awake until midnight, then two men in three. And they would wait.

FETTERMAN AND HIS PATROL dashed across the Ho Chi Minh Trail and nearly leaped into the jungle. There was a shout behind them and a burst of fire from an automatic weapon. But they plunged onward, heading east, trying to run away from the Trail and the men who were now chasing them.

Krung sprinted ahead, taking the point without being told, but in the fading light of the setting sun he had to slow down. The spreading blackness was beginning to mask the pitfalls.

There was more shouting in Vietnamese and more firing. Fetterman dived for cover, nearly tripping over one of the Tai. Tyme was crouched beside a large palm, his scoped M-14 pointing back the way they had come.

"On your feet," Fetterman ordered. "Krung, get back on the point. Move it! We stay here, we die!"

As they got up and began to run again, firing erupted all around them, but it seemed poorly directed. None of the rounds was hitting anything near them, and Fetterman figured the VC were trying a recon by fire to see if they could induce Fetterman and his patrol to shoot back.

Instead of shooting they ran. They ran as fast as the jungle would let them. One of the Tai stumbled and cried out, falling to his face. Fetterman grabbed him under the arm, jerking the man to his feet.

"You hurt?" he asked. When the man failed to respond, he ordered, "Move it. Run!"

But Fetterman knew that headlong flight wasn't the best way for a military unit to retreat. It might put distance between the enemy and the patrol, but it gained nothing in the long run. He knew they had to do something to slow the enemy's pursuit, but at the moment there wasn't much he could do. His patrol was getting scattered throughout the jungle, the gaps among the men widening as they fled the VC.

He caught up to Krung on the bank of a shallow stream. Tyme was leaning against the trunk of a palm, breathing rapidly and watching the trail behind them.

"What now?" he said, gasping.

"Ambush," said Fetterman. "We cross the stream and ambush them."

With that he stepped into the center of the stream and leaped up on the other bank. He disappeared into the jungle as the men of the patrol followed him. He pointed out positions to each soldier, telling him to fire only when he had a good target and warning that no one was to shoot until Sergeant Tyme did. He set them in two lines, one behind the other. The first, with Tyme in the middle, was to surprise the enemy with a fusillade and then fall back, allowing the VC to cross the stream. Then the second would open fire, causing more casualties and therefore making the VC more cautious in their pursuit.

The men waited tensely, oblivious to the staggering humidity and the clouds of mosquitoes that descended on them when they stopped moving. For a moment everything around them was quiet, and then they heard a faint sound coming from the jungle in front of them, the noise of a branch sweeping across the canvas of a VC backpack.

Fetterman wanted to whisper to the men to be patient, to wait for the enemy. But he didn't dare move. All he could do was sit tight, letting the sweat drip from under his helmet and run down his face, making his skin itch.

The VC appeared suddenly, rising out of the trees on the other side of the stream. Tyme tossed the grenade he had been clutching, and when it exploded, the Tai with him opened fire. Two of the enemy fell, one into the stream, but the others did not retreat. They attacked, leaping the creek to land among Tyme and his men.

Tyme got to his knees as one of the VC jumped up in front of him. The American swung the butt of his rifle upward in a low arc so that it hit the man in the crotch. There was a shriek like tires on concrete as the man collapsed. Tyme shot him in the face and turned in time to see another enemy soldier. He thrust with his rifle, trying a vertical butt stroke, but the VC countered, his AK connecting with the ART scope mounted on Tyme's rifle, shattering it.

Tyme ducked, kicking out with his foot and hitting the enemy in the knee, snapping it. As the man fell, Tyme fired twice.

Then the shooting all around him tapered, and over the noise he heard Fetterman shouting in English and French for them to fall back. Tyme glanced to the right and saw one of the Tai struggling with a VC. In a moment he was on them and hit the enemy in the back of the head with his rifle butt. As the Vietcong dropped, the Tai shot him. Then, backing up, firing into the trees near the stream, Tyme and the Tai retreated.

They passed Fetterman and Krung, who waited until their men were clear and then opened fire. Fetterman didn't have a target, and he just pumped out rounds to slow the enemy advance. He emptied a magazine, dropped it from the weapon and jammed a new one home, firing it single shot, almost as fast as he could pull the trigger.

Finally he turned to run, Krung right beside him. It was almost completely dark, and Fetterman could barely make out the shapes of Tyme and his men in front of him. He tried to close the distance, gaining a little.

They headed east, away from the Ho Chi Minh Trail and the enemy soldiers. They ran until their hearts pounded and their lungs ached. They ran until each step was a test of will. They would run a hundred steps and walk fifty and run a hundred more. They ran until they were sure they were out of Cambodia, until they could hear nothing but the sounds of their own breathing and the pounding of their own hearts in their chests.

Then they stopped. Stopped to rest because they could not go farther. And even then Fetterman put out security. Two men in front of the patrol to look for the enemy and two behind it in case the VC were closer than he suspected. Then Fetterman dropped to the ground and pulled his canteen, drinking deeply and spitting, trying to get the cotton out of his mouth. Finally he took a measured swallow and felt it spread in his stomach. He took another and waited, his breathing slowing.

Fetterman then took out his map, covered himself with the poncho liner, making sure the edges touched the ground all around, and pulled his flashlight. He studied the map for a few minutes, looking for landmarks he might have passed. Once he switched off the light, stood and studied the black landscape around him. He looked at the stream and the swamps on the far side of it. Behind him was the stretch of jungle they had just traveled through. He tried to think back, starting with the location of the second VC camp, their direction of travel, the point where they reached the Ho Chi Minh Trail and the stream where they had ambushed the VC.

He thought he knew where they were and believed he could find Gerber and the patrols, if Gerber had followed the schedule established in the camp. Just then he heard one of the men run up.

"VC. Beaucoup VC."

"Where?"

The man turned and pointed in the direction they had come from. "There. Close."

Fetterman's first instinct was to run again, just as they had earlier. Then he thought about it. Am ambush was no good because it would allow the enemy to catch up. Gerber and his men should be only four or five klicks away to the north. He could try to lure the VC into an ambush there. But he had to be careful because he couldn't just run up to Gerber's patrol in the dark. He had to let the VC do that.

He rounded up his men and told Tyme to take the point. He told him to run north about three klicks and stop. Fetterman would have to identify their location more precisely then.

For forty minutes they ran, first through the jungle, then along paddy dikes. They crossed open fields, running even faster to get out of the clearings before the VC saw them. They ran by a farmer's hootch with a single lantern light in the window. As they entered the trees again, they heard a burst of fire from an automatic weapon. Fetterman figured it was the VC shooting at the light, and that put them about three minutes back.

Suddenly Tyme stopped. Fetterman, who had been the rear guard, slid to a halt, but didn't need to ask what the problem was. They were on the edge of a gigantic open area where the jungle gave way to paddies and swamp. A half klick away was another tree line, and Fetterman was sure that Gerber and the strikers were there.

Silently Fetterman moved his men along, keeping to the cover of the trees near the edge of the rice fields. They came to a bend in the tree line so that they could look over open fields, back at the jungle where they had been. Fetterman stopped his men, using the available cover of bushes, palms and the eighteen-inch paddy dikes. He told each of the men to wait for him to fire first and then to crank out the rounds as fast as they could.

Once they were in position, Fetterman took the tiny earpiece from the PRC-10 he had been carrying and keyed the mike. "Zulu Six. Zulu Six. This Zulu Rover, over."

A second later a voice boomed back, "Rover, this is Six. Go."

Fetterman turned down the volume and reported, "Six, be advised that we are in the vicinity."

"Acknowledged."

Then there was nothing to do but wait. Fetterman switched magazines in his M-1 carbine, substituting one that contained tracers. He wanted Gerber's men to see the source of his firing, and the ruby tracers would identify him and his people. The VC used white and green tracers.

Minutes slipped by and nothing happened. Fetterman had just begun to wonder if he'd lost the enemy with his rapid trip through the jungle when, outlined in the paddies in front of him, he saw something moving. A dark-gray shape was silhouetted against the lighter gray of the sky and the horizon. The lone shape was soon joined by a second and a third, until there were fifteen or twenty men in the open, all moving slowly forward.

Fetterman muttered, "Wait for it. Wait for it. Let them get away from the protection of the trees."

As the men of the enemy patrol pulled away from the trees, Fetterman set his chin on the butt of his rifle so that he was looking over the sights on the barrel in the best traditions of U.S. Army night-fire training. It allowed him to aim the weapon without restricting his vision in the sights.

When he had the M-1 lined up, he pulled the trigger and watched the tracer stream toward the enemy. The others with him opened fire on cue, until the night was filled with the rattle of small arms, the flashes of the muzzles and the bouncing tracers as they struck the ground.

Two of the VC went down quickly, and the other dived for cover behind the paddy dikes. One or two fired back, their rounds wide.

But that was enough to give away their position to Gerber's men, and they began raking the paddies with devastating fire. There was the pop of an M-79 grenade launcher, followed by an explosion in the paddy.

Slowly the shooting tapered off. Then, suddenly, five of the VC stood up and threw Chicom grenades. As they detonated, all the VC were up and running, trying to gain the safety of the jungle behind them.

Fetterman had been waiting for that. He opened fire again, pulling the trigger as fast as he could. The men with him joined in, shooting at the fleeing shapes, watching them fall. The jungle where Gerber's men hid seemed to erupt, the muzzle flashes sparkling in the dark. The red tracers danced across the paddies, some of them bouncing through the night.

At that moment a parachute exploded into brilliance, lighting the ground in a wavering yellowish glow that pinned the VC against the trees. With targets plainly visible, the machine gunners opened fire with their M-60s.

And then the targets were gone. Fading into the jungle or falling into the paddies. The firing ceased as the flare burned itself out. A second one went off, but it caught no one in the open. After that there were only a few random shots as someone fired at the shadows.

There was a crash of thunder overhead that sounded like someone had channeled it into a single, thin line. It rattled teeth before it blossomed into fire in the paddies in front of them, momentarily lighting the ground with mushrooming flame. A second shell exploded closer to the trees, and the third dropped in the jungle at the edge of the clearing.

Six quick explosions followed, flashing briefly as the rounds detonated, throwing shrapnel through the air like a thousand darts that could rip a man apart. There was a brief calm then another six rained in as the American artillery men in one of the fire-support bases got the rhythm, and then silence.

When the firing stopped, Tyme crawled to Fetterman and asked, "What now?"

"We keep our eyes open and wait for morning. Then we join the captain."

At dawn Fetterman used the radio to announce that he was coming in and for the men to hold fire. He was told to throw smoke and then to come ahead. Gerber was standing with a small group of strikers when Fetterman appeared out of the trees and walked across a short section of the paddies.

Fetterman saw the captain, broke out of the group and said, "We've succeeded with Crinshaw's body. The man is down."

"Fine," responded Gerber. He wanted to say more, but it wasn't the time nor the place to get into a long conversation. It was possible that the VC would have left a sniper.

He turned to Anderson and said, "Cat, I'd like a patrol to sweep across the paddies and see what we might have hit last night."

"Excuse me, Captain," said Fetterman, "but I'd like to take that patrol."

"Any particular reason?"

"Yes, sir. Those guys chased my butt all the way from the Ho Chi Minh Trail, and I would like to get a look at them."

"Thought your guys would like a rest," said Gerber.

"I'll take part of the platoon here. And Boom-Boom."

"Take three squads. Hurry it up because we'll want to get out of here and head back to the camp."

"Yes, sir." Fetterman turned, saw two of the squad leaders and said to them, "Get your men up and on-line to sweep through the paddies." He spotted a third and gave him the same instructions so that he had thirty-six men standing side by side just inside the tree line. Fetterman took his position in the center and sent Tyme out of anchor the left side of the line. On his order they all stepped into the open, then spread out until there were five or six feet between each of them as they moved forward.

They stayed off the paddy dikes and walked through the paddies instead. Most were dry, having been drained after the farmers had harvested the crop.

As they approached the area the VC had defended the night before, they saw the first body. It was lying facedown, the helmet touching the dirt in front and hiding the head. There were no obvious signs of injury except for the ragged rust stain on the ground. As the men walked up, Fetterman stopped long enough to pick up the weapon and check the body. There was a single bullet hole in the face. A neat, round hole, the edges slightly bruised, just below the right eye. The helmet had hidden the real damage. The exit wound. A fist-sized chunk of the skull was gone. When Fetterman kicked the helmet out of the way, he could see the gray brain matter that had been jellied by the impact of the bullet.

Farther on they came to the area the artillery had hit. They couldn't tell how many of the VC had been killed there because they could only find tiny pieces of bodies. A finger on the side of a dike, a foot still in the boot, most of one arm and some of the shoulder muscle, a single undamaged lung. Adding all the pieces together would almost add up to one man, but Fetterman knew that the artillery had probably landed among nine or ten people to leave the evidence he was finding.

At the tree line they found another body that was nearly whole. The cloth of the uniform was burned by the white phosphorus of the marking rounds the artillery had used. Most of the equipment was gone, taken by the survivors.

In the forest they found a couple of blood trails, indicating there were some wounded who had managed to escape the artillery fire. Standard procedure was to follow the trails until a dead soldier was found or the blood vanished. Fetterman didn't have the time. He'd seen what he wanted to, and now he turned the men around and headed them back to the main body of the patrol. It was time to return to the camp.

The trip back to the base was uneventful. Rather than follow the patrol pattern that had been laid out days before, Gerber turned the patrol directly to the east, cutting across rice fields and through fingers of jungle that reached out to break up the open ground.

Gerber had requested airlift support, but it was denied in Saigon because of other priorities. Since they were no longer in contact and had no casualties, they would have to walk.

By three o'clock that afternoon they were working their way through the perimeter wire. Bromhead and Bocker met them at the gate and helped organize the cleanup detail, weapon check, equipment inspection and storing of the extra ammo in the bunker. Then the strikers were released for the rest of the day.

As soon as he could get close to Bromhead, Gerber asked, "When did all our company leave?"

"Crinshaw and his boys left early this morning. The Vietnamese general decided that he didn't like the way we roughed it out here. No women. No good food. No women. No entertainment. And no women. He pulled out yesterday. His people found the dead rangers and worked it so that an Army Aviation shit hook flew the bodies out. I guess they were pretty ripe."

"What about Robin Morrow?"

"She's still looking for the story to end all stories. She got to Crinshaw at one point, and he made sure to tell me that she was to get anything she wanted. Within reason, of course."

Gerber shook his head. "I'm surprised by that. You'd think Crinshaw would have a fit about a woman here."

"The media, Captain," Bromhead reminded him. "She has a public forum from which to relate our general's daring exploits. He's not about to do anything to piss her off. Especially since she conned him into signing that order authorizing her visit in the first place."

"Yeah, that's right." Gerber thought for a moment and then said, "I want you to take out a patrol, say ten, twelve men, and make a wide sweep south of the camp. Look for signs of the VC moving in close. But organize it so that you're back by dusk. I don't want anyone outside the wire tonight."

"Any reason you want me back by dusk?" he asked.

"Only that we've kept everyone up for a couple of days, and it's time to stand down for a day or two. If you don't find anything around us, that is."

"Yes, sir. I'd like to take Bocker with me. He seems to get stuck here all the time."

Gerber nodded. "Have Anderson take over the radio watch. Check with me before you move out."

As Bromhead headed for the commo bunker, Gerber spotted Fetterman sitting on the short sandbagged wall near the south gate unlacing his boot. As Gerber approached him, he said, "You and I should get together with Kepler and tell him about the patrol."

"I had the same thought, sir. Besides, I want to tell him about the Ho Chi Minh Trail. That thing is unbelievable. Twenty, thirty yards wide and damn near paved."

"Well," said Gerber slowly, "we'll want to be careful what we say about the Trail. The only way you could have seen it was by being somewhere you weren't supposed to be."

Fetterman finished unlacing his boot and took it off. He held it upside down and shook some red dirt out of it. "I'll think of something. Maybe one of Kepler's trusted agents can report it."

"When you've finished here, find Kepler and report to me in my hootch. We'll go over all this then."

GERBER WAS WAITING for them when Fetterman knocked on the door. After he'd invited them in and told them to sit down, he picked a bottle of Beam's off the littered desk, pulled the cork and took a deep swallow. Then he handed the bottle to Fetterman, who did the same and passed it on to Kepler. Kepler gave it back to Gerber, who took another drink, corked the bottle and said, "That's smooth."

"Why don't you fill us in on the mission now," Gerber said as he sat down.

Fetterman nodded and began telling them about the trip to Cambodia. He stopped once to spread a map on the desk so that he could show them his routes of march, locations of the enemy camps, and the point on the Ho Chi Minh Trail that he crossed. He speculated on a couple of the infiltration routes, the points where the Trail disintegrated as it crossed the Cambodian border into Vietnam.

Sitting down again, he told of the shooting of the Chinese officer, the loads they had used and the distance from which the kill was made.

At that point Kepler stopped him and asked, "Are you sure you got the right guy? We never really got a good look at him, and you said Tyme made the shot from over seven hundred meters."

Fetterman didn't reply right away. It was true he had never seen the Chinese officer up close. But he had seen him as he ran for Cambodia and had seen him from nearly the same angle as he walked through the camp. Fetterman nodded once and then said confidently, "Yeah, I'm sure. It was the right guy."

"Okay," said Gerber, "Tony, you and Derek get together and work out that report on the Ho Chi Minh Trail. We'll have to be very careful with it." He didn't tell them that he would have to go to Saigon the next day to report the success of the mission to the CIA.

THIRTY MINUTES LATER Bromhead found Gerber still sitting in his hootch, his feet propped on a table and a can of beer in his hand. Bromhead, now in full field pack and carrying a full load of ammo, walked in.

"We're ready."

"Who all are you taking?"

"I've Bocker as senior NCO. Lieutenant Bao is going out with a couple of the Tai. Sergeant Tam and six of the Viets are going, too."

"Remember to be back by dusk. And check in by radio every hour."

"Yes, sir. Anything else?"

"Just be careful out there. Don't do anything stupid."

"I'll be careful."

Bromhead had his patrol at the south gate when Robin Morrow ran up, carrying her camera bag and wearing a field harness with a canteen and large bowie knife on it. She was wearing khaki pants, a khaki bush shirt and a large Australian bush hat.

"Say, Lieutenant," she said, "mind if I go along? Captain Gerber said that it was all right with him, if you didn't mind."

Bromhead hesitated. It didn't sound right to him, not after some of the negative things Gerber had said about the press. How the media were always searching for a good story, one that was visual, exciting and who the hell cared for the facts. Damn the facts if they got in the way. Still, she had Crinshaw's ear and doing everything to please her probably wouldn't upset the general, and that would make the captain happy.

"You sure that Captain Gerber said it was okay?"

She pointed over her shoulder toward Gerber's hootch. "You can ask him if you want," she said.

Bromhead looked at Bocker, who shrugged slightly and glanced at his watch. "Okay," said Bromhead. "You stay close to Sergeant Bocker and do whatever he says. We're not going to slow down or go easy to suit you. You have to keep up and listen to everything I say."

"No problem. You won't know I'm here."

Once they were through the gate and into the deep elephant grass outside the last strand of the perimeter wire, Bromhead picked up the pace. The patrol moved rapidly to the south, down toward the river where the ground turned soggy and spongy and where the footing was dangerous. Since he wasn't particularly interested in sneaking through the area, Bromhead didn't mind the splashing or the sucking pop they made as they walked through the mud. And when Morrow lost her balance, falling sideways into a water-filled shell crater, he laughed. To make it funnier, Bocker had leaped toward her to keep her from falling, but had only saved her camera bag.

"Welcome to Vietnam, Miss Morrow," Bromhead said as she stood in water up to her knees.

Bromhead quickly deployed the men of his tiny force for security. Bocker lifted Morrow to her feet and even produced a large OD towel from his pack so that she could try to dry off. That done, she tucked her blond hair up under her bush hat and said she was ready to go.

They continued, weaving in and out of the trees, bending the patrol to the west along the northern bank of the river. They moved quietly and cautiously now, realizing the VC might be anywhere.

Morrow danced off the trail a couple of times, trying to get pictures of men at war. She tried for sunlight streaming through the branches of the trees, with the leaves obscuring some of the foreground. She caught the men, both American and Vietnamese, silhouetted by shafts of sunlight, their weapons held at the ready. She photographed their faces, young, determined, staring ahead warily, their eyes searching for the enemy. She wanted close-ups that showed the strain on the young faces, dark circles under the eyes, the dirt smeared on their skin as they hunted the VC. She tried to capture the moment. Young men engaged in the greatest adventure of all—the hunt for other young men.

She took dozens of pictures. She photographed Bromhead as he talked on the radio carried by one of the Vietnamese strikers, the antenna held in his hand so that it bent over the top of his head. He didn't want it sticking up to signal his location to the enemy.

She got a picture of Bocker as he reached out to help one of the Vietnamese over a fallen palm. And one of the point men as he crouched near a large bush, pointing forward, as if spotting the enemy for the men at his rear.

Finally she stepped close to Bromhead and asked, "Can we stop for a minute? I want to change a lens."

"Miss Morrow, we're on a military mission here and not a goddamned walk through the park," Bromhead said sternly. But he called for a ten-minute break anyway.

While sitting with her back against a large teak tree, Bocker crouched near her and said, "Miss Morrow, I wouldn't go stepping off the trail and crashing through the jungle. Charlie has begun to booby-trap this area pretty heavily. You have to be careful or you'll blow yourself up."

She smiled up at him as she snapped her camera bag shut. "Don't worry about me, Sergeant. I'm being careful and I've been through that course on booby traps the Army gives its men when they arrive in Vietnam.

"Yes, ma'am. Except that class isn't as thorough as it could be. You'll find the VC are a little better at it than the Army gives them credit for. Thought I should say something because we don't want to lose you."

"I appreciate the concern," she said, getting to her feet. "But I do know what I'm doing."

Bocker didn't move. "I'm not sure that I know what I'm doing," he said, "and I've been here ten months. Charlie is tricky, and just when you think you've got it all figured out, he throws something new into the game. First he has small booby traps with trip wires across the trail. We learn to look for those, and he then begins to bury single bullets, their primers against a nail so that they detonate when you step on them, firing the round into your foot or, if you're unlucky, up the inside of your leg. You have to understand the nature of this war. It isn't just soldiers killing soldiers, but terrorists killing innocent people so that the government will capitulate."

"I understand that, Sergeant. I really do."

"Yes, ma'am," Bocker said, straightening. "Except that if you get hurt out here, it's going to cause the captain a great deal of trouble."

"Because I'm a woman?"

"No. Because you're a reporter."

Bromhead looked back at them. Seeing both of them on their feet, he said, "If you're ready, we'll get going."

There was only an hour of sunlight left when they found the VC. The point man stopped, dropped to the ground and waited for the rest of the patrol to catch up. Bromhead crawled forward and saw the solitary enemy soldier sitting with his back to a palm tree, his AK-47 leaning next to him.

Bocker, who had come up behind him, made a motion with his index finger across his throat, asking if they should kill the man.

Bromhead shook his head and pointed to the rear, indicating they should fall back the way they had come and then head straight for the camp. They had the information they wanted.

It was then they both heard the whirring pop of the motor-driven film advance of a 35 mm camera as it cranked through a dozen or more shots. Morrow had managed to get into a position where she could photograph the enemy, unconcerned about the noise her camera was making.

It looked, for an instant, as if they had gotten away with it. Then, springing suddenly to life, the VC rolled to his right, grabbed his rifle and started spraying bullets into the trees to the left of where Morrow was crouching.

Bromhead and the Tai striker who had been walking point both opened fire at the same time. The rounds from the striker hit the tree high, peeling bark and shredding leaves. Bromhead fired low, kicking dirt up in great brown splashes.

The VC rolled to his right, to the cover of a large bush. When he leaped to his feet, Bromhead hit him with rounds in the shoulder, the back and the hip. The Tai striker added to the damage, scoring hits in the lower back and both legs. The enemy dropped to the ground, rolled over a couple of times and then was still. There was a spray of blood where one bullet had exited his chest, severing an artery. A second spray, not as high as the first, followed and then a third that was little more than a bubbling. The VC was dead.

Bocker and two of the strikers ran forward, one of them grabbing the AK-47. Bocker checked the body and then pointed to the north and pumped his arm twice, telling the striker to hurry to the flank in case there were other VC.

Bromhead was on his feet immediately, and in three running strides was right in front of Morrow. She was looking more than a little shaken, but he was unable to stop himself from teeing off on her.

"You stupid, goddamned bitch," he yelled. "Just what the hell did you think you were doing?"

"I was just—"

"I don't give a fuck," interrupted Bromhead. "Of all the stupid stunts! We're out here trying to find the enemy and work around him, and you've got to go advertise that we're here. That guy could be the point for a whole company of VC for all we know. We've got to get out of here because of all the shooting. When Bocker returns, you stay with him. You stick to him like glue. You don't get more than three feet from him, and you keep your goddamned camera in the fucking case. You got that?"

Before she could answer, Bocker appeared at Bromhead's elbow. "He was alone, sir."

"Okay. Put someone on point and head them to the camp via direct. You take charge of Miss Morrow and see that she doesn't cause us any more trouble."

8

U.S. SPECIAL FORCES
CAMP A-555

As the returning patrol moved through the gate, Bromhead didn't suspect anything was wrong. He saw Gerber standing near the command bunker on the south wall only thirty feet away, but Gerber was often there when a patrol came in.

Just inside the gate Bromhead turned to face the patrol and gave the order for the men to clean their weapons. Then he looked back at Gerber.

"I'll want to see you in my hootch just as soon as you're free," Gerber said as he walked up to Bromhead.

Since it was said casually, Bromhead didn't think much about it. Gerber liked to hold a debriefing session after a patrol had returned. Then he looked into Gerber's eyes and saw that they were cold. He also noticed Gerber's mouth was set in a hard line, and suddenly Bromhead knew he had been wrong in letting Morrow go on the patrol. It took a physical effort to keep from moaning.

He turned the job of checking the patrol's weapons over to Bocker, and as soon as he entered Gerber's hootch he saw that he was in trouble. Gerber was sitting behind his desk, a stack of papers in front of him. "Just come in and close the door," was all he said.

As soon as Bromhead closed the door, Gerber was on his feet shouting, "What the fuck is going on in your mind?"

"Sir?" said Bromhead, sure now about why he was there.

"Don't play dumb with me," cautioned Gerber. "What kind of stupid play was that? Who told you to take a reporter on patrol? A female reporter at that."

"She said that she'd checked with you and that you'd said it was up to me."

Gerber collapsed into his chair, rubbed a hand through his hair and stared at his subordinate. "Oh, come on, Johnny. Don't be naive."

Bromhead unbuckled his web gear and sat down. The sweat stains on his jungle jacket and around his waist were apparent. "I guess I should have known that you didn't give her permission, but she did say for me to check it out with you and knew where you were. Besides, since she has Crinshaw's ear, I thought you might have figured it would be good for us. Crinshaw would appreciate us doing all we can for her."

"Just use your head. We don't need having a reporter killed, especially a woman." Gerber stopped and waved a hand through the air, as if to erase a slate. "Now, suppose you tell me what happened out there?"

ACROSS THE CAMP Fetterman and Tyme were in Fetterman's room, seeing just how fast they could empty a case of Coors beer. Tyme had just taken a large swig out of his and slammed the can on the tabletop.

Fetterman, showing the first signs of becoming drunk, was speaking with a precision that he normally ignored. "It was a damned good mission, Boom-Boom. A damned good one."

Tyme nodded, bobbing his head up and down in an exaggerated movement. His face was getting numb. "It's nice when things work out as well as they did."

Finally Fetterman said, "How are you doing?"

Tyme stared at the older man and then asked, "What do you mean?"

"I mean, how are you doing now that the mission is over? After what happened on the Ho Chi Minh Trail?"

Tyme stood up, drained his beer and walked over to the table where a half dozen full cans waited. He opened one with a bayonet, took a deep drink and then turned back to face Fetterman. Tyme wasn't sure how he felt about it. He hadn't really thought about it, and at the moment he wasn't sure he wanted to think about it.

"I thought we had gotten beyond worrying about what happened there," said Tyme.

"I don't think you have," responded Fetterman. "I saw the look on your face. We didn't have time to talk about it then, but we do now. And we've both had enough to drink to be able to talk about it."

"There's nothing to talk about, really."

"Come on, Boom-Boom. This is your old master sergeant. I know better than that."

"I was just surprised that it was a woman. That's all. I hadn't expected it."

"Justin. Talk to me."

Tyme took a deep breath. "Shit, she was so young."

"And carrying a weapon, along with supplies for the VC, so they could go on killing our people."

"But she thought she was safe. She wasn't paying any attention to what was happening. She didn't have a chance."

Fetterman finished his beer and crushed the tin can effortlessly with one hand. He tossed the remains into the corner of his hootch.

"Okay. I see we're not going to get anywhere on this, so I'll just throw out a few comments for general consumption.

"First of all, I know that you wouldn't have been greatly upset if the enemy soldier had been male. Even if he had been young. I suppose you can make a case for the woman not being on the Ho Chi Minh Trail because she wanted to be there. She was probably drafted and ordered to be there. But that's the same as it is for a lot of men who fight wars. If it were left to choice, very few men would ask to fight in a war. But no one ever gives you a choice.

"So we can ignore that argument. She was there, in the wrong place at the wrong time, and it's too bad that she had to die. But it was better than your dying in her place. Tough on Co Cong is just tough on Co Cong. The VC use lots of women. We've killed them before. We've seen their bodies lying on the—"

"That's not the point," said Tyme, interrupting.

"That's precisely the point my boy," said Fetterman. "She was an enemy soldier doing a job for the enemy."

"But I came up behind her and cut her throat."

"As we have a number of times."

"But those were men."

"So what? Fetterman nearly roared. "There is no difference between a man and a woman when she is wearing the enemy's uniform and carrying the enemy's rifle. You think she would hesitate if she had the chance to stick the knife into you?"

"No, but—"

"There are no buts about it. Killing an enemy soldier is killing an enemy soldier. If you're going to fight a war, people are going to die. If you're going to fight a war, you've got to be prepared to kill people. There is no other way to do it. If you're not prepared to kill people, then you have no business being here."

Tyme nodded, sipping his beer. "I know you're right. It still bothers me."

"Let me ask you a question," said Fetterman. "Are you bothered by the other people you've killed? Did you enjoy any of it?"

Tyme remembered the first man he had killed in hand-to-hand fighting. There had been an exhilaration about it. Not the killing, but the fact that he had been in a death struggle, and Tyme had won the fight. He didn't enjoy the act of killing. It was the contest. The fight to the death.

He regretted taking the human life. It was such a permanent act, something that, once done, could never be undone. But he had chosen to be a soldier, and with that choice came the territory. He wasn't sure that he had the right to take a human life, but somehow, by risking his own, it became almost right. If he were willing to put his own life on the line, then it became right for him to take the enemy's, and if he lost his, he had no complaints. He understood the rules.

Fetterman had been watching Tyme. Finally he said, "Justin, if you weren't bothered by this, I would worry about you. If you get to the point where you live for the killing, I'll transfer you out of here immediately. And if you hesitate to use your knife when you have to, I'll have you out of here on the next flight.

"We walk a fine line, and we have to stay on it. If we fall off, to either side, then we stop the game and go home. Sometimes in a box."

The private party of Fetterman and Tyme continued until 2:00 A.M. when Tyme, trying to stand up as he announced that he was going to his room to sleep, fell flat on his face. Fetterman nearly laughed himself sick, picked Tyme up to make sure he wasn't hurt, then went out to take a shower.

The water in the fifty-five-gallon drum perched on the roof of the shower had been refilled after sundown and was probably cold. It was a gravity-fed system and never got too warm with only the sun to heat it. But it was a shower, and that made it better than bathing in the river or in one of the water-filled shell craters. Fetterman didn't mind. He got wet, soaped and rinsed in less than three minutes. Then, feeling better than he had since he arrived in Vietnam, he went to bed.

It took only four minutes for him to fall asleep. But in that short time he felt the elation of a well-planned, well-executed mission. He couldn't ask for anything better. No one killed or wounded on his side, and the enemy had suffered.

IT WAS JUST AFTER TWO when Gerber walked into the team house. Morrow was sitting at one of the tables, her notebook in front of her next to a can of beer. Her eyes were closed and she was tapping her chin with a yellow pencil. Her damp hair hung straight down, and there was sweat on her forehead and upper lip. She had unbuttoned her khaki shirt to her navel.

"Thought everyone was asleep," said Gerber to announce himself.

Morrow jumped, as if she had been jabbed, and snapped, "Don't do that. You scared me to death."

"Sorry," he said. He turned to the coffeepot, but it was empty. He stepped to the refrigerator and pulled it open. A lone can of beer sat in it, but when he picked it up, he discovered it had already been opened. He gave up looking for something to drink and sat down opposite Morrow at the table.

"I thought maybe we should talk," said Gerber.

Morrow took a deep swallow from her can of beer, as if steeling herself. "Talk about what?"

"You conning my exec into letting you go on his patrol."

"Nothing to talk about. I wanted to go along, and I knew that you would never allow it if I asked you, so I short-circuited the system and got to go. Simple as that."

"Simple as that," repeated Gerber. "Jesus, Robin! What the hell were you thinking of? Nothing is as simple as that."

"Well, listen to the hypocrite," she said. "Nice job, Robin. Way to con Crinshaw, Robin. But when it's you who gets conned, it's a different story."

"Okay," said Gerber, holding up a hand to stop her. "I deserve that. I haven't been fair. But you could have done some real damage if anything had happened to you."

"Don't worry about it, Gerber," she said, suddenly angry. "I was just doing my job."

Gerber watched her, wondering when he had lost control of the situation. He had thought it would be a good chance to talk to her about conning her way onto the patrol, and suddenly he was on the defensive, as if he had done something wrong.

As he stared at her, he saw she was an attractive woman. She looked a little the worse for wear, away from the luxuries of hot showers, air conditioning and good food, but still damned attractive. If she didn't look so much like her sister, he would have made the effort to talk to her, to be with her sooner. Now he had gotten off on the wrong foot.

He smiled at her and said, "Can we start this again? I don't think I handled it quite right."

"Okay, Captain, we can start again."

"Let me put it this way," he began and then stopped, wondering why he was trying so hard not to insult the woman. She had duped one of his men into taking her on a patrol when she should have been in the camp. "Next time you want to do something like go on patrol, have the courtesy to ask me. I'm responsible for everything that happens here, and I'd like to know what's going on."

"All right, Captain," she said. "I apologize." She stood and walked around the table so that she was facing Gerber. She pulled a chair out and sat down, slowly crossing her bare legs.

Gerber tried not to stare at her, but he couldn't help himself. He wanted to keep the relationship on a professional level. Camp commander and military officer to journalist. But then he said, "I thought we had gotten beyond that captain nonsense."

"I'm always formal when I'm chewed out."

"I wasn't chewing you out. I was merely asking for a little courtesy."

"I stand corrected," she said, leaning forward slightly so that the edges of her shirt pulled apart, revealing the sides of her breasts.

Gerber wanted to reach out and touch her, but restrained himself. He didn't want to get involved with a woman, any woman, at the moment. Especially one named Morrow. He had done a good job of forgetting about Karen in the past few days, even with an almost exact replica of her in the camp.

Morrow reached down and scratched her knee and then drew her fingers along the inside of her thigh, her nails leaving light-red marks on her flesh. She glanced at her leg and then looked back at Gerber.

"So, Mack Gerber, how did a nice guy like you get stuck in a hole like this?" she asked, not realizing it was nearly the same thing she'd said to Bromhead a couple of days earlier.

"I don't see it as being stuck," he said automatically. "I'm doing an important job here."

Morrow edged closer to him. She touched his knee and repeated, "An important job?"

"Yes," he said and then realized she didn't want to hear about the mission of the Special Forces in Vietnam. She had left her notebook and pencil behind and was now talking to him on a personal level. The professionalism he was trying to maintain was slipping away fast.

Something seemed to shift in the team house, and the heat and humidity of the Vietnamese night slipped away forgotten. The journalist was gone, replaced by a desirable woman in sweat-stained clothes.

Gerber wanted to touch her, to kiss her. He wanted to ease the shirt from her shoulders and the shorts from her hips. But he didn't move. He sat there looking at her as the thoughts swirled through his head and the memories of her sister intruded.

Morrow seemed to feel it, too, because she took Gerber's hand in hers, lifting it from the table.

"This isn't the right time," he said quietly, "or the right place." There were too many other people around. Not in the team house itself but in the camp, and there were almost no doors that locked. But it went beyond the inconvenience of the location. It had to do with Karen and the way she had left.

"You sure?" she asked.

He didn't want to hurt her, but he wasn't going to be forced into something that he didn't want. He withdrew his hand and said, "For now, I'm sure. But just for now."

She stood. "Okay," she said, "I can be patient, too."

AT 0600 Anderson, who was guarding the radio, got a call from Big Green announcing that he, along with two additional helicopters, would be landing in less than ten minutes. Big Green expected Gerber to meet him at the pad.

Anderson acknowledged the call, told the young Vietnamese NCO there to stay alert and then hurried out to find Gerber.

Gerber was on the helipad before the helicopters were in sight. He asked Anderson if there had been any more to Crinshaw's message.

The big sergeant shook his head. "No, sir. Just that he was coming in with three ships and that you should be there."

"Okay. Why don't you go get Sergeant Fetterman and Lieutenant Bromhead up here, too. And find Minh and tell him that Crinshaw is inbound."

As Anderson disappeared, Bromhead walked up, buttoning his fatigue shirt and carrying his rifle. "What's happening?"

"Damned if I know. Crinshaw is inbound with another fleet of helicopters."

Gerber turned and saw that Fetterman was heading toward the pad. Behind him were Smith, Bocker and Tyme. When Bocker was in earshot, Gerber said, "What are you people doing out here?"

Bocker shrugged. "Don't know, Captain. Just seemed like we should be."

Gerber noticed they all were carrying their weapons. Then, behind them, Minh and a squad of the Vietnamese appeared, and near the commo bunker a group of Tai, led by Bao and Krung, was forming.

"I don't like this," said Gerber to Bromhead, indicating the armed men who were beginning to surround the helipad. "I don't like this one bit."

The popping of rotor blades interrupted him. All heads turned so that they could watch the aircraft dropping toward them. Anderson tossed a yellow smoke grenade onto the center of the pad, and the lead aircraft shot its approach to the smoke, then hovered beyond it, giving the helicopters behind room to land. As its skids touched down, the cargo door slid open and two big sergeants dressed in freshly starched jungle fatigues leaped out, each carrying an M-16.

As the other helicopters landed, a squad of military policemen, each man wearing a ceremonial black helmet polished to a high gloss with a large white MP painted on it, jumped to the ground and spread out.

Behind him Gerber heard rather than saw his men doing the same. Tension filled the air like electricity just before a thunderstorm. There was no reason to suspect any trouble, but apparently everyone did. Gerber didn't like this one bit.

The whine of the Huey turbines seemed to die as one, as the pilots of each of the aircraft shut down the engines. For a moment the three groups of men stood staring at each other as opponents at an armed camp. Gerber's Green Berets stood around the forward edge of the pad, while the MPs filled the sides and rear. All around them were the Vietnamese and Tai. Everyone was armed.

Crinshaw appeared in the doorway of the lead helicopter and stood, bent at the waist, looking out. Then he stepped down slowly, glanced around and moved to Gerber.

Gerber saluted and said, "Welcome to the camp, General."

"Cut the shit, Gerber."

"General?"

"What are all these men doing here?" demanded Crinshaw.

"Part of the welcoming committee," said Gerber.

"Well, get them out of here."

Gerber looked at Bromhead, who had taken a step to the rear. Then he turned to Fetterman and saw the hard look on his face.

"What's this all about?" asked Gerber, turning back to Crinshaw.

"Don't go asking me questions, boy. You get these men out of the area and we'll talk."

Behind Crinshaw the MP lieutenant had drawn his .45, but was holding it with the barrel pointed downward.

Gerber looked at Minh and said, "Captain, why don't you get your people some breakfast." He raised his voice and repeated the instruction for Lieutenant Bao.

Slowly the Vietnamese and Tai began to drift away. Only Minh and two of his NCOs remained behind. None of the Green Berets made any move to depart.

When all the Vietnamese were gone, Crinshaw waved to another officer who had been standing near the lead helicopter. The man wore clean fatigues and held an attaché case. He had short dark hair trimmed so closely around the ears that it looked like the whitewall haircuts given recruits prior to basic training. He was badly sunburned, as if he had only recently arrived in Vietnam, and wore wire-rimmed glasses. Gerber saw no signs of weapons or field gear.

The man stepped forward, stopping one pace behind Crinshaw, who nodded to him and said, "Read it!"

"Yes, General." The man set his case on the ground and unfolded a sheet of paper. He looked at Gerber and said, "I am informing you, as camp commander and commander of this A-Team, that charges of murder have been filed against two of your men."

For just an instant Gerber felt like laughing. But Crinshaw was not known for his sense of humor; this couldn't be a joke.

"They will also be charged with violation of various other military regulations and Vietnamese and international laws."

Gerber ignored the man with the attaché case and looked directly at Crinshaw. "What kind of crap is this?"

"No crap, Captain. Fact. Your Sergeant Fetterman and Sergeant Tyme are going to be arrested for the murder of a foreign national in a neutral country. I told you that you would go too far and I'd be there to hang your butt. Now here I am."

Abruptly Crinshaw stopped talking. He saw Robin Morrow coming around the corner of a hootch. He pointed at her and demanded, "What the fuck is that civilian still doing here?"

"Looking for a story," said Gerber, almost smiling.

"Have her look somewhere else," Crinshaw shouted hoarsely. "Now you get Fetterman and Tyme here. Tell them to bring their gear because they'll be staying at Long Binh for a while."

Suddenly something changed. The situation that had only seconds before seemed tense now escalated beyond that. Then Gerber identified the triggering element. He heard the slide of a .45 being pulled back so that a round could be chambered. Somewhere behind him he heard one of his men jack a round into his weapon. There was a rattling of weapons as others, on both sides, followed suit.

A couple of the MPs stepped back to take cover behind the helicopters. Some dropped to one knee. The Green Berets did the same, each one of them taking whatever cover was available, some near the pile of sandbags that were used for the ammo bunker, one behind the fifty-five-gallon drum used for burning trash for an emergency light on the helipad and one falling back to the commo bunker entrance. As it now stood, a wrong word would set off a fire fight between the Green Berets and the MPs.

"Captain, you had better do something before you are all in trouble."

Gerber turned, taking it all in. His men crouching around the pad, the MPs near the helicopters and Morrow near the corner of a hootch, her camera out, taking pictures as fast as the automatic advance could feed the film. All this because he had allowed Fetterman to pursue the war a little more enthusiastically than Crinshaw thought it should be done. All this because politicians and civilians didn't understand the nature of war and thought you could limit it by putting restrictions on your own side that the enemy wouldn't follow.

Gerber turned and looked at his team sergeant. Fetterman was standing where he'd been when Crinshaw had gotten out of his helicopter. He had his weapon pointing at the general. The safety was off.

Quietly Gerber said, "Tony, you think you could get your gear together?"

"Certainly, Captain. No problem. And Boom-Boom?"

"Him, too. Make it snappy."

"Yes, sir."

Gerber turned to Bromhead, who was crouched near a pile of sandbags that were going to be used to reinforce the ammo bunker. "Johnny, take the rest of the men to the team house."

"Sir?"

"Do it."

"Yes, sir." Bromhead moved off toward Sully Smith and Sam Anderson. He spoke to them and they reluctantly stood. Together they walked to a couple of the other men.

"You might want to have your MPs relax," Gerber said to Crinshaw.

Crinshaw nodded to one of the NCOs, who in turn went off to talk to the MPs.

Ten minutes later Fetterman and Tyme returned to the helipad, each carrying a duffel bag full of extra clothes, shaving kit and other personal items. Fetterman had hidden a bottle of Beam's disguised as shaving lotion deep in the bottom of his. He wasn't sure he could sneak it by the guards at the stockade, but he was sure as hell going to try.

At the aircraft Crinshaw was sitting in the cargo compartment smoking a pipe. The MPs were standing at ease, waiting.

Fetterman whispered to Gerber, "Captain, you get us out of this. We're counting on you to get us out."

"I'll get you out," Gerber replied. "Don't worry." If he had to, he'd testify he had issued the orders to the two men. That way they couldn't be held ultimately responsible.

Four of the MPs came forward, two of them carrying handcuffs. Crinshaw jumped down from the helicopter to follow.

With one hand in the air, Gerber stopped them. "You have no need for those," he said, pointing to the handcuffs.

"Regulations, Captain," said the MP lieutenant.

"Not on my men."

"We have your word they won't try to escape?" asked Crinshaw.

"Of course you do," snapped Gerber.

The general waved off the MPs. "Let's get out of here," he ordered.

The MPs separated Fetterman and Tyme, putting one on the second aircraft and the other on the third. Crinshaw turned and waved a hand over his head, telling the pilot of the lead aircraft to start his engine.

Just before he boarded, Crinshaw leaned close to Gerber and said, "Don't think you're in the clear on this deal, Captain. I suspect that once we start taking testimony, you'll be coming in to keep your men company."

Before Gerber could respond, Crinshaw climbed on board. Gerber stepped back as the pilots wound the helicopters up to full operating RPM. The noise increased to a steady roar from the turbines that was replaced by the popping of the rotor blades as they began to lift off. The wind from the rotors swirled around the pad, threatening to blow away everything that wasn't tied down. Gerber put a hand on his beret to keep it from blowing away and turned his back to the red dust that had begun to sandblast him. A moment later he felt the hot blast from the turbines as the helicopters maneuvered before taking off to the south.

Gerber watched as they climbed out, gaining altitude rapidly and then turning to the east toward Saigon.

"What are you going to do now?" a soft voice asked.

Gerber turned to look at Morrow. She had her camera clutched in one hand and held the other to her eyes to shield them from the bright sun.

"I'm not sure. But I'm going to have to do it fast."

9

LONG BINH JAIL, LONG BINH, REPUBLIC OF VIETNAM

The helicopters didn't fly to Saigon and Hotel Three, but diverted to the north to land at the airfield at Long Binh, where they were met by a convoy of jeeps and three-quarter-ton trucks. Crinshaw got into one of the jeeps and was driven from the field toward the headquarters building at Bien Hoa situated to the west. Fetterman and Tyme were put into the covered back of one of the three-quarter-ton trucks with two MPs sitting near the tailgate.

The thick canvas that covered the framework behind the cab absorbed the heat and held it in, making it uncomfortably hot in the back. Tyme sat on a fixed low bench on one side of the truck, with his head bowed and his hands clasped around his knees.

Fetterman sat on the opposite side, watching the two MPs, who were looking out the back. He used the sleeve of his fatigues to wipe the sweat from his forehead and hoped the ride to LBJ would be short.

They bumped along in silence for a while, the fumes from the truck's exhaust blowing back into the bed, where it mixed with the damp tropical air making it hard to breathe. Fetterman slid along the bench to get closer to the opening where the air wasn't quite as foul.

He looked at Tyme and said, "Hey, Boom-Boom, take it easy. It could be worse."

Tyme turned so that he could see Fetterman and said, "I don't understand why the captain let them arrest us."

Fetterman glanced at the MPs, as if to tell Tyme that it wasn't the place to discuss the matter. He then sat back and closed his eyes, waiting for the ride to end.

But he wasn't nearly as relaxed as he wanted Tyme to believe. He knew exactly how serious the charges were and wasn't sure that Gerber would be able to do anything to get them out. Crinshaw's information was right on one point. They certainly had crossed the border and Army regulations and international law prohibited it. A case could be made for smoking the Chinese officer since he was helping the enemy. A strong case. If the man had been in South Vietnam when he had been shot.

The fly in the ointment was that the man had been in Cambodia, where technically he wasn't fair game. Fetterman smiled to himself when he realized Crinshaw had missed on a couple of charges. He had forgotten conspiracy. They all had conspired to kill the man. And he had forgotten about being out of uniform, a fairly minor charge when compared to the rest of them.

Still, he had faith in the Army system. They couldn't find him guilty of murder if he'd only been doing his job. And then he realized he was guilty. The difference between doing his job and murder was an imaginary line, and Fetterman had crossed it.

Tyme stood a chance of getting off since he was the junior NCO on the mission, except that he had pulled the trigger. Their only defense was that they had been following orders, and that defense had not worked for the Nazis after World War II. If there had been an officer on the patrol, then that ploy might have worked, but not the way the thing developed. When it came right down to it, they were guilty as hell.

The truck rumbled to a halt in a clatter of grinding gears and squealing brakes. The driver came around to drop the tailgate, and as it fell away, the two MPs stood up.

"Let's move it," said the larger, darker of the two.

Fetterman stood and dropped to the ground, blinking in the bright sunlight of midday. Even with the temperature hovering at about ninety, Fetterman found it cool compared to the stifling interior of the Army truck.

Tyme appeared and handed down his duffel bag and then Fetterman's. He stooped, put a hand on the bed of the truck and dropped to the ground.

"You men leave your bags here," said a third MP who had appeared from inside the stockade. "Someone will pick them up later so they can be searched. Follow me."

Fetterman turned and stared at the building surrounded by a twelve-foot-high double chain-link fence that was topped with concertina wire. There was a gate in front of them, flanked by a white guard hut where an MP armed with an M-16 watched without interest the activity outside the fence.

The main building was a flat, white, two-story structure that reflected the bright sunlight. The windows of the upper story, where the prisoners were kept, were barred, but the ones on the bottom, where the administration offices and storage were housed, were not.

The MP who had spoken led them past the guard and through the gate to the double doors that led into the building. There they were met by an MP lieutenant who was six feet tall and extremely thin. He had very short blond hair and a long nose. He held a clipboard in his hands, a sheet of paper folded over the top.

"Fetterman, Anthony B.," he read from the clipboard.

"Yes, sir."

"Tyme, Justin."

"Yes, sir."

"You will follow me into the holding room until someone can be freed to take your fingerprints and finish the processing. Cause any trouble and you might just disappear into the jungle around here." He flipped the paper back and turned, entering the dim recesses of the building.

The inside was incredibly clean. The floors showed no sign that anyone ever walked on them. The bulletin board beside one of the doors had several documents posted on it, but all were new. One demanded that soldiers wear their ribbons proudly.

They walked past a Coke machine to an office that was divided in half by a waist-high wooden counter. The counter was painted a bright green that rivaled the verdant jungle. Two MPs sat at desks behind it while a man wearing gray clothes with a big white P on the back of the shirt pushed a broom lazily around the floor.

The lieutenant stopped long enough to request the key for holding room two, and one of the seated MPs pulled it from a lockbox mounted on the wall.

The lieutenant ushered them out a second door and into another hallway. He stopped in front of a metal door, unlocked it and reached inside to turn on the lights. "You men will wait here until someone comes for you," he said as he stepped back out of the way.

Fetterman entered first. The room was brightly lighted and contained a single fixture recessed in the ceiling and protected by a metal cage. Fetterman looked at the chairs carefully and saw they were made of metal and bolted to the floor. There was nothing else in the room.

When Tyme had entered, the lieutenant shut the door with a dull metallic clang and locked it from the outside.

Within five minutes the door was unlocked and opened. A staff sergeant wearing the black armband of an MP told them they were to follow him. In the hallway were three more MPs.

Fetterman and Tyme were taken to a small room where they were photographed, front and profile. Next they were fingerprinted. As they were cleaning the ink from their fingers, another MP arrived and asked Fetterman to follow him. Tyme was to be taken back to the holding room to await the arrival of his defense counsel.

Fetterman was escorted to a room on the second floor. Inside, a man in rumpled jungle fatigues was waiting. He had silver captain's bars pinned to the collar of his uniform, but wore no other insignia or patches. He had longish brown hair, blue eyes behind black, horn-rimmed glasses and skin that was fairly tanned. Although he was slim, he didn't seem to be thin. He was tall and had large, bony hands. He put a large black briefcase on the table and pulled a large bundle of papers out of it. He read them over for a moment and then turned to Fetterman.

"You're in a shit load of trouble," said the man.

"Thank you," said Fetterman. "Would you be good enough to tell me who you are?"

"Oh, of course." The man set the papers down and held out a hand. "I'm Dennis Wilson. I've been appointed to act as your defense counsel."

"You're a lawyer, then?" asked Fetterman, shaking Wilson's hand.

"I'm assigned to the Adjutant General's Office and have had a year of law school."

"Great!" said Fetterman. He hadn't expected Clarence Darrow, but this kid probably didn't have enough qualifications to be a law clerk, let alone a defense attorney. "You want to tell me a little more about what's been happening here?"

Wilson dug through his stack of papers. He grabbed a file folder, opened it and said, "According to this, on or about the twelfth of this month, you led a patrol consisting of yourself, Sergeant First Class Tyme and a couple of the indigenous personnel on a border-crossing expedition that violated a dozen international agreements. While on that illegal patrol you did conspire to murder an individual of another nation not engaged in the conflict in South Vietnam. Having completed that assignment in the foreign country, you did return to South Vietnam."

Fetterman sat back in his chair and laughed. "Well, that about sums it up. If all that is true, then why didn't they arrest Captain Gerber? He would have had to approve our operation."

"As of now there is no proof that Captain Gerber knew that you were going to cross the border and murder a foreign national. If testimony or evidence show that Captain Gerber knew of this mission, then I suppose his arrest will be forthcoming. Now, would you like to tell me your side of the story?"

"You mean somebody is actually interested in that?"

"You're not helping yourself with that attitude, Sergeant."

"And what do you expect? Yesterday I'm in the field fighting the Communists, and today I'm arrested for doing that job a little better than someone thinks I should. Besides, I don't know you, who you work for or how much of what I tell you will remain privileged. You could be setting me up for someone."

Wilson took off the horn-rimmed glasses and began to polish the lenses with an OD handkerchief he pulled from the top pocket of his fatigues. "I can understand your reluctance to talk to me, but I assure you that anything you tell me will not go beyond this room. My job is to help. That's the only reason I'm here."

"You know," said Fetterman, smiling, "that 'I'm here to help you' is one of the three great lies, like 'the check is in the mail' and 'I won't come in your mouth.' "

"I could give you a written pledge," Wilson said with a touch of exasperation.

"What good would that do me when this is over and I'm in jail because you violated that trust?"

"As I said, I can understand your reluctance. All I can say is that Sergeant Tyme is currently with his counsel."

"If Boom-Boom is telling that man anything, I'll be extremely surprised."

"Then you refuse to cooperate?"

"Did I say that? All I said was that I had no guarantee that anything you say is true, or that anything I tell you will stay in this room. If you're going to get me out of this, however, I suppose you need to know what happened."

Wilson brought a large yellow legal pad and a ballpoint pen out of his briefcase. "Yes, I do. We have the Article 32 hearing tomorrow afternoon, so I'll have to know everything."

GERBER WASN'T WORRIED. He didn't like having his men arrested by MPs and spirited to Long Binh Jail, but he wasn't worried. Jerry Maxwell had told him not to get caught, but he didn't think the CIA would let Fetterman and Tyme go down in flames. He would speak to Maxwell, who would speak to his boss, who would talk to someone in Washington, who would then order someone in the Pentagon to tell Crinshaw to quietly drop the charges. That would be that. No problem at all.

As he had done too many times in the past few days, he packed his knapsack with a change of clothes and got ready to leave for Saigon. He left the knapsack sitting on his cot and headed for the commo bunker, where Bocker and his Vietnamese counterpart were sitting at the chart table playing cards.

"Have we got anything scheduled in here this afternoon, Galvin?" asked Gerber.

"Resupply chopper from Tay Ninh should be here in thirty or forty minutes. Nothing else. Why?"

"I need to make a trip into Saigon about a couple of things, and I'd like a ride."

Bocker tossed his cards facedown on the table and said, "I can rustle up something sooner if you would like, sir."

"That won't be necessary. I can wait for the resupply ship. Just don't let it get out of here without me."

"No, sir." He hesitated for a second and then asked, "What's going to happen to Tony and Justin?"

Gerber smiled. "Don't worry about them. I won't let anything happen to them." Without another word Gerber left, heading back to his hootch. Once there he opened his wall locker and took a bottle of Beam's from the bottom shelf. He pulled the cork and took a deep drink, breathing through his mouth after he swallowed to ease the fire in his throat.

"Mind if I join you?" asked a feminine voice from the doorway.

Gerber turned and saw Robin Morrow silhouetted against the light. She was dressed in much the same fashion as she had been the night before. Khaki shirt unbuttoned all the way, but now she had the tails knotted together. She wore Khaki shorts and jungle boots. There was sweat on her forehead although her hair was pulled back into a ponytail. A camera hung around her neck.

Gerber held out the bottle and said, "It's warm and I don't have any mixers."

Morrow stepped inside and took the Beam's. "Why cut the effect with mixers?" She took a long drink, her throat working convulsively as she swallowed. She lowered the bottle, blinked her eyes rapidly and said, "Wow."

"You don't have to kill yourself with it," he said.

She handed the Beam's back and sat down in one of the lawn chairs. "What are you going to do about the men who were arrested?"

"Personal question or professional?" asked Gerber.

"A little of both."

"I plan to go to Saigon as soon as the resupply chopper arrives and talk to some people I know there. I think we can straighten this whole thing out before it goes to trial."

"Uh-huh," said Morrow. "Operations into Cambodia. Murder of foreign nationals. Quite a story as I see it."

"Alleged operations and murder," said Gerber quietly.

"Alleged doesn't mean shit," said Morrow. "Just how are you going to spring them from charges like that? Who are you going to talk to?"

Gerber was suddenly frightened. The one hope he had for getting Fetterman and Tyme out of LBJ was to keep everything quiet. To keep the press out of it. But Crinshaw, spouting off about cross-border operations while Morrow stood there and took pictures, might have sunk the whole deal. Gerber corked the bottle and sat down on his cot. "What are you going to do?" he asked.

"I'd like a ride into Saigon with you to talk to a few people of my own. Besides, I should check in at the bureau and file a couple of stories."

"But nothing about Fetterman and Tyme," said Gerber, a little too quickly.

"Not yet, anyway. I don't have all the facts. You going to give me a lift or not?"

Gerber hesitated before replying. Hell, if he didn't give her the ride, she would find another way to Saigon. He couldn't keep her prisoner in the camp. Too many people knew where she was.

"Sure," he said.

"Good," she said as she stood. "I'll buy you dinner."

He watched her leave, wondering if it might not be too late to save Fetterman and Tyme. Too many people seemed to be in on this one. As he thought that, he suddenly realized Crinshaw shouldn't have had any idea of what had happened. No one on his team would have told Crinshaw a damned thing about it. And Crinshaw hated the Vietnamese so it didn't seem likely that he heard it from them. Besides, other than Minh, none of the Vietnamese actually knew anything other than that Fetterman and Tyme had gone out on a mission.

Yet Crinshaw did know something; otherwise he couldn't have arrested Fetterman and Tyme. One of the first things he would have to do when he got back to camp was find out who had been talking out of turn and stop them.

He retrieved the Beam's and poured a healthy slug into his canteen cup. Then he sat on his cot and leaned back against the wall and slowly drank the bourbon. The nature of war was different than what he had read in history books. No masses of brightly dressed men marching to save king and country. Here there were only tired, dirty men who were arrested for fighting the war a little too effectively.

Several minutes later he heard the sound of the approaching chopper and downed the remainder of the Beam's in a single swallow. He set his canteen cup on the papers piled in the center of his desk, picked up his knapsack and reached for his M-14. Then he put it down, deciding it was too much trouble to carry the weapon to Saigon. Instead, he stuffed his M-3 grease gun into the bottom of his knapsack. Next he stripped off his fatigue jacket and strapped on a shoulder holster containing a .45 automatic. He put his jacket back on and walked toward the helipad.

Morrow was already there, standing well back so that the chopper would have room to land and she wouldn't be in the rotor wash. She had changed into jungle fatigues and had a suitcase and her camera bag at her feet.

Gerber was nearly to the pad when Bocker ran out of the commo bunker and tossed a green smoke grenade onto the center of it so the pilots would have a landing point. He saw Gerber, waved and ran back.

Gerber stepped next to Morrow and yelled over the noise of the landing chopper, "You taking all your clothes with you? That mean you're not coming back?"

"I'll be back," she shouted at him. She turned to watch as the helicopter flared to stop its forward motion and then settled to the center of the pad, sucking the green smoke up in the rotor wash and swirling it toward her.

The crew chief leaped from behind his M-60 machine gun in the well of the Huey and trotted to Gerber. He pushed the boom mike of his flight helmet out of the way and yelled, "We've got some supplies to leave here."

Gerber turned to look at the commo bunker, wondering if Bocker had arranged for someone to assist the helicopter crew with the unloading, then saw Anderson approaching from the direction of the team house. Gerber pointed at Anderson, and then the crew chief nodded his understanding. He asked, "You the passenger for Saigon?"

"That's right." He indicated Morrow. "She needs a lift, too."

"No problem, Captain."

Anderson stopped beside Gerber, leaned close and said, "Are you going to help Fetterman and Tyme?"

"I'm going to try, Cat," said Gerber.

He nodded and moved to the cargo compartment of the helicopter. The crew chief slid two boxes containing batteries for the night-ranging weapons, sniperscopes and PRC-10s across the deck of the helicopter. On top of that he tossed a bright-orange bag containing the personal mail for the Americans. Anderson picked it up and, lifting it clear of the chopper, stepped back.

"Good luck, Captain," he yelled as Gerber helped Morrow into the chopper.

Gerber held a thumb up to acknowledge Anderson's remark as the crew chief set Morrow's luggage in the cargo compartment, sliding it under the troop seat. Gerber sat down on the red canvas troop seat that was next to the housing for the transmission and buckled his seat belt. He glanced at Morrow, who sat right next to him, leaning against his arm.

The engine noise increased, and the chopper lifted to a hover, hanging in the air three or four feet above the pad. It turned slightly toward the runway, then the nose dropped and the helicopter raced along the ground without climbing. Suddenly the nose came up and the chopper shot into the air, leaving Gerber feeling as though his stomach remained behind on the ground.

They reached altitude and turned toward Saigon. Gerber glanced to his left and could see the top two buttons on Morrow's shirt were unfastened. He watched the rise and fall of her breasts as she breathed.

She turned and looked at him and smiled. She leaned against him so that her lips were next to his ear and her breast was pressed against his arm. Over the whine of the turbine, she yelled, "How long is the flight?"

He turned his head and put his lips against her ear. "Should take about forty minutes."

She nodded, but didn't move away from him.

They flew on in silence for a couple of minutes, Gerber aware of the pressure of her breast on his arm. He wondered if she knew that he could feel it and decided she had to be able to. He also felt the warmth of her hip as it pressed against him. He thought about shifting his weight to see if she would move with him, but decided to let her play out the game the way she wanted to.

As they neared Go Dau Ha, she grabbed his arm, pressing closer and pointing out the cargo-compartment door. She yelled in his ear, "What's that?"

He liked the feeling of her warm breath on his ear. He said, "Bridge at Go Dau Ha or, as we call it, Go To Hell. Every time we get it built, the VC drop it back into the water. That's why it looks like a cement triangle sticking out of the river and not like a bridge."

"I thought it was some kind of religious structure."

As they continued, Gerber realized she hadn't let go of his arm. She kept the conversation going by asking him about the hamlets they flew over or the military bases they passed. He pointed out the big swamp area south of Highway 1 that was a free fire zone.

He wondered what the flight crew thought of the attention she was paying him, but when he looked, both pilots were staring ahead, watching their instruments and the sky in front of them. There were a lot of other aircraft in the friendly sky—flights of helicopters circling, single ships popping up and dropping down, small propeller-driven airplanes buzzing by and squadrons of jets going to and coming from missions.

The crew chief, hidden in his well on one side of the helicopter, and the door gunner on the opposite side kept watch of the sides and rear. No one had time to worry about the Army captain they had picked up. Gerber was surprised they didn't pay more attention to Morrow.

Gerber sat back to enjoy the flight, realizing it was the best one he had been on. Morrow was making all the difference. She was trying so hard to make him aware of her that Gerber had to smile to himself. Maybe that was why the flight crew seemed to ignore her. They didn't want to be frustrated because she was so obviously trying to attract Gerber's attention. And she was having a great deal of luck doing it.

It was late in the day when they landed at Hotel Three. The crew chief helped Morrow from the chopper and then handed down her suitcase and camera bag. He smiled at her and she yelled her thanks over the engine and rotor noise.

Gerber grabbed his knapsack and leaped to the ground. He took Morrow's suitcase from her, and she shouldered her camera case. They walked across the grass of the heliport to the terminal building.

As they entered, Morrow said, "What's the plan?"

"I've got a number of calls to make and some people to see," answered Gerber.

"Mind if I tag along?"

"Yes. Besides, it's going to be very boring. Nothing that great stories are made of."

"That makes me suspicious," said Morrow. "Anytime I'm assured there's nothing interesting happening, I figure that there is."

"You still can't go with me," Gerber replied. "Where do you want to eat this dinner that you promised to buy?"

"Nice try, Mack, but I know you're trying to change the subject." She smiled at him.

"You're still not going with me," he said.

"I'll let you win this one," she responded. "Besides, I can ask you at dinner tonight."

"Which will be where?"

"The Caravelle, downtown. Help me get a taxi," she said.

Finding a taxi outside the air base was no problem. They got in the back of a beat-up old Ford that might have been blue once. The driver shot off into the traffic before he even knew the destination, weaving in and out of the bicycles and motor scooters. But the palm-lined streets were wide, and the driver knew the best route to the Caravelle after Gerber had shouted the name to him.

When they pulled up in front of the hotel, Gerber said, "Get me a room when you check in. I shouldn't be more than an hour or so."

"I hope you brought some civilian clothes," said Morrow.

"I brought a clean uniform and I'm afraid that's it."

She got out, lifted her suitcase and camera bag out of the cab and shut the door. She leaned back in the window and said, "I'll get the reservations. Hurry back because I want to eat."

He smiled and said to the driver, "Let's go."

They took off in a squeal of tires and blaring of horns. As soon as they were away from the hotel, Gerber said, "MACV compound, and when we get there, I'll want you to wait."

They pulled up in front of the MACV HQ, and Gerber got out. He flashed his ID at the MPs stationed at the doors and went inside. He walked down the nearly deserted corridors, located the stairwell and descended to the basement level. He told the guard at the bottom that he wanted to see Jerry Maxwell.

"Sorry, sir, he's checked out for the day."

"Did he say where he was going?" asked Gerber, trying not to sound irritated. In fact, he was mad as hell.

"No, sir. Would you care to leave a message?"

"Yes. Tell him that Mack Gerber would like him to call tonight. I'm at the . . . No, that's not such a hot idea. Tell him I'll see him at nine tomorrow."

The guard nodded. "Mack Gerber. Nine tomorrow."

Gerber went back upstairs and left the building. As he got into the cab, he instructed the driver to take him back to the Caravelle, and once in front of the hotel, he paid the driver, grabbed his knapsack and went inside. At the desk he asked for his room key and went upstairs, found the room and went in. He dropped his knapsack on the double bed and looked in the bathroom.

The telephone rang, and Gerber picked up the receiver.

"Hi, Mack. You ready to eat?" said an exuberant voice at the other end.

"I'll assume that it's Robin," Gerber said with a laugh. "No, I'm not ready. I just got in. Give me about twenty minutes."

"I'm in the rooftop bar and way ahead of you on the booze. You'd better hurry or I'll be too drunk to eat and too good to resist."

"Sounds like you want me to slow down," he said.

"Suit yourself," she responded. "See you in a few minutes."

Gerber hung up and looked around the room. Lamps on bedside tables flanked a large bed, and there was a tall wood wardrobe in the corner instead of a closet. A ceiling fan spun lazily overhead while a small air conditioner stuck in the room's only window wheezed faintly as it fought a losing battle to cool the room. Gerber dropped into the one chair to take off his boots. It was better than his hootch, he decided, and certainly cooler.

Opening his knapsack, he set out his shaving kit on the side of the bathroom sink. He tested the taps that hung over an old Victorian bathtub and rejoiced at the feel of hot and cold running water.

He shaved quickly and went back to change into his clean fatigues.

Gerber took the elevator to the rooftop bar and restaurant. The doors opened on a crowded bar and a wall of loud music. Most of the people inside were in civilian clothes, with just enough military uniforms sprinkled around to remind everyone of where they were. Gerber was the only one in fatigues, though. He pushed his way in toward the bar at the far side of the room, weaving among the tables, looking for Robin Morrow. To his right were a couple of steps that led to French doors and a rooftop terrace that overlooked Saigon. The doors were open, letting in the humidity that the air conditioners on the lower floors were trying to keep out.

To the left was a wall of windows, the blinds partially drawn to obscure the sun sitting on the horizon. A gigantic crystal chandelier that contained a hundred light bulbs threw a soft but bright light over the room.

At first Gerber couldn't find Morrow. She was lost in the crowd of diplomats, embassy workers, journalists and civilian contractors. Then, in a corner near one end of the French doors, he saw her stand and wave. He ducked around a massive man in an Air Force uniform wearing the eagles of a colonel.

"I thought you'd never get here," she said as he approached.

"I didn't think I'd find you when I saw the number of people in here. You sure you want to eat here?"

"It has passbable food, and besides, anywhere else would be just as crowded," she answered.

Gerber sat down and looked across the table. Morrow was wearing a white silk dress that was cut low in the front. She had washed her hair and then brushed it until it reflected the light from the chandelier and sparkled with the oranges and reds of the setting sun.

She leaned forward slightly, her elbows on the table, and reached for Gerber's hand. He saw a bead of sweat between her breasts and noticed that her hair was damp where her bangs brushed her forehead.

"Not terribly cool in here," he said.

She smiled at him, showing her white teeth. "No. Not very." She locked her eyes on his and held them there, staring intensely at him. She held his hand in both of hers.

There was something about the look that Gerber didn't at first understand. When he did understand it, he wanted to break the eye contact, but found he couldn't. He felt himself respond to the look. His mind raced, and he knew everything that he wanted to say, but could not find the words.

Robin didn't move. She stuck the tip of her tongue between her teeth and slowly licked her lips. She squeezed Gerber's hand in hers. Gerber knew he was no match for her.

"Would you care to order?" asked a waiter who had appeared at their table.

Gerber exhaled as if he had suddenly just remembered how to breathe. With a physical effort he tore his eyes away from Robin's. "What?" he asked. Then added, "Not yet. We'll order in a minute."

As the waiter left, Morrow said, "We don't have to eat, you know."

"I thought you said you were starving," Gerber replied. But he knew exactly what she was talking about. Now, however, with the mood broken he could see only trouble on the horizon with her. She was a journalist who was looking for a story. She was a woman who could leave Vietnam and him the minute she felt like it. She wasn't trapped by Army regulations and orders. And to top it off, she was Karen Morrow's sister.

Gerber wondered if his reluctance to have anything to do with Robin was because of Karen. Was it the lies that Karen had told, or was it just that he didn't want a woman to complicate his life?

Suddenly he asked, "Are you married?"

She laughed at that. "Not even going steady. Yet."

He opened his mouth to ask her to go to his room and instead asked, "You care to dance? Some people are dancing."

"Anything you say. Anything at all."

He stood and came around the table, holding out his hand. He saw a flash of her thigh as she swung her legs out from under the table. The tight skirt that kissed her knees had a long slit up the side.

On the dance floor he held her loosely, carefully, as if she might break. He had his left hand on her bare back, and her skin was damp with a light coat of perspiration.

She moved with him for a moment and then pulled him close, holding him tightly. She rubbed herself against him, slipping a leg between his. When she looked up, she put her lips to his ear and said in a low voice, "You really want to stay here?"

"No," he said. "Not at all. Let's go to my room."

She took his hand and pulled him toward the elevator. Gerber asked, "Your purse?"

"I've nothing at the table."

As soon as the elevator doors closed on them and they were alone, Morrow turned and kissed him, forcing her tongue into his mouth, probing quickly, hungrily.

When the bell rang signaling they had arrived on the right floor, Morrow broke the kiss. "We're here," she said breathlessly.

At the door to his room, Gerber fumbled for the key, found it and opened up. Morrow pushed past him and then nearly dragged him in as she kicked the door shut. She kissed him again savagely. Gerber brought his hand up until he could feel her erect nipples beneath the cool silk of her dress.

She stepped back, staring straight into his eyes. Then she reached behind her and drew the zipper on her dress down slowly. She smiled and let her hand fall away. The dress slipped from her shoulders, revealing her to the waist.

Gerber moved to her and kissed her throat. Then he kissed her shoulder and chest, finally licking away the sweat that beaded between her breasts. At the same time he slipped the dress from her hips so that it pooled around her feet.

Her breath was coming in short bursts, as if she couldn't get enough air and had forgotten how to breathe. She clung to him.

Gerber lifted her up and carried her to the bed. He set her down and smiled. Under her dress she had only worn panties. No bra or stockings.

She reached up and unbuttoned his fatigue jacket. When she saw the shoulder holster, she said nothing; she just tugged on it until he helped her remove it. He took off his T-shirt and tossed it to the floor.

Morrow sighed and kissed his stomach as she tried to unfasten the waistband on his fatigue pants. She slipped her hand inside and squeezed gently.

"Will you make love to me?" she asked quietly.

"I'm not sure that I'm ready for this," he whispered. "I'm not ready to love someone."

"Doesn't matter. You will be."

For a moment he hesitated, letting his emotions run wild as he considered everything. Suddenly he realized that she was right. It didn't matter. He pushed his thumbs under the waistband of her panties, and as she lifted her hips, he slid them to her knees. Now he bent over her so that he could kiss her, his tongue deep in her mouth.

She laid back, her blond hair spread on the pillow, and said, "I love you, Mack."

10

MACV HEADQUARTERS, SAIGON

Gerber arrived at the headquarters building shortly before nine and went immediately downstairs, where the MP on duty logged him in and opened the gate. The door to Maxwell's office opened before Gerber could reach it, and Maxwell stepped out long enough to grab Gerber by the arm and haul him inside. Maxwell then looked out the door to see if anyone other than the MP was standing there.

"I don't have a lot of time this morning," Maxwell said. "I've got to brief the commander in an hour and a half, and I still don't know what I'm going to say."

Gerber fell into the chair beside the littered desk and noticed there were more Coke cans on it. There were also more manila folders, but none of them were stamped Secret. For his part, Jerry Maxwell didn't look very good. He was pale as if the blood had drained from his face. The dark circles under his eyes stood out in vivid contrast to his skin color. Gerber wondered if the man were going to fall over.

"I won't take much of your time," said Gerber.

"That's good." Maxwell took off his suit coat and hung it on the back of his chair. He took his pistol, a Swenson .45 Auto Custom, from his shoulder holster and put it in the middle drawer of his desk. Then he sat down and tried to look calm.

"Now, what can I do for you?" Maxwell asked.

"You remember that problem we discussed the last time I was here?" Gerber said.

Maxwell looked startled, but quickly covered it up. "What problem?" he replied.

"We talked about a Red Chinese operating out of Cambodia and how he was hurting our operations."

"Now hold it right there," interrupted Maxwell. "There are no Red Chinese in Cambodia. You never mentioned that."

"What the hell do you mean I never mentioned that?" Gerber spoke in a cold voice. "We sat right here and talked about Phoenix and the elimination of the top cadre on the enemy's side."

"Mack, I just don't know what you're talking about. You were never here. I never heard of this Phoenix." Maxwell picked up one of the Coke cans, shook it and said, "Damn!"

Gerber opened his mouth to respond, then changed his mind. It suddenly dawned on him what was happening. Maxwell and the CIA had stepped into something, and everyone was denying they knew anything about it. And he and his men were caught in the middle.

"I've got two men at LBJ charged with murder," said Gerber quietly. "They went on the mission that you and I discussed here because you said that such an operation was within the new guidelines issued by MACV."

Maxwell slammed a hand to the desktop. "You just won't get it, will you? You sit here pretending that you don't understand. There was no conversation in this room about any mission into Cambodia. There was no conversation about Phoenix. Nothing."

"There are logs proving I was here," said Gerber. Even in the air conditioning of the basement he was beginning to sweat. He felt it under his arms and trickling down his sides, but it wasn't the temperature that was causing it.

"There are no logs. You're on your own on this one. There is nothing that I can do and very little that you can do."

Gerber looked at the floor in front of his feet and then turned his gaze on Maxwell. "You bastard. You're going to sit there and let my men go down? You're going to do nothing to help?"

"I told you then that a nice quiet mission into Cambodia would be overlooked," said Maxwell. "I said *quiet* and if there was trouble you were on your own. Now there's trouble. More than I care to think about. Your boys weren't quiet. There's a stink all over Saigon, and you're going to have to live with it. You make too much noise in the wrong place, and you're going down, too."

"But—"

"There are no buts, Gerber. I'm giving you the facts of life, which, I might add, I shouldn't be doing." Maxwell opened one of the file folders that was lying in front of him. "Now, if you're through, I have work to do."

"Then you plan to do nothing?"

"About what?" asked Maxwell. "I have no idea what you're talking about. Now, don't take this personally, but would you kindly get the fuck out of here? I have work to do."

Gerber got to his feet and stared down at the CIA agent. Maxwell didn't meet his gaze. He felt sorry for the man. Felt sorry for him because he had to cave in to the pressure and had to do things that he might not like. Gerber could tell this game they were playing was eating him up, but he knew Maxwell well enough to know he wouldn't jeopardize his own career to save Fetterman and Tyme.

"There is one thing you might do," said Gerber. "Get two passports made out. One for Fetterman and one for Tyme, but don't use their real names."

Maxwell snapped the folder shut and sat staring at the wall. "You're asking for trouble. Now get out."

Outside, Gerber caught a ride back to the Caravelle with an Air Force major who was on his way to Tan Son Nhut, but didn't mind the detour. Robin was not in his room when he got there, and when he tried to find her, he discovered that she hadn't even registered in the hotel.

"That's just great," he said aloud. Maxwell wouldn't help get Fetterman and Tyme out of LBJ, and now Morrow had deserted him. He walked into the bathroom, jammed his shaving gear into the kit and then stuffed it into his knapsack. He took a quick look around the room and then went to the door. When he got to the front desk downstairs to pay his bill, he learned that Robin had taken care of it.

On the street Gerber waited for a taxi, passing up the chance to ride in a lambretta that contained two old women and a young man. He didn't feel like riding in the open air. He wanted the solitude of the back seat of a taxi.

The doorman finally got him one, and Gerber took it to the gate at Tan Son Nhut. He paid the driver, giving him a large tip for not talking, and headed toward Hotel Three. Then he had a better idea and changed direction so that he could see Bates before he went back to camp.

When Gerber got to the outer office of Bates's domain, a Spec Four told him to cool his heels while he checked with the colonel. Gerber sat down in one of the metal chairs that lined the perimeter of the room. There was a potted plant stuck in one corner and a table littered with back issues of *Stars and Stripes* and the *Army Times*. The wood floor was bare, and there was nothing hanging on the walls. The room was, however, air-conditioned, and a ceiling fan revolved slowly, trying vainly to stir up the air.

The Spec Four reappeared quickly and said, "Colonel Bates will see you."

Gerber got to his feet and entered the inner sanctum. It wasn't as fancy as Crinshaw's nor as severe as Gerber's. Somewhere in between. The desk was wood and recently polished. There was a blue couch along one wall and two blue armchairs in front of the desk. A rug that was little more than a bamboo mat was spread between the armchairs and the desk. Blinds on the window would kill the rays of the late-afternoon sun, but had nothing to do in the morning. Out the window Gerber could see part of the street and another building. He could hear the aircraft on the airfield, but it was a quiet sound, deadened by the distance.

"Morning, Colonel," he said.

"Have a chair, Mack." Bates leaned to his right as if to look around Gerber and raised his voice. "Petersen, I don't want to be interrupted. And close the damned door." He turned back to Gerber and said, "What's on your mind?"

"Simple question. How much do you know about what's happening?"

"Probably more than you think. General Crinshaw advised me of the arrests of your boys and the charges. He didn't bother filling in all the details. I was going to fly out this morning and see what I could do."

"Crinshaw briefed you?" asked Gerber, surprised.

"Somewhat. He didn't tell me all that much. You want to go over it now?"

For a moment Gerber hesitated. The mission that Fetterman had led was supposed to have been quiet. Now, it seemed, everyone was aware of what had gone on. Gerber couldn't see how telling Bates could make anything worse. Besides, he needed an ally. One who had access to the inner circles of Army politics in Saigon.

Quickly Gerber outlined what had happened, starting with the ambush of the Vietnamese ranger patrol, and continued right up to his most recent meeting with Maxwell. He left nothing out.

When Gerber finished, Bates said, "I'm not surprised."

"Now what the hell does that mean?"

"Think about it, Mack. Yours is not the only A-Team I have in the field and not the only one that works with the CIA. Who else do you think they sent out on Phoenix? You just happen to be the only one with your tit in the wringer."

"Why is that?"

Bates leaned forward and clasped his hands. "I would guess because of the target. Everyone else took out Vietcong and NVA cadre. Not Chinese, and not in Cambodia."

"So what do we do?"

Bates looked at his watch. "I think that maybe we should sit in on the Article 32 hearing. That might give us an idea of how much Crinshaw and his people know. Although, from what you've told me and what I've seen from Crinshaw's office, there doesn't seem to be much that they don't know. All the sessions are going to be classified, but I don't think we'll be excluded since we already know what's going on."

"And then what?"

"Then we can plan a strategy." Bates got up and walked around his desk. "I've got my jeep outside. We can drive it over. It's getting too hot to walk."

As he stood, Gerber said, "Where's this being held?"

Bates opened the door. "In Crinshaw's new building. He's emptied one of the conference rooms and set it up for the trial board. He's treating it as an unimportant case, and he's trying to keep the journalists from showing up."

Outside, they climbed into the jeep that Bates had signed out of the motor pool and rode across the base in silence. Outside Crinshaw's blue, two-story building, they pulled into a parking slot reserved for visitors. There were four MPs flanking the double doors of the entrance, but Bates and Gerber had no trouble getting by them. On the second floor there were two more guards stationed outside the trial room, and they wouldn't let either Bates or Gerber through without additional clearances.

"I would suggest, then," Bates told the MP staff sergeant, "that you get your boss over here, and I mean right now."

The sergeant stared at Bates for a second, wondering what he should do. Bates was a lieutenant colonel and seemed to know what he was doing. The sergeant turned to the corporal with him and said, "Go get the lieutenant."

The corporal ran off and returned a few minutes later with an officer carrying a clipboard. "What's the problem here?" he asked.

"No problem," said Bates. "Just tell your people to open up and let us go in."

"Ah, yes, sir," said the lieutenant. He read the names off both Bates's and Gerber's fatigues and flipped through the papers on the clipboard. "You're not on the list, sir."

"Then you had better get your list updated because we are going in there," said Bates.

The MP lieutenant folded the sheets over the top of his clipboard and read through the names a second time and then said, "If you'll wait here for just a moment, I'll make a call." He turned and trotted down the hall to a room near the stairway. A minute later he reappeared and said, "Let them in."

The staff sergeant stepped aside and opened the door. He said unnecessarily, "You may go right in, sir."

Gerber stopped just inside the room. On the far wall was a single window letting in the bright light of the early-afternoon sun. On either side of it stood flags, one the American stars and stripes and the other the South Vietnamese flag. In front of the window were five high-backed chairs for the members of the trial board, and in front of them was a long table of polished mahogany.

On the left side of the room, off by itself, was a small table and a single chair. There was a closed book on the table, and Gerber could see that it was a copy of the *Uniform Code of Military Justice*. The trial officer, the man who was supposed to make sure that military regulations weren't violated and that the law was followed, would sit there.

In front of the table for the trial board was the chair to be used for the witnesses. Farther into the room were two more tables separated by six or seven feet. Behind one were two chairs and behind the other were three. These would be used by the prosecutor and the defense. It wasn't quite what you'd find in *Perry Mason*, but it was a courtroom nonetheless.

Separated from the rest of the room by a flimsy wooden rail that looked as if it had just been erected was a group of chairs meant for the observers. There weren't many chairs, and with all the trouble he and Bates had had getting in, Gerber wondered who Crinshaw was expecting.

Bates and Gerber took seats in the back and waited. In a couple of minutes people began arriving. First there was an enlisted man who checked the trial officer's table and then set manila folders in front of each of the chairs of the trial board. The trial officer, a major wearing a dress green uniform, entered and sat down at his table. He glanced around quickly and then opened the book sitting in front of him.

Moments later Fetterman and Tyme entered, each escorted by two MPs. Fetterman stopped and leaned toward Gerber "Glad to see you, Captain. How are things?"

"I should be asking you that," said Gerber. "They treating you all right?"

"Just fine," said Fetterman.

Gerber turned his attention to Tyme. "Anything you need, Justin?"

"Just get us out of here," he said.

Just before they moved off, Fetterman said, "Thanks for coming."

The defense counsel followed a moment later, and the prosecutor after that. Gerber recognized the prosecutor as the major who had been with Crinshaw when Fetterman and Tyme had been arrested.

After they all had found their seats, the door opened again and one of the MPs announced, "Gentlemen. General Crinshaw."

Crinshaw, with four other officers, all colonels and all unknown to Gerber, swept into the room and headed for the trial board table. Crinshaw took his place at the center, picked up the gavel and banged it once.

"This is a preliminary hearing and is now in session," he said.

"Can he do that?" asked Gerber.

"If you mean start the hearing, yes," said Bates quietly. "If you mean act a senior officer, I think that technically he can. That is, if he didn't bring the charges. He may have directed that someone else do it so that he could preside."

"Hardly the impartial judge we would have wanted," grumbled Gerber.

Crinshaw looked at Gerber and Bates and said, "You have no authority to be here, and if you insist on disrupting this hearing, I will have you ejected."

When he had everyone's attention, Crinshaw said, "This is an Article 32 hearing to determine whether there is sufficient evidence to charge either or both of the accused men. It will be conducted in a manner set forth in the *Uniform Code of Military Justice*. All questions about procedure will be directed to Major Winston, who will act as the trial officer. Now, Major McKowen, would you care to proceed?"

Major James McKowen, the prosecution officer, stood and said, "I would like to call Lieutenant Le Phouc Khai."

Fetterman turned in his chair and shot a glance at Gerber.

Gerber shrugged in answer and leaned close to Bates. "Well, that explains part of it," he said. "It's one of Minh's strike company commanders trying to make a name for himself. He can't know too much."

Khai, wearing a new tailored uniform that displayed all of his various badges, ribbons and insignia, entered the hearing room looking straight ahead. He was tall for a Vietnamese, about five-foot-eight or-nine, thin and had short black hair. Like most Vietnamese he had a rounded face, dark-brown eyes and a small nose. He moved straight to the witness chair and was sworn in.

The trial officer, Winston, came from behind his table and asked, "Would you like a translator?"

"No, sir. I am fluent in English, as well as French and Spanish," said Khai in an accented voice that was almost impossible to understand.

"All right, Lieutenant," McKowen began as Winston returned to his seat. "For the record, would you please give us your name, rank and your current assignment."

"Yes, sir. I am First Lieutenant Le Phouc Khai, and I am Strike Company A commander and at the Special Forces camp designated A five, five, five."

"How long have you held that position?"

Khai looked at the prosecutor and then at the trial board. "Six months," he said. "I replaced Captain Minh, who was elevated on the death of Captain Trang."

"You said that you are the A Company commander. Would you tell us exactly what that entails?"

"I am responsible for the command and control of the company. My duties include assigning the men to details, overseeing the supply function, paying the men, coordinating the training and the patrols."

McKowen smiled and asked, "So you are aware of all the patrols?"

"Yes, sir."

"And you work closely with the Americans?"

"Yes. I act as a liaison between them and the Vietnamese assigned to me."

"All right," said McKowen, summing up. "Then it would be fair to say that in your capacity as company commander, you know what is happening in the camp on a day-to-day basis. You know who is detailed to accomplish what. You might say that there are no missions, no patrols, no operations accomplished without assistance from you."

"That is correct."

"All right, Lieutenant. Would you please tell us what prompted your report?"

Wilson jumped to his feet. "Objection. We have no knowledge of a report."

Crinshaw glanced at the trial officer, who nodded and said, "Counsel is correct. Major McKowen, you seem to have leaped over some ground here."

"I was trying to save a little time," he responded.

"Don't save it," snapped Wilson. "These men aren't going anywhere, and we all have plenty of time."

"That will be enough from you," said Crinshaw. "Watch your mouth, boy."

McKowen returned to his table and picked up his legal pad as if to check it for instructions. He said, "You recently became aware of some unusual activity near your camp?"

"Yes, sir. I knew that the Americans had run a cross-border operation."

"Objection!" shouted Wilson.

"Overruled," said Winston before Crinshaw could get a word in. When Wilson made no move to stand down, the trial officer added, "You can object to everything the prosecutor says when introducing his evidence, but we must assume that a report was made. Otherwise, none of us would be here. Therefore, the question stands."

"Thank you," said McKowen. He looked back at Khai. "The Americans were running an operation across the Cambodian border?"

"Objection," said Wilson. "A leading question. It hasn't been established as the Cambodian border."

Before the trial officer could respond, McKowen asked, "Which border?"

"The Cambodian border," Khai replied.

Crinshaw spoke up. "You see, boy? All your objecting is just drawing this thing out. We all know what border he was talking about. Now you just watch what you're doing."

Wilson didn't say a word.

McKowen proceeded to get Khai to talk about his knowledge of the operation that Fetterman had run into Cambodia and of the VC base he found there. Gerber was stunned as Khai talked about the mission as if he had an intimate knowledge of it, describing some things about it he couldn't possibly have known.

During the questioning Bates leaned close to Gerber and asked, "How could he know all this? Somebody on your team talking out of turn?"

"No one," whispered Gerber. "I can't figure it out. No body on my team would have told him this, and he won't talk to the Tai."

And then Gerber did know how Khai could have such detailed information. There was one source other than Fetterman and his patrol. The enemy. The VC at the Cambodian camp knew exactly what had happened and knew when it had happened. Khai would have seen Fetterman and Tyme leave, he might have seen them zeroing the weapon or loading the special ammo for it, and he had seen them return. He could have put two and two together and figured it out. That is, if the VC intelligence system was good enough to get the information to Khai, and Gerber knew that it was. The conclusion was obvious to Gerber. Khai, one of Minh's strike company commanders, was a VC. The trouble was, how was he going to prove it?

The questioning went on for nearly two hours, and when it was finished, Crinshaw asked if the defense had any questions for the witness. Wilson stood up, moved to the witness chair and stared down at Khai.

"Lieutenant," he said, "were you on the operation that you just described in such detail?"

"No."

"Then how do you know so much about it?"

"I saw Sergeant Fetterman and Sergeant Tyme leave the compound. I saw Captain Gerber and a strike company leave, and I saw them all return. I heard from many people exactly what the mission was. There is no doubt."

"Who are these many people? Were they on the mission?"

"I have names."

"Would you share some of them with us?" asked Wilson.

Now it was McKowen's turn. "Objection."

The trial officer flipped through his book rapidly and then said, "The names do not have to be introduced at this time. The defense, however, has a right to those names outside of this proceeding."

Wilson nodded and then asked, "You didn't see any of the mission that you described."

"No, sir. But I talked to people who did."

"Then what we have is hearsay evidence. You can't actually testify that—"

"Objection," McKowen said loudly. "The witness has answered the question. His position gives him knowledge of the activities of the unit and allows him to testify about the activities of the unit."

"That is not entirely true," snapped Wilson. "Many military operations take place without large numbers of people knowing about them, especially company commanders who are not directly involved. Just because he was on the Special Forces camp doesn't mean that he knows what was happening."

"Don't be naive," snorted McKowen.

There was a sharp bang as Crinshaw rapped his gavel for order. "That will be enough of that. Captain Wilson," he said, "you have asked your question, and it has been answered. Is there anything else that you want to talk about?"

Wilson stood staring, first at Crinshaw, then at McKowen and finally at Khai. At last he walked back to his seat and said, "No further questions."

"Major McKowen, do you have anything more?" asked Crinshaw.

"No, sir."

"You may step down, Lieutenant," said Winston.

"Major Winston," said Crinshaw, "what is the next step?"

"You have to ask if defense has anyone they want to put on the stand. I might remind counsel that this is not a court-martial, merely a hearing to determine if there will be one."

Gerber watched as Wilson quietly discussed something with Fetterman and Tyme. Gerber stood up and stretched, realizing that he had missed lunch. He sat down again and waited.

As Wilson got to his feet, he said, "The defense has nothing to present at this time."

Crinshaw smiled and glanced at Winston, who asked, "Do either of the men wish to make a statement?"

"Not at this time," said Wilson.

Crinshaw rapped the table with his gavel and said, "We will adjourn for a few minutes to deliberate."

"General," said Winston, "I believe you wish to call a recess."

Crinshaw waved a hand. "Whatever. You just keep everyone in here while we go talk about this."

As soon as Crinshaw was out of the hearing room, Gerber asked Bates, "What the hell kind of kangaroo court was that?"

"I think it was supposed to be some kind of arraignment hearing. I'm not sure myself."

"They'll never get away with it. A bunch of kids playing trial could have done a better job. It will never stand up on appeal. There were so many violations of Fetterman's and Tyme's rights and trial procedures that it'll get thrown out. Hell, even I can see that."

"I think," said Bates, "what the general has in mind is not so much legally proving that Fetterman and Tyme are guilty. He seems content with destroying their military careers. Even if everything is thrown out on appeal, there will always be the stink of it in their records. Everyone will know they were cleared on a technicality. Actually, it's a brilliant maneuver. He doesn't have enough to convict them, so he rigs it to get a conviction that is thrown out. It wouldn't matter if they were innocent. All that matters is they were arrested and tried."

Gerber ran a hand through his hair. "That doesn't make sense."

156 *Vietnam: Ground Zero*

"Sure it does. Lizzie Borden was acquitted in the ax murder of her parents, but look at the schoolchildren's rhyme. It says she was guilty, and nearly everyone believes it. Hell, even Fetterman's record can't save him. The people at his new post will figure he's some kind of rogue that can't be trusted in a peacetime assignment. And Tyme is through immediately, no matter what."

"Okay," admitted Gerber grudgingly. "It's a brilliant maneuver. But what does it gain him?"

"First, it removes your team sergeant and a damned good weapons expert. Next, he brings you up on charges because you're the commander. If you didn't know they went to Cambodia, then you're incompetent. If you did know, then you're as guilty as they are. In the end you're destroyed, too."

"That's all providing that Crinshaw has a trial. It might end here and now."

"Mack, don't you be naive, too."

They lapsed into silence. Gerber watched Fetterman and Tyme talking together quietly. Wilson had gone over to Winston and was talking to him. McKowen was at the window, his hands on the frame as he stared into the bright afternoon sun.

A few minutes later the door opened again and Crinshaw reappeared. He went immediately to his seat. The other four officers followed and sat down. None of them looked at either Fetterman or Tyme.

Crinshaw banged his gavel for attention and said, "After a careful review of what we have heard today, and taking into account that Lieutenant Khai's testimony is open to some question, we find that we do have reason to proceed to trial."

Wilson was on his feet immediately, but before he could speak, Crinshaw shouted, "The decision has been made, Captain!"

Tyme turned toward Gerber with a scared look in his eyes and said, "Captain?"

"Sergeant Tyme, let's have your attention up here," demanded Crinshaw.

"I didn't think he'd actually go through with it," said Gerber. "I thought this would be enough for him."

Crinshaw started giving instructions. He told Fetterman and Tyme that they would be returned to LBJ to await their court-martial. The defense would have two days to prepare the case.

Gerber sat there feeling as badly as he'd felt since he'd arrived in Vietnam. A half dozen irrational plans flashed through his mind, but none of them stood a chance of working. He had to get out of the room and into the field where there might be something he could accomplish. He got to his feet and walked over to Fetterman and Tyme. "Don't worry," he said. "We're working to get you out of this."

Then Crinshaw began banging his gavel and shouting for order.

Bates stepped close to Gerber and said, "Let's get out of here. There's nothing more to be done."

"Yeah," said Gerber. "I know." As Bates left, he hesitated long enough to say to Fetterman and Tyme, "If there is anything you need, you let me know." With that he turned and walked out of the room.

Gerber caught up to Bates in the hallway, and together they walked to the first floor and stepped out into the blast furnace of the afternoon.

"Well, that was just fucking great," said Gerber.

"What are your plans now?"

Gerber climbed into the jeep and stared through the cracked windshield. "Head back to camp."

Bates started the jeep. "I think he has you boxed on this one, Mack. I can't see a way out, and he's holding all the cards."

Gerber smiled at that and said, "Then we've got to find a new deck." He remembered a couple of things that had been said in the hearing and what he had been told by Maxwell. All of it led to one point, and Gerber was beginning to see that point. It wasn't a full-blown idea yet, but the details were beginning to fill in. His head swirled with them, and it was now only a question of sorting them all out.

11

HOTEL THREE, TAN SON NHUT AIR FORCE BASE, SAIGON

Gerber lifted his knapsack out of the back of the jeep and said, "Thanks for the lift. I'll be in touch."

"Mack," said Bates, "be careful on this one. Crinshaw is looking to hang you, too. Don't go off half-cocked."

"I won't. I think I know what I have to do, but I'll check it out carefully before I act. You watch out for my boys."

"I will. Just be careful." Bates shifted into first, turned the wheel and stepped on the gas.

When he was gone, Gerber entered the terminal building to check on the flights out toward Tay Ninh and his camp. He was halfway to the wooden counter when he heard someone call his name. He stopped and looked around. Finally he said, "Robin. What the hell are you doing here?"

"Nice greeting, Gerber. What the hell do you think I'm doing here? I'm waiting for you."

"I thought you'd found another assignment," he said. After the empty room at the hotel, he had assumed she had split for something else. Besides, he'd had other things on his mind. He was happy to see her now, but what could he tell her about his troubles? Hell, she was a journalist, and this was a big-time story. A Pulitzer prize story if ever there was one.

"Are you crazy?" she demanded. "The big story is going on with you."

"Suppose I say you can't go back to the camp."

She stared at him, looking straight into his eyes. She smiled and said, "All you can do is keep me off the aircraft that you take back. I'll grab the next one. They'll let me fly out of here because I still have the letter of authorization from General Crinshaw. I suppose that you could put me bodily on a helicopter to return me, but I'd just come back."

"There are people I could call. People at MACV headquarters and at the embassy."

"And I could tell Crinshaw that you refuse to cooperate. I could ask him what's going on because you refuse to cooperate," she said harshly.

Gerber glanced around the terminal building. This late in the day there weren't more than two dozen people in it. A couple of very young sergeants in old, faded jungle fatigues wanting a flight back to their unit caught his eye, as did an Army nurse with first lieutenant bars pinned to the front of her fatigue jacket, scissors stuck in the pocket and black hair piled on top of her head.

Gerber took Morrow's arm and led her to the corner where there were a couple of beat-up chairs for the passengers to use while they waited. He sat down with her and leaned close so that he could speak softly. "I really wish that you'd reconsider your decision."

"Which decision is that?" she asked.

He looked at her closely. She was dressed in a khaki bush jacket and pants. She wore jungle boots, the new ones that had a green nylon panel on them that let the feet breathe. A camera was hung around her neck.

He thought about the night they had spent together and wondered why he was trying so hard to send her away. Anyone else in the Army would probably be trying to convince her to come with him. It was just that the timing was so lousy, and timing was turning out to be everything.

"Which decision?" she asked again.

"Coming out to the camp. There's no story there."

"This is probably the biggest story I've ever come into contact with out there."

"But you can't use it," said Gerber sternly.

"Why the hell not?" she demanded.

"Let's talk about this later," said Gerber. "I've got to check in at the counter to see what's scheduled through. I'll put your name down, too."

"Don't bother," she said. "I already took care of that. If something comes in that's headed in the right direction, they'll let me know."

Gerber dropped back into his chair. He took off his beret and set it on the table next to him. He wiped a hand across his forehead and then rubbed it against his chest.

When he didn't say anything, Morrow asked again, "Why can't I use the story?"

"Because there isn't one."

"You have two men arrested for crossing into—"

"Robin, will you shut up," interrupted Gerber. "This is not the time or the place to go into this. There are too many people around who could hear too much. All right?"

"We're not through with this discussion yet," she warned him.

"We'll take it up at the camp when we have the chance," he said.

Just at that moment the clerk who had been working behind the counter approached and said, "Ma'am, I've an aircraft from Tay Ninh that's going back now, if you'd still like a lift."

She smiled and said, "Yes, thank you. Captain Gerber will be going, too."

"That's fine." He leaned down so that he could point through the window. "It's the one with the knight's shield on the nose sitting on Pad Five."

They landed at the camp about an hour later, having had to stop in Cu Chi to pick up another passenger. They also touched down outside of Go Dau Ha to drop off mail. At the camp Morrow grabbed her suitcase and camera bag and headed to her hootch without talking to anyone.

Bocker pretended not to notice. Gerber told Bocker that he wanted to see Kepler right away and that he needed to talk to Captain Minh. With that he went to his hootch to wait.

Minh was the first to arrive. He knocked once and entered when Gerber yelled for him to come in. Minh sat down in one of the lawn chairs and said, "Welcome back, old boy."

"I'm afraid you won't think that way after I tell you what I've learned." Gerber took the chair behind his desk and leaned forward.

"Yes?" said Minh.

"Your Lieutenant Khai is a VC," he said abruptly.

"What? How do you know?" Minh was surprised, but unflappable.

"He knows too much about Fetterman's last mission. If you didn't tell him and I didn't, there is only one source he could have used. The VC."

"Can you prove that?"

"No. No, damn it, I can't."

Minh stood up and walked around his chair. He stopped and faced Gerber. "But you are sure? No mistake?"

"No mistake. What are you going to do about it?"

"Don't worry, Captain, I'll handle it quickly and quietly."

"I must warn you that Khai has an important role in the upcoming trial. You'll have to allow for that."

Minh nodded. "So there will be a trial, after all. What do you plan to do about Fetterman and Tyme?"

"I'm not sure yet. I have a couple of ideas." He looked up at the knock on his door. "Enter," he called.

Kepler stood there wearing dirty fatigues that were badly stained with sweat. "You wanted to see me, sir?" he asked.

"I've some things to do," said Minh. "I'll meet with you later, Captain, to finish our discussion.

When Minh was gone, Gerber said, "Have a seat, Derek. I've got a couple of questions to ask you."

"Yes, sir."

"First, do you have any information about the Red Chinese in Cambodia?"

"You mean officially?"

"Exactly."

"Nothing officially. There seems to be a tacit agreement among all the combatants to ignore the Red Chinese. No one wants to admit that the Chinese are helping the North and the VC. I think that if we had a body dressed in a red Chinese uniform hanging in the wire, no one would take notice of it." Kepler smiled at that.

"Which means?" asked Gerber.

"Which means there are no Red Chinese in Cambodia. In other words, the man smoked by Fetterman and Tyme must have been a civilian."

"Oh, for Christ's sake."

"Yes, sir. Exactly," said Kepler. "If we were to obtain hard evidence of the Red Chinese in Cambodia, there will be a real effort to bury it."

"Okay. Second," continued Gerber, "what is the extent of the Ho Chi Minh Trail? How far south does it go?"

"The latest evidence I have suggests that it turns to the east just north of Highway 1, and, in fact, might incorporate portions of the highway," answered Kepler.

"Then if Sergeant Fetterman had gone far enough to the south, he could have avoided crossing the Trail?"

Kepler rubbed his chin. "I'm not sure, sir. Our information on it is sketchy at best. It may run all the way to the Gulf of Siam. I'm just giving you the latest that I have."

Just then there was another knock on the door. Gerber opened it and found Sergeant Bocker holding up a small package. "This arrived with the afternoon supplies, Captain," he said. "I thought you might want it."

"Thanks, Galvin," said Gerber. He took the package and turned it over to look at the return address. It had come from Maxwell in Saigon, according to the coded return address. "I'll want you back here in about an hour. Spread the word. Find Lieutenant Bromhead and have him meet me in thirty minutes." Gerber turned to Kepler. "You be here, too."

"BEFORE WE START this briefing," said Gerber, "I thought you would all want to know that Sergeant Fetterman and Sergeant Tyme are going to face a court-martial murder. Crinshaw and his kangaroo court decided that this afternoon."

"Jesus!" said Bocker.

"Exactly," said Gerber. "The purpose of this meeting is to determine what we can do to get them out of LBJ. I've made a few preliminary plans and want to get some feedback from you people on this."

Gerber crossed the room to the map he had tacked to the wall. He pulled the cloth that covered it free and said, "Our mission is to return to the VC camp that Sergeants Fetterman and Tyme discovered and gather evidence that the Red Chinese are there."

Bromhead nodded as he studied the map. He said slowly, as if formulating a plan as he spoke, "To prove Fetterman's innocence, we have to show that he was chasing an enemy soldier into Cambodia. But I can't see where this is going to help us."

"Ah, Johnny, my boy," said Gerber, almost mocking the way Fetterman sometimes talked to Tyme, "it can't do anything but help us, even if Fetterman is not innocent. He, or rather Sergeant Tyme, did shoot the man. And they did cross the border. The important question is, what had our Chinese friend done just prior to crossing the border back into Cambodia?"

A smile spread across Tyme's face. "The South Vietnamese rangers."

"Exactly!"

"And suddenly," said Bromhead, "Crinshaw begins to get pressure from all over to end the trial. Fetterman and Tyme were avenging the deaths of the South Vietnamese. They showed poor judgment crossing the border, but who could blame them after what they had just seen."

"And," added Gerber, "we have our government wanting the trial to end because the victim was a Red Chinese, and that is going to come out. The last thing anyone wants is for the Red Chinese to have an excuse to get into the war on an overt level. Not with nearly a billion of them on the other side of the North Vietnamese border."

"A masterstroke of intrigue," said Minh, "but for one flaw. What are you going to do to put pressure on the brigadier?"

Gerber turned and looked at the Vietnamese officer. "I'm not going to have to. That will come from above."

"You have all your ducks lined up, but for one," said Minh. "You waltz into Crinshaw's office and present this to him, but he has no incentive to let your Sergeants Fetterman and Tyme go. He still has them in jail."

"We tell him," said Gerber, "that we are prepared to go public with this. Give the information to the press. That is, as a final resort."

"You could go him one better," said Minh. "Take Miss Morrow with you."

"That's definitely out," said Gerber. "I'm not going to take a reporter, a woman no less, into Cambodia, for any reason."

"Oh, but you must," maintained Minh. "She can provide the one thing that you can't. She can go to her publisher with the evidence and be believed because she has no ax to grind. With her help you can tell Crinshaw that if Fetterman and Tyme don't get off free, the world will learn exactly who they shot."

"I said that was out. We can do this without bringing her into it."

"What's the plan, Captain?" asked Bromhead.

"The mission is simple. We go to Cambodia and gather evidence of the North Vietnamese, the VC and the Red Chinese. We establish the exact location and size of the camp and document it with photographs. We find out exactly who is using it. Remember that we need the evidence as a lever. It doesn't have to be proof that would stand up in court, only sufficient to raise questions.

"Johnny, I'm afraid that you're going to have to remain here in camp, covering our rear." He saw that Bromhead was going to protest and held up a hand. "I know. It stinks, but somebody has got to hold down the fort. If I stay, then I can be arrested. If I'm out on patrol, then Crinshaw can't arrest me until he can find me. I'll leave T.J. and Cat here with you, so you'll have someone to talk to."

Reluctantly Bromhead nodded.

"We don't want to engage the enemy," continued Gerber.

"We are an intelligence-gathering operation. We are going to find the evidence of the involvement of the other Communist parties so that we can force Crinshaw to drop the charges.

"We leave in the morning. We'll spend the first day moving carefully toward the border, so that any surveillance of our activity won't tip our hand. We cross at night."

"Will this be a sterile mission?" asked Kepler.

"No. We're going in carrying our own equipment and as American soldiers. I'm getting a little tired of fighting the war as if it doesn't exist. The only important point to remember is that no one gets left behind."

"How long are we going to be out?" Kepler continued.

"It better be less than a week. We can't spend too much time screwing around out there, or Crinshaw is going to have the trial over and Fetterman and Tyme shipped to Leavenworth.

"If there are no other questions, then everyone is dismissed for now. Detailed briefing at 2200 hours."

MINH AND ROBIN MORROW CAUGHT Gerber outside the team house as he was heading there for dinner.

"I have taken the liberty of suggesting that Miss Morrow talk to you about the patrol coming up," Minh said.

"Captain Minh," said Gerber, "I don't like being put on the spot like this."

"I'm sorry, old boy, but I believe I'm right on this one. The only way you'll win is by having a helping hand from the local newspaper."

"And I don't understand," Morrow nearly shouted, "what the big deal is."

"The big deal," Gerber shouted right back, "is that you are a reporter and a woman."

"What difference does that make?"

Gerber took a deep breath. "I think you can figure it out."

"You worried about me getting killed?"

"That's the least of the problems. If you get killed, it will probably mean that the rest of us are dead, too, and there would be nothing Crinshaw could do to us. Although getting a reporter killed out here wouldn't do us a whole lot of good when the news was released back home.''

Morrow ran a hand through her hair. "Then what's the big deal?"

For a moment Gerber hesitated, wondering how to phrase it. Finally he just blundered ahead. "What happens if you're captured? There would be no way we could protect you, and you surely can figure out what that would mean."

"Are you talking about rape? Are you suggesting that I not be allowed to go along because I might be raped?"

"Well, that's one good reason," admitted Gerber.

"Look, Gerber," said Morrow, "I don't want to be put in the position of saying that rape isn't traumatic for women, but I will say there is nothing that the enemy can do to me that is any worse than what they can do to a man. My sex doesn't make me any more vulnerable to torture.

"I had this fight with my editors when I wanted to come over here. They told me about the hardships. Living out of a suitcase or a knapsack. A lack of privacy. That I could be killed, captured or raped.

"And my response was always the same: if a man is killed, is he any less dead? If a man is tortured, is he any less hurt? I think I could handle the trauma of rape. I might be wrong, but that's no reason to leave me behind. How well could you stand up to torture or homosexual rape? Huh?"

She stopped speaking because she could feel the anger swelling in her again. Anger because she was not allowed to do her job. Anger because men were holding her back, protecting her from imagined problems.

She felt a knot form in her stomach and her knees shaking. She took several deep breaths trying to rein in her emotions so that she could tell them all what she thought of their reason for holding her back.

She turned to Gerber and said, "I've been through some of the training that you had to go through to get here. I stomped through swamps full of snakes and alligators. I went without food because we couldn't find any, and when we captured the cute little bunny, I made the men let me cut its throat to prove to them that I had the stomach to do it. Some of the training I had to take to prove to my editors that I could do it, and some of it I took because I wanted to know what it was like to be in the Army.

"So I won't fall down because we've walked a long way. I won't cry because of the horror I see out there. At least I won't until I get back here. I won't endanger your patrol by slowing you down or stepping on twigs, or even slapping an insect that is crawling on my neck."

"Or letting the motor of the film advance on your camera announce our presence."

"I learned my lesson there," she said, her face coloring slightly. "And I want to know where it says that men are somehow better able to handle combat. I want to know why anything that happens to me will be that much worse than anything that happens to the men. If you could tell me that men somehow held up better, and you could prove it, I would pick up my camera bag and go home. But you can't."

Gerber held up a hand, trying to stop her.

Morrow kept right on talking. "In Korea ten percent of the prisoners couldn't handle being captured and just rolled over and died. They didn't deal with it very well."

Minh, who had been standing by watching and listening to the entire tirade with an amused smile, said, "You know, some of the best armies ever seen have included women. Even in combat roles. May I remind you, Captain, that the Vietcong are an equal-opportunity army?"

"Damn it, you're supposed to be helping me," said Gerber.

"Why?" demanded Morrow. "You should listen to him."

"Now, old boy," continued Minh, "the reason for taking Miss Morrow with you is to document everything. She has a forum for publication if your plans fail. And I will tell you right now that anything you get is going to be buried by either your government or mine. Robin will be able to get it released, which is the only threat that is going to work."

"I don't know," said Gerber. He had to admit that Minh's arguments made sense. But that still didn't get Morrow on the patrol. Even if he could logically understand what was being said, emotionally he couldn't handle it. It just wasn't...what? Normal? Right?

"Captain Minh is right," Morrow said. "Suppose you gather your information and give it to Crinshaw and he classifies it all by claiming national security. Then what do you do? If I'm there, I can go to the network."

"Let's, for the minute, say that you're right," Gerber said. "There's still a problem. This is a hell of a story. What's to stop you from printing it, anyway? We help you gather it, and then you stab us in the back by using it even if it's not needed. The only reason for this mission is to get Sergeant Fetterman and Sergeant Tyme out of jail."

"Captain," said Morrow, her voice softening slightly, "I'm as interested in freeing your men as you are. Sergeant Fetterman never treated me as anything but an equal. He helped me when I needed it. He doesn't deserve what has happened to him, and I'll pledge to you that anything I see out there will not be used by me while it can still hurt any of you, or until you tell me that I should go to the network with it. Besides, after last night I thought you knew me better than that. I just didn't fully understand what was going on here. Captain Minh made it clear."

Gerber looked at Minh. He didn't want Morrow on the patrol for a number of reasons, a couple of them personal, but all the arguments made sense. Especially the one about needing the extra leverage to spring Fetterman and Tyme.

Reluctantly he said, "Okay. You go. But we can't compromise anything for your convenience. You have to hold up your end."

"Did you hear me ask for a compromise? Did you hear me say that I couldn't hack it?"

"There'll be a briefing tonight at 2200 hours. You be there. Without your notebook or tape recorder. We don't want anything written down that would suggest we planned this out."

"Understood, Captain," said Morrow, "You won't regret this."

AT 2200 HOURS all the Americans left in the camp were in the team house. Bocker, who had left one of the Vietnamese on radio duty so that he could attend, was handing out beer from the tired old refrigerator. Anderson had taken two and given one of them to Kittredge. They sat together at one of the rear tables. Kepler had a map of his own and was sitting near the front so that he would be close to Gerber and could verify what the captain was saying. He had checked his intel files before coming to the meeting. Mc-Millan and Washington, the two team medics, sat eating sandwiches at a table to the left, and Bromhead stood at the door watching. He was to make sure that no one approached too close once the briefing began.

Gerber stood at the front of the room with a large map of the immediate area tacked on the wall behind him. On it he had traced a route. He checked his watch once, saw that everyone was present and began.

"After talking to Krung and a couple of the other Tai, and coupling that information with the aerial recon photos that Sergeant Kepler reviewed, we have pretty well established the exact location of the new camp. If we leave here at 0600 hours tomorrow, we'll have all day to get to the border. We rest there, cross in the dark and keep moving until morning. Given the distances and the route we're going to use, it should take three days."

Gerber went on, detailing the plan over the next fifteen minutes. He showed them the route of march, outlining probable areas of danger based on the latest information that Kepler had gotten from Special Forces headquarters in Nha Trang. He talked about the supplies they would take, the weapons they would carry and then explained the necessity of taking Robin Morrow. There were a few raised eyebrows, but no one commented. When he finished, he answered questions and then explained in greater detail why it was necessary for Morrow to accompany them.

By 2300 hours they had finished the briefing. Gerber dismissed the men, telling them to get ready to move out at first light. Then he drew Bromhead off to one side.

"Johnny, there is one thing that you're going to have to do. I wouldn't ask you to do this except that there's no way I can lead the patrol and take care of it."

"Doesn't matter, Captain. I'll do what I have to do."

"You'll have to keep a watch on that trial in Long Binh. If it looks bad for Fetterman and Tyme, you'll have to get something to them. There's a package in my hootch containing new passports for both of them. You might have to deliver them."

"No problem, Captain."

"You might want to think about this for a couple of minutes before you agree. Do you fully understand what it means?"

"If I'm caught sneaking passports in to them, I'll be arrested."

"Exactly."

"Doesn't matter, Captain. I'll do what I have to do. If it comes to that, I'll get them out of there."

"I'm sorry to have to put you on the spot like this, Johnny, but someone has to be available to do it."

"It's all right. We're getting a little short for this shit, but I'm happy that you feel you can trust me to spring them."

12

SOUTH GATE OF U.S.
SPECIAL FORCES CAMP
A-555

The patrol had gathered at the gate just before six. Gerber set his pack down near a low sandbagged wall that was a second line of defense if the VC got that close, and pulled the map from his pocket. He folded it so that the area they would be marching through would be on top and showed it to Krung and the three Tai who would be going on the mission with them.

Morrow stood to one side, watching. She was dressed in a camouflaged jungle suit borrowed from Minh. She didn't have a steel pot, but wore a boonie hat pulled down low to hide her blond hair. She had a pistol belt around her waist that held two canteens, a large bowie knife and a small first-aid kit. She had a small pack containing her C-rats, a poncho liner and a roll of toilet paper scrounged from the team house. And she had a small camera bag for the single 35 mm that she carried.

The other Americans on the patrol—Smith, Kepler, Bocker, Kittredge and Ian McMillan, the team senior medic—all carried three canteens. They also carried a pistol each, extra ammo, grenades, combat knives and flares. Bocker had the additional duty of carrying the PRC-10, and McMillan had his medical kit. Kittredge was responsible for the M-60 machine gun and two belts of ammo for it. Smith had an M-79 grenade launcher strapped to his back. All that was in addition to their rifles. Each carried an M-14 because it used the same 7.62 mm ammo as the M-60.

Gerber sat down in front of his pack, eased the straps over his shoulders, buckled it and stood up, shifting the weight so that it rode high on his back. He leaned forward, moved the pack around and then stood straight. He reached up to where his Randall combat knife was taped upside down to the harness of his web gear, making sure it would come free in a hurry without hitting the other equipment he carried.

Gerber checked the sky and saw low-hanging black clouds swirling to the west, indicating the possibility of rain sometime soon. Back to the east the sun was climbing in the sky. It all meant that the day would be very humid. Gerber was already beginning to sweat, and all he had done was stand up.

"Sergeant Smith," he said, "take Sergeant Krung and walk point."

"Yes, sir."

"Johnny," said Gerber, turning his attention to the young lieutenant, "I'm counting on you in case things go bad for Fetterman and Tyme."

"I understand, Captain."

Before he could say more, T.J. Washington, the big black assistant medical NCO, appeared from between two of the hootches in the Tai area. He shouted, "Captain. Hold up."

"What's up?" asked Gerber as the man halted in front of him.

"Radio message out of Saigon. They've got someone coming out to talk to you this morning."

"No call sign?" asked Gerber.

"Came through the Operations section of one of the helicopter units down there. Didn't say who the passenger was, only that he would be out here this morning and that you should meet him at the pad."

Gerber shook his head. "I'm on patrol. You tell him that I wasn't here when the message came in."

"He's going to want to know why I didn't radio the information to you, sir," said Washington.

"Because we're on radio silence and you couldn't see any reason to break it. Once he gets here, if he insists, you ask Lieutenant Bromhead about it." Gerber glanced at Bromhead. "I trust that you'll deny him permission."

"Can't have people calling all over on the radio when we have a patrol out on an ambush assignment," said Bromhead, grinning. "Might tip our hand."

"Very good, Johnny. I'll see you again in about a week." He raised his voice. "Sully, let's move them out."

They wormed their way through the wire and into the elephant grass south of the camp. Once clear of the final defenses, the booby traps that Sully Smith had hidden as the first obstacle for attacking VC, they turned to the west, along the bank of one of the smaller canals. Trees and bushes provided them with some cover, but the vegetation wasn't too thick so the going wasn't tiring. They crossed the remnants of roads, one of them having been paved sometime in the past but now little more than broken chunks of concrete that were slowly disintegrating.

They passed a number of abandoned hamlets, the mud and thatch structures falling down. They skirted the edges, avoiding walking through them. Morrow took pictures of them as they went by, almost as if to document the route they had taken. They also crossed several streams, but since it was the end of the dry season, it hadn't been difficult.

At noon they halted in a stand of huge trees that had one time hidden a farmer's two-room hootch. The remains of a mud wall and fence that had been the pen for a water buffalo were evident. To one side was a short domed structure that was an outdoor oven. Gerber allowed the men to build a fire in it to heat their C-rations for lunch. He was surprised that the canned food tasted so much better if it was heated slightly. But to admit that was to admit that your taste buds were ruined for life.

Before they began the afternoon march, Gerber asked Morrow how she was doing.

She sat with her back against a large palm tree, the remains of her lunch scattered in front of her as she scraped at the ground so that she could bury the cans. Her hair was hanging around her face, damp with sweat. She was pale, as if she were about to pass out.

She smiled weakly and said, "I'm doing just fine. Just fine." She glanced at the others, who seemed not to have noticed how far they had walked. "What time do you plan to make camp this evening?"

"Depends."

"Mack, the worst thing is not knowing how long we're going to be moving. If I have a goal, I can make it, but if it is just some time in the future, I'm going to fold up. I have to have that goal."

"We've made good time this morning," said Gerber. He took his map from the side pocket on his fatigue pants and studied it for a moment. "It's maybe ten, twelve klicks to the border from here. That's a couple of hours away, unless we rest frequently."

"You don't have to go slow because of me," she snapped.

"I know that. I just don't want to get too close to Cambodia in the daylight. Anyway, I suspect we'll be camped by four or five this afternoon." Gerber looked at Morrow closely. She was sitting with her legs flat on the ground and her hands by her sides. Her head was slightly bowed. She looked totally exhausted. "You sure that you're all right."

"Yes. Would you worry this much about one of the men?"

"Yeah, I would. Anyone having heat stroke is going to slow us down. Maybe cause us to cancel the mission if we have to call for a medevac. Did you take your salt tablets?"

Morrow shook her head. "I'm not convinced that salt tablets are a good thing."

"Neither am I," said Gerber, "but they do seem to prevent the heat from sapping all your strength. Take a couple of them. And drink some of your water. We're going to move out in about ten minutes."

Gerber got to his feet and walked over to where McMillan sat eating the Army's version of fruit cocktail. He crouched near the medic and said, "You want to keep an eye on Miss Morrow? The heat seems to be getting to her."

"No problem, Captain."

"If she gets into trouble, or you think she's getting sick, let me know, but don't let her know what you're doing."

"Understood. She going to slow us down?"

"I'm not sure that it matters today, Ian. We made good progress this morning, and we're not that far from where I want to cross the border. I was going to slow us down, anyway. You just keep an eye on her."

"Yes, sir."

Gerber then moved over to where Bocker was sitting, listening to the radio. "You hear anything on the radio from the camp?" he asked.

"No, sir. Well, not for us, anyway. Heard T.J. talking to someone a little while ago about resupply. Think it was an incoming chopper."

"We move out in a few minutes."

"I'll be ready."

After lunch Gerber avoided the fingers of jungle that meandered toward Cambodia, opting for a path that headed nearly due west. He followed the canal to the northwest of Long Khot, keeping on the edge of the swamp and staying in the paddies. The water in some of them was nearly knee-deep, and there were no young rice plants to walk on so the feet of the patrol were sucked at by the mud, making it tiring to walk and slowing them down. They arrived at the Cambodian border at a point about seven klicks due south of Svay Rieng. Gerber knew the enemy camp he wanted was north of there. By swinging this far south, he hoped to avoid the southern end of the Ho Chi Minh Trail.

Gerber scattered his men, making use of the little cover available. There was a clump of trees that provided a good field of fire for a hundred meters in all directions, and he put the majority of his tiny force there with Morrow in the middle of them. He set two men about fifty meters to the north, almost in Cambodia, hidden in a depression that had a large bush growing in the center. From there they would be able to see anyone approaching and could alert the others.

Once security was set, Gerber moved back to the stand of trees. The men and Morrow rested, a couple of them sleeping, even though it was the hottest part of the day. Sweat rolled off them, soaking their uniforms as completely as if the rain that had threatened in the morning had finally fallen. Morrow had collapsed near a tree, removed her pack and then rolled onto her side, her hands under her head. She seemed to be asleep, but her breathing was rapid and shallow. She seemed to be exhausted, and Gerber wondered if she was going to make it.

Gerber sat down and took out the canned bread that came with his C-ration meal. He opened the tin and used his knife to cut the bread into halves. Then he opened the can of grape jelly and spread it all on one half of the bread. He squeezed the two pieces together and ate it. The bread was dry and the jelly runny, but Gerber didn't care. Then, opening a can of boned chicken, which he salted heavily, he ate his dinner while studying his map, looking for landmarks that he would be able to spot in the dark. The most obvious were the large river on the east side of Svay Rieng, the bridge over that river and Svay Rieng itself. It seemed to be a large town compared to most of the hamlets in the area and would probably have lights that could be seen from a couple of klicks in the dark.

When he finished eating, Gerber sent and briefed Kittredge and Krung on the route they would follow after dark. They could easily get north of Svay Rieng in the dark, and they could lay low for the day. That done, he went to check on Morrow. She was sitting up, her legs crossed Indian fashion, eating peaches from an OD can.

"You look a hundred percent better," Gerber told her.

"I feel better," she said with a smile. "Just needed a little nap." She held up her can. "You want some peaches?"

"No, thanks. I've eaten." Gerber sat down next to her. "We're going to be on the move most of the night," he warned her.

"It'll be cooler without the sun," she said. "It was the sun that was getting to me. I'll be all right."

Gerber nodded and got up, putting a hand on her shoulder. She looked up at him, and Gerber could see that she was afraid. He walked off to check on the rest of his men and make sure they all had eaten something. Then he sent two men out to relieve the men in the clump of bushes. When he'd finished all that, he sat down off by himself and carefully cleaned his rifle. He didn't think it was dirty, but it couldn't hurt to clean it. Besides, it was something to do.

BRIGADIER GENERAL BILLY JOE CRINSHAW stood in front of his ornate desk and stared at McKowen. He slammed his fist down hard on the desktop.

"I don't give a shit about your stupid rule book. I want everything moved up. I want the trial to start in the morning. You tell that defense puke that national security comes before the accuseds' rights, and if he has a real problem with that, we'll find someone who doesn't."

McKowen opened the briefcase sitting on his lap and flipped through the papers. He said, "That won't give us time to assemble all the witnesses and interview them."

"Look," shouted Crinshaw, "the men are guilty. All this legal maneuvering is designed to get them off. I want them nailed."

"It doesn't matter how guilty they are if we go on violating their rights. You're pushing this too hard, General. If we're not careful, they'll get off scot-free."

"I want this finished. We can bury it under national security. I don't want you telling me why something can't be done. I want you to find a way to do it. You got that, boy?"

McKowen flipped through more of his papers as he tried to think of something fast. Finally he muttered, "Yes, sir."

Crinshaw walked around his desk to the blinds on the window. He pulled them open and looked out, but saw nothing that interested him. Then he moved over to the air conditioner and turned it down a notch so that it was blowing more cold air.

"I'm telling you the truth, Major," said Crinshaw as he walked to his desk. "Somebody causes a stink, we tell them that it's national security. We wear that like a cloak, and we can do anything."

McKowen stuffed the papers into his briefcase and stood up. "I can be ready tomorrow, but I'll tell you right now, General, the defense is going to ask for a continuance."

"You let me worry about that. I'll see that they don't get it. Anything else you need, Major?"

"No, sir. that should be it. I'll be ready tomorrow at nine."

IT HAD BEEN DARK for over an hour when a light rain began to fall. Gerber decided that the conditions for crossing into Cambodia would never be any better. They left the trees, worked their way slowly to the bushes that concealed the two security men and then headed straight for Cambodia. Kittredge, still on point, consulted his compass frequently to make sure they weren't diverting too far to the west. In the dark and rain the patrol was grouped closely together so that not more than a meter separated them from one another.

They were moving over open ground, through paddies and clear fields, and since they were now in Cambodia, it gave them a feeling of being naked. But the jungle had shriveled to scraggly tree lines that were broken frequently by streams.

To the left was a tree line that ran almost north-south, and Gerber had Kittredge veer toward it. He wanted the cover it would provide, and it would give them an opportunity to take a break. Besides, Gerber was tired of the feeling at the base of his spine where he imagined an enemy sniper was aiming. He knew there were no snipers behind him, but he couldn't shake the feeling. He wondered if he ever would.

They were nearly to the trees when there was a stuttering burst from a machine gun, and in the mist of the falling drizzle, two men went down. There was a piercing scream from one of them, but nothing from the other. Gerber dived to his right, rolling in the mud, and aimed his M-14 over the paddy dike at the muzzle-flash of the enemy RPD machine gun. He glanced right and left, but in the dark and falling rain could see no one nearby.

All at once a dozen new weapons joined the machine gun, the green-and-white tracers from the VC positions slashing through the air overhead, or kicking up dirt and splattering mud in the paddies and along the dikes. Rather than use his M-14, which would only pinpoint his location for the enemy gunners, Gerber reached for one of the grenades he carried. He raised his voice and said, ''On three, we toss the grenades before we attack the trees. McMillan, you stay here with Morrow and keep her head down.''

Gerber didn't wait for any of his men to acknowledge as he began counting off, shouting over the rattling of the enemy weapons. As he shouted the last number, he lobbed the grenade as far as he could. He knew that he wasn't following the Army standard of throwing it like a baseball, but in Army training he'd never been pinned down by Russian RPDs and AK-47s.

As the grenades detonated in a flaming burst of light like the flashbulbs of a camera, Gerber was on his feet shouting at the top of his voice, ''Let's go! Let's go!'' He ran forward, dodging right and then left, firing five-shot bursts from the hip, watching his tracers disappear into the blackness of the tree line.

Then he was in the trees among the VC. Out of the corner of his eye, he saw movement and turned to fire. Just as he pulled the trigger, something snapped down on the barrel of his rifle and the ruby tracers buried themselves in the jungle floor. Gerber didn't try to see what knocked his weapon aside, he just kicked sideways with his foot, but connected with nothing. He then dived forward, rolling to his back so that he was suddenly facing the VC who had struck his rifle. The man turned and lunged with his bayonet, but Gerber blocked the blow with his own weapon, forcing the blade to the side. At the same time he kicked out, snapping the enemy's legs out from under him so that the man fell to his side. Gerber pulled the trigger on his M-14, but nothing happened.

He rolled to the right toward the enemy soldier and grabbed the barrel of the AK-47, twisting it away from him. As the man tried to stand, Gerber jerked the knife from his harness and slashed at the enemy. The VC screamed in pain, and Gerber felt himself splashed with blood. He thrust again, driving the knife to the hilt in the man's side. The VC went into a spasm, jerking the blade from Gerber's hand.

As Gerber got to his hands and knees, someone leaped on his back and an arm circled his throat, lifting his head. Gerber reached for the VC's elbow, dropped his shoulders and flipped the enemy to the ground. He grabbed the steel pot from his own head and used it to club the man, hitting him three times rapidly, hearing the sickening crunch of breaking bone as the VC's skull splintered.

As Gerber got to his feet, he heard the rattling of weapons around him as the two sides searched for each other in the dark. Gerber pulled his pistol from the holster and moved to the right. Charlie seemed to rise out of the ground in front of him, and Gerber jammed his weapon into the man's stomach and fired twice. He turned quickly and saw another VC running in the trees. Dropping to one knee, he emptied his .45 at the fleeing shape.

Suddenly the American force began taking heavy fire from the left flank. Gerber fell to the ground, rolled to his left and reached for a grenade. There was an explosion far in front of him, twenty or thirty meters away, the flash outlining the enemy machine gunners. Gerber threw a grenade, but it was long, detonating behind the enemy. Before he could try again, there was another explosion right in front of the enemy machine gun that bent the barrel upward toward the sky. The firing from that position ended abruptly.

The shooting tapered off to an occasional bang, but all of it from American-made weapons. Gerber couldn't hear any firing from AKs or SKSs. He eased back, out of the trees and away from the dead men, pausing long enough to retrieve his M-14. He worked the bolt and dislodged the round that had jammed it.

"Cease fire! Fall back!" he yelled.

In the paddies he found McMillan crouched over one of the Tai who had been hit in the initial burst. Morrow was beside him, shaking out a field dressing so that she could give it to McMillan.

"Wounded?" asked Gerber.

"Just him. Other one's dead. Took a round through the chest. Right in the heart. He had to be dead before he hit the ground."

"Who was it?"

"Le Khan."

"You okay, Robin?" he asked.

"Fine. A little shaky, but fine."

Kepler appeared at Gerber's side and said, "Sir, we've got three prisoners."

"What? Prisoners?"

"Yes, sir. Three of them surrendered as Kittredge blew up the machine gun. Just stood up, threw down their weapons and started yelling in Vietnamese. I'm afraid we killed the fourth before we realized what was happening. I've got the men sweeping through the trees to see what else they can find."

"Any of the others hurt?"

"Not really. I think Kittredge has a nasty cut on the arm, but he did it to himself with his own knife. He's more pissed than hurt."

Gerber stood up and took Kepler off to the side. "The last thing we need is prisoners. There's no way we can head deeper into Cambodia with a bunch of VC prisoners."

"You don't understand, sir. One of them's Chinese. A Chinese NCO, I think."

Gerber felt a tickle of excitement as his adrenaline began to pump. He tried to keep his voice calm as he asked, "Chinese? You're sure?"

"Yes, sir. Doesn't seem to understand Vietnamese, and he's definitely wearing the uniform of a Chinese." Kepler wiped the rain from his face with his arm.

"Christ, I don't believe it." Gerber turned and looked at the tree line, but could see nothing moving in it. "Get the men recalled," he ordered. "Get the prisoners subdued, collect the weapons."

"Yes, sir," Kepler replied.

Gerber turned back to McMillan. "Ian, can we move the wounded man?"

"I've got the bleeding stopped and given him a shot of morphine. The wound isn't that bad. Grazed the shoulder and went through the fleshy part of the upper arm."

"Derek, have your boys cut us some bamboo for poles to make stretchers. Let's snap it up. We've got to get out of here."

Gerber then got down and stretched out on the ground. He put a poncho over his head and used his flashlight to study his map. He saw that the shortest way out of Cambodia was the way they had come. The border near the Parrot's Beak whipped east and west before turning south again. He snapped off the light and folded up his map before he rolled up the poncho.

Kepler had returned with four lengths of bamboo. Gerber watched as Kepler laid two of the poles, separated by eighteen inches, in the center of a poncho. He then folded the excess material over top of the bamboo to create a stretcher, then repeated the exercise for the second stretcher. They put the wounded Tai on one of them and the dead man on the second after tying his body into a poncho liner.

When they were ready, Gerber said, ''Steve, take the point. Keep Krung with you. Move due south and hurry it up. We want to get to the border as quickly as we can. And Galvin, you're going to have to guard the prisoners.''

''No problem.''

They moved out with Kittredge and Krung leading, followed by the two stretcher teams, Bocker and his prisoners and finally Morrow and Gerber. The pace was slower now because of the stretchers, and everyone was tired. The light rain that had aided them earlier finally stopped, and they could hear the sounds of the insects. The mosquitoes attacked them relentlessly. It was hard going, but they continued until they had recrossed the border and were in South Vietnam.

Gerber was tempted to stop in the clump of bamboo and palm trees they had used earlier, but knew that was the quickest way to get ambushed. Army training had taught him to not double back on his own trail except for an ambush or in very unusual circumstances, and not to use the same rest stops. He forced his team to the south, away from the border, until they reached Kinh Bay Thuoc. Then, as the first faint evidence of dawn began to appear, Gerber found a stand of trees that made an ideal camp.

As soon as he had the perimeter established, he looked at the prisoners. They sat huddled in the center with Bocker watching them warily. Kepler stood off to one side observing.

As Gerber approached his intel officer, he said, ''Derek, what do you think?''

''I think we've got them dead to rights. There's no way to argue that he isn't here. We have the proof that the Red Chinese are here. I'll need some time to talk to them, but I think we've got it.''

Next he went over to talk to McMillan about the wounded man. McMillan told him that a rest would probably be good for him, rather than undergoing the constant rocking movement of the stretcher. The man was in no danger.

He turned and saw Morrow sitting on the ground leaning on her pack, her eyes closed. He walked over to her and asked, "How are you doing?"

She opened her eyes and wiped the perspiration from her forehead. "Just fine."

"We're going to hold here for a while. I'm going to try to get us airlift out of here so we don't have to walk back to the camp."

"You think you'll have any luck with that?"

"Should. I have wounded and I have prisoners." He looked at her carefully and added, "You look a little flushed. You take your salt tablets?"

"Yes, sir," she said in a mocking voice.

Gerber sat down next to her and took off his helmet, setting it on the ground beside him. In the growing light of day, he could see it was stained with the blood of the man he had killed with it. He turned it so that he didn't have to look at the stain.

"Listen," he said, "I just wanted to say that you've held up your end just as you said you would. You've done a hell of a job."

Morrow turned so that she could see him better. She wasn't sure what to say. She brushed at the damp hair that clung to her forehead.

"You mean that?"

"Yeah. I just wanted you to know that anything I might have said was nothing personal. Hell, after the night in Saigon, you should know that. I'm just trying to do what's best for everyone."

She started to reach out to touch him, but stopped. She smiled and said, "I understand." She didn't speak for a moment and then, as if to change the subject, said, "You think we have what we need to spring Fetterman and Tyme?"

"Yeah, I think so. If I didn't, we'd still be in Cambodia. but I think the Chinese soldier is going to be the one thing we need to underscore this whole mess." Gerber looked at his watch. "Why don't you take a few pictures of our Chinese guest and then get some rest. It'll be a few hours before I can arrange airlift out of here.''

13

TAN SON NHUT AIR
FORCES BASE, SAIGON

It was shortly after nine when Fetterman and Tyme were brought into the trial room. The trial officer sat at his table, the *Uniform Code of Military Justice* sitting in front of him. McKowen sat behind his table, and two assistants, both young second lieutenants, sat just behind him on the other side of the rail. As soon as they were seated, the trial officer announced the entrance of the board. Everyone stood again while Crinshaw and the four other members of the board entered.

When everyone was settled, the trial officer, at the direction of the presiding officer, General Crinshaw, said, "Charges and specifications. One. That on or about Twelve June 1965, Master Sergeant Anthony B. Fetterman did willfully, and with malice aforethought, conspire to cause the death of a foreign national while operating illegally in a neutral country.

"Two. That Master Sergeant Anthony B. Fetterman did illegally enter said neutral country in violation of Army regulations, government policies and the law of the land."

He went on for another minute, outlining a list of minor charges and offenses, the worst of which seemed to be causing his subordinates to violate regulations. When he finished reading the charges against Fetterman, he read the ones against Tyme, which were virtually the same. When he finished, he sat down and waited, almost as if he expected applause for his performance.

Crinshaw banged his gavel unnecessarily and asked, "How do you plead?"

Wilson rose, repeated the charges against Fetterman and said not guilty after each one. He then went through the same routine with the charges against Tyme.

Again Crinshaw rapped his gavel on the table and said, "Is the prosecutor ready to proceed?"

"If it pleases the court," interrupted Wilson, "I have a motion."

Crinshaw looked immediately to the trial officer. "He has that prerogative," said Winston.

"Go ahead, then," said Crinshaw.

"Sir, I would like to move that the case be delayed by one week so that I may better prepare the defense."

"Denied."

"Sir, I would like to have Sergeant Tyme tried separately from Sergeant Fetterman because Sergeant Tyme is required by military regulations to obey the orders of his senior sergeant and is therefore not responsible for his actions. Had he failed to obey those orders, he could have been charged with making a mutiny."

"Denied."

"May I have a clarification?"

"National security," said Crinshaw, falling back to the position he'd planned to use. "We can't afford to have another trial after this one. It does not prejudice the case against Sergeant Tyme to have him tried at the same time. Anything else?"

Wilson looked at the yellow pad sitting on the table in front of him. He scratched out the motions that Crinshaw had denied. "That's all," he said.

"Is the prosecution ready?" asked Crinshaw.

Mc Kowen stood and said, "I am prepared to proceed."

"Then please do."

Mc Kowen checked his legal pad sitting on the table and said, "I would like to call Sergeant John Happel."

"Who's that?" asked Wilson, leaning close to Fetterman.

Fetterman shrugged. "I haven't the faintest idea."

Happel, a short, fat sergeant wearing an ill-fitting uniform that couldn't hide the massive gut hanging over his belt, walked into the trial room. He had black hair that had been cut short, thick eyebrows and a large nose that dominated his face. He was sworn in and sat down in the witness chair, facing Crinshaw and the four colonels of the trial board.

"All right, Sergeant," began McKowen, "for the record, please state your name, rank and unit of assignment."

Happel ducked his head twice instead of nodding and said, "John C. Happel, staff sergeant for the 205th Resupply Company here at Tan Son Nhut. I'm the supply sergeant."

"Have you had any dealings with either Sergeant Fetterman or Sergeant Tyme?"

"Yes, sir."

"Were all these official dealings?"

"Sir?" asked Happel.

"What I mean, Sergeant, were all your dealings with them in the proper channels with the proper forms?"

"Oh, no, sir. Lots of them were what you might call midnight requisitions. They would want something, come down to me and trade for it. They rarely had the proper supply forms."

"What sort of equipment were they obtaining?"

"Objection!" said Wilson, leaping to his feet. "This line of questioning is producing nothing."

"It is establishing that both Sergeant Fetterman and Sergeant Tyme are renegades who have no respect for the Army or the Army system," responded McKowen heatedly.

"What?" asked Wilson. "Because they sometimes went outside of official supply channels to obtain the equipment that they needed?"

"Exactly."

Wilson shook his head in disbelief. "In the interest of saving time," he said, "we are prepared to stipulate that both Sergeant Fetterman and Sergeant Tyme used unofficial channels to gather the material and information they needed to fulfill their duties." Out of the corner of his eye. Wilson saw McKowen open his mouth. Wilson added hastily, "On the condition that the prosecutor will stipulate that it is a common practice throughout the Army and not indicative of poor soldiers."

"That's ridiculous," said McKowen.

"In that case I object again. And I plan to refute this testimony by bringing in other soldiers who are known for their abilities to gather material outside of normal supply channels. Every unit has one. They trade their surplus around so that everyone ends up with what they need. These talents are not those of bad soldiers, but of dedicated and loyal ones who are ingeniously completing their mission."

"Counsel is summing up," protested McKowen.

"Mr. Trial Officer," interrupted Crinshaw.

"The objection is sustained unless the prosecutor can establish quickly the relevance of this line of questioning," Winston stated.

Fetterman looked at Crinshaw and could plainly see the general was not happy with the way Winston had ruled.

The prosecutor turned his attention to the fat sergeant sitting on the witness chair. "I have no further questions in that case."

"You may step down," said Crinshaw.

"Wait a minute, General," said Wilson. "I have a couple of questions for this man."

Crinshaw shot an icy glare at Wilson, but said nothing. Wilson turned and walked back to the defense table and picked up his legal pad. He read it for a moment while the tension built.

"I have only one question for the witness," he said. "I want him to describe Sergeant Fetterman to me."

The sergeant began to turn, his elbow on the back of the witness chair. Wilson jumped between him and the defense table. "No, Sergeant," he said. "I want you to describe him without looking at him. If you've had as many dealings with him as you claim, and if all of them were the under-the-table operations you've mentioned, you should know what he looks like."

The sergeant stared at the trial board, as if he expected them to help him. He was quiet for a moment and then said, "I'm not very good at describing people."

"A general description will do. Nothing elaborate. Tall or short. Thin or fat. Blond hair or brown. Flattop? Just a general description."

"Well, I think he's on the tall side."

"That will be all," snapped Wilson. He went back to the defense table and sat down.

The prosecutor watched the fat sergeant leave the room. He sat there for a moment waiting. Then he shrugged and said, "I would like to call Lieutenant Khai to the stand."

The MP at the door opened it, spoke to someone outside and a minute later Khai entered. He was sworn in and then began describing the same things that he had talked about during the Article 32 hearing. He mentioned that a specific man seemed to have been the target and that Fetterman and Tyme had been bragging about killing the man who had engineered the deaths of the South Vietnamese rangers.

"I have never bragged about killing a man," Fetterman told Wilson.

"Don't worry about it," said Wilson. "We'll get our chance in a little while."

IT WAS NEARLY NOON before Gerber could arrange for airlift. Using the PRC-10, he contacted Crusader Operations in Tay Ninh, alerting them that he needed travel from his present location to his camp. He was told that airlift was not available and that all the aircraft were tied up in a mass combat assault into the Hobo Woods and Iron Triangle area.

"Roger," said Gerber, his voice harsh. "Be advised that I have wounded."

"Understand that you have wounded. Are they critical?"

"Negative, Crusader Ops. I say again, negative."

"Zulu Six, Crusader Six advises that he can supply three ships for airlift in approximately one hour."

"Understand. Advise Six that I have three POWs. And thank him for the lift."

"Roger, Zulu Six. Crusader Six will radio when flight is one five minutes from your location."

It was actually less than an hour. Gerber heard the call and told Bocker, "Acknowledge and throw smoke."

Bocker keyed the handset and said, "I will throw smoke."

"Roger Zulu Six."

Gerber found a smoke grenade and flipped it to Bocker, who pulled the pin and tossed it into the open. It billowed into a green cloud that drifted back to the west.

"ID Green," said the voice on the radio.

"Roger green."

Gerber got to his feet and said, "Let's get into the field. Kittredge, I want you and Kepler on one aircraft with the prisoners. They try anything stupid, you shoot them. Ian, you get on one chopper with the wounded and the dead. You need to divert to Dau Tieng or Tay Ninh for the medical facilities, you do it. The rest of us will get on the last ship."

They filtered out of the trees in the open rice fields. Gerber spaced the loads so that they were thirty feet apart. The incoming aircraft would be able to land close to the group that it was to pick up.

He watched the helicopters approach from the north, dropping from the sky slowly as they got nearer. When they were a hundred meters from the LZ and still about thirty or forty feet in the air, they flared, slowing their forward momentum, one aircraft settling toward each group.

The patrol was hit by the rotor wash that threatened to knock them to the ground, and Morrow staggered a couple of steps. Gerber grabbed her arm, steadying her.

As the skids touched the ground, Gerber was moving, leaping into the cargo compartment, reaching out to lift Morrow in after him. Smith tossed some of the captured equipment in and then scrambled up after it. Gerber held a thumb up as Krung and Bocker climbed in, yelling to the pilot that he was ready.

They lifted off immediately, the nose of the chopper dropping suddenly as the pilot tried to increase his airspeed as they flashed across the paddies toward a tree line. He leveled off, and as they were about to collide with the trees, he pulled back on the cyclic, popping over them and then settling back so that they were flying only three or four feet above the ground, first to the south to gain speed and then turning to the east so that they were on the way back to the camp.

Gerber was fascinated as they climbed slightly to fly over tree lines, or farmers and their oxen in fields. He was grinning from ear to ear, enjoying the feeling of speed that he was getting from the flight. To the right, level with them, was another helicopter, and next to it the third, leading them. The door gunners and crew chiefs all sat behind their weapons, aviation-modified M-60 machine guns, ready to return any enemy fire they received.

He glanced to the left and saw Morrow gripping the edge of the troop seat in both hands, her knuckles white. She had her eyes closed and her lips were working as if she were praying silently.

Just beyond her, almost on a level with them but in the distance, he saw a rice farmer's hootch. He thought he saw someone jump inside, but couldn't be sure. A moment later there was a splash in the water of one of the paddies near them, as if someone had fired a single round at the flight. But none of the door gunners shot back, and Gerber wasn't sure that he had seen anything.

From the other side of the cargo compartment he heard a whoop and looked over. Smith was leaning forward, straining the seat belt, holding his steel pot with one hand as if the wind rushing through the open doors would be strong enough to tear it from his head. He turned, smiled at Gerber and gave him a thumbs-up sign.

The aircraft seemed to slow and began to gain altitude until they were at the normal cruising height of about fifteen hundred feet. Off in the distance Gerber could see the telltale square on top of the slight rise that was his camp. A cloud of bright yellow rose from the northern side of the camp where the helipad was.

They came screaming out of the sky, approaching faster than normal, and as they neared the ground, all three helicopters flared at the same time, stopping in a swirling cloud of red dust and yellow smoke.

Smith unfastened his seat belt, grabbed his equipment and leaped to the ground, rushing to the side of the pad. Gerber tapped Morrow on the shoulder, startling her. She snapped her eyes open and screamed, but the sound of her voice was lost in the whine of the turbines and the popping of the rotor blades. Gerber laughed and pointed to the ground. She nodded and reached down with a shaking hand to unbuckle her seat belt. Once out of the aircraft, she ran from the helipad toward her hootch without looking back.

Gerber got out and ran to the second chopper. McMillan was grinning as he helped unload the wounded man, who had been lying on the floor of the cargo compartment. The man was semiconscious as the morphine that McMillan had given him earlier began to wear off. McMillan held up a thumb to tell Gerber that the man was all right. He would be taken to the dispensary for treatment. The body of the dead striker was taken off, and two Tai carried it toward their area.

Kepler and Kittredge escorted the three prisoners from the lead helicopter. They moved rapidly from the pad toward the redoubt, heading straight for the team house. That would separate the prisoners from the rest of the compound and give them an extra barrier to cross if they had any escape plans.

Almost as the last of the patrol hit the ground, the choppers picked up to a hover, sending the people on the pad scrambling. They hovered to the west, to the runway, and then took off down it. They climbed out slightly so that they would clear the bunkers and wire on the south side of the camp. Once over them they dropped down, flying with their skids just above the elephant grass, the rotor wash clearly visible as it whipped through the vegetation.

As soon as the helicopters disappeared, Minh, who had been watching the show from the commo bunker, walked up. Gerber immediately said, "Where's Johnny?"

Minh waved the question aside and asked, "Who was wounded?"

Gerber explained about the ambush and then said, "I really should go tell Bao that one of his boys was killed before Sergeant Krung does. Where's Johnny?" he asked again.

"Don't really know, old boy. A Major Dumont arrived shortly after you departed and demanded, in no uncertain terms, that you be recalled from the field. Lieutenant Bromhead refused, following your instructions to the letter. After waiting most of the day, Dumont insisted that the lieutenant return with him to Saigon.''

"Well, that's just fucking great!" Gerber said angrily.

"The lieutenant wanted to make sure I told you that he had the package that you had mentioned to him."

"Shit!" said Gerber. "I hope he doesn't do anything rash."

"Such as?" asked Minh.

"Just some special instructions I gave him." Gerber was worried. In his message Bromhead was obviously referring to the package containing the two false passports Maxwell had gotten for Fetterman and Tyme. Gerber was afraid that Bromhead might give them to Fetterman too soon.

"You heard anything about the trial?"

"Not really. Only that they moved everything up."

Gerber slapped a hand on Minh's shoulder. "I'll have to hope that Johnny can take care of himself in Saigon for a few hours. I'll find him tomorrow when I take the results of the patrol in to show Crinshaw."

"You think you found enough?"

"I'm not sure. I hope I can force Crinshaw's hand, but I just don't know."

Before they got away from the pad, Kepler and Robin Morrow returned. Morrow complained, "Sergeant Kepler doesn't want me with him while he interrogates the prisoners. I think he's afraid I'll see something he doesn't want me to see."

"It's not that at all, sir," Kepler said. "Psychologically I don't think it's such a good idea. Miss Morrow's presence might make them clam up."

"Sounds like bullshit to me," she said.

Gerber couldn't help himself. He burst out laughing. "You may be right, but let's let Sergeant Kepler have his way for now. I want you to get some pictures of the prisoners, but that will be later."

An hour later Kepler found Gerber working in his hootch, his shirt hanging on the back of his chair as he sat at his desk. "Something I think you should know, Captain," he said.

"What'd you get?"

"Well, the Chinese guy won't talk to me. I think he's claiming that he doesn't speak English, and the Vietnamese told me they couldn't speak Chinese."

"I suppose we could have killed the interpreter."

"Yes, sir. Anyway, I talked quite a bit to the VC. They told me something that I think might end our problem. I think they're telling me that Fetterman and Tyme dusted the wrong guy."

"What?"

"From what I can gather, the officer who led the patrol that ambushed the Vietnamese is not the guy they shot."

"Oh, shit!" said Gerber. "I don't believe it."

"Well, sir," Kepler began, "Fetterman never got a good look at the guy."

"No. No," said Gerber. "All this trouble and we hit the wrong guy."

"How's this going to affect the trial?"

Gerber scrubbed at his face with both hands. "That I don't know. I use that little gem right, and it might crush the case."

FETTERMAN WAS SURPRISED when he received a visitor after his evening meal. He was surprised that Crinshaw would let him have a visitor and he was even more astonished when it turned out to be Bromhead. The young lieutenant stood at the far end of the second floor of the Long Binh Jail near an iron door with bars in the window, arguing with a corporal. The enlisted man finally nodded and backed away, allowing Bromhead to pass.

At the cell door Bromhead said, "Well, Master Sergeant, I see that you've finally gotten yourself into a mess that you can't get yourself out of."

"That's right, Lieutenant," responded Fetterman, "whatever that means."

"Corporal," Bromhead shouted, "open this door."

The man trotted over, took a large key ring holding two dozen keys from his pocket, selected one unerringly and unlocked the door. As he locked Bromhead in, he said, "Let me know when you're ready to go, sir."

When the corporal was gone, Fetterman said, "What's happened to the captain?" He thought about that and then said, "Which isn't to say that I'm not glad to see you, sir."

"Captain Gerber is out with a patrol, trying to find something to get you out of here."

"So, how are things at the camp?" asked Fetterman. He sat back on the single cot in the cell. There was a toilet stool a couple of feet away with a partially used roll of paper next to it. Only the back wall was solid. The rest were made of bars that ran from floor to ceiling. That allowed a guard at the door at the far end of the building to see into each of the cells.

"Things are fine. Listen, Sergeant, the captain asked me to come and see you if things got grim. I would have been here earlier, but I had to hang around with a major named Dumont. He finally went to talk to Crinshaw, and I came up here."

Bromhead looked around carefully. The corporal was at the far end of the room, out of easy earshot. There were a couple of privates sitting at a table, but they were more concerned with their card game.

"The captain gave me a final instruction before he left on patrol." Bromhead stopped talking and looked sheepish. "I don't really know how to phrase this, except to say if you, ah, would like a pistol and a passport, they're available."

"You got them with you?"

"Yes. If you want them."

"Lieutenant, I have been raked over the coals today. I've watched a court-martial that was more like a circus. I've watched a general officer subvert a system that was designed to protect the rights of the innocent. I'm tired of it all. I don't want to wait around to see if someone at a high level is honest or not."

"What about Sergeant Tyme?"

"I'll take him with me. Can't leave Boom-Boom behind. He's like a babe in the woods."

"I've got a passport for him, too. Don't have a weapon for him, though."

Fetterman shook his head. "Just give me the passports, sir. If I have the pistol, I'll be tempted to use it, and I don't want to hurt any fellow GIs, even if they are MPs."

"Won't you need the pistol to get out?"

Fetterman grinned. "Really, Lieutenant, give me some credit. These rear-area jailers won't be hard to fool. They never make jailers out of the top-of-the-line troops. I'm as good as out of here."

After looking one last time to see where the MPs were, Bromhead reached into his jacket pocket and pulled out the two passports. "I don't know how the captain got them, but they're current and made out in false names."

Fetterman picked up one of the passports and opened it. It was a standard United States passport with a dark-green cover indicating that it wasn't issued to a government employee. It was the kind given to regular citizens. Inside were the proper entrance stamps showing that the passport holder had entered Vietnam legally four weeks earlier. It also contained the proper stamps for entering and leaving Japan. Fetterman read through his false travel itinerary in the fake document.

Bromhead stood. "I'd like to stay here, I mean in Long Binh or Saigon tonight, in case I could be of service to you. But I really should try to return to camp."

Now Fetterman stood and held out a hand. "Thanks for your help, Johnny. I enjoyed working with you."

"The same, Master Sergeant." Bromhead stood, his eyes locked on Fetterman's. He was remembering the first time he had talked to Fetterman, telling him to call him Johnny because everyone did. Fetterman had said to call him Master Sergeant because everyone did. But then it had been Fetterman who had bailed him out when the west wall had nearly collapsed as the VC tried to overrun the camp. They had shared some life together, but more important, they had defeated death together.

"It's a rotten deal, Master Sergeant. I wish there was something more I could do."

"You did what you could," he said. "Mrs. Fetterman and the kids would appreciate all that you've done."

That was Fetterman's highest praise.

14

U.S. SPECIAL FORCES
CAMP A-555

Gerber spent the night organizing his reports so that he would be prepared when he confronted Crinshaw in the morning. He asked Morrow to take more pictures of the prisoners and to develop them as soon as she could, and had Kepler continue his interrogation of the prisoners in case they had any more information that would be useful. Bocker arranged for a helicopter to take him to Saigon in the morning.

· After a hasty breakfast of powdered eggs and reconstituted orange juice, he checked with Robin Morrow. She had been up all night developing the pictures. She told him that the hootches weren't completely lightproof and that her lab technique might leave something to be desired, but the pictures clearly showed all that they wanted shown. She said she would be ready when the chopper arrived at nine.

As Gerber stood in his hootch, his knapsack on his cot, he was interrupted by a quiet knock on the door. "Enter," he said.

Minh walked in, a grim look on his face. "Lieutenant Khai returned to camp last night," Minh reported. "He said that his part in the trial had been concluded and that he was reporting for duty."

Gerber sat down on his cot. Before he had gone on his patrol, he had been so sure that Khai was a VC. He knew many of the ARVN units were infiltrated by the Vietcong so to have one in a strike company on the camp wasn't totally unexpected. The evidence against him was circumstantial, but it seemed to be overwhelming. "You think we should talk about this now since he's back?"

"No, I don't think that will be necessary. I investigated the problem last night and regret to inform you that Lieutenant Khai took his own life when confronted with the accusation.

"My God!" exclaimed Gerber.

"It is of no consequence, old boy. The man was a traitor." Minh rubbed a hand over his face. "No, that is not fair. He was an enemy soldier and a spy, but I don't believe he was a traitor. He was loyal to his government. It just wasn't mine."

"Are there going to be any repercussions?" asked Gerber. He was suddenly aware of how tired he was. He wanted desperately for this to be over.

"I think not. My people in Saigon believe he was killed in action, and the men here know the truth. The situation is now resolved."

Gerber got to his feet and retrieved the bottle of Beam's from the bottom of his wall locker. He uncorked it and said, "I know there is nothing I can say to make this easier. To say that it is the nature of war is no help. I'm sorry for the way it turned out."

Minh took the Beam's and drank deeply, breathed and drank again. As he handed it back, he said, "It's not your fault. I'll get back to my duties. Good luck in Saigon."

Gerber sat down on his cot again when Minh left and took another drink of Beam's. At the moment there seemed to be nothing else to do.

Bocker looked in a moment later and said, "Chopper will be here in a few minutes, Captain."

"Thanks," said Gerber. "Please inform Miss Morrow."

"Yes, sir. Good luck, sir."

Within five minutes Gerber was at the pad with Morrow, watching the Huey approach from the distance. As it came in, he said to her, "This is it." He was echoing the words said by a million different soldiers before they entered a thousand different battles.

A little before noon they were in Crinshaw's outer office, facing the same old master sergeant who sat behind the same old desk. He stopped them before they could enter Crinshaw's inner office because they didn't have an appointment. The room was cooler than it had been the last time Gerber had been there. A new air conditioner had been built into the wall just under the window. The blinds were drawn so that there was no glare from outside, and that meant the lights had to be on. The walls of the office were made of dark stained paneling so even with the overhead lights and three lamps—one on each of the two end tables and the third on the old sergeant's desk—it was still dim inside. A coffeepot on a small table had been added, along with Styrofoam cups, sugar and creamer. The sergeant didn't offer any coffee to Gerber or Morrow. There were pictures scattered around the walls in wooden frames, watercolors of local scenes and one of F-4s sitting in sandbagged revetments waiting to take off on new missions.

The sergeant reached for the field phone, spun the crank and spoke into it quietly for a moment. Then he gestured at the new beige couch. When he hung up, he said, "Please have a seat. The general will be ready to see you in a couple of minutes."

When they were seated, Gerber said, "Now you wait here while I start this. I may be able to get through it without having to bring you in."

"I don't understand your reluctance to go in with everything you have."

"It's simple. We're supposed to clean our own dirty laundry without having to resort to outside forces. The man who calls a senator because he feels he has been treated shabbily has his records flagged with a note that says there is Congressional influence. It's not a good career move. Likewise, someone who goes to the papers has his record marked. He's labeled as a maverick, a troublemaker."

"Then why do all this?"

"To get my people out of jail."

Before he could say more, there was a buzz from the field phone, and the sergeant pointed to the closed door. "The general will see you now, Captain," he said.

Gerber stood up. "It'll be a while before I need you, but if I holler, it's going to mean that I'm in a hole."

"Good luck, Mack."

"Thanks." He took a deep breath, hesitated for a second with his hand on the doorknob and then went in.

As usual, it was so cold in the office that Crinshaw was wearing a field jacket. Like the outer office, the curtains were drawn, giving the impression of late evening. The captured weapons were still mounted on the wall, and Gerber thought that a couple of new ones had been added. Gerber knew Crinshaw collected them by telling subordinates that trophy hunting was career suicide. The general sat behind his mammoth desk that was bare except for a green blotter, a couple of pens in a shiny brass holder and a single manila file. The file was open, and Crinshaw was reading the top page.

"Boy, you are in a heap of trouble," Crinshaw began. He held up a hand to stave off any protest that Gerber might want to make. "You are lucky that you came in before I sent out the military police to arrest you. I've already locked your lieutenant up in LBJ for helping Fetterman and Tyme escape. I should also tell you that you'll be arrested just as soon as I can get the MPs over here."

"Before you make any precipitative moves, General, I think you'd better hear what I have to say."

"Don't go telling me what I better do, boy. And before you open that smart mouth of yours again, let me remind you of your rights under Article—"

"Cut the shit, General. You don't intimidate me by reading my rights to me. You are not in possession of all the facts in this case. You had better hear what I have to say or you can kiss all our careers goodbye."

Gerber was going to say more, but Crinshaw had stood and was trying to speak. His face had gone a deep purple and his mouth was working, but there were no sounds coming out of it. He clutched his chest, and for a moment Gerber thought the older man was having a heart attack.

Finally Crinshaw got his breath back. His voice was strained, but quiet. "Talk to me," was all he said.

Gerber moved closer to the large desk. He handed a package of pictures across as Crinshaw collapsed into his chair and said, "First, maybe you'll want to look at these. They are proof that the North Vietnamese and the Red Chinese are operating both here in South Vietnam and in Cambodia."

Without a word Crinshaw grabbed the pictures and thumbed through them. He saw pictures of a couple of men in NVA uniforms sitting in Gerber's team house at the camp. He hesitated when he came to the one showing a man in a khaki uniform sitting at a table while Derek Kepler stood by, but all he said was, "So?"

"General, you have my men in jail for committing crimes in a neutral country. I'm showing you the country isn't all that neutral."

"Makes no difference what you have there. The entire army of the People's Republic of China could be in Cambodia, and it wouldn't matter. The Soviet Union could have giant bases there, and it wouldn't matter. Your people crossed the border illegally."

"All right, General," he said. "If you'll look at that last picture again, you'll see that it is of a man wearing the uniform of a Red Chinese NCO. You'll also notice that he is in the team house at my camp. In other words, he is currently a prisoner of war. Positive proof that the Chinese are assisting the North Vietnamese. He was captured after he participated in an ambush against one of my patrols. He was fighting the war.

"You'll further note," Gerber said conversationally, "that reports from all my operations in the last month have been appended to the photos. You'll note that there is an order signed by you stating that I am to allow one reporter, Robin Morrow, free access to everything I have, including participation on patrols—"

"I never said that she was to be allowed on patrols," countered Crinshaw.

Ignoring the interruption, Gerber continued, "And you will see a copy of an order, again signed by you, sending us out to look for a missing Vietnamese patrol and to do everything in our power to find it. That can be interpreted to mean we were to sweep into Cambodia if necessary. In other words, it's possible that my men were in Cambodia on your orders."

"That's really stretching things, Gerber," Crinshaw replied. "I never meant for you to violate Cambodia's neutrality and you know it. You're grasping at straws there. If that's the best you can do, I'll just call the MPs now and save us all some trouble."

"I have witnesses, both American and South Vietnamese, who can testify you hinted strongly that a recon into Cambodia would be permissible if the patrol was not found."

"That's not what I—"

"You wanted to convict Sergeants Fetterman and Tyme for the murder of a foreign national," Gerber continued, ignoring Crinshaw's protest. "Except that the foreign national was a soldier who had participated in a number of actions against us."

Now Crinshaw felt that he was on firmer ground. "Makes no difference. You can't go around smoking Red Chinese, especially when they are in Cambodia. All your arguments make no difference to me. The man you claim is a Red Chinese NCO does nothing for you or your men. You just don't get it, do you, boy? Fetterman and Tyme did cross the border into Cambodia, and they did shoot the man. We all know that."

"Then you admit that this case is about the killing of a special Red Chinese," said Gerber.

"Among other things," admitted Crinshaw. He leaned back in his chair. He laced his fingers behind his head and looked at the ceiling.

"The man you are referring to," said Gerber, "the one supposedly dusted by Sergeant Tyme, is, in fact, still alive and well."

Crinshaw slammed his fist to the desktop with so much force that the penholder flew to the floor. "Now how in the hell can you know that?"

"Interrogation of one of our other prisoners, a North Vietnamese regular. We talked to him for quite a while. He told us that the Chinese officer who normally ran patrols into South Vietnam had been recalled to China three days after he eliminated the South Vietnamese ranger patrol."

Now Gerber held up his hand. "I know what you're thinking. But our prisoner told us all about it, including the story of a marvelous pistol the Chinese officer picked up as a trophy. I'm sure you'll be able to confirm that one of the South Vietnamese ranger officers was carrying a special weapon.''

"Think you're pretty smart, don't you, boy? Think you boxed old Billy Joe pretty good with all your reports and pictures and interrogations and all, don't you? Well, you got one big problem. They still killed a Chinese, and they did it in Cambodia. I have them dead to rights, and they will be convicted the moment we catch them—and then we'll try them for desertion. When we're done with them, you'll be next. You sent them out to do that.''

Gerber was suddenly tired of it all. He didn't like this one little bit. Vietnam was a war zone, although some of the newspapers liked to call it an undeclared war. But it was war nonetheless. Everyone was supposed to stick together with an eye on defeating the enemy. Personal hatreds and personality conflicts were supposed to wait until the enemy was defeated. Crinshaw wasn't interested in any of that. He wanted to destroy the Special Forces for some reason that Gerber just couldn't understand.

He sat down uninvited. It was something that his military training told him never to do. But now it didn't matter. He had already violated a dozen unwritten rules and about half that many that were written. Sitting down without permission certainly couldn't make things any worse than they already were.

Crinshaw was right on one point. Fetterman and Tyme were guilty of crossing the border and shooting a Red Chinese. They had done it because the CIA had said that other teams in other locations were eliminating Vietcong cadre and North Vietnamese leaders. The only real difference was that all the other activity was taking place in South Vietnam. Gerber's men had gone into Cambodia.

"Why don't you save us all some trouble, boy," said Crinshaw, "and meet the MPs outside. I don't want to look at you anymore."

"Because I don't think I'm going to jail," responded Gerber.

"One thing I should mention," said Crinshaw, rocking forward in his chair so that he could lean both his elbows on the desk. "None of what you have said will leave this room. This is national security and I've just classified it. You've got nothing. I'll give a call to MACV, and they'll pick up your prisoner and see that he gets back to the proper place. They'll keep it quiet, so that you don't even have that."

Gerber shook his head. He had used it all. He'd tried everything he had, and Crinshaw showed no signs of caving in. He had an answer for everything. Minh had been right about that. The fact that Fetterman and Tyme had shot the wrong man made no real difference. They had shot someone.

"The CIA at MACV headquarters is fully aware of the mission," said Gerber. "We discussed it before the men went into the field."

"The CIA and MACV deny all knowledge of such activities," Crinshaw shot back. "You just refuse to understand. You're all alone on this. Now why don't you just get out of here, you dirty son of a bitch."

Gerber stood, but made no move to leave the room. "If you continue to do this, I take you down with me."

For just an instant Crinshaw thought Gerber meant to kill him. His face drained of color, and he rocked back in his chair. Then he realized what Gerber meant. He said, "There is nothing you can do."

It was time to play the last card. The one that Minh had insisted would have to be used. Gerber was suddenly glad that he had allowed himself to be pushed into taking Morrow on the patrol. "A story has been written and is on its way back to the United States," he said softly. "It outlines everything that has happened. It points fingers at you for ordering the mission, for covering up and for obstructing justice. It proves that the Red Chinese are involved in Vietnam. It covers it all, every bit of it, and when it's published, we all go down."

Crinshaw burst into laughter. "That's old, boy. That's really old. It's got whiskers on it."

"It's not a bluff, General."

"You try something like that, you're going to be in jail for a long time."

"From what you've already said, General," countered Gerber, "I'm heading there for a long sentence, anyway. I've nothing to lose. You overplayed your hand."

"Why don't you just get the fuck out of here."

Gerber moved to the door and opened it. Robin Morrow was on her feet and inside before Crinshaw could say a word.

"She filed her story this morning before we came over here," he said. "A story that contains all the things that we've just talked about."

"I can stop the story, General," she said. "But without my word it gets printed and syndicated and broadcast. It's already on the plane heading home, with lots and lots of pictures."

"One call," said Crinshaw. "I can stop it with one call."

"It's too late," said Morrow. She looked to the right at the wing chair, walked over and sat down. "Far too late."

"I'm sure that I can convince your editors to withhold the story," said Crinshaw, smiling. "In the interests of national security, that is. They are reasonable people."

"I can stop it," said Morrow, "but you can't."

"Go ahead," blustered Crinshaw. "Print it. I'll get by, but you, Captain, you'll be court-martialed. And so will all of the men you're so damned proud of. Every last one of them. You'll all end up in jail or worse."

Morrow looked at Gerber, her eyes questioning, wondering if Crinshaw could make good his threat.

But Gerber knew he had won. Crinshaw had made his threat with no conviction in his voice. It was as hollow as a drainpipe. He said, "Make your calls, General. I've got to get my people back to the camp. I've got my senior demolitions man in charge right now. There's not an American officer within fifty miles of the place."

"There is still a regulation covering insubordination," said Crinshaw. "You're getting a little too smart in your tones. And I believe we have a directive covering who is to be left in command of units in the field."

"Yes, sir," said Gerber. "But this is an extraordinary set of circumstances."

Crinshaw slumped in his chair. He stared at the two people in front of him. The whirring of the air conditioner was the only sound as it continued to blast an icy breeze into the room.

"You say that you can stop the story," he finally said to Morrow. "It won't look suspicious to your people?"

She shook her head. "They won't even look at it without my say-so."

"Everything stays in this room," said Crinshaw. "Everything."

"Of course," said Gerber, suddenly wanting to laugh, to shout or scream.

Crinshaw turned to Morrow again. "I let you go out there and you do this to me."

"I'm sorry about that, General, but—"

"Never mind," said Crinshaw harshly. "It all stays right here. You have no story. No pictures. Nothing."

"Until you approve it for publication," she said.

"Don't hold your breath on that," he said. "It'll never see the light of day." He turned his attention to Gerber. "What do you need from me?" asked Crinshaw, his voice subdued.

"First, call Long Binh and get my executive officer out of jail. Then call the judge advocate, or whoever, and order all copies of the trial proceedings brought here so you can destroy them. Then issue the appropriate orders so that neither Fetterman nor Tyme will be arrested for a jailbreak."

Crinshaw nodded dumbly and sat staring at the bright-green blotter, as if in a trance. Then he shook himself. The color came back to his face and the anger flared in his eyes. "All right, Captain. You've made your point. Now get the hell out of here."

"Yes, sir."

"One thing, General," said Morrow. "Just before I came in, two MPs arrived, and I think they wanted to arrest Captain Gerber."

Crinshaw picked up the phone. He grumbled into it and then said, "You're in the clear. Now get the hell out of here."

At the door Gerber stopped. He turned back and said, "One more thing, General. What do I do with the Chinese NCO?"

"That's your problem now, hotshot. You deal with it."

"Yes, sir."

Outside, the sergeant was telling the MPs to fade away. Morrow stopped at the couch to pick up her camera bag. She turned toward Gerber and broke into a smile, giggling almost helplessly. "You did it!"

"We did it," said Gerber, laughing. "Without you, it would never have worked. I had to have it all. If I had missed a single piece, Crinshaw might have been able to get out from under it. If it hadn't been for the threat of public exposure, Crinshaw still might have beaten it, but with the public in on the case, Crinshaw would have fallen, too. It had to be the whole package, or we would have lost." He laughed again, but more from relief than anything else.

"I do have just one question," said Robin. "What *are* you going to do with the Chinese guy?"

Gerber pushed a hand through his hair. "Hadn't thought that much about it. I suppose I'll turn him over to the CIA and let them worry about it."

"What will the CIA do to him?"

"I would imagine they'll question him and then send him home with a nasty-gram to the Chinese about keeping their people out of the war."

"You think that's fair?" asked Morrow. "After all, he helped you, even if he didn't mean to."

"Yeah, but he's also an enemy soldier. Besides, if the CIA sends him home, we'll get something in return."

"What about him?"

"What about him?" repeated Gerber.

"When he gets back to China, if the CIA sends him, won't they shoot him? Aren't you worried about that?"

"I doubt seriously that they would shoot him. But even if they did, why should I care? He's an enemy soldier, and if we met on the battlefield, I would be obligated to shoot him. For that matter, he would be obligated to shoot me. Hell, for all I know, he tried to. I'm not going to lose any sleep over an enemy soldier. I have too many friendly soldiers to worry about."

"Like Fetterman and Tyme?" she asked.

"And Bromhead."

15

OFFICERS' CLUB, TAN SON NHUT AIR FORCE BASE, SAIGON

It had taken less than an hour to get Bromhead out of Long Binh Jail. Crinshaw's phone call had arranged it, and when Gerber walked into the jail, he found the young lieutenant waiting in a downstairs office, talking to the MPs about the war in the field. They had then driven back to Saigon and the Tan Son Nhut officers' club. Gerber had found a secluded table in the back that was away from the late-afternoon diners. He had asked for a bottle of Beam's and then ordered three drinks, neat, to take to the table for Morrow, Bromhead and himself.

"You know," said Gerber, "you make me sorry for some of the things I've said about journalists. You prove that there are some who have a sense of responsibility, who won't violate trust or human feelings, in search of the almighty story."

"I don't know whether I should thank you or stomp out of here," Robin replied.

"I meant it as a compliment. I do appreciate all that you did for us."

"Mack," she said quietly, "I think you know why I did it."

Bromhead looked from one to the other and said, "Did I miss something?"

"You must have," said Gerber. "Jail will do that to you."

Robin picked up her drink and swirled it around. She had her eyes fixed on Gerber.

For a moment there was silence between them, but it was an easy silence with no pressure. Gerber sat there relishing it because it was the first time in several weeks he'd been able to relax. He didn't have to worry about patrols, or the disposition of troops, or where Bromhead was. In three or four hours he would have to get back to camp, but right now Minh would have to handle it. Smith was there to oversee it, and Charlie hadn't tried anything for a couple of months.

The only real problem was how to find Fetterman and tell him that everything had changed during the past twenty hours. He and Tyme could return to the unit with the charges against them dropped. Better than dropped. They had been erased. Gerber was sure Fetterman would check in, but figured he would receive the message while at the camp. Then he would tell him to bring Tyme home.

Morrow cut into his thoughts. "So now what? Is your general going to cause you any more problems?"

"That's going to be a very interesting situation. He could cause a lot of trouble for us, just by making us sign forms—in triplicate—for everything we need. Or by denying us air support and sending us the worst men for replacements. He could probably have the Vietnamese pull Minh and a couple of the top strike companies out and replace them with crooks. He could, but I don't think he will."

"Why not?"

"It would be like cutting his own throat. We've got a good record out there, and that makes him look good. No, I think he'll just look for ways to cut us down without hurting himself. We've made a real enemy, but not one who will let himself be destroyed to get us."

There was more to say, and more questions that Morrow wanted to ask, but it wasn't the time or the place for them. Now was the time to celebrate before they had to catch the flight back to the camp.

Gerber turned his attention to Bromhead. "I think you may have jumped the gun a little," he said, laughing. "Gave Fetterman the passports a little too soon, although it doesn't matter."

Bromhead had ordered another round of drinks when the waitress came by. "They were as good as convicted," he said in his own defense, "and the way the general was shoving everything through, I figured he'd have them on the way to Leavenworth by morning. I got them out as quickly as I could."

"I'm not criticizing you, Johnny, other than to say you shouldn't have let them catch you."

"I'll buy that," he said.

They were interrupted again, this time by the PA system in the bar. "Captain Mack Gerber, you have a call in the main office. Captain Gerber, telephone in the main office."

As he got up, Gerber said, "Just who in the hell could that be! If the waitress makes a swing past us again," he added, "get me a steak, rare, with a baked potato."

Gerber asked the bartender where he could take the call and was directed to a phone. He picked it up, listened for a second to the open line and said, "Gerber."

"Afternoon, Captain," said Fetterman. "How's the world treating you?"

"Tony! Where in the hell are you?"

"Bangkok, Captain. An aptly named little burg. Ol' Boom-Boom is living up to his name, too. Right now he is in the company of a young Oriental lass with the most beautiful black hair you could imagine. And, for contrast, he has found a blond lady. He's entertaining both of them with stories of derring-do that raise my hair."

Gerber laughed. "Bangkok! You old son of a bitch. How'd you get there?" He thought for a moment and then said, "More important, how'd you know to call me here?"

"Figured that after the young lieutenant sprung us, he'd get his ass in a sling and you'd have to rescue him. Then you'd head over to the club for a quick one before heading home. Besides, when you're a master sergeant, you have to know these things."

"I find that extremely difficult to believe."

"Yes, sir. Actually, I managed to get through to the camp, and they told me where you had gone. I called Colonel Bates and he suggested that I try the club."

"Speaking of which," said Gerber, "everything has been cleared at this end. The general has been convinced that a grave mistake was made, and the slate is now clean. You can return anytime you want."

"Well, now, Captain. That might be a problem. Me, I would be back immediately. Only get myself in trouble with Mrs. Fetterman and the kids by hanging around here. But Boom-Boom, he doesn't have such mundane worries. He wants to see the sights, entertain the ladies and have a good time. Figured that you might see your way clear to letting us have a couple of three-day passes, or maybe granting a little extra leave time."

"That's no problem, Tony."

"What about the escape, Captain? They can't be real happy about that."

"All I can tell you is that Lieutenant Bromhead is here in the club with me sucking down the Beam's like he was told that he'd better drink it fast or somebody else would get his share. Seriously, the theory here is: if there was no trial, then there was no arrest, and if there was no arrest, then there couldn't have been an escape. You're in, free and clear."

"Okay, Captain. We'll come on back in a couple of days. You might have to arrange for transport from Tan Son Nhut out of the camp."

"There is one other thing, Tony. We had some trouble with Crinshaw's body. They shipped the wrong one for burial. You understand what I'm telling you? We got the wrong body."

"Yes, sir. I get the message. Me and Boom-Boom will be there by 0900 tomorrow."

Gerber hung up the phone carefully. Two or three weeks would soon be wiped out. Totally gone. In the morning things would be back to normal, and he would be back at the camp. Tomorrow they would start the war again.

GLOSSARY

AC—An aircraft commander. The pilot in charge of the aircraft.

AK-47—Assault Rifle normally used by the North Vietnamese and the Vietcong.

AO—Area of Operation.

AO-DAI—A long dresslike garment, split up the sides and worn over pants.

AP ROUNDS—Armor-piercing ammunition.

ARVN—Army of the Republic of Vietnam. A south Vietnamese soldier. Also known as Marvin Arvin.

BAR—Browning Automatic Rifle.

BEAUCOUP—French for many. Boonie rats usually pronounced this word boo-coo.

BODY COUNT—The number of enemy killed, wounded or captured during an operation. Term used by Saigon and Washington as a means of measuring progress of the war.

BOOM-BOOM—Term used by the Vietnamese prostitutes in selling their product.

BOONDOGGLE—Any military operation that hasn't been completely thought out. An operation that is ridiculous.

BOONIE RAT—An infantryman or grunt.

C AND C—The Command and Control aircraft that circled over-head to direct the combined air and ground operations.

CARIBOU—Cargo transport plane.

CHICOM—Chinese Communist.

CHINOOK—Army Aviation twin-engine helicopter.

CH-47—Also known as a shit hook. See *Shit hook*.

CLAYMORE—An antipersonnel mine that fires 750 steel balls with a lethal range of 50 meters.

CO CONG—Term referring to the female Vietcong.

DAI UY—Vietnamese Army rank the equivalent of captain.

DCI—Director, Central Intelligence. The director of the Central Intelligence Agency or CIA.

DEROS—See *Short-timer*.

DONG—A unit of North Vietnamese money about equal to a penny.

FIVE—Radio call sign for the executive officer of a unit.

FNG—a fucking new guy.

FRENCH FORT—A distinctive triangular structure built by the hundreds by the French.

GARAND—The M-1 rifle that was replaced by the M-14. Issued to the Vietnamese early in the war.

GREENS—The Army Class A uniform.

HE—High explosive ammunition.

HOOTCH—Almost any shelter, from temporary to long-term.

HOTEL THREE—A helicopter landing area at Saigon's Tan Son Nhut Air Force Base.

HUEY—A Bell UH-1D, or its successor, the UH-1H, helicopter. Called a Huey because its original designation was HU, but later changed to UH. Also called a Slick.

IN-COUNTRY—Term used to refer to American troops operating in South Vietnam. They were all in-country.

KABAR—A type of military combat knife.

KIA—Killed in Action.

KLICK—A thousand meters. A kilometer. Roughly five-sixths of a mile.

LBJ—Long Binh Jail.

LEGS—Derogatory term used by airborne-qualified troops in talking about regular infantry.

LIMA LIMA—Land line. Refers to telephone communications between two points on the ground.

LLDB—Luc Luong Dac Biet. The South Vietnamese Special Forces.

LP—Listening Post. A position outside the perimeter manned by a couple of people to give advance warning of enemy activity.

LZ—Landing Zone.

M-14—Standard Rifle of the U.S. Army, eventually replaced by the M-16. It fired the standard NATO 7.62 mm round.

M-16—Became the standard infantry weapon of the Vietnam War. It fired 5.56 mm ammunition.

M-79—A short-barreled, shoulder-fired weapon that fires a 40 mm grenade. These can be high explosive, white phosphorus or canister.

MACV—Military Assistance Command, Vietnam. Replaced MAAG in 1964

MEDEVAC—Also called Dustoff. Medical evacuation by helicopter.

MP—Military Police.

MPC—Military Payment Certificates. GI play money.

NCO—A noncommissioned officer. A noncom. A sergeant.

NEXT—The man who said he was the next to be rotated home. See *Short.*

NINETEEN—The average age of the combat soldier in Vietnam. During World War II the average age was twenty-six.

NOUC-MAM—A foul-smelling (to the Americans at least) fermented fish sauce used by the Vietnamese as a condiment. GIs nicknamed it "armpit sauce."

NVA—The North Vietnamese Army. Also used to designate a soldier from North Vietnam.

OD—Olive drab.

P-38—Military designation for the small, one-piece can opener supplied with C-rations.

PRC-10—Portable radio.

PRC-25—Standard infantry radio used in Vietnam. Sometimes referred to as the "Prick-25," it was heavy and awkward.

PROGUES—A derogatory term used to describe the fat, lazy people who inhabited rear areas, taking all the best supplies for themselves and leaving the rest for the men in the field.

PULL PITCH—Term used by helicopter pilots that means they are going to take off.

PUNGI STAKE—Sharpened bamboo hidden to penetrate the foot, sometimes dipped in feces.

R AND R—Rest and Relaxation. The term came to mean a trip outside of Vietnam where the soldier could forget about the war.

RF STRIKERS—Local military forces recruited and employed inside a province. Known as Regional Forces.

RINGKNOCKER—A ringknocker is a graduate of a military academy. It refers to the ring worn by all graduates.

RPD—A 7.62 mm Soviet light machine gun.

RTO—Radio-Telephone Operator. The radio man of a unit.

RULES OF ENGAGEMENT—The rules that told the American troops when they could fire and when they couldn't. Full Suppression meant they could fire all the way in on a landing. Normal Rules meant they could return fire for fire received. Negative Suppression meant they weren't to shoot back.

SAPPER—An enemy soldier used in demolitions. Used explosives during attacks.

SIX—Radio call sign for a unit commander

SHIT HOOK—Name applied by the troops to the Chinook helicopter because of all the "shit" stirred up by the massive rotors.

SHORT—Term used by everyone in Vietnam to tell all who would listen that his tour was almost over.

SHORT-TIMER—Person who had been in Vietnam for nearly a year and who would be rotated back to the World soon. When the DEROS (Date Of Estimated Return From Overseas) was the shortest in the unit, the person was said to be Next.

SKS—A Simonov 7.62 mm semiautomatic carbine.

SMG—Submachine gun.

SOI—Signal Operating Instructions. The booklet that contained the call signs and radio frequencies of the units in Vietnam.

STEEL POT—The standard U.S. Army helmet. The steel pot was the outer metal cover.

TAI—A vietnamese ethnic group living in the mountainous regions.

THREE—Radio call sign of the operations officer.

THREE CORPS—The military area around Saigon. Vietnam was divided into four corps areas.

THE WORLD—The United States.

TWO—Radio call sign of the intelligence officer.

VC—Vietcong, called Victor Charlie (Phonetic alphabet) or just Charlie.

VIETCONG—A contraction of Vietnam Cong San (Vietnamese Communist.)

VIETCONG SAN—The Vietnamese communists. A term in use since 1956.

VNAF—South Vietnamese Air Force.

WILLIE PETE—WP, White Phosphorus. Called smoke rounds. Also used as antipersonnel weapons.

That damned noise again!

I'm not imagining it, Smith thought. But what the hell could it be? Leeches falling off the ferns? Some kind of jungle cat? Vietcong looking for me? VC!

He heard the noise again. Definitely VC!

Smith moved his sweaty hand forward along the dirt-encrusted stock of the Garand M-1 with agonizing slowness. His entire left arm felt as if it were made of lead. When his fingers finally reached the trigger guard, he had to push a leech out of the way before he could ease the safety off. He barely had the strength to do it, but the adrenaline was pumping again. Not much, but enough. He'd manage somehow. They weren't going to take him without a fight. His other hand found the fore end of the rifle, steadying the heavy weapon against his shoulder. The humidity in the jungle was oppressive. Just another enemy.

All right, I'm ready for you sons of bitches, Smith thought. I'm not going to die in Vietnam.

To Captain Humbert Rocque Versace
and Sergeant Kenneth M. Roraback,
who resisted to the end.

And to Ellie, who waited patiently
through the long months.

VIETNAM: GROUND ZERO
P.O.W.
ERIC HELM

A GOLD EAGLE BOOK
London·Toronto·New York·Sydney

All the characters in this book have no existence outside the imagination of the Author, and have no relation whatsoever to anyone bearing the same name or names. They are not even distantly inspired by any individual known or unknown to the Author, and all the incidents are pure invention.

All Rights Reserved. The text of this publication or any part thereof may not be reproduced or transmitted in any form or by any means, electronic or mechanical, including photocopying, recording, storage in an information retrieval system, or otherwise, without the written permission of the publisher.

This book is sold subject to the condition that it shall not, by way of trade or otherwise, be lent, resold, hired out or otherwise circulated without the prior consent of the publisher in any form of binding or cover other than that in which it is published and without a similar condition including this condition being imposed on the subsequent purchaser.

ISBN 0 373 62702 5 (Pocket edition)

*First published in Great Britain
in pocket edition by Gold Eagle 1987*

© Eric Helm 1986

*Australian copyright 1986
Philippine copyright 1986
Pocket edition 1987*

**This OMNIBUS EDITION 1988
ISBN 0 373 57467 3**

8810
Made and printed in Great Britain

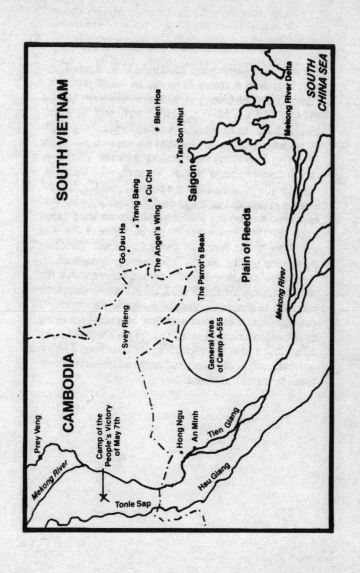

AUTHOR'S NOTE:

On or about September 25, 1965, U.S. Army Captain Humbert Rocque Versace, an Intelligence advisor with the Military Assistance Advisory Group (MAAG) at Ca Mau (Quan Long), and Sergeant Kenneth M. Roraback, a communications specialist with the U.S. Army Special Forces camp at Hiep Hoa (Ap Tan Hoa) were executed by the Vietcong. According to Radio Hanoi, Versace, who was captured while accompanying a patrol from the Special Forces camp at Tan Phu, and Roraback, who was captured during the Vietcong attack on Hiep Hoa, both in 1963, were executed in reprisal for the shooting in Da Nang of three suspected Vietcong prisoners by the South Vietnamese government. Roraback's name evidently caused some trouble for the Vietcong, as the Radio Hanoi announcement referred to him as Sergeant Coraback, apparently a contraction of his first and last names. According to the radio announcement, both men were shot by a firing squad at ten o'clock in the morning. The exact date, time, location and method of their executions remains unknown.

PROLOGUE

CAMP OF THE PEOPLE'S VICTORY OF MAY 7TH, CAMBODIA

The camp sat about a dozen kilometers inside Cambodia, some forty-odd kilometers east of Takeo and a bit farther south by southwest of Prey Veng. It was situated between the Tonle Sap Thaot and Mekong River, almost due north of the point where they crossed the border into South Vietnam and became the Song Hau Giang and the Song Tien Giang. Despite the official "neutrality" of the Sathearnak Roath Khmer and the Sihanouk government in Phnom Penh, the camp was a Vietcong operation and training camp.

Major Vo Dinh Tien stared out the doorway of the tin-roofed grass hut that was his office, his bedroom and the center of his life and tried to penetrate the late-afternoon rain that looked like a curtain as it fell just beyond the overhang of the tiny bamboo porch. It was a wasted effort. He couldn't see more than half a meter beyond the porch, and for one insane moment he wondered vaguely whether the camp was still there.

Perhaps it has all been washed away by the rain, thought Vo. Perhaps it is all gone now: the radio shack that houses the old French radio that never works, the longhouses or barracks of bamboo where the men sleep, even the kitchen where the miserable excuse of a cook prepares indigestible meals. Perhaps all these things are no more forever.

And then Vo carried the dream one step further. Perhaps not only were these things no longer there, but maybe they had never been there at all.

Suddenly Vo was no longer standing in a hut in the middle of the Cambodian jungle. He was back once more in his home in Hue, listening to the rain beat upon the tin roof and watching the people outside scurrying by the window, struggling to stay dry beneath their parasols. The vivid colors of the parasols reflecting brightly but without shape on the wet asphalt, the effect reminding Vo of an artist's watercolor.

Vo could hear his young wife, Tam, singing softly as she prepared an early supper for them in the tiny kitchen of their three-room flat. Both were students at the Imperial College for Administration, she majoring in classical Chinese literature, he in the political history of Western Europe. They had met one day by accident while both were walking along the bank of the Song Huong, the Perfume River. It had been love at first sight, love such as Vo had believed occurred only in storybooks. But their love had been real. It had lasted almost three years now and seemed to grow greater every day.

They had married at the end of the first year despite some misgivings of their parents. But there were advantages in coming from financially secure families with good connections other than being able to attend college. Tam's father was a dentist in Hue, Vo's father a career bureaucrat in the French Colonial government in Hanoi. Both had become exposed to Western ideas through the influence of the French in Indochina. Had they been Vietnamese traditionalists, marriage while still in college would have been impossible. But then, had they both been Vietnamese traditionalists, college itself would have been out of the question.

Vo laid aside the book he had been reading, a history of the French Revolution, pushed back his chair and stood. Two short steps carried him to the window, and he looked down the street toward the bus stop where a young French soldier dressed in khaki and a blue overseas cap was attempting to offer his trench coat to a Vietnamese woman who looked to be about thirty. The soldier's offer was not being very graciously received. The rain had ruined the woman's parasol and her expensive French hairdo. It had also soaked through her white silk dress and plastered it to her body in such a fashion that, even from where Vo stood, it was obvious that the woman had gone out without wearing a bra. This startling revelation had attracted the attention of several onlookers, to the woman's obvious embarrassment, and the young soldier, in a show of French chivalry, was apparently offering her his coat to spare her further embarrassment. The woman evidently had misinterpreted the offer, however, and an argument ensued that ended when she struck the soldier with her parasol and strode off down the street. The young soldier stared after the woman for a few moments, then shrugged in Gallic fashion and struggled back into his coat before walking in the opposite direction.

Vo laughed out loud at the spectacle because it was good.

One week later it all came to an end. At two o'clock in the morning, a peremptory knocking heralded the arrival of a half-dozen French paratroopers dressed in camouflage fatigues and carrying MAT-49 submachine guns. Before he could even ask what it was about, Vo was punched, kicked, handcuffed and thrown into the back of a French army truck. His only clear memory of the arrest was hearing the screams of his young wife coming from the bedroom before he was dragged outside.

For nearly two weeks Vo was a guest of the French military authorities. During that time he was seldom fed, frequently beaten and endlessly questioned. The French interrogator, a lieutenant with the unlikely name of Krause, was very polite. Never once did he threaten Vo or strike him. Lieutenant Krause left that unpleasant chore to other soldiers, who were only too willing to oblige. Lieutenant Krause merely asked the questions. He was, after all, trying to help Vo out of a serious predicament, the good lieutenant explained. But there was little he could do for him if Vo did not cooperate and answer the questions.

On the fourth or fifth day Lieutenant Krause greeted Vo with his usual pleasant smile at the start of their session. He even offered Vo a cup of coffee and a cigarette, a Galois. Lieutenant Krause explained to Vo that he was in a good mood that day. During the night, Krause further explained, Vo's wife had admitted being a Vietminh agent and was now cooperating fully with the French in their investigation of the Communist terrorist organization. Lieutenant Krause even hinted that Vo's wife would be released as soon as she had finished making her statement. Perhaps, the lieutenant theorized, she would be released as soon as that afternoon and be home in time for supper. Now, surely, the lieutenant suggested, Vo would also want to cooperate with the French in their investigation, especially since his wife was being so cooperative.

Vo told Lieutenant Krause that he was very pleased to hear that his wife was going to be allowed to go home and that he would like very much to cooperate with him, especially if it meant that he would not be beaten again. But there was really nothing he could tell the lieutenant since he did not know anyone who was a Vietminh. Vo told the lieutenant for the thousandth time that of course he had heard of the Vietminh and the Vietnam Cong San. But he did not know anyone who was a Vietnamese Communist. He was only a student, and his father was a loyal employee of the French Colonial government in Hanoi.

"You say that you do not know any Vietcong," said Lieutenant Krause. "But your wife is a Vietcong. She had told us that she is a Vietminh agent. Surely you do not expect us to believe you do not know your own wife?" Lieutenant Krause looked at Vo from behind his desk, and his smile grew even wider.

Vo replied that he could only repeat what he had already told the lieutenant.

"I see," the lieutenant said pleasantly. Then he got up from his chair and walked around to the front of his desk. He took the cigarette from Vo's mouth and dropped it into Vo's coffee. Then he set the coffee cup carefully upon the desk and, still smiling, nodded slightly to the two soldiers who were standing on either side of Vo, holding hard rubber truncheons.

The remainder of Vo's stay with the French military authorities was a blur of more beatings, most questioning and an illuminating introduction to what a field telephone could be used for other than communication.

And then one day the French grew tired of the game and let him go. They did not bother to officially release him; they couldn't since he had never been officially arrested or charged. They simply let him go.

A guard came and unlocked the steel door of Vo's cell and left it open. Vo, suspecting a trick of some kind, remained where he was for over an hour. When it finally became obvious to Vo that no one was coming to get him or to relock the door, he got up from the floor of his cell and shuffled slowly to the doorway. He cautiously looked outside.

The long hallway was empty. Vo walked slowly toward the concrete stairs, past the other cells. Most of the steel doors were locked. A few, like his own, stood open, but the cells were empty, waiting for the arrival of new guests.

At the top of the stairs, Vo stumbled along a hallway painted a sickly yellow-brown whose only remarkable features were a series of wooden office doors set on either side. Vo did not try to open any of those doors. When he got to the end of the hallway, he tried the door he found there, which opened easily and let him out into the booking room of the military police station. Timidly Vo approached the bored-looking sergeant sitting behind the high desk.

"What is happening?" Vo asked.

"You may leave," said the sergeant.

"I am free? You are releasing me?" Vo asked incredulously.

"You may leave," the sergeant repeated. He said it in a tone that indicated to Vo it would be better if he did not ask any more questions.

Vo walked unsteadily to the door, fully expecting at any moment to be seized by soldiers and dragged back to his cell, but nothing of the sort happened. He pushed open the heavy doors and made his way shakily down the steps. It was late afternoon, and the street was alive with bicycles, motor scooters and lambrettas. No one paid him the slightest attention.

Sure that there would be a sudden cry of alarm behind him or that he would be struck down by a bullet in the back, he walked along the sidewalk away from the military police station. Vo went several blocks before he realized that no one was going to come running after him and walked a few more blocks before he realized where he was and that he was going in the wrong direction.

He was shirtless and barefoot, and his pants were torn and filthy. Except for a few mildly curious glances from passersby, however, nobody seemed particularly interested in Vo Dinh Tien or where he had spent the past twelve-and-a-half days.

Vo walked several blocks out of his way to make sure that he stayed well clear of the military police station, and then he went home to the apartment near the Imperial College. He had no money for a pedicab or the bus, and the trip took him nearly an hour and a half. When he arrived, there was a padlock on the door.

Another hour's walk brought him to the house of his father-in-law. There was no padlock this time, but the door was still locked, and no one answered his knock. Vo was in despair. He had no money, no place to go and no hope. He paced aimlessly in front of the house for some minutes, then finally sat down on the step and began to weep softly.

After a while a neighbor woman whom Vo had met once or twice approached him cautiously, looking about nervously as she crossed the street. She invited him in and gave him some food and one of her husband's old shirts and a pair of sandals that were too small for Vo's feet. She explained that Dr. Cao and his wife had gone to stay with relatives in Da Nang because the French suspected them of being Communist sympathizers. They had left her an address in Da Nang and some money should she see him. They were not staying at the address, but he could get a message to them there. Did he wish the money and the address?

"Yes," said Vo. "I will take them. Have you any news of my wife?"

"Only rumor," said the neighbor woman.

"What do the rumors say?" asked Vo.

"They say that your wife is dead," said the woman.

Strangely, Vo found himself unsurprised to hear the news. Too much had already happened. His system was already numb with shock.

"Do you know how she died?" he asked quietly.

The woman did not answer him.

"How did my wife die?" he shouted at the woman.

"They say she was tortured to death by French paratroopers of the counterterrorist unit," she answered. "Now, take your money and your address and go. Please. You must go before the French come and find you in my house."

Vo took the money and the address and left. But he did not go to Da Nang, nor did he go to his father's home in Hanoi. He went instead back to the Imperial College and began asking questions of his friends. Most of them were reluctant to talk to him and eager to see him leave. But eventually he found one who introduced him to a classmate who might know someone else who could possibly introduce him to a man that could tell Vo what he wanted to know.

When Vo was finally introduced to the man that could answer his questions, Vo realized with a shock that Lieutenant Krause had been at least partially right. Vo did know someone who was a Vietcong. The man was Vo's history professor.

Three months later Vo was with a Vietminh guerrilla patrol in the Iron Triangle northwest of Saigon when it ambushed a small column of French soldiers. When the shooting stopped, the guerrillas walked out onto the road and bayoneted the survivors before stripping them of all their weapons, equipment and clothing. It was the first time Vo had killed anyone. Afterward he laughed because it was good.

Years had passed, and Vo had become a battalion commander of a main force unit of the Vietcong Army of Liberation of the National Liberation Front. The French soldiers were gone, replaced by the Americans, to whom the French had transferred both the task of propping up the Saigon government and the penchant for wearing berets and to whom Vo had transferred his consummate hatred of the French. By hating the Americans, Vo continued to hate the French by proxy. His hatred was the one thing that continued to give meaning to his life.

Almost reluctantly Vo turned away from the rain and peered into the dimness of his hut. Dau, the political commissar, and Major Ngoi, the NVA advisor, were staring at him expectantly, but Vo ignored their stares and looked past them at the Chinese advisor who stood apart, quietly smoking a filter-tipped American cigarette.

"All right, Comrade Major," said Vo, addressing the Chinese officer, "tell me. What is this brilliant new advice that the People's Liberation Army is so anxious to impart to me? What is this great new idea that judging by the look on their faces, has already been discussed with and met with the approval of my faithful advisor from the North and his political expert?"

It was a serious insult to all three men, but only the two North Vietnamese frowned, and Vo did not greatly care if they were insulted. They were seldom helpful and always putting on airs, as though being a part of the NVA made them somehow better than the Vietcong. Vo, having been born in Hanoi himself, was unimpressed with their smugly superior attitude.

The Chinese officer remained unruffled, however. He puffed briefly on his cigarette, then held it out in one hand and studied the glowing tip as he spoke.

"It is really very simple, Major Vo," he said, intentionally avoiding the Party-approved use of the title Comrade. He knew that Vo had become a Party member largely for convenience rather than conviction, much the same as he himself had done. They were both professional soldiers and ignored politics as much as the Party would allow them to do. "What I have in mind is a plan that will permit us to destroy the U.S. Army Special Forces Camp A-555 and regain domination over our entire operational region."

Vo emitted a derisive snort. "May I remind you, Comrade Major, that that has already been tried on numerous occasions, ever since the Americans built their cursed camp across the border, and the results have been uniformly disastrous."

"You may remind me if you feel it is necessary, Major Vo. But I am already well aware of these facts. Please do not forget that I was the area advisor here for a long time before you became the area commander."

"Yes. And as such you helped plan many of the previously mentioned disasters, no doubt. Why should this time be any different?"

The Chinese officer remained unperturbed. Despite Vo's abrasive manner, the Chinese had a secret liking for the man. Vo was a real fighter, unlike many of the VC and NVA he had worked with; he was an unorthodox tactician and leader. Further, Vo harbored a hatred for the common enemy that was personal rather than political, and that, in the Chinese officer's mind, made him far more reliable than any card saying he was a member in good standing of the Communist Party.

The Chinese major drew languidly on his cigarette before answering. "This time is different, Major Vo," he said, "because this time we shall not attack the body of the dragon. This time we shall cut off its head."

"You speak to me in Chinese puzzles," said Vo sourly. "Can you not tell me what you are talking about in language that a poor, dumb Vietnamese peasant can understand?"

The PLA advisor could not suppress a thin-lipped smile. He knew that Vo was not dumb and had never been a peasant.

"Certainly, Major Vo," said the Chinese. "As I said before, it is really very simple. I have devised a plan that will deliver into our hands the twelve members of Captain MacKenzie K. Gerber's U.S. Army Special Forces A-Team. How would you like to have twelve Green Berets as your guests for an extended period of time?"

There was a lengthy moment when the only sound was the hammering of the rain on the tin roof of the hut, and then, slowly, Major Vo returned the Chinese major's smile.

"Yes," said Vo. "Yes, I believe I would like that. I believe that I would find having these twelve Americans as my guests very entertaining indeed. I think, Comrade Major, that I would like to hear this plan of yours. Tell it to me."

Without further preamble the Chinese advisor unfolded his maps and began outlining his plan. He talked for forty-five minutes without interruption, and when he had finished, he carefully refolded his maps and lighted another cigarette.

"Well, Major Vo," he said at last, "does the plan meet with your approval?"

Vo got up silently from his chair and walked back to the doorway to stare once again at the rain. Then he threw back his head and laughed a deep, throaty laugh. He laughed for a very long time. He laughed because it was good.

1

THE MARKET OF AN MINH, REPUBLIC OF VIETNAM

Sergeant First Class Derek Kepler of the United States Army's Special Forces Detachment A-555 stood in the mud at the edge of the squalid hamlet and stared hard at the three old women, one old man and six very small children who had suddenly seemed to find one of the tiny settlement's communal cooking fires the most interesting thing in the entire world.

Kepler's fatigues were soaked with sweat and slimed with patches of rust-colored mud, which was already beginning to crust over in the heat of the midmorning sun. When he shifted his balance slightly as he transferred the heavy M-14 rifle from his left hand to his right, his feet squished softly in his jungle boots, where his toes were awash in the excrement-laden water from the rice fields to the northwest of the village. A couple of flies buzzed noisily about his head, and one of them picked Kepler's right cheekbone for a landing zone. Kepler hardly noticed. Slowly he raised his left arm to about the height of his pistol belt and, with a butterfly motion of his hand, waved his troops into the village.

The old women and the man studied the fire even more intently. They were trying very hard not to see Kepler or any of the dozen Tai strikers who had accompanied Washington and him on the patrol. Even the children were absorbed by the fire, except for one naked toddler who twisted around in the arms of the woman holding him to see what everyone else was so carefully ignoring. He stared at the soldiers in open curiosity until the woman hissed at him, and then he started to cry.

The Tai slid wordlessly past Kepler, going about the routine business of war in Indochina, the two with BARs taking up covering positions on either flank while the other ten moved down the rows of thatched bamboo huts lining either side of the red mud trail that was the hamlet's only street. With the same wordless efficiency they searched each hootch in turn, two soldiers to each hootch, one covering while the other looked for any sign of weapons, contraband or recent visitation by the Vietcong. When they got to the end of the street, they left two soldiers with grease guns at the edge of the hamlet and the other eight worked their way back toward Kepler, this time moving more slowly and checking more thoroughly, looking under grass sleeping mats for tunnel entrances, checking beneath woven blankets and iron kettles for trapdoors to spider holes, moving carefully the odd bit of strangely positioned crockery or earthenware jug that might conceal a hiding place or be wired to a booby trap.

Kepler watched the scene unfold with stoic detachment. He'd seen the same scene played out at least a hundred times before in at least half a hundred hamlets and villages, any of a dozen of which might have been this very same hamlet or at least its twin. Kepler knew that the two soldiers with submachine guns at the end of the street were unnecessary. There were another six men in the high grass out along the paddy field dike, and they had a .30 caliber Model 1919 Browning machine gun with them. The assumption was that the villagers didn't know they were out there, however, and Kepler intended to keep it that way. Things that the villagers knew about, the Vietcong had an unpleasant habit of finding out.

Kepler couldn't decide if the scene was good or not. When you went into a village and the people were going about their business and then stopped at your approach to come forward to be friendly and chatty, that was a good sign. That sort of thing didn't happen often in this part of South Vietnam. The Vietcong had a way of making those kinds of villages disappear. It was when you went into a village and everybody was just a little bit too friendly and polite that you had to be really careful. That was when you started feeling relaxed and got careless and stupid and got your ass zapped. But you could usually spot those situations by the absence of the children, who the villagers would have hidden someplace relatively safe from bullets and shrapnel. One like this was hard to figure. It could mean the men of fighting age had all slipped away to escape recruitment by the Vietcong, or they were off a klick or so up or down the trail, industriously preparing an ambush for you to walk into.

"Well, what do you think?" a voice said at last from somewhere behind Kepler. It was Washington. Kepler shot a quick glance in his direction.

Staff Sergeant Thomas Jefferson Washington, T.J. to his friends, was a large black man with a wistful smile that all by itself managed somehow to convey the impression that he would have been happier playing fullback at a Big Ten university than he was practicing medicine without a license amid the jungles, swamps and hills of Southeast Asia. He was the A-Detachment's junior medical specialist.

"Hell, I don't know," replied Kepler. "There aren't any men, and there are too few women, but they haven't hidden the kids. It ought to be all right, but one never knows . . ."

"No, my man, one never does. Which is what keeps life interesting and McMillan and me in the doctor business. Let's go see what ails these folks today, shall we?" As he spoke, he slung his rifle and opened his medical bag.

The two Americans walked slowly toward the Vietnamese, who continued to ignore them, even when the Americans were standing next to the fire.

Kepler looked down and noticed that one of the women had an angry red welt on the back of her hand, extending up her arm until it was hidden by the sleeve of her coarse white blouse. Kepler knelt, staring at the welt until finally the woman turned her head enough to look at him out of the corner of her eye. When she did so, Kepler gave her his best see-what-a-swell-guy-I-am grin. After a moment the woman grinned back, showing crooked teeth stained a deep blackish brown from chewing betel nuts. Kepler categorized it as an excellent example of see-I'm-friendly-too-you-bastard-so-what-the-fuck-do-you-want grin. It was a beginning, though, and he switched to a warmer, softer smile.

"*Chao ba. Chung toi la ban. Dung so, chung toi muon giup cac ong,*" said Kepler, pointing to the woman's arm.

She gave him a look that said she didn't entirely believe him.

"T.J., do you want to take a look at this?" asked Kepler. "Looks like this woman has a pretty bad burn on her arm."

Washington crouched near the woman but made no move to touch her. Flashing a mouthful of bright teeth, he indicated her arm and said, "How about letting me take a look at that, ma'am. I think maybe I can do something about that burn." When the woman didn't move or speak, Washington tried his own limited Vietnamese. "*Dung so. Chung toi muon giup cac ong.*" He still got no response. Finally, in exasperation, he pointed to himself and said, "*Bac si,*" then reached out and carefully took hold of her arm. The woman flinched, but didn't pull away.

Washington held the woman's arm gently as he examined it. It was a boney arm, the skin almost paper-thin yet tough and leathery. Washington pushed the sleeve up to the woman's shoulder and examined the burn. It appeared to continue onto her back. Finally he nodded and said, "Uh-huh."

"Uh-huh what?" asked Kepler impatiently.

"Uh-huh, she's got a bad burn, that's what. And I don't think it was an accident."

"Are you saying somebody did that to her on purpose?" asked Kepler.

"People burn people on purpose all the time, man. Especially in war. We do it to Charlie with napalm and foogas. He does it right back with white phosphorus and Molotov cocktails. Sometimes to us, sometimes to these people here. Although in this woman's case, I'd say somebody heated up an iron rod until it was good and hot and ran it along the poor lady's arm. If you're asking if it was Charlie or an irate husband who caught her with another man, I don't know the answer to that one." He considered the woman's appearance for a moment. "Well, okay, probably not an irate husband."

"Can you do anything for her?" asked Kepler.

"For her? No, man. The arm maybe I can fix. Half these people have got tuberculosis or plague or dengue fever. The other half have got all three. The kids we might be able to save if we could get 'em out of this stinkin' country, but out here, by the time you hit forty, you're livin' on borrowed time."

"We're all living on borrowed time out here," said Kepler. "What about the arm?"

Washington shrugged. "The burn itself isn't all that bad. What makes it a bad one is that it covers so much area and it's about three days old. If I could have caught it just after it happened, I could have wrapped it up in plastic, given her some antibiotics and not been too worried about it. Now about all I can do is put a topical antiseptic and a clean dressing on it, have you tell her to keep it clean and hope for the best. Infection? Who knows? If it's gonna get infected, it probably already is. If it is, she'll probably lose the arm. Hell, Derek, out here she'll probably die."

"What's this about wrapping it in plastic?" asked Kepler.

"Little trick I learned from McMillan," said Washington, rummaging in his kit. "Doc says it goes against protocol, but it works. With a bad burn the body loses fluid, mostly blood plasma, out of the injured tissues. Because the integument is damaged, it also lets bacteria get into the wound and cause infection. It's the fluid loss and the air getting to the raw nerves that causes the pain. If the burn's bad enough, the nerves will be burned completely away, and it won't hurt at all until the tissue starts to grow back, but the fluid loss can be a real killer. Gets you before you even have to start thinking about infection. The plastic keeps the fluid in and the germs out. Oh, here it is." Washington fished a small tube of ointment out of his medical kit and dabbed some of it on the burn, carefully spreading it around the injury. Then he took a couple of sterile dressings and covered the burn, wrapping the entire arm with a gauze bandage to hold the dressing in place.

"What's an integument?" asked Kepler.

"Skin, man. Just skin. An integument is a covering. We medical professionals like to use big words. Keeps you laymen on your toes." He tied the ends of the bandage. "Ask her if there's anything else, will you?"

Kepler spoke briefly in Vietnamese to the woman and she rattled off a long speech, smiling as she spoke and pointing at the black medical sergeant. Kepler decided the smile was genuine this time.

"What did she say?" asked Washington.

"She said to tell you thank you for your kindness. That her arm felt suddenly cool. She wants to know if there is anything she can do to repay you."

"Just tell her to try to keep that bandage on and keep those dressings clean. Tell her that will be repayment enough." Washington smiled at her again, then got up and moved over to see if there was anything he could do for the old man.

For a moment Kepler didn't move, just continued kneeling there on one knee, watching the old woman stir the pot of boiling liquid. Finally he said, "Where is everyone? *Nguoi lang o dau?*"

The woman threw him a furtive glance and went back to stirring the liquid. It was a minute or two before she spoke. "Tending the fields," she said in Vietnamese. "They're all out tending the fields. No one's here but us."

"I don't think so, Mama-san," said Kepler softly. "I think they're hiding somewhere, but I don't think they're hiding from us." Kepler continued to press the woman. "Where is the head man of the village? *Lang truong o dau?*"

"Tending the fields," the woman insisted.

Okay, fine, thought Kepler. If that's the way you want to play it, we'll let you take us to them. *"Xin chi doung den cho do."*

The woman glanced at him again, and Kepler saw either fear or apprehension in her eyes. He gave her his best winning smile and said in Vietnamese, "Look, now, we've tried to help you. How about being honest with us? We both know the men are not in the fields. They're hiding somewhere. I don't even care where they are if you don't want to tell me, but at least tell me why they are hiding. Are they afraid of us?"

It took the better part of another five minutes, but Kepler finally extracted from the woman that all the young men and women of the village had gone into hiding in the distant hills because a Vietcong recruiting platoon was expected to come through looking for fresh converts to the cause of Marxist-Leninist world revolutionary struggle. A small Vietcong squad had been through the hamlet three days earlier and had boasted of their alleged recent victories over the puppet ARVN troops and their running dog American allies. They had also told the villagers of the recruiting patrol and warned them that An Minh, like all other villages, was expected to contribute both food and fighters to the cause. After the VC squad had left, the young people had all gone to the hills to hide. They would hide for at least a week, she explained, since no one was sure when the Vietcong were coming.

Kepler did his best not to appear excited by the news. He asked the woman how she had burned her arm. She looked at the ground, but did not speak. She had, however, stopped stirring.

"Please tell me," Kepler persisted in Vietnamese. "I really would like to know what happened."

The woman was silent for a moment longer, then she said, "VC." She spat the words out and spat on the ground after them.

Kepler had half expected the answer but hadn't really thought it would be given. "Why?" he asked at last.

The woman did not look at him. "They wanted to take my daughter with them," she said. "She did not want to go, and I did not want her to go. First they did this." She moved the burned arm slightly. "Afterward my daughter went with them." The old woman spat on the ground once more. "VC," she said and spat again.

When the Tai had finished their fruitless search of the hamlet and Washington had completed his MEDCAP visit, Kepler moved the patrol out of An Minh, first walking south but turning to the northwest once they were out of sight of the huts. After walking about half a klick in that direction, Kepler halted the patrol to await the rendezvous with the machine gun squad that had remained in concealment along the paddy dike to cover the patrol's withdrawal from the hamlet. While they waited, Kepler used the PRC-

10 to contact Camp A-555, or Triple Nickel as the men liked to call it, to file a request for airlift support back to the camp. Since the request had to pass through Big Green, the logistics and support command in Saigon, it was denied as usual. Kepler sighed and ran down the antenna on the heavy backpack radio. The stupidity and pettiness of the Saigon command used to disgust him. Now he had grown so used to the routine denials of support and supplies that he found them more amusing than anything else. The airlift denial was typical. He'd have been surprised if Big Green had okayed it. As soon as the machine gun squad had joined them, Kepler got the patrol moving again. It was a long walk back to the camp, nearly eight klicks over miserable terrain. It wasn't really all uphill, Kepler knew. It only seemed that way. You can't walk uphill for eight klicks when it's nearly all swampland, he thought, at least they'd have good walking for the first three-quarters of a klick. Kepler's feet squished softly in his boots as they moved off through the scrub.

As THE AMERICAN AND TAI PATROL moved out, it was watched through binoculars by four Vietnamese clad in camouflage uniforms of the type normally issued only to Red Chinese snipers. One of them was, in fact, a very good sniper. His name was Sergeant Doan, and he had fifty-six confirmed kills to his credit. Nearly twice that many probables. He had been trained by some of the top marksmen in North Vietnam and China and had been a student of a famous Russian woman sniper, herself a hero of the defense of Stalingrad. But Sergeant Doan and his security team were not there today to kill Americans or Tai, although Doan had little doubt that he could kill both Americans easily. Today Sergeant Doan was there merely to observe. His orders had been quite explicit on that point.

"It is time to leave," Doan said simply to his men after the Americans and Tai had moved out of sight. "We know what we wanted to know. They know."

KEPLER PACED BACK AND FORTH in Captain Mack Gerber's tiny office. There wasn't much room for pacing amid the makeshift furniture, the ammunition-box filing cabinets and the metal cot with the wafer-thin mattress, but Kepler was too excited to sit down despite his aching feet. First Kepler stared out the open doorway, past the sandbagged redoubt and the fire control tower toward the helipad that lay beneath the sun like a huge black wrestling mat with a large yellow H painted on it. A sandbag on each corner held the net down. Beyond the helipad was the worse than useless pediprimed runway. Kepler then stared at the map tacked to the wall of Gerber's hootch and finally back at his thirty-year-old commanding officer.

The captain appeared unimpressed with Kepler's information. He was sitting back in his folding steel chair with his hands behind his head and his feet up on the small desk he'd hammered together from old ammo crates and scrap lumber. Finally he spoke.

"I just don't know about this, Derek. It sounds just a little bit flaky to me. The old woman, for instance. Just how sure are you that she was telling you the truth?"

"Christ, Captain, I saw the burn. T. J. treated it. Why would she lie after they'd done something like that to her? If it was an act, it was an awfully good one, and I just don't see where she'd have any percentage in telling us a tale like that if it wasn't true. It's the first hard intelligence we've gotten in the last month on VC movement in the area. If you'll pardon my saying so, sir, I don't understand your reluctance to pursue the matter."

Gerber gave no indication of being annoyed by the last remark.

"Come on, Derek, it's not hard intelligence, and you know it," said Gerber. "It's a good beginning, but that's all. We've heard nothing else about a recruiting platoon from any of the other villages and nothing from your network of agents. Right now all we've got is some old woman's story that may be nothing more than the boasting of some VC soldier's overactive imagination. The whole thing just seems a bit thin to me."

"Captain, it could be that the information is so new that none of the other villages have heard about it. Besides, Charlie doesn't normally send out engraved invitations announcing an upcoming recruiting drive."

"My point exactly, Derek. Doesn't it strike you as just a little bit funny that this time he's giving advance notification?"

"It wasn't advance notification, Captain. The guy was bragging and he screwed up. The old woman said that one of the other VC got all over his case for mentioning it," Kepler insisted.

Gerber let his feet drop to the floor and leaned forward. "I still don't like it. Maybe we should just pass the information on to Nha Trang and let it go at that. Let them decide what they want to do with it. You know, we're getting awfully damned short here to be going off on something half-baked."

Kepler quit pacing and stopped in front of Gerber's desk. "Just because we're getting short doesn't mean that we've stopped being soldiers, does it?" he asked bitterly.

"Of course not, Derek. You know me better than that. It just means things have changed a little. We don't have the time left in-country to follow through on everything. It also means that now is not the time to start getting stupid. We've got one old woman's say-so about a VC recruiting platoon that might not even exist, and her story is unsubstantiated by any other intelligence source. That's pretty thin stuff to justify putting an operation into the field, maybe having one member of the team run out of luck, step on a mine and go home minus a foot or worse."

"What's to follow through on?" Kepler persisted. "We know where they're going to be, and we've a pretty good idea of when. We even know the approximate strength of the enemy unit. It'll only take a couple of hours to put together the operation and get some people into the field. By tomorrow or Wednesday it could all be over."

"I still don't like it," insisted Gerber. "There's something about it that just doesn't feel right. I still think we should just pass this on to Intel in Nha Trang and let them deal with it. If they think it's good, they can get up a special operation to deal with it. Maybe make some use of the Mike Force."

"Captain," Kepler pleaded, "we haven't gotten anything like this information in a long time. It would be a good way to go out, sir. A sort of final parting victory. What have we got to lose? Really, sir, I just don't understand your reluctance to take these guys!"

Gerber rubbed his chin. Kepler was getting hot, and Gerber knew he had to cool him down. "I don't really understand it, either, Derek. I've just got a bad feeling about this one. I must be getting short-timer's jitters." He was silent for an instant, then said, "Find Lieutenant Bromhead and Master Sergeant Fetterman and come back here. We'll talk it over and see what they have to say about it."

Now Kepler grinned. Bromhead, the team's young executive officer, was fast becoming a real tiger. Kepler knew that Bromhead would be in favor of any mission that might make contact with the enemy. And Fetterman, the team sergeant, was a real old pro. The man had been fighting in a war someplace or other ever since he lied about his age and shipped out to France back in the Deuce. Once the captain said to find them, Kepler knew the mission was on.

"Yes, sir," said Kepler. "I'll have them here in ten minutes." He went out the door of Gerber's hootch whistling a merry little tune.

By the time everyone was gathered, Gerber had already roughed out a working plan. Bromhead sat on the folding cot shoved against the wall, Fetterman collapsed into one of the lawn chairs and Kepler sat on one of the stray ammo crates arranged haphazardly about the dirty plywood floor. Gerber reached into the bottom drawer of his desk and pulled out a bottle of Beam's Choice. "Before we begin, why not a touch of Beam's?"

"Why not, indeed," grunted Fetterman.

Gerber took a long pull, then passed the bottle around. When it got back to him, Gerber took another pull, swallowed and put a finger to his lips. "Smooth as ever." As he put the bottle away, he said, "Derek has some interesting information he'd like to share with us about enemy troop movements. Derek?"

Kepler took the floor and briefed them about the VC recruiting platoon. When he'd finished, Gerber picked up the thread of the conversation without waiting for anyone else to say anything.

"I would think that we'll need about a company for the op," said Gerber. "An ambush platoon, two platoons for a blocking force and one for a ready reserve and field HQ."

Fetterman, who had fought as a teenager in France and Germany and later as a slightly older and much wiser man in Korea, immediately saw what the captain had in mind. "The object of the ambush platoon is not to annihilate the enemy but to force him to withdraw along a specific route so that he runs smack into the blocking force."

"Brilliant," said Bromhead. "A classic military maneuver."

"If they stand and fight," continued Gerber, "their forces and the ambush platoon should be about evenly matched in manpower, although the ambush team should have an edge in automatic weapons and the advantage of surprise. This, of course, assumes that the old woman was telling the truth about the VC unit being platoon strength and that she knows what a platoon really is."

"Captain," interrupted Kepler, "I don't think the recruiting squad will really be up to platoon strength. It's much more likely to be a squad or two at most. My hunch would be one or two political cadre, a couple of noncoms to keep the new recruits in line and a small security detachment—probably won't be more than ten or fifteen VC in all, unless this turns out to be the tail end of their recruiting trip. In that case, they might have a pretty good bunch of conscripts with them, not all of whom will be exactly crazy about the idea. I would think that most of the conscripts would break and run as soon as the shooting starts. Besides, the VC's table of organization and equipment is structured for slightly smaller platoons than ours are, and we're talking about a recruiting team, not a combat patrol Any way you look at it, we should have them outgunned."

Gerber nodded and moved to his map. "If the information the old woman gave Sergeant Kepler is correct, we can expect that the VC will move through the area tomorrow or Wednesday. We'll figure on keeping the troops in the field until Saturday morning to allow for the VC being late. If we don't have contact by then, we'll give it up as a lost cause. I don't think the Vietcong are going to wait more than a few days after letting the information slip to the villagers, and that was three days ago. I also think it unlikely that the VC who broke security about the recruiting trip to the old woman would have picked up that kind of scuttlebutt much more than a week in advance of the recruiting team's visit so, if we haven't turned up anything by market day, we'll take our marbles and go home. Understood?''

There were nods from the group of men.

"Now, an ambush set up here," Gerber went on, pointing to a spot on the map, "will allow for limited options by the enemy. If he stands and fights, we'll be able to reinforce quickly, either from the blocking force, or the reserve force, putting the squeeze on the Cong from both ends. If Charlie decides that discretion is the better part of valor, the only real avenue for withdrawal will be along this thin tree line, which will dump him right into the laps of the blocking force. By moving through this area of swamp, the blocking force should be able to sneak into position without tipping our hand. It's going to be a really crummy job, trying to cross this swamp and get into position unobserved, the blocking force is going to get very wet, very muddy and undoubtedly develop a close relationship with a wide variety of interesting fauna, mostly leeches.'' Gerber looked pointedly at Bromhead.

Bromhead smiled wryly and said, "Sounds just peachy. Why, I'd be delighted to volunteer to lead the blocking force through a leech-infested swamp, Captain. Can't think of anything in the whole wide world I'd rather do than lead a blocking force through a leech-infested swamp. You know how fond I am of leeches, sir.''

Gerber smiled back. "That's nice, Lieutenant. I was hoping you'd feel that way about it.''

"Captain, who's going to lead the ambush platoon?" asked Fetterman.

"I'd sort of figured that would be the kind of assignment you'd be interested in, Master Sergeant. Who do you want to take with you?''

"I'd like a platoon of Lieutenant Bao's strikers, sir," said Fetterman. "They have better fire discipline than the PFs do in an ambush situation. Maybe Sergeant Krung as senior Tai NCO. His English is getting pretty good, and I think he'd probably enjoy the opportunity to add to his trophy collection.''

"Christ!" said Bromhead. "I'm beginning to think you're spending too much time with Krung. I suppose next you'll start keeping one of those damned disgusting trophy boards yourself."

Like all the other Americans, Bromhead was aware of Sergeant Krung's "trophy collection," as the man called it. Two years earlier the Tai NCO's family had been murdered in a particularly brutal fashion by the Vietcong. They had been impaled on sharpened bamboo stakes. It had taken three days for Krung's older brother to die. The Vietcong had killed all of Krung's family except his youngest sister. The VC had been content with merely raping her. In fact, forty or fifty of them had been content with merely raping her. Later the humiliation had driven her to commit suicide. The ugly lesson had been intended by the Vietcong to be a demonstration of what happened to families who supported the Saigon government. The Vietcong had made one serious mistake, however. They had missed killing Krung. Krung's people were Nung Tai, and among them there was a fierce sense of honor that demanded a blood code. Krung had carried that tradition one step further and vowed not to rest until he had killed ten VC for each member of his family. He kept score by cutting off the genitals of the male enemy soldiers he had personally killed and nailing them to a plywood board in his hootch. Krung had had a large family.

"Why, Lieutenant," said Fetterman earnestly, apparently offended by Bromhead's suggestion, "you know I would never do anything like that, sir. I'm a professional soldier. Besides, I probably couldn't fit a board that big in my quarters."

Everyone laughed, but Bromhead had the uneasy feeling that Fetterman wasn't joking about the size of the board. Especially when you considered that the man had been in the Second World War and Korea. Fetterman had already done two tours in Vietnam, as well as some side work for the CIA in Laos before being assigned to A-Detachment 555 as a replacement for the unit's original sergeant, Bill Schattschneider, who had been killed within a month of his arrival in South Vietnam. And Fetterman had accrued thirty-two confirmed kills in the short time that Bromhead had known him. That number represented only the number of confirmed personal kills. It didn't consider the probables and the assists, and it didn't count any of the master sergeant's previous tours or previous wars.

For a moment Bromhead had difficulty reconciling that image with the picture of the short, thin, balding man with the gentle face who sat in a brightly colored lawn chair near the door of Gerber's hootch. A face that belonged to a man who was kind to small children and stray dogs and had, in fact, initiated the paperwork that would allow Fetterman and his wife to adopt a Vietnamese orphan boy. Fetterman was one of the gentlest men Bromhead had ever known and the most deadly.

Bromhead felt a momentary uneasiness, then remembered his own record. Eleven kills and seventeen probables, a pretty damned good record for a first tour. A pretty good record? thought Bromhead. Christ! He felt an inward shudder. Mixed with it was a curious sense of guilt and pride.

"All right," Gerber was saying, "that leaves the reserve force."

"Captain, if it's all right with you, I'd like to head that one," said Kepler.

Gerber considered for a moment, then shook his head. "Sorry, Derek. I know it seems like a dirty trick, since the whole thing was your idea, but I'll want you here to coordinate this thing from our end. Besides, you're going to be busy the next couple of days trying to confirm the information from other sources and helping me convince Nha Trang that we're doing the right thing. Anyway, I can't have all my best people running around out in the field."

"How about Sergeant Kittredge, then?" offered Bromhead. "He's been complaining that he never gets a chance to go out on patrol. Says all he ever gets to do is sit up there in the fire control tower, and correct other people's mistakes. Besides, sir, he is cross trained in demolitions and medicine."

"Steve's been complaining we aren't working him hard enough, has he?" Gerber smiled. "Okay, I guess we can spare him for this one. I wouldn't want him to think we don't appreciate his efforts. He might drop a short round on the latrine or something. I'll brief him myself in a few minutes. Anything else anybody can think of?"

"Only when do we leave?" said Fetterman.

Gerber looked at the map again. "Lieutenant Bromhead has the longest distance to go over the worst terrain. Johnny, I think you should plan to move out within the next hour. Tony you go out as soon as it's good and dark. I'll send Kittredge along about an hour and a half after that. Any further questions?"

"Sir, what about the Vietnamese?" asked Bromhead. In the excitement of planning the operation, the issue had almost been overlooked.

"I'll take care of that," said Gerber. "I'll have to tell Captain Minh, but given some of the problems we've had with security among the PFs lately, I think he'll be willing to keep this an all-Tai operation. Anything else?"

Each man silently shook his head.

"Okay, then," said Gerber, "that's all. I'll see each of you before you go out."

They all stood up, and Gerber reached for the bottle of Beam's again. "A last drink, to the success of the mission." Even as he said it, Gerber couldn't shake the feeling that he was making a mistake.

2

THE SOUTH GATE, U.S.
ARMY SPECIAL FORCES
CAMP A-555, SOUTH OF
THE PARROT'S BEAK,
RVN

Dusk had come and gone and with it Bromhead's platoon. They had exited the south gate of the camp as the sun kissed the horizon in flaming oranges and reds, and Fetterman and Tyme began coordinating their patrol. Now that it was night, the oppressive heat of late afternoon had broken slightly but the humidity remained high, making it impossible for the soldier's sweat-dampened uniforms to dry. It was nearly pitch-black because of low-hanging clouds and all the lights in the camp were hidden behind thick, heavy curtains. Gerber wouldn't even let the men smoke outside when the night was this dark.

Gerber found Fetterman by process of collision when he nearly walked into the small master sergeant. "You ready, Tony?"

"Of course, Captain. Did the lieutenant get out on time?"

"More or less. He's now ass deep in that swamp but claims to be making good progress."

"You going to provide any cover fire for us?"

"Don't think it will do any good, Tony. Besides, even if you're observed leaving, the VC aren't going to know exactly what you're doing."

Sergeant First Class Tyme quietly stepped up behind them. He was a young man in his mid-twenties with sandy hair and a passion for weapons. Even though he was the light weapons specialist, he was as knowledgeable about howitzers as he was about pistols. He said, "The equipment is check complete. We're ready to go when you are."

"You going on this boondoggle, too, Justin?" asked Gerber.

"Yes, sir. Wouldn't miss it for the world."

Fetterman, pointing at the strangely shaped pistol that was just barely visible in the darkness, said, "Now what in the hell is that, Boom-Boom?"

"Second World War flare gun called a Very pistol. Got it off an Air Force pilot down in Saigon. Fires a twelve-gauge shotgun shell, although I do have a couple of flares that came with it."

"You've replaced your Remington hand howitzer with that?" asked Fetterman, somewhat aghast.

"Only for this mission. It's a little more versatile, given what we're planning. My shotgun won't fire flares."

Gerber shook his head slowly. "I just got a directive from Saigon about unauthorized weapons, and that is about as unauthorized as anything I've seen. How safe is it?"

"For whom?" responded Tyme. "For me, it's no problem. I've tested it a couple of times, and it works quite well. Accuracy after about three feet goes all to hell, but in the jungle I won't be shooting at anyone very far away."

"And your backup weapon?" asked Gerber.

Tyme automatically glanced down at his rifle. It was made of high-impact black plastic with a lightweight barrel that was a dull, dark gray. The weapon had a rear sight that looked like a carrying handle. "I've got one of these new M-16s. I'm not really happy with it, but I think it'll be okay. It's got field problems that come from the efforts to step down the cyclic rate of fire, causing it to jam."

Gerber turned his attention back to Fetterman. "How many of your people are carrying M-16s?"

"Only a couple."

"Doesn't that increase the amount of ammo you have to take? You've got 7.62 for the M-14s and M-60s, plus other ammo for the M-1s and the .45 caliber rounds for the pistols. Now there's the 5.56 for the M-16s," Gerber said. "Hell, we're supposed to be soldiers, not munitions suppliers to the Third World."

"We're not going to be out too long," Fetterman replied. "And we've stripped the packs down to the bare essentials, such as a couple of C-ration meals, and left out spare socks, ponchos and the like. Besides everyone is carrying some of the ammo for the M-60s. The advantage of the M-16 is that the ammo and weapon weighs less than the M-14. We can carry more rounds."

"Okay, okay," said Gerber. "You can move out whenever you're ready. I'll send Kittredge out in about an hour."

"Thank you, Captain," said Fetterman. "See you Wednesday or Thursday."

"Good luck, Tony. You too, Justin. Be careful and remember we're all getting pretty short."

"Yes, sir," said Tyme. "Can't get involved in any long conversations. No time left to finish them."

"Yeah, yeah," answered Gerber. "I've heard them all. Can't check books out of the library because you're too short. Anyway, good luck."

"Justin, take the point and get us out of here," Fetterman said. "Stop in about fifteen minutes and we'll regroup."

With that the patrol, consisting of nearly fifty men from the First Tai Strike Company, left through the flimsy gate in the south wall and began to wind its way out of the camp through the six wire barriers. They headed south through the tall, dry elephant grass that made travel difficult toward a large clump of palm and coconut trees that they often used as a staging point. Once there they regrouped, checked the maps and then moved out to the northwest, walking along the rice field dikes and skirting the swamp that now shielded Bromhead and about eighty other strikers.

GERBER STOPPED by the team house for a cup of coffee. Sitting down at one of the tables, he dumped sugar into the brew without realizing what he was doing. He was very worried. For nearly a year they had been extremely lucky. He had lost only a few of his men, and one of those had been with the unit only a short time. He had pulled off a couple of victories that had amazed the people in Saigon. He had gotten out of trouble a couple of times by being prepared with the proper answers. Brigadier General Billy Joe Crinshaw, an officer who had managed to insert himself into the chain of command, had tried to convict two of his men for murder and had failed when Gerber had shown up with evidence proving they were ordered to violate the Cambodian border. It was a constant war with the brass hats in Saigon, but he had always felt confident. Now it was different.

He tried to tell himself that it was because they were short. In just a few weeks they would be going home, and because that goal was now within reach, he was getting jumpy. He had almost moved his cot into the commo bunker for the added protection of the heavy sandbags and beams that would stop mortar rounds, but decided against it when he found both Smith and Kittredge had already moved in. The whole team had talked about extending for six months, which would give them a month's leave in The World, but they hadn't begun the paperwork yet. A couple of clerks in Saigon had told Gerber it was too late, but he knew that if he and his team really wanted to extend, the clerks and the Army would find a way to make it happen. No one was about to turn down a volunteer's offer to stay in Vietnam.

Idly Gerber stirred his coffee and looked around the team house. It wasn't much, but it had been home for nearly a year. There were several tables with four chairs at each in the building that doubled duty as a mess hall and dayroom. Near the door was an old refrigerator that labored to keep its contents slightly below room temperature. Next to it was a coffeepot that was kept busy twenty-four hours a day. Across one end of the room was a counter, and behind that was a galley used by a Vietnamese woman to cook the meals. On one of the plywood walls someone had drawn a fireplace in a sudden burst of Christmas spirit. A ceiling fan suspended from the rafters at least put the heat in motion. Over everything was the film of red dust that became synonymous with Vietnam in the mind of every American soldier.

He looked up when he heard a noise. Robin Morrow, a journalist that Crinshaw had saddled him with, stood in the doorway. She knew her job, had learned a great deal about Special Forces tactics since she had arrived weeks earlier and had even helped save Fetterman and Tyme from the hangman. She was a tall, slender woman with long blond hair cut in bangs that brushed her bright green eyes. She was dressed in khaki pants and a partially unbuttoned khaki shirt. Her hair was damp with sweat.

"You looking for some coffee?" asked Gerber.

Morrow sat down next to him, fanning herself with her hand. "What I'd really like is a cold beer. That is, if you have one around."

"We always have beer. What I don't know is if I can give you a cold one. The refrigerator is acting up again."

Morrow stared at him as if she wanted to kill. "For this I gave up my air-conditioned room in Saigon that had hot and cold running water, indoor plumbing and room service."

Heading for the refrigerator, Gerber said, "The room service I can provide, if all you want is a beer. I could also provide air-conditioning of a sort, but that's about it."

Morrow accepted the beer that Gerber handed her. She pulled a church key hanging on a chain around her neck from under her shirt and opened the beer. After drinking deeply, she sat back with a sigh. "Warm. Maybe cool. But definitely not cold. Now what about the air-conditioning?"

Gerber picked a magazine off the table and fanned her with it. The slight breeze didn't stir her wet hair.

"How come the heat doesn't bother you?" she demanded.

"I'm used to it by now. Haven't had the opportunity to sit in air-conditioned rooms ruining my acclimatization. After three or four months you just get used to having your clothes wet all the time."

"Great. Just the encouragement I needed to hear."

"I can whistle up a chopper for you anytime you want. You can be back in Saigon by noon tomorrow, sitting in a tub washing off the dirt, while room service sends up a seven-course meal."

"Nice try, Captain," she said, draining the beer quickly. "But I saw those patrols go out, and it looks like an interesting mission.

Thought I'd hang around long enough to find out what it's all about.''

"To be honest with you, I'm afraid that it's not such a big deal. More or less routine." But her remark bothered Gerber. If a reporter who hadn't been in Vietnam very long could see the significance of the size of the units sent out, surely the VC would understand. One more thing for him to worry about.

"I have learned," said Morrow, getting up so that she could get another beer, "that, any time someone starts a sentence with 'to be honest,' they are usually less than honest."

"It really is routine," protested Gerber. "With luck we might pull off something interesting. I doubt that it will be interesting to the press because we're hunting an enemy unit of fewer than forty men, but if we find them, we strengthen our hold in the area."

Morrow collapsed into her chair and rubbed the can against her forehead. She pulled the front of her shirt away from her chest so that she could blow down it. Sweat was beaded on her upper lip and dripped down the side of her face. Finally she said, "If it wasn't for the humidity, I could take this heat a lot easier."

"Only advice I have," said Gerber, "is to take a shower. Wash off the sweat. Makes you a little more comfortable. I'll even stand guard for you."

She smiled for the first time. "Stand guard, huh? And who'll guard you?"

"I could call Anderson over. Or maybe Doc McMillan. Or maybe even Kepler."

"And who will guard them?"

For some reason Gerber was suddenly annoyed. "We'll all keep our backs turned," he snapped.

But Morrow kept on smiling. "And what if I don't want you to keep your back turned?" she asked, almost innocently.

Gerber remembered a night in Saigon they had spent together just after he had met her. A night she engineered so that they would have to be together. He had let it take its natural course, but he sometimes wanted to let it stand as a night with no past and no future. He just wasn't sure that he wanted anything to do with Morrow because of her sister, Karen, who had once been a good friend, a lover and who had never mentioned that she had a husband. Now he sat across from Robin and found himself staring at the beads of sweat that formed between her breasts and wished that he was on patrol with Bromhead or Fetterman.

Morrow tried to prod him. "Well?"

He knew that he had to say something fast, but Gerber felt as slow as an Iowa summer. He turned and looked at her carefully. "Your timing in incredibly bad," he said.

Not sure what he meant, she asked, "My timing is bad?"

"I've got nearly a hundred men in the field with a real possibility that they'll be in contact within a couple of hours. I need to stay loose."

"Then the patrol is not routine."

"Yes, it is routine, but the situation is fluid. You understand, don't you?" He badly wanted her to understand.

She reached out and touched his hand. "I really do understand," said Morrow, realizing that the patrol had very little to do with Gerber's agitated state. "But I'll still need someone to guard me while I take my shower."

Gerber pushed his chair back and stood. "I'll give it a try, but if I yell for you to grab your towel it's because I'm going to desert my post."

"You've got a deal."

BEFORE HEADING to the makeshift shower situated near the team house and Gerber's hootch, he walked to the south gate where Sergeant First Class Steven Kittredge and Sully Smith, the stocky Italian-American who, at twenty-two, already had one complete tour in Vietnam, were waiting. Smith was the senior demolitions expert. Kittredge, although older than Smith and with more Army service time, was only now completing his first tour in Vietnam, as were most of the members of the A-Team.

Gerber found them ready to move out, their weapons and equipment checks complete. He gave them the same speech he had given Fetterman and Tyme. In the back of his mind, he still felt uneasy about the mission and the timing, but tried to write it off as a short-timer's nerves.

"Don't worry, Captain," Smith said. "I'm not about to do anything stupid out there. Not after spending so much time here already."

"Steve, you know the route. You're there to support Fetterman if he needs it. He might also call on you to provide a blocking force. Remain flexible."

"No problem, sir."

"Okay. Good luck. See you when you get back in."

As Kittredge left the compound, he turned his troops to the northwest, parallel to Fetterman's trail. They moved slowly through the elephant grass, with Kittredge breaking the trail by twisting his foot as it touched the ground. That broke the elephant grass and pushed it aside so that the man following found the walking easier. But even with the sun gone, it was still hot, humid and tiring.

They moved into the tree line on the western side of the camp, and Kittredge thought that he detected movement ahead of him. He signaled everyone to drop and then crawled forward slowly, watching the trees and brush in front of him. Within a minute Sully Smith was beside him.

Kittredge pointed to the right and made a flanking motion with his hand. Smith nodded his understanding and began easing off in that direction. As he moved, he slipped off the safety on his M-14.

Kittredge held his position and looked off to one side, trying to pick up movement with his peripheral vision. For a long time nothing moved. There was no sound except the distant popping of artillery as it shelled someone somewhere.

Smith crept toward a large teak tree and then peeked around it. At first he, too, saw nothing. He felt the breath rasp in his throat and the sweat trickle down his sides as he watched and listened. Then he heard a faint rattling and turned toward the noise. There was the briefest motion, as a bush blowing in a light breeze. Only there was no wind, and in the shadows Smith could now see a human shape.

Smith wasn't sure what to do. He didn't want to tip his hand, but he didn't want to leave a known enemy on his lines of communication. He didn't think that one man would present much of a problem, but where there was one enemy soldier, there usually were more.

Of course, if the enemy knew that he had been spotted but not engaged, it might make the VC more cautious. Smith's only course of action was to kill the soldier. Smith set his rifle aside, then thought better of it. He didn't know for sure that there was only one of them, and he didn't want to get caught in the open without his main weapon. He safetied and slung it, and pulled his Randall combat knife. The blade's dull surface wouldn't reflect light.

Quietly he moved around the tree, keeping to the available cover, never taking his eyes off the enemy soldier. And then Smith let his gaze wander, suddenly afraid that his staring would somehow warn the VC that he was near. Smith wasn't sure that he believed in ESP, but he figured that there was no sense in taking chances. He glanced back at the Vietcong to make sure that he hadn't moved, but he no longer stared.

The enemy never heard him. Smith cupped a hand under the VC's chin and over his mouth and nose. With a whisper like silk being cut, Smith drew his knife along the Vietcong's throat as he jammed his knee into the soldier's back. Then he pulled back, dragging the body and wrapping his legs around the VC so that the man would not have a chance to make a noise. He sliced at the throat again with so much force that the enemy's head broke away from his trunk, and there was a spurt of blood that splashed over Smith, soaking him.

Just as he rolled free from the dead soldier, dropping the head, another man rose out of the darkness, walking straight toward him. From his attitude Smith didn't think that the man knew what was happening, but Smith couldn't take the chance. He thrust out with his knife, driving it deep into the man's chest just under the breastbone. Smith twisted the blade, trying to rupture the heart and penetrate the lungs. He felt warm blood wash over his hand as the VC's heart burst.

As the enemy soldier died, he fell backward in a spasm, wrenching the knife from Smith's grasp. The VC fell with a thud that sounded like an elephant crashing through dried grass, drumming his heels on the soft, moist earth of the tree line. There was a shout in Vietnamese, followed by a burst of gunfire that raked the trees above Smith's head with emerald tracers.

With all the noise Smith dropped flat, covering his eyes momentarily to avoid ruining his night vision by looking into the muzzle flashes of the enemy weapons.

"Sully!" shouted Kittredge. "You all right?"

Smith, unsure of the locations of either the strikers or the enemy, didn't want to reveal his position so he didn't answer. He rolled to the left, unslinging his rifle, wishing that he could find his knife. It had cost him too much money to lose now, not to mention all the time that he had put into customizing it.

From the rear came a sustained burst from an M-60. The ruby tracers lanced through the night, skipped on the ground and bounced into the sky. There were a couple of answering shots from an AK and an explosion from one grenade, the flash lighting the area like the strobe of a camera, and then Kittredge was kneeling beside him.

"You okay, Sully?"

Smith got to his knees and tried to brush the dirt from the front of his jungle fatigues. There was blood caked on his jacket and staining his web gear. He realized just how wet he was and knew that not all of it was from enemy blood. Part of it was the sweat brought on by the fright and his nerves. He took a deep breath and said, "I'm fine. I killed two of them, but the last one or two eluded me."

One of the Tai strikers came up then. "We find one body, one weapon."

"Maybe we got them all," whispered Kittredge.

"Either that," responded Smith, "or the survivors didn't get the chance to pick up the weapons before they split."

Kittredge moved off to the RTO, calling the base to report the brief encounter and to say that he had no casualties. Smith crawled off in search of his knife. They would proceed from there.

3

THE SWAMPS
SOUTHEAST OF U.S.
ARMY SPECIAL FORCES
CAMP A-555

Bromhead was unhappy. Unhappy, wet, tired, and the splashing by the Tai as they moved through the swamp seemed to be enough to wake the dead. For three hours they had been stumbling through water that was at times chest high. There had been no place to take a break since he had found the high ground earlier. That had been a series of small islands of mud that allowed them to get out of the water. There had been no real cover on the islands, just some grass that masked the deep holes and the wreckage of a South Vietnamese plane that helicopter crews used for target practice during the day.

After twenty minutes in which they used Army issue insect repellent to coax some of the leeches to drop off, Bromhead had reluctantly ordered his men back into the swamp that looked like a giant grassy plain. The hidden swamp water quickly soaked through everything, and in the heat of the afternoon that might have provided some welcome relief, but now, long after midnight, it was merely cool, clammy and uncomfortable. It filled a man's boots, weighing him down and sucking at his feet, sapping the strength of his legs. It slowed the platoon and stole their energy. It made them sloppy. They stumbled, splashing each other and adding to their misery.

The grass was no help. Sometimes it was only waist-high, other times it reached higher than the heads of the men. They lost sight of one another and tripped over hidden logs and stumps. They soaked their equipment and lost some of it. If that wasn't dried quickly, they knew that there would be rust by late afternoon the next day.

Bromhead could hear his men breathing hard with the effort of moving through water that was ankle-deep, knee-deep or waist-deep, depending on the rise and fall of the land. There was rattling of equipment as the men grew tired, but there was no way that they could rest while they were in the swamp. Then, in the distance, not more than a couple of hundred meters away, he could see a tree line that suggested they would soon be able to take a rest break.

He turned to look at the men and saw that they had begun to bunch up again. He was going to order them to spread out when he heard the telltale pop of a mortar being fired. He waved an arm and yelled, "Scatter! Scatter!"

Bromhead was going to dive for cover, but in the swamp there was no cover. Only water and grass. He slumped to one knee, the water lapping at his chin as he held his rifle over his head and studied the trees. He saw the flash of the mortar tubes and heard shouting in Vietnamese as the mortar rounds rained down on them. But the mortars weren't very effective against troops in a swamp. They didn't explode on the surface but dropped through the water to detonate on contact with the mud. The water absorbed most of the shrapnel.

The mortars were followed by concentrated fire from several RPD machine guns. Bromhead heard the rapid chattering and watched the green tracers flash by. He saw fountains of white where the bullets hit the swamp. Some of his men slumped into the water, floating in spreading stains of red barely visible against the darkness of the water.

Still Bromhead hesitated. He thought about charging the enemy position, just as the infantry manual directed, but he would have to move his men nearly half a klick without the benefit of cover. The machine guns would cut them to ribbons, and if anyone survived the assault, they would be in no condition to engage the enemy. An enemy who had mortars and machine guns and assault rifles.

There was a sporadic return from the weapons of the strikers, but it was ineffective and only served to identify by the muzzle flashes their locations for the VC gunners. About three hundred meters to the left, there appeared to be some high ground and cover. No enemy fire originated from that location and it would allow them a chance to regroup and to assess the situation.

"Cease fire!" ordered Bromhead. "Follow me. Let's move it."

Most of the men turned with Bromhead, happy to have someone in charge with some kind of plan. Bromhead wasn't happy because he felt that he was maneuvering into a trap. He was moving to the only high ground and cover available, but he was certain that the VC would have thought of that, too. It seemed highly improbable that the Vietcong would not see the advantage of putting another ambush on that ground. He hoped that he could get close enough before they opened fire so that he could mount a successful attack.

The firing from the tree line increased as AKs and SKSs joined the machine guns, their white tracers joining the green. Bromhead let some of the men get in front of him and then tried to urge the others to run. He screamed at them to hurry, which was difficult in the waist-deep water. He pushed at the backs of some and grabbed the web gear of others, trying to force them forward. He knew that, if he could get them moving with a goal in mind, he would be able to keep them moving in that direction, even if the enemy had taken the high ground. Once a man was running a certain way, he tended to keep running that way. If he was walking without a goal, it would be easy to turn him—to chase him back into the swamp where he could be killed.

Bromhead fell back with a couple of the grenadiers and attempted to lob grenades into the ambush to slow down the murderous fire. The water all around them was kicked up into a white froth, and the white-and-green tracers from the enemy weapons laced the night sky. Streams of red flashed back into the trees from his own men, the paths of the bullets crisscrossing in the dark.

The explosions of the grenades, like brilliant yellow fireworks among the trees, caused some of the VC to back off, and the fire from the tree line tapered off slightly. The surge through the swamp had carried the American force within a hundred feet of the high ground. It was then that the second ambush was sprung.

The first five or six men disappeared into the water. A couple dived out of the way, letting the water close over them for a few seconds. Bromhead instinctively ducked and then fell to one knee, bringing his rifle to bear on the enemy soldiers. A few others did the same.

Bromhead realized that he had let his advance falter and that could be disastrous. He grabbed one man by the shoulder straps of his pack and tried to push him forward. He screamed at them, "Get the fuck moving! Let's go!"

This time he led the charge himself, firing from the hips, burning through his magazine. He ejected it into the swamp and slammed another home. The Tai, seeing the big American forcing his way toward the high ground, joined him in the charge, shooting and yelling and cursing. There was an increase of enemy fire, but it was poorly directed, passing overhead. It seemed to irritate the Tai, and they yelled louder, fired faster and ran harder.

Suddenly the water dropped away, and Bromhead found himself standing on land. Around him were a dozen or so of the Tai. He saw where the enemy was dug in and turned toward their position, running in a crouch, firing his weapon from his hip. He didn't call to the Tai or give orders. He simply expected them to follow him. He didn't realize that he was screaming like a Sioux warrior.

All at once, as he leaped a small stone wall that marked the perimeter of a Vietnamese peasant's graveyard, Bromhead found himself standing among the enemy. There were three VC squatting behind gravestones. One of them stood to meet Bromhead, brandishing a bayonet attached to his AK-47. Bromhead used his rifle barrel to push aside the bayonet and then swung the M-14 butt upward, hitting the VC under the chin and flipping him backward. He heard the snapping of the man's jawbone and the shattering of his teeth.

Bromhead kicked outward, knocked the second VC to the soft earth and then dropped to one knee on the man's chest, pinning him to the ground. As the third turned, Bromhead shot him three times in the chest, the bullets ripping into the man just below the collarbone and blowing out his back. He dropped without a sound. Bromhead then turned his rifle on the VC he held down and shot him in the head as the man tried to reach the combat knife strapped to his thigh.

All around Bromhead the Tai were engaging other VC in hand-to-hand combat. Pistol shots punctuated the melee, and men were screaming in anger and pain. From the far tree line the VC machine guns continued to fire into the swamp and mortars continued to explode among the Tai trying to reach land. Bromhead attempted to rally his men so that he could consolidate his position and take stock of how things stood. But then there was an enemy counterattack, launched from the trees about fifty yards away.

The Tai grenadiers had been well trained. They didn't allow themselves to be engaged in the hand-to-hand fight but stayed back. When they saw the enemy charge, they began lobbing 40 mm rounds as fast as they could reload their weapons. The explosions, accompanied by fountains of sparks mushrooming among the rear elements of the VC attack, cut down the enemy enough to break the first assault. The VC fled to the safety of the trees.

About that time the Cong who had been part of the ambush on the high ground tried to break contact and retreat. There was a sudden increase in the firing as the two sides separated.

Bromhead crawled to the rear, looking for one of the Tai officers or NCOs and trying to find a radio. He found a second lieutenant, pointed to the left and shouted, "Get the men there set. Have them deploy to receive an attack from the trees. Get the machine guns emplaced. Use the gravestones for protection. You understand all that?"

The Tai nodded in response.

"You seen any of the radio operators?" Bromhead added.

"No. No see a one," the Tai replied as he moved.

Next Bromhead found a Tai sergeant who had been grazed by a bullet. His shirt was badly ripped, and there was blood dripping down his arm. One of the Tai was wrapping a bandage around the wounded man's chest.

"You okay?" Bromhead asked.

"Yeah," the sergeant said as he looked up at Bromhead. "It looks worse than it is."

"I want you to find a radio. We need to make contact with the camp. And I want a head count. I have to know how many men we lost in the fight."

As the Tai sergeant was helped to his feet, Bromhead started to place the men he could find so that they could support the machine guns. He put a couple of men behind them as a rear guard and equipped them with the grenade launchers. He didn't expect the VC to try to cross the open swamp. If they attacked again, he figured it would be from the trees. Once all of that was done, he checked on the injured. The men who had been hit were only slightly injured; the ones who had been seriously hurt had been left in the swamp where they had probably drowned.

FETTERMAN WAS DRAWING close to his ambush point when he heard distant firing. At first it was just the crump of mortars and then machine gun bursts and finally a thunderous swelling of automatic weapons. He knew that it was Bromhead. Kittredge and his men would be to the east and north of where the shooting was coming from.

Fetterman halted and listened, wanting desperately to know exactly what was happening. As long as there was shooting, Bromhead and his force were still alive. At least that was something.

Finally he moved back to the radio operator and called the camp. Nothing had been reported and they had heard no shooting. As far as they knew, the plan was proceeding according to the timetable.

ON THE HIGH GROUND Bromhead had organized his force into a circular perimeter, anchoring it on one side with the gravestones of the Vietnamese cemetery. The machine guns could cover anything and could be moved to the area of the strongest attack with a minimum of effort. The wounded were being cared for in the center of the perimeter.

Once he was set, he crawled around the perimeter, encouraging the men and looking for a radio since the Tai sergeant had been unable to locate one. Apparently neither of the radio operators had made it out of the swamp. He had lost all communication with the camp.

He was about to ask a couple of Tai if they would help him go out to look for the radios, although he thought they would probably be waterlogged, when firing broke out. Bromhead turned and saw about fifty men leave the trees and run across the open ground. A bugle sounded behind them, and a shout rose among them.

Bromhead didn't have to give command to fire. The Tai began to shoot as soon as they saw the enemy. The red tracers of the M-60 machine guns crisscrossed the green of the VC's tracers.

Bromhead thought that the attack would break before it reached his lines, but suddenly the Vietcong were there, overrunning the machine guns to engage the men behind them. Again Bromhead used his rifle butt on an enemy's head, hearing it split like a ripe melon.

Another VC came at him with a machete held high, as if he wanted to chop Bromhead into pieces. Bromhead didn't even blink. He put two bullets into the man's stomach, and as the enemy doubled over, he put a third into the top of his head. As Bromhead turned, a VC loomed out of the dark, swinging a machete as if it were a baseball bat. Bromhead grabbed the barrel and the butt of his rifle and blocked the blow. He stepped close to the enemy, moving inside, and shoved, knocking him to the ground. The man rolled and lunged with his blade, trying to impale Bromhead. The young lieutenant sidestepped the VC and kicked at his arm, snapping his elbow. The VC howled in pain as his machete went spinning into the dark. He grabbed Bromhead around the ankle with his hand, but Bromhead stomped down, smashing the bones of the man's forearm. As the enemy continued to scream, Bromhead swung his rifle butt, hitting the man in the head and ending his wailing.

Around him the fight raged. He saw another VC with a machete lop the head from one of the Tai. Then the VC was bayoneted from behind by another Tai. A third shot the VC seven or eight times.

Someone fired a flare, and it burst into the brightness overhead, throwing a yellowish light on everything. Bromhead could see the individual fights in the shifting shimmering shadows of the eerie half-light. Men struggled with men until one or both fell to the muddy earth. He heard calls for help, cries of pain. The firing was sporadic in the clash of rifle barrel against machete and bayonet. Bromhead ducked like a quarterback dodging a blitzing linebacker as a VC tried to knock him to the ground. He whirled and shot the man in the back, the impact slamming the enemy into the mud. Ragged firing came from the perimeter, and a couple of flashing grenades almost blinded the combatants in the semidarkness. A bugle sounded, was answered by another and was joined by a whistle. Bromhead expected another assault, but the VC who were still standing slowly tried to disengage, falling back until they could turn and run for the safety of the trees.

With the close of the fight, Bromhead made a quick check of the men. More than half his force had been killed or was missing. Another quarter had been wounded, a couple of those seriously. He made the check again, as if he couldn't believe how badly his force had been mauled by the VC. There was no way he could complete his mission. Worse, he couldn't contact the camp to tell them, and they would be unable to warn Fetterman, who would operate under the assumption that Bromhead had a Tai strike force close at hand.

AT THE CAMP Gerber was standing next to the tiny shower, staring into the night sky. Behind him he could hear the water splashing. It was ridiculous, he thought. A woman in the camp caused all kinds of extra problems. They'd had to build a separate latrine and then screen it. Whenever she wanted to take a shower, one of the men had to stand by to make sure that no one walked in on her. Not that he was worried about his men taking advantage of the situation. Sure, they'd peek if they could, but they wouldn't go out of their way to see, especially when, without much difficulty they could get a night in Saigon to visit the various strip clubs, massage parlors or bordellos.

Gerber was surprised that Morrow was still with them. She had tricked Crinshaw into letting her into the field in the beginning, with the request for a reporter to view U.S. Army Special Forces Camp A-555 made by R. Morrow. Crinshaw had naturally assumed that the request had been made by a man. Of course, when Crinshaw had realized his mistake, he had let it stand. When she'd said that she wanted to stay, Crinshaw didn't object.

"Captain!" said Anderson as he rushed up, breaking into Gerber's thoughts. "I just received a call from Sergeant Fetterman saying he heard some shooting in the vicinity of Lieutenant Bromhead's patrol. We tried to raise the lieutenant but couldn't get a response."

"Okay, I'll be with you in a minute." He turned, looking over his shoulder, and said, "That's it, Robin. I'm going to desert my post."

"Wait a second!" she said frantically. "I'm covered with soap."

"Hurry it up," he ordered.

A moment later Morrow appeared, an OD towel wrapped around her body, her wet hair hanging in her face. One hand swiped at her hair while the other tried halfheartedly to keep the towel in place. "You're a lousy guard."

"Sorry. Duty calls. See you in the morning." He watched her walk away, the towel not quite covering her rear. For just a moment he wished that he didn't have to go to the commo bunker.

In the commo bunker Gerber saw Bocker behind the plywood counter hunched over one of the radios. He was speaking into a hand-held microphone and twisting the gain knob on the front panel of the Fox Mike. He turned at the sound behind him and shrugged.

"You think there's a problem?" Gerber asked.

"Don't really know, Captain. Haven't been able to raise Lieutenant Bromhead, but you know the trouble we've had with the radios, especially when we're operating near water."

"Just what exactly did Sergeant Fetterman say?" asked Gerber.

"He used our standard code to say that he had heard some firing in the area where the lieutenant was supposed to be operating. Said that it sounded like a sustained firefight. I haven't been able to reach the lieutenant, although I did make contact with Kittredge and his people."

Gerber moved to the map posted on one side of the bunker. In the dim light he could barely see it. He leaned across the wooden table for a closer view and confirmed that Bromhead was in an area full of swamps. The probable cause of the radio silence was that the radios were wet and wouldn't work. It seemed ironic. Gerber was nearly overwhelmed by the red dust in the commo bunker, and Bromhead was probably ass deep in water.

"There's nothing we can do tonight. Galvin, call Saigon and lay on a chopper for tomorrow at first light. We'll make a recon flight and check out the situation. In the meantime keep trying, but don't overdo it. We don't want the VC to know we're worried, if they happen to be monitoring our freqs."

"I seriously doubt they will be, sir. We changed all our operating frequencies just before the patrols went out."

Gerber clapped Bocker on the shoulder. "Good work. See you in a couple of hours."

SINCE THE LAST ATTACK no one had moved from the trees, and there had been no incoming fire. Bromhead didn't like it. He was afraid that it meant the VC had slipped away, and that meant Fetterman would be walking into an area where there was a lot more of the enemy than he thought.

Bromhead wasn't worried about his position, however. The tree line where the Vietcong had hidden was nearly a hundred yards away. The ground was nearly flat, and the short grass could not conceal the VC if they tried to crawl forward. Although it was night, the overcast had begun to break up so that the moon showed, giving him some additional light. A dew was beginning to coat everything and everyone, making them even more uncomfortable. His men were dug into the soft, damp earth around the perimeter he had created earlier, creating shallow foxholes with bottoms that quickly filled with swamp water. They set their machine guns behind the gravestones. The wounded had been tended, and no one was in danger of dying soon. Bromhead was sure that, in the morning, Gerber would have choppers up looking for him. He hoped that the helicopters would find him before Fetterman got into trouble.

He thought about sending out a runner, someone who could look for Fetterman to tell him that the blocking force had been ambushed and chewed up. The trouble with the plan was that he didn't have any lowland Vietnamese with him, only Tai strikers who were smaller and darker than the Vietnamese and didn't speak the same language.

The big advantage was that they were near Cambodia and some of the Cambodes looked like the Tai. The only thing to do was send a few of them out with instructions to alert Fetterman.

Bromhead crawled around until he found one of the Tai NCOs that he trusted. He told the man to pick two others, slip into the swamp and work their way to the northwest to the trail being followed by Fetterman. They were to tell the American sergeant that he would not be receiving all the support that he thought he would get and to act at his discretion.

The Tai nodded his understanding, and Bromhead watched the three men work their way back into the swamp. He heard a quiet splashing and then lost sight of the men. He hoped that they would succeed.

He sat for a moment, wiping the sweat from his forehead as he stared into the night. He hadn't done too well in the fight. He had lost most of his men, and he knew the shock of that would set in soon enough. He was hot and tired, and he didn't want to think about the next few minutes or the next couple of hours. He just wanted Gerber to bring out some choppers and get him out. He shook his head, realizing that it wouldn't happen that way and that he had things to do. He had to check the men once more to make sure that they were all alert. And he had to see if there was a radio lying around. He was sure that he would have found one of the radio operators by now if either of them had made it out of the swamp. With a deep breath he forced himself to his feet and began checking things out.

BEFORE THE SUN ROSE, Gerber heard the faint sound of a helicopter. He headed to the helipad, saw the aircraft's lights in the distance and turned on a strobe for a guide. Then he stepped back and turned his head in anticipation of the swirling dust and debris from the rotor wash.

The chopper touched down, bounced slightly as if the pilot had been a little too fast in dropping the collective and then settled to the pad. The aircraft commander leaped out. He was a tall, skinny man who had not taken off his flight helmet or his chicken plate. The helmet hid his hair, but the flowing mustache that was completely outside Army regulations and a trademark of helicopter pilots was black. He said, "Good morning, Captain."

"Ramsey, isn't it?" responded Gerber, studying the man. "Charles Ramsey?"

"Yes, sir."

"Thought after the last time you wouldn't be back."

"No, sir," said Ramsey. "You've provided the only good missions I've been on. When the operations officer asked who'd like the ash-and-trash flight with the Special Forces, I jumped at the chance."

Gerber looked at his watch. "You can shut down and grab some breakfast if you want. Be a half hour or so before it's bright enough to see."

As Gerber left the helipad, the other pilot, a very young warrant officer named Randle, said to Ramsey, "You know that guy?"

"Yeah. Worked for a couple weeks out here with him. Had five other aircraft. I thought you'd been here."

"I just flew in and out once or twice, ferrying a lieutenant to Saigon," said Randle as he followed Ramsey away from the helipad and toward the team house.

Gerber reappeared at the helicopter thirty minutes later, accompanied by two of his NCOs. He laid a map in the cargo compartment and said, pointing to a place on the map, "We've got to search this general area. We're looking for a good-sized force so it shouldn't be hard to find them." He took off his beret and wiped the sweat from his forehead. He put a hand to his eyes and looked to the east. "It's going to be a hot one today," he added.

Ramsey nodded and climbed into the left seat as Randle took the right. Ramsey leaned across the console, set the flight idle detent button, glanced through the windshield and yelled, "Clear!"

Randle looked out his side window to the right and then held up a thumb. From the rear both the crew chief and gunner shouted, "Clear!" The crew chief tapped Gerber on the shoulder, pointed to Gerber's seat belt to indicate he should fasten it and then handed him a spare flight helmet that contained a headset so he could talk to the pilots.

A moment later there was a quiet whine that built slowly until it was a hot roar. The blades began to swing faster and faster. Ramsey sat upright, his eyes focused on the instrument panel, watching the gauges. He rocked the cyclic around and then began to ease in the pitch until the helicopter trembled and jumped into the air. It hung about three feet above the pad, oscillating slightly, and Ramsey used the pedals to turn to the south. He dropped the nose and the chopper began to slide forward, gaining speed as it rushed down the runway, leaving a trail of swirling red dust and flying debris behind it.

They climbed out to the south, leaving the heat and humidity of the ground behind, and turned west over the swamp. The clouds were high and scattered. The ground was partially veiled in a whirling mist that obscured detail and then blew away to reveal it. At first they could see a trail through the light grass, but as the water became deeper, they lost sight of it. Gerber continued to consult his map, trying to guess the route Bromhead would have taken. They overflew the small clump of high-ground islands, and they could see from the crushed grass and churned-up mud that someone had been there recently.

They continued flying at about fifteen hundred feet to keep out of effective small arms range, trying to locate the column. As they veered toward a tree line, where it was possible that Bromhead had holed up for a rest, there was a short burst of AK fire. Ramsey circled, and the door gunner returned fire, his M-60 machine gun mounted on the side of the Slick pumping out rounds. Gerber could see the red tracers slam into the trees. There was a second burst from the VC, and Ramsey broke down and away.

Over the intercom, Gerber said, "We go on?"

"Not that way, Captain. Enemy soldiers there."

"What are you going to do about it?"

"Call our Operations and let them know we took fire and the location. Also tell them that it was only one weapon."

"How can you be sure that there is only one guy?" asked Gerber.

"Because," answered Randle, who looked over the seat into the back, "if there was more than one down there, they would have shot at us, too."

"Oh," said Gerber, feeling a little silly. "And we continue?" he added.

"Of course. No reason not to," Randle replied.

But just as he finished speaking, another weapon opened fire. It was followed by another and another and then the rapid chatter of a .30 caliber. The green tracers, seeming smaller in the daylight, danced skyward, disappearing into the clouds. Ramsey dropped the collective, diving toward the ground, away from the enemy weapons as both door guns began to return the fire. He felt three or four rounds smash into the side of the helicopter as they skimmed the grass in the swamp, trying to stay as low as possible until they were well away from the enemy weapons.

Randle had switched on his UHF radio and was trying to make contact with Cu Chi Arty to tell them the location of the enemy. Gerber could hear him giving the coordinates, the type of fusing and the type of terrain the artillery would be hitting.

"Can you spot?" asked the voice from Cu Chi Arty.

"Negative. We have sustained combat damage."

"Do you need assistance?" asked the man on the radio.

"Negative. Just give him hell for us."

"Roger. Hell."

Ramsey glanced at the instrument panel and saw the oil pressure begin to drop. He looked at Randle and then back at the instruments. "Let's get out of here," he said.

"We're heading back?" asked Gerber.

"Have to," responded Ramsey. "Took a couple of hits and we're losing oil pressure. It goes and we'll lose the engine. I can get another aircraft out here for you."

Gerber shook his head and thought, *I didn't like this mission in the beginning. Damn!* Over the intercom he said, "Head on back."

4

SOUTH OF THE
PARROT'S BEAK, SOUTH
VIETNAM

Fetterman wasn't overly concerned about the lack of radio contact with Bromhead. It had happened often enough before. He remembered the trouble they had had with their equipment during the river operations, and they hadn't had to move across great expanses of open water. Those radios had become waterlogged just by being close to the river. No, he wasn't concerned. Just annoyed.

The shooting that he had heard early in the morning bothered him a little more. He knew that Bromhead could take care of himself, and his force was large enough to deal with any threat that the VC could mount. At least the intelligence reports suggested that Bromhead could handle anything. The Vietcong weren't supposed to have much in the area.

At sunup Tyme, who had been sleeping under a large tree, crawled over to Fetterman. "You find out anything else?" he said.

"No. The camp hasn't heard a word."

"We going to proceed?"

Fetterman studied the younger man carefully. "Don't really see any reason to cancel," he replied. "Even if we can't coordinate with the lieutenant, we should be able to handle anything they throw at us. The lieutenant was being set up to catch anyone who might get away from us."

"I don't like this. Somebody was shooting out there last night, and now we can't make contact with one of our patrols. Our biggest one at that."

"Don't sweat it. See that the men get something to eat and then we'll move into the final positions. After that, I don't want anyone moving about until we spring the ambush."

"You talked to Kittredge?"

"Not directly. He called the camp about the shooting, too. I heard part of the message, but he was breaking up pretty badly. All I really could tell was that it was Kittredge."

"Another great mission," said Tyme. "Going out to attack the enemy and we can't even talk to the friendlies."

"You know, Boom-Boom, you're becoming a real worrywart. Didn't anyone ever tell you that nothing ever goes according to plan? Once you begin, you have to be flexible."

"It's just that I'm getting too short to be very flexible."

When they finished breakfast—canned C-rations for the Americans, rice and fish heads for the Tai—Fetterman moved them a half klick to the west. He found a well-used trail through the jungle that was lined with bushes and palm, banana and coconut trees. The trail meandered around stands of bamboo and touched the bank of a shallow stream before bending away from the water toward Cambodia. The trail itself was packed earth, three or four meters wide. The bamboo and trees rising steeply at the trail's edge provided good cover, and there were several escape routes through the jungle.

Fetterman had deployed the Tai into a modified U-shaped ambush so that his men lined both sides of the trail. No matter which way the VC broke, they would run into more shooting. He had Tyme anchoring one leg and Krung anchoring the other. He knew Krung well enough now to believe that Krung would watch the entire army of North Vietnamese walk by without shooting if he was ordered to do so. But, once given permission to fire, he would kill every enemy soldier he could see.

Fetterman had taken the base of the ambush where he could control the claymore mines set to rake the trail. Once those were detonated, the men of the ambush would begin pouring rifle bullets into the enemy. Each man had been given a specific field of fire so that he wouldn't be shooting men on the other side of the trail. Now all he had to do was wait for the recruiting platoon to walk into the death trap.

They had just gotten set when they heard distant firing. Fetterman knew that it had to be Kittredge and his men. It rolled to him like thunder diminished by distance. There were periodic explosions and the rise and fall of small arms fire. Suddenly Fetterman felt like Custer and then remembered the stories that he had heard as a little boy. His great-great-great-grandfather, William J. Fetterman, had lead a group of eighty cavalrymen and infantrymen into an ambush arranged by Sioux warriors. In less than forty minutes his entire command had been wiped out. Fetterman suddenly knew how his ancestor had felt.

Fetterman turned to his RTO. "I've got to raise the camp," he said.

AT THE CAMP Ramsey and Randle stood looking at the bullet holes in the side of the helicopter. There were two through the tail boom, peeling the light skin of the fuselage back to reveal bright silver metal. There was one on the left side that had penetrated the window of the cargo compartment door where it was locked back against the chopper. The bullet had smashed into the engine and the deck there was covered with oil. A couple of the wires to the turbine had also been severed.

"That should take care of it," said Randle. "Wouldn't be such a good idea to fly this out of here."

"Yeah," agreed Ramsey. "Maintenance is going to be pissed. Told me not to break the airplane."

Randle laughed. "Wonder if I should flunk you on your check ride. Flew into enemy fire and broke the airplane."

"Extremely funny."

Gerber broke into the conversation. "Then you're down for the day?"

"We're not going to fly this out of here, if that's what you mean. The engine oil is leaking all over the deck. We could get airborne, but I doubt we could stay that way for very long. Maintenance may fly in to try to fix it, or they may just call in a shit hook to lift it out. If we're lucky, we'll get a replacement."

Gerber did not look pleased. "Let me know what you learn. I've got to get over to the commo bunker," he said.

Gerber left the helipad, crossed the northern end of the compound and entered the commo bunker. It was a large, heavily sandbagged structure that sprouted a half-dozen antennas. The interior was dark and the air was slightly cooler than it was outside, although it was still extremely humid. Bocker was sitting behind the counter, his feet propped up, sipping a Coke and reading the latest *Stars and Stripes*.

"Any news?" Gerber asked as he walked in.

Bocker dropped his feet to the dirty plywood floor and set his Coke on the counter. "No, sir. Been real quiet except for traffic on Guard. Somebody lost a chopper up near Go Dau Ha. They're all out picking up the crew."

At that moment they heard Fetterman's voice slice through the static on the Fox Mike. "Zulu Base, this is Zulu Main."

Gerber stepped around and took the microphone from Bocker and said, "Zulu Main, this is Zulu Six."

"Roger, Six, say status of Zulu Five and Zulu Reserve."

For just a minute Gerber wasn't sure how to answer. Their codes didn't really cover the situation he now found himself in. He knew that radio operators sometimes made up the codes as they went along. Once he had been told that the grid coordinates were up five from Jack Benny's age. The thinking was that the VC would have no idea what it meant, but every American would know that the base number was thirty-nine. Gerber had never been convinced that these tactics fooled the VC.

They had just changed the frequencies so the odds were that the Vietcong could not monitor their radio transmissions. He took a chance that the VC, even if they were monitoring the Green Berets' frequency, wouldn't know the police ten codes.

"Ah, Zulu Main, we have ten seventy-seven with Zulu Five. Recon has not succeeded. We have not attempted to reach Zulu Reserve."

"Roger, Six. Understand. Please advise as soon as you can."

"Will do. Are you planning an advance to the rear?"

"Negative, Zulu Six. Have no reason to make a move now."

"Roger, Main. Will advise. Out." Gerber held on to the mike for a moment before handing it back to Bocker. "I have a very bad feeling about this," he said. "Very bad."

KITTREDGE FOUND a good location for his reserve force. He held what little high ground there was. It was grassy and fell gently away to the jungle below. Bushes were scattered around the slopes along with a couple of tall palms and a single banana tree. From his vantage point he had a limited view of the surrounding countryside. He could see a single hootch about half a klick away through a series of breaks in the jungle vegetation. A little farther to the east he could see the water of rice fields flashing and shimmering in the morning sun. The jungle nearest him was thin enough that he would be able to see anyone approaching and could bring them under fire. With the M-60 machine guns and two 60 mm mortars to support him, he didn't worry about sneak attacks.

Kittredge made a radio check to let both the camp and Fetterman know that he was in position. Then he told his men to go to half alert so that some of the men could eat and relax. The force was spread out in a circular formation with the crest of the hill in the center. Smith and one of the Tai sat there eating their breakfast. The Tai was sharing his fish heads and rice with Smith, who had given the man a can of ham and lima beans. Looking around, Kittredge didn't have the feeling that anything was going to happen.

Just after sunup one of the men reported movement in the trees to the south. Kittredge thought that it was probably a farmer heading for the rice fields a klick or so to the east. But, to be safe, he edged to the side of the perimeter to watch.

The pop of several mortars took him completely by surprise. He yelled, "Incoming!" as he rolled to the ground and tried to spot the flashes through the jungle.

The first of the rounds dropped short, exploding in the high grass on the southern slope and throwing up small clouds of dust and dirt. The next volley landed closer to the lines, and the third landed among his men. Kittredge ordered them to keep their heads down. He leaped to his feet, sprinted toward the middle of the perimeter and dived for cover. He got to his knees and saw the mortar crew huddled together, ignoring their weapon. He hesitated for a moment before running toward them to begin a counter-mortar duel and as suddenly as the mortar rounds started falling, they stopped.

On the other side of the perimeter, Sully Smith rolled into a shallow depression where he bumped into a couple of the Tai strikers who were huddled at the bottom. Smith got to his knees, looked around and dived out of the hole to land behind a rotting log. From there he could see the entire northern approach to the perimeter.

Kittredge got up and ran to the right until he found Saut, the Tai NCO who was working with them. He whispered to him, "Get ready to repeal an assault. I think we're about to be attacked."

Saut turned and began yelling quickly in Tai to the men. There was a rattling of weapons as the Tai strikers made sure that they had rounds chambered.

"Sully," yelled Kittredge, "keep your eyes open. I think they're coming at us."

Smith left his position and crawled across the perimeter. He whispered to Kittredge, "You call the camp?"

"Was about to. Let me find the number two RTO."

Together they crawled off. The RTO was lying on his back, blood running from a dozen wounds in his chest and head. His dead eyes stared at the rising sun. There was a stubble on his chin where he needed to shave.

"Shit," said Kittredge as he turned the body over. He could see the hole in the PRC-10's canvas cover. He pulled the handset out, keyed it and tried to raise the camp. When that failed, Kittredge opened the canvas, saw the hole in the radio and asked Smith, "You cross trained in commo?"

"Hell, no," said Sully. "But I do know something about radios—sometimes they come in handy to blow things up."

"Then see if you can fix this before it gets really ugly out here."

They were interrupted by a single bugle call, followed by a couple of whistles and a sudden surge of enemy small arms fire.

"Here they come!" yelled Saut.

"Fix it, Sully! Fix it quick! This wasn't supposed to happen," Kittredge shouted. He crawled off to see fifty or sixty black-clad VC running through the grass and up the slope toward them, already too close for the mortars to be effective. The VC had their bayonets out and were firing their weapons from the hip as they shouted and screamed. The enemy outnumbered them at least two to one.

As the firing increased, kicking up the dirt in the center of the perimeter and ripping apart the Tai's makeshift cover, the enemy soldiers closed with them. Smith worked feverishly to open the radio. He found that the shrapnel had not penetrated very deep, but had severed a couple of wires. Using his combat knife, he stripped the insulation from the wires, glanced at the onrushing enemy, looked at the wires and connected them. He heard the shout from the VC, shot another glance at them and twisted the broken wires together. He turned the PRC-10 on and heard the hiss of the carrier wave indicating that the radio was now operational.

But Smith had no time to make any calls. He pushed the radio out of the way, trying to protect it behind a log, and then turned to meet the coming threat. He was stunned to see that the VC were already inside the perimeter.

Off to the right Kittredge was trying to direct the fire of the machine guns, but the assistant gunner wasn't interested in feeding bullets into the machine gun. He wanted to shoot at the Vietcong so the machine gun jammed. As it did, the VC swarmed up that slope, too, overrunning the American and Tai lines. The mortar crews had abandoned their weapons, picked up their rifles and were using them.

Kittredge jumped to meet the enemy. He had one of the short bayonets attached to the front of his rifle, and as one of the enemy soldiers ran toward him, Kittredge parried and thrust. The bayonet penetrated the silk of the black pajamas and entered the man's stomach. There was a spurt of blood as the VC stopped suddenly, leaped backward and turned so that he could shoot at Kittredge. The American dropped to one knee and fired his own rifle. The bullet slammed into the VC's chest, throwing him back into the tall grass, and he died with a look of surprise.

As that happened, another enemy jumped at Kittredge from the side, knocking him to the ground. Kittredge rolled over, pain flaring in his back and side. He kicked out, cutting the VC's feet from under him. As that man fell, Kittredge squeezed the trigger twice, and he saw the body jerk as the bullets hit. Blood blossomed on the man's chest and spurted from his throat. The VC dropped his rifle, one hand clawing at his neck as if he couldn't breathe. The enemy thrashed around, pounding his heels on the soft ground, his hands raking his neck as he slowly died. When the man was dead, Kittredge got shakily to his feet, turned and saw the battle raging around him. Suddenly he was aware of the noise. Of the shooting. Screaming.

Smith was fighting two of the VC, holding them off with his rifle that lacked a bayonet. He was swinging it back and forth between the two, shouting at the top of his voice. One of the VC hesitated at the wrong moment, and Smith clubbed him with the rifle barrel, smashing into the man's skull. As the other moved in, Smith dropped his rifle and kicked upward, hitting the man in the crotch. The VC shrieked in pain and doubled over. Smith kicked again, snapping the Vietcong's head back with an audible crunch, killing him.

As Smith bent over to pick up a weapon he felt someone leap onto his back. Reaching over his shoulder, Smith grabbed the loose material of the enemy's black pajama top and slammed him to the ground. The American followed through with a punch to the neck, crushing the VC's throat.

Just as the fighting looked as if it could get no worse, the enemy vanished. It seemed that one moment there were Vietcong all over them and the next they had disappeared. Bugle calls and shouts filled the air as the enemy retreated to the trees. It meant that Kittredge would have a moment to regroup.

FAR AWAY, FETTERMAN HEARD the first sounds of the enemy as they moved toward the ambush. He'd been worried about all the shooting that he'd heard, apparently from Bromhead's group and then Kittredge's, but now he ignored that as the Vietcong began to close in. He could no longer afford to worry about anyone else.

AS SMITH PICKED UP his rifle, Kittredge crawled over to ask, "What the hell happened?"

"I don't know. It jammed somehow." He worked the bolt and saw that one of the rounds had not stripped from the magazine properly. The nose of the round was pressed into the top of the breech. Smith reached in and flipped the shell out of the way, worked the bolt and discovered that the next round was crooked. Smith pulled the magazine from the rifle, checked it, reseated it and saw that it was now working correctly.

"You get the radio working?" Kittredge wiped the sweat from his forehead with the sleeve of his fatigues. He had lost his helmet during the fight.

"Yeah," Smith replied. "Couple of wires broken, but I didn't have time to make any calls. Got kind of busy."

"Okay," said Kittredge. "Advise the camp that we've run into trouble. Maybe they'd better pull Fetterman out. I'll check to see what kind of damage has been done."

There was a single shot, and the ground between them erupted. Kittredge rolled sharply to his right and yelled, "Sniper! Anyone see where that came from?"

One man pointed toward the trees.

"Then return fire, for Christ's sake. Don't let them get away with that shit. Kill the son of a bitch!" He glanced back at the mortar crews and yelled, "Use the fucking tubes."

But before anyone could take the sniper under fire, another enemy charge flooded across the open grounds, accompanied by a sudden eruption of shooting and yelling. There was a hesitation by the Tai and then they began firing, but the VC didn't waver.

A couple of the Tai stood to meet the charge and were cut down immediately by sniper fire. One fell back, his right arm hanging loose at his side as the blood cascaded from a shoulder wound.

And then the enemy was there among them, using bayonets and machetes to chop and slash at the Tai, hacking at them as if they were trying to clear vines from a jungle trail. The Tai fought back with their rifles, bayonets and pistols. They lobbed grenades at the VC, but the enemy kept coming, pouring out of the trees like someone had opened floodgates. Smith and Kittredge were kneeling near the center of the perimeter, shooting the VC as fast as they could pull their triggers. A dozen of the enemy fell, but then the VC swarmed past the first line of defense and spilled into the center with Smith and Kittredge. Both men stood up back-to-back, covering one another.

Using their rifles, bayonets and finally knives, they kept the enemy bodies piling up around them. Kittredge grabbed the barrel of an enemy rifle as the man tried to impale him. The American jerked the weapon forward, pulling the enemy soldier toward him and then slashed with his knife, slicing into the soft skin under the man's jaw. Blood spurted, washing down the front of the VC's uniform, staining it crimson. He collapsed to his knees and pitched forward into the grass as the rest of his life pumped out.

Another VC ran at Kittredge, his rifle hip high, bayonet extended. Kittredge turned so that his right side faced the man, jumped back and plunged his knife to the hilt into the man's chest. He twisted it and jerked it free as the man shrieked and died.

The shooting died in the mass confusion of soldiers, VC and Americans fighting hand-to-hand for their lives. There was shouting and screaming without intelligent thought. Men grunted and fell, and all the while the bugles kept blowing and the whistles kept shrilling.

Surprisingly, the VC swept past the center of the perimeter and grabbed the mortar tubes, shooting and stabbing the crews as they ran into the line on the other side and down the opposite slope. It was as if the attack had been planned that way—sweep through, kill as many of the Americans and Tai as possible, capture the mortars and then get out.

With the lull in the fighting, Kittredge checked the perimeter. Bodies were scattered up the grassy slope, and where the enemy had encountered the perimeter force, there were piles of bodies. Dead men dressed in black pajamas and khaki uniforms. Dead men dressed in the olive drab of American-made uniforms. Men with rust-colored stains on their clothes and in the grass around them. Blood that was soaking into the earth, turning the dirt to mud.

Weapons were strewn over the battlefield. Brown craters dotted the slope and the hilltop. Dead men lay near them, some of them broken, the white of bone contrasting with the red of torn flesh. Pieces of the dead littered the ground. Kittredge bent to pick up an undamaged boot and then nearly threw up when he found that there was a foot still inside it.

Still holding the boot, Kittredge slowly turned, counting the bodies, no longer caring that there were snipers. Of the fifty men he had started with, thirty-two were dead, including Sergeant Saut. More than half his men were dead. Twelve others were wounded, and of those, five were in danger of dying from their wounds. One just barely clung to life, an Army belt drawn tightly around the stump that had been his arm. His blood had dyed the side of his fatigues red.

That left him with just six men ready to fight. Seven of the wounded could hold rifles and fire into the VC when they began the next assault, but they would be useless if the enemy penetrated the perimeter. And the VC had yet to fail to do that.

Kittredge crawled to the radio, turned it on and found to his surprise, that it was still working. First he tried to call Fetterman to tell him that the reserve force no longer existed, but he couldn't reach him. Next he tried to call Gerber at the camp to let him know, hoping that he would be able to relay a message to Fetterman. Only after he failed to make contact with the camp did he realize that he could have asked them for help if he could call them. Maybe helicopters to swoop out of the bright deep-blue sky to save them. Or artillery. He could call in artillery support. Something that could be there in seconds, if he could get a radio call through.

Standard procedure, if the radio was operating and you failed to make contact, was to call in the blind, hoping that anyone who heard would answer.

Kittredge, now sitting in the center of the perimeter with his tiny command dead around him, keyed the mike and in a voice that was lifeless with shock said, "Anyone listening, this is Zulu Reserve calling in the blind. How do you hear, over?"

"Zulu Reserve, this is Black Sabbath One One. I roger your transmission."

Just as he received the response from the Army Aviation helicopter, he heard the sound of bugles and the yelling of the VC as they sensed victory. There was a rattling of rifle fire as Smith moved all the men to one side of the perimeter to deal with the threat of attack.

For a moment Kittredge stared into space. He saw the gently sloping hill with the scattered bodies of his men. Beyond them were thirty or forty dead VC lying near the trees. Kittredge knew that he and his men would not survive another assault. There were simply too many of the enemy coming. All he could do was take as many of them with him as possible.

Over the radio he said, "Black Sabbath One One, please relay to Cu Chi Arty that I have a fire mission. Over."

"Understand fire mission."

"That is correct and please hurry."

To Smith, Kittredge yelled, "Sully, we've had it! We're not going to get out of this one. I'm calling for artillery."

With bullets hitting the ground all around him, Smith wormed his way back to Kittredge and asked, "What the hell good is that going to do?"

"I'm bringing it down on us. We'll take some of the bastards with us!"

Smith looked at Kittredge's eyes and saw that he meant it. He glanced over his shoulder and saw that the VC were running up the slope and screaming, the sound of their bugles filling the air.

"You do what you have to. I think we better tell the Tai and give them a chance to bug out."

Kittredge shook his head. "Wait for the first rounds to fall. That might give them a chance to reach the trees behind us, but I doubt it."

The radio crackled to life as the Army pilot tried to contact Kittredge.

"Roger, One One," said Kittredge. "Tell Cu Chi Arty we have a reinforced VC company attacking across open ground from a tree line. Grid X-ray Sierra two five six four. Request area fire, quick fuse." He hesitated and warned, "You'll be dropping it danger close."

The pilot relayed the message and then asked, "Can you spot?"

Kittredge grinned at the radio. "I will as long as possible. The VC are about to overrun us."

Just as he made that statement, the first of the artillery rounds slammed into the trees. A plume of white from the smoke round sprouted skyward, fire spreading from it. There was agonized screaming from the VC where it had landed. A few jumped up to run, fleeing from the white phosphorus of the round.

"Drop twenty five and fire for effect." Kittredge yelled at Smith, "They'll come in groups of six. After the sixth one has hit, have everyone fall back to the north."

Firing erupted all around them as VC machine guns and grenades from the trees joined battle. When the VC were twenty yards away, the first of the artillery rounds fell. The ground all around the VC exploded into geysers of brown soil, red blood and obscured the jungle as the artillery continued. Fifteen of the VC died in the detonation of one 105 mm howitzer shell.

Then it seemed as if the entire planet was exploding as the artillerymen at the unseen fire support base got into the rhythm of loading and firing their weapons. The VC assault slowed—neither attacker nor defender wanted to stand in the midst of the artillery barrage. Everyone hugged the ground, trying to disappear into it so that the shells wouldn't kill them.

When the sixth round had hit, Smith leaped to his feet and shouted, "Scatter! Run! Let's get the fuck out!"

The Tai and the Americans got up and began to run to the north, away from the main VC assault. They were on the downslope side when the next artillery volley began to fall. They hit the dirt as the ground all around them blew up, throwing tons of deadly shrapnel through the air. Smith turned and saw Kittredge standing near the crest of the hill. He was firing at the VC as if unaware of the artillery, shooting at anything that moved as the 105 mm shells landed. Then he disappeared in a fountain of earth. Smith closed his eyes tightly, breathed deeply and counted to six again. Then he was on his feet, surrounded by the few survivors, running for the supposed safety of the jungle, away from the hilltop and the VC.

He dived to the ground as the third volley landed, and defenders and attackers alike died.

5

U.S. ARMY SPECIAL
FORCES CAMP A-555

Cat Anderson left the commo bunker and walked across the compound toward the helipad, where Gerber stood talking to the chopper pilots. When he was close, he said, "Say, Captain, we just got the strangest call. Helicopter crew asked if we had anyone in trouble."

"Don't look at me," said Ramsey. "I've been here the whole time."

"You get a call sign?" asked Gerber.

"Black Sabbath One One."

Gerber looked slightly irritated. "I mean, did they get a call sign from our group?"

"Oh, yes, sir. I think it was Kittredge's people. One One said they called in artillery. The pilot claimed it sounded like they were calling it down on themselves, but Kittredge wouldn't do that," said Anderson.

Gerber felt the blood drain from his face. "Good God!" he said. "You tried to contact them, didn't you? Really tried?"

"Of course. Couldn't raise them, but with the way the radios have been working, I'm not surprised."

"You talk to Fetterman about this?"

"Not yet, Captain. Wanted to advise you first. See what you thought about it. I thought it pretty strange that Kittredge would be calling artillery in on his own position. The pilot said he wasn't sure about that, but it sounded like it." Anderson was repeating himself because he refused to believe that Kittredge was dead— which was what the radio call meant if taken at face value.

"Okay," said Gerber, thinking rapidly. "Try to let Fetterman know and suggest that he pull back. Next, get hold of Crystal Ball and advise him and ask for immediate airlift. Ten choppers. Let me know as soon as you learn anything else. And keep trying to get Kittredge."

"Yes, sir."

As Anderson took off running, Gerber said to Ramsey, "How long before your replacement is here?"

"Twenty minutes at the most."

"No way you can get this airborne?" he asked, pointing to the helicopter.

For a moment Ramsey said nothing. Then slowly he confessed, "Given the situation, we could get it up, but I can't guarantee how long it'll stay up. We've got the leaks plugged, but we lost a lot of the oil. Engine could quit quickly."

"But you could get airborne?"

"Yes, sir. In an extreme emergency."

"Then please consider this an extreme emergency."

Ramsey shot a glance at Randle, who nodded gravely. "Yes, sir," Ramsey said.

Gerber stood staring at the helicopter. He felt sick. He hadn't liked the idea when Kepler had come up with it, and now it sounded as if his feelings were justified. Kittredge was in deep trouble, and Bromhead was out of contact, too. It all seemed to be too much. Not a coincidence. Bromhead and Kittredge apparently ambushed. It *had* to be a coordinated plan designed to inflict losses on the men of his camp.

"Listen, Ramsey, get ready to take off. I mean now," Gerber said. "I don't think we have time to fool around. I've got to get to the commo bunker, but I'll be back in a minute."

Ramsey looked at the helicopter as Gerber took off at a dead run. The oil still glistened on the deck, but the lines were patched with hundred-mile-an-hour tape. He reached over to jiggle the wires and lines and then said to Randle, "Let's crank it up and hope for the best."

"I'm not thrilled about trying to fly this sucker out of here," Randle replied. "We're taking a real chance."

Ramsey looked oddly at his copilot. "We don't have a choice," he said.

FETTERMAN LISTENED to the artillery shells exploding near where Kittredge and his men were supposed to be. He'd tried to raise Kittredge on the radio with no luck. Now he had his own worries. He could see the lead elements of a VC unit and knew that he would have to spring the ambush in less than a minute.

Just at that moment there was a crackle from the radio and the beginning of a message. Fetterman shut it off. The VC had entered the killing zone. Fetterman tossed a grenade, and as it detonated, he fired the first of the claymores as the enemy's lead elements broke and ran toward him.

From the far end he heard Tyme shout and the Tai open fire, raking the trail with a devastating fusillade. Bullets smashed into the soldiers, cutting them down. Dirt was kicked up, and the trees rained splintered bark and bits of leaf. There was a momentary confusion while a dozen enemy soldiers dropped and others turned to flee.

Fetterman thought that the ambush had gone quite well. The VC had been surprised and had reacted like amateurs. They had fled in terror rather than attacking the ambushers. It was then that the mortars began to fall, first on the trail, killing the wounded VC in almost festive puffs of gray smoke and brown earth, and then among the trees, forcing the ambushers to hug the ground. Shrapnel from the enemy weapons whined through the air, ripping into everything in its path.

From somewhere came a wailing call from a bugle followed by whistles and shouts as the VC rallied and assaulted the ambush. The enemy swarmed out of the jungle, firing their weapons from their hips, screaming curses at the ambushers. The mortar barrage lifted as the enemy soldiers scattered along the trail, spreading out so that the Americans and the Tai couldn't bring them under a concentrated fire. There were at least five times more VC than Fetterman had expected.

But the American sergeant was prepared for the worst. He picked up the controls for his claymores and detonated them simultaneously. A curtain of steel balls blew along the trail, cutting men off at the knees, at the waist or at the neck. Shattered bodies bounced on the ground as blood from about fifty men spurted onto the jungle floor. There were shrieks of pain and the groans of the dying.

The claymores broke the attack, but the firing from the enemy crouching in the trees kept pouring into the ambush. Mortars began dropping again, walking along the trail and into the ambush site. They were not well aimed, but they were taking their toll as the shrapnel tore at the Tai.

Fetterman realized with a feeling of frustration and anger that the enemy strength in the AO had been badly underestimated. Suddenly he knew that both Bromhead and Kittredge had been ambushed and there would be no help. Firing from the enemy increased, the green tracers from the AKs and the SKSs pounding into the jungle around him. The mortars were joined by Chicom grenades and it seemed as if the jungle were alive with weapons firing and exploding. There were shouts from his own men, and he heard Tyme trying to rally the Tai like a cheerleader at a football game.

Suddenly Fetterman knew that to stay where he was would be disastrous. The VC would assault them again and probably overwhelm them. Fetterman ordered the first section to fall back, telling them to "Go to E and E plan two."

As the Tai, led by Sergeant Krung, began exfiltration, Fetterman moved along the northern side of the ambush. Out of the corner of his eye, he saw his men helping each other, one man leaning on the shoulder of another. It was a coordinated withdrawal, some of the men trying to cover the others, firing their weapons into the jungle. One or two threw grenades at the VC positions. The bodies of the dead lay sprawled where they had fallen.

When he found Washington, the medic's hands were covered with someone else's blood and his fatigues stained with it. He was tending a wounded Tai striker who had taken a rifle bullet in the shoulder. Then, just as Washington was tying off the bandage, he shifted the man and saw a second wound that had opened the entire stomach. The Tai's entrails spilled onto the soft jungle earth.

"We've got to pull out, T.J.," Fetterman said. "Kepler got his information wrong. I think we've been set up."

Washington looked down as the Tai opened his eyes wide, as if surprised by something in the sky overhead. The wounded striker reached up, his right hand bright red with his own blood and his fingers clawing at the air. He shuddered once, kicked his foot and died without saying a word or making a sound.

The American medic shook his head, then grabbed the dead man's rifle. He and Fetterman crawled along the north side of the ambush, checking the bodies of the Tai. Three had been killed by rifle fire and the rest hit by shrapnel. They crept past the bodies, using the bushes and trees for cover as the firing continued. The sharp, flat bangs of the AKs and the crack of M-16s filled the air.

At the far end of the ambush, they found Tyme. He lay on his side, gasping for breath. His helmet had come off, and blood congealed in his sandy hair. His eyes were closed, and he'd dropped his rifle.

Enemy mortar rounds still fell to the east, where the anchor of the ambush had been. Rifle firing was sporadic, and then there was shouting from the VC and someone was blowing a whistle. It sounded as though the Vietcong were rallying for a final assault.

"Second section, pull out now!" ordered Fetterman. "Go!"

Washington had rolled Tyme to his back, had pried back an eyelid and was peering into the unfocused eyes.

Fetterman just reached down, twisted Tyme's ear and was rewarded with an angry shout.

"What in the hell are you doing?" Tyme yelled.

"Come on, Boom-Boom, I think we've overstayed our welcome. We've got to bug out."

Tyme struggled to sit up and said, "Help me to my feet." He shook his head as if to clear it and grinned at Fetterman. "We sure blew that one, didn't we?"

"I think," countered Fetterman, "that we walked into the whole North Vietnamese army. We've got to make tracks."

Tyme, Fetterman and Washington, along with six Tai, fell back from the trail. Using palm and coconut trees to shield their retreat, they moved carefully away from the scene. Running through a tree line, they emerged on the dike of a paddy field. Fetterman halted for an instant and looked around. Behind him he could hear the RPD machine guns still firing and the bursting of mortar shells. In the distance he saw the ruins of a farmer's hootch. He turned toward it, running quietly through the light trees that bordered the paddy field. "Head over there. We've got a chance to regroup," he called to Tyme.

About that time the mortars stopped falling—the VC were moving back into the ambush site. They would quickly discover that it had dissolved, and Fetterman grinned to himself, thinking that it was nice to have reversed the tables for a change. Usually it was the VC who sprung an ambush and faded into the jungle. The only problem was that Fetterman didn't have dozens of tunnels, bolt holes and spider holes to use. He only had his wits.

GERBER CURSED AS HE FAILED to raise Fetterman. He threw the mike at the sandbagged wall, watched it bounce to the floor and said, "That fucking tears it. It really does."

Both Bocker and Anderson tried to stay out of his way. He pointed at Bocker and said, "You get back to Crystal Ball and tell Bates that I need ten helicopters out here and I need them yesterday. Anderson, you get to Captain Minh and have him get two of his strike companies ready. One should stand by at the helipad, and the other has to be ready to move out on foot."

"That's going to leave us awfully thin here, Captain," said Bocker. "We've already got a bunch of people out."

"Shit! We've got to do something!"

Surprisingly, the helicopters landed less than ten minutes later in a gigantic cloud of blowing red dust and swirling debris. Nine of the ships touched down along the runway while the lead chopper broke off to land on the helipad set on the northeast side of the strip. Lieutenant Colonel Alan Bates, the B-Team commander stationed in Saigon, had found an aviation unit that had just completed one mission and had been heading to Dau Tieng. He had them diverted to the Special Forces camp, telling the flight leader that he would have to pick up the camp commander for the C and C role. They would recon the area as the rest of the flight worked on getting the strike company organized for the lift.

At the helipad Gerber, sweating heavily in the hot sun and carrying only his M-14 and a bandolier of spare ammo, found Anderson. "Cat," he said, "you're going to have to take charge down here. Get these guys organized, check the weapons and equipment."

"I say, old boy," said Captain Minh, the Vietnamese camp commander, "aren't you forgetting about me?"

"No, Captain, I'm not. But we find ourselves in that bizarre situation again with both American officers off the camp. You have to stay here. You're the only one who can."

"Of course," agreed Minh. "Just didn't want you usurping my authority."

Gerber had to smile at Minh's British accent. It seemed so out of place—yet Minh had opted for an education in Great Britain rather than France like most of his contemporaries.

"When I've located the LZ, Cat, I'll let you know. Shouldn't take long to find it."

The big Special Forces sergeant was slightly confused. "Who are you looking for, Captain?"

"Kittredge. I know where he was supposed to be, and we have a report that he was definitely under attack. We should be able to find him quickly."

"And then?"

"We'll try to tie up with Fetterman and withdraw to here."

"What about Bromhead?" asked Minh.

"Once we get the others taken care of, we can begin looking for Bromhead again. We'll just have to trust Johnny to take care of himself for now. One more thing, we'd better get Doc McMillan, too. I'm sure his services will be needed."

With that Gerber ducked beneath the spinning roto blades of the chopper and trotted across the helipad to the lead ship. He leaped into the cargo compartment, and before he could even sit down, the aircraft lifted to a hover, turned to the north and began a rapid climb out. Gerber fell onto the red canvas troop seat and pulled his map from the side pocket of his fatigues.

Using the grid coordinates given by Black Sabbath One One, Gerber found the remains of Kittredge's patrol in less than fifteen minutes. He had the pilot of his aircraft fly over the battlefield a couple of times, looking for signs of life. He could see none. At Gerber's insistence the pilot descended and flew slowly over the hilltop.

Now Gerber could see only too well. He could see bodies in khaki, black and olive drab scattered like toy soldiers around the top of the slight hill. He could see equipment, rifles, machine guns, helmets and packs strewn everywhere. Some of the trees in the jungle surrounding the hill were still smoking from the fire caused by the artillery barrage. Others were stripped of their leaves. Everywhere he could see the fresh brown craters made by the artillery scarring the landscape like newly opened wounds. But he could see no sign below him that anyone was alive.

He had the pilots withdraw to the north, and in a voice emotionless with the shock of seeing the reserve force's remains below him, he called for the strike company. They approached from the east, landed on the hilltop among the bodies and rubble of the battle and swept downward into the trees. That done, they fell back to the hill and established security. After they had finished, they had the opportunity to examine the battlefield.

Ten minutes later Gerber landed and found Anderson standing in what must have been the center of the defense perimeter. He was turning slowly, taking it all in. As Gerber approached, Anderson said quietly, "They're all dead. Doc couldn't help any of them, but they put up one hell of a fight. There's forty or fifty enemy dead lying around here and in the trees. Quite a few weapons left behind, too."

"You found Kittredge and Smith?"

Anderson couldn't meet Gerber's gaze. "Yes, sir. That is, we found Sergeant Kittredge, or most of him." Anderson's voice trembled as he spoke. "Artillery must have got him. We can't find six or seven of his men, including Sully. Artillery must have got them, too."

"Shit! Just fucking shit." Gerber took off his helmet and ran a hand through his hair as he stared into space. "I didn't like this mission from the beginning. Not at all. You know that."

"What'll we do?"

"Get the bodies of our men lined up so that we can get them out of here. Detach a squad, maybe twenty men, and sweep around the whole area but not more than two or three hundred meters into the trees. They run into trouble, they get out. And we call in the fucking artillery."

"What about the VC?"

"Pick up the weapons and check for papers. Leave the bodies. If their own people didn't give a fuck about burying them, I sure as hell don't."

In less than an hour they were back at the camp; the bodies of the dead were stacked like so much cordwood near the helipad. Each body had been wrapped in an OD poncho liner that had been tied at both ends. Blood had soaked through some of the liners, staining them a dark red. A light breeze stirred the loose ends, providing a macabre movement among the dead.

The lead pilot wanted to be released so the helicopter unit could return to base, but Gerber didn't want them to go just yet—they might be needed to locate Bromhead and his men, or Fetterman and his patrol. There was still no word from either group. Gerber told the pilots to go and refuel and hurry back. He was afraid that the disasters for the day were just getting started.

"What now," Anderson asked as the helicopters disappeared.

"We try to identify the dead and get a list of the missing for the report in Saigon," Gerber replied. "They have to know that we stepped in some shit out here in case someone else steps in it. They'll be able to adequately evaluate the situation."

Anderson took a step backward and dropped onto a couple of sandbags. He lowered his head and put a hand over his eyes as if to shade them from the sun. He looked up, blinking rapidly and said, "This sure happened fast."

"Yeah. Too fast. I should have taken more time to study Kepler's information. It was just too good, and it gave us no time to think. Just time to react."

From behind them Gerber heard the sound of the motor-driven film advance of a 35 mm camera. He spun and saw Morrow taking pictures of the bodies and the men standing around them. "Christ!" he shouted at her. "Don't you have any fucking sense at all? Stop that."

Morrow let the camera fall from her eye and stared at Gerber. "What are you talking about?"

"Robin, we've just come back from the field with the bodies of our friends. We don't know exactly what happened, except that they were all killed. Then you stand around taking fucking pictures."

"The people have a right to know."

"Shit! I don't want to get into that now. Just don't take any more pictures, okay?"

She was going to argue and then saw the hard look in his eyes. "Okay, Mack, I understand. I'm sorry. I wasn't thinking."

"Forget it."

Then from near the commo bunker came a shout. "Captain Gerber! Quick!"

Gerber broke into a run, coming to an abrupt halt in front of Bocker. "What? What is it?"

"South gate, sir. They say there is a group of men moving toward it. They think it might be Lieutenant Bromhead."

Without a word Gerber spun and took off toward the south gate. Before he got there, he could see the green smoke from the trees in the distance before the men revealed themselves. He stood by impatiently as the men worked their way through the elephant grass and began to wind their way along the concealed and irregular path that had led through the rolls of concertina wire protecting the wall.

Gerber could see Bromhead leading them. He looked dirty and tired. One sleeve of his uniform was badly ripped, but he didn't seem to be injured. He was followed by some of the Tai and then a couple of men being helped along by their friends. Four men carried two stretchers with bodies on them. Several of the men had large blood-stained field dressings wrapped around their heads or shoulders or chests. But there weren't nearly enough of them. They had been badly shot up.

As soon as Bromhead was within talking distance, Gerber said, "What happened?"

Bromhead stepped beside Gerber, but before he answered his commanding officer's questions, he waved his men past and told the senior BCO, "Get a weapons check made and a muster. I want a roster in ten minutes of the men who came in with us. I also want to know who's missing and who's wounded and how badly they're hurt. You understand?"

"Yes, sir," the man said with a nod.

"You get together with Lieutenant Bao and have him help you," he said as the man ran off.

"Johnny, what happened to you?" Gerber repeated.

"They were waiting for us, Captain. They seemed to know exactly where we were going and how many men we had. The ambush was set perfectly. I think they underestimated our resolve to get out of the swamp. Otherwise, I think we would have all been killed. But they had everyone placed perfectly. I don't think we could have set it any better."

"Okay, Johnny," said Gerber, studying the younger officer. He could see the strain on his face and in his eyes. "Let's head to my hootch and get a drink. Then you can tell me what happened."

"How are the others? How's Fetterman?"

Gerber stopped walking and stared at his executive officer. "I think it's bad all over. Kittredge is dead. Sully's missing, but I think he's probably dead, too. We haven't been able to talk to Fetterman. It's getting fairly grim."

"God, Captain. It seems that we've been had."

IN THE SMALL HOOTCH hidden deep in the Cambodian jungle, Major Vo, Commissar Dau, Major Ngoi and a Chinese officer sat around a rough wooden table hammered together by a long forgotten rice farmer. The hootch had a dirt floor, a single window with no glass and a doorway with no door. The thatch of the roof was in poor shape. The mud walls were crumbling and did nothing to keep out the heat, or the humidity and the insects.

Standing at one end of the old table was a young Vietnamese covered with sweat and breathing hard. He had just run a long distance to bring news of one of the counterambushes. He looked longingly at the cigarettes that burned in the ashtray made from half a coconut shell but did not ask for one. He was frightened by the North Vietnamese officers and he directed his comments at Major Vo because Vo was the one man that he knew and was his commanding officer.

Slowly he told of the fight between the Green Berets and their puppet soldiers and the Vietcong and NVA. He told how they had made a final charge toward the perimeter and how they had penetrated the defense of the Americans and the Tai when the artillery barrage began.

"The Americans must have made a mistake," the young soldier reported as the sweat dripped from his face and stained the collar of his already wet shirt. "The shells began exploding all over the hillside, killing them as well as us."

The Chinese officer, who had been partially hidden in the shadows of the hootch, leaned forward and put out his cigarette. "I think not," he said. "I believe it was a deliberate act by the Americans. An act to prevent their capture."

"It gained them nothing," said Dau.

"It denied us the prisoners we sought," said Vo bitterly. He turned his attention to the Chinese. "You have promised me prisoners. You didn't expect the Americans to die rather than be captured."

"You forget, Major, that there are other teams in the field, each in contact with the Americans. You will have your prisoners yet."

A lizard scurried across the dirt floor, scrambled up the mud wall and disappeared into the rotting thatch. Vo watched the creature until it disappeared. He said to the Chinese, "And what if each group does the same? What if each group denies prisoners to us by sacrificing themselves?"

"It was a fluke," said the Chinese. "We shall have our prisoners." He pointed to the runner and said, "You searched the field after the battle, of course." It was a statement rather than a question.

"When the shells stopped exploding, we began to search, stripping the dead, but enemy helicopters appeared, and we were forced to abandon the search."

"Abandon the search," repeated Dau. "You abandoned the search?"

The young Vietnamese looked at Vo for support and then turned his attention back to the commissar. "Yes, comrade," he said. "We were told that it was very important that we not be engaged by other Americans and to abandon the field if the helicopters came."

"Why was that?" asked Dau.

"Because," snapped the Chinese officer, "to let the Americans engage our troops takes the initiative away from us. We do not let them catch us in the field. We catch them."

"How many were killed?" asked Ngoi.

"We found the body of one American and nearly forty of their puppet soldiers."

"Only one American?" asked the Chinese officer.

"Yes, comrade."

The Chinese smiled shyly. "Major Vo, it is my experience that the American soldiers do not work alone. There should have been a second American body. Possibly more, but certainly more than one. I believe that one American escaped. You must capture him."

Vo got to his feet and stepped to the door to order his men to prepare for another patrol. Outside, he could see three of his NCOs crouched near a small fire barely visible in the bright sunlight. Behind him he heard the Chinese officer say, "It is only a matter of time before we have the prisoners we need for the next phase."

6

SPECIAL FORCES CAMP
A-555

It was only early afternoon, but the day had already been a disaster. Gerber sat in a hard wooden chair and stared at his executive officer. Bromhead's uniform was sweat-stained and torn in a dozen places. There was mud caked on it, some of it obscuring the left breast pocket and the patch that read U.S. ARMY.

Gerber waited for Bromhead to speak, and when that didn't happen, he reached into a drawer for his bottle of Beam's. Wordlessly he handed it to Bromhead and watched as the young lieutenant drained nearly half the remaining liquor.

As Bromhead handed the bottle back, he asked again, almost as if seeking confirmation, "How are the others?"

"Kittredge and Smith were ambushed and wiped out. Kittredge is dead and Smith is missing," Gerber replied.

Bromhead nodded, dazed. "What about Fetterman?"

"No word from him for a couple of hours. Just as soon as the helicopters return from refueling, we're going out in force to look for him." Gerber paused, letting the weight of what had happened sink in. Then he said, "Sounds like you did everything you could."

"You mean I didn't get wiped out," Bromhead said in a deadpan voice.

"There is that. But I was thinking more of the way you handled the ambush. You did the only thing you could think of and it worked. You got as many of your people out of the swamp as you could."

Bromhead stared at the Beam's. "What are you going to do about Fetterman?" he asked.

"Like I said, go get him. Troops are standing by." As Gerber finished his sentence, he heard the sound of helicopters in the distance. "In fact," he said, standing up, "I'm going to get him now."

"Mind if I come along?"

Gerber stopped at the door and thought. "No, Johnny, you've got plenty to do here. Check on your men, see who needs to get evaced. I'll leave McMillan here with you. Washington is out with Fetterman."

"Yes, sir," Bromhead said forcefully.

As he walked away, Gerber wondered how much Bromhead held him responsible for what had happened.

FOR THE MOMENT THEY WERE SAFE, or as safe as they could be. The farmer's hootch had no roof and one wall had collapsed. There were the remains of a bunker in one corner of the hootch and a disintegrating bamboo mat on the dirt floor. Tin and thatch from the roof littered the inside.

The hootch was nestled inside a small grove of coconut and banana trees. It might be dilapidated, but it offered some protection, maybe even sanctuary. For now it provided Fetterman and the few men with him a chance to figure out what to do.

As soon as they were inside the hootch, Washington made Tyme sit down. He examined him closely and found a lump on the side of his head where a bullet had grazed it but had not broken the skin. He also had a gigantic bruise on his chest as if he had been hit with a large rock, probably thrown up by a mortar shell exploding.

Washington moved off to look at the Tai. Only one of them seemed to be badly hurt, and he was not in danger of dying. The wound in the man's thigh, although deep, had formed a scab and the bleeding had stopped. Washington dusted the wound with sulfa powder to combat infection and covered it with a large, clean field dressing. There was little more he could do. He didn't have the equipment or the time.

Fetterman posted his security and then sat back. He took one drink from his canteen. Like the others, he was tempted to drink it all, and normally he would have finished off the water to prevent it from sloshing in the canteen as he tried to sneak through the jungle. But he knew that as the day progressed, he would need the water. He saw a couple of the Tai drink their canteens dry. Maybe they figured there wouldn't be too much of the day left for them.

When he saw Tyme staring at him, Fetterman smiled and said, "How you doing, Boom-Boom?"

"I'm fine." Tyme gingerly touched the side of his head and asked, "What do we do now?"

"Hang loose. The captain will be looking for us before long, and if he doesn't, we'll just have to make our way home."

"You sure this is a good place to hole up?" Tyme asked, gesturing at the hootch.

"It's lousy, but it's better than anything else I saw. We have a good field of fire, some protection in the packed mud walls, and if we have to bug out of here, there are a couple of ditches and that mud wall over there to use for cover. Lots of ways out."

Suddenly there was a snap from the jungle, and a single bullet struck one of the inside walls, showering dirt everywhere. Fetterman grabbed one of the Tai and threw him down before he could return fire. He stopped two others and whispered, "Hold it. They may not know we're here and are trying a recon by fire. Just hold it."

A moment later a single mortar round exploded in a puff of gray-white smoke and was followed by four VC rushing from the trees. Fetterman could see no point in letting them advance. He raised and fired his M-14 as fast as he could pull the trigger. The first two VC went down in a burst of blood and bone. The third was staggered by the heavy 7.62 mm round and dropped his weapon, but he kept running. The fourth turned to flee, threw himself behind the mud wall, hesitated and then leaped to his feet. Fetterman cut him down as the staggering man collapsed in front of the hootch. There was a wail of pain and then silence.

From the jungle came a sustained burst of RPD machine gun fire that was quickly joined by a dozen AKs. Fetterman ducked quickly as the walls of the hootch began to disintegrate from the machine gun bullets ripping into it. When the enemy firing started to taper off, Fetterman and a couple of Tai popped up and returned it. They had no visible targets so they just hosed down the trees in front of them, hoping to keep the VC pinned down.

Tyme kept an eye on the jungle behind the shelter and watched a dozen or more VC rush from the cover. He shouted a warning, but the others didn't seem to hear him over the staccato of their own weapons.

Tyme fired his M-16 on full automatic and several of the enemy soldiers fell, bullets in their chests or heads or stomachs, spreading stains of red dying their khaki uniforms. But the others kept coming, and Tyme quickly emptied his weapon. He fumbled for a new magazine, pulling at the pouches on his pistol belt, but somehow he seemed to have lost them all.

Tyme threw the now worthless weapon to one side and pulled his Very pistol. As three of the VC jumped over the short wall, Tyme pulled the trigger. The noise from the weapon was tremendous, as was the recoil, but all three of the Vietcong fell as the number four buckshot pellets spread and drove into them. Two VC were screaming in pain.

Two more VC leaped the wall, and Tyme was ready for them with his combat knife. He had dropped his pistol to the floor of the hootch, when there was a burst of rapid firing beside him as one of the Tai soldiers turned and fired. One of the enemy went down, a bullet blowing away half his face. The other dived for cover, popped up to shoot and ducked again. When he jumped up to flee into the jungle, the Tai striker was ready. He pumped four rounds into the man's back.

Quiet descended around them. For the moment the VC assault was over and Fetterman used the time to check his men. Two more had been wounded. One of the Tai had been shot in the stomach, and he was holding himself, moaning quietly and asking for water. The other had been clipped by shrapnel or flying rock that had torn through his right hand. Washington was wrapping a bandage around the man's hand. Tyme sat with his back against the wall and wiped sweat from his face. He was breathing hard, as if he had just sprinted a mile. He drained one of his canteens.

As he reloaded, Fetterman said, "They'll try a little finesse during the next round. I don't think they'll mount any kind of frontal assault. Time is on our side."

Washington was trying to help the Tai with the stomach wound. There wasn't much he could do, given the medical supplies that he had brought with him. He used sulfa powder, trying to limit the infection, and knew that they would have to evacuate the wounded man quickly, or there would be no way to save him.

As Washington glanced up, he saw nearly a dozen VC. "Here they come again," he yelled as he dropped his medical bag and picked up his rifle. He fired single shots, carefully picking out his targets until the whole open area in front of him seemed to be crawling with VC. Then he switched to full auto.

Tyme set his rifle down, leaning it against the mud wall of the hootch and got out his last four grenades, lining them up in front of him. Then deliberately he pulled the pin of the first, threw it, got the second ready and threw it. After the first two explosions, he popped up and threw the third and the fourth.

The attackers seemed to waver, then regroup, and the VC surged forward, screaming and shouting. Tyme picked up his rifle and began killing the VC. More of the enemy fell while others scrambled for cover.

Fetterman was directing the fire of the Tai who could still hold a weapon. Two of the others were now unconscious because of blood loss from wounds. Another one had been so badly shot up that, although he was conscious, he couldn't sit up.

They were all firing on full automatic, but the attack didn't seem to be slowing. It reached the mud wall and a couple of the VC hurtled it, but they were quickly cut down, tumbling into bloody heaps. The remainder of them seemed content to hide behind the wall, afraid to either attack or retreat. The two sides were now separated by only about thirty yards. It seemed that each side had found some momentary protection.

As the last of the firing died away, Tyme looked over his shoulder at Fetterman and asked, "And now what?"

"Doesn't seem like we're going to get a reprieve until dark," said Fetterman. He looked at the men with him as they crouched behind the flimsy protection of the crumbling mud walls and rotting thatch. Shell casings littered the floor. In some places they were a couple of inches deep. To his right the man with the stomach wound moaned quietly, semiconscious. "I suppose we'd better see if we can't get out of here."

"We can't move the wounded," countered Washington.

"Yeah, I know," said Fetterman. "But I sure as hell don't want to be captured, either."

"That's okay, Tony," responded Washington. "I'll stay behind, hold off the VC as long as I can and then surrender to them. We might be able to get some medical help for the men."

"That idea stinks. I don't want any martyrs or medal winners here," Fetterman replied.

"You have an alternative? We can't hold this place much longer. It makes no sense for all of us to be captured," argued Washington.

Fetterman peeked over the wall and saw that the VC hadn't moved. He shifted his attention to Tyme and said, "What's it look like back there, Boom-Boom?"

"Clear right now. I haven't seen anyone moving in the trees. We might be able to sneak off."

"If we can get to the trees, we should be able to get clear," Fetterman said. He turned his attention back to Washington. "Look, T.J., I'm sure the captain is trying to get in here, but there's no way we can hold out. I'm not leaving anyone here who can travel. You've got one wounded man who won't survive until nightfall and two more who might live to be evaced if we had a way of doing it."

"And I'm not going to leave the wounded," said Washington. "There is no way that I can leave the wounded."

Fetterman shot a glance over the top of the wall again. He could see a couple of the VC running through the trees in the distance. He ducked again and said, "T.J., I want you to make the wounded as comfortable as possible. Give them everything you have in your medical bag of tricks. Leave the bag. The next time the VC rush the front of this place, we throw up a cloud of steel for a couple of minutes and then E and E out the back. Everyone understand?''

There were nods all around except for Washington. "I said that I can't leave the wounded."

"You have two choices, Sergeant Washington," said Fetterman with a hard edge to his voice. "You can either treat the wounded as best you can and prepare to leave them, hoping that the VC will have a doctor, or you can watch me shoot them right now."

Washington held Fetterman's gaze for a few moments and then dropped his eyes, "You won't shoot the wounded," he said.

"No, maybe not," agreed Fetterman. "But I'll fucking drag you out of here."

Washington didn't say anything. He merely nodded.

"Okay," said Fetterman, "I don't know how well this is going to work, but it's the only plan we have."

WHEN THE HELICOPTERS LANDED, Gerber issued his instructions. Minh would be in command of the assault troops, and Bromhead would be responsible for the camp's defenses in the event of an enemy counterattack. Gerber told them that, as soon as he had learned something, he would call.

The helicopter lifted off, coming to a hover and then racing along the ground to gain airspeed. The pilot hauled back on the cyclic, turned to the nonthrust and began a low-level flight along the path that Fetterman was supposed to have followed. All the time Bocker sat in the commo bunker trying to raise Fetterman on the radio.

On the ground around them, Gerber could see nothing. He trusted the pilots to follow the route he had shown them on the map, and looking out, he could see many of the landmarks, canals, roads and abandoned hamlets. But the ground was rushing by too fast for him to spot anything of significance. If Fetterman had come this way, he had been very careful not to leave any sign.

As they neared the operational area, there was a burst of firing from the ground and the green tracers of the enemy flashed far to the left of the aircraft. The pilot broke in the opposite direction and was immediately taken under fire by a .51-caliber Soviet-made antiaircraft machine gun. The door gunner opened fire, but the rapid chatter of the M-60 made no impression on the enemy, who kept hammering away and trying to walk the tracers into the helicopter.

They dived away from the antiaircraft fire, trying to put a tree lie between the helicopter and the enemy. They raced to the north and then turned back to the west, low-leveling toward the camp. Over the intercom Gerber shouted, "We can't go back to the camp!"

"Captain," said the pilot, "I understand what you need, but if I get shot down, what good will that do you? If I go down and they come out to rescue us and the rescue ship goes down, how does that help? We need to get an air strike to suppress the antiaircraft fire. The bad guys have some big shit in here."

Gerber didn't like what he was hearing in the least. Time was wasting, and everything he did seemed to take more time, but none of it moved him any closer to the answers he needed. He wanted to get in there and learn the fate of Fetterman and his patrol, but he could see the point being made by the pilot. It would do no good to get shot down.

"Can we spot for the air strike?"

"Yes, sir. Sure can. I've got the request in, and we can direct the artillery in there now if you want."

"Okay, put the artillery in. Can you put me through to my camp?"

"You bet. Hill, you want to set the captain up to make his call?"

The crew chief turned the selector switch on the radio control head to the number two position so that Gerber could talk on the radio. The pilot had already dialed the proper frequency into the radio. A moment later the crew chief yelled to Gerber, "Press the button when you're ready to transmit."

"Zulu Base, Zulu Base, this is Zulu Six."

"Roger, Six. Go."

"We have taken heavy fire. Will be directing LZ prep. Get the flight off the ground. I say again. Get the flight off the ground."

"Roger, Six. Will do."

The aircraft commander came on the intercom. "What are you planning on doing?"

"Insert my people as close to Fetterman's position as possible and walk in. We're not that far from him."

"Captain, I might remind you that we'll have an air strike coming. It might be quicker to wait for that and insert closer to their location."

Gerber looked at his watch. It was now after two. Fetterman had been out of touch for nearly five hours. In that time Gerber had learned that Bromhead had been ambushed and Kittredge killed. He felt that he had to act quickly but couldn't see the point in getting more people killed through unnecessary haste. He had been running almost since sunup. He sat in the back of the helicopter, shaking because he was forced to sit in one place. He wanted to be on the ground doing something. Again he thought about the information that Kepler had provided that had started the mission. Too much, too fast, and it was getting worse.

"How long until the jets arrive?"

"Maybe ten minutes."

Gerber nodded but didn't speak. He had to make himself relax. He took a deep breath and closed his eyes. He forced himself to concentrate on what he was going to do when he got on the ground. He would have a company of strikers. About the size of the force that Bromhead had had the night before. Bromhead hadn't been able to do much with them, but then Bromhead hadn't really been expecting trouble. Gerber had the advantage there. Not to mention air mobility. If he walked into trouble, he could get out of it quickly, or he could get reinforcements quickly. And he had all kinds of radios that were working.

The one thing that he had to guard against was making a mistake by hurrying. The adrenaline was pumping through him, making him nervous. He needed to think everything through carefully. He had to remember that he had the time to make intelligent decisions. It would do no good to fly off half-cocked and get another company ambushed. He would have to be patient.

At the moment, there wasn't much for Gerber to do. The whole flight was airborne but still fifteen minutes away. Artillery was falling on the antiaircraft positions they had identified, and the Air Force was coming. He tried to get the pilots flying in an ever-expanding search, looking for Fetterman. Unfortunately they couldn't fly too far to the north for fear of fouling the gun-target lines of the fire-support bases. And they couldn't fly too far west because they kept encountering enemy antiaircraft. All they could do was fly east and south, and there was nothing that Gerber wanted to see in either direction.

THE SHOOTING STARTED AGAIN after a fifteen-minute break. It started slowly with one VC firing a single shot. He was quickly joined by several others using a full auto until the RPD opened up. Fetterman emptied a whole magazine at the VC, then tossed a grenade over the mud wall to stir them up. Three or four tried to jump up, but Washington gunned them down. The others escaped into the jungle. Fetterman picked off the stragglers, but he wanted the others to make it to the trees. He didn't want to waste ammo keeping them pinned down behind the mud wall.

When the VC had escaped and the enemy shooting was coming from the jungle, Fetterman whispered, "That's it. Let's get out."

Washington checked the three badly wounded Tai. The man with the stomach wound looked at him and grabbed the front of his uniform. Slowly, carefully, Washington peeled the Tai's fingers free and laid the man's hand beside him.

Tyme crawled to the rear, pushed two of the unwounded Tai forward and pointed toward the jungle. He turned and glanced at Fetterman, who waved him forward. Tyme pushed another of the Tai out as Fetterman joined him.

Together Fetterman and Tyme began crawling along the ditch, keeping their heads down. Behind them they heard the firing increase and then heard a bugle call. There seemed to be a shout from the jungle. Fetterman looked in time to see a dozen more of the enemy rush the hootch.

Ahead of them came more firing as the Tai ran into a couple of VC. As Tyme rose out of the ditch, he was shot once in the shoulder. He cried out in surprise and pain, fell back and rolled to the bottom of the ditch out of sight.

Fetterman crawled to him, shook out a field dressing and pressed it to Tyme's shoulder. He reached down, took one of Tyme's hands and pressed it to the dressing. He saw the young sergeant try to smile. Then Fetterman crept past him to the end of the ditch where he got to his feet. He rushed to the jungle's edge and leaped into the trees. He spotted a VC who was drawing a bead on one of the Tai. Fetterman clubbed him with the butt of his rifle, and as the enemy fell, Fetterman shot him, the round penetrating the VC's back.

The fighting on that side of the clearing degenerated into hand-to-hand combat. Fetterman pulled the short bayonet from its scabbard and fixed it. He whirled in time to see a VC running among the trees. Fetterman fired from the hip and turned the man's head into an explosion of red mist as the high-velocity bullets connected.

Spinning to his right, he saw another VC. Fetterman lunged and was surprised when the Vietcong parried and thrust. Fetterman jumped back, faked a thrust and came around with a vertical butt stroke, smashing the side of the enemy's head. The man fell to one knee but tried to ram his bayonet into Fetterman's stomach as he fell forward. Fetterman knocked the rifle from his hand and then jabbed the bayonet into the man's neck. He ripped the blood-stained blade free and spotted still another enemy soldier. He fired once and the VC was thrown forward, his rifle flying from his hands. Then Fetterman ran forward, halted and waited. He saw two Tai attack one VC, killing him. Both of them then fell to the ground and fired into the jungle as if they had suddenly seen more enemy soldiers.

Fetterman ran to them, saw that they were shooting at shadows and ordered them to stop. He found two others and told them to establish a tiny perimeter so that they could guard one another.

"I have to go back to see about Boom-Boom," he said. "He went down wounded. You wait here."

There was still some shooting near the hootch as Fetterman cleared the jungle and entered the ditch. He could see Tyme lying on his back, staring into the sky. He had dropped the field dressing and now clutched his rifle in both hands so that it was across his chest. He looked as if he held it at port arms.

"Boom-Boom," he whispered, "you okay?"

"I'm hurt, Tony. I'm hurt."

"Can you move?" Fetterman asked.

"Yeah. I think I can move. Just help me get out of here."

He reached Tyme and looked at the bullet hole in the fatigue shirt. He took the first-aid kit off Tyme's pistol belt and used Tyme's knife to cut the shirt away. He pressed the bandage to the bleeding wound. He held it there for a moment, released the pressure and saw that the bleeding hadn't slowed.

"I've got to get you out of here so that I can work on you."

Tyme didn't respond. He stared upward.

"Give me your rifle and then hold the bandage in place. You've got to apply pressure, or you'll bleed to death."

"Okay," he replied absently.

"I'm going to have to drag you out. I'm afraid that it's going to be painful."

"Okay."

Fetterman took the rifle and used the sling. He grabbed Tyme by the collar of his jungle fatigues and pulled. Tyme used his feet to push and lifted his wounded shoulder off the ground, sliding on his other. They had almost reached the safety of the jungle when the shooting suddenly stopped. Fetterman glanced toward the farmer's hootch but saw nothing. Then he heard the unmistakable sound of a bolt slamming home.

At that moment Fetterman looked up into the barrel of an AK-47 and the grinning face of an NVA lieutenant. Fetterman held the lieutenant's eyes, thinking that he could kick the man's feet out from under him. Then he saw three VC and knew that there was nothing he could do. He smiled at the lieutenant and let go of his rifle that he held in one hand. Then he shrugged his shoulder so that Tyme's rifle slipped to the ground.

THE ARTILLERY LIFTED, but the Air Force still hadn't arrived. Gerber tapped the helicopter pilot on the shoulder and said, "We don't have any more time to waste. Let's try again."

The AC nodded. "Okay. I think they might have silenced that big gun."

They turned back to the west and descended so that they were only a couple of feet above the trees, dropping close to the ground whenever there was a large clearing. They circled one area, saw nothing and took no fire.

Then, as they were drawing close to the place where Fetterman should have been, they were taken under fire again. This time it wasn't just a couple of weapons, it seemed like a hundred. The AC broke away, fleeing the heavy fire.

Over the intercom, he said, "There's no way to get a flight in there, Captain. They'll all be shot down before they can land."

"Head back to the camp," he said. Gerber shook his head. This was deep shit. "We'll rendezvous with the flight and find an LZ somewhere else. We'll have to walk in."

"I may be talking out of turn, Captain, but it seems to be a very large enemy force in there."

"I appreciate your concern. We'll work something out."

Far in front of them, Gerber spotted the other helicopters. His own chopper joined the flight and turned back to the west. Gerber told the lead pilot where he wanted to go, that the arty prep had been completed and that there was still a possibility that an air strike would be going in if they encountered resistance of any kind.

But as they approached the area, firing erupted around them again. The door gunners returned it, but that didn't seem to slow it down. The VC were swarming all over the area, and since Cambodia was less than ten klicks away, they could reinforce their troops quickly or pull them out.

With the amount of antiaircraft fire increasing, Gerber realized that he was badly outnumbered and outgunned. To land anywhere near Fetterman would spell disaster.

He gave the order to return to cover.

At the camp he was met by Bocker, Anderson and Kepler. As Gerber got out of the helicopter, they all began shouting at him.

"What the fuck are we going to do?" Kepler asked.

"We got people out there. We've got to do something," Anderson chimed in.

"I know all that," Gerber shouted right back at them. "Now, if you people will join me in my hootch, we'll try to work something out."

Bocker looked at Anderson, who shrugged. "Yes, sir," said Bocker. "I'll see that Lieutenant Bromhead is there, too."

"That's fine."

"What's the plan, Captain?" the lead pilot asked as he got out of the helicopter.

"You guys need to hang loose for a while. Shut down and I'll get with you in a moment."

"We have orders to get out of here as soon as you've finished with us. We do have other commitments."

"I understand that. But I still have fifty people in the field that I can't find. And a hell of a lot of Vietcong who may have already found them."

"Yes, sir."

In his hootch Gerber found Anderson, Bocker, Bromhead and Kepler. They were waiting patiently for him, none of them speaking, each man staring at the floor.

"First things first," said Gerber by way of preamble. "We couldn't land because I could tell by the amount of antiaircraft fire we were encountering that we wouldn't survive very long on the ground. The size of the enemy force is a lot larger than estimated." He turned significantly to Kepler.

"All I had, Captain," Kepler replied, "was the one report from that old woman. A recruiting platoon would be moving through. But without being allowed to move into Cambodia to gather data, the VC could move an entire division in there and we wouldn't know it."

"What about reports from Nha Trang?" asked Bromhead.

"I know what you're thinking," Kepler continued. "The recon flights over the area showed nothing significant, but the short distances the enemy have to travel would allow them to move into position in just a couple of hours. The overflights showed no significant movement or buildups. The first indications we have are the ones we're running into."

"Okay," said Gerber. "We've got to think of something. Fetterman and his people are still missing out there, and until we find out what happened, we've got to keep moving."

"We could put out two strike companies from here," said Bromhead slowly, as if he were working out the details of the mission as he spoke. "Maybe get a couple of others moving into the area from other bases."

"No good, Johnny. Not enough time to coordinate it. I just don't want things to break down any further than they have. We've already taken more casualties today than we have since the VC tried to overrun the camp six months ago."

"What are we going to do?"

"I'm not sure yet," answered Gerber. "But I know that I'm not going to send a bunch of people out to get killed for no good reason. We're going out but not until we have a definite plan that will allow quick reinforcements and air and artillery support. I'll speak to Colonel Bates."

7

SOUTH OF THE
PARROT'S BEAK, RVN

Fetterman climbed slowly to his feet, still smiling and holding his hands open, palms down, away from his body. He glanced over his shoulder and saw Washington, his hands in the air, walking toward them.

"You my prisoner now," said the NVA officer. Fetterman's captor stood about five-and-a-half feet tall. He had straight jet-black hair. His oval face was shiny with sweat, and his uniform was stained with it. One knee of the trousers was torn, and there was mud caked on the front. He was grinning as he said, "You do as I say, or I shoot you."

"I understand, sir," said Fetterman, nodding gravely. "We will give you no trouble."

"See that you don't, Yankee dog."

Washington, who now stood with them, asked, "What about the wounded? Some of the men have been badly hurt."

"We will take care of your wounded as soon as we finish treating our injured," said the officer with a contemptuous smile.

"You speak remarkably good English," commented Washington.

"Yes. I was forced to take training in the United States at your Fort Benning. I found it necessary to learn your harsh and uncomfortable language."

"Christ," muttered Washington, "we trained the son of a bitch."

Fetterman shot him an angry glance but said only, "You learned your lessons quite well, sir."

"Shut up!" He pointed at Fetterman. "You help your friend now, or we will have to shoot him."

Fetterman crouched and checked Tyme's bandage. He saw that the bleeding had slowed considerably. Fetterman tied the bandage and said to Tyme, "Can you sit up?"

"I think so," Tyme replied, looking at the NVA officer and the VC who surrounded him.

"Okay. We'll take it easy now. If you feel woozy, you speak up. I don't know what these guys have in mind, but I think you'll probably have to walk ten, twelve klicks to get out of this area and into Cambodia, where they think they'll be safe."

"You stop that talking," commanded the NVA officer.

"Yes, sir," responded Fetterman. "I was trying to determine the state of mind of Sergeant Tyme."

Tyme was horrified by Fetterman's use of his name, but Fetterman said, "Don't sweat it. We'll have to give them names anyway." He lowered his voice. "If we make it look like we aren't real sharp, things might go a little easier."

"I would like to check on the wounded," said Washington.

"You are a doctor?" asked the NVA, studying the big, black American soldier. "You have medical supplies?"

"No, ah . . ." He hesitated.

Fetterman spoke up. "He's a medic. Probably could assist your doctors or your medics."

Now it was Washington's turn to be amazed. He tried to catch Fetterman's eye, but Fetterman was busy working on Tyme. Washington crouched, examined Fetterman's work and nodded his approval.

"I have some medicine in my bag," said Washington, pointing back toward the dilapidated farmer's hootch. "I left my stuff there."

"My men will find it," said the officer. "I will give it to my men."

"What about our wounded?" asked Fetterman.

There was a burst of machine gun fire followed by three quick pistol shots. The officer turned toward the sound, smiling, and then said, "Your injured have succumbed to their wounds. I'm afraid nothing more can be done for them."

GERBER WAS UP AND PACING. Inside his tiny office were all the Special Forces men still on the camp—Bromhead, Bocker, McMillan, Kepler and Anderson—and Captain Minh. They were sitting on Gerber's cot, on the floor or in the lawn chairs that he had gotten in Saigon. Minh was leaning against the wall, his arms folded across his chest. They were all trying to work out a plan.

"We've only got four, maybe five hours of light left," said Gerber, checking his watch. "What's the status of the choppers?"

"They're here until we release them," said Bocker. "Oh, and Ramsey said to let you know that he was off. Chinook airlifted that broken helicopter. Ramsey and Randle went with it."

"I suppose that we've heard nothing from Fetterman on the radio."

"No, sir. He hasn't checked in."

"Christ!" said Gerber. "We're really working in the dark on this one. No idea of the size of enemy forces or where they are."

Kepler felt that he had to say something. "We had no indication of enemy movements or buildups. But we do know where some of them have been operating, based on our troubles." He bent over the map spread out on Gerber's flimsy desk.

"Don't sweat it, Derek," said Gerber. "Right now we've got other things to do."

"What are we going to do, old boy?" asked Minh.

"I think we need to put a strike company into the field near the place Fetterman was supposed to set up the ambush and let them sweep through the area. We'll have a second company on standby here in case they need reinforcements and coordinate with Henderson's people in case we need more people than we have. He's running the Mike Force now.

"Galvin," Gerber continued, "I'm going to want you to head over to the commo bunker and start the coordination efforts. Alert the various fire-support bases about the possibility of some fire missions. Call Bates and have him start working on the air support. Also, call Henderson and see what kind of shape he's in.''

"Yes, sir.''

"I understand that two of your strike companies are ready,'' Gerber said, turning to Minh.

"And waiting,'' Minh replied.

"Good. Strip the defenses as best you can and see if you can scrape together a third. Some of the stragglers from Bao's strike company can augment if necessary. Is your new exec very good?''

"I'm afraid that I don't trust him very much, considering he was recommended by a general in Saigon. I just don't know him that well, old boy. I suppose that he's probably as good as anyone,'' said Minh with a shrug.

"Leave him in charge from your end. I'll leave Johnny here, too.''

"Wait a minute, Captain,'' Bromhead protested.

"No, Johnny. You wait. You were out all night. You'll be of more help here.''

"Yes, sir,'' said Bromhead bitterly. He understood Gerber's statement, but he didn't have to like it.

"Cat, I'll want you on the first shift. Derek, you and the doc should be on the second. Captain Minh, I think you should be with them, too, if you approve.''

"Sounds fine to me.''

Gerber turned and walked over to one of the maps. He studied it carefully and then pointed to an area south of the Parrot's Beak. "There are a couple of good LZs right in here. We'll go into one of them and sweep northwest into Fetterman's ambush location. If we run into trouble, we'll call for the backup. We'll make a radio check every fifteen minutes, and if we don't, it means that we need help.''

"And then I come to the rescue?'' asked Minh.

"Yes, if you think it wise. Any questions?''

When there were none, Gerber said, "All right. I'll want to see Minh and Bromhead in the commo bunker before we take off.

We'll mark the LZs on the maps there. As soon as that's done, we're going in.''

The flight lifted off twelve minutes later with the pilots staring into an orange sun that was dropping toward the horizon. Gerber sat on the right side of the helicopter, his eyes moving back and forth over the terrain shooting under him. He could see nothing that told him what to expect—just the rice fields, the swamps, the groves of coconut or banana trees and the scattered hootches of the farmers. He saw abandoned hamlets, some of them smashed by American artillery or VC rockets and mortars. There were only a few people visible. Old farmers in their black pajamas or khaki shorts and coolie hats, working their fields and refusing to look up at the American helicopters that flashed by.

Gerber, using a set of headphones and boom mike given to him by the crew chief, finally asked the pilot, ''Are we getting close?''

''Yes, sir,'' said the AC. ''Took some fire in this area last time we passed by.''

But they flew on without being shot at by anyone. Now they had gunship cover, provided by the armed helicopters assigned to the helicopter company—C-Model Hueys loaded down with 2.75-inch rockets and machine gun bullets. One of them had the new mini guns that could crank out six thousand rounds a minute and put a slug into every square inch of an area the size of a football field with a single ten-second burst. High overhead was a C and C containing the air mission commander. He had wanted Gerber to stay up with him, but Gerber preferred to be on the ground with his men. Air and artillery support could be coordinated through the C and C, as could reinforcements.

Using his map, Gerber had told the C and C where he planned to land. In turn, the air mission commander called the gun team leader and told him. Together, from altitude, they flew by the LZ and took no fire. They relayed the information to the flight.

Gerber acknowledged the information with a grunt. He was thinking how complex the mission had become and yet how quickly he had gotten all the assets he needed. The men in the helicopters were highly trained professionals, and if he let them do their jobs they would give him an edge. He didn't have to understand the operations of an assault helicopter company. All he had to do was tell them he wanted to make a combat assault into a certain area, and they would take care of their end of it.

All at once he saw a Charlie-model Huey appear in front of him. Over the radio he heard the pilot of the oncoming aircraft contact the AC of the flight lead. As the contact was established, the gunship turned, diving back toward the ground as if leading the Slick.

"We're making our approach, Captain," said the aircraft commander. "Please get your people ready."

From the open cargo-compartment door Gerber saw another gunship dive beyond them, firing rockets two at a time into the trees. He saw bursts of smoke at the sides of the chopper and two bright lights that were the flames of the rockets. Seconds later there were bursts of black smoke and orange fire below. On the other side of the flight, another gunship used its mini guns to rake the trees. The sound from the Gatling-type machine gun sounded like a buzz saw, and the tracers reached down like a red ray. The gun team leader led the flight to the LZ, flew through it, and two small objects tumbled from the cargo compartment. The smoke grenades fell to the center of the LZ.

Over the radio Gerber heard the AC say, "ID yellow."

"Roger, yellow. Negative fire."

Gerber stripped his headset, tossing it on the console between the two pilots. As he donned his steel pot, he heard both door guns open fire as the men behind the M-60s began a routine suppression. He checked the magazine of his M-14 and then worked the bolt.

As the helicopter touched the ground, its nose hidden in the billowing cloud of yellow smoke, Gerber leaped into the grass being flattened by the rotor wash of the chopper and fell to his knees. Around him, the men of his company jumped from the other ships, which took off as soon as they were unloaded. It was a classic air assault into a cold LZ.

Immediately Gerber signaled his men forward toward the trees, forming them into squads. Anderson and a couple of Tai hurried forward as a point and slack. As they entered the trees, the last of the men fell into a rear guard.

They held their interval well and had a couple of flankers out on both sides because they were using a trail. Gerber didn't like walking on a trail, where he could easily be ambushed or trip any number of booby traps, but he felt that speed was important.

Thirty minutes later they stopped. Gerber crawled forward to see what was wrong. Anderson held his map out and whispered, "I think we're getting close."

Gerber checked his compass and consulted his map. He nodded to Anderson and said, "You're right. I don't hear anything, do you?"

"No, sir. I sure don't."

Gerber waved at the RTO, who carried the heavy PRC-10. He called the C and C. The gunships had been crisscrossing the area, looking for a target or trying to draw enemy fire, but not a shot had been fired at them. It was as if all the VC had pulled out.

Having confirmed that nothing had been seen by the helicopters, Gerber waved his men forward. They spread out carefully now, watching the ground near them for signs of booby traps. The advance was slow and it was another twenty minutes before they discovered the first evidence of what had happened to Fetterman's ambush. They found the body of one of the Tai strikers. The VC had taken his weapon, his clothes and anything else the man might have carried. Then they had mutilated the body. Some of the mutilation was obviously trophy taking. There were no fingers or ears. And some of it was obviously designed to terrorize the other strikers. There was a gaping, bloody hole in the man's chest where his heart should have been. Gerber turned and looked at his strikers. What he saw wasn't terror or fear; it was anger.

Now they began a leapfrog advance, half the men covering the rest as they moved forward. Once they had deployed, the remainder of the strike company moved up and took positions. It slowed the advance but made if safer.

A few minutes later they found a second body. The Tai had been shot fifteen or twenty times, but only a couple of wounds would have been fatal. It looked as if the man had been captured alive and then shot to pieces as a form of torture. Once he was dead, he had been stripped and mutilated. He was missing one hand, three fingers from the other and his head.

They found several more bodies near a trail. From the evidence—trees riddled with bullets and shrapnel, craters in the ground from exploding grenades and mortars and the remains of claymore mines—Gerber knew that they had found the ambush site.

They swept through it, looking for signs of the enemy. They saw more bodies, all stripped and mutilated. But there were no weapons or booby traps. Nor did they find the bodies of Fetterman, Tyme or Washington. Once they knew that the area was clear, they began a detailed inspection to determine what had happened.

Gerber could tell from the evidence of the mortar craters that Fetterman had run into something a lot larger than he had expected. Fetterman had apparently been able to hold his position for quite a while. Again it was the evidence left behind—the damage to the trees where the bullets had slammed into them, the number of mortar craters, the blood trails and the large pools of blood—that suggested that many of the NVA or VC soldiers who had been killed had been dragged away. They also found the body of the RTO, the remains of his radio shot full of holes. Anything that was of value had been stripped from the carcass of the radio.

"Now what?" asked Anderson quietly. It was the second time in less than twelve hours that he had stood looking at a battlefield.

"We sweep through again to see if we can find a trail to follow," growled Gerber. "Fetterman and the rest of the strikers have to be somewhere."

"It will be getting dark soon, Captain," said Anderson.

"Yeah, Cat, I know. But according to the map, there's a good LZ about half a klick from here. We can use it. That means," said Gerber, consulting his watch, "that we can stay here another twenty or thirty minutes."

The search failed to turn up anything useful. They found a couple of dead strikers a hundred meters behind the ambush. Once again the bodies were stripped and mutilated. Each had had the heart cut out. The heart of one of them had been set on a nearby log as if it were some kind of warning. Behind the dead Tai they found still another body, also mutilated, but this one wasn't a striker. From the remains of the khaki uniform, they could tell that it was an NVA NCO.

"Looks like they didn't find all their dead," commented Anderson.

"And from the mutilation," said Gerber, "it appears that our Sergeant Krung survived the ambush and managed to escape in this direction."

"You think he's still out there?" Anderson asked, looking into the dense vegetation.

Gerber smiled. "Knowing Krung, he's still out there carrying on his private war. We could probably find him by following a trail of dead NVA and VC who were mutilated. I think all we have to do us wait for him. He'll show up at camp carrying a bagful of trophies."

"What about Fetterman?"

"That, Cat, is the question. I can't see Tony getting himself captured. I suspect that he's faded into the jungle."

"Do we continue to look?"

Gerber shook his head. "Not now. We've got to get out of here. Tomorrow we organize a battalion-sized sweep through the area and see what we can find. Right now we've got to get back to camp."

Gerber turned to his RTO, grabbing the handset of the PRC-10. He radioed the flight and asked that they use the small LZ to the west of the ambush site. The VC or NVA had probably escaped to Cambodia.

The flight back to the camp was somber. Although the whine of the Huey turbines and the roar of the engines made conversation difficult, the men usually joked with one another at the completion of a mission. But not this time. Too many friends were dead and too many were missing. He would have Bocker try to arrange aviation support for the next day. Gerber knew that he had to divert some of his assets the next day to collect the bodies. The Tai expected it and the Vietnamese demanded it. If the dead weren't picked up and buried properly, Gerber knew that he would no longer be able to count on the Tai or the Vietnamese in a fight. He made a mental note to coordinate with Bates and have Bao command the detail, with Bocker or Anderson to advise.

The mood in the camp was not happy. Bao and his strikers were mourning their dead in their own way. Gerber and most of the Americans that were left were in the team house. Bocker had added to the gloom by telling them General Crinshaw had denied airlift, explaining that the LZs were within walking distance and the aviation assets were needed elsewhere. No one spoke too much. A bottle of Beam's sat on one of the tables and periodically someone would take a swig from it.

Morrow came in about an hour later and saw them all sitting around. She went directly to the refrigerator, took a barely cool beer out of it and held it up. "Anyone else?"

"I'll have one," growled Anderson.

"Me, too," said Gerber.

As she handed the beer to Gerber, she asked, "Shouldn't you be doing something?"

"Such as?"

"Planning your operation?"

"Right now the operation is off. We have orders from Saigon. Crinshaw to be exact. We don't have an airlift."

Morrow sat down next to Gerber and popped her beer using the church key she wore around her neck. "And you're going to let that stop you?"

"Of course not!" said Gerber. "It's just that there isn't a whole lot to do right now. Bocker is still trying to get us one helicopter for recon. Bromhead is out organizing the men. I thought it would be good training for him. He's getting to be fairly senior and will get promoted to Captain soon. And I don't know why I feel compelled to explain all this to you."

"Maybe you're feeling guilty," she said and then wished she could bite her tongue off.

But Gerber just smiled. "No. Not guilty. We received some information and acted on it. By the time we hit the field, the information was outdated. Now we're trying to recover from that. But right now there's nothing we can do but wait."

8

MACV HEADQUARTERS, SAIGON

"Thank you for seeing me at this late hour, General Hull," said Lieutenant Colonel Alan Bates, saluting the tall, thin, balding man behind the heavy steel desk. As he did so, Bates couldn't help comparing Hull's office to that of Brigadier General Billy Joe Crinshaw's.

Crinshaw's office was opulent, the floor newly carpeted, the mahogany-paneled walls lined with bookcases or decorated with weapons captured in battle from the Vietcong, none of which, Bates knew, had been captured by General Crinshaw. Crinshaw had used his influence as a general officer to make himself a very comfortable inner sanctum, where he held court from behind his massive oak desk, resplendent in his Class A blouse bedecked with several rows of ribbons, the most important being a Bronze Star without V device. That is, he was resplendent in his Class As when he wasn't huddled in a field jacket to protect himself from the icy blast of his new air conditioner, which would have been sufficient to handle the walk-in freezer at the Tan Son Nhut Officers' Club.

Major General Garrison Hull's office was spartan by comparison, the walls painted a light shade of restful green, the desk the regulation military issue in battleship gray, topped with a small green blotter and two OD metal in and out trays that seemed always to be full. There were stacks of papers and file folders neatly arranged along one edge of the desk and a single black telephone and photograph of General Hull's wife and daughter along the other edge. On one painted wall hung a picture of Eisenhower before he had become President, talking to some troops in the field. Hull, then a captain, stood second from the left in the line of soldiers. A second photograph, this one autographed, showed Hull as a major, receiving the Army DSC from General Patton. The other wall held a large map and a Renoir print of a young girl who bore a striking resemblance to the general's daughter. Bates noted that the map, unlike the one in Crinshaw's office, was covered according to regulations. Behind Hull was the officer's one concession to the privileges of rank—a large set of double windows stood open to the night air, which an ancient ceiling fan stirred languidly, the faint, warm air currents providing the illusion of a breeze.

"No problem, Al. I was catching up on some back paperwork anyway," said Hull, returning the salute. "Besides, I usually figure when you want to see me it's about something important. Have a seat and tell me how I can help." He motioned to a battered armchair set near the window and turned his own chair so that he could face Bates without the desk being between them. Then he leaned back in the chair and dug into the pocket of his OD jungle jacket for his pipe and tobacco pouch. It was a bit early for the single bowl of Whitehall he allowed himself in the evenings, but the paperwork was getting monotonous, and he welcomed the break created by Bates's visit.

"Thank you, General," said Bates, taking the offered chair and then leaning quickly forward, sitting on the edge to avoid sinking into the overstuffed cushion as the worn springs creaked loudly. He considered how different this meeting was from the one he'd had earlier in the day with Brigadier General Crinshaw. Both Crinshaw and Hull were USMA graduates, both career soldiers, yet there the resemblance ended. Major General Hull was a man that Bates admired, respected and liked, someone he trusted and as much of a friend as a lieutenant colonel could be friends with a major general. Crinshaw, on the other hand, was the perfect example of the kind of officer that Bates despised—a loudmouthed garret trooper leg, who still thought wars could be fought and won using the kind of tactics employed at the Battle of Hastings.

"Well, General," began Bates, "as you probably know by now, Mack Gerber's A-Detachment stepped into it in a big way out by An Minh early this morning."

Hull nodded. "I was just reading the initial report before you came in. Gerber's a good man. Has he located all his people yet?"

Bates suddenly felt very tired. "He's located some remains he believes to be those of Sergeant First Class Steven Kittredge. He was the team's heavy weapons specialist. It appears that he called artillery fire in on his own position as he was being overrun by the Vietcong."

Hull stopped sucking on his pipe in middraw and slowly lowered it. "The poor bastard. Did he have any family?"

Bates nodded. "He left a wife and a four-year-old daughter."

Hull turned his head toward the desk and stared at the photograph of his own wife and daughter. The silence stretched out for several seconds before he asked, "What about the men with him?"

"The strikers were slaughtered to a man, stripped and mutilated. Staff Sergeant Sully Smith was with Kittredge as second advisor. He's listed as missing at this time. He was—is—the team's demolitions specialist."

"And the rest of the operation?" asked Hull, still staring at the picture. He sensed that the worst was yet to come.

"Well, you'll know from the preliminary report that Lieutenant Bromhead made it back to camp with what was left of the blocking force. Sergeant First Class Tyme, the team's light weapons specialist, and Staff Sergeant Thomas Jefferson Washington, the junior medical specialist, were with the ambush party under Anthony Fetterman, the team sergeant. All three are missing. Same story as before with their strikers—no survivors. Except possibly one. Captain Gerber indicated that he had reason to believe one of the senior Tai NCOs may have escaped. He didn't say what the reason was."

Hull seemed not to have heard the last part. "Tony Fetterman? Wiry little guy, mild mannered, claims to be descended from the Indian fighter, or sometimes Aztecs?"

"That's the one. I didn't realize you knew the master sergeant," said Bates with some surprise.

"And I didn't know he was even still in the Army. Take another look at that picture of Eisenhower before you leave, Al. The skinny little short kid to the far right with the corporal's stripes. That's Tony Fetterman. He carried me five miles through German lines one night in France. I don't remember too much of the trip because I had a sucking chest wound and kept passing out. I found out later that Fetterman had been shot through the left shoulder and thigh, and he carried *me* out. I owe Tony Fetterman, and now you tell me he's missing in action."

"I'm sorry, General, I didn't know. I knew you knew Captain Gerber from Korea, but I didn't know about Master Sergeant Fetterman. Which doesn't make the next part of what I have to tell you any easier. Captain Gerber suspects, and given the absence of bodies—" Bates broke off, immediately regretting the turn of phrase. "What I mean to say, General, is, given the absence of evidence to the contrary and the massacre of the strikers, Captain Gerber suspects, and I'm forced to agree with him, that all four men may have been captured by the Vietcong."

It was an obvious statement but one that had to be made.

Hull nodded slightly. "What's being done to get them back?"

"Captain Gerber took two companies into the field late this afternoon to search for survivors. They were forced to abandon the search at dusk because of a lack of adequate supporting fire and a suitable night defensive position. There was also a high probability of a large VC force in the area."

"And in the morning?" asked Hull.

"And in the morning, nothing," said Bates quietly.

"What the hell do you mean, nothing, Al?" snapped Hull.

"Captain Gerber had planned to strip the camp and conduct a battalion-sized sweep of the area. I was going to loan him Dave Henderson's Mike Force as well, but the plan has been scotched."

Hull was incredulous. "Why on earth would Nha Trang do that?"

"SFHQ would never do that, General. Special Forces takes care of its people. Colonel Andekker's even offered a couple of companies from the Moc Hoa area." Bates had bristled at the implication, then shrugged it off before continuing. "The problem isn't in Nha Trang. It's here in Saigon. General Crinshaw—"

Hull practically exploded. "God damn the man! I should have suspected Billy Joe was making an ass of himself again the minute you walked in. What's the mental midget done this time?"

Bates couldn't have agreed more with Hull's assessment of Crinshaw, but he also couldn't express his agreement. Lieutenant colonels didn't speak that way about general officers, especially not in the presence of another general officer. Not even if that other general officer said so first.

"We need airlift support to mount an operation of this size," Bates began carefully, "and I'm afraid that General Crinshaw..."

"Who has a certain amount of say-so over the allocation of aircraft in such matters, has denied the airlift," Hull finished for him. "Am I correct?"

"Yes, General."

"And did Brigadier General Crinshaw give you a reason for his decision?" asked Hull, his voice dangerously calm.

"Yes, General. He said that other requirements of the military assistance effort prevented the allocation of the numbers of aircraft necessary for an operation of this size at this time, that the very nature of such an undertaking constituted an inefficient waste of manpower and that, in any event, an operation of this magnitude would take at least three weeks to coordinate with the ARVN staff."

"By which time our boys will be in northern Cambodia, enroute for Hanoi, or dead. Well, by God, I'll not let the silly bastard get away with it. If those men are going to have any chance at all, we've got to find them, and I mean quickly."

"Yes, sir. That's pretty much the way Captain Gerber and I have it figured."

As the conversation had developed, Bates had watched Hull grow increasingly angry. Now the major general was almost trembling with barely controlled rage.

"Alan, you call your Captain Gerber and you tell him to have his people ready to move at first light. Where can I reach you later this evening?"

Bates was exhausted. He had been planning to go to his quarters to try to get some sleep, but this put things in a different light.

"I'll be in my office, General. No, on second thought, I'll be at the B-50 TOC. You can reach me at B-Detachment Tactical Operations Center anytime after, say, thirty minutes from now."

"All right, Alan, I'll call you as soon as I can. Just make sure Gerber and the Mike Force are ready. I'll find you some goddamned helicopters if I have to go all the way to Westmorland to do it."

SPECIAL FORCES STAFF SERGEANT Sully Smith lay shivering in the darkness beneath the low, drooping limbs of a thicket of broadleaved giant ferns and fought hard to slow the pounding of his heart and quiet the wheezing of his breathing. The night air had turned cool, chilling him as the almost undetectable breeze evaporated the perspiration from his skin and sweat-soaked fatigues. But he knew the trembling was more the result of the adrenaline coursing through his bloodstream than anything else.

Smith wasn't afraid. Indeed, he'd felt a curious sense of calm detachment ever since he'd seen Kittredge die. The image was still clear. He'd glanced back to see where Steve was when he'd realized he wasn't running beside him, and he'd seen the heavy weapons specialist standing calmly upright, as if he were trying to get a better view of the onrushing enemy, the handset of the PRC-10 radio still held to the side of his head. Then the next salvo of artillery had landed on the slope of the tiny knoll, and Kittredge had disappeared in a big geyser of mud, water and bodies. After that, it had seemed as though that entire region of swamp had started blowing up, and it had become a highly unhealthy neighborhood. There had been no point in going back. Steve Kittredge was dead. Smith hadn't seen any point in compounding the situation with his own death.

There had been a brief, fierce firefight when he'd reached the tree line with four or five strikers and run smack into a VC squad. He remembered shooting a couple of VC. Then it had gone hand-to-hand and somebody had smacked him on the side of the head with a rifle butt. He thought that he'd killed the man with his knife, but he couldn't remember for sure. Things had gotten pretty confusing after that. When his head had cleared, he'd been a few hundred meters away from the fight. He'd lost his rifle somewhere but had picked up one of the old heavy Garand M-1s and most of a bandolier of eight-round clips. Presumably he'd taken them from a dead striker. The strap of the bandolier had been cut, and he had the loose ends and his knife clenched in one hand, the semiautomatic rifle in the other. Two large demo bags were strapped over his shoulders. He'd also had a splitting headache, with occasional blinding flashes of white light before his eyes, and blood streaming down the right side of his face and neck.

Smith had spent most of the afternoon running as fast as he could. Several times he'd risked the few trails he'd come across, hoping that the better footing would allow him to put more distance between himself and the short-legged Vietcong. Smith knew that at least some of the trails would be mined or booby-trapped, *dap loi* toe poppers if nothing else. But he'd taken to the trails when the sixth sense a soldier develops in combat told him that the enemy was closing in on him, then broken off into the jungle again when that same sixth sense told him that he'd stayed on the trails too long.

At one point he'd realized with horror that he was leaving tracks along a section of trail where the packed earth had turned soft from the recent rains, his Panama-tread jungle boots leaving painfully obvious footprints that even the greenest VC recruit couldn't fail to spot. Smith had turned the situation to his own advantage, stepping off the trail and doubling back to string the trip wire of a pair of claymore mines that he dug out of one of the demo bags he carried. He set the mines to rake the trail in both directions. It had cost him seven minutes to rig the trap and another fifteen minutes of struggling through the dense growth flanking the trail before he'd dared come back to it, but it had been worth it. He'd still been within earshot when he'd heard the mines blow.

"That ought to slow the bastards down a bit," he'd muttered through clenched teeth and then he'd run on.

Sometime during the afternoon the bleeding had stopped. A bad contusion from the feel of it. He probably had a mild concussion, too, but he couldn't be bothered with trivialities. He was still alive, and as long as the Vietcong didn't get hold of him, he had a chance of staying that way. If the VC caught up with him, chance wouldn't enter into it. Not with all the plastic explosives and other goodies he was carrying in his shoulder bags. There had been some instances down in the Camau Peninsula, near the Rung U Minh— the Forest of Darkness—where Special Forces men or MACV advisors had been captured by the Vietcong. What had been left of them when the bodies had been found wasn't nearly as pleasant to think about as the prospect of blowing yourself to bits and maybe taking a few VC along with you.

He wasn't, however, in any hurry to rush the situation. When the time came, he'd pull the pin on a detonator or pop the spoon off a grenade, but until then old Victor Charlie was going to have to work like hell if he was going to get the best of Francisco Giovanni Salvatore Smith, and he wasn't going to get one damned bit of help from Franchesca Smith's little boy, Sully, in doing it.

Sully Smith had not come to Vietnam to fight and die for his country. He had come to fight and live, and let some other poor dumb bastard die for *his* country. That was why they all had come. Only Kittredge had forgotten.

Smith jerked his head upright, causing another of the blinding flashes as his temple began pounding once more. His mind had been wandering, and he'd nearly dozed off. He couldn't afford to do that. It wasn't just because the Vietcong might find him. He didn't know how serious the concussion might be. If he let himself fall asleep, he might never wake up.

He would have to rest, but he couldn't sleep. He was too tired to go on, despite the adrenaline telling his body it should be running. But it was too damned dark to tell where he was going. He would have to find some way to occupy his mind. That was the trick. Let the body relax, but keep the mind alert. If only he could concentrate . . . But he was so tired.

Think, you stupid bastard, Smith swore at himself. You want to stay alive, you've got to think so use your mind. He could feel the leeches crawling across his hands and face, but he was too exhausted to brush them away. Wouldn't do any good anyway. The underside of the ferns must be thick with the bloodsuckers. Some had already fastened themselves into place, but he didn't dare light a cigarette to burn them off. Someone might see the light. Tomorrow he might risk it, after he was another klick or two closer to the camp, if any of his cigarettes were still dry enough to light. His head nodded, and he snapped it back up. The pain helped. Now he needed something to occupy the old gray matter, and his mind turned to what he knew best....

The individual tetrytol M-1 chain demolition block is two inches square by eleven inches long and weighs two-and-one-half pounds....

He heard a sudden sound, and his senses were jerked into alertness. Was somebody moving out there? he wondered. He listened hard, swearing he could hear something, then telling himself he was imagining things. He was getting tired, but he had to stay awake. Had to keep alert.

Composition C-4 is a white plastic explosive, more powerful than TNT, but with no offensive odor. It is plastic over a wide range of temperatures, and has about the same sensitivity as...

He stopped. There was that damned noise again! He couldn't be imagining it. But what the hell could it be? he asked himself. Leeches falling off the ferns? Some kind of jungle cat? VC looking for him? VC! Definitely VC!

Smith moved his sweaty hand forward along the stock of the Garand M-1 with agonizing slowness. His entire left arm felt as if it were made of lead. When his fingers finally reached the trigger guard, he had to push a leech out of the way before he could ease the push-through safety off. It seemed as if he barely had the strength to do what was needed. But the adrenaline was pumping again. Not much, but enough. He'd manage. Somehow. They weren't going to take him without a fight. His other hand found the fore end of the rifle, steadying the heavy weapon against his shoulder.

All right. I'm ready for you sons of bitches now, Smith thought. Come on, you bastards, it's time for fun and games. Then he heard it. So quiet that at first he was not sure that he'd heard it at all, but after a few seconds it came again. This time there could be no mistaking it. A soft, whispering voice. He shifted the rifle slightly so that it was pointing in the direction of the voice and strained his ears, trying to catch the words.

"Sergeant Sully," the voice said in heavily accented, broken English. "Sergeant Sully, you there?"

9

THE JUNGLE NEAR
HONG NGU

Fetterman had a pretty good idea where he was, despite the blindfold and all the marching back and forth that the VC security team had put him, Tyme and Washington through in an effort to confuse the Americans. It had started as soon as the Green Berets had been blindfolded and turned around several times, but Fetterman had judged that he was still facing more or less the same direction when they'd finished as he had been before they'd started. He'd simply paid attention to the number of times a hand had touched his left shoulder to turn him and had ignored the other touches. The touch of the hand had felt the same each time—first the heel of the palm striking his biceps, then the fingers curling behind the arm to jerk him around to the right. Since the hand grabbed him in the same fashion and at the same location each time he felt its touch, Fetterman reasoned that it belonged to the guard in front of him and was therefore a useful indicator of the general direction in which he was facing. He'd had a pretty good idea of his directions before they were caught, and after that it was just a matter of noting turns and counting paces as the VC hustled them along a series of trails.

Fetterman was concerned about the other two prisoners, particularly Tyme. Washington had only been allowed to glance quickly at Tyme's pressure dressing before the VC lieutenant had slapped his hand away.

Fetterman was also concerned about Washington's mental state. When they'd heard the gunfire indicating that the VC had killed the wounded strikers, Washington had thrown himself at the VC officer, intent on wringing the man's neck. The big medical specialist would likely have succeeded had not Fetterman pulled him off. The master sergeant had seen a second VC soldier raise his rifle to shoot. Washington had not. Afterward they'd each received a vertical butt stroke from the lieutenant for their trouble and had had their wrists and elbows bound tightly behind their backs. The VC lieutenant had then taken the time to kick Washington in the groin and had admonished Fetterman with, "Master Sergeant, you keep your men in line, or I shoot them. Then maybe I shoot you, too."

The VC had, of course, immediately taken their weapons and equipment belts; their floppy jungle hats, helmets, wallets and wristwatches had disappeared at the same time. They had been allowed to keep their boots until they stopped at a tiny hamlet of not more than half a dozen hootches. Fetterman estimated the time to have been around 2200 hours, based on the 40,259 steps he had taken since they'd been blindfolded following their capture.

The VC marched them into the village, made them kneel in front of one of the huts and then removed their blindfolds. Fetterman was relieved to see that the others were still with him, and although he couldn't tell if the bleeding from Tyme's wound had stopped entirely, the young sergeant seemed to be doing fairly well considering the situation. Tyme nodded in Fetterman's direction and flashed him a tight grin but was kicked between the shoulder blades when he'd tried to speak.

Fetterman then took in his surroundings and was a bit surprised to find the huts. He didn't recognize the ville, and hadn't realized there were any settlements quite that small in the area. What really surprised him, though, was the lights. Each of the huts had a kerosene lantern burning, either inside or hung outside the door. A light like that in the jungle at night was an invitation to either get shelled or bombed, now that the American pilots had begun flying some of the combat missions. Unlike the VNAF, the Americans weren't hesitant to fly at night and frequently had an O-1 Bird Dog out looking for likely targets for Puff or the fast movers out of Saigon. Fetterman couldn't decide if it meant that the VC felt the tiny village was secure, or if it was all an arranged show, designed to impress the Americans with how safe the VC felt here.

The villagers were all paraded by, were given a chance to look at the despicable Yankee dogs and were encouraged to shout insults and spit at them. Then the VC lieutenant came forward and ordered the prisoners to stand. After they had struggled to their feet, the VC officer nodded to one of the other Vietcong, who untied their arms and gave each of them a cigarette. Fetterman noted with amused interest that the cigarettes were American, Chesterfield Kings, Tyme's brand, and undoubtedly had been taken from him earlier.

"You see," said the VC lieutenant, "you think the Front is your enemy. But we are not your enemy. It is the people who hate you, not the Front. The Front gives you your lives rather than kill you in the battle. But the people hate you because they do not want you in their country. Your presence here helps to prop up the puppets of the corrupt Saigon regime, and the people rightly hate you for this and would kill you. You must learn the error of your behavior and correct it if the Front is to continue to protect you from the people and keep you safe until you have learned the wrongness of your ways and can be returned home to your families again."

It was the biggest speech he'd heard so far, and Fetterman replied humbly, "Thank you, sir, for your lenient treatment of us and for the cigarettes. And please accept our thanks to the Front for sparing our lives."

It was difficult to say who wore the most stunned expression, Washington, Tyme or the VC lieutenant. It was obvious that, whatever they had expected the master sergeant's reaction to be to the VC lieutenant's canned propaganda speech, this wasn't it. But Fetterman knew the rules, and rule number one was do not antagonize your captor.

The VC officer was quick to recover. He smiled and stepped forward to light Fetterman's cigarette. Fetterman recognized the lighter but said nothing. It was his.

"You see, we are not so bad," the VC said easily. "We all want to be reasonable. But you must learn to understand the wrongness of your position here. Soon you will be taken to a camp where you will begin school to teach you the truth of our revolutionary struggle. How soon you can be returned to your families will depend upon how soon you learn the lessons of your mistakes. I urge you to study hard when your classes begin and learn your lessons quickly so that the generosity of the Front may return you to your families in the shortest possible time."

The lieutenant knew his stuff. He kept referring to the men's families. If you make a man sentimental, you make him weak. If he's weak, he's already yours. Fetterman wondered how many other Americans the lieutenant had used to perfect his routine.

"Thank you for your advice, sir," said Fetterman. "I'm sure we all want to go home as quickly as possible. I know that I'm very anxious to get back to my family. Do you suppose the Front would mind if we used these cigarettes to get rid of a few leeches, sir?"

Tyme was so disgusted that he felt nauseated. He just couldn't believe the way Fetterman was caving in to this guy. The team sergeant was absolutely the last person he'd ever expected to knuckle under to the VC, no matter what the situation. Yet the sergeant was practically kowtowing to a slimy VC bastard. Tyme wanted to kick the VC in the nuts the way the VC had kicked Washington. He wanted to spit in the man's face. Goddamn it, they were professional soldiers, and the Code of Conduct was very clear. They were to resist the enemy by whatever means possible. If captured they were to continue to resist, by passive noncooperation if nothing else.

The VC lieutenant checked his new watch—Fetterman's watch—and seemed to consider for a moment. Then he nodded his assent. "The Front grants its generous permission for you to remove the leeches. You may help each other."

"Thank you, sir," Fetterman replied. He moved toward the other two Americans, feeling the tingling burn of blood pumping through his arteries and veins as the circulation returned to his forearms and hands. The VC soldier who had tied him up, using a split bamboo thong at both wrists and elbows, had been a little too enthusiastic about his work, and Fetterman fumbled the cigarette as he held it between clumsy fingers.

"What's the big idea, Fetterman?" whispered Tyme. "I thought for a minute there you were going to kiss that son of a bitch's hand."

"I'd kiss his ass if I thought it would keep us alive, Boom-Boom," answered Fetterman. He used his cigarette to burn off some of the leeches clinging to Tyme's arms and legs, while Washington checked the bandaged shoulder. Tyme's face was ashen, and he was highly diaphoretic.

"Damn it, Tony, what about the Code of Conduct? Do you have to be quite so helpful to them?" Tyme spoke with his words strung out, breaths interspaced between them, as if each word were costing him considerable effort.

"Come on, Boom-Boom. I haven't told them anything they don't already know or won't figure out pretty quickly. Besides, you know what these guys think of the Code and the Geneva convention. I can't see where it's going to hurt us to be polite to them. It might buy us some time, and it isn't going to help our situation any if we piss them off."

"Time for what?" Washington asked.

"Who knows? We've been out of contact with the camp for a long time and missed three routine radio checks. Captain Gerber will have people out looking for us by now. Best thing we can do is try to stay alive and see what happens." Fetterman glanced at Washington, who shook his head.

"I think part of the bullet is still lodged in there. I need a chance to dig it out and get some antibiotics in him. If it stays in, it's going to get infected."

"I'll see what I can do," Fetterman said. "Just don't either of you guys get that VC lieutenant pissed off again."

"No whispering!" snapped the VC officer. "You talk, you speak so I can hear you."

"Yes, sir," said Fetterman. "I was just asking Sergeant Washington about the condition of Sergeant Tyme's wound. He believes the bullet is still lodged in Sergeant Tyme's shoulder and needs to come out. We were wondering if the Front would be generous enough to return Sergeant Washington's medical bag long enough for him to remove the bullet and give Sergeant Tyme some medicine."

"No!" the Vietcong said adamantly. "Your man is responsible for his condition. Besides, I need all the medicine for my own wounded. We must go on in a short time to camp. The doctor there will treat your man if he needs medical attention."

Fetterman tried another approach. "Sergeant Tyme has been greatly weakened by his wound. Sergeant Washington is concerned that he will not be able to continue to walk to your camp if it isn't treated soon."

"No medicine until we reach camp. If your man cannot walk, we must leave him behind." The lieutenant's voice had the ring of finality.

Fetterman didn't like the sound of that. He had no doubt that if they had to leave Tyme behind, the VC would care for him in the same manner as they had the wounded Tai strikers.

"We understand your concern for your own men must come first," Fetterman told him. "I'm sure that Sergeant Tyme will not mind waiting until we reach your camp to have his wound looked at by your doctor."

"He must be able to walk when we are ready to move. If he slows us down, we will have to leave him behind."

Fetterman shot a doubtful glance at Tyme, who returned it with a tight grin that twisted his face into a grimace.

"It's okay, Tony. Tell the representative of the Front I'll be fine until we get there," said Tyme, gasping and swaying uncertainly on his feet.

At that point another VC came up and said something to the Vietcong officer, who checked his new watch again and nodded to the VC who had given each of the Americans one of Tyme's cigarettes. He came forward, passing out fresh ones and taking away the half-smoked ones. A group of civilians was arranged around

the Green Berets, all smiles this time, and the VC officer stepped
up and struck the flint of Fetterman's lighter, holding it out toward the cigarette that Washington, who was at the end of the line,
held. Another VC appeared, equipped with a 35 mm camera and
flash, and started snapping pictures. When he had taken a dozen
photographs, the VC soldier that had passed out the smokes collected the still unlighted Chesterfields and tucked them back into
the pack. The man with the camera disappeared, and the three
Americans had their wrists and elbows tied together once more and
their blindfolds replaced. Shortly after that someone came and took
their boots and socks away.

They marched steadily throughout the remainder of the night,
pausing only twice to rest briefly before continuing. The narrow
jungle trails would have been bad enough without the blindfolds.
With them it was a nightmare. Vines and fallen branches crisscrossed the trails, and Fetterman stumbled over logs so many times
that he lost count, pitching facedown onto the jungle floor, unable
to break his falls because his arms were bound behind his back.
Each time it was a bigger struggle than the last to get back to his
feet, and the only help offered by the VC was an occasional kick or
a gun butt. His feet were past aching and full of thorns. Snakes and
venomous insects were things he tried not to think about. There
was an old joke about Vietnam having one hundred varieties of
snakes—ninety-nine were poisonous, and the last one could swallow you whole. Fetterman hoped he wouldn't get the chance to put
the theory to the test.

As bad as it was for him, Fetterman knew that it must be worse
for Tyme. The young sergeant hadn't looked good at all back in
the village, but Fetterman was encouraged by the fact that there
had been no gunshot.

After it began to get light, the going wasn't quite so bad. The
blindfold, which seemed to be made of an old strip of burlap,
hadn't been tied all that well, and Fetterman discovered that he
could see just a bit of ground if he pitched his eyes steeply and
peered out from under the bottom of it. By tilting his head, he
could see a short distance in front of his feet, only a foot or so but
enough to prevent him from stumbling over any more vines or

branches. Once, his new sight saved him from stepping squarely on a scorpion that was apparently late getting home and a bit slow scurrying out of the way.

In spite of the very difficult terrain, Fetterman stubbornly continued to keep track of the number of steps he took and a general sense of direction. He estimated that they had come only about four-and-a-half klicks from the village when the VC lieutenant called a halt.

For about twenty minutes nothing happened. Fetterman stood waiting, swaying slightly on tired legs, feeling the oppressive heat that always signaled the start of a new day in the land of eternal summer. He could barely see his feet beneath the blindfold and wished he couldn't. They were filthy and covered with scratches and cuts from the brambles and thorns, a real invitation to infection. And that was only the tops of his feet. The soles, he knew, would be even worse. He wondered how many thorns and pebbles he would find embedded there if he got the chance to examine them. What parasites could you pick up from the soil? His feet were beyond pain now. There was only a dull, tired throbbing, much the same as followed any long march, suggesting to him that the nerve endings in the outer layers of skin might possibly have abraded.

As he waited for whatever was going to happen, he flared his nostrils and strained his ears, trying to catch some scent or sound that would give him a clue to their surroundings. Curiously he thought he could detect the faint odor of a cooking fire, but the only sound he heard was a dull thud, like someone dropping a sack of potatoes. He stood there, part of his mind searching the environment, while another part continued to assess the organism.

Feet bad, need boots. Legs weak, but probably okay. Something crawling up the left thigh toward the groin, probably one of the ubiquitous leeches. Try not to think about it; nothing can be done right now. Hands numb again—try to work fingers and keep blood flowing past bamboo thong. Shoulders ache but don't seem dislocated.

The assessment was interrupted by the sudden removal of the blindfold, leaving him blinking in the bright sunlight filtering through an open space in the jungle canopy overhead. He was facing east and thought that Camp A-555 would be about fifteen klicks east by southeast. He judged the time to be about 0900 before glancing quickly to either side. To the left he could barely see the dim outline of a camouflaged hootch across a small clearing, maybe twenty meters away. To the right was a packed mud wall with punji stakes pointing inward, distance perhaps fifteen meters, with a punji moat in front, width about four meters. Beyond the moat and wall was the jungle. About halfway to the moat Washington was sprawled facedown. His body was in a small mud puddle, but his head was out of the water. His upper body was rising and falling, indicating that he was breathing heavily. Closer to Fetterman, only five or six feet away, Tyme lay on his side, his face turned toward the master sergeant, looking like death. His breath came in short, jerking gasps. His eyes were closed, and his skin was the color of a corpse left too long in the water.

"Gentlemen. Welcome to your new home."

The words startled Fetterman. They had been spoken in English, and although they had a rusty, creaking tone about them as if the speaker had not used English in a long time, the grammar was more precise than that which had been spoken by the VC lieutenant. The voice brought Fetterman's attention back to the front. He had to squint to see in the strong sunlight, but there were two groups of men in front of him.

A little to one side stood the VC lieutenant and a couple of the guards. The other group was made up of four men, two wearing the dark green uniforms of the NVA and the other two wearing the khaki and green uniforms sometimes worn by Main Force Vietcong units.

"My name is Major Vo," said one of the men in khaki and green. "And you men are my prisoners. No doubt Lieutenant Trang has filled your head with a lot of nonsense about your being prisoners of the Front. Permit me to dispel any notions that may have arisen from his zealousness. You are not prisoners of the Front. You are my prisoners. I am the commander here, and you men belong to me.

"Later we will have much to talk about. I will ask you questions, and you will give me answers. There is much that I want to know about your camp and your Captain Gerber, and I know that you will want to answer all my questions because I am very good at asking."

Another man, one that Fetterman had missed in the glare of the sunlight, emerged from behind the two NVA soldiers, casually lighting a cigarette. Fetterman felt himself stiffen. The man was dressed in the full khaki uniform and Sam Browne belt of a Communist Chinese officer.

Hello, thought Fetterman as he stared at the man's face. I've seen you before, old friend. Over the sights of my rifle. You just keep making a nuisance of yourself, don't you? Like a toothache.

"Major Vo, if you would permit me to interrupt," the Chinese officer suggested mildly. "Perhaps before you begin questioning your prisoners, you should have your doctor take a look at this man." He pointed toward Tyme. "Otherwise, I believe he may well bleed to death before he can even tell you his name, rank and serial number."

Major Vo glared at the Chinese, then gave a deprecating gesture with his hand. "Trang! See to it! We must not allow one of our guests to leave us before we are ready for him to do so."

The VC lieutenant spoke briefly to his men, and the two guards grabbed Tyme under each arm and dragged him roughly toward the camouflaged hootch. Lieutenant Trang brought up the rear.

"Now, then, as I was saying," continued Vo, addressing Fetterman directly, "I want to welcome you to your new home. We have spent a great deal of time preparing it especially for you. I think that you will find that our preparations have been more than thorough. Actually, I must admit that we had expected to entertain a few more of you. But do not despair, gentlemen, I am sure that the rest of your team will be joining us shortly. I especially look forward to many long conversations with your Captain Gerber.

"I trust you will find the accommodations adequate. I do not think that it would be quite fair to call them comfortable. Still, for the moment at least, you will have plenty of rooms to choose from.

I do hope you will enjoy your stay, gentlemen. Because you will never leave.''

Vo made a quick motion of his hand, and Fetterman crumpled under a blow to the right kidney, delivered by an unseen guard behind him.

"Sergeant Bat! Take our guests to their rooms, please. And do be more careful with the older one. After all, we must show appropriate respect for our seniors."

Then Vo threw back his head and laughed. He laughed at the new day and the spectacle before him. He laughed at his own little joke. He laughed because it was good.

10

THE JUNGLE NEAR
AN MINH

"Sergeant Sully, you better now? You maybe want another drink from canteen? Want another C-rat?"

Sully Smith smiled happily at the diminutive Tai striker and had his smile returned with Krung showing two rows of teeth filed to even points, which was an improvement over the four rows he'd been seeing earlier.

"No, thanks, Krung. I'm just fine now. I've have plenty to eat and drink, and I've had five-and-a-half hours of sleep. But, best of all, you don't have a twin brother anymore."

Krung looked puzzled. "What you mean? I never have a twin brother. I had brothers once, but VC kill them all. You know that."

Smith was instantly sorry for his choice of metaphor. "I'm sorry, Krung. I know. What I meant was, when I looked at you earlier, I saw two of you because of the bump on my head. But now I can see that there is only one Sergeant Krung, and it makes me very happy. It means the injury wasn't as bad as I thought it was."

Krung squatted next to the stocky Green Beret demolitions man and digested this information for a few minutes. Then he shook his head.

"Sergeant Sully, what you say make no sense to Krung. I think maybe knock on head shake something loose inside. Make you say funny things. Maybe you rest some more, okay?"

Smith chuckled. "I'm okay, Krung. Really." He gingerly felt the bandage on the side of his head. "You're partly right. It did knock something loose, but I'm fine now. Let me have my rifle, will you?"

Krung reached behind himself and passed the heavy Garand to Smith, who unloaded the weapon, checked to make sure that the bore was clear and that the rifle was functioning properly, and then inserted a fresh clip.

"Well, I guess we'd better be going. Captain Gerber will want to know about what happened to Sergeant Kittredge and the others, and we've still got a long walk back to camp."

Krung wasn't totally convinced of Smith's condition yet. "How about you rest here another thirty minutes before we go? Krung go make recon, scope out area, make sure no VC follow Sergeant Sully and Krung's tracks. Then when come back here, we go on to camp. Okay fine?"

Smith chuckled again. "Okay, fine. Only let's make it twenty minutes. We don't want to keep the captain waiting."

Krung glanced at his wristwatch, a U.S. Army-issue OD plastic model that Smith had given him some months before. "Twenty minutes, okay." With that he picked up his carbine and moved off, disappearing into the jungle as quietly as he'd arrived.

While he waited, Smith checked his resources. There were five full clips for the Garand in the bandolier, plus the full one in the rifle and the five rounds from the partial that had been in the M-1, fifty-three rounds in all. Not the sort of load a man wanted for a serious firefight. He still had his .45 pistol and three mags, plus one up the spout, making twenty-two rounds. But the .45 was essentially a close-in defense weapon, and he didn't want the situation to get down to that.

There was still his knife. But if they got into it again before they made it back to camp, they were going to have to break contact damned fast and run like hell. Of course, there might be a way of slowing their pursuers down a little.

Smith rummaged in his haversacks, looking for anything that might prove useful. Ten pounds of plastic explosives, always handy to have around but not very useful in this situation. A fifty-foot roll of det cord; might be able to do something with that, he thought. A small roll of safety fuse and a couple of fuse lighters. An assortment of electric and nonelectric blasting caps. A pressure release device, two pull release devices and a fifteen-second delay detonator. Crimpers. Two more claymores and two WP grenades.

With all that and the three frags he still had on his webbing, he thought he should be able to do something, certainly with the grenades and claymores—if there was time to set it up right. The rest of his gear wasn't particularly useful for killing people. He still had his LBE, a few more rations, a compass, map and his nickel-plated whistle, which he sometimes used to spring an ambush or for signaling. That and two smoke grenades, one green, the other yellow.

Smith considered ditching the yellow smoke. He couldn't see it as anything but extra weight, and it might be smart to leave it and part of the C-rations behind to lighten his load. He'd already donated his poncho and liner to the jungle landscape during yesterday's marathon run. He'd need the green smoke to signal the perimeter guard when they got back to camp.

It seemed to be taking Krung a long time to get back. Smith glanced at his watch and saw that Krung's twenty minutes were not yet quite up. Worrying over nothing again, he told himself. The man would be on time. They'd evaded the VC this long, and another three or four hours would put them back at the camp.

That was something that Smith wasn't really looking forward to. While making it back to the camp represented safety from the Vietcong, at least of a sort, it also meant that he'd have to explain to Gerber about Kittredge and the others, and he wasn't looking forward to that.

He also wasn't happy about all the questions that would go unasked by the rest of the men, both the strikers and the team. He could see their silent, questioning glances already, the looks from eyes that would be quickly averted when he returned their stares.

"Sully, old boy," the looks would be asking, "tell us, please, just how is it that you're the only one who made it back while Steve and all the rest of them died?"

It wouldn't be as though any of them really believed that he'd turned tail and run away to avoid a fight. They all knew him too well for that, and the head injury would confirm that he was no coward. But there would still be that little niggling doubt.

"Sully, wasn't there *something* you could have done to help Steve? Anything, Sully? *Anything at all?*"

How could he tell them that there was nothing any of them could have done but run away? That they'd underestimated the cleverness of the enemy and got caught with their butts hanging out in the breeze? That the VC had been better equipped and better led than ever before and had been waiting for them with a vastly numerically superior force. And that they'd all just walked into it, fat, dumb and happy, and found themselves up to their necks in deep shit?

The enemy had been waiting for them. Kepler wasn't going to like that. He wasn't going to like that at all. The mission had been his idea, and it hadn't just gone sour. It wasn't just a chance encounter with a big VC unit that had happened to be in the wrong place at the right time. The VC had been waiting for them. Kepler had been had. They'd all been had. And Kittredge and all the strikers had died because someone had guessed wrong. It wasn't a question of someone being stupid or making a mistake. Military disasters were seldom that simple. It was a question of guilt by association, and no one involved would escape the blame. Not in a fiasco this size.

The brass hats back in Saigon would try to hang the captain out to dry because he'd authorized the mission instead of just passing the information on to Nha Trang, where it could work its way up through the chain of command and be useless by the time anyone decided whether to act on it. Then they'd try to hang Kepler because he was the one who'd gotten the information in the first place and conceived the mission. Then they'd probably hang Smith and Krung for having been unfortunate enough to survive the massacre. After all, they must have done something wrong, or they'd have died like everyone else, right?

Well, at least we're alive to be hung, thought Smith. And Christ only knows what happened to Fetterman's bunch and Bromhead's group. I hope to good God that they didn't get clobbered the same way we did. Goddamn it! Those bastards *knew*. They knew we were coming, and they waited for us to do it and then closed the trap. How did they know? How could they have known? Security had been tight on this one. Real tight. There was no way they could have known.

Unless they had known all along. Unless they had always known, known from the very first. *Unless they'd planned it.*

GERBER WAS PUSHING HIMSELF too hard. They all were, but he was being especially hard on himself. He'd had six hours' sleep in the last forty-eight, and the last of that had been over thirty-five hours ago. The Benzedrine tablets that McMillan had reluctantly prescribed for him when he had refused to rest were still in the left pocket of his jungle fatigues. He knew that he'd have to take them soon if he was to keep going, but he also knew they'd only prop him up for so long, and when he crashed off the bennies, he'd be out of it for a long time. McMillan had warned him that he might sleep for two or three days straight once the pills ran out and he came down. And Gerber had a hunch that McMillan wouldn't be willing to prescribe a second batch for him, no matter what the situation. So Gerber continued to hoard the bennies until he absolutely needed them, functioning now on sheer willpower and helped by strong GI coffee. He didn't know how many cups he'd had. He'd lost count somewhere around forty.

Bates's call had come in around 0100. Bocker had found Gerber working at his makeshift desk, trying to rough out plans for the ground search that he intended to mount in the morning. Bocker had noted that Robin Morrow, the young photojournalist who seemed to be trying her best to attach herself permanently to the captain, had curled up under a poncho liner and gone to sleep on Gerber's bunk. Bocker hadn't quite figured out yet if she was interested in Gerber in a boyfriend-girlfriend fashion or just thought the captain made good copy for her readers back in the World. He also figured it wasn't really any of his business, but he couldn't help wondering. It was common knowledge among the team members that Gerber and Morrow's sister, Karen, an Air Force flight nurse, had once been lovers. There were no secrets in so close-knit an organization as the Special Forces A-Detachment. Bocker was concerned that the captain had enough on his mind right now without the complication of a romantic involvement with a former lover's sister. Still, if it was an affair, it was the captain's affair and not his place to bring it up. Besides, maybe I'm just a little bit envious, Bocker thought.

"What is it, Galvin?" Gerber had asked, looking up from his work and rubbing his eyes.

"Crystal Ball is on the horn, sir," Bocker had answered him. "He asked to speak to the Actual."

"Bates wants to talk to me? At this hour? The colonel's keeping some pretty late hours," Gerber had replied.

"Yes, sir," Bocker had told him. Then had come the carefully not expressed implication that Bates wasn't the only one keeping long hours. "I told him you might be asleep, sir, but he said to wake you."

"You told him I was asleep?" Gerber had seemed puzzled.

"Yes, sir," Bocker had finished, not quite so subtly the second time. "I'd hoped you might be, sir."

"Uh-huh," Gerber'd grunted, finally picking up the hint. "Any idea what it's about?"

"No, sir. Just that the colonel said it was important."

It had been. Bates had informed Gerber to have the two Tai strike companies and one of the PF companies ready to move at first light. General Crinshaw, it seemed, had been induced to modify his position on the denial of airlift support.

The helicopters had come in shortly after dawn, two flights of CH-47 Chinooks, each accompanied by a two-ship Huey gun team. Dave Henderson's Mike Force had come with them.

Gerber had been so busy pumping his old friend's hand and thanking him for the added help that he failed to notice the other passenger until Henderson hitchhiked a thumb over his shoulder.

"Good morning, Captain Gerber. Hope you won't mind my tagging along. After all, I did convince Billy Joe to give you the helicopters." Standing there in his old but still highly shined paratrooper boots and chin-cup helmet and armed with an M-1 carbine with a folding stock was Major General Garrison Hull.

Gerber was stunned.

"Had to bring him along." Henderson grinned. "You ever try to say no to a general when he wants you to take him somewhere?"

"No," admitted Gerber, "I don't believe I've ever tried. To what do we owe the honor of this visit, General?"

"You know how stuffy it can get in Saigon—conferences one minute, briefings the next, paperwork sandwiched in between. Just thought I'd get out in the country and get myself a bit of air," said Hull flippantly. "Truth of the matter is, Mack, that Al Bates told me you were having trouble locating Tony Fetterman and a couple of the boys, and I really was getting bored around the old office so I thought I'd come out here for a day or two and give you a hand. I scrounged myself a couple of air assets and rounded up Henderson's bunch for a security team—we generals aren't supposed to go out in the field without a security team, you know—and here I am."

Gerber's expression said he didn't believe a word of it, but he couldn't very well call a general a liar. Especially one he'd known and been friends with since Korea.

"It's good to see you again, sir, but I can't really say that I'm happy to see you," Gerber said truthfully. "We've apparently got a large, well-directed Vietcong Main Force unit operating in our area. I'd hate for anything to happen to you while we were out looking for the others."

"Mack," said Hull, raising one eyebrow and lifting his carbine slightly. "I used to be pretty good at looking out for myself with this little popgun, and I haven't forgotten how to use it. I'm not here to take over and try to run things. This is your show. Just think of me as a useful adjunct if you have any trouble getting support, say from Cu Chi Arty or Stinger Ops. In the meantime just put me anywhere you can use an extra pair of eyeballs and a weapon, and I'll keep my mouth shut until you ask me to open it. Tony Fetterman is an old friend of mine from the Deuce. I'd like to help, that's all."

Gerber looked at Henderson, who gave him a shrug and a grin. "See what I mean? You say no to the guy if you want to. I can't."

"Well, General, I must say I applaud your judgment in selecting a rather large security detachment. Have you completely emptied Saigon of Special Forces personnel, or is somebody still minding the shop back at B-Detachment?"

"Colonel Bates is still coordinating things back at B-Team TOC," said Hull. "He'll be mad as hell when he finds out I came out here without him."

They all laughed at that, and somehow the laughter seemed to drain the tension that had permeated the entire camp since yesterday's disaster. For a moment Gerber even felt less tired. Then he saw Morrow walking across the camp toward them.

"All right, sir. I guess I don't know how to say no to a general, either. I've got my executive officer supervising the loading. He'll be coming out with the second lift. I'd have had to put him in the stockade to keep him from coming along. It's not SOP, but Captain Minh is a very competent officer and he'll be in charge here while we're out. If I could impose on Dave to introduce you to him and my XO, I think I'd better go deal with our representative from the press. She's going to be real happy with me when I tell her she can't come with us."

Hull raised a quizzical eyebrow again, and Henderson gave him a blank look. "She? As in female-type reporter?"

Gerber moved his head slightly in Morrow's direction. "Morrow, Robin E., shade tan and blond, eyes green. Seriously she's a damned good journalist, and she isn't going to like being left in camp one bit."

"Morrow? I don't think I like the sound of this. Any relation to your lady friend the nurse?" asked Henderson.

"Ex-lady friend," said Gerber sourly. "This one is her sister."

"I definitely don't like the sound of this. General Hull, maybe we'd better make ourselves scarce for a bit."

"Somebody want to tell me what all this is about?" asked Hull.

"No," said Gerber.

"How about that! He can say no to a general," said Henderson. "This way, please, General. I think we ought to let Mack wing this one on his own."

Hull shot Gerber another questioning glance, noted the correspondent's approach and acquiesced. "Lead on McDuff. I'm not looking for any literary entanglements."

They turned and walked off down the flight line, moving quickly but casually.

Morrow's walk was purposeful, determined. She was close enough now for Gerber to see the fine line of her jaw, which was set. He knew this wasn't going to be easy.

It wasn't. Morrow started in when she was still fifteen feet away.

"All right, you male chauvinist bastard, what's all this bullshit about not letting me go out with the search party? I spent half the night sitting up with you, then I dragged my ass, my camera and my notebook down to the far end of the runway to find out from Lieutenant Bromhead where I'm supposed to ride, and Bromhead told me you say I can't go. And after all I've done in the past for you and Fetterman and all the rest of the guys. This is a good story, and I'm not going to miss out on it. I'm going so you'd just better think again."

"Sorry, Robin. Not this time. That's the way I want it."

"The hell with that noise. I'm going."

"No, you're not. And that's final."

"You can't stop me. I'm a member of the press."

"I can stop you," said Gerber, "and I have. You're not going on this one. Not even if I have to put you in the stockade to keep you here."

"You wouldn't dare!" she muttered.

"I will if you make me."

"Why, for Christ's sake?"

"Because it's safer here."

"Oh, that's just great. I'm supposed to tell my editors that you made me stay in camp because it's safer here? Since I've been here, I've been sniped at, mortared, gone on a secret mission into Cambodia and had the wonderful experience of finding a cobra in my sleeping bag. And now you tell me I can't go out and help look for

Fetterman, Smith, Washington and Tyme because it's safer if I stay in camp? How in the hell am I supposed to do my job if you won't let me?"

"That's exactly the point. How am I supposed to do my job if I'm spending all my time worrying about what might happen to you? We don't know how big a force we're up against. I've already got one of my team killed and four missing, and I will not allow you to be put in a position where you might be joining them."

"You won't allow . . . Just who in the hell gave you the right to be my keeper, Mr. Supersoldier? Wait a minute. Oh, you rotten SOB. You're doing this because I'm Karen's sister, aren't you?" She was almost shouting in his face now. "When will you get it through your thick head that I'm not her, I'm me?"

She swung an open hand at him, but Gerber saw the slap coming and caught her wrist before the blow could land. He pulled her in close to him, snaked his right arm around her shoulders and grabbed the back of her head. He kissed her hard.

She tried to pull away and pounded on his back with her other fist, but slowly her resistance subsided. Gerber could feel the anger ebbing out of her body as he held her until finally she returned the kiss. He broke the embrace and held her at arm's length. The expression on her face was a mixture of surprise and confusion. Gerber wondered briefly what his own expression must look like.

"Yeah," he said quietly. "I'm doing it in part because you are Karen's sister. But not for the reason you think. Robin, I'm confused about us right now, and I need time to think things through. But I can't do it right now. My first responsibility is to my men. If you go out in the field with us, I'm afraid I won't be able to do my job right. That will put you in danger, me in danger and my men in danger. I'm not talking about the kind of day-to-day dangers we all face out here. I'm talking about the kind of avoidable, preventable, unnecessary danger that results when the commanding officer hasn't got his mind on the job. I don't want anything to happen to anybody else because I was thinking about you instead of doing my job. Is that what you want?"

"No, Mack. Of course not," she said softly. Her eyes searched his face, trying to see into his mind to understand what had just happened.

"Then just this once do this one thing for me. Stay here, where I know you'll be relatively safe, and I can concentrate on finding my men. We'll talk about it when I get back."

Morrow was in a state of confusion. Something had happened between them, something more than had taken place on that last night in Saigon over a month ago. It was something that she'd been trying hard to bring about during the last two months that she had known Mack Gerber, but it had somehow remained one-sided until now. It had taken her almost a week to fall in love with her sister's old boyfriend, and she'd been miserable ever since knowing that although Gerber liked her, maybe even cared for her, her love wasn't returned because Gerber's love still belonged to Karen, even though Karen had gone home to her husband in Seattle.

But that had all changed. She'd felt it, and there was no mistaking it. She knew that, at least for the moment, Gerber loved her, too. It left her with a curious sense of undeserved guilt and with a feeling of awe and wonder. And fear. She now had what she'd wanted so desperately. Now she was desperately afraid of losing it. Of losing him. She'd been worried about his safety at times in the past, but this was real fear, and she understood for the first time what Karen had meant when she'd told her that she was going back to Seattle because she couldn't handle the fear of falling in love with Mack Gerber. Robin didn't know if she could handle it, either.

"Okay, Mack," she heard herself say quietly. "I'll stay."

Gerber turned away from her for a moment, and when he turned back, his eyes were red and moist. Morrow could feel a tear working its way slowly down her own cheek and brushed angrily at it with the back of her hand. Now was no time for weakness. She had to be strong so that he could be strong, too.

"Robin," he began, "there's something I have to tell you. I want you to know that I—"

Quickly she put her hand to his lips. "Shhhh. Not now. Don't say it now. Don't even think of me now. Wait until you come back to me. I'll stay here and I'll wait, and I'll be just fine. Don't worry about me at all. You just go out there and do your job. You find Fetterman and the rest and bring them home safe, and I'll be waiting here for you. I love you, Mack. I always will. And I promise I won't ever go away or let you down. Just do what you have to do and come back to me safe. That's all I ask. Do that for me, and we'll worry about the future later, okay?''

She kissed him again, quickly, then stepped back. ''Now go on, soldier. Get the hell out of here, will you, and let a poor working girl get back to her business. I've got a deadline to meet, and I don't even know what story I'm going to file yet.'' Then she turned and walked away from him across the compound toward the team house.

Gerber stared after her, then turned away himself and went to find Henderson and General Hull.

11

VC P.O.W. CAMP NEAR HONG NGU

The rooms were okay, Fetterman decided. He'd stayed in worse accommodations in France and Korea, but the service and the attitude of the staff left a lot to be desired.

Fetterman had mentally christened the camp the Jungle Hilton because of Major Vo's continual references to them as his guests. That, he figured, made Vo the manager, with Lieutenant Trang the concierge or keeper of the keys and Sergeant Bat the bell captain. He hadn't figured out who the head waiter was yet, and he had a hunch that he wouldn't either, because so far the VC had shown no inclination to feed their prisoners or give them any water.

The camp was situated among the trees and was virtually invisible from the trail. Fetterman had been able to glimpse only the one hootch from the clearing, apparently a guard shack of some kind, and had almost missed it because of the camouflage. A well-trained soldier looking for something might or might not notice it. Fetterman had little doubt that a passing peasant would have small likelihood of spotting it and even less interest in investigating it. Besides, it was undoubtedly well inside a defensive perimeter of some kind. At the very least they had to have a few pickets or patrols out beyond the clearing.

There wasn't much chance of being spotted by an aircraft passing overhead, either. The thick, leafy tree branches formed an almost impenetrable canopy overhead that effectively screened the camp from air observation and cast the compound into a kind of twilight world. The reduction in light had the curious effect of making things warmer, not cooler, since the closeness of the trees also effectively blocked any breeze. In addition it brought the mosquitoes out in hordes, the bugs' biological clocks oblivious to the fact that it was midmorning.

It was hard to get a really accurate idea of the camp. The ground had been cleared only where absolutely necessary, and the remaining trees and ground cover made it impossible to see more than one or two dozen yards in any direction. It made for effective camouflage both outside and inside the camp.

In addition to the guard shack at the edge of the clearing, they had passed two longhouses on the way in that were apparently used as barracks for the camp's garrison, a small hootch without windows and with the door wired shut, which Fetterman thought to be a storage hut of some kind and a third longhouse with a packed mud fireplace at one end, apparently the mess hall for the guards. All of the structures were set on stilts or earthen mounds, which suggested seasonal flooding of the area, and that, in turn, indicated the nearby presence of a river or major canal.

All the structures in the camp had a new but solid look to them, suggesting that, although the camp had only recently been constructed, it had been built with long-term occupancy in mind. There was even the beginnings of a system of elevated bamboo walkways paralleling the pathways within the camp, a further indication of seasonal flooding and that the Vietcong intended to occupy the camp for some time to come. Fetterman noted that most of the cut bamboo used in construction was still green.

Major Vo and his Chinese friend had obviously planned to have several guests in residence at their little jungle hotel. Fetterman counted eight "bungalows," with three more under construction. There could have been more, but his view was blocked by the trees.

Each of the "guest cottages" consisted of a bamboo cage measuring about five feet wide by ten feet long, with a thatched roof around five-and-a-half feet high at the center ridge that sloped to about four feet above ground level. The roof overhung one end of each cage by about a meter, making a sort of floorless porch over the doorway. The door itself was a cross work of bamboo with wrapped wire hinges, secured by the simple expedient of being wired shut after the prisoner had been placed inside. The precaution was hardly necessary, however, because of the clever arrangement of leg irons.

The leg irons illustrated the VC penchant for making do without benefit of the more sophisticated devices and techniques used by Westerners. They consisted of a long iron rod bent into a large loop at one end and a small hole drilled through the rod at the other end. A pair of U-shaped iron pieces with loops bent into each leg of the open end of the U were fastened at the bottom. The U-shaped pieces could be placed about a prisoner's ankles and the rod inserted through the small loops in them. The large loop kept the prisoner from slipping them off that end, and the smaller end could be inserted through a hole drilled through a large wooden stake that had been driven into the ground outside the cage and then wired to it. The result was even more effective at limiting motion than a set of Peerless leg irons, didn't require a padlock or key, which could be lost, and assuming that it had been made from scrap materials, cost zero to build. A series of stakes, driven at intervals along one side of the cage, made it possible to lock up more than one prisoner in the same cage, limit the prisoner's movement as punishment, or, with a second set of irons, stretch the prisoner out spread-eagled on the floor of his cage. Fetterman appreciated the ingenuity of the leg irons's inventor, but under the circumstances he really couldn't say that he found the man's inventiveness admirable.

The VC didn't start to work on them right away, and Fetterman was thankful for that. It gave him a chance to assess their situation and plan a course of action. The basic situation did not look good. He had no doubt that Vo had meant it when he'd said that he would ask the questions and they would be glad to give him the answers.

They were prisoners not just of the VC but of a man who had made it clear that he did not consider them to be prisoners of the National Liberation Front, but rather his own personal property. Vo had also made no pretense of concealing a clearly sadistic bent of mind.

Fetterman knew the assumption among Special Forces personnel had always been that, if they were captured and were not killed outright, then they would be taken to one of the VC sanctuaries in Cambodia. And that, he knew, was what Gerber would expect, too. If the captain had been able to mount any kind of rescue operation at all, he'd be looking for them along the border itself, not here, well inside Vietnam and, at the most, a day or two's forced march from Camp A-555. That would give the VC plenty of time to work on their prisoners, and he had no doubt that Major Vo would have a number of highly original persuasion techniques in mind. The permanent-looking nature of the camp suggested that Vo had anticipated having plenty of time to employ his methods as well. Sooner or later, Fetterman knew, those methods would produce results, though just what Vo hoped to learn from them, he didn't know. The man already seemed unusually well informed about them. He had known they were from Camp A-555 and that Gerber was their commanding officer. Deducing they were from the camp wouldn't have been any real trick, but how had the man known Gerber's name?

"I will ask you questions, and you will give me answers," Vo had told them. *When ya got 'em by the balls, their hearts and minds will follow.*

The Vietcong had placed the prisoners in separate cages but left them within sight of each other. Fetterman recognized the tactic. It was a way of isolating the Americans so that they couldn't help each other. But at the same time it provided a visual reminder that, if you weren't cooperative, the same sort of thing that had just been done to the other guy could happen to you. From a psychological standpoint, Fetterman wasn't sure that it wouldn't have been better, from the VC's point of view, to have completely isolated the prisoners. That would have left considerable doubt in each of the American's minds as to what had happened to the others, giving each a feeling of total dependency on the Front for their continued existence. It might also have been a better softening-up technique. But then, he reminded himself, they weren't prisoners of the Front. They were Vo's prisoners, and somehow he didn't seem to be the type to go in for subtle psychological interrogation techniques.

Washington's cage was about fifteen meters away and partially screened by trees and brush. Tyme was somewhere out of sight, presumably still being seen to by the camp's doctor. While he waited for some sign from the others, Fetterman amused himself by taking stock of his own condition.

His feet were an absolute mess. They were cut, bleeding, full of thorns and the wounds were filled with dirt and pebbles. For the first time in his long military career, Fetterman was thankful that he'd kept his immunization record up to date. He might die of infection, but at least he wasn't going to have to worry about tetanus. The raw flesh and oozing blisters were things that he tried not to think about.

He did, at least, have the use of his hands again. One of the guards had seen fit to cut through the split bamboo thongs at Fetterman's wrists and elbows after they'd got him safely locked up in the leg irons, and sensation was beginning to return to his fingers.

The wrist thong had bit deeply into the flesh over the radius and ulna, and the ragged edge of the bamboo had caused some cuts. Fetterman noted that the blood flow was a slow oozing of bright red, indicating capillary bleeding. It would be sore as hell tomorrow and was another outstanding opportunity for infection. He wasn't in any danger of bleeding to death, and although his fingers tingled and were clumsy, it didn't seem as though any permanent damage had been done.

Fetterman's back ached all the way into his groin from the blow that Sergeant Bat had delivered to his kidney, and he didn't know if he was hemorrhaging internally or not. His pulse seemed normal. And although he knew it was the poorest of tests, considering that he had to judge for himself rather than being evaluated by an unbiased observer, he hadn't noticed any decrease in his own level of consciousness or mental ability, which was one of the early symptoms of hypovolemic shock. As far as he could tell, if he was bleeding inside, it was a slow bleed.

Fetterman worked his trouser leg up until he found the leech. It was happily sucking away. The VC had pretty well gone through his pockets, including the thirty-odd ones sewn all over the outside of the camouflaged jungle jacket that he'd had custom made in Cholon, and he didn't have any insect repellent, salt or matches to encourage the nasty little slug to let go. Pulling on it wouldn't work. That would only leave the head firmly embedded in his thigh, enhancing yet another risk of infection. All he could do was try to encourage the little bloodsucker to let go, and he could only think of one way of doing that.

Bending painfully forward, Fetterman picked up the leech's tail and bit the slug in two, spitting out the rear part and tossing it clear of the cage. The leech didn't care for that. It thrashed madly about on his leg for a bit, finally loosening its grip enough for Fetterman to pull it free without leaving the head behind. He tossed it out after its tail.

Fetterman checked himself over as best he could without finding any other injuries or leeches. The mosquitoes, which seemed to number in the thousands, had discovered his raw feet and were having a picnic. Fetterman plucked out what rocks and thorns he could reach and squashed a few hundred mosquitoes in the process, getting a few flies as a bonus. Clearly, though, the jungle had more mosquitoes to offer than he could hope to deal with in so direct a fashion, and he finally struggled out of his jungle jacket and used it to cover his bloody feet, figuring that his upper body could stand the bites better. In the unlikely event that an escape opportunity presented itself, his most valuable equipment, outside of a well-trained and inventive mind, was going to be those feet. Bad as they were already, he couldn't afford to let them get any worse.

After that, there was nothing to do but wait and see what happened next. That and periodically smash a few of the mosquitoes that were finding his face interesting, now that the more attractive meal of his feet had been covered up.

About half an hour later Fetterman saw Washington slowly sit up in his cage. When he finally spotted Fetterman, the big medical specialist flashed him a weak smile and gave a brief nod of his head between ineffectual swipes at mosquitoes. Fetterman returned the grin and winked. It was his way of telling the staff sergeant that he was okay. Washington responded by giving him a quizzical look and scratching his head. The seemingly innocent gesture was plain enough to Fetterman. He shrugged his shoulders in the universal gesture and silently mouthed, "I don't know where Tyme is."

Neither man attempted to speak. Although they could see no guards, it was likely that some were nearby and might overhear the conversation. Fetterman knew that at least Vo and Trang spoke English, and it was possible that some of the others did as well. He didn't know if Washington had been conscious enough to have heard Vo's little welcoming speech or not, but Washington knew about Trang and was playing it safe as well.

A long scream answered the question of whether Tyme was still alive. There was really no way to be certain that the scream belonged to the weapons specialist, but it was a pain-filled, animalistic protest that reminded Fetterman more of a puma's cry than a human being's. It was followed a few moments later by a second much longer scream and then finally a third, very weak this time.

About ten minutes later a couple of guards dragged Tyme's limp body down the trail and dumped him unceremoniously inside a cage about five meters from Fetterman's cell. They didn't even bother with the leg irons, just wired the door shut, then disappeared back up the trail, laughing and sharing a cigarette between them. When the sound of their voices faded, Fetterman cupped his hands to his mouth and risked a low whisper.

"Boom-Boom! Can you hear me?"

There was no answer, and he tried again, slightly louder. "Boom-Boom! It's me, Fetterman. Can you hear me?"

This time there was a faint response.

"Tony? I'm okay, I think."

"What did they do to you? Did they hurt you?"

"Stupid question. Of course it hurt. Oh, you mean... No. That was just the doctor performing a little minor surgery. He got the bullet out but couldn't control the bleeding so he had to cauterize the wound. He wanted to give me some morphine from Washington's kit, but there was some officer there that wouldn't let him. Bastard seemed to find the whole business very funny. Kept laughing every time it hurt too much and I had to scream.''

"That would be Major Vo, our host. The camp commander," Fetterman told him.

"Nice guy, I'm sure. You'd better hope you don't get sick 'cause the doctor here is just some kid who was in his first year of medical school in the North when the Front drafted him."

"How'd you find that out?"

"He told me. Didn't seem like a bad kid for a VC. I think he was sweating more than I was."

Tyme's voice was coming in ragged gasps now; the effort of speaking was costing him a great deal.

"Tony? You still there?"

"I'm here, Boom-Boom."

"Tony, I'm sorry I screamed like that. I couldn't help it."

"I know, Boom-Boom. It's all right. Don't worry about it."

"I tried not to, but I couldn't help it when he stuck that poker in my shoulder."

"I said it's all right. Forget about it. It couldn't be helped."

"Tony... There's something I've got to tell you... I want you to understand...."

"Forget it, Boom-Boom. I understand. I said it's all right."

"No. You don't understand.... I've got to...tell you we're...not alone...."

Tyme wasn't making any sense.

"Listen to me, Boom-Boom. You're weak. You've lost a lot of blood. I want you to be quiet now and rest."

"No! You don't understand! We're not alone...not alone here.... There are others."

"Other what, Boom-Boom? Other guards? Other prisoners?"

"Americans...other Americans here."

Fetterman sat up straighter.

"Americans? You mean there are other American prisoners here?"

"Got to understand... Yes. Other American prisoners...here."

"How many, Boom-Boom? How many other prisoners are there?"

Tyme was silent.

"How many, Boom-Boom? Tell me how many there are."

Still no response.

"Sergeant First Class Tyme," said Fetterman a bit louder, trying to break through the other man's increasingly befuddled state, "I order you to tell me how many other prisoners there are here!"

"Two... Washington and..."

Christ! thought Fetterman. The kid's delirious. He means Washington and me.

"Washington's okay, Boom-Boom. I've seen him. Is that what you meant about there being other prisoners here? Is it?"

"Washington fine? Yes. No. Not you and Wash... Others, Tony. There are two others."

"What two others? Did you see them? Where are they?"

"Didn't see...didn't see them, Tony. Heard...Vo and that lieutenant nabbed us...heard them talk...talking. Two Americans brought here last night."

"Boom-Boom, this is very important. Think. Did you hear who they were? Were they part of our team?"

"No. Not our...guys. No. Rock...Rockford...Rock somebody. Can't remember...Rock something and Corbett. I think the other guy's name was...Corbett. I...Sorry, can't remem..."

"Okay, Boom-Boom, that's fine. You just rest easy now. We'll talk more about the other guys later."

"No time...no time for that. Fetterman...you don't unders... Damn it! Shoot them. The VC..."

Fetterman felt a chill run up his spine despite the heat.

"Shoot who, Boom-Boom? Shoot the VC? Are the VC going to shoot us? Are they going to shoot the other prisoners? Who's going to shoot whom?"

"The other guys. Vo's going to shoot...the other guys."

"When? Can you still hear me? When is he going to shoot them?"

"Tomorrow... maybe day after tomorrow. He's... waiting."

"What's he waiting for, Boom-Boom? Why is he waiting to shoot them?"

"Waiting for word from... from..."

"From where, Boom-Boom? He's waiting for word from where?"

"Hanoi."

Fetterman tried for several minutes more to get Tyme to talk to him, but there was no further response. He didn't know if the young soldier had passed out or died. There was no way he could check and no way he could reliably communicate Tyme's information about the other two Americans to Washington without running considerable risk of being overheard by one of the guards, who might or might not understand English but who would certainly understand that the prisoners were not allowed to talk to one another. Right now there didn't seem to be anything that he could do but wait. He didn't have to wait for very long.

Three VC soldiers, two carrying carbines and one carrying an M-14 that might have been Fetterman's own rifle, came down the trail and unwired the door to Fetterman's cage, as well as unwiring his leg irons from their attachment to the wooden post.

"*Di!*" one of them shouted at Fetterman. "*Di di mau lien!*"

Evidently Fetterman didn't move fast enough to suit them. One of the guards stepped into the cage and rapped Fetterman on his head with a carbine while one of the others yanked viciously on the rod of the leg iron arrangement, drawing the narrow end through the bars into the cage, scraping the skin from the backs of Fetterman's ankles in the process. They shoved Fetterman out the door, and he pitched face first onto the path. One of the guards clubbed him again, on the back this time, then two of them grabbed him by the arms and dragged him along the trail until they came to a small bamboo hootch with an overhanging porch roof, similar to those on the cages but bigger.

Fetterman wasn't a large man. He was short and thin but surprisingly strong for his size. This was not the time to exhibit that strength, however, so he simply let himself go totally limp, making things as difficult as possible for the guards. Even so, the VC, who were nearly as big as Fetterman, had little difficulty half holding him up between them. One of them got a hand under Fetterman's chin, after trying unsuccessfully to find any hair long enough to grab on to, and tilted the master sergeant's head back so that he was forced to look up the two small steps to the entrance to the hootch. A smiling Major Vo looked down at him. Behind Vo, Fetterman could see the Chinese officer seated on a folding canvas chair inside the hootch. He was smoking and appeared to be reading something, showing a total lack of concern for what was going on outside the hootch.

"Good morning again," said Major Vo. "Or perhaps I should say afternoon. It is a few minutes past the twelve o'clock I see by my new watch."

Fetterman noted the watch on Vo's wrist. It was Fetterman's. Evidently Vo had relieved Lieutenant Trang of the responsibility of looking after it for the Front.

"The time has come for us to have a little talk," Vo continued.

"Of course," said Fetterman mildly. "I'll be happy to tell you whatever you want to know."

Vo looked genuinely surprised, and Fetterman noticed that the Chinese officer straightened and turned partway toward the door before catching himself. It confirmed that the Chinese advisor also spoke English.

Vo was quick to recover, however, and wasn't about to be deprived of his entertainment by a cooperative prisoner.

"Yes, of course. I am sure you will be happy to tell me whatever I want to know. There has really never been any doubt of that." Vo smiled. "But first, I think, we shall have a little lesson, shall we say. In order to ensure the honesty of your cooperation."

He gave a quick nod, and the two guards dropped Fetterman on his face and bound his hands behind him.

"You will be interested to know, I am sure," continued Vo, "that I have devised a number of means that are very effective in ensuring the honesty of cooperation of my prisoners."

Vo addressed his remarks to the guards but kept them in English to make sure that Fetterman understood. Evidently one of the guards spoke English, or they knew the drill.

"Take the prisoner to the hanging tree," said Vo, still smiling. "And string him up." Then he turned and walked back into the hootch, laughing loudly, as though someone had just told him a very funny joke.

Christ! thought Fetterman. I am in a world of shit.

12

THE JUNGLE NEAR
AN MINH

"Sergeant Sully, we are in a world of shit," said Krung, pushing breathlessly through the vegetation to Smith's side.

"What is it, Krung? What's the matter?"

"Krung make bad mistake, Sergeant Sully. Me see three VC come along trail look for us. Kill two, but one get away. Shit!" He spat. "Krung must be getting old."

"What happened?" asked Smith.

"Krung go take look, like we say. Check back trail, hear someone come, so hide quick to watch. Only one of VC see me when stop to take piss. Me move quick, but not quick enough. Shit!" He spat again. "Krung getting slow in old age."

"I didn't hear any shots," said Smith, struggling into his gear.

Krung looked at him aghast. "Krung no rookie trooper. Know better than to draw big crowd of VC with shot. Use knife, but not quick enough to get all three."

"You tried to kill three armed VC with your knife?" said Smith, then wondered why that really didn't amaze him somehow. After all, he was talking to Sergeant Krung.

"No biggie," said Krung. "Besides, one have dick in hands. Not hard for Tai to kill three Vietnamese when one have dick in hands. Only Krung fuck up, let one get away. Krung getting too old for this shit." He spat. "Krung very sorry."

Smith picked up the heavy Garand rifle and pushed himself to his feet. "Why didn't the VC shoot?"

"Two VC no have time to shoot," said Krung matter-of-factly. "Third VC drop rifle and run away. Fucking garret trooper. Krung chase, but not catch. Think maybe better stop chase before chase right into beaucoup VC. Think maybe best come back tell you what happen. Krung sorry let one get away, Sergeant Sully. You no think Krung dumb leg for make this FUBAR?"

Smith clapped the little tribesman on the shoulder. "No, Krung, I don't think you're a dumb leg. You did as well as could be expected under the circumstances. Are you sure these guys were looking for us? Maybe it was just a couple of local guerrillas out wandering around with their guns to get away from a nagging mama-san."

"They look for us," said Krung definitely. "One who stop to piss have this under arm." He reached behind him and pulled a bundle from beneath the H-straps of his web gear. It was a poncho and blanket liner with Smith's name and serial number neatly stenciled in one corner.

"In that case," said Smith, tucking the poncho and liner into his own web gear, "they've got to have a bunch of friends around here somewhere, and I don't think we ought to hang around waiting to be introduced. I think we'd better di di most rickey-tick. You want to take point? I'll try to hang back about a hundred meters and see if I can't figure out some way to slow them down a bit."

Krung nodded and moved toward the trail.

"Try not to get too far ahead," Smith called after him. "I may need a little time to set up a surprise. We'll follow the trail about a klick and see what happens, then decide whether to stay with the trails or make our way through the jungle to the camp."

Krung nodded vigorously and waved to show that he had heard, then disappeared quickly down the trail.

Smith considered the possibilities of the trail, but it really wasn't conducive to booby-trapping. Not in this particular area, anyway. He could rig a simple trip wire to one of the grenades. The enemy would be excited and in a hurry to catch them, and the trip wire might be overlooked until it was too late. If they hit it, it was sure to make them cautious and slow them down a bit, which was the general idea, but it wasn't enough. Smith wanted something that would bring the VC to a screeching halt and hurt them. He wanted something massive.

He ran for almost a full klick and had nearly caught up to Krung when he found the perfect spot.

The trail had widened a bit, becoming almost as wide as a single lane road, which made it possible for soldiers to bunch up three or four abreast. Based on Smith's experience, he knew that that was exactly what the average soldier tended to do when he was in a hurry. And the VC would be in a hurry. Further, there were two deep ditches on either side of the trail, providing exactly the sort of cover a soldier would instinctively seek when fired upon, and there was a small side trail leading off to the south that would look like a good escape route to anyone wanting to run away. The whole setup was, Smith decided, perfect for a Sully Smith demolitions extravaganza.

Smith moved rapidly ahead to find Krung, knowing that he'd need someone to cover him while he set up the fireworks. Krung also had the one piece of equipment that would add the finishing touch to the plan. He'd seen it thrown over the Tai tribesman's back when he'd moved out—a PPS-43 submachine gun, which the Tai had taken from one of the VC in his earlier encounter.

Krung didn't like the idea of doubling back on their trail, wasting time when they could be putting more distance between themselves and the pursuing Vietcong, but when Smith explained his idea for killing many VC, Krung happily agreed. If there was one thing in life near and dear to Sergeant Krung's heart, it was killing many VC.

As he worked feverishly to set the trap, Smith explained to Krung how he hoped the firing chain would operate once the VC activated it. For Krung, it was a detailed lesson in the complimentary arts of mayhem and death. For Sully Smith, it was all just part of a day's work, doing what he liked to do best—making things go bang.

"I figure it this way, Krung," said Smith, pausing to wipe the sweat from his brow with the back of his hand before crimping a length of time fuse into a blasting cap. "Those three VC you ran into were either an independent search element of a larger unit, say fifteen or twenty men to a platoon, or they were a point element for a really big unit, maybe company size.

"If they were a search team from a platoon, the one who got away will hotfoot it back to the RP, and they'll collect all their buddies before coming after us. If they were point for a company, their CO will send the lead platoon after us while he tries to get the rest of his troops in front of us. He'll then use the lead platoon to locate and fix our position while he maneuvers the rest in for the kill, like drawing the string shut on a bag.

"Either way, we can reasonably expect about a platoon of Vietcong to come charging down this trail in short order. If those guys are even half-assed trackers, they've got to know that they're only chasing a couple of guys. They'll put speed ahead of caution, figuring two guys won't be dumb enough to try to ambush a whole platoon of Vietcong. That's where they're wrong, and that's how we're going to kill them. You set this claymore up at the end of this ditch," Smith said as he pointed to his left. "Then take this spool of wire and run me about three sets of trip wires lengthwise down the ditch for about fifteen meters or so. Just stake them out at the far end. Make the wires about a meter apart. I'll show you how we'll tie them all together when you've finished."

Smith finished his work and moved across the trail to the other ditch to deploy the second claymore.

"The trick is to get all of them, or at least as many as we can, into the killing zone. Since we can't guarantee the VC will cooperate with us, what we have to do is set up a killing zone big enough to sucker them all into it, then make sure none of them can get out.

"The first step is to bait the trap properly. I wrapped my extra smoke grenade up in my poncho and liner after removing the pin. If they pick it up the wrong way, or unroll it, the yellow smoke will drop out, and the grenade will pop about a second and a half after the spoon flies off. The idea is the VC won't know it's only a smoke grenade and will dive for cover. The only good cover is the ditches, and when they hit them, they'll hit the trip wires, triggering the claymores. With luck, we might get five or ten of them right there."

Smith made sure the claymore was properly sighted, then began stringing the second set of trip wires.

"We can't be sure they'll do that, however, so we'll improve the trap. Farther up the trail we'll string a trip wire across the trail itself and attach it to a pull release detonator inserted in a block of C-4. We'll put another blasting cap in the other end of the C-4, tape it to a twelve-meter piece of det cord with another blasting cap on the far end and insert that into a second block of C-4. We'll open up all our C-ration cans and fill them with pebbles from that little stream over there, then pack them around the C-4 blocks to create a shrapnel effect. Well, almost all of the cans. I'll need a couple for the grenades, but I'll explain that later. The first block of C-4 goes up—'Boom!'—throwing the rocks out in a circular fan-shaped pattern about knee-high, the det cord tears up the middle of the trail in a fast ripple, mangling anybody still on the trail, then sets off the second C-4 and shrapnel bomb, smack in the middle of the VC. Surviving VC once again seek shelter in the ditches, and our claymores, if they haven't already claimed a few, get put to good use."

Krung had finished staking out his trip wires, and Smith showed him how to attach them to the claymore so that a pull on any of the three wires would trip the mine, filling the ditch and raking the edge of the trail with a hail of seven hundred and fifty steel balls.

"Got the idea?"

Krung nodded a vigorous affirmative.

"Okay. You finish the other one while I work on the rest of our little surprise."

Smith cut a piece of safety fuse with his knife, lighted the fuse and timed its burning with his watch.

"Thirteen seconds... that's a little long." He cut a slightly shorter piece and crimped it into a pull fuse igniter.

"The pull on the trip wire attached to the pull release device will also activate this fuse igniter and light this piece of fuse. When it burns through, it will release a wire attached to a fifteen-second delay detonator attached to another piece of det cord, which is in turn attached to a third shrapnel-surrounded block of C-4 placed just about five meters short of the point where the back trail narrows, creating a natural bottleneck.

"If all goes well, the first two explosions, three counting the det cord between the C-4 blocks, clear the trail of the advance element of VC. The survivors in the middle jump into the ditches where the claymores take care of a few more of them. Whoever is left runs back the way they came, right into the third block of C-4, or the tail of the VC unit coming forward to reinforce the point takes the third charge in the face."

Krung reported that he had finished with the second claymore, and Smith set him to work preparing the C-ration cans.

"When you've finished with the cans, gather four or five helmetfuls of rocks. Try to get mostly small ones, about the diameter of your thumb, but don't waste time looking. If you can't find real small ones, take whatever's there. The more rocks we have, the more VC we'll kill.

"I'm going to go a little way down the side trail and string another trap—trip wire designed to drop a Willy Pete grenade out of a tree onto the trail. I'll string it so the grenade drops in front of the man who triggers the wire, and also tie it into a second piece of fuse and igniter so that it will drop a couple of frags onto the path at the mouth of the trail about seven seconds later. That ought to catch anybody that the Willy Pete misses and stampede them back toward the main trail. I'll splice a twelve-second piece of fuse into the end of the seven-second fuse, cap it and connect it to the rest of the det cord, tying it into the third C-4 and shrapnel bomb. That way, even if they check the side trail first, it'll trigger the whole firing chain in reverse.

"When you've got the rocks, fill all the C-ration cans but one. Save me one of the long cans. Then pack the cans and the rest of the loose rocks around the C-4 and cover them with dirt. I've scooped out a shallow hole around each of the C-4 blocks so they won't be quite so obvious. Try not to mound the dirt up too high or the VC may spot them. If the Vietcong show up before I get back, fire a warning shot and take off. Can you find your way back to camp from here without me if you have to?"

Krung gave Smith an insulted look in reply.

Smith nodded. "Sorry." Then he moved about three dozen meters down the side trail, found a good spot and began rigging the secondary mechanical ambush. When he returned, Krung was putting the finishing touches on concealing the C-4 and rock bombs.

Smith inspected the Tai's handiwork briefly, nodded his approval and asked him for the submachine gun, noting as Krung handed it over that it bore Chinese markings. The weapon was, in fact, a Type 43, a Red Chinese copy of the M1954 variant of the PPS-43, which had been developed during the Second World War by the Soviet military engineer Alexei Sudarev, rather than the original Russian weapon that Smith had at first assumed it to be. Smith would have preferred a PPSh-41 with its larger, 71-round drum magazine over the 35-round box of the Type 43, but beggars could not be choosers. Besides, he had a hunch that it would be enough.

"Sergeant Sully, why you want burp gun?" asked Krung.

"It's the icing on the cake," Smith explained. "We'll put it up the trail, near the point where the pathway bends to the left, and tie it to a tree. Then we'll wrap a wire around the C-ration can you saved for me. We'll wrap the wire in two different directions and tie a rock to one end. The rock is held up by a forked stick attached to the trip wire and pull-release arrangement. When the wire is tripped, it pulls out the stick, allowing the rock to descend. As the rock lowers, the turning of the can lets wire out in the other direction, releasing pressure on a bent branch so that it will pull a wire loop with a slipknot in it down tight against the trigger and the grip, causing the weapon to fire. The submachine gun will continue to fire until the magazine is empty and will spray the trail with bullets. Most of the rounds should impact just about where we're standing now. With luck, one or two of them might even kill somebody. But that's not important. What is important is that the sound of the firing will convince the VC that this is an ambush, not just a few booby traps. And that will make them very nervous. Perhaps nervous enough to panic. If they do that, we might kill a whole lot of them with our booby traps before they figure out that they're the ones setting off the explosions.''

Krung grinned, showing his sharply filed teeth. ''Good.''

13

VC P.O.W. CAMP NEAR
HONG NGU

Fetterman tried hard to find something good about the situation that they were in. It wasn't an easy thing to do.

At least I'm still alive, he told himself, then whispered it softly, as if the sound of his own voice would reassure him that it were true. "At least I'm still alive."

Fetterman had fully expected that not to be the case. He'd expected to be cold and dead by now, the rigor mortis stiffening his limbs as the ants made an early supper of his eyeballs and the flies crawled in and out of his dead mouth.

Vo had told his men to take Fetterman to the hanging tree and string him up. That cheerful news, coupled with Tyme's information that there were two other Americans in the camp that the VC were preparing to execute, had led Fetterman to believe that he could expect to be hung by the neck until dead. Instead, the VC tied his elbows together behind his back and hauled him up by his wrists, hanging him by his hands a few feet above the ground until he was thoroughly miserable.

The experience was unique, to say the least. Fetterman could not recall a time when he had felt such pain, including the times during the Second World War and Korea when he had been wounded. The pain was so exquisite that he hardly noticed the severe beating that two of the guards administered to him with split bamboo poles as he hung helpless from a tree branch. He couldn't remember if he had screamed or not but decided that he probably had. It was not the sort of punishment that even a man in good physical shape could stand up to for long, and Fetterman could hardly have described his physical condition as good following the long bootless march through the jungle to the camp. Sometime during the process his left shoulder was dislocated, although Fetterman couldn't say if the dislocation had been caused by the beating or by being hung up.

Every few minutes Major Vo stepped out on the porch of his hut to inspect the proceedings, making sure that the beating was progressing at a satisfactory rate and intensity. On one such occasion the Chinese advisor put in a brief appearance, gazing at Fetterman, cigarette in hand, with a look somewhere between mild curiosity and recognition, before turning wordlessly and reentering the hut.

Fetterman fainted sometime after that. He didn't know how long he remained unconscious. He'd been awakened by having a bucket of liquid thrown in his face. It wouldn't have been fair to have called it a bucket of water. Fetterman strongly suspected that the bucket had been used as somebody's chamber pot. It was sufficient, however, to bring him back far enough to something like consciousness to see Vo's laughing face swimming nauseatingly before him. After that he'd passed out again.

Sometime later he'd regained consciousness a second time, and one of the guards had gone to summon Vo. The Vietcong major stood before him, positively beaming with delight.

"Ah, Master Sergeant Fetterman, I see that you have rejoined us. How good of you to do so," said Vo. "I trust that my staff have now properly welcomed you and that you did not find the accommodations too uncomfortable."

Fetterman wondered how Vo could know his name and rank. As a matter of course, the Special Forces advisors wore neither rank insignia nor name tags on their uniforms when in the field, and practically no one in Vietnam bothered with dog tags except Saigon commandos. They were a nuisance, no one used them for anything and they had an annoying habit of clinking together at the wrong time while on patrol unless they were taped together. It was simpler just to leave them in camp.

"Unnecessary," Fetterman managed to whisper between cracked, dry lips.

"I'm sorry. I could not hear you," said Vo mildly. "What did you say?"

Fetterman worked hard, trying to form enough spit to frame an answer. "Unnecessary," he finally got out. "I'll answer your questions."

Fetterman had already carefully constructed what he hoped was a highly creative tale that still contained enough elements of the truth to be believable. He figured that Vo wanted information on Camp A-555's defenses, and Fetterman hoped to give him the kind of information that would cost Vo a few dozen of his men when the time came for the VC to check out that information. He also hoped that, by appearing to cooperate with the Vietcong, he might be able to keep Washington, Tyme and himself alive long enough to be able to figure a way out of this mess—or for Gerber to find them. He knew that it was a long shot, but it was the only game in town at the moment.

Vo flashed him a warm, almost friendly smile. "Of course, Sergeant. You see..."

He was interrupted by the hasty approach of a Vietcong messenger, clamoring for his attention. Vo wheeled on the man and fixed him with an icy stare.

"How dare you interrupt me when I am interrogating a prisoner! You will show proper respect for your superior officers in the future, or I will have you reduced in rank, Corporal. I could have you shot for such an insubordinate display of ill manners."

The messenger blanched, and Fetterman noticed from beneath half-closed eyelids that the man's lower lip trembled slightly.

"Yes, Comrade Major," the messenger said. "I confess that my behavior has been inexcusably rude, and I am truly sorry for the dishonor I have brought upon the Front and our just Revolution by it, but I bring you important news. Good news."

"Well? What is it, then?"

"Comrade Lap's patrol reports that they have made contact with the missing American Smith and one of the hired mercenary dog Tai. They are following their trail and should apprehend them soon."

Vo's countenance softened. "Excellent. Excellent indeed. You may go now. I order you to spend one hour in self-criticism for your unprofessional behavior."

"Yes, Comrade Major. Is there any reply for Lieutenant Lap?"

"Only that the American is to be brought straight here to me immediately upon his capture. Lieutenant Lap may dispose of the Tai as he sees fit. Now go."

"Yes, Comrade Major." The man went.

Vo turned back to Fetterman. "As I was saying, Sergeant, of course you will answer my questions. But you see, I haven't asked you any questions yet. It is a question of propriety. You cannot answer my questions until I have asked them, and I am not ready to ask them yet. I think, perhaps, that it will be some time before I am ready to ask you anything at all. A very long time perhaps. But take heart, Sergeant, take heart. Soon you will have yet another of your men here with you to share your misery. Won't that be nice?"

Then he turned to one of the guards. "You may let him down now and take him back to his cage. I think, perhaps, that we shall entertain the black soldier this afternoon. After all, we don't wish to tire any of our guests too early. And prepare another guest cottage. I think we can expect a new visitor soon."

As he walked back into the hut, Vo threw back his head and laughed. Today it had been very good indeed.

LIEUTENANT LAP TUNG LUONG considered the evidence in the middle of the trail before him. While it would, in truth, not be entirely fair to say that they had found the enemy, they had certainly made contact with him. The flies swarming over the blood-encrusted bodies of the two Vietcong soldiers lying lifeless before him were solemn, mute testimony to that fact.

"Private Lim, tell me once again how it is that your two comrades, Privates Chi and Rho died."

"As I said, Comrade Lieutenant, we were surprised and ambushed by the enemy. We put up a heroic fight, but there were too many of the devils. I was lucky to escape with my life and be able to inform you that we had found them."

"I see. You put up a heroic fight, but there were too many of the devils." He knelt and picked up the two Mosin-Nagant rifles that had been left lying near the bodies, opened the bolt of each in turn and checked the rounds in the magazines. "If there were so many of them, why do you suppose they did not take these rifles with them?"

"I have no idea, Comrade Lieutenant. Perhaps they were afraid I would bring back help and defeat them. Besides, the Americans and their Tai have better weapons. Perhaps they did not want the rifles," Lim finished lamely.

"And perhaps you are exaggerating the truth?" Lap asked calmly.

"No, Comrade Lieutenant. We tried to fight, but there were too many of them. And see, they took the submachine gun that Rho carried," Lim finished hopefully.

"You tried to fight. Liar! Then why have neither of these weapons been fired? Why are there no spent brass casings on the ground? Do you expect me to believe that the enemy took the time to pick up all the spent casings, both theirs and yours, and left behind two rifles? Do you think that I am a fool? There is not even a single bullet wound in either of the bodies! Your comrades were killed with a knife, not a gun!" He grabbed Lim roughly by the cloth of his black pajama top and shoved him toward the bodies. "Look! Look at them! Look at their wounds! You allowed the enemy to take you by surprise and kill your two comrades, and you did not even so much as fire a single shot while they were being knifed to death! You are both a coward and a liar!"

Lim said nothing.

"You fought heroically, but there were too many of them, were there?" Lap continued angrily. "Then why is there only one set of footprints made by the crosshatched pattern that the Americans and Tai wear? One rather small set of boot prints at that? Oh, fine, brave soldier of the Front! You and your comrades allowed yourselves to be surprised by a single enemy soldier, a small, filthy animal Tai at that, and you let them be killed because you ran away. And then you compound your cowardice by lying about it. I should have you shot. I should shoot you myself."

Lap's hand drifted downward toward the pistol holstered at his belt, and for a moment Lim was afraid that his lieutenant might do exactly that.

"You let your two comrades be killed, and then you come to me with a wild story claiming to have found the American we seek. There is not even any sign that the American was ever here."

"But the poncho!" Lim tried desperately. "We found the American's poncho. It had his name on it."

"Are you telling me that you can read American now? I was not even aware that you could read Vietnamese."

Lim shrugged. "Rho could read Vietnamese. He said it was not a Vietnamese name."

Lap looked dubious.

"I see no poncho, Private Lim. Where is this poncho with this American name?"

"Perhaps the enemy took it with him," said Lim quickly. "After all, they took Rho's submachine gun."

Lap still looked skeptical. "What was this American name that was on the poncho?"

Lim shrugged again. "I do not know, Comrade Lieutenant. I cannot read American."

"Bah! You are lying again."

Lim noticed the hand straying toward the holster again.

"No, Comrade Lieutenant! No! It is true, I swear. I can remember what it looked like. I can sketch it for you." He knelt and began drawing in the dirt of the trail with a stick.

When he had finished, he stood up and Lap examined his handiwork. It said: THE IRVING AIR CHUTE COMPANY, INC.

Lap stared at the strange symbols and scratched his head. One thing was certain. It was not a Vietnamese name.

"Sergeant Nguyen," said Lap abruptly to his senior NCO, "take your best tracker along the trail for two hundred meters and see if you can find any evidence that the American came this way.

It is just possible for once that this excremental excuse for a soldier is telling the truth. I will await your report here.''

The two men returned within ten minutes.

"Comrade Lieutenant," said Sergeant Nguyen, "approximately one hundred and fifty meters from this spot we found a partial boot print and evidence that the trail had been swept with a branch to hide other boot prints. The size of the partial print we found was much wider than the prints here. A short distance beyond we found other prints, the same size as the ones here."

"Very good, Sergeant. Thank you."

Lap turned toward Lim, tossing one of the rifles at him. The VC private failed to catch it but hurriedly picked it up.

"Private Lim, your story is still in doubt. I have decided, however, to give you a chance to redeem your unworthiness in the eyes of your comrades. You will take the point."

Lap glanced at the two emasculated bodies lying in the trail. They were not the first such bodies he had seen since their ambush of the American and Tai unit the day before.

"You should have no difficulty locating these enemies of the Front. This Tai particularly is not a hard man to follow. He leaves dead bodies wherever he goes."

FETTERMAN LAY ON THE FLOOR of his cell feeling the sweat bead on his forehead and run down the side of his face and neck. He was amazed that there was enough moisture left in his body to sweat. His lips felt cracked and dry and his mouth felt like some one had stuffed it full of cotton balls.

Fetterman had lain on the floor of the cage for an indeterminable time after the guards had thrown him unceremoniously back inside and wired the door shut. They hadn't bothered with the leg irons, and the leg irons hadn't been necessary. Fetterman drifted in and out of consciousness repeatedly before his mind finally cleared enough for something like coherent thought. He didn't know how long he'd been out of touch. It might have been only minutes. It might have been days.

When he tried to move, there was a sudden, blinding pain in his shoulder, and a wave of nausea washed over him. He turned his head quickly to one side in order to keep from aspirating his own vomit. There wasn't much despite the racking spasms, and he realized how truly dehydrated he must be. If the VC didn't water their prisoners pretty soon, they might not have to worry about beating them to death.

Still nauseous, Fetterman used his right hand to explore his injuries. Tilting his neck only slightly, he moved his head as little as possible to minimize the urge to vomit again. His right side hurt when he breathed, but his fingers found no obvious deformities so he suspected that he only had a couple of cracked ribs, information he regarded as good news. Well, at least better news than broken ribs.

His upper body was covered with yellowish-purple bruises and crisscrossed with long but fairly superficial lacerations from the beating that the guards had given him with the split bamboo poles. The trousers of his jungle fatigues hung in tatters, revealing cut and bruised legs. His entire body ached and his testicles felt swollen, although he couldn't remember being struck there. Aside from the possible rib damage and the dislocated shoulder, however, most of his injuries seemed to be more discomforting than disabling.

Fetterman knew that, if he was going to have any chance at all of making a success of what he now hoped to do, he was going to have to do something about the dislocated shoulder. He knew that reducing a dislocated shoulder was a job for a doctor, but as it seemed unlikely that Vo would allow Washington to take a look at it for him, Fetterman didn't see that he had any choice. Moving carefully and with infinite patience, Fetterman inched his way across the floor of the cage until he could reach his jungle jacket. He wadded up one of the sleeves and stuck it in his mouth to give himself something to bite down on and help muffle the scream of pain that he knew would come with what he must do, then worked his way to the side of the cage and grasped one of the bamboo bars with his left hand.

He was perspiring heavily now and felt faint, but he did his best to ignore both the faintness and the persistent nausea as he bent his legs and drew them up, placing his battered feet against the bamboo bars of the cage wall. He felt the shoulder with his right hand, making sure of the position of the dislocated joint, and took in several deep breaths through his nose. Then, when he was ready, he set his feet and pulled until the head of the humerus popped back into the socket of the acromial-clavicular joint. He was hardly aware of the scream when it came.

When it was over, Fetterman lay quietly on the floor of the cage, his chest heaving from the effort, the injured ribs causing him pain with each breath. But the pain was not so bad now. Not at all like the pain of the dislocation. Carefully he checked to make sure that the procedure had not impaired his circulation by pinching the nail beds of his left hand with the thumb and forefinger of his right. The capillary refill might have been just a bit slow, but that was to be expected under the circumstances. There was no numbness or tingling to indicate that he had pinched a nerve in the process of reducing the dislocation. He moved the arm slightly to check the range of movement. It still hurt, but it worked okay. Finally Fetterman turned himself onto his injured right side. It seemed to make breathing a little easier and would allow for fluid drainage from his mouth should he vomit again. Only after that did he permit himself the luxury of fainting.

14

THE JUNGLE NEAR
AN MINH

"You know, Krung," said Sully Smith as he put the finishing touches on the triple-triggered, booby-trap firing chain, "the one thing I'm kinda sorry about is that we won't be around to see this baby when she blows. If it works right, we ought to take out a whole bunch of Cong."

"Yes," agreed Krung, sharpening his M-3 combat knife. "That would be good."

The Tai sheathed the knife and unslung his M-1 carbine, slipping out the long, curved banana magazine to check the loads. He tested the spring tension of the magazine follower against his finger, hefted the magazine in his hand and decided it was about half empty. He tucked the partial magazine into a pocket of his tiger-striped jungle fatigues, removed a full magazine from one of the canteen covers on his belt that served as an ammo pouch and snapped the new magazine into place. Then he rechecked the safety.

"But me think, Sergeant Sully, that this one time even Krung believe it's best we don't hang around to wait see what happen. Think maybe best we *di di mau* back to camp. Only *dien cai dau* soldier hang around when odds twenty to one and low on ammo. We make beaucoup too much time here already now."

"I couldn't agree with you more, old friend. But first I've got just one more thing to do. The pièce de résistance. Hand me that last C-ration, will you?"

Krung did as he was asked, and Smith took the can, noting that the meal consisted of ham and lima beans, a military gastronomic delicacy best described as tasting like bits of truck tire mixed with pieces of greasy cardboard—unless you had the opportunity to heat it up. Then it tasted like warm bits of truck tire mixed with pieces of greasy cardboard.

"Beans and motherfuckers," muttered Smith, almost happily. "Offhand, I can't think of a better use to put this to." He pulled out the P-38, which was tied to the bootlace fastened to his belt, and began opening the can.

Krung stared at him aghast. "Sergeant Sully, what you do? This no time to eat. We go now."

"I know, Krung. I know," Smith answered. "I'm just making it a little easier for the VC to be sure to come the way we want them to."

Smith cut the lid most of the way around and bent it back. Then he peeled the plastic spoon out of its cellophane wrapper and stuck the spoon with some difficulty into the unpalatable mass. He set the can down just to the right of the middle of the trail and carefully poured the remaining contents of the combat meal onto the ground next to it, adding a handful of dirt to the empty cardboard carton so that it wouldn't blow away. Then he took the shiny, nickel-plated whistle on the lanyard from around his neck and hung it on a low branch overhanging the trail just above the pile of cans, envelopes and box that made up the combat meal. The main trip wire was about six feet away, with the poncho and smoke grenade bait another ten feet or so beyond that. Smith wanted to be sure that the VC saw what appeared to be the hastily abandoned remains of a meal soon after they saw the poncho. It would add urgency to their pursuit and give them plenty to think about other than trip wires. The poncho and smoke grenade might well initiate the firing chain that Smith had laid out, but he was betting on one of the trip wires to actually do the job. A pull on any of them would initiate the entire firing sequence in a timed order depen-

dent upon which wire was tripped first. Even if the VC had somehow gotten ahead of them and came down the trail from the wrong
direction, the initial couple of explosions would probably claim a
few and the burp gun rig would hit them from behind.

Smith made his final check and was about to speak when Krung
suddenly held up a hand and motioned for him to be quiet, cup-
ping a hand to his ear to indicate that Smith should listen.

Smith strained his ears, at first hearing nothing, then faintly, in
the distance to the southwest toward the Cambodian border, he
could hear them. Helicopters. Big ones, and a lot of them from the
sound of it. It sounded as if a large operation of some kind were
underway, but Smith couldn't figure out what it could be. He
nodded at Krung.

"Sounds like we're not the only members of the VC Hunting
Club out this morning," said Smith. "I hope those guys have bet-
ter luck than we did yesterday. Too bad they aren't coming our way.
I wouldn't have minded a ride back to the camp or a little help.
Come on. Let's get out of here."

They moved down the trail past the burp gun trap. A few yards
farther they turned off the trail into the jungle. The dense foliage
made the going slower, but it was safer than the trail. It would be
harder for the VC to track them. Smith had decided that, if they
encountered any other trails, they would follow them only as long
as they were headed in the right direction. When he reasoned that
they were within a klick of the camp, they would leave the trail
system entirely and proceed carefully on an indirect course through
the jungle. He didn't want to risk being ambushed at the last moment. As he stepped off the trail into the brush, Smith checked his
watch. It had taken nearly twenty-five minutes to booby-trap the
trail. The Vietcong could not be far away.

HAD SMITH ONLY KNOWN IT, the help he had wished for was not
far away, either.

Acting on a hunch, Sergeant First Class Derek Kepler had persuaded Captain Gerber to let Sergeant Anderson and himself take
a small reconnaissance patrol to the vicinity of An Minh while the
main search effort was being conducted farther west along the

Cambodian border. The nine-man patrol had spent most of the night and a good part of the morning walking to the area from the camp. Airlift support hadn't been available at the time, but Kepler had considered stealth more important than a comfortable ride.

Corporal Phung, one of the better Tai NCOs, and Specialist Shoong, a Tai medic trained by Doc McMillan, walked with them while a Tai with an M-79 grenade launcher brought up the rear. The command group was preceded by a BAR team, and a hundred meters in front of them was Private Krak, one of the best trackers in the Third Independent Tai Strike Company. Between Krak and the BAR team a seventh striker picked up the slack, checking the compass and pace.

Kepler wasn't sure what he hoped to find. The battle areas to the southwest and east of the village had been well searched the day before without finding any sign of the missing men, and the village itself had been checked and found temporarily deserted. It was a common enough occurrence in Vietnam whenever there had been a sizable fight near a small hamlet before the operation had even started.

Still, Kepler couldn't shake the feeling that this time the villagers were hiding from the Americans and the Tai and Vietnamese PF strikers from Camp A-555. The old woman had indicated that they were hiding from the Vietcong when he and Washington had been there only a few days ago for the MEDCAP visit, but Kepler was no longer sure that he believed the old woman. The men sent out to ambush the VC recruiting patrol had themselves been ambushed by a large, well-organized VC force. That couldn't have been the work of local guerrillas. It had to be the result of a Main Force VC unit, and it would have been the most improbable of coincidences for the strikers to have simultaneously blundered into the VC unit in three different widely separated places. That left only one highly unpleasant alternative to think about. They had been set up.

Kepler didn't know if the old woman had been a VC agent or had been duped by the VC. It was hard to imagine her allowing herself to be subjected to the kind of burn that the old woman had exhibited. Still, some of the Vietcong could be most fanatical in their dedication to the Front. In the final analysis it didn't matter. The Americans had been suckered and had paid a heavy price for it. Kepler felt that he'd been suckered most of all, and he didn't like the feeling.

The whole setup had seemed so perfect, such an easy way to strike a sharp blow at the VC's prestige in the region, for the A-Detachment to finish its tour with a final parting victory. It had been too perfect, too easy. Maybe that was what Gerber had sensed and why he had been opposed to the operation. But Kepler had argued in favor of it, finally persuading the captain to his point of view. Steve Kittredge and a lot of strikers had died because of him. Fetterman, Washington, Tyme and Smith were missing. The only person they'd found any evidence to suggest might have survived was Sergeant Krung, and if the VC found him, he wouldn't survive for long.

Kepler couldn't shake the feeling that it was all his fault. He'd made his recommendation to Gerber based on what appeared to be good information, but he'd underestimated the cunning of the enemy. It was a bitter pill to swallow.

A lot of the strikers had wanted to put An Minh to the torch yesterday afternoon, especially after they'd found the bodies of the men that the Vietcong had so obviously executed after they were wounded. For the Tai, the philosophy of the war was a simple one. Let me win your hearts and minds, or I'll burn your damned huts down. And why not? The Vietnamese had been doing it to them and all the other ethnic minorities for years. As little as a year ago, VNAF pilots had had standing orders to drop any unexpended ordnance on Montagnard villages.

Kepler had sympathized with the Tai. But there was no proof that the villagers had betrayed them. Even if some of them had, what good would burning down the villagers' homes do? Prove that the Americans and Tai who worked with the ARVN were no better than the Vietcong? It would have been playing right into Charlie's hands. The VC would have pointed a finger at the warmongering Americans and their hired Tai killers, and the leftist liberal press would have had a field day hyping it up back in the World.

Yet Kepler had felt that there still might be something to learn at the deserted village, some evidence or clue as to what had gone wrong and what had happened to the other members of the team. The villagers had a way of knowing when the Vietcong were around, and the villagers were making themselves conspicuously absent. Kepler knew that he was reaching but it was just possible that if the villagers were staying away, the Vietcong might still be around. And if the VC were still around, it might be possible to capture one of them and pump the prisoner for information about Fetterman and the others. Kepler wanted some answers. He knew that, if they were lucky enough to grab a human intelligence resource, his field interrogation technique might leave a lot to be desired as far as the Geneva Convention was concerned, but that was just going to be tough. He didn't have time to fool around. Wherever they were, time had to be running out for the others.

AS HE CREPT CAUTIOUSLY along the trail with agonizing slowness, keeping first to one side, then the other, Private Lim of the National Liberation Front could feel the fear twisting his intestines like a bad case of dysentery. The sweat ran down his face and sides in rivulets, and the ancient, heavy Mosin-Nagant bolt action rifle felt slippery in his hands. For a moment he considered that it might have been better to have been killed with the others than to know such fear, but he immediately dismissed such an idea. As bad as his situation might now be, there was, he knew, no such thing as a fate worse than death. Death was the final ultimate insult to the body. Once you were dead, there was no means of escape, no more *nouc-mam* or rare letters from your family. There was only the long silence of the grave.

Lim considered ideas such as heroism and bravery foolhardy notions that had little practical application in life and were best left to the philosophizing of political cadres. What good did it do to say that a man was brave when he was dead and there was no one to earn a living and build a house for his family? Bravery did not feed or shelter the family, and the man who was dead was beyond caring whether others thought him brave or a coward. Was it not better to be a live coward than a dead hero? Evidently Lieutenant Lap did not think so. Or perhaps he did in his own way. After all, had he not sent Lim to walk the point while he stayed back, safe with the main group?

Lim had been a Vietcong soldier for a little more than a year. In all that time he had never seen anyone die until today. He had seen people who were dead, of course—casualties brought back to their camp in Cambodia following raids on the ARVN and their American advisors. He had seen the bodies of the dead policemen following the raid on the South Vietnamese Nation Police outpost at Tan Chau, a raid in which he had participated and actually fired his rifle a few times, although not actually *at* anybody. But he had never really seen anybody *being* killed until the Tai striker had suddenly materialized out of the jungle growth alongside the trail and killed Chi and Rho with his big knife. Lim had stood momentarily frozen at the horror of witnessing death at such close proximity as Rho died before his very eyes. Only a low grunt had escaped his friend's mouth. Then Lim had run away, moaning in terror.

Lim would have liked to have helped his fallen comrades. But in that one brief moment he had discovered an inner truth about himself. He lacked the emotional strength, the inner resolve, to take another man's life. There are some people who simply cannot bring themselves to take another's life, and Lim was one of them. He did not know if that made him a better human being than someone who could kill or a worse one, but he did know that it was a poor survival trait for a soldier to possess. He wished that Lieutenant Lap could understand that as he himself did.

There was a hissing sound behind him, and Lim spun about, his heart pounding in his chest, nearly stumbling and falling in the process.

A short distance back along the trail, he could see Sergeant Nguyen, annoyingly motioning for him to continue. With the utmost reluctance Lim moved along the trail to the accompaniment of Sergeant Nguyen's frantic gestures for him to hurry up. Nguyen's vigorous exercising of his hands and arms were, for the most part, lost on Lim, who couldn't see much sense in hurrying to catch up to someone who was likely to kill you.

It was near midday and insufferably hot, as were all middays in the delta region. Even the animals had enough sense to rest during that time of the day. The only things foolish enough to be moving around in such heat were Americans and Tai and Lieutenant Lap, who was chasing them with his patrol. Perhaps Lap dreamed of promotion or of a decoration. Hero of the Revolution Second Class or whatever it was that the big shots in Hanoi handed out these days. Or perhaps he merely feared the wrath of Major Vo should they fail in their mission to capture the American.

Whatever his reasoning, it made little difference to Private Lim as he walked the point for the patrol. If he found the enemy, it seemed reasonable to suspect that he would die as his friends had, and if he did not, it also seemed reasonable to suspect that Lieutenant Lap would shoot him for cowardice and insubordination. The intricacies of the dilemma would have appealed to Lim's sense of humor had he not been the object of the dilemma.

Ahead the trail broadened, and Lim approached the wider pathway as though it were the most dangerous piece of real estate in all of Indochina. The sound of a startled bird suddenly taking flight with a great flapping of wings caused him to feel as though an invisible hand had closed about his heart and was squeezing it within his chest. When that was followed by a loud grunt and the sound of some animal, probably a wild boar, crashing through the underbrush after being disturbed by the bird, Lim nearly fell to his knees as his legs became rubbery and unwilling to support his weight. And then he saw it.

As his gaze swept along the trees lining one side of the trail, then darted across to sweep down the other side, a glint of light caught his eye. It was there for only a fraction of a second and then gone, but it brought his focus back to the center of the trail, and there, a few dozen meters ahead of him in the middle of the pathway, lay a familiar bundle. A few yards beyond it was a pile of something. It might have been cans or it might have been grenades, that and some kind of box. And above it, again, that brief glinting flash of sunlight.

Lim squatted on his haunches along the side of the trail, and slowly brought his rifle across his knees and would go no further.

He waited for what seemed an eternity, feeling the sweat roll down his body. His bladder was full and felt as though it might burst at any second, but still he did not move. At long last he heard the voice of Sergeant Nguyen behind him.

"Private Lim! What do you think you are doing? You are holding up the entire patrol."

Lim inclined his head toward the objects lying in the trail by way of answer. His mouth was too dry to speak.

Nguyen followed Lim's gaze until he, too, saw the objects. He immediately brought his rifle into the ready position and scanned the sides of the trail for any sign of a trap.

"What is the problem, Sergeant?" asked Lap, coming forward.

"There is something on the trail, Comrade Lieutenant," Nguyen answered.

"I can see that, Sergeant. What is it?"

"I do not know, sir," replied Nguyen. "It appears to be a bundle of some sort."

"It is death," whispered Lim softly.

"What? What did you say, Private?" Lap demanded.

"It is death," Lim repeated. "All those who touch it die. I have touched it, and now it has come back to tell me that it is my time to die."

Lap stared down the trail at the object.

"What utter nonsense. It's nothing more than a poncho. It must be the one you spoke of, the one belonging to the American. Perhaps you will yet redeem yourself if you desist from making these fatalistic statements, Private Lim. Go and fetch it. I want to examine it."

"No," said Lim softly.

"Are you refusing to obey my order?" Lap spoke sternly. "Go and bring it to me at once!"

"No, sir," said Lim. "I will not go and fetch it."

"Bah! You cowardly fool. Sergeant Nguyen, go and bring me that poncho."

Nguyen looked dubious. "Comrade Lieutenant, do you think it wise? Perhaps it is a trap of some sort."

Lap exploded. He had already been irritated by Lim's continual delays in pursuing the enemy, and he was in no mood to put up with such nonsense now, further delaying them while the enemy slipped through their fingers.

"Am I surrounded by incompetents? Are all my men afraid of just one American and one filthy little Tai? I shall inspect it myself. Sergeant Nguyen, bring the men. Now, Sergeant."

"Yes, sir," said Nguyen reluctantly.

Lap strode boldly up the trail, his eyes fixed on the poncho, his gait almost swaggering. He knelt next to the bundle and stared at it curiously, tilting his head first one way, then another, to view it from different angles. It was a rolled-up poncho, all right, although a bit thick as though there might be something else rolled up inside it. A blanket perhaps. Lap examined it carefully. He could see no wires or strings that might lead to a booby trap. Gingerly he lifted the poncho and turned it in his hands. There was writing on it. The strange American name that Lim had spoken of. He read it carefully. These Americans had very long names apparently. There was even more to it than what Lim had sketched.

Lap stood, holding the poncho in his hand and waving the men forward to show that there was no danger. It was at that moment that a brief flash of light caught his eye. He turned and looked up the trail, seeing the items in the middle of it for the first time. Lap recognized the containers as American food. He had seen such items before, once in the field and once for sale on the black market in Saigon. If they had disturbed the enemy at his meal in such a fashion that he had not had time to take it with him, then they could not be far behind, he reasoned.

Lap started forward, and the glint of light caught his eye once more. He could almost smell the success. They had surprised the enemy at his meal, and now they would capture him, but they must hurry before the enemy could escape. He called to the men, urging them forward, then strained his eyes to see what had caused the flash. There! Something was hanging over the trail, a little bit to one side. As he approached it, Lap could see that it was a small metallic object hung on a cord that allowed it to swing freely beneath an overhanging branch. As he neared it, he stretched out his hand to touch it, allowing his grip on the poncho to relax. The poncho slipped in his fingers, and he partially dropped it, allowing it to unroll. As it did so, a small, olive drab can-shaped object dropped out of it and onto the trail next to him. Lap heard the *spoing* as the safety lever flew from the grenade.

"Cover!" yelled Lap.

He attempted to take one quick step away from the grenade before throwing himself to the ground. As he moved, he felt his foot snag on the thin, almost invisible wire strung an inch-and-a-half above the trail. Then his world exploded.

A huge geyser of dirt and stones erupted before Lap's face, and almost simultaneously a second explosion rippled back down the trail beneath him, hurling him into the air and setting off a second shattering explosion in the midst of the lead squad, flinging men and pieces of men in all directions. As the second squad dived for cover in the ditches alongside the trail, two more explosions filled the air with whining steel as the claymores were tripped, their hundreds of steel balls cutting men off at the knees, the waist, the neck, and giving the more distant Vietcong a fatal case of measles.

For just a moment all was quiet. Then, up ahead on the trail, a machine gun opened fire, spraying a long stream of bullets down the packed dirt pathway. The men in the fourth squad panicked and ran back in the direction they had come from, just in time to be met with a barrage of rocks propelled at supersonic speed by the third charge of plastic explosive.

The men from the third squad, caught between the explosions, took the only route of escape left open to them—down the side trail. Their squad leader died screaming in the white-hot glare of Smith's WP grenade as burning bits of phosphorus inexorably ate through the skin and muscle tissue of his face, shoulders, arms and chest, searching for the bone beneath. Those not killed or injured with the leader ran back toward the main trail and were shredded by the two fragmentation grenades dropping abruptly in their midst.

For less than a minute absolute pandemonium reigned in the jungle. The air was filled with explosions, shouts, the yelling of contradictory commands, screams of pain and shrieks of unreasoning terror. The cough and clatter of several hundred rounds of ammunition fired blindly at an unseen, unpresent enemy over-shadowed the crashing flight of panicked jungle animals, drowning out even the startled screech of the ubiquitous monkeys. Then, as suddenly as the cacophony had begun, there came perhaps thirty seconds of absolute silence.

Private Lim picked himself up from the dirt of the trail, where he had been knocked by the flying body of a fellow VC soldier, and stared in numb silence at the incredible scene of mass carnage before him. Scattered over nearly a hundred meters of jungle terrain were dead bodies, dying bodies and bits and pieces of bodies. Hanging like a pall over this vast open-air charnel house was a sickly shroud of yellow smoke.

For a moment Lim thought that he had been struck deaf, so utterly complete was the silence. A sound even more dreadful began. The cries and moans of the wounded rose from the jungle floor in a climbing, tortured wail that crescendoed until it became a shrieking howl, like the demented cry of some lost dweller of the spirit world. Lim clapped his hands over his ears to shut out the sound, but it was useless. When the noise finally subsided to a sonorous lamentation, he dropped his hands. The left one came away red and wet. Part of his left ear was missing.

Lim shuffled through the maze of broken, twisted humanity, his expression the blank, unseeing countenance of a zombie, yet he saw. Here was a man whose life blood pumped out onto the ground from a severed leg, his eyes glassy, unfocused. Beside him lay a man with no face, yet the rising and falling of his chest indicated that he was not quite dead. Over there was a man with a hole in his side the size of a sun helmet, his intestines strung out for half a dozen meters among the bushes lining the side of the trail. He was sitting upright with his back against a tree, and as he looked at Lim, he smiled and winked incongruously before he died. Hands, fingers, sneakers with feet still in them that were no longer attached to a body, were strewn over the ground. A torn and shredded pair of lungs was draped limply over a tree branch, and a human heart lay in the dusty trail beneath them, still beating with a curiously quivering rhythm. Nearby lay the unmoving figure of a young soldier, the jagged end of a shattered femur driven through his throat by the force of one of the explosions.

Lim did not venture down the side trail, but he did cast a look down it. He could see the blood-soaked, sodden uniforms of several men, a few of them still moving. Beyond them were the still smoking bodies of the men who had been hit by the white phosphorus grenade. One of them screamed as the phosphorus continued to burn inside his body.

Lim turned his attention back to the main trail. A few of the men were sitting up now. Some were trying to help the more seriously wounded while others tried with equal futility to stanch the flow of blood from mangled stumps that had once been their own arms or legs.

As Lim walked among the bodies and the wounded, he found the still form of Sergeant Nguyen. The Sergeant's face was set in an expression of outrage and accusation. Lim wondered who he had been angry at during the moment of death. There was a hole the size of a beer can in the center of his chest and an exit wound the size of a melon in his back.

Lim searched through the carnage for several minutes before locating the remains of Lieutenant Lap. It was not an easy process. In the end he succeeded in matching the lieutenant's severed head with his crushed and mutilated body on the evidence of his leather pistol belt. Lying next to it were the tattered remains of a familiar object. The largest piece of it was about a forearm's length square and contained the strange writing that Lim had seen earlier. He stared down at the odd words, wondering once again at the profoundness of their meaning. MANUFACTURED BY THE IRVING AIR CHUTE COMPANY, INC. CEDAR RAPIDS, IA. Above that, in a slightly different lettering, was F.G.S. Smith, S/Sgt., R.A. 438/02/4551.

Lim did not know what the words meant, but he understood their meaning and marveled at the complexity of the American language.

"It is a very long name for death," he said.

It was only then that he noticed that, at some time during the ambush, he had pissed in his pants.

SMITH AND KRUNG HAD no trouble hearing the explosions when they occurred, even though they were over a kilometer away. The jungle muffled the dull crump of the grenades, but there was nothing dull about the sound of the C-4 or the det cord.

"I think we just bagged ourselves a few Cong," Smith gasped to Krung as he pulled up panting beside the Tai at the entrance to a side trail.

Krung, who wasn't even breathing hard after their three-quarter-mile run, smiled brightly at Smith and gave a quick nod of his head. "Cong blow up real good, Sergeant Sully."

Smith nodded in reply. "Real good," he agreed. "How come we stopped?"

Krung indicated the side trail.

"This come out near An Minh. We take, mean we have to cross couple hundred meters elephant grass near backside of village, but save maybe two, maybe three klicks we get back Camp A-Triple Nickel. What you think? Okay fine?"

Smith considered the trail. It would be a dangerous crossing. The swaying of the high, tough grass was sure to give their position away to any observer. Further, the trail that Krung had indicated wasn't on Smith's map, but then the map had been made by the French over twenty years ago. It might be worth the risk if it would save them a couple of hours getting back to camp.

"Are you sure this comes out near An Minh?" Smith asked dubiously.

Krung looked hurt. "Sergeant Sully, Krung no give bum steer. This the straight poop. No shit."

"Okay," said Smith with a shrug of his shoulders. "We'll give it a try. Only I'll take the point this time. The pace you're setting is killing me."

The Tai sergeant looked puzzled. "Krung no hurt Sergeant Sully. You okay fine? Krung not understand."

"It's an expression, Krung, that's all. It means you're going too fast for me. I can't keep up with you so I want to take the point for a while. You cover our tail, okay?"

Krung nodded and they moved down the trail. Forty-five minutes later they came to the edge of the tree line. Spread out before them, at the foot of a small, gentle slope, was a veritable sea of elephant grass. In the distance off to the right, Smith could see a cluster of huts and part of a mud and bamboo fence. To the left of the fence were a series of paddy field dikes.

"An Minh," said Krung authoritatively.

It didn't look like An Minh to Smith, but then he'd only seen the village once before and that had been from the other side.

"We cross that way," said Krung, pointing to their left. "Beyond second paddy dike is shallow canal, and we follow to trees way over there. Trail start again there, head toward camp."

Smith got out his compass and shot an azimuth on the distant paddy dike. He estimated the distance to be just under three hundred yards.

"Okay," he decided. "We'll crawl it. We don't want to stir the grass up any more than absolutely necessary. And that way at least we'll be low if we run into trouble."

They slipped down the hill and into the grass, Smith in the lead, Krung barely in sight to his left rear. They were about halfway through the grass when Smith thought he heard a rustling ahead of them. He held up his hand. Krung saw it and both men froze.

For a moment there was nothing, and then it came again, directly ahead of them. Smith motioned Krung farther to the left, but the sound shifted with them, getting slightly closer as it did so. Disgustedly Smith tried to flank whatever or whoever was ahead of them to the right, but again the sound shifted to match their direction. It had to be VC. Nothing else made any sense.

Slipping his last fragmentation grenade from his web gear, Smith showed it to Krung, then pulled the pin and held the grenade ready, the spoon trapped in the web of his hand. He was just about to throw it when he heard a voice not three feet away from him.

"You know, Sully, Derek's gonna be awfully pissed if you throw that thing at him."

The nearness of the voice startled Smith so much that he nearly dropped the grenade.

"Anderson? Cat, is that you?" Smith was incredulous.

"Unless there's two of me and I'm somewhere else."

"Where the hell are you? What the hell are you guys doing out here?"

Anderson pushed forward out of the grass slightly to Smith's right. "Right here. Sorry about sneaking up on you. We been stalking you for the last twenty minutes. Thought you were VC. Don't you think you ought to put a pin back in that thing before somebody gets hurt?" he added, nodding toward the grenade.

Smith glanced down at the grenade absently as though he had forgotten about it. He reinserted the pin, then grinned sheepishly at Anderson.

"Christ, Cat, it sure is good to see your ugly face again. Just what the fuck *are* you guys doing out here?"

"That should be obvious, even to a dumb bastard like you, Sully," said Kepler, pushing through the grass directly in front of him. "We came to take you guys home."

"Well, it's about fucking time you got here," said Smith, aiming a good-natured jab at Kepler's shoulder.

"Fucking-A time," agreed Krung. "We out here fighting whole fucking war by selfs."

"Is that Krung with you? How many men have you got?"

"That's it, Derek," answered Smith solemnly. "We're all there is. Kittredge and the others didn't make it."

Kepler nodded. "I know about Steve. We checked the hillock out in the swamp. Sorry, Sully. Have you heard anything from Fetterman's bunch?"

"Fetterman? Is he missing?"

"Afraid so," said Kepler. "Washington and Tyme with him. The captain got on to Colonel Bates, who got on to General Hull, and the two of them have got about a battalion out looking for all you guys along the border."

"Along the border? Why would they look along the... Oh! You figure maybe they've been . . ." Smith didn't want to say it.

"Captured. I'm afraid it kind of looks that way. Captain Gerber figured the VC would take them across the border into Cambodia as soon as possible."

"Oh, man. They are really in some deep shit."

"You don't know the half of it. Saigon shot three VC suspects up in Da Nang the other night, and Radio Hanoi had been promising to shoot a couple of American P.O.W.s if Saigon followed through with the executions. I guess I don't need to tell you Green Berets aren't likely to be invited in for tea and crumpets by the VC. They shot three Victor Charlies in Da Nang, and we're missing three Green Berets."

"You don't have to draw me a picture." Smith frowned at Kepler for a moment. "Say, do you suppose we could get the hell out of this Goddamned grass before Charlie comes along and puts the bag on the rest of us?"

"I thought you'd never ask." Kepler grinned, trying to break the tension. "Stick with me, old buddy, and we'll have you home in about twenty minutes."

"Twenty minutes," Smith snorted. "Unless I've seriously miscounted, we're still several klicks from camp. You got a pair of seven league boots in your backpack?"

"Nope, but Anderson does. Show him your boots, Cat."

Anderson produced the handset of an PRC-25 radio and keyed the transmit button on the handset.

"Zulu Six, this is Zulu Two, over."

"Zulu Six," the radio crackled faintly with Gerber's reply.

"The recon has born fruit. We have located the mad bomber and his trophy-collecting friend. They say their feet hurt. Can you send us a ride, over?"

There was a long pause, then the radio crackled again.

"Roger Two, the ride is on the way. Give coordinates. Over."

Kepler looked at Smith and grinned. "See. Seven league boots."

Twenty minutes later they were all laughing and downing Carling Black Label beer in the team house.

15

VC P.O.W. CAMP NEAR
HONG NGU

Fetterman could have used a beer, but he would have happily settled for a glass of water. In fact, a gallon of water would have been just about right, he decided. Two or three gallons and a couple of hamburgers would have been even better. Even ham and lima beans was beginning to sound good to him.

Anything sounded better than the occasional screams coming from the direction of Vo's hootch. By Fetterman's reckoning, which could have been off by a couple of hours or more due to his lapses of consciousness, Major Vo had been entertaining Washington since around 1500. It didn't sound as though Vo's new guest was enjoying the entertainment much.

It was oppressively hot in the cage. The hottest afternoon that Fetterman could remember experiencing in the Land of Eternal Summer, but then, in Vietnam, you swore that each afternoon was the hottest that you could remember. This one was like being in an oven. It was too hot even for the mosquitoes, who had abated their banquet, except for a few dozen grimly determined diners still droning languidly about his head. Fetterman wondered idly how many thousands of mosquitoes it would take to make a meal. There'd be enough of them after the sun went down if he could figure out a way to catch them.

Another scream brought Fetterman's mind back to Washington. It didn't have the same rhythmic quality to it as the beating that Fetterman had taken this morning. Was it only this morning? But whatever they were doing to him, it must have been pretty rough to get that kind of noise out of the big, ex-junior college football tackle. Washington was known as a man of few words, a man who entertained the striker's kids around Camp A-555 by putting out candle flames with the palm of his hand. He had once walked five miles on a broken leg without mentioning it to anybody. Then, on his return to camp, he had strolled calmly down to the infirmary and said to McMillan, "Hey, Doc. Take an X ray of this thing, will ya? I think I busted the distal end of my fibula." He had.

Fetterman tested his relocated shoulder joint gingerly. It still hurt but then so did almost everything else. It worked and that was all that mattered.

He tried to talk to Tyme again but could get only a moan or two and a bit of incoherent babbling out of the young soldier. After fifteen minutes, he gave up trying.

Then there was nothing to do but lie on the floor of the cage and wait for nightfall, moving as little as possible to try to conserve whatever body fluids that he might have left. Everything would depend on what kind of security arrangements the VC made at dusk. If they decided to hang a lantern over his cage and place a guard outside the door, that would be the end of it. But Fetterman didn't think that they'd do that. There'd been a lot of air traffic in the area during the day, most of it a bit to the south of the prison camp, and a light in the jungle at night stuck out like a wart on the end of a beauty queen's nose. Even with all the tree cover, Fetterman didn't think that they'd risk giving away the location of the camp like that. Not this close to the Special Forces camp and not this soon after the capture. Captain Gerber would have mobilized some kind of search party, and Vo wouldn't want to risk being deprived of his entertainment so soon. Not while he was enjoying himself. It wasn't as if the prisoners might actually be rescued, Fetterman knew. It was simply that Vo would execute them if there was any danger of a rescue attempt being successful. It wouldn't do to leave behind prisoners who could testify that they were tortured by the Vietcong.

Washington screamed again.

Fetterman lay listening to the scream, feeling a cold rage growing inside him. It wasn't hatred. Hatred was a hot, violent, unreasoning emotion. This one could be better described as a thirst for revenge.

"Some people in this world simply need to be killed," Fetterman muttered to himself. "And two of them are in this camp. Every time we've gotten our tails twisted in the last year, that Chinese bastard has been behind it, and Vo is a psychopathic sadist. I don't know exactly how I'm going to do it, but I'm going to get out of this hellhole, and when I do, I'm going to come back and kill both of those mothers."

For the rest of the day, Fetterman lay quietly, conserving his strength and developing various contingency plans. He still had a few tricks up his sleeve. Literally. His situation might be far from ideal, but he wasn't beaten yet. Not by a long shot.

At midnight he made his move.

IT WAS A BEAUTIFUL MORNING when Vo awakened and pushed aside the mosquito netting over his sleeping platform. At least it was as beautiful as any morning can be in the Delta. There was a faint breeze coming through the open window of the hut, and while it was not exactly cool, neither did it carry with it the stifling heat that would come later in the day.

Vo rose and took his shirt and trousers from the back of the lashed bamboo chair, slipping them on and buckling his Sam Browne pistol belt and holster about his waist before pulling on his boots. Then he walked over to a corner of the hut and fired up the tiny single-burner kerosene stove, putting the kettle on to make tea.

Looking through the window, Vo could see that it had only just begun to get light. He decided that he would go for a short walk through the camp while he waited for the water to boil, perhaps check on his guests and see if they were resting comfortably this morning.

Vo chuckled to himself at the thought of that. Resting comfortably. Soon they would rest in peace. But not just yet. Not for a week or two. Not until he had a few new guests to take their place. After that they could join the other two Americans, Versace and Roraback, who had been brought in three nights ago.

The PLA advisor had not been pleased with that development. He had argued that their presence here jeopardized the security of the operation in progress against Camp A-555, but the orders had come from Hanoi, and there was nothing that he could do about it.

Vo had agreed with him that it was a stupid thing to do, but then Hanoi often ordered stupid things to be done. So what if it would have been simpler to shoot them at the camps where they had been held? They had provided Vo with two days of entertainment before the arrival of the other three Americans. If Hanoi wanted Vo to shoot them, that was fine with him. He would have preferred a slower means of execution, but perhaps if the firing squad was careful, the two might not die at once. And they had been most entertaining while they had been Vo's guests.

The order had come from Hanoi last night: proceed with the executions at the date and time specified. At ten o'clock this morning Versace and Roraback were to be shot.

As Vo was leaving the hut, he met the camp's duty radio operator coming up the steps.

"Good morning, Major Vo. I have received an urgent signal for you from Hanoi," the man said, handing over a small scrap of paper. "Will there be any reply?"

"Permit me to read it first, Corporal. Then I will be able to tell you whether or not there will be any reply."

"Yes, sir. I'm sorry, sir."

Vo unfolded the scrap of paper and read the message with a combination of disbelief and anger. It instructed him to delay the executions until the morning of the 26th of September and at that time to execute all prisoners under his control.

"Have you read this message, Corporal?"

"Yes. Of course, Major Vo. I received it and copied it down myself."

"Has anyone else seen this?"

"No, sir."

"Good. Did you acknowledge receipt of it?"

"Yes, Major Vo. That is standard procedure."

"That is not so good. Did you repeat the message back?"

"No, sir. That was not requested."

"Excellent. Now listen to me. This message was garbled in transmission. Further, I was in the field at the time and never received it. Do you understand?"

The duty radio operator looked extremely puzzled. "No, Major Vo, I do not understand. The message seems perfectly clear to me, and you are standing right here."

"You do not understand because you are not meant to understand. This message does not say what it appears to say. It is a special code intended only for me. Now do you understand?"

"No, sir. I mean, yes, sir." The doubtful expression on the corporal's face made it plain that he, in fact, did not understand.

Vo tried again. "This is a special code which only I know. It informs me that the executions of the two Americans will proceed as planned. The others will be retained for a time until we have completed the questioning. It was sent to me in code because we have a traitor in our midst who would thwart our plans if he knew what they really were."

"If you say so, Major Vo."

"I do say so, Corporal. And I further say that, if you mention one word of our conversation or say anything about this message to anyone, you may very well be joining the Americans before the firing squad as a traitor to the Front. Now do you understand?"

The corporal understood that all right. "Yes, sir!" he replied crisply.

"Very well, Sergeant. Thank you. You may carry on."

"Sergeant? No, sir. I'm a—"

"I said you may carry on, Sergeant. Thank you, that will be all."

"Thank *you*, Major Vo."

The duty radio operator hurried away to ponder the meaning of his new promotion.

Vo stood on the porch until the man had disappeared from sight. Then he took a Zippo lighter from his pocket and put the flame to a corner of the paper. When the fire had burned almost to his fingertips, he dropped the paper to the ground. After the fire had burned itself out, he crushed the ashes beneath his boot and watched them blow away on the faint morning breeze.

It was the first order of the Front that Vo had disobeyed. At least, it was the first order of any significance, and if it was found out, the consequences would be most severe. Yet Vo had taken the risk because he was unwilling to let Hanoi deprive him of his entertainment. What difference could it make if the Americans were executed tomorrow or a week from tomorrow after he had had his fun with them? It was unfair of Hanoi to take away his entertainment in this fashion, and he would not permit it. He would execute the two prisoners according to his original orders, but he would not execute the three new ones until he had completed his entertainment. The two prisoners who had been transferred to his control were burned-out shells of men who had already served their purpose, and the Front could do with them as it pleased. But not the three new ones. They were his guests, his prisoners, and he would do with them as he pleased and to hell with the Front. The Front could have them when he was done with them, not before.

I think I shall start with this small older one, this Master Sergeant Fetterman, again today, thought Vo. I must not overtax any of them right away. The black soldier will need a chance to regain his strength before I have him entertain me again, but he is big and strong. I think that perhaps by this evening he will be sufficiently recovered. And this other one, the wounded one, he is not yet strong enough. Perhaps I will even have to feed him. We must not let him expire before he has amused us. So it must be this little man with the balding head. He interests me anyway. He always says that he is willing to talk, yet it does not seem to arise out of fear. He withstands pain even better than the big black. I wonder what his game could be? Well, this morning perhaps I shall ask him why he pretends to be willing to cooperate with us. That will be very good because it is not the sort of question that he will be expecting.

Vo walked down the trail to the cages and inspected the prisoners. He came first to Versace and Roraback. They were asleep or unconscious. It did not matter. By lunchtime they would be dead. Then he walked the trail in the opposite direction. The black soldier did not look well this morning. The burns covering his thighs and groin had a nasty, oozing, pustulant appearance, and his burned eyelids were nearly swollen shut. And the young wounded soldier was a pale, ashen, gray color. Vo might have thought him dead already if it were not for the erratic rise and fall of his chest.

Vo turned away from Tyme's cage and walked toward Fetterman's. He stared down at the small figure, wondering if today he should try the field telephone connected to the genitals or the bamboo shoots beneath the finger and toenails. He stared again. This could not be. The body in the cell, although turned facedown and partially covered with the many pocketed, tiger-striped jungle jacket, was a Vietnamese! Master Sergeant Anthony B. Fetterman had vanished!

A cry of anger arose in Vo's throat, climbing in pitch and volume until it became an animalistic howl of fury that awakened the rest of the camp and sent men running to the cage to see what the trouble was. A roll call revealed three men dead.

One of the inner perimeter guards had a dark discoloration about the eyes, a broken, swollen nose and a thin trickle of frothy pink fluid, now mostly dried, leaking out of one ear. A member of the outer perimeter patrol had had his throat expertly cut, severing both carotid arteries, the jugular vein and the trachea. They had to unwire the door to the cage to check the body of the third man. Except for a large purplish bruise on his throat, there was not a mark on him.

A check of the possessions of the dead men revealed that all three had been stripped of their M-1 carbines and ammunition, although two of the weapons were later found, their barrels bent at ninety-degree angles, bolts and firing pins, springs and operating rods missing.

Also missing from the guards' barracks was an M-14 rifle that had been captured from one of the prisoners, three magazines of ammunition and a couple of grenades.

Screaming at the top of his lungs, Vo pushed, prodded and kicked his men into action until he had dispatched nearly two hundred soldiers into the bush to look for the escaped prisoner. Only then did he turn to glare at the PLA advisor.

"Well, Comrade Major," Vo demanded of the Chinese officer, "what is your assessment of the situation?"

The Chinese officer gave Vo a thin smile and very calmly lighted a cigarette, his first of many for the day.

"It is my assessment, Major Vo," said the PLA advisor, "that Master Sergeant Fetterman is an extremely resourceful man. I have the feeling that I have met him before. I also have the feeling that eventually he will come back, although not, I think, in the company of your men."

"And your advice in this matter, Comrade Advisor?" asked Vo sourly.

The Chinese officer puffed languidly on his cigarette.

"That's easy," he said. "Pray to Buddha that he does not."

16

SPECIAL FORCES CAMP
A-555

Captain MacKenzie K. Gerber sat in the folding steel chair behind his desk and rubbed at his puffy, reddened eyes. A heavy china mug of steaming black coffee rested between his elbows, and his head, leaning forward, rested between his hands. The skin of his face looked pale and drawn, and the lines around his eyes and mouth were deeply etched.

For the third straight night Gerber had not slept. Despite the minor celebration caused by the return of Sully Smith and Krung, he still had too much on his mind to sleep despite his exhaustion.

Fetterman, Tyme and Washington were still in the field and unaccounted for.

Steve Kittredge was gone. What could be found of his remains had been flown away in an olive drab body bag in the back of the mail run Huey. Gerber hadn't yet been able to bring himself to sort through Kittredge's belongings and package them up for shipment back to his family or to write the requisite letter expressing his sorrow at their great loss. He didn't know if that would mean much to Kittredge's young wife and daughter. He hoped that the Medal of Honor would. Gerber had written the recommendation last night, and General Hull had already affixed his signature to second it.

Sully Smith had been recommended for the Silver Star. He had probably done as much, if not more than Kittredge, to deserve the MOH, but regulations required that a recommendation for the Congressional medal be accompanied by a witness statement of the action, and Smith didn't have a witness. His witness had called artillery fire in on himself as he was being overrun. In the infinite wisdom of the U.S. Army, it was easier to get a Medal of Honor for a dead hero than it was for a live one.

And then there was the problem of what to do about Robin Morrow. Robin had made it very apparent that she had fallen in love with Gerber, but until yesterday Gerber still nurtured feelings for her sister Karen, despite Karen's final rejection of him and her return to the States. Hell, maybe he was in love with both women. Logically it should have been an easy choice to make. Robin was here, loved him, and he loved her. Karen had gone home to her husband. It was enough to drive a man crazy, he thought.

"Good morning, Mack," said Hull, coming into Gerber's hootch. "You look like shit this morning. Get any sleep?"

Gerber gave him a lopsided smile and pushed himself up from the desk with some difficulty, listening to the joints in his knees crack. He felt like an arthritic septuagenarian. "No," he answered truthfully. "Did you?"

"Not as much as I like," Hull confessed, "but enough to get by on. What's the game plan for today? We going to go over the same ground again?"

"I thought we'd try a bit farther to the southwest, today, General. Check the area between Nha Bang and Chau Phu."

"You think the VC could have taken them that far by now?"

Gerber shrugged. "Who knows? I just don't know what else to try. They could have gone northeast toward Moc Hoa and crossed near Kompong Rau, or due north toward Svay Rieng. If they did either of those, they're probably already in Cambodia by now. You got any other ideas? I'm open to suggestions."

"Nothing that sounds any better, I'm afraid. Choppers should be here in about twenty minutes. You had breakfeast yet?"

Gerber shook his head. "Didn't feel like eating."

"Well, you're going to. Come on along and I'll buy you some pancakes. Sergeant Kepler says they're about as light and fluffy as a manhole cover this morning, but we got sausage from the World via Saigon to go with them."

"Excuse me, Captain, General," said Bocker, poking his head in the doorway. "Fire control tower reports green smoke southwest of camp. Thought you'd want to know."

"I don't understand," Gerber said. "We don't have anybody still in the field, do we? Outposts should have come in just after dawn."

"That's right, sir. LPs came in just after first light. We don't have anybody in the field. Except," he added, "Fetterman's bunch. They're still in the field, sir."

Gerber grabbed his helmet and snatched up his rifle. "Keep the men on the wall, Galvin, but have them stand down from their weapons. We don't want some nervous striker firing off a round and everybody letting loose. General Hull and I will be at the south gate immediately."

"Yes, sir." Bocker vanished.

"Do you suppose it's possible?" asked Hull, slinging his carbine.

"Possible? Hell, yes, it's possible. Where Fetterman is concerned, anything is possible. Let's go."

Bromhead met them at the gate, binoculars hung around his neck.

"What's happening? Can you see them yet?" asked Hull.

"Nothing yet, sir. So far just the smoke." He trained his binoculars on the distant tree line. "Movement to the right, Captain. Black pajamas. Must be a Vietcong."

"Why would he show himself? What's he doing?" Gerber demanded.

"It looks like he's surrendering, sir. He's taking off his shirt and waving it over his head, and now he's holding something out to one side in his left hand. Looks like a couple of rifles."

"All right," said Gerber. "Everybody just stand easy till we find out what this is all about. Don't anybody shoot."

"He's walking toward the camp," reported Bromhead. "Now he's waving something white. He seems to be having difficulty.... He just fell. Now he's getting back up and waving the white thing again. He keeps stumbling around. It looks like he's hurt or something. Now he's ... Good Christ, it's Fetterman!"

"What? Are you sure?"

"Here, Captain. Take a look for yourself. I'd know that chrome dome of his anywhere."

Gerber snatched the field glasses and stared hard through the eyepieces. "All right. Stand down! Everybody get off the wall! Johnny, get a squad together and go get him. Where's Doc McMillan?"

"Right here," said a soft voice behind him. "Saw all the excitement and thought I'd come have a look. I brought my bag."

"All right, Doc, you go with them." Gerber glanced around. "Goddamn it! NCOs, get your people down off that fucking wall. Now!"

"WELL, DOC, HOW IS HE?" asked Gerber.

"Surprisingly well, considering what he's been through. He's got contusions and abrasions over forty percent of his body, along with one broken and three cracked ribs. He's suffering from severe dehydration and a dislocation of his left shoulder that he reduced himself while in the field, fortunately without doing any further damage as far as I can tell. His feet look like raw hamburger, and he's got a fever from a low-grade infection. And there are about a billion mosquito bites over eighty percent of his body."

"Anything else?" asked Gerber quietly.

"Yes," said McMillan, cracking a smile. "He's hungry and he wants a beer."

"He'll live, then?"

McMillan laughed. "He'll live, all right. Although right now he needs rest and fluid replacement. I've got two IVs running, but I think that, when they're through we can let him have that beer. Sometimes I think Fetterman could live through a B-52 strike." Then he turned serious. "He wants to talk to you, Captain. I don't think you're going to like what he has to tell you."

"What is it? What's the matter? The others . . . ?"

"They're alive, sir. At least they were the last time he saw them. I think I'll let him tell you. I don't believe I care to hear the story again."

Filled with a mixture of curiosity and foreboding, Gerber pushed through the doorway into the tiny, twelve-bed ward of the dispensary. The only other patient, a Tai striker recovering from an appendix operation, was at the far end.

"Christ! Master Sergeant, you look like death warmed over."

"Damned glad to see you, too, sir," Fetterman answered cheerfully, although his voice was a bit harsh. The sound reminded Gerber of the rattle of an old piece of paper that had been left lying out in the sun too long.

"The doc says you got something you want to tell me."

"Yes, sir. It's about Tyme and Washington."

"Where are they, Tony?"

"VC prison camp near Hong Ngu."

"Hong Ngu? You mean they're still in South Vietnam?"

"Yes, sir. We were captured just about the time Kittredge and the lieutenant stepped into it. When we sprung the ambush, the enemy counterattacked. Must have had seven or eight times as many guys as we did. We had to break contact and escape and evade. We got separated from the main group, and Justin was wounded. I was bandaging him up when the VC put the bag on us."

"You were all captured together?"

"More or less. Washington was trying to help some wounded strikers when they got him. The VC executed the strikers, sir."

"I know," said Gerber. "We found the bodies."

"Captain, Sergeant Krung, was he . . . ?"

"Krung made it okay. He found Sully and brought him in."

Fetterman leaned back and gave a sigh of relief. "Good. I'm glad to hear that." Then he noticed that Gerber had not mentioned the others. "What about Kittredge and the lieutenant's bunch?"

"Steve didn't make it, Tony. I'm sorry. Bromhead came through okay, though. His group took a real beating, but they were able to break contact and get back to camp. He was with the squad that came out to pick you up.''

"Sorry, sir. I don't remember that too well. Thank him for me, will you?"

"Consider it done."

"I'm sorry about Kittredge, too. He was a good man. Never saw a man who could lay a mortar tube like he could. Best heavy weapons man I've seen in ten years with the Special Forces."

Gerber merely nodded. He couldn't see any point just now in telling Fetterman how Kittredge had died. "I'll tell you about it later when I bring you your beer. McMillan says you can have one as soon as you've finished your IVs."

"Damned nuisance, if you ask me," snorted Fetterman, shrugging both arms. "Wouldn't be so bad if he could figure out how to put a couple of beers in the damned things."

"Sorry," said Gerber. "Doc says you'll have to wait." There was a pause, and then Gerber said, "Tony, about Washington and Tyme . . ."

"Yes, sir. Like I said, they marched us all night through the jungle. We were blindfolded most of the time, but I counted pace and had a pretty good idea of where we were. They took us to a camp just a little north and east of Hong Ngu. I confirmed the location when I escaped."

"You escaped? How?" Gerber felt like an idiot. Of course the man had escaped. That was obvious. But for some reason or other it seemed so unlikely that it hadn't fully sunk in yet.

"I had one of those new, plastic-coated escape and evasion maps, a button compass and a small survival kit sewn into the lining of my jungle jacket. The VC missed it when they searched us. There was a time or two when I could have slipped away before we got to the camp, but of course I couldn't do that, sir."

Gerber was confused. "You could have escaped before you got there, but you didn't try? Why in God's name not?"

"I could have slipped away, sir, but not with the others. I had to wait until we got to the camp to find out where it was if we were going to have any chance of rescuing Washington and Tyme."

"You allowed yourself to be taken to the camp so that you could help the others escape?"

"No, sir. So we could go back and rescue them. Tyme would never have made it in an escape attempt, sir. He's too weak. He took a hit in the shoulder and lost a lot of blood. I was hit in practically the same place once, and his was worse. I figured the only thing to do was let them take all of us to the camp so I could pinpoint its location and then bring back help. It's a big camp, sir. Looks like Charlie was figuring on doing a lot of business in the P.O.W. area. They had a lot of cages. I didn't see them, but Tyme said there were two other Americans already there, Rockford or Rock somebody, and a guy named Corbett. Ever hear of them?"

"Don't think so. Did Tyme actually see the other prisoners?"

"No. He overheard the VC talking about them. He said the VC talked like they were planning to shoot them."

"Did they?"

"I don't think so. At least I didn't hear any shots before I left. Tyme thought the camp commander was waiting for word from Hanoi. Boom-Boom was pretty incoherent, but from what I could gather, the executions weren't supposed to take place until today or tomorrow."

Gerber felt sick. The men could already be dead. They might all be dead by now.

"Captain," said Fetterman, "there's something else. The Chinese guy was there."

Gerber stared at him in disbelief. "Come on, Tony. For Christ's sake. The man can't be everywhere. You're becoming obsessed with him. The Chinese probably pulled him out of the area right after that little hunting trip you and Tyme took into Cambodia. We haven't had any reported sightings of Chinese advisors in the last two months. Anywhere in Vietnam."

"Captain, I tell you he was there. I recognized him, and he seemed to recognize me. It was the same man. What's more, they knew everything about us, our names, our ranks, who you were. I'm telling you, sir, it *was* him. And I'll tell you something else. We were set up, and he's the bastard who did it. I don't know how. He must have a spy in the camp or something."

"Only one?" said Gerber cynically. It was well known that the Vietnamese component of the Strike Force was infiltrated with Vietcong agents. Knowing who and proving it was another matter.

Fetterman ignored the comment.

"Captain, the guy was there. He knew me. He knew all about us. We were set up, and he did it. The SOB knows we were after him on the Cambodian raid, and this is his way of getting even. Call me paranoid if you like, but I know what I'm telling you. I can't prove it, but I *know*."

It seemed a pretty farfetched idea, almost as farfetched as the idea they'd put into practice a few months ago when Gerber had sent a hit team into Cambodia to assassinate the Chinese advisor to a group of VC who had been causing them a lot of trouble. Maybe Fetterman was right.

"How did you escape, Tony?"

"It wasn't easy, sir. Like I said, I had the little E and E kit sewn into my jungle jacket. When it got dark and I realized the guards weren't paying any particular attention to us, I sawed my way out of the cage with this."

Fetterman reached over to the tiny nightstand next to his cot and picked up a small knife. It was a piece of electric hacksaw blade that had been ground and sharpened into a small knife blade, with the hacksaw teeth still on the top edge, and a handle of split bamboo, wrapped with wire.

"I made the handle out of one of the bars I cut out of the cage and used part of the wire from the leg irons. Of course, once I got out, I had to find a body to put in the cage, and I had to fix the bamboo bar so they wouldn't notice I was missing."

Gerber stared at Fetterman in amazement. "Of course," he said. "What's this about leg irons?"

Fetterman explained the arrangement of U-shaped pieces and rod and how he had gotten out of them by sliding the U-shaped shackles along the rod, once he could squeeze out of the cage, until he was able to unwire the rod from the stake and slip the shackles off over the end.

"After that I found myself a passing VC and traded places with him," Fetterman concluded matter-of-factly. "With any luck at all, they didn't discover I was missing until this morning. I had to kill two other sentries on the way out, and I suppose they might have noticed that one of them was missing before morning, but I doubt it. Anyway, after I got through their perimeter patrols, I made my way into Hong Ngu and stole some fisherman's boat. I figured that, if the VC did notice I was missing, they'd expect me to make straight for the camp through the jungle so I headed away from camp, and came down the Song Tien Giang to just north of Cho Moi. Then I came overland to the camp, approaching from the southwest rather than the northwest. We've worked that area a lot, and I know the trails. Also figured the VC would be less likely to look for me there."

Gerber shook his head in amazement, then snapped it up suddenly. "Where'd you get the smoke grenade?"

"Oh, that. It was nothing. Slipped into the guards' barracks before I left and took it back from the VC who took it from me. Got my rifle back, too, but I couldn't find Boom-Boom's or Washington's. Picked up three carbines on the way out, but I couldn't carry it all so I destroyed two of them."

"Ah, now, Tony, that's just too much. How could you possibly have known it was your rifle?" said Gerber, grinning.

"I checked the serial number." He paused. "Captain, I wish I had a photograph of your face right now."

Gerber gave a long snort, then both men broke into laughter. When it finally subsided, the conversation turned serious again.

"Tony, I've got about a battalion of men waiting to go get T.J. and Boom-Boom. Can you pinpoint that camp for us on the map?"

"Can but won't," said Fetterman. "Not if you're going in there with a battalion."

"What! Why?"

"Captain, that camp is run by a VC major named Vo. The guy is a real sadist and absolutely loony tunes besides. He talks like a hotel manager, calls the prisoners his guests and refers to torturing them as entertainment. I'm telling you, the guy is as crazy as a March hare. You go trying to put a big-assed air assault into that place, and he'll kill Boom-Boom and Washington for sure. Besides, he's got a couple of hundred men in there with him. Got to have, given the size of the force that hit us and what I could see of the size of the camp. You go in there making noise with a bunch of choppers, and your battalion is likely to find itself up against his battalion. While the two of you are slugging it out, he'll either off the prisoners or slip across the border into Cambodia. It's not all that far away, you know."

"Tony, be reasonable, will you. They'll damned sure hear us coming if we try to walk in with a battalion."

"Yes, sir, that's true. But I don't think they'll hear anything at all until it's too late if you let me take a squad of men in first, say about ten minutes before the helicopters, and spring our boys."

"Master Sergeant, are you out of your mind? You were captured by the Vietcong and escaped. That's your ticket out of here. We're sending you home, man. Back to Mrs. Fetterman and the kids. Your war is over."

"Not yet it's not. Not until I get Boom-Boom out and take care of the Chinese and that bastard Vo."

"You don't seem to understand me, Tony. You are going home."

"And you don't seem to understand me, Captain. I can lead a patrol in there and spring them. I can get them out if they're still alive. Your way, they're dead for sure."

In exasperation Gerber yanked back the sheet and pointed to Fetterman's feet. They had so many bandages wrapped around them that they looked like a poor imitation of Mickey Mouse's feet.

"And just how are you going to do it? How, Sergeant? Answer me that one, will you? How are you going to take a patrol in there with your feet looking like that? In a wheelchair?"

Before Gerber could stop him, Fetterman yanked the IV catheters out of his arms, swung his legs over the side of the cot and stood facing Gerber. The master sergeant's face was etched with pain, but his voice was icily calm when he spoke.

"Are there any more questions, sir?"

"Tony, please," begged Gerber. "Lie down."

"I walked on them this far, sir, and I can walk on them all the way back. Just get me as far as Hong Ngu, and I'll crawl if I have to. I can do it, sir, and I want this one. Please, Mack."

Gerber ran his left hand down the side of his face. His eyes felt as if they were full of sand, and he wanted to cry. He could tell that Fetterman was in pain, but the man was determined not to let it stop him. And he realized something else. It was the first time ever, in their nearly full year together in Vietnam, that Fetterman had called him Mack, despite Gerber's continual assurances that it was okay to do so.

"All right, Master Sergeant," said Gerber. "We'll see what can be done, but that's all I'm promising. It depends on what Mc-Millan says about your fitness for duty. Damn it, Fetterman, at least sit down, will you?"

"Yes, sir. Thank you very much, sir." Fetterman eased himself back down on the edge of the cot.

"What's all the yelling about in here?" asked McMillan, sticking his head in the doorway.

"The captain and I were just having a little discussion," said Fetterman breezily. "He was trying to convince me that my feet hurt, and I was trying to convince him that they're my feet."

"He wants to lead the rescue party going after the others," said Gerber.

"What! Fetterman, you can't be serious!" McMillan exclaimed.

"That's what I told him," Gerber continued. "But he's too much of a bullheaded Apache to listen to reason."

"Aztec, sir. Aztec. Not Apache. We Fettermans have been Aztecs for centuries."

"I give up," said Gerber, throwing up his hands. "You try to talk some sense into him, Doc. I'm going to go out and get that beer for him, and then I'm going to sit down and drink the damned thing myself."

Gerber got up to leave.

"Well, if you two are done *discussing*, the patient has a couple of other visitors. And then the patient's doctor thinks he needs some rest."

"Tell him he's in no shape to be running around the jungle, will you, Doc?" Gerber persisted.

"Fetterman, you're in no shape to go running around the jungle," said McMillan sternly. Then he turned to Gerber. "See how easy it is?"

"Say, Doc," said Fetterman, "remember that time you and I went into Saigon to pick up some medical supplies and you said, 'First let's stop over at the Blue Parrot and see that dancer and have a quick...' Say, Doc, what was her name? I've kind of forgotten, but I think it's all starting to come back to me now. Co Bang, that was it, wasn't it, Doc?"

McMillan cleared his throat noisily. "No, that was not her name. I've never been in the Blue Parrot in my life—it's an off-limits bar as you well know—and anyway, there was plenty of penicillin to spare that month. And so help me, Fetterman, if you ever mention it again and word gets back to Louise Denton, I'll fill your IV bottles full of formaldehyde and saltpeter, and you'll wind up with a limp prick that will last forever."

"Does that mean I can go?" asked Fetterman.

McMillan turned to Gerber and shrugged. "Like he says, Captain, they are his feet."

"I'll be back with the maps," said Gerber sourly. "Then you can show me this great, harebrained scheme of yours."

"Thank you, sir. I knew you'd understand once you realized I have the highest enthusiasm for the mission."

"The highest enthusiasm. Why I ought..." Gerber shut up. He could tell that he'd lost the argument, and he decided that he'd better get out before he lost another one.

"Now, can I show in the other guests?" asked McMillan.

"I'd appreciate it, Doc, if you wouldn't use that term."

McMillan looked puzzled. "All right, visitors, then."

"Male or female?" joked Fetterman.

"One of each, actually."

Now Fetterman looked puzzled.

"Miss Morrow is outside with her camera and notepad in hand," McMillan said with a laugh. "She wants to ask you all sorts of questions about your miraculous escape."

"Oh, no!" groaned Fetterman in mock horror. "The insatiable curiosity of the press. Will they never leave me alone?"

"But first there's someone else."

"Has she got better legs than Morrow? If she has, send her in," quipped Fetterman.

"My guess is that he's got really ugly legs, but I'll bet they're a lot stronger than Morrow's." He turned to shout at the door. "You can come in, now, General."

"Hello, Master Sergeant," said Hull, stepping into the room. "I guess I can't call you corporal anymore, can I?"

The face was older, more creased and gaunt, the head balding like Fetterman's own, but Fetterman would have known the man if he'd bumped into him wearing a disguise on a New York subway.

Fetterman half rose from the cot.

McMillan pushed him back down. "You want to go back out into the field, you stay off your feet for now. Doctor's orders."

"Captain—I mean, General Hull. It's an extreme pleasure to see you again after all these years, sir."

McMillan looked at the two men and was surprised to see that both had wet eyes. He cleared his throat again.

"I've got lots of other patients to tend to," McMillan lied. "So if you two gentlemen will excuse me, I'll leave you alone to talk over old times."

As he went out, he closed the door softly.

17

THE JUNGLE NEAR
HONG NGU

The Huey UH-1D made five landings in five widely spaced LZs west and northwest of Tan Chau shortly before dark. Four of the passengers were dressed in gray-and-black-striped tiger suits. The fifth wore a many pocketed, sleeveless vest of black material over an all-black ninja costume that covered him from head to toe. All five got off at the second LZ, just northwest of Tan Chau, a few hundred yards from the Mekong River.

The men's faces, covered by camouflage makeup paint or the close fitting hood of the ninja suit, were invisible in the darkness, except when one of them smiled briefly, showing a quick glimpse of teeth filed sharply into points.

The men carried a wide variety of unusual weapons with them as they moved quickly into the trees lining the edge of the landing zone. Three Karl Gustav Model 45-B 9 mm submachine guns, widely known as Swedish Ks, with large sound suppressors fitted to the barrels, were augmented by a similarly silenced .45-caliber M-3A1 grease gun, and a likewise quieted Mk IIS Sten gun of Second World War vintage. The man in the ninja suit wore a Czechoslovakian-manufactured Skorpion machine pistol, also suppressed, in a shoulder holster beneath his left armpit. Two of the other men carried silencer-equipped .380-caliber Beretta semiautomatic pistols, the squat 1934 model. A much noisier U.S.-

made M-79 40 mm grenade launcher, a locally made crossbow and a Soviet-made RPD light machine gun, captured a few months earlier from the Vietcong, along with a varied collection of fragmentation, white phosphorus and concussion grenades, rounded out the collection of military oddities.

The ninja carried a few other items familiar only to followers of the martial arts, all of them with the potential to kill silently. He had begun his study of the martial arts in the United States shortly after the Second World War when he was twenty years old and stationed in California with the U.S. Army. Later he had continued his interest in unarmed combat and the arts of kendo, akido, kenjutsu, kung fu, jujitsu, tae kwon do and finally ninjitsu during overseas duty tours with the Army in Honolulu, Korea, Thailand, Okinawa and Japan. At one time he taught hand-to-hand combat to students at the Ranger School in Fort Benning, Georgia. A member of no orthodox martial arts school, he blended his skills and knowledge of pressure points and nerve pathways into a nononsense killing art devoid of the formalized postures and flowery movements that characterized traditional forms and Hong Kong karate movies. He had learned to kill with the pressure of a single finger, and to control his own pain through willpower and Zen philosophy. He was an unlikely-looking karate killer and quite possibly, at that moment, the deadliest man in Southeast Asia. His name was Master Sergeant Anthony B. Fetterman.

No words were spoken by the five men. There was an occasional tap on the shoulder or a nearly invisible gesture of the hand to indicate that someone should go a certain direction or perform a certain task. But as far as speech was concerned, the men might never have realized that language had been invented. They hid, unmoving, just inside the tree line until it was completely dark, then the owner of the crossbow and sharply filed teeth, Sergeant Krung, led them through the woods to a place where they could observe the fishing boats working the evening catch out of the Tan Chau docks.

By 2200 the boats had all been brought in and the fishermen had gone home, except for one elderly gentleman who insisted on remaining to fish off the dock when everyone else had sense enough to go home to bed. It appeared as though he intended to make a night of it.

The old fisherman might perhaps have simply been a dedicated angler or a henpecked husband seeking to escape from his nagging mama-san for the night. Or he might have been a Vietcong agent, set to watch the river for interesting traffic. Fetterman could neither afford to take the chance nor wait for the old man to leave. With Krung and Kepler covering, he silently stalked the man, taking nearly fifteen minutes to cross the open dock area behind the fisherman without making the slightest noise to betray his presence.

When he was directly behind the old man, Fetterman waited patiently for him to bend down, extract a grub from a tin can and rebait his hook. Then, as he straightened to cast the line back into the water, Fetterman snaked an arm around the old man's neck and squeezed, putting pressure on both carotid arteries.

When he felt the man slump into unconsciousness, Fetterman immediately relaxed the pressure of his judo choke. Another few moments of continued pressure, Fetterman knew, would have caused brain damage followed rapidly by respiratory and cardiac arrest. It was not Fetterman's intention to kill an old man who might be nothing more than what he appeared to be. He left the man tied to a corner post of the dock, his hands bound behind him with nylon parachute cord and his shirt stuffed into his mouth for a gag. He would regain consciousness in a few minutes and spend an uncomfortable night, but he would be alive to be found when others came to fish in the morning. Fetterman and his men would be long gone.

When he had satisfied himself that the activity on the dock had not been observed by any late-night passersby, Fetterman signaled the others, who came down to the dock. They searched through the boats tied up there until they found one suitable for their purpose and then helped themselves.

It took nearly two hours to travel the eight miles to Hong Ngu, mainly because they kept in the shadows along the bank on the Tan Chau side until they had passed the island separating the two cities. When they were south of the point of the island, they poled their way across to the Hong Ngu side and hid the boat in a patch of reeds just below the town. After checking their equipment, primarily to make sure that the radios were still operating after the water crossing, they moved into the swamps and jungle to the northeast, heading for the area where Fetterman believed the P.O.W. camp to be located. It would have been a great deal simpler to have had the helicopter insert them below Hong Ngu. It also would have been a great deal noisier.

Almost immediately they encountered a Vietcong patrol but were able to avoid detection by quick action and the use of available tree roots as a backdrop. Twenty minutes later they encountered a second patrol, and a short time after that a third.

"Jesus!" Kepler whispered in Fetterman's ear after the third patrol had passed them by. "I didn't realize there were this many VC in all of Vietnam. Where the hell did all these guys come from?"

"A few may be local guerrillas," Fetterman told him, "but most of these guys are all wearing some sort of uniform. They're Main Force. I would guess that they are from the camp."

"So what are they all doing out here wandering around in the swamps?"

"I would guess," Fetterman answered, "that they are looking for me. They've had time by now to discover I'm gone, try the direct route between here and Triple Nickel and figure out I didn't go that way. Now they're looking for clues closer to home."

"That's a lousy break," whispered Kepler. "The woods are full of them. I don't see how we'll ever get in and out undetected."

"On the contrary," Fetterman replied, "it's an excellent break. It means the camp is still here. They didn't get excited and move the prisoners after I escaped. Watch and learn, Derek, and I'll show you how to become invisible before your enemies' very eyes."

"Great. 'Cause otherwise I don't see how we're going to get in there without being spotted."

"Relax," Fetterman reassured him. "Prison camps are designed to keep people in, not out. You'll see."

In all they encountered six patrols before finally reaching the outer perimeter of the camp. But those patrols were looking for a lone, injured, escaped prisoner, not a well-equipped, well-concealed five-man raiding party. Each time Fetterman's little group was offered ample warning by the noisy approach of the Vietcong patrols. They succeeded in remaining undetected.

At 0200 Kepler used the primary radio to signal the precise location of the P.O.W. camp to Gerber and the main assault force. Then he switched the PRC-10 off. The radios would now be used for communication only in an extreme emergency. They didn't want a stray burst of static giving their position away once they were inside the camp.

Getting in was fairly easy, as Fetterman had predicted. The VC guards, for the most part, were alert for another escaping prisoner, not an infiltrating assault. Two were encountered whose positions made the party's advance awkward, but they were conveniently killed by Anderson and Krung and offered no more problems. The bodies were carefully hidden by submerging them in one of the punji moats, all the stakes of which faced inward, and then they quickly crossed the moat on a hinged plank that Fetterman had assembled and brought along for that purpose.

By 0330 they were in position. They had completed their reconnaissance of the camp, pinpointing Vo's hut, the radio shack with its hand-cranked generator, the one longhouse, which still seemed to contain a few sleeping men, and the prisoner cages. It wasn't hard locating Washington and Tyme. The cells were where Fetterman remembered, and each now had a small kerosene lantern with a leaf shade hung inside the enclosure. An armed guard, who seemed reasonably awake and alert, stood outside each door. While they found many other cages designed to hold prisoners, they found no others that were occupied. Of the other two Americans that Tyme had mentioned to Fetterman there was no sign.

At precisely 0445, Krung shot the guard in front of Washington's cage through the throat with his crossbow.

At the same instant Fetterman snapped a piano wire garrote down over the head of the second guard, crossed the wooden handles over each other as he turned his back toward the guard's and pulled the wire taut, bending forward at the waist to lift the man off his feet as the piano wire cut into the man's throat from bottom to top, front to back. The only sounds were a short clatter as the man dropped his burp gun and a low, burbling noise as his blood flowed out.

Krung and McMillan immediately came forward and opened the cells by using a combination of end and side cutters on the wire closure.

The shackles were quickly cut away with a large set of bolt cutters, and McMillan made a quick assessment of each of the patients, making sure that they were still alive and could be safely moved.

"Fetterman?" Tyme whispered the question hoarsely and with obvious disbelief. "They said you'd been shot."

"Then they're either lousy shots or lousy liars. Be quiet, Boom-Boom. We've come to get you out."

Tyme nodded weakly. "I knew you'd be back."

"Listen, Boom-Boom, we can't find those other two Americans you told me about. Do you know where they are?"

Tyme shook his head. "Sorry. I never saw them. I heard some shots around midmorning. After that Vo came and told me you'd been shot trying to escape. Didn't really believe him because he had too many guys still out looking for you."

"They still are. Come on. Let's get you out of here."

As they loaded Tyme and Washington onto two folding stretchers, Anderson suddenly appeared out of the shadows, the sling of the RPD draped over his mammoth shoulders so that it hung in front of him, a Swedish K in his hands.

"All set on the claymores. Ready anytime you are, Master Sergeant."

Fetterman nodded and glanced at the plastic wristwatch he'd picked up back at camp. The time was exactly 0450. In the distance he could faintly hear the sound of approaching helicopters.

They carried Tyme and Washington to the edge of the small clearing that Fetterman had seen when he had first arrived at the camp, pausing only long enough to permanently ensure the quiet of the two guards in the well-camouflaged hut near it.

Anderson set up the RPD to provide covering fire, should it be necessary.

"Derek, you still got the strobe unit?" asked Fetterman.

"Right here," answered Kepler, "although if it gets much lighter, a smoke grenade will probably work better."

"Okay. You're in charge. If I don't make it back in time for the evac chopper, you get everybody out of here. Don't worry about me. I'll catch a ride back with the main group."

"Just where in the hell do you think you're going?"

"Got a little unfinished business to attend to. I'll be back."

"Fetterman, for Christ's sake . . . Fetterman!"

But Fetterman was gone.

The sound of the helicopters was getting louder. Enough to be plainly heard by anyone who cared to listen. Fetterman moved quickly back into the camp and hurried down the trail. As he did, a VC stepped out into the pathway directly in front of him. Reacting instinctively, Fetterman pulled a shuriken from a pocket. The throw was only about five yards, and the heavy, razor-sharp throwing star embedded itself nicely in the VC's forehead. Fetterman hadn't even broken stride.

Fetterman moved past the guards' barracks and through the camp, past Vo's hut to the radio shack. He stepped quickly up the low step to the doorway. The suppressed M-3 made a low, guttural coughing as he hosed down the interior, killing the two men inside and riddling the radio equipment with bullets.

Fetterman didn't dawdle to admire his handiwork. He changed magazines on the grease gun, then raced back into camp toward Vo's hut. The sound of the helicopters was becoming quite loud now, and people were beginning to come out of their hootches to see what the noise was all about.

As he ran toward Vo's hut, Fetterman caught sight of a flash of familiar khaki and loosed a long burst at it. The Chinese dived back into a hut, and Fetterman tossed two grenades, one fragmentation and the other white phosphorus, in the open doorway behind him. Fetterman couldn't wait to check their effectiveness, but he heard both grenades go off and felt the heat of the WP. A moment later he heard two sharp explosions ahead of him as someone hit a trip wire outside the guards' barracks. The helicopters were beating the air into submission now, and Fetterman could hear the door gunners laying down suppressive fire along the edges of the LZ.

As he reached Vo's hut, Fetterman lobbed his second WP grenade inside, found cover and waited for the blast. The explosion seemed to lift the roof from the hut, setting the entire structure on fire.

A moment later a figure ran from the hut, his clothing aflame, screaming in pain as he beat ineffectually at the burning cloth and pieces of phosphorus with his hands. It was Major Vo. Fetterman watched the spectacle with an abstract detachment until the man fell to the ground and lay still. Then he walked over very calmly and emptied his grease gun into the smoldering corpse.

18

SPECIAL FORCES CAMP
A-555

A very tired Tony Fetterman sat in the team house, finally drinking the beer that McMillan had promised him. His feet were propped up on the table, and they hurt like hell, but he had a curiously warm feeling inside.

Tyme and Washington were on their way to a hospital in Saigon, and Doc McMillan was keeping them company on the trip. They both had a good chance of complete recovery.

Lieutenant Colonel Bates had arrived from B-Team Headquarters, and Gerber was regaling him with the tale of how General Hull had leaped out of the C and C ship when the air assault had inserted, fired twice at a fleeing Cong and had another pop up out of a spider hole directly in front of him only to discover that his carbine had jammed. The general, thinking quickly, had pulled off his own helmet and had beaten the VC to death with it.

"That's the way John Wayne would have done it." Bates laughed.

Gerber didn't bother to tell them that what made it such an excruciatingly funny story was that that was exactly the way that he had done it a month earlier when his M-14 had jammed.

Morrow was there, too, alternately snapping away with her motor-driven 35 mm camera and chugging down large gulps of beer. She paused occasionally to stare at Gerber with a look that made Fetterman feel happy for the captain but a little bit uneasy about the possible consequences.

The mop-up operation had taken the rest of the morning and most of the afternoon but had been a success. They had inflicted heavy casualties on the VC with a confirmed body count of forty-two and had suffered only light casualties themselves. The enemy had been scattered, unable to mobilize reserves or organize to fight effectively with their radio command center knocked out and their commanding officer dead. The VC plan to cut off the head of the American dragon had backfired.

There were only two dark notes. They had been unable to find the two Americans that Tyme had spoken of, and the Chinese had somehow escaped Fetterman once again. No body had been found in the smoking remains of the hut that Fetterman had seen him duck into.

Anderson had tuned in Radio Hanoi, which was blaring out rock tunes, and everybody seemed to be having a good time. Then the music was interrupted by the strains of *Vietnam muon nam*, and the announcer broke in with the evening propaganda newscast. His first story was the announcement that a Captain Humbert Rocque Versace and Sergeant Kenneth M. Roraback had been executed at ten o'clock in reprisal for the execution in Da Nang of three Vietcong suspects.

For a moment everyone was very quiet. Could they have come so close, yet been so far away? Then Fetterman heard the click-whir-click-whir of Morrow's camera as she photographed the stunned faces of the men around her.

For a moment everyone glared at her, then the tension was broken by an insane chuckle from Fetterman.

"Lady," he said, "I thought I was hard, but you are one tough cookie."

"Damn it, I feel for them and their families, too," Morrow protested. "It might have been any of you. But I'm still a reporter. I'm just doing my job."

"Miss Morrow, that's all any of us are doing," said Fetterman.

Then they all laughed.

Because it was good.

GLOSSARY

AC—Aircraft commander. The pilot in charge of the aircraft.

ACTUAL—The actual unit commander as opposed to the radio-telephone operator (RTO) for that unit.

AK-47—Soviet assault rifle used by the North Vietnamese and the Vietcong.

AO—Area of Operation.

AO DAI—Long dresslike garment, split up the sides and worn over pants.

AP ROUNDS—Armor-piercing ammunition.

ARTY—Artillery.

ARVN—Army of the Republic of Vietnam. A South Vietnamese soldier. Also known as Marvin Arvin.

BAR—Browning Automatic Rifle.

BEAUCOUP—Many.

BISCUIT—C-rations or combat rations.

BLOWER—See *Horn*.

BODY COUNT—The number of enemy killed, wounded or captured during an operation. Used by Saigon and Washington as a means of measuring the progress of the war.

BOOM-BOOM—Term used by Vietnamese prostitutes to sell their product.

BOONDOGGLE—Any military operation that hasn't been completely thought out. An operation that is ridiculous.

BUSHMASTER—Jungle warfare expert or soldier skilled in jungle navigation. Also a large deadly snake not common to Vietnam but mighty tasty.

C AND C—Command and control aircraft that circles overhead to direct the combined air and ground operations.

CARIBOU—Cargo transport plane.

CHICOM—Chinese communist.

CHINOOK—Army Aviation twin-engine helicopter. A CH-47. Also known as a shit hook.

CLAYMORE—Antipersonnel mine that fires 750 steel balls with a lethal range of 50 meters.

CLOSE AIR SUPPORT—Use of airplanes and helicopters to fire on enemy units near friendlies.

CO CONG—Female Vietcong.

DAI UY—Vietnamese Army rank equivalent to captain in the U.S. Army.

DAP LOI—Single-shell booby trap, sometimes a 50 mm round, with a nail for a firing pin. Small and virtually undetectable, it could put a round through a trooper's foot.

DCI—Director, Central Intelligence. The director of the Central Intelligence Agency.

DEROS—See *Short-timer*.

DI DI MAU—Vietnamese expression meaning "get the hell out."

DIEN CAI DAU—Vietnamese. Literally "off the wall." Used to refer to a person who is crazy."

DONG—Unit of North Vietnamese money equivalent to about a penny.

FIIGO—Fuck it, I've got my orders.

FIVE—Radio call sign for the executive officer of a unit.

FNG—Fucking new guy.

FRENCH FORT—Distinctive, triangular-shaped structure built by the hundreds by the French.

FUBAR—Fucked up beyond all recognition.

GARAND—M-1 rifle that was replaced by the M-14. Issued to the Vietnamese early in the war.

GARRET TROOPER—Rear-area pogue; a fat cat, someone who doesn't get out and fight in the war.

GUARD THE RADIO—Term that means to stand by in the commo bunker and listen for messages.

GUNSHIP—Armed helicopter or cargo plane that carries weapons instead of cargo.

HE—High-explosive ammunition.

HOOTCH—Almost any shelter, from temporary to long-term.

HORN—Term referring to a specific kind of radio operations that used satellites to rebroadcast messages.

HORSE—See *Biscuit*.

HOTEL THREE—A helicopter landing area at Saigon's Tan Son Nhut Air Force Base.

HUEY—A Bell UH-1D, or its successor, the UH-1H, helicopter, called a Huey because its original designation was HU, but later changed to UH. Also called a Slick.

IN-COUNTRY—Term used to refer to American troops operating in South Vietnam. They were all in-country.

INTELLIGENCE—Any information about the enemy operations. It can include troop movements, weapons capabilities, biographies of enemy commanders and general information about terrain features. It is any information that would be useful in planning a mission.

KABAR—A type of military combat knife.

KEMCHI—Korean foul-smelling cabbage delicacy.

KIA—Killed in action. (Since the U.S. was not engaged in a declared war, the use of the term KIA was not authorized. KIA came to mean enemy dead. Americans were KHA or killed in hostile action.)

KLICK—A thousand meters. A kilometer.

LBJ—Long Binh Jail.

LEGS—Derogatory term used by airborne qualified troops in talking about regular infantry.

LIMA LIMA—Land line. Refers to telephone communications between two points on the ground.

LLDB—Luc Luong Dac Biet. The South Vietnamese Special Forces. Sometimes referred to as the Look Long, Duck Back.

LP—Listening Post. A position outside the perimeter manned by a couple of soldiers to give advance warning of enemy activity.

LZ—Landing zone.

M-14—Standard rifle of the U.S., eventually replaced by the M-16. It fired the standard NATO 7.62 mm round.

M-16—Became the standard infantry weapon of the Vietnam War. It fired 5.56 mm ammunition.

M-79—Short-barreled, shoulder-fired weapon that fires a 40 mm grenade. These can be high explosive, white phosphorus or canister.

MACV—Military Assistance Command, Vietnam. Replaced MAAG in 1964.

MEDEVAC—Medical evacuation. Also called Dustoff. Helicopter used to take the wounded to medical facilities.

MEDCAP—Medical Civilian Assistance Program.

MIA—Missing in action.

NCO—Noncommissioned officer. A noncom. A sergeant.

NEXT—The man who says he's the next to be rotated home. See *Short-Timer.*

NINETEEN—Average age of the combat soldier in Vietnam, in contrast to age twenty-six in the Second World War.

NOUC-MAM—A foul-smelling (to the Americans, at least) fermented fish sauce used by the Vietnamese as a condiment. GIs nicknamed it "armpit sauce."

NVA—North Vietnamese Army. Also used to designate a soldier from North Vietnam.

O-1 BIRD DOG—Single-engine recon aircraft (usually a Cessna) used for forward air control and artillery observation. Their pilots were called FAC pilots.

OD—Olive drab; standard military color.

P-38—Military designation for the small, one-piece can opener supplied with C-rations.

PF—Popular Forces; Vietnamese soldiers drawn from the local population.

P.O.W.—Prisoner of war.

PRC-10—Portable radio.

442 P.O.W.

PRC-25—Standard infantry radio used in Vietnam. Sometimes referred to as the "Prick 25," it was heavy and awkward.

PROGUES—Derogatory term used to describe fat, lazy people who inhabited rear areas, taking all the best supplies for themselves and leaving the rest for the men in the field.

PUFF—A prop plane carrying enough flares to floodlight a mile radius and capable of firing 6,000 rounds per minute. Also called Puff the Magic Dragon and Spooky.

PULL PITCH—Term used by helicopter pilots that means they are going to take off.

PUNGI STAKE—Sharpened bamboo hidden to penetrate the foot, sometimes dipped in feces.

R AND R—Rest and relaxation. The term came to mean a trip outside of Vietnam where the soldier could forget about the war.

RF STRIKERS—Local military forces recruited and employed inside a province. Known as Regional Forces.

RINGKNOCKER—Graduate of a military academy. It refers to the ring worn by all graduates.

RP—Rally point.

RPD—7.62 mm Soviet light machine gun.

RTO—Ratiotelephone operator. The radio man of a unit.

RULES OF ENGAGEMENT—The rules that told the American troops when they could fire and when they couldn't. Full Suppression meant that they could fire all the way in on a landing. Normal Rules meant that they could return fire for fire received. Negative Suppression meant that they weren't to shoot back.

SAPPER—Enemy soldier used in demolitions. Used explosives during attacks.

SIX—Radio call sign for the unit commander.

SHIT HOOK—Name applied by troops to the Chinook helicopter because of all the "shit" stirred up by the massive rotors.

SHORT—Term used by a GI in Vietnam to tell all who would listen that his tour was almost over.

SHORT-TIMER—Person who had been in Vietnam for nearly a year and who would be rotated back to the World soon.

When the DEROS (Date of estimated return from overseas) was the shortest in the unit, the person was said to be "Next."

SKS—Simonov 7.62 mm semiautomatic carbine.

SMG—Submachine gun.

SOI—Signal Operating Instructions. The booklet that contained the call signs and radio frequencies of the units in Vietnam.

SOP—Standard operating procedure.

STEEL POT—Standard U.S. Army helmet. The steel pot was the outer metal cover.

1077—Police call code indicating negative contact.

TAI—Vietnamese ethnic group living in the mountainous regions.

THREE—Radio call sign of the operations officer.

THREE CORPS—Military area around Saigon. Vietnam was divided into four corps areas.

THE WORLD—The United States.

TOC—Tactical operations center.

TWO—Radio call sign of the intelligence officer.

VC—Vietcong. Also called Victor Charlie (phonetic alphabet) or just Charlie.

VIETCONG—Contraction of Vietnam Cong San. A guerrilla member of the Vietnamese Communist movement.

VIETCONG SAN—Vietnamese Communists. A term in use since 1956.

VIETMINH—Vietnamese who fought the French; forerunner of the Vietcong.

VNAF—South Vietnamese Air Force.

WIA—Wounded in action.

WILLIE PETE—WP, white phosphorus. Called smoke rounds. Also used as antipersonnel weapons.

XO—Executive officer of a unit.

ZAP—To ding, pop caps or shoot.

Gerber knew the man

He was the Chinese officer they had been chasing for a year. The one who had marked them for death more than once. The man who had failed each time he ran into Gerber's Special Forces squad.

He was shorter than Gerber had expected. In his mind the officer had taken on gigantic proportions. The man stepped into the room and pointed the pistol at the American's head.

"If I had any intelligence at all," the Oriental said, "I would shoot you dead this minute."

For a moment everything seemed to stand still. Gerber was afraid to move. He felt closer to death than he ever had before because he knew that the officer was right. The quickest, smartest thing to do was shoot him. If the situation was reversed, Gerber doubted he would hesitate.

Instead of shooting him, the officer walked toward the desk. He sat behind it, then placed his pistol on the top. Indicating the chairs opposite, he spoke again.

"Sit down, Captain Gerber, and let us talk about Vietnam, the war and your death."

VIETNAM: GROUND ZERO
UNCONFIRMED KILL

ERIC HELM

A GOLD EAGLE BOOK
London · Toronto · New York · Sydney

All the characters in this book have no existence outside the imagination of the Author, and have no relation whatsoever to anyone bearing the same name or names. They are not even distantly inspired by any individual known or unknown to the Author, and all the incidents are pure invention.

All Rights Reserved. The text of this publication or any part thereof may not be reproduced or transmitted in any form or by any means, electronic or mechanical, including photocopying, recording, storage in an information retrieval system, or otherwise, without the written permission of the publisher.

This book is sold subject to the condition that it shall not, by way of trade or otherwise, be lent, resold, hired out or otherwise circulated without the prior consent of the publisher in any form of binding or cover other than that in which it is published and without a similar condition including this condition being imposed on the subsequent purchaser.

ISBN 0 373 62703 3 (Pocket edition)

*First published in Great Britain
in pocket edition by Gold Eagle 1987*

© Eric Helm 1986

*Australian copyright 1986
Philippine copyright 1986
Pocket edition 1987*

**This OMNIBUS EDITION 1988
ISBN 0 373 57467 3**

8810
Made and printed in Great Britain

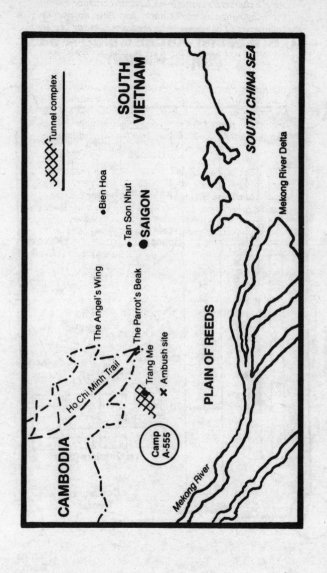

U.S. Special Forces Camp A-555
(Triple Nickel)

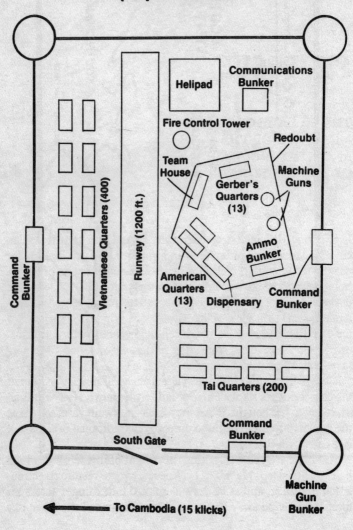

PROLOGUE

THE VILLAGE OF TRANG ME, SOUTH OF THE ANGEL'S WING, WEST OF THE CAMBODIAN BORDER

U.S. Army Special Forces Sergeant First Class Ian McMillan crouched in a stand of bamboo and watched. He was looking for movement among the collection of mud hootches, fences of woven branches and broken-down water buffalo pens that made up the darkened village. Since he had scattered his patrol of twelve Vietnamese strikers in a loose defensive ring an hour earlier, a little after dusk, he had seen no movement and heard nothing unusual except for the rustle of leaves and symphony of sound from nocturnal creatures.

The village, only a hundred meters ahead of him, was quiet as the few residents slept. There shouldn't be any activity until almost dawn, he thought. Then the mama-sans would awaken, light the cooking fires and begin to prepare the traditional breakfast of rice cakes and fish heads.

McMillan rose slowly, taking the weight off his left leg, which had gone to sleep. He flexed his knee, trying to restore the circulation in his leg, and as he drew a crooked index finger across his forehead to wipe away the sweat, his palm grazed the three-day growth on his face. Then he slipped back down and relaxed, keeping his eyes focused on the Vietnamese hootches.

But he wasn't really seeing anything. His mind had glided back to his four-day, in-country R and R taken at the Special Forces compound in Nha Trang. He had had a choice of a couple of places, but Louise Denton had been in Nha Trang and she had been excited about the chance to see him again.

In fact, she had been so happy about the opportunity that she had promoted a jeep and met him at the airfield, anxious for the C-130 to land and taxi. Even before it had stopped moving, she drove out on the field while a master sergeant stood near the tower and screamed at her.

The spinning propellers threw swirls of red dust that blew toward the terminal building; then the troop doors opened and the passengers began deplaning. Denton positioned her jeep so that McMillan could not miss it, but when he failed to appear among the disembarking crowd, she was afraid, she had told him later, that she had misunderstood his instructions. He was the last one out.

As his feet hit the blistering PSP, he turned and yelled something up to the flight crew. Then, carrying his duffel bag in his left hand and with his M-14 slung over his shoulder, he held up his right hand to his eyes to shade them from the bright, early-afternoon sun.

Denton roared up, skidded to a stop in a tiny cloud of dust and yelled, "Hey, soldier, want a ride?"

McMillan looked around, pretending that she was talking to someone behind him. Seeing no one there, he pointed to himself and said, "You talking to me?"

"Yeah. I'm talking to you. You want a ride or not?"

He tossed his bag into the back of the jeep, shrugged his rifle from his shoulder to place it beside his duffel, climbed in the passenger's side and put a foot up on the dash. He turned to look at her and said, "Yeah. I want a ride."

Without another word she slammed the jeep into gear, missing first once and then grinding the gears loudly before she roared off the field. As she sped past the master sergeant, who tried to yell at her again, she flipped him the finger.

"You got to watch out for these sergeants," she shouted over the whine of the jeep's engine and the rush of the wind. "Think they run the army."

"Yeah," agreed McMillan.

Denton drove off the base and after a few minutes they approached a run-down building. "I took the liberty of getting you a room in the Jockey Club." She indicated the hotel with a nod of her head. "Lots of Green Berets hang out around here. I don't like it much, but it'll give us some privacy, and I figured we could put up with it for a few days."

Before he got out of the jeep, McMillan stared at the place. It was a relatively small building with a decided French flavor. The facade was flat with dozens of ornate windows, many of them without screens and nearly all of them open. The old stone was weathered to a dirty brown that contrasted with the rich tans of the beach behind the building. Dark streaks ran down the front where the monsoons had washed pitch from the roof. On the ground floor a porch led into the building.

McMillan could see a couple of Vietnamese girls in exceptionally short skirts lounging around in what passed for a lobby. He could tell from their attire that they were hookers. He shifted his gaze to Denton, whose fatigue shirt had its sleeves and a couple of buttons missing. She was wearing shorts cut off from fatigue pants and scuffed, gray combat boots. McMillan found her much more sexy in her ragged, sweat-stained clothes than he did the Vietnamese in their short skirts and skintight blouses.

"This may not be such a great idea," he said.

She turned off the engine. "Why not? We won't be bothered here."

"Looks like a pretty seedy joint."

"Well, I understand that it has hot and cold running water and electric lights that work most of the time. And you can get a passable meal."

McMillan looked at the hotel again and said, "Okay, if you don't have a problem with it, I guess I don't, either."

"Why don't you get checked in officially and meet me on the beach?"

It took McMillan fifteen minutes to get a key, retrieve his luggage and rifle from the jeep, then climb the stairs to the room. It was small, and made even more so by a double bed that occupied its center. Four large posts rose from each corner of the bed, stopping just short of the ceiling; they had been designed to hold the thick OD mosquito netting. An oak wardrobe with a hole punched in one of the doors, maybe by some drunken GI, McMillan figured, was jammed between the shaded windows, which were closed and made the room extremely hot and dark. A fan suspended from the ceiling turned lazily but did little to dissipate the heat. McMillan wondered why the Jockey Club's operators kept these windows closed, since there wasn't anything worth stealing. The bathroom contained a toilet with its tank resting on top of a pipe that traveled up the wall. From the right side of the reservoir hung a pull chain with a large ring attached to it. Along another wall stood a rust-stained tub on clawed feet, and there was no sign of towels or toilet paper.

McMillan dumped his duffel on the bed and set his M-14 in a corner so that it was almost out of sight. Then he moved back to the bed and opened the bag. He rummaged through it until he found some of his civilian clothes and changed into his beach wear. Finally he shut the bag and stored it on the bottom shelf of the wardrobe. McMillan had thought about taking a quick shower, but he wanted to see Louise too badly to wait any longer. He left the hotel wearing some swimming trunks he had bought during one of his trips to Saigon, a boonie hat to keep the sun out of his eyes and rubber shower shoes to protect his feet from the hot sand.

Denton was sitting on an OD towel on the beach, watching the surf. Wordlessly McMillan dropped beside her and began to study her carefully.

Her tan had darkened a little since he had seen her before Nha Trang. Her red hair, damp and slightly curly from sweat, now hung below her shoulders, and beads of perspiration glistened on her upper lip. She had kicked off her boots, which she had obviously worn because she had to drive a jeep.

Squinting, McMillan shifted his gaze to the calm waters of the South China Sea and the azure sky above it. There were some storm clouds building to the east, but they would probably stay out to sea. A couple of birds windmilled about high overhead.

"When do you have to go back on duty?" he asked.

"Not until after you leave," she said without looking at him.

"How in the hell did you manage that?"

She turned and smiled. "Major Acalotto seemed sympathetic to my needs. Said to take a few days off and have a good time. Now how long are you going to keep me on this beach?"

McMillan reached over and took her hand. "I've seen enough water to last me for a couple of days. Let's go inside."

"I thought you'd never ask," she said, getting to her feet.

Once in the room, Denton moved to the window, pulled up the shades and then the window itself. She turned and began unbuttoning her shirt. "We should get a little breeze off the ocean."

McMillan was still near the door. He leaned against the wall and watched as she slowly stripped. She did it casually, but managed to put a lot of suggestion into it. When she was down to brief panties, he felt like applauding.

"Well," she said, moving to the bed, "You going to stand there all day?" She raised an eyebrow in question and then, watching his face, slowly rolled the panties down her thighs.

McMillan moved across the floor and took her in his arms. She had straightened with her panties still at her knees. She moved her legs, and they fell to the floor. McMillan lifted her and deposited her on the bed. As he crawled on with her, she reached up and slipped her thumbs into the waistband of his trunks. When he was free of them, he moved closer to her, leaned down and fiercely kissed her hungry mouth.

"I'm sorry about this," she whispered, "but I've missed you. I've wanted you."

"Nothing to be sorry about," he said, moving closer. "Nothing at all."

A sudden crashing in the bush nearby, as if some small night animal had sensed a human presence, brought McMillan out his reverie. He blinked a couple of times to clear the perspiration from his eyes, then removed the canvas flap that covered the luminescent dial of his watch to check the time.

It was twenty minutes before sunup, and McMillan was beginning to worry. He felt that something was wrong in the village but didn't know exactly what it was. It seemed as if the settlement were deserted, that the residents had abandoned it during the night, although that couldn't be true. He had seen the villagers the night before, and no one had stirred since sunset.

He was loathe to dismiss his thoughts about Louise and his leave in Nha Trang but knew that he had better concentrate on his surroundings. It wasn't a good idea to let thoughts of women or home or anything else intrude while on patrol. In fact, he shouldn't have let his mind wander as far as it had.

Still, something gnawed at his gut. Without thinking about it, he slipped his combat knife from its sheath. He couldn't explain that move, either, because the M-16 he held was the deadlier of the two weapons. But it was also noisier.

He turned his head slowly so that he could scan the jungle around him. He strained his eyes as he peered between the broad leaves of the bushes and among the teak, mahogany and palm trees, trying to see anything as the sky began to brighten and the ground changed from black to light grays enshrouded by early-morning mists. He thought he detected a slight movement, but with a steady breeze stirring the bush, he couldn't be sure. Suddenly he was uncomfortable. Not with the humidity of the Vietnamese jungle or the heat of the early morning, but the feeling that there were enemy soldiers nearby.

Without warning, a VC dropped onto McMillan's back and struggled to shove a knife into his chest, but the Special Forces sergeant was faster. He released his M-16, shrugged his shoulder, grabbing the man's wrist and flipping him to the ground. In the same motion McMillan's knife flashed, nearly severing the enemy's head in a splash of blood that stained his sleeve. McMillan paused then, breathing hard, his heart hammering in his chest and the breath rasping in his throat.

A second VC leaped, but McMillan caught the movement out of the corner of his eye. He spun to meet his adversary, scrambling to his feet as he turned. He grabbed the man behind the neck and jerked him forward. The Vietcong's arms shot out straight, elbows locked and braced against McMillan's shoulders. The sergeant dropped to his knees, snagging his attacker's belt and yanking him forward.

The enemy soldier lost his balance and fell forward, impaling himself on McMillan's knife. He twisted the blade and forced it upward, slicing through his opponent's abdomen almost to the breastbone. The man shrieked, an errie sound in the morning stillness, and fell to his knees, grabbing at his stomach, trying to hold in his guts as they spilled out of the open wound. He pawed at them, his face turning pale as blood gushed from his belt to his thighs. He groaned low in his throat and fell forward onto the pile of steaming intestines.

McMillan sprang to his feet, staring at the back of the dead man's head, noticing the telltale stubble where the razor had cut the hair on his neck, which identified him as a VC soldier. He glanced at his blood-covered hand as a third VC came at him. The soldier leaped, slamming into McMillan and knocking him to his side.

A fourth VC, who had been crouched near the edge of the fight, slashed at McMillan when he fell. The swipe missed everything vital but cut McMillan on the upper arm, and the sudden pain, dulled by the adrenaline pumping through him, seemed to slow the action to a snail's pace. McMillan reached out with one hand to stop his fall and lost his knife as he hit the ground. As he tried to roll, he grabbed his M-16 and swung it up. But the VC stepped to the side of the barrel, snatching it and trying to wrench it free as he kicked at McMillan's crotch.

McMillan turned and took the blow on the thigh. He twisted and tried to rise so that he could get a clean shot at the enemy; but he felt a pressure in his back that blossomed into pain as a hot liquid splashed down his side. Ignoring the searing agony, he jerked the rifle to free it from the grasp of the VC, realizing that the weapon was his only chance of survival; however, the lightweight barrel bent under the strain. McMillan struggled to his feet, aware now that he was bleeding profusely. Light-headed, he swung the rifle around and pulled the trigger. Nothing happened.

Hearing movement behind him, McMillan whirled to face a new threat. He clubbed the man there with the useless rifle. The VC dropped to his knees, but before McMillan could turn again, he heard a shot. He was aware of fire in his side as if a white-hot poker had been jammed against his bare skin. There was a buzzing in his head, and he thought that his heart was going to burst.

Something hit him in the back again, the blow like a sledgehammer in the spine, and everything began to fade. He didn't realize that he was falling forward and didn't put out his hands to break the fall.

His last thought was of Louise and how upset she would be not to get another letter from him. He wanted her to know that it wasn't his fault. He wanted to shout something, a warning to the men with him, but didn't have the strength. As the blood pumped from his wound, he didn't know that he was dying.

1

The party being held in the team house at the Special Forces camp was rather subdued. The team house, a hootch that served as day-room, mess hall and briefing room, was made of plywood, screen and sandbags, and topped by a corrugated tin roof. Tables with four chairs each were scattered around the dirty plywood floor. An old, unreliable refrigerator stood next to the hootch's entrance, and a bar that separated the kitchen from the rest of the hootch dom-inated one side of the room.

Each of the men not on duty held a can of beer, and there were empties already stacked high on one of the tables. No one talked much and no one laughed at all. It was too soon after they had freed their friends from a POW camp, recovered the body of another of their friends after he had been forced to call artillery in on himself, and too soon after a series of ambushes had been directed at them.

Robin Morrow, the journalist that a press-loving general in Sai-gon had saddled them with, sat by herself, one can in her hand and another on the table in front of her. Blond hair hung to her shoul-der blades and was brushed into bangs that tickled her eyebrows. She was tall and slender with green eyes, straight even teeth and an infectious grin. But right now she was as solemn as the others because she had been on the camp long enough to get to know each of the men.

Captain MacKenzie K. Gerber, wearing his last clean set of jungle fatigues, the sweat stains just beginning to appear under his arms and in the center of his back, sat across the room, as far away from her as possible. He cast an occasional glance in her direction, marveling at her resilience. On the whole she seemed to be almost untroubled by the experiences of the past month or so. He, on the other hand, felt responsible for everything that had happened. It had been his decision that had put the plans in motion and had caused the deaths and the captures of some of the team members.

As Gerber watched, Lieutenant Jonathan Bromhead, the team's executive officer, entered. Bromhead was a tall, thin kid who still retained his freckle-faced look of innocence, even after completing nearly a year's tour in Vietnam. He studied the silent group briefly, then moved directly to the beer tub. He fished one out of the cold water and then ambled toward Robin Morrow. He crouched in front of her so that he could look up into her eyes.

"How's it going?"

She smiled and shrugged. "Kind of a dead party."

"Yeah, I see what you mean," he answered, looking around. He reached out and touched her bare knee. "You okay?"

"Johnny, you don't have to be so concerned. I'm not going to break," she nearly snapped. "Okay?"

Without a word he reached for the church key that she wore on a chain around her neck. She bowed her head slightly so that he could open his beer.

"Okay, so what are we going to do to liven up this group?"

Robin was trying to watch Gerber without his knowing it. She let her eyes drop back to Bromhead. "I don't know. Maybe some music?"

"Yeah! Music. I'll go get my radio and see if AFVN is still on the air. Who knows what we might hear."

"Good idea." She watched the young Green Beret officer almost run from the team house in his enthusiasm. She thought he was a good-looking young man and could tell that he liked her. She wished that she could return his affection, but there was something about him. Maybe it was just his youth. He seemed to exude self-confidence, sure that he had the answers to everything but that no one would listen to him. There were only two sides to an issue in Bromhead's mind. He saw no shades of gray.

As Bromhead disappeared, Morrow got up and slowly walked across the floor. She stopped and said something to Fetterman, the diminutive team sergeant who alternately claimed an Aztec heritage and a Blackfoot Sioux ancestry, then continued until she was standing in front of Gerber. Her bare midriff, where the tails of her khaki shirt were knotted, was right in front of his face. He pretended that he hadn't seen her coming.

Without looking up, Gerber said, "When did you want to go back to Saigon?"

Her immediate impulse was to dump the beer on his head, but she reined in her anger. She jerked a chair away from the table and flopped into it.

"How long are you going to act like this?" she demanded.

"Act like what?" he said, genuinely confused.

"Oh, never mind. I suppose you all will eventually learn that you can still talk to me. I don't hold any of you responsible for what happened. I'm the one who demanded that I be allowed to ride with the convoy. I'm the one who wanted to watch as the villagers built the school. If it hadn't been for that, I would never have been in the middle of that ambush. Hell, if it's anyone's fault, it's mine. I wouldn't leave when I had the chance and then insisted on riding with the trucks rather than fly in with the helicopters."

Before Gerber had a chance to reply, Bocker entered. He was the team's communications sergeant and spent most of his time in the heavily sandbagged commo bunker that held the radios, field phones that tied into the network out of Saigon, and the tactical situation maps. He held up an envelope so that Gerber could see it and dodged around the others.

"Got the rest of the mail over at the commo bunker," Bocker said. "Afternoon chopper brought it in a while ago. This one looked official. I think it's the one you've been waiting for."

"Where'd Johnny go?" Gerber directed the question to Morrow.

"Went to find his radio to see if we couldn't liven up this group. God, I've never seen a deader bunch. Everyone just sitting around swilling beer as fast as they can." She added, "Well, I'll get even. As soon as the music starts, Mack, I expect you to dance with me."

He was about to tell her that he couldn't and then had a better idea. "You'll owe the first dance to Captain Bromhead." Gerber nodded and raised his voice to include the others. "I've just received confirmation of Johnny's promotion to captain."

"He doesn't know?" asked Morrow.

"He knows it's coming, but he doesn't know when."

"All right." She clapped her hands and rubbed them together. "Now we've got something to celebrate."

Gerber suddenly saw the advantage. The party had seemed like a good idea, but no one was really in a festive mood. Too much had happened. But now, with everyone trying to make Bromhead feel good about his promotion, they would loosen up. Maybe with luck they would be so busy trying to make sure Bromhead had a good time that they would forget everything themselves. Maybe it would work out.

"No one say anything when he returns. We'll kind of spring it on him," ordered Gerber.

Fetterman nodded his approval of the announcement. "The lieutenant's a good man. He deserves it."

"Make that the captain," Gerber reminded him.

"Of course," said Fetterman, grinning. "And of course, now has to pay for all this."

"Sully," said Gerber, addressing his senior demolitions expert, Staff Sergeant Sully Smith, "hotfoot it over to my hootch and see if you can find that bottle of Beam's I have stashed away. This seems like a good time to break it open."

"Right, Captain." Smith slid to a halt near the door. "Say, you wouldn't want some fireworks for the celebration, would you?"

At first Gerber was going to point out that a series of explosions on a military base in Vietnam might confuse some of those not in on the celebration but then decided that he had to let the reins go. Anything to break the mood.

"Just what do you have in mind, Sully?"

"Nothing too spectacular, sir. Maybe a couple of star cluster flares, a parachute flare or two, some tracers and three or four willie petes from the mortars."

"Arrange it," Gerber said. He smiled and added, "But don't use too much of the camp's ordnance. And as a courtesy let Captain Minh in on the gag."

For a spontaneous celebration, it was coordinated beautifully. Smith got back with the Beam's before Bromhead returned with the radio. As soon as the sergeant dropped off the booze, he ran out again.

Bromhead noticed that something had changed during the few minutes he had been gone. The moment he entered, he help up a package that had arrived on the mail chopper. He shouted over the noise that was bubbling around him, "You're not going to believe this." When no one noticed him, he yelled again, "You're not going to believe this!"

Bromhead held up a plastic bag, waving it like a banner. "My folks finally came through. I got the spark plugs for the boat."

"What boat?" asked Fetterman, momentarily forgetting the speedboat they had stolen a couple of months earlier, which now rested at the bottom of the Mekong River.

"Our patrol boat. It would be great, if we still had it."

He tossed the bag of spark plugs onto the table and crouched to plug in the radio, then turn it on. Almost before he could get back to his feet, Morrow was beside him asking if he wanted to dance.

The last thing he wanted was to be the center of attention. But he wanted an excuse to hold Morrow so he pretended that they were alone.

As the music ended, Gerber walked up to him and said, "Let's step outside for a minute."

Bromhead didn't know what to make of the order but followed anyway. He noticed that the rest of the Special Forces men were also leaving the team house. When the last of them was standing in the fading light of the evening sun, there was a pop to the right followed by six others. Overhead, a green star cluster flare exploded. Even before it burned out, a red one burst, followed closely by more red and green so that it seemed that the heavens had broken into plumes of color.

Then a single M-60 opened fire, the red tracers stitching the sky. It was joined by a second and a third, the rounds crisscrossing upward. M-16s, apparently loaded only with tracers, joined in until it looked as if the whole east section of the camp was shooting, a crimson waterfall climbing upward instead of cascading to the ground. From the corners came the hammering of the .50-caliber machine guns, their tracers defining the edges of the waterfall.

From the mortar pits came the unmistakable pop of the weapons firing. Moments later white phosphorus explosions dotted the horizon, the brilliant flashes of fire splintering into flaming debris that rained into the rice fields.

When the parachute flares, followed by more red tracers from the .50-cals, exploded, Bromhead said, "What's all this?"

"You haven't figured it out?"

"No, sir."

Gerber unfolded the paper he had received earlier. "Got this in the mail, *Captain*."

"Cap— It came? It really came?"

Fetterman, who had had the presence of mind to carry the bottle of Beam's outside, opened it and said, "A celebration drink?"

Bromhead grasped the bottle, drank from it, then handed it to Gerber, who followed suit. When everyone, including Morrow, had taken a swig, the bottle was returned to Bromhead, who took a final swallow, emptying it.

"God, that's smooth," he said.

At that moment the heavens seemed to open up again. Gerber knew that Sully had given the order to start the fireworks, which were purchased in Saigon weeks earlier. Giant bursts of color ranging from deep red to golden yellow to emerald green exploded over the camp, lighting it in flickering, multihued, dancing glows. For nearly five minutes the sky exploded into a riot of color.

"Now for the bad news." Gerber turned to watch more of the flares and tracers leap skyward as the last of the fireworks burned out. "With your promotion will come a new duty assignment. You'll probably receive orders within the next few days to a week."

"Well, sir—" Bromhead grinned despite himself "—I was afraid of that, but I guess I must continue upward."

"Hardly a speech about missing old friends and mixed emotions," said Fetterman.

"Yeah, don't get all mushy on us, Lieuten—ah, Captain," said Anderson.

Morrow edged closer to Bromhead and took his hand. "Congratulations, Captain. You deserve it."

"Don't I get a kiss?"

"Of course." She got up on her tiptoes and kissed him, forcing her tongue into his mouth.

Bromhead was pleasantly surprised and responded with enthusiasm while the team stood around, at first watching in silence and then with wild cheers.

Before the shouts ended, Smith ran over. "That about exhausts the show," he reported.

Gerber, ignoring both Morrow and Bromhead, said, "Let's get back inside."

"Ah, in a moment, Captain," said Sully. "I said it about exhausts the show. I've got one more surprise."

"Let's have it," growled Gerber.

Taken aback at Gerber's new tone, Smith shot him a quick glance. "You okay, Captain?" he asked quietly.

Gerber turned his gaze on the NCO. He nodded almost imperceptibly. "Sorry, Sully. I'm just a little depressed about losing my exec, and I'm more than a little worried about Ian's patrol."

"You ready?"

"Okay, do it, Sully. Do it."

Smith picked up the tiny generator that would detonate the explosives he had rigged. He turned the handle three times to ensure a powerful current, then swiveled his head to watch. The first explosion wasn't too impressive, but it detonated a willie pete round that threw brightly burning magnesium high into the sky. At the same time several barrels of foogas erupted into gigantic orange fireballs, illuminating the ground almost to the horizon.

This fiery panorama was punctuated with the flat bangs of detonating C-4, the shock and heat waves hitting about the same time.

Gerber took an involuntary step backward. "Wow!"

"Yes, sir. Wow."

"Come on, let's go inside," Gerber said.

The party was finally in full swing, with everyone now chattering animatedly and having a good time. Morrow had given up dancing with the men and was alone in the corner, swaying to the music and clutching a beer in each hand. Foam ran down her arms, and she tried to lick it off without losing the beat of the music. Bromhead sat nearby, watching her.

Bocker had to miss the party because it was his turn for radio watch. He hesitated at the door, saw Gerber and walked over to him.

"Sorry to bother you, sir. Thought you'd want to know that McMillan has missed another radio check."

"You think there's a problem?"

"Well, sir, McMillan is pretty good about sticking to the schedule. I don't think he'd let a broken radio keep him from calling in. I mean, he'd get word to us somehow."

"Well, I'm not worried yet. We've had this happen before, and nine times out of ten it's because the radio broke."

"Yes, sir. Just thought I'd let you know that McMillan was out of touch."

"Thank you, Galvin. If you hear anything, please let me know."

Across the room Bromhead was trying to convince Morrow that they should leave. He could see that she was nearly soaking wet from the exertion of her dancing. Her hair hung damply, and she had unbuttoned her shirt all the way. She had even rolled her shorts higher, trying to cool herself.

"At least there is a breeze outside," Bromhead told her.

Morrow picked up a new can of beer and said, "Let's go see how Mack is doing. He's been sitting there by himself long enough."

Bromhead didn't really like the idea but agreed.

As they approached the table, Captain Minh, the Vietnamese camp commander and Gerber's counterpart, entered. He stopped at the door only long enough to spot Gerber.

"I say," said Minh, his British accent sounding completely out of place in the American camp, "some of our chaps are returning, saying they were ambushed. Thought you might want to meet them at the gate."

"You mean McMillan's patrol."

"That's right."

"Oh, shit." He looked at Bromhead. "We're going to the gate. You stay here and keep the party rolling for a couple of minutes. I think it's going to be bad news."

"I'll go with you, Captain," said Morrow.

Gerber shook his head. "Why don't you wait here, Robin. It'll be for the best."

2

THE SOUTH GATE OF
U.S. ARMY SPECIAL
FORCES CAMP A-555

As Gerber approached the gate, an opening in the south wall flanked by sandbagged bunkers containing .50-caliber and M-60 machine guns, he could see the men of the patrol as they stood waiting for their officers and NCOs. Five feet inside the gate a couple of them sat on the sandbagged wall, which was a second line of defense. They were clutching their weapons with the butts resting on the ground between their feet.

One soldier was rummaging through his rucksack, which lay in the red dust of the compound. Bags of rice and fish rations, a clean shirt and dry socks were scattered on the ground near him.

The men were all carefully looking at the six strands of concertina wire that surrounded the camp or the bunkers near the gate or their own equipment. Even though it was now dark, the full moon threw a dim light over the whole camp, and Gerber could see the Vietnamese strikers trying to ignore a poncho-wrapped body lying in the dirt. What he couldn't see scared him more. There was obviously no American standing with the Vietnamese.

Minh, walking beside Gerber, knew what he was thinking. "Not to worry, Captain. Your chap is probably heading for the team house, old boy," he said.

Gerber glanced out the corner of his eye at the shorter officer and knew he didn't believe it, either. Instead, Minh hurried forward, looking for one of his sergeants.

Before they had gotten very close, one of the strikers said in poor English, "I sorry about this."

Then Minh was there, speaking rapidly in Vietnamese, asking questions, but the speech was too fast for Gerber to follow. He could pick up a couple of words but couldn't really understand what was being said. Instead, Gerber moved to the body and crouched beside it. Without having to look, he could tell that it would be McMillan. There was a stained green beret lying next to it.

Carefully Gerber lifted the corner of the poncho so that he could see the face of the dead man. McMillan looked amazingly peaceful, as if he didn't have a care in the world. There was a dark smudge on his chin, but in the dim light from the moon, Gerber couldn't tell if it was dirt or blood.

Gerber opened the poncho farther looking for the wounds, but he couldn't find them. There was a large stain on the side of McMillan's fatigue jacket, and Gerber thought that it was blood. Finally he looked up at Minh, who had stopped talking.

"What the hell happened?"

Minh shrugged as if he didn't know what to say. In a quiet voice he said, "I believe the VC jumped them just before sunup. No one heard anything until Sergeant McMillan fell. By the time anyone could do anything, the VC were gone."

Gerber didn't speak. He just stared.

"I know what you're thinking, old boy. But these chaps didn't let it happen. They heard nothing. They're good boys."

Gerber closed the poncho and then stood. "I know it, Captain. I wasn't really thinking that they could have saved him. I know they would do everything they could."

As they turned to head back to the team house, Gerber stooped long enough to pick up McMillan's beret. "We better tell the others," Gerber said, trying to mask his emotions. But there was a slight tremor in his voice.

It was strange. He kept losing men, but he never got used to it. Maybe it was because the unit was so small that they got to know each other too well. A general commanding a division couldn't possibly know each of the twelve to fourteen thousand men in his unit. If some of them or a thousand of them or even five thousand of them died, the general would see it only as numbers on a chart or names listed on the casualty reports. Gerber knew each of his men very well.

Somehow it seemed worse now because they were so close to rotating home. It was only a couple of weeks until they would all be back in the World and the heat and misery of Vietnam would be unpleasant memories. If only Gerber hadn't felt the need to send McMillan out on patrol, then things would be different.

Gerber checked himself, realizing that he shouldn't accept any blame. Just because they were close to DEROS didn't mean, as Kepler had reminded him not long ago, that they should stop being soldiers. They had to patrol. They had to search for the enemy. It was too bad that McMillan . . .

He stopped that line of thought also because it was more than too bad. It was tragic, but nothing could be done about it.

They stopped outside the team house, yellow light leaking from the open door and from the screen that was wrapped around the top half of the building to let the air circulate but keep the insects out. Sandbags hid part of the lower wall. "Are you going to be all right, old boy?" Minh said.

It was the second or third time that night that someone had commented on his emotional state. He realized he was doing a poor job of masking his emotions, not that it mattered that much.

"I'm fine," he said, wiping a cold sweat from his forehead. He could feel it under his arms and trickling down his back. He hesitated before saying, "As fine as I can be. Let me tell the team about this alone. Okay?"

"I understand, Captain," Minh said. "I shall check the perimeter and see that the guard is properly mounted."

Inside, Gerber could see that the party had slowed quite a bit. Everyone had sensed that something was wrong, and the moment Gerber entered the room, they knew it was going to be bad news.

Without a word from him, they fell silent. Kepler leaned over and turned off the blaring radio.

Fetterman took a single step forward, stopped and said, "Ian?"

Without realizing it, Gerber was twisting the beret he held in his hands. He didn't remember picking it up. This was the first time he had to announce to the team that someone had died. In the other cases, everyone had known that one of them had died because it had been in heavy combat or on patrols into enemy territory. This time it was a routine patrol that wasn't supposed to run into the VC. It was an attempt to provide some medical assistance to the villagers who never saw anyone with medical training.

"I'm sorry," said Gerber, unsure of what he should say. "Sergeant McMillan was killed earlier today. I don't have all the details, but apparently it was some kind of ambush."

"The Viets?" asked Tyme. "What about the Viets?"

"They're all okay."

"That's not what I meant," said Tyme. "Where the hell were they while Ian was getting killed?"

"I don't have all the details. Captain Minh is still trying to find out exactly what happened, but he doesn't think they ran and left him."

"What are we going to do now, Captain?" asked Fetterman.

Gerber moved to the table and sat down, pushing a couple of beer cans out of his way. He set the beret in front of him and turned it so that he could stare at the flash. "First thing in the morning we begin a patrol."

He stopped for a moment to look around him. The others stood staring at him. One or two held forgotten cans of beer. Morrow was leaning against the far wall. There were only Americans in the room.

"First patrol," said Gerber, "will be squad-sized. It will be poorly run with no noise discipline and will follow the path Ian took."

"And?" asked Fetterman.

"The second, a company-sized patrol, will follow about an hour later under the tightest discipline. It will be in position to offer assistance if the first gets into trouble. Maybe we can draw the enemy out. If we can, then we'll have a unit of sufficient size to stop anything sent after us."

"Is there a reason for this?" asked Fetterman.

"We do have to explore the area where Ian was killed. I believe the minor deception might give us a chance to hit the VC who attacked Ian, if they're still around. I can't see any reason for them to have faded away."

"Captain," said Bromhead, "I would like to lead the small patrol."

"No, Johnny. I want you to take the company. It'll be good experience for you, especially now that you're a captain. I'll take the small unit."

"And both American officers will be off the camp at the same time," said Fetterman.

Gerber shot a glance at him and said, "It won't be the first time we've had that situation." He then looked at Morrow, wondering what he should do about her because she was the only American woman there.

She shrugged. "I could go with you," she said hopefully.

"No, Robin. You stay here." Gerber turned his attention back to Fetterman. "Besides, we're not taking all the Americans out. Just a few of them. This is something we have to do."

Fetterman nodded. "Fucking A, Captain. Something we've got to do."

GERBER SAT IN THE MAKESHIFT OFFICE that also served as his living quarters. A map was spread out on the desk that he had built from old ammo crates and bamboo scrounged from the trash pile. Behind him was a metal cot with a paper-thin mattress, and next to the cot stood a nightstand made from an ammo crate. A Coleman lantern and a nearly empty bottle of Beam's rested on the makeshift table. In front of the desk were two lawn chairs that Gerber had bought in Saigon. On one corner of the desk, out of the way, sat a half-finished can of beer that was rapidly growing warm. He reached for the can and took a swig from it, setting it back down as he studied the map.

He heard a shuffling sound at the door and looked up to see Morrow standing there. She was dressed as she had been in the team house earlier but her face had that well-scrubbed look, as if she had just stepped from the shower.

She waited at the door for a moment but didn't step in. "Can we talk?" she asked.

Gerber pointed at one of the chairs opposite his desk, then leaned back, lacing his fingers behind his head. "What do you want to talk about?"

Morrow slipped into the chair and then leaned forward to pick up his beer. As she reached, Gerber could see the tops of her breasts. He wondered if she knew that he could see them and decided that she must.

"I think I would like to talk about the mission tomorrow," she said.

"I don't think there is anything about it that we need to discuss. Unless there is something that I'm not aware of."

Morrow stood and turned her back. She drained the beer and tossed the can out the door. "Mack? I don't want you... I think that you..." She stopped talking and then faced him. Her eyes searched his, but all she said was "Why do they call you Mack?"

"It's the army," said Gerber, trying to avoid her stare. "Anyone with a name like mine is going to be called Mack. When I was a kid, I went by my middle name. Used my first initial. I guess I thought it sounded more mature to be known as M. Kirk Gerber."

"M. Kirk, huh? I think I like that." She moved back to the chair and sat down again, crossing her legs slowly.

"I don't think you came here to discuss my name," said Gerber quietly.

"Well, you're right there." She laughed self-consciously. "It's that damned patrol tomorrow. I don't think you should go." She stared at him and then added as an afterthought, "Any of you."

"Why not?" Gerber didn't really care why because he knew that he had to go, had to see if he could find out what happened to McMillan. But he wanted to hear what she said.

"Why?" she repeated. "You've done your part here. You're almost ready to rotate home. All of you. You shouldn't be taking risks now that you're so close to being out of this. I don't want to see you, ah, any of you get hurt now."

Gerber let his hands fall to the desktop. He let his eyes wander to her shirt where he could see the rise of one of her breasts only partially hidden by the khaki fabric. He then studied her legs, trying to see them without her realizing that he was looking at them. Suddenly he realized that he had forgotten about the map, the patrol and what might happen in the morning. She had forced herself into his thoughts in a way that he had believed could not happen for quite a while. It was the last thing he wanted, especially when he remembered what her sister, Karen, had done to him.

"We haven't stopped being soldiers, and our job demands that we make contact with the enemy if we can."

"Mack. Kirk. It's just that . . ."

Gerber stood and moved to her. He reached out and took her hand, pulling her to her feet. "Robin, don't make this any harder than it is. If you're worried about being left on the camp, we can get a chopper here for you in the morning."

She pulled her hand free. "That won't be necessary. I'll wait here for your return. Might make a good story." Her voice was harsh and slightly strained. Without another word she stormed out.

For a moment Gerber thought of following her, to try to explain why he had acted as if he hadn't understood what she was trying to say. He wanted to tell her that it was wrong for the two of them to feel anything for one another as his men went into the field to die; for he and Robin to find pleasure together while his men sweated, fought and died in the jungle. He remembered their night in a Saigon hotel when he had no longer worried about such things, had forgotten about Karen for a few hours. He recalled the bliss he had found with Robin. But that had been a momentary aberration, one that he was determined not to repeat. It complicated his life too much to have a woman on the camp, one to whom he had an emotional attachment. Maybe he should go and tell her why he had seemed to become so cold and distant. But the longer he sat contemplating the action, the dumber he thought it was. If he let her go, she would quickly get over her hurt; but if he followed, she would interpret it as a positive response on his part, that there was something more to their relationship than the army officer-journalist one that existed now. Existed at his insistence.

GERBER WAS AWAKE AT DAWN. He hadn't slept well and had spent most of the time with his hands behind his head staring into the darkness at the ceiling. He had heard the occasional pop of the artillery from one of the new fire support bases now surrounding his camp. Once or twice he had heard aircraft fly over. With the coming of the sun, he had gotten up, found his weapon, opting to take one of the new M-16s that had finally been issued to his unit, and headed outside.

At the south gate he found the patrol waiting. Fetterman had already finished making a weapons and equipment check. Bromhead, his new captain bars pinned to his collar, stood to one side, watching as Tyme and Anderson checked each other.

As Gerber approached, Bromhead said, "You sure you want to take this one? I can handle it."

"Johnny," said Gerber, "this is something I have to do. You have your assignment. In a couple of weeks you'll be able to tell others how to run their unit, or rather your unit, but right now this is mine. I'll lead this."

"Just thought I'd mention it," said Bromhead.

"No problem. You seen Bocker or Smith this morning?"

"Galvin was in the common bunker playing with his radios and complaining about being left behind while we got to have all the fun."

Gerber glanced at his watch and then at the horizon where the sun was just making its presence known. "Listen, I don't have time to run him down. I want you to tell him and Sully to make sure that one of them keeps an eye on Morrow all the time."

"Of course."

"And remember, the timetable isn't all that strict. You follow in about an hour."

Bromhead grinned and said, "Don't worry, Mack, I can handle it."

For an instant Gerber was taken aback by Bromhead's use of his first name and then grinned back at him. "Feeling the first power of your new bars, Captain?"

"Thought I would see how they work."

"Don't let it go to your head, Johnny. You're still my exec."

Fetterman appeared then with one of the Vietnamese in tow. "Captains, this will be our guide. He'll try to re-create the route followed by McMillan. He was on the patrol."

Gerber studied the small man. He looked like so many of the other Vietnamese: short, a slight build, black hair chopped off raggedly and very dark eyes. There was nothing to distinguish him from any of the others.

"You know the route?" asked Gerber, first in English and, when there was no immediate reply, in Vietnamese.

The man nodded rapidly and pointed to the west. "I know the way," he replied.

"Okay—" Gerber slapped the Vietnamese on the shoulder "—let's do it. Johnny, tell Minh we're off and we'll see him in a couple of days."

"Yes, sir."

The patrol wormed its way through the six strands of concertina wire surrounding the camp, broke to the west away from the river and entered the high elephant grass. Although the sun was still low on the horizon, the humidity was already making itself felt. They were sweating heavily before they had gone more than a hundred meters. Gerber knew that by midday it would be unbearably hot. The humidity was bad enough, but then they would have the sun to contend with, as well, and even if they were into the jungle, the shade would provide little relief.

After only an hour and a half Gerber called a halt to let the men rest. He had filled four canteens before he left the camp and wondered if he had enough water. The moment security was established, Gerber opened a canteen and took out a couple of salt tablets. He didn't like taking them, but he was already sweating so heavily that he was afraid the heat was going to get to him. He couldn't remember it being so hot and humid before.

It seemed as if they had just sat down, but by his watch Gerber knew that fifteen minutes had passed. He hoped Bromhead would keep the pace slow, trying not to wear the men out before they got into the ambush area. Besides, he didn't want the new captain to catch up. His job was to stay a klick or so behind the squad in case the VC were watching.

Trying to ignore the heat, Gerber signaled the men back to their feet, and they started forward again. The point slid off to the right, and Gerber was forced to chase him back to the proper course. When the pace slowed to something that approximated a crawl, Gerber passed word to the point man to speed it up.

An hour before noon there was a sudden crash in the jungle as if a grenade had detonated. Through breaks in the trees and gaps in the brush, Gerber saw a cloud of black smoke and reddish-brown dust. He dived to one side, his weapon ready, but there was no firing. Only the single explosion.

Without waiting, Gerber leaped to his feet and had to consciously suppress the urge to run forward. Instead, he carefully worked his way in the direction of the explosion, his eyes searching the ground and the jungle around him, looking for other booby traps. Finally he could see Fetterman crouched on the ground, a large bandage in his hand as he worked on one of the Vietnamese strikers.

As he approached, Gerber asked, "Status?"

Fetterman kept working and spoke over his shoulder, his eyes on the wounded man. "Tripped a grenade booby trap. Charlie didn't rig it quite right so the grenade went off with a tree absorbing most of the shrapnel. It should have killed the point man, but it detonated too soon. He's got some pretty bad wounds but nothing really serious, if you know what I mean."

"He need a medevac?"

"No, sir. I would think we can give him a shot or two and let someone take him back to the camp. I've got most of the bleeding stopped already."

"Tony," said Gerber quietly, "if he was an American, would you medevac him now?"

Fetterman turned his head so that he could stare up at Gerber. "I'm not sure I like the implication of that question, Captain."

"Sorry. I wasn't thinking. Listen, let's have our guys take a lunch break and wait for Johnny's group to catch up. He can dispatch the stretcher team and an escort back to the camp, and then they can eat their lunch while we carry on."

"Yes, sir. Aren't you worried about both units being together? Might tip our hand."

"I'm not totally convinced that Charlie doesn't already know what we're up to. He may have had spies in the area who saw both patrols leave the camp. Anyway, I don't think it will hurt."

"Fine, sir, I'll pass the word."

As Fetterman stood, giving some quick instructions in Vietnamese to one of the other strikers, Gerber said, "Tony, I'm sorry about that remark. I should have know better."

IT WAS MORE THAN AN HOUR before they got moving again, into the sweatbox that the jungle had become. Before long, Gerber's shirt was soaked. His hands had become slippery, and it was difficult to hang on to anything. The men were tiring fast, the heat rapidly sapping their strength, and by midafternoon most of the Vietnamese had finished their water. One of them drank from a paddy field they passed, leaving the tree line for a moment. Gerber knew it would make the Americans sick to drink that water but wasn't sure that the strikers couldn't. They hadn't grown up in the germ-free environments that were the pride of American mothers.

By late afternoon they had slowed to a crawl with the men ignoring some of the fundamentals of patrol. They had been trying to follow the trails that Gerber was certain would be booby-trapped. He instructed Fetterman, along with the guide, to take the point. He told Fetterman that he wanted the rest of them to arrive safely, not to take any chances but to speed it up.

Just when Gerber decided to call a halt for the night, the patrol stopped. As the strikers automatically took up defensive positions, Gerber slipped forward to find out why Fetterman had halted. As he approached the hiding spot of the master sergeant, Gerber could hear voices speaking Vietnamese in the distance. There was the unmistakable odor from a fire and the slight breeze carried the obnoxious smell of nouc-mam to him.

Gerber crouched beside his team sergeant. "Is this it?"

Nodding at the Vietnamese soldier who was the guide, Fetterman said, "This is the village. Nuyen here says that McMillan had come out a little farther to the north and set up his perimeter there."

"He's sure about this?"

"Yes, sir. I thought I'd see what's happening in the ville and then Nuyen and I could swing north. We've got an hour or so of light left. Nuyen should be able to pinpoint the ambush site pretty closely, and it shouldn't take us that long to find some physical evidence."

"Okay, Tony. Go to it. We'll stay here."

"Sure, sir. You and the boys rest while the old master sergeant goes off and does your job for you."

"And snap it up, Tony," said Gerber, smiling as he dropped his pack.

3

OUTSIDE THE VILLAGE
OF TRANG ME NEAR THE
CAMBODIAN BORDER

It took Fetterman and the guide less than ten minutes to find the ambush site. The evidence that he had mentioned to Gerber was obvious in the trampled vegetation gouges in the soft, moist earth and the traces of blood that the hot, damp weather and jungle creatures had failed to conceal. Slowly Fetterman examined the site, aware that the VC often booby-trapped such areas because they knew the Americans would come back to try to learn what had happened.

McMillan's position in the jungle was obvious because he had been the only one attacked.

Fetterman shed his pack at the edge of the ambush site. He stripped his web gear, dropping it on top of the pack and then took a deep, long drink of the warm water from one of his canteens. He kept his weapon with him as he got to his hands and knees and began to inspect the site, trying to piece together the fight.

The jungle around the village wasn't the thick triple-canopy type that was found farther north but a thin, almost landscaped, forest. Short grass and bare ground surrounded the tall teak, mahogany and palm trees that threw a spotty shade. Fetterman crawled around, using his left hand to pat the grass as if searching for a dropped coin. He advanced toward an area of crushed grass that was stained a rusty color. He knew it was dried blood.

Nearby were a couple of smaller patches of blood and part of a trail that pointed into the jungle. He could find nothing to tell him why only McMillan had been attacked or how the VC had stumbled upon him and not the rest of his patrol. Nor could he figure out how the enemy soldiers had escaped without any of the strikers actually seeing them. The strikers had reported hearing a scream, and they had fired a few random, unaimed shots into the trees, but the attack on McMillan had been so swift, they hadn't had time to react.

His search completed, he picked up his equipment and worked his way back to Gerber through the light forest, keeping to the shadows so that the villagers wouldn't be aware that he was near.

Gerber was sitting deep in the trees, his back against a palm, his pack in front of him. He was staring at it as if it would somehow provide him with answers. To one side, Fetterman could see a couple of the Vietnamese smoking American cigarettes, but he could hear no talking from them. They, too, were well back, using the broadleafed bushes, the trunks of coconut palms and the shadows to conceal themselves.

"I've found it, Captain," he whispered.

"And?" asked Gerber.

"And nothing. I can't tell what happened. Some evidence of a struggle. Looks like Ian might have killed or wounded a couple of them, given the blood smears. But I don't know how the VC got there or how they got away."

Gerber turned so that his pack was now at his back. He struggled into the straps and stood up, taking a hasty step to the right to maintain his balance. To Fetterman he said, "Let's set up our night location near the ambush site. Tomorrow we can move into the ville and see if they can shed any light on this."

They spent a quiet evening cautiously watching the villagers, almost all old or very young, go about their chores. The women circulated among the mud hootches, stopping to talk briefly or to pick up some food or leave some. All were dressed in rough blouses, which were the tan of undyed cotton, and black pajama bottoms.

Some wore sandals made from old tires, and some were barefoot. The old men were dressed in the same fashion, except that one of them wore an old U.S. Army fatigue shirt with the sleeves hacked off at the elbows.

The cooking fires were extinguished as the sunlight faded, and although there was noise from the ville after sunset, it quickly faded. They heard the discordant music of a stringed instrument for a few moments, but that ended almost as soon as it started. Gerber made the rounds at dusk, telling his men that they would be on half alert throughout the night: they were to pair up, and every other man was to stay awake.

At midnight, in keeping with the standard operating procedures, Gerber used his radio to contact the camp and tell them that all was well. He heard Bromhead check in, too, and, from the strength of the signal, knew that he was close. But Bromhead had done a good job of moving into position because Gerber had seen nothing to indicate that a large unit was nearby. When it was dark, he could see no lights from Bromhead's men, which meant that they had eaten unheated C-rations and that Bromhead was not letting them smoke. Extraordinary discipline to expect from the Vietnamese strikers and even more extraordinary that the new captain was getting it. Gerber was pleased. It demonstrated how much Bromhead deserved his promotion and command of an A-team.

In the moments before dawn, Gerber came awake suddenly, sensing that something had changed, as if a kind of warning had alerted his subconscious mind. He lay with his eyes closed, concentrating on the sounds surrounding him, but could hear nothing other than the noises of the jungle creatures as they moved through the bushes or in the tops of the trees, and the rapid breathing of one of the strikers asleep near him.

For a moment, Gerber berated himself for his paranoia. He wondered if he was doing the same things that McMillan had done in the last minutes of his life. Listening to the surroundings, trying to hear the enemy slipping up on him or feeling, with an almost extrasensory ability, the VC sneaking up on his position. He knew that the sweat coating his body was not from the humidity of the jungle but from the fear that had crept up on him. Without thinking about it, Gerber pulled his weapon closer and took the safety off. He could feel the flesh at the back of his neck crawl as he waited for someone to grab him from behind. And then he realized that his fears were unfounded. All the sounds around him were the natural activity of the jungle creatures, the monkeys calling to each other, the birds screaming and the rustling of the night predators as they raced for their lairs. Gerber knew that he was keyed up because this was the same time of day when McMillan had died.

After a quick cold breakfast of C-ration scrambled eggs that looked pale and tasted plain, a hint of egg flavor in the cardboard mess, Gerber broke camp. He stood for a moment looking at the light mist, which hung close to the ground near the palms and coconuts and signified the coolness of the morning. Overhead, through breaks in the light green canopy, Gerber could see a deep blue sky with only a few high, wispy clouds. The day would get hot quickly, and the humidity would climb rapidly. He would have to watch the pace to make sure that they didn't overexert themselves.

He left half the squad with Sergeant Tyme to search the ambush site again, looking for anything that Fetterman might have missed. But Gerber doubted that the master sergeant would miss anything of importance. He planned to enter the village with the rest of the men and question the people there. Gerber had already coordinated the effort with Bromhead on the radio so that the newly minted captain would keep his men out of sight nearby.

As the six men entered the tiny ville, coming from the north and moving between two mud hootches with rusting tin roofs, the mama-sans working at the cooking fires suddenly disappeared into their hootches. This was not a reaction that Gerber expected, and suddenly he was worried.

The villagers usually ignored the Americans and their Vietnamese counterparts, taking great pains to pretend they couldn't see the soldiers. These women had leaped up the moment they spotted the Americans.

Without a word Fetterman took half of the squad and drifted to the right so that he could cover Gerber and the point element. As they sought the little cover available to them in the village—near the corner of a hootch with a thick thatched roof, behind a fence of woven branches cut from thorn bushes or at the base of a palm tree—Fetterman took the safety off his weapon. He crouched behind the remnants of a mud wall, near the corner of a deserted hootch.

Gerber waved a hand behind his back, signaling the men with him to spread out and prepare to withdraw. He continued walking forward, angling toward the corner of a hootch, thinking that he could use it for cover if they were forced to fight. He didn't plan a retreat because he knew that Bromhead would attack the instant he heard shooting.

For ten long minutes the situation remained static. Fetterman and a couple of the men behind Gerber and the rest waited for something, anything, to happen. When the villagers didn't reappear, when no old men came out to learn what was happening, Gerber moved toward the one hootch where he knew there were some people hiding. Rather than enter uninvited, he stood outside it and called in Vietnamese, "We mean you no harm."

From the left Gerber heard, "Won't do you any good, Captain. They're afraid of us. We'll have to go in and get them."

Gerber turned and saw Fetterman standing there. He hadn't heard the master sergeant walk up. To him, Gerber said, "I hate to violate their homes like that. Probably why they ran in the first place."

"I don't know, sir. I don't like this at all. Usually they just stand around and let us do what we want. They rarely flee unless they're VC."

"All right. Take a couple of men and bring the villagers out. We've got to talk to them, but treat them kindly. We don't want them joining the VC because of our actions."

"You beginning a new career of telling me my job, sir?" asked Fetterman, grinning.

"No, Tony. I'm just making sure that you'll instruct the men to treat the villagers with some dignity. It'll pay off for us."

It didn't take Fetterman long to get the people into the center of the village. Then, rather than have all the villagers stand around being interrogated, the Americans let some of them go back to the cooking fires, and when one of the old men complained that his fields were being neglected, Gerber ordered that he be allowed to leave, wondering if he was making a tactical mistake. The man could flee into the jungle in search of the VC.

As the man disappeared into the trees, Fetterman asked, "You sure that was a good idea?"

Gerber shrugged. "I doubt that he'll cause any trouble, and besides, we've got Bromhead around here with a company. Also, there's no evidence of any VC force. Thought maybe a little kindness would win us some friends. It's worked for us before."

Slowly and carefully they moved among the villagers asking questions about what had happened. After an hour Fetterman had pieced together a story. He reported to Gerber that it appeared as if the VC had entered the village about an hour before McMillan's patrol had settled in for the night. They had been shadowing McMillan and his strikers for most of the afternoon and had been looking for an ambush site but hadn't found anything that would allow them to set up the way they wanted to.

Gerber raised an eyebrow at this and said, "The VC let all that slip to the villagers?"

"I gather they were pretty talkative," said Fetterman. "Felt omnipotent and were discussing the afternoon among themselves as they forced some of the women to cook them an evening meal."

"Ian didn't see all the extra people?"

"He wouldn't know if there were extra people. Besides, the VC stayed out of sight. I haven't gotten to the best part."

"Sorry. Go ahead."

"Seems that this place was once a VC stronghold. The villagers were rabid sympathizers. Government airplanes bombing them all the time. Shooting the water buffalo for target practice and that sort of thing. Then one night the VC came and demanded some young men and young women for recruits. Said that the village owed it to them. The head man refused, saying they needed the young people to harvest the crop for the next few days and the recruiting would have to wait. The VC said no, it had to be right then, and somehow a fight broke out. When it was over, about half the villagers were dead and the rest were marched off into the jungle."

"Then who in the hell are these people?"

Fetterman shrugged. "I think they were moving from another area, found the empty hootches and just moved in. Learned later what had happened."

"The point of all this, Tony. The point?" Gerber wiped a sleeve across his forehead to mop up the sweat.

"Tunnels. The area is crisscrossed with them. They lead from the hootches into the jungle. From the bunkers hidden around into the jungle. From the jungle back to here. The whole village. Dug by the old villagers and the VC over a period of years. These people have kept them in repair because we brought the war back into this zone."

"I see," said Gerber, nodding. "The tunnels lead into jungle and right into the middle of the area where McMillan's patrol was."

"Yes, sir. Dead into the middle."

While Fetterman continued to question the villagers, Gerber took the rest of the men and entered one of the hootches. There was little inside except a wooden chest, obviously made by the owner because of the rough construction, and some woven bamboo sleeping mats in the corner. By moving one of the mats, they found an entrance to the tunnel system. It looked like an ordinary hole in the ground, but from a different angle they could see that it turned. There was a wooden door covering the entrance.

Gerber wanted to drop down and explore the inside, but he was too big. Instead, he pointed to one of the Vietnamese strikers and watched as the frightened man, clutching a pistol in one hand and a flashlight in the other, climbed into the hole. He pushed on the wooden door, which swung out of the way. The man looked back, sweat covering his face, his eyes wide with fear, but when Gerber nodded, the man disappeared into the tunnel.

Fifteen minutes later the striker, covered with red dust, reappeared shaking his head and chattering rapidly. Gerber didn't understand much of it but thought he was being told that there was nothing of interest down there.

Gerber wasn't satisfied with the answer. He didn't think that the tunnel system would be as barren as the striker indicated and suspected that the man had learned from past experience that, if he found anything, the Americans would require him to search for hours. The only solution was to send one of the team down. Fetterman was the only one whose size didn't make it dangerous. He was only slightly bigger and stockier than the Vietnamese. Gerber decided to wait until Fetterman finished with the questions.

Outside the hootch Gerber saw the master sergeant standing to one side, alone, clutching his weapon in both hands. He was covered with sweat, ragged stains down the front of his shirt and under his arms. There was something peculiar about his posture, and as Gerber approached, he saw the look on Fetterman's face. It was one of disbelief.

"Tony," said Gerber. "What is it?"

Fetterman turned and saw Gerber, and in an instant his face became as passive as if he had just completed a Sunday stroll through the park. "Nothing at all, Captain. Picked up an interesting bit of intelligence."

"And?"

"Brief you on it just as soon as the possibility for real security presents itself."

Gerber was going to demand to be told but decided that Fetterman knew what he was doing. If it was something that would affect the mission, Fetterman would tell him right away, and if Fetterman wanted to wait, it was something that could wait. Still, the captain was more than a bit curious.

Changing the subject, Gerber said, "I'd like you to explore the tunnels a little. See if there is anything down there of interest, and see if there is a way to destroy them without blowing up the whole damned village."

Fetterman dropped his pack outside the hootch. He took the Randall combat knife that was taped upside down to the harness. Carefully he slipped it into his boot where he could get it quickly. Next he took two grenades, and slipped one into each of the front pockets of his jungle fatigue pants.

Silently Gerber handed him a .45, and Fetterman released the magazine, checking to make sure that it was fully loaded. He slammed it back home and racked the slide once, chambering a fresh round. That done, he dropped the magazine again, replacing the round that was now in the chamber of the pistol. He took three spare magazines, placing one in a front pocket of his jungle fatigue jacket, one in a side pocket and one in the top of his other boot.

"Won't that be uncomfortable?" asked Gerber.

"Damned uncomfortable, but you never know when something like that will come in handy. Now if I have to, I should be able to reach at least one spare mag."

"Anything else?"

"Let me see that flashlight." Fetterman took it and turned it on, looking directly into the beam. He shook it twice and banged it against his hand but didn't see the beam flicker. The batteries seemed to be new.

Finally he peeled off his watch and handed it to Gerber. He rolled down his sleeves, buttoning them tightly around his wrists so there would be no excess material to snag on any obstructions in the tunnel. He checked himself one last time. "That should be it."

"I don't suppose I need to tell you to be careful."

"Always am. Wouldn't want to do anything to upset Mrs. Fetterman and the kids. I'll be down there for a while, Captain, so don't get nervous."

"It may not help," said Gerber, "but if you get into trouble and need us, fire three quick shots."

"I'll keep that in mind."

Inside the hootch Fetterman sat on the edge of the tunnel and played the beam along the sides and bottom. He looked at Gerber and said, "You know, Captain, I really am getting too short for this shit."

"We all are, Tony."

"Yes, sir." Fetterman dropped to the tunnel floor, stopping there long enough to study the walls around him. They were smooth, almost as if they had been bored rather than dug. He felt the side, but the earth was packed hard and it took the point of his knife to scrape any dirt free. This was a new experience, one that he hadn't trained for. During his career Fetterman had signed up for the most outlandish Army schools, figuring that someday, somewhere, one of them might come in handy. But no one, nowhere, had ever designed a course on how to explore an enemy tunnel system. One that had literally been clawed out of the ground.

Fetterman did know, from his experience on the surface, that the VC would booby-trap nearly everything. Each of Charlie's own soldiers using the tunnel system would know of the traps, but an enemy penetrating the system would fall victim to them. Fetterman didn't think there would be much to worry about once he got deep enough, but near the surface he would have to be extremely careful, even though a striker had gone in before him.

He had dropped down carefully, gingerly placing his feet on the bottom, waiting for a sudden shift that would tell him that he had stepped on the pressure trigger of a mine, but that didn't happen. He pressed on the wooden door and felt it swing back so that he could crawl forward slowly, at first with the pistol in one hand and his flashlight in the other. He quickly realized that he would need one hand to feel his way. He lowered the hammer of the .45 and slipped it into his belt, then switched the light to his left hand and began moving forward again, feeling for hidden protrusions and trip wires.

The floor of the tunnel was packed hard and smooth to the touch with no loose dirt on it. The walls were of red clay with very little bracing. The roof of the tunnel was also hard-packed clay with wooden supports spaced liberally around it. Fetterman was concerned that it would collapse on him and then reminded himself that the Vietnamese Air Force had bombed the village without destroying the tunnels. The odds were that he would stumble across a booby trap long before the tunnel fell on him.

There was no litter on the floor and no recessed niches that hid papers or weapons. The light from the tunnel entrance dissipated rapidly, and Fetterman was nearly overwhelmed by the musty smell. An odor of freshly dug earth was everywhere. Fetterman took a deep breath of the astonishingly cool air, expanding his chest, but the tunnel was large enough to accommodate him. He was surprised that the air wasn't stale and realized that the system would have to be well ventilated. He continued forward, blinking rapidly as his eyes adjusted to the almost total darkness of the tunnel.

He hadn't gone very far when he came to a ladder that led deeper into the tunnel. It forked off to one side, but Fetterman couldn't see much in that direction and knew that anything interesting would be found lower in the system. Using the slightly enlarged area, he turned around so that he could climb down the ladder. If he was going to run into any booby traps, it would be at that point. He kept his feet next to the rails of the ladder, putting as little pressure as possible on the rungs and carefully avoiding the center of them.

When he reached the bottom, instead of stepping to the floor, he turned and used his light to examine the earth. He saw no trip wires, no glints of metal suggesting the firing mechanisms of mines and no slight depressions showing where a pressure plate might be buried. He stepped off the ladder to the side, then crouched so that he could examine the new tunnel.

This one was larger, the roof being nearly five feet above the floor. And it was wider, almost six feet across, and cut into the sides were niches. Fetterman moved to his left and looked into the niche nearest him. There was a wooden platform in it covered with straw. A human stink to the place overpowered the odor of moist earth that he was becoming used to. He couldn't identify what was human about the smell. It seemed to be sweat mingled with urine.

"I'll be damned," he mumbled to himself. "A goddamned barracks."

He worked his way through the barracks and had to stoop to enter the next phase of the tunnel. Crawling along it, still looking for trip wires and booby traps, he felt his way with the fingers of his right hand as he swept the flashlight beam back and forth. He was now finding more evidence of human occupation. An old can from stolen American C-rations. Two almost new rounds for an AK-47. A loop of copper wire that didn't seem to have any function because it was so short. And papers, many of them Chieu Hoi leaflets dropped in large numbers from American and South Vietnamese airplanes, some of which had been used as toilet paper.

Again the tunnel opened up so that it was ten feet wide and five feet high, the sides braced with four by fours supporting wooden beams on the ceiling. Lightbulbs were suspended from wires looped along the beams. The floor was covered with a thin wooden veneer, slatted to let water seep into the ground, although the tunnel was extremely dry. The human odor had given way to the musty, dirty smell of a freshly dug grave.

This was not another barracks area. This time he found an arms locker. At first he didn't think much of it, figuring that the VC and NVA had to store their weapons somewhere, then he realized what he had found. There were three .51-caliber machine guns, what the Communists designated as 12.5 mm. One of them had the huge circular sight on top that was used for antiaircraft weapons and stood on a solid metal tripod. There were several mortar tubes, a couple of them of American manufacture. Off to one side was a rack of AK-47s, most of them Chicom but a couple obviously Soviet made because of the Russian lettering on them.

Then at the far end he saw a weapon that nearly bowled him over. He couldn't believe it. A fully assembled ZSU-23. A goddamned 23 mm antiaircraft gun that contained twin barrels, with wheels folded under and which could be erected and used to tow the weapon. There was a seat near two hand cranks for the gunner. It had to have been brought down in pieces and reassembled; to get it out, the VC would have to take it apart again.

Fetterman moved closer and reached out to touch it as if he didn't believe his eyes. He sat in the gunner's seat and twisted the cranks that would move the weapon. It was fully operational. He shook his head in disbelief.

For several minutes Fetterman sat there and stared. It was such a strange thing to find. An antiaircraft gun underground. It was of no use there, other than for the practice of taking it apart and putting it back together. It wasn't like the other weapons that could be carried easily to the surface. Even the .51 cals could be taken to the surface intact, once the tripods were removed.

Finally Fetterman decided that he had seen enough. It was time to get back to the surface. He could leave his grenades behind as booby traps to cause some confusion among the VC when they returned, or he could carefully withdraw and hope that the enemy wouldn't discover that his tunnels had been penetrated.

As carefully as he entered, Fetterman left the tunnel system. He kept his eyes open for anything that he might have missed, but the upper levels were still clean.

When he approached the entrance to the hootch, he shouted up, "I'm coming out."

Gerber answered him with a quick, "It's clear."

As rapidly as he could, he explained that they had found a VC base camp. He didn't think that the villagers had any idea of how extensive it was. He suggested that they had only seen a couple of soldiers at a time use the entrances in the village but was sure that there was access to the system from far outside the ville, hidden in the jungle.

"They could put a regiment down there, and the villagers wouldn't know it, Captain," he said.

"What do you recommend?"

"That we pull out of here as quickly as possible so that we don't tip our hand. Then we should brief Nha Trang about this. Let them put an infantry battalion with engineers in here to blow it all up. Hell, there's so much stuff down there we couldn't carry it all out in a month."

"Maybe we should just blow the entrances," said Gerber.

"We'd never get them all, sir, and then Charlie would move all his stuff out before we could do anything about it. I only had an hour down there and didn't see even a fraction of it. I mean there is a fucking arsenal down there."

"You didn't steal yourself a souvenir?"

"No, sir. As I said, I didn't want them to know that I had been down there and I don't know how good their accounting system is." He grinned. "But those Russian AKs were mighty tempting. You don't see many with Russian lettering on them."

Gerber glanced at his watch and saw that it was nearly two in the afternoon. There was absolutely nothing they could do about it that day. If they headed back to the camp, they wouldn't get there until dark. If they waited until the morning, they could watch the ville from the jungle and see if the VC showed up, then leave at first light. By dusk he or one of his men could be in Saigon or Nha Trang passing along the information.

"Okay, Tony, take a while to catch your breath. We'll pull back to the ambush site and explore it again. Camp for the night and return to base in the morning."

Fetterman dropped to the ground and said, "Sounds good, sir."

Gerber stood and started to move away but stopped. "I wonder if we're not being a little too clever about this."

"Meaning?"

"The villagers know that we've found some of the tunnels, and they're sure to mention it to the VC if they come back soon. Now if we don't try to destroy the system, the VC might abandon it anyway. But if we drop a couple of grenades down the holes we've found, which would only do superficial damage, it might make the bad guys think that we think we've ruined their complex."

"Or we could be outsmarting ourselves."

"I know, but I just don't feel right about leaving this untouched. I know we can't really destroy the entire complex, but we should try."

"Perhaps we should discuss this some more with the rest of the team back at camp," said Fetterman.

Gerber continued to look at the master sergeant without really seeing him. After a few moments the captain nodded.

"Okay," he said.

4

U.S. ARMY SPECIAL
FORCES CAMP A-555

Gerber waited for everyone on the team to find a seat. It was the first time in months that they had all been together in a single meeting.

Fetterman and Tyme sat together at the table closest to the refrigerator. Tyme, who was recovering from a wound received during an ambush that had gone wrong, was sipping a beer. He had only recently returned to the camp. He was a tall, sandy-haired man in his mid-twenties. He was normally quiet, except when someone asked a question about weapons, and then he was all too happy to talk to him for hours.

Sam Anderson, the huge, blond demolitions sergeant, stood in the corner closest to the bar, eating a sandwich he had made himself. He kept his hair cut so short that he looked bald, and his eyes were such a light blue they looked gray. He had an open, friendly face with a boyish smile and the whitest, straightest teeth that anyone had ever seen. Next to his sandwich plate stood a glass of milk.

Galvin Bocker sat at a table with Sully Smith and Derek Kepler. Sully Smith, whose real name was Francisco Giovanni Salvatore Smith, had an American father and an Italian mother. He was on his second Vietnam tour because, like Anderson, he loved to watch things explode, especially when he got to wire the charges. Short and stocky with the olive complexion of the Italians, he was from Dayton, Ohio.

Kepler was the strangest of the team. He had once arrived at camp drunk, but with a 90 mm recoilless rifle that Gerber had spent weeks trying to have sent to him through official channels. Kepler would never tell anyone where he got it, except to say that the men who had it didn't need it. He had been dressed in a nurse's uniform complete with a bra and stockings. He hadn't explained that, either. His expertise at supplying equipment that couldn't be found via normal channels had earned him the nickname of Eleven Fingers. Since he was the intelligence specialist for the team, they expected bizarre behavior, but Kepler seemed to have made it into a fine art.

Thomas Jefferson Washington, the twenty-one-year-old medic whom the others called T.J., sat by himself, staring at his beer, drinking it steadily and quietly. Until the day before yesterday, he had been the junior medic, a position he loved because McMillan was teaching him so much. They had operated on wounded strikers, removing bullets that would have killed them had McMillan not ignored regulations preventing medics from performing surgery.

McMillan's death had hit him the hardest because he had worked the closest with him. T.J. was a big black man with the fine features that suggested his ancestors had come from the eastern side of Africa rather than the West Coast.

Once they were all present, seated or standing at the back and quiet, Gerber stood. He drew a hand across his forehead, looked at the sweat in his palm and wiped it on the front of his dirty fatigue jacket. He said, "We've got a couple of things to decide and a few things to discuss prior to me getting on the chopper to Saigon."

Before he could say anything else, the door opened and Robin Morrow stood there, holding a couple of cans of beer. "Anyone interested in something cool to drink?" she asked.

"No," said Fetterman, "but you can come in, anyway."

From the other side of the room, Bromhead said, "Are you sure that's a good idea?"

"Shouldn't matter, Johnny," said Gerber. "You won't tell anyone what's said in here, will you, Robin?"

She pulled a chair out and sat down. "You should know me better than that."

"Then you can stay." Gerber turned his attention back to the rest of his team. "I think the one thing that you all should know is something that Master Sergeant Fetterman said to me only a few minutes ago. Something he discovered, and when put together with some of the other things we know, makes a lot of sense."

He stopped talking and studied the faces of the men of his team. After nearly a year in Vietnam, they were all veterans. They all knew the score now, what combat was like and what men did when faced with death. These were all men who could be trusted to do their jobs, to die doing their jobs if it came to that. These were men whom Gerber would trust with his life.

He turned his eyes momentarily to Morrow. She was the real enigma. Although she was a journalist who had tricked a Saigon general into letting her come out to the camp, she had volunteered to hold back a story to help them. She had even helped get Sergeants Tyme and Fetterman out of trouble. Now she put up with hardships, staying at the camp for some reason that Gerber refused to understand, and which caused him undue distress.

He had spent a night with her in Saigon that involved little talking. Now he avoided her when they were alone, afraid of what might happen. He avoided any eye or body contact, and tried to exclude her from his thoughts. He felt that they had worked out an arrangement that was satisfactory to them both. He believed the one night in Saigon, with her protestations of love, had been just one night in Saigon. She had been lonely, maybe afraid. He had been lonely, hurt by Robin's sister and reluctant to get involved in any lasting relationship. He was attracted to her, of that he had no doubt, but believed the attraction was because of her amazing resemblance to her sister. His feelings for her were a direct result of his rejection by Robin's sister. He didn't want to explore it any further so he avoided the problem as best he could. Because he had once loved Morrow's sister, Gerber was overly obtuse when dealing with Robin.

"While interrogating the villagers," Gerber began, almost physically shaking himself to put the thoughts of Robin Morrow out of his mind, "Sergeant Fetterman learned something that is shocking. First, though, I should explain that, from the evidence we could find on the field, there is no indication that the Vietnamese strikers left Ian to die. He was killed in an ambush that was set to kill him. There is really nothing the strikers could have done. It happened too fast and too quietly. By the time they were alerted to the problem, Ian was dead, and the VC were escaping."

Again he stopped talking, wondering if he believed what he had been told and deciding for the twentieth time that he did. "It seems that Ian was the target of the ambush. Just him. Not the patrol or the Vietnamese, but Sergeant McMillan."

Before anyone could say anything, Gerber continued. "I know what you're thinking because it's the same thing I thought when I was told. The VC don't know McMillan and, therefore, wouldn't try to kill him. Well, that's right, but McMillan was the target of the ambush.

"If one of us had been with him, we would have been a target, too. The VC are interested in killing us all. Those of us here who ruined their master plan to rid the area of the Saigon government's presence. The ones who built a camp in their backyard and who have been able to maintain that camp no matter what they have thrown at us. We're the ones who have shown that the VC aren't the omnipotent soldiers everyone thought they were."

Smith interrupted. "That would mean we're all the targets."

"Right," Gerber nearly yelled to underscore the point. "We have been singled out for assassination by the enemy. Master Sergeant Fetterman might have something more to say on that point."

Fetterman stood. "Before we all go off half-cocked, let met say that what the captain just explained should be no surprise. We have hurt Charlie here. We have pushed him and prodded him and forced him to do things that he didn't want to do. He has tried to take the camp from us and has failed to do it. He has tried to put a propaganda cadre into the area to explain the failure, and we destroyed that. Each time he has moved a force into the region, we have met him and defeated him. Now he wants us all dead. Ian, unfortunately, was the first victim of this new campaign because he was in the wrong place at the wrong time."

"So who cares?" yelled Anderson. "We all rotate out of here in a couple of weeks, anyway. We'll beat Charlie because of the way the war is being run."

Now Gerber took over from Fetterman. "The Cat has a point. All we really have to do is sit tight, and our tours will end and we'll go home. We're all extremely short. But that doesn't end the problem."

"What the captain is saying," said Fetterman, "is that we'll pass the problem along to the team that replaces us here. Charlie doesn't care who he kills, just as long as he takes out one of our teams. Kill all the Americans on one of the teams, even if he has to do it one at a time. The people in the villes won't know it was a different team."

"Sounds like you're suggesting that we extend," said Smith, laughing. "Stay for an extra six months."

"Before we get into that," answered Gerber, "there are one or two other things you should know. Tony?"

Fetterman began to address the group again. "I've talked to Eleven Fingers about this, and he's checked with his informants. There is a bounty on us. A thousand bucks apiece for you low-ranking sergeants, fifteen hundred for me because they don't re-alize how valuable I am and two thousand for each of the offi-cers."

"Say," said Smith, "how do we collect?"

There was a bark of laughter, which Fetterman stared down. "I believe we have to supply the bodies. If they just wanted insignia, we might be able to find a way to tap into it. We can get all the in-signia we need."

"I'll check into it," said Kepler seriously. "I know that some VC units are paying for the wings of helicopter pilots. Don't need the bodies, just the wings. And the warrant officer bars. They're paying for those, too."

"We are not selling any insignia to the damned enemy," said Gerber. "Tony. Finish it."

"Yes, sir. Sergeant Kepler and I confirmed through some of his sources that the Chinese officer is behind all this. It was his plan we wrecked. He was trying to get even for our assassination attempt on him, and when that blew up in his face, he decided to put his people into the field to take us out."

"Jesus Christ!" said Bromhead.

Ignoring that, Gerber said, "I plan to meet with Colonel Bates tomorrow and tell him that I want to extend for six months. I know the clerks in Saigon are going to have fits because of the paperwork involved, but I doubt the Army is going to tell someone who is here and who has survived for a year that he cannot continue to fight the war."

"Come on, Captain," said Anderson. "This is crazy. We can't stay here for an extra six months."

"He's right, sir," said Bocker.

"I expected you to at least listen, Galvin," replied Gerber. "Of all the men, I thought you would be the one to listen to the plan before rejecting it."

"I'll listen to anything. You know that. But extend to see if we can't shoot some Chinese guy? Hell, sir, we've never even seen him." Bocker looked at the other men in the hot, sticky team house, trying to gauge their reactions. Nervously, he wiped the sweat from his forehead.

"Not true," said Fetterman. "I've seen him a couple of times. Once real close. He's out there and he's very good. And he'll kill our replacements before they have a chance to do anything. I want that bastard, and I want him badly."

From the back came a new voice. Everyone turned to see Morrow standing there. "I've listened to enough of this. It's all crazy. You guys have put in your year. You deserve your DEROS. You shouldn't stay because of some perverted view of war. You don't owe anyone anything, except a good briefing on what is going on here."

"Miss Morrow," said Gerber, "I appreciate your concern, but you really don't have a voice in this. If you want to return to Saigon, just say the word, and we'll have you out of here in an hour."

"Sorry, Captain," she said. "I don't want anyone making a mistake that they may live to regret. Providing they get a chance to live."

"I'm staying," said Gerber, "because it is our responsibility to take care of the Chinese officer. We're the ones who have hurt him, and it's us he wants."

"I'm staying, too," said Fetterman. "For the obvious reason. I want that bastard."

The debate raged for an hour. Several of the team members, having planned on their homecomings for a year, were reluctant to change their plans on such short notice. Gerber explained that Army regulations provided everyone who extended with a thirty-day leave before the start of the second part of the tour; they could still have their leave but then would be back doing an important job. They wouldn't be garrison troopers in the World, reading about the war or watching it on the six o'clock news.

Bromhead convinced almost all of the holdouts to extend when he volunteered to give up his promotion so that he could stay to help find and kill the Chinese officer. Only Kepler insisted he was going home. He had classes to attend because he wanted to become an officer.

"Derek, my boy," said Fetterman, "I won't argue with a man who has aspirations toward becoming an officer because someday he might be a general and I could find myself in an awkward position serving under him. But I will say this. If Captain Bromhead can offer up his promotion, I would think that you could wait six months. Besides, it would look good on your records. Volunteered for an extension of his tour to help make the world safe for democracy."

"You'd really give up your promotion?" Kepler asked Bromhead.

"It's a moot point," answered Gerber. "We won't let him."

"I would," answered Bromhead, anyway. "This is something that we should all do together."

"All right," said Kepler. "I can put my plans on hold for six months."

"Okay," said Gerber. "Tomorrow I will see Bates and tell him what we have in mind. I'll explain the situation to him. With luck, I can bring the papers back with me."

"I don't believe it," shouted Morrow. "You have all lost your fucking minds. To stay in this godforsaken hole for one extra day because of some abstract belief is insane! And you people want an extra six months?"

"Miss Morrow!" snapped Gerber. "I don't expect you to understand. I don't expect you to stay, either."

"No, I guess you don't, Captain," she said with obvious anger. "Sometimes you are so blind I wonder how you've managed to live this long. You think of this as some great crusade. Some great adventure. Save the world from Communism and make it safe."

"That's enough, Morrow," Gerber ordered.

"Don't take that tone with me," she shouted back. "I'm not one of your Boy Scouts. I live in the adult world."

"The adult world of journalism?" said Gerber sarcastically. "You really think of that as an adult world?"

"I don't have to take that shit from you, Gerber." She whirled and stormed from the team house.

Momentarily embarrassed and a little surprised by her anger, Gerber tried to cover it by saying, "What got into her?"

"I think it's more a case of what didn't," said Fetterman with a straight face. But everyone understood his meaning.

THE FOLLOWING MORNING Gerber hitched a ride to Saigon on the mail chopper. As the aircraft skimmed the jungle and muddy rice fields of Three Corps, he thought about his men. The team had finally decided they would stay in Vietnam an additional six months for the sole purpose of eliminating the Chinese officer. Once that was done, they would take their next rotation home. No one mentioned that they were really staying to avenge the death of McMillan because the Chinese officer was responsible for it. In fact, he was responsible for most of the bad things that had happened to them during their tour in Vietnam.

Gerber tried to tell himself that he was operating on a higher plane, and that his reasons for staying, while influenced by the death of McMillan and the operations conducted by the Chinese officer, were somehow more moral. He was staying to finish their job. In rare moments he knew that the real reason was to make sure the Chinese bastard drew only a limited number of breaths.

Gerber's mind replayed the orders he had left with Minh and Bromhead. The most important of them called for a platoon-sized operation in the area of the VC base at Trang Me. Gerber had been prepared to take a larger role in the surveillance but figured that Minh knew what he was doing and that Bromhead could use the experience. So Gerber just made sure they understood that someone should be watching the enemy camp until he could get to Nha Trang and pass the intelligence along. He expected one of the infantry divisions recently deployed to Vietnam to send in a battalion or two to take out the VC camp within a week.

That off his mind, Gerber had thrown some spare clothes into an overnight bag and had headed for the chopper. It was sitting on the pad on the northern end of the runway, the blades spinning, the cloud of red dust created by the landing slowly dissipating in the light morning breeze. To the west, storm clouds, that threatened rain later in the day, were swirling above Cambodia, but the bright sun overhead was baking the ground, making it hot and miserable in the open. He had no sooner climbed aboard than he saw various members of the team strolling toward him as if they wanted to be sure that he got on and the helicopter took off safely. Conspicuous by her absence was Morrow. As the noise of the chopper engine increased to a steady, earsplitting roar and the blades began to pop rhythmically, Gerber wondered if she was just pissed off about the whole episode of the night before or afraid that, if she was around, he would order her off the camp. Not that he particularly cared one way or the other. He settled back to enjoy the ride.

SINCE HE HADN'T TOLD Bates that he was coming, there was no one to meet him at Hotel Three. Carrying his overnight bag, with only his pistol safely hidden in his shoulder holster beneath his freshly laundered but unstarched fatigues, Gerber walked along the world's largest PX, a post exchange that would rival any of the department stores in the World. To one side, he could see a movie marquee proclaiming that a Paul Newman film was showing. Gerber passed it, thinking that someday he should try to see a movie there. He caught the odor of fresh hot popcorn drifting from the open doors of the cinema. As he neared the door of the PX, guarded by two Air Force MPs, he decided to enter on a whim.

Just inside, there was an eight-by-eight cubicle that passed for an entrance foyer, which was made of unpainted walls and had a dusty concrete floor. He was told that he would have to leave his overnight bag in one of the open lockers. The MP assured Gerber that his gear would be safe. Gerber nodded, not really caring because the bag contained only some clean underwear and a set of jungle fatigues. If somebody wanted to steal them, Gerber figured they could have them.

The first thing he noticed as he left the foyer and entered the PX itself was a large display of fur coats and diamond jewelry. Gerber looked at the coats, thinking that the last thing someone in Vietnam needed was a full-length mink coat. But he knew they were really meant for wives and girlfriends back in the World.

The main part of the PX was like a warehouse divided into sections for different types of merchandise. He saw everything that anyone could possibly want: stereos, color televisions, civilian suits, food, books and magazines, and on and on. In one corner was a lingerie selection that featured little that was practical but a lot that was interesting.

Two Vietnamese girls were modeling some of the more sedate costumes, wandering among the GIs and talking to them before moving on. For a moment Gerber had an urge to buy something for Morrow. In fact, he headed toward the section, seeing a black lace garter belt with black stockings that he liked, but then he realized what he was thinking and detoured away from it.

Finally he decided that he had wasted enough time and started back toward the door. He collected his bag and stepped outside into the early-afternoon sunlight. A wall of heat slammed into him, and it was only then he realized that the PX had been air-conditioned. In seconds he was through the gate that separated Hotel Three from the rest of Tan Son Nhut. It was a short walk from that gate to the

Air Force Officers' Club where Gerber called the Army motor pool and got a jeep and driver to take him over the Bates's new office.

There was only a slight delay in Bates's outer office. Gerber stood in front of the clerk's desk, taking in the metal chairs that lined the room's perimeter, the potted plant stuck into a corner and the low table that held tattered copies of *Stars and Stripes* and *Army Times*. The clerk, newly promoted to Spec Four, waved Gerber into an inner area where Bates was only mildly surprised to see him.

"What can I do for you, Mack?" he asked, waving Gerber into one of the two blue armchairs that sat in front of his wooden desk. There was a matching blue couch against one wall and blue blinds on the window, which killed the rays of the afternoon sun. A bamboo mat was spread between the chairs and the desk. On the wall, paneled in plywood and painted a dull gray, was a single Army picture labeled *The Wagon Box Fight*. There was a quiet hum from an air conditioner in a corner that did little to cool the office.

"I want to extend," said Gerber.

"Oh, you do not," said Bates, grinning. Bates was a stocky man of medium height with graying blond hair, which he wore in a flat-top. Laugh lines bracketed brown eyes in a round, tanned face. He was wearing starched, pressed jungle fatigues that held his jump wings and a combat infantryman's badge with two stars above the left breast pocket. "Now, what can I really do for you?"

"I said I want to extend. So does the rest of the team. We need more time to finish what we've started."

Bates stood up and came around his desk. He sat on the corner of it, letting one foot dangle. Gerber noticed the new jungle boots with the green nylon panel on the sides that allowed the foot to breathe. The boots had been polished but not spit shined. Bates clasped his hands and said, "Too late, Mack. Can't get the paperwork done in time. Orders have already been cut. Replacements have been slated, and your exec has been given an A-detachment."

"Let's stop dancing around this one, sir," said Gerber. "I want to stay on and so does my team. We've good reason for it, and I can't believe you'll take an experienced man out of the field to replace him with someone new."

Bates passed a hand through his graying hair and said, "What brought all this on?"

"You have some time?" asked Gerber.

"Plenty." Bates walked around his desk and sat down there. He pulled open the bottom drawer, propped his feet up on it and then laced his fingers behind his head and looked at the ceiling. "Tell me all about it."

For the next hour Gerber explained everything that had happened in the past few weeks, including the speculations about the assassination of McMillan. Gerber talked about his belief that the whole thing was being orchestrated by a Chinese officer, the same one they had discussed time and again. Now it had become more than a conflict of geopolitical ideologies. It had become a personal war between the Special Forces men from Camp A-555 and the Chinese officer who worked with the VC and NVA stationed just across the Cambodian border from them.

When Gerber stopped talking, Bates said, "And you now want to go after this man?"

"Wouldn't be the first time," Gerber smiled. "But, no, all we really want to do is destroy his unit."

"You have a plan?"

"No. But with six months to play with, we can plan some way to get him."

"Without operating in Cambodia again?"

"Listen, Alan," said Gerber, violating military protocol and presuming on friendship, "this man has targeted my team for extinction. He has now started the game, hell, he might have started it a month or more ago, and I don't want to be pulled in the final quarter because of some bureaucratic rule. If I don't destroy him, he is going to destroy my replacement. And that's a fact."

"Okay, Mack, let me ask you one question. Did your team volunteer to stay without any coercion from you?"

"We discussed it for several hours, but after that we were all in agreement. Even Captain Bromhead."

"Say, that's right. Bromhead finally got his orders. I'll have to hit him up to buy me a drink or ten at the club next chance I get."

"He's so happy about the promotion, I think if he was here he would have gone broke buying drinks for everyone."

"Okay," said Bates. "I'll get my clerk to type up the papers for you to sign. You can take the ones for the rest of the team back when you go."

"One other thing," said Gerber. "McMillan had a friend in Nha Trang. I need to go tell her that he was killed."

"The Army will notify his family."

"She's not family. She's just a friend, but I think they were quite close. I would like to tell her."

"I don't know. You're asking for an awful lot here, Mack. An extension this late and now a trip to Nha Trang."

"Well," said Gerber, "there *is* something else. I told you about the VC base at Trang Me. I need to go to Nha Trang to let the SFOB know about it so that they can get something in there to destroy it."

Bates stood. "That information can be forwarded from here."

"Of course it could. I could be debriefed by one of the Intelligence officers here, but I would really appreciate it if I could go to Nha Trang. Louise deserves it."

"Louise?"

"Sergeant McMillan's friend. She deserves better than hearing about his death via the grapevine. We're supposed to take care of our own, and she is one of ours."

"I'll get you on the afternoon flight and have the papers dispatched to your camp as soon as they're typed. You'll need to get them back as soon as you can."

Now Gerber stood. For a second he hesitated, studying the older man. Gerber had caused him a dozen problems in the past few months, but Bates had always been there when he needed help. He had protected Gerber and the team from Crinshaw and the other brass hats stationed in Saigon.

"Thanks, Colonel," said Gerber. "I knew I could count on you. You've been a big help."

"Sure," said Bates. "Get out of here before I change my mind."

5

ABOARD AN AIR FORCE
C-130 EN ROUTE TO
NHA TRANG, RVN

Gerber sat in the red webbing that formed the seats along both sides of the C-130's fuselage and wondered exactly what to say to Louise Denton. With the roar from the four Allison T56 turboprops and the lack of soundproofing inside the aircraft, it was almost impossible to carry on a conversation with any of the other passengers. As they were boarding, the flight engineer or the loadmaster had handed out earplugs. That virtually isolated the passengers from one another.

Sitting on the ground in Saigon with the doors open and the ramp down had been hot and miserable. Gerber was belted into his seat between two perspiring, overweight sergeants. They had leaned across him, mumbling apologies, and then carried on a long-winded, extremely loud argument about the relative merits of the hookers they had shared the night before. Gerber tried to ignore them and finally got up to move away from them. Moments later the loadmaster had shut the doors and closed the ramp, and they had bounced down the runway for takeoff.

Once airborne, the air in the cabin had turned so cold that the crew was forced to use the heaters. Now Gerber tried to figure out how to break the news to Denton. And then he wondered where he should tell her. He wasn't sure that the relationship between

Denton and McMillan was quite as close as he had led Bates to believe but thought he owed it to her to tell her in person. That left all the questions that were swirling around.

In case her reaction was bad, he wanted her away from the others so that she would have time to compose herself. The hospital would be the wrong place, as would the club or a downtown Nha Trang restaurant or bar. Everything was wrong because it was all too public. Maybe he should just find a jeep and tell her there. Tell her quickly, and then let her decide what she wanted to do.

Of course, if she wasn't as in love with McMillan as Gerber thought, none of it would matter. He could tell her in a hospital corridor, or call her on the phone or let her learn about it from others.

And none of it gave him the words he needed to tell her. That was what he really dreaded. How do you break the news to someone that a person close to them is now dead? It wasn't completely unexpected because the Special Forces lived on the edge all the time, but that didn't make the task any easier. Nor did it give him the words. He didn't want to blurt it out, and then he realized that people always drew out telling good news. They tried to make it seem bad. Tried to make it a joke. But bad news, really bad news, was told in as few words and as quickly as possible.

For a moment Gerber stared at the men across the aisle from him. They were all young and all looked scared. Three or four were Army and the remainder were Air Force, and all were wearing new fatigues. He could tell they were new by the bright green color. They hadn't had time for the sun and repeated washings to bleach them to a light green. It meant the military was drafting men younger and sending them to Vietnam quicker.

Gerber realized he was trying to distract himself from the problem at hand. Where to tell her? How to tell her?

He supposed the best thing was to just say something like, "Louise, I have some very bad news. Ian was killed in action." There was no way to soften the blow. Let her ask questions if she wanted more information. Let her take it from there, and he could react to her. Louise could set the tone.

There was a jeep waiting for him at Nha Trang. It sat in the shade next to the tower, the windshield down, and as Gerber approached, he saw why. Both sides were badly cracked, the driver's side looking as if it had been hit by bullets. The driver, who was a regular Army sergeant, was leaning back, one foot on the dashboard, his hat pulled down over his eyes. As the passengers walked down the ramp of the C-130, the sergeant sat up and started the engine, heading for the only person wearing a green beret. He pulled up next to the officer and leaned over to yell, "Captain Gerber?"

"Yes."

"I've been sent over to give you a lift."

Gerber threw his gear in the back.

As soon as he had climbed in, the sergeant gunned the engine, and they roared off in the direction of the Fifth Special Forces Headquarters. Here Gerber spent the rest of the afternoon filling them in on the VC base camp they had found. He talked to Major William Houston, the Intelligence officer, a couple of other staff officers and three NCOs who made copious notes and checked a dozen separate maps. Every few seconds Gerber would remember the real reason he was there and would feel his stomach turn over. As he finished the debriefing, he realized that he would have to call someone at the hospital to make sure Louise was still there. He was not looking forward to the next hour.

Outside the debriefing room Gerber found a clerk's office with a phone and then found the number of the hospital in a mimeographed phone book that had most of the numbers crossed out. New ones had been scribbled in the margins. He had spent weeks trying to forget the number after Karen Morrow had left Vietnam.

After nearly ten minutes someone located Louise Denton and got her on the phone. When she answered, it sounded as if she had run through the ward. "Ian, is that you?"

"No, Louise," said Gerber carefully. "This is Mack Gerber. You remember me, don't you?"

"Of course, Captain. Are you here in Nha Trang?" There was no suspicion in her voice.

"Yes, for the day. I thought we might get together for a while."

Her voice suddenly turned cold. "No, Captain, I don't think that would be a good idea."

"No, wait! I'm afraid you don't understand. I'd like to meet you for a few minutes when it's convenient." Gerber was aware that his own voice sounded strained and unnatural. He tried to lighten the mood slightly by saying, "I'll buy you a drink. Anything you want."

There was a long pause before she said, "I get off at six. There's a small club that the medical people use. Do you know it?"

"Yes, I know it." All too well, Gerber thought. Karen Morrow had taken him there a couple of times when he had been in Nha Trang, and he wasn't sure how he would react to being in it again. It was filled with memories of his affair with Karen, and it was a place that he had planned to avoid. Although she didn't know it, Louise was making this harder than necessary.

"I'll meet you there a little after six."

"That'll be fine." Gerber hung up, thinking she had totally misunderstood why he called. She had sounded as if he were trying to date her, and although they had had some interesting discussions while she was at his camp with a medical unit, he had never done anything to suggest that he was interested in her as a woman.

With some time to kill, he decided to head over to the PCOD lounge for a couple of drinks. Something to relax him for the coming ordeal. He didn't want to see Louise because he knew what was going to happen.

SHE WAS SITTING with two other nurses at a table at the rear, out of the way. The club was small, only a couple of tables surrounded by chairs, with a bar stuck in one corner. There were four stools in front of it and a small mirror behind it. Denton had her back to him, but he recognized the red hair piled high on her head, to conform to Army regulations. She was wearing jungle fatigues but there was no mistaking the feminine shape. Gerber knew that she had brought the other two nurses so that he couldn't try anything. He wondered how he could separate her from her reinforcements.

He walked up behind her and placed a hand on her shoulder to get her attention. She turned her head, looked up and smiled briefly. Then she saw the look on his face. She stared into his eyes for a moment and then shook her head as if she had seen a ghost. The blood drained from her face, and Gerber realized that she knew.

She looked at the two nurses with her and said, "Would you excuse us?"

Neither moved.

"Please. It's all right."

As the two women left the table and headed for the empty stools at the bar, Gerber slipped into a chair and took Denton's hand. She squeezed in response and said, "Please," without realizing she had spoken again.

"Would you like to get out of here?" asked Gerber.

She bit her bottom lip, gripping it in her teeth, then closed her eyes and shook her head. "When?"

"Two days ago, about dawn."

"I knew it," she breathed. "I felt it. Do you know what happened to him?"

"Louise, I'm very sorry about this. I didn't know how to do this. I haven't had to do it before."

She held herself together as long as she could. The tears that had been burning her eyes spilled over, running down her cheeks. She dropped her head to her arms and rested them on the table.

Gerber stood and reached out, lifting her from the chair and guiding her out of the room. One of the nurses who had been with Denton half rose, and Gerber shook his head, telling her that it was all right. The woman hesitated, saw Denton take Gerber's hand and dropped back to her stool.

Outside, they turned right and walked rapidly to the corner of the building where the shadows would hide them. Gerber twisted her shoulders so that she faced him, then put his arms around her. She clung to him and mumbled something that Gerber couldn't understand. She began to shake as she cried harder. Finally she regained control of herself. She leaned her cheek against his shoulder and said quietly, "We got married, you know. When he was here. Just went downtown and got married. It didn't mean anything to the Army, but it did to us."

Gerber hadn't counted on this. The revelation about the marriage caused him even more distress. He was at a loss for words. Everything he thought of would sound trite, he realized. Everything would sound insincere. He had felt this before and hadn't found an answer to it. He wondered how ministers could talk to the relatives of the recently dead. What could they say that would relieve the pain? Everything seemed so inadequate.

"Is there someone you would like me to call?"

She didn't answer right away. Then she said, "Do you know what happened?"

"We've managed to put some of it together. He was ambushed while on patrol. I know it'll mean nothing to you, but we put him in for a Silver Star."

"It'll make his parents happy," she said. "Now, if you don't mind, I would like to go back into the club and drink heavily for about three hours and then pass out."

"Tell you what," he said, a little too cheerfully. "I'll buy the first one and then leave quietly."

"No. Please. Drink with me. No one here knew Ian, and I want to think about him a lot tonight. No one here will understand."

"Louise, Ian was special to all of us. He had a talent that we're going to sorely miss. I think a little of all of us died with him, and I would be more than happy to drink with you tonight. Anything you want, you've got. We, meaning the team and I, owe him that much. You're one of us, too."

Denton slipped her hand into his and nearly dragged him back into the club. She stopped at the bar long enough to order a bottle of Scotch, but when the bartender set it in front of her, she pushed it away. "Not Scotch," she said. "Beam's. A bottle of Beam's."

"You can drink anything you like," said Gerber.

"And tonight I want to drink Beam's."

"Good choice. You want a mixer?"

"Straight. I want it straight, and I want a lot of it."

Three hours later Denton's eyes were unfocused, and she was weaving back and forth in her chair as if she were having trouble sitting up. She couldn't speak in full sentences, and what she did say made little sense. She had finished most of the bottle herself and had ordered a second.

At midnight Gerber decided that it was time to get her back to her room. He corked the remainder of the bourbon, stuffed the bottle into one of the side pockets of his jungle jacket and stood. Denton looked up and smiled. "What's this?"

"Time to go. You've had enough."

"I don' thin' there's any such thin' as enough."

"Sure there is. You think you can find the way?"

"The way where? To room? You have ta help. You have ta take me."

Gerber led her from the club, keeping her upright with great difficulty. At the door to the nurse's quarters, she stumbled and fell and ended up sitting on the floor, giggling helplessly. She couldn't stand up, and she couldn't stop laughing. Gerber bent and picked her up. She wrapped her arms around him and buried her face in his neck. "Nice," she mumbled. "Real nice." The word sounded like "nahce."

"Where to?"

"Right. Go right and don' fall."

To Gerber's horror, Louise Denton lived in the same building where Karen Morrow had lived, except on a different floor. But each one mirrored all the others, and Gerber had an uncomfortable feeling of déjà vu. The only way he could find Louise's room was by walking up and down the hall, reading the signs on the doors listing the occupants.

To make matters worse, when he found her quarters, he learned that she lived alone in a room that duplicated the one Karen had lived in. Denton's roommate had DEROSed. He was alone with her in her room.

He set her on the bed, a standard Army cot with a thick mattress, and OD blanket and worn cotton sheets. As he moved to the wall switch so that he could turn on the light, Denton stood up and began to undress. She dropped her fatigue jacket to the floor and was struggling with the buttons on her pants.

"Help me!" she demanded. "I canna get them."

"Louise, go to bed."

"Wha's wrong, Cap'n Mack. You don' like me?"

"I like you just fine, but in the morning you wouldn't like yourself. The best thing for you is to go to sleep. You're set for it now."

"I don' wanna sleep. I wanna play." She continued to try to unbutton her pants, weaving around until she lost her balance and fell again, landing on the small area rug that lay on the painted plywood floor. She finally tugged at her pants with all her might and scattered the buttons. Then she wiggled from side to side on her bottom, all the while sliding the pants over her hips. She kicked her legs until the trousers had slipped to her ankles, then sat quietly for a moment. Suddenly she bent forward and pounded the floor with both fists, demanding, "Why?"

Gerber sat beside her and put his arm around her but didn't say anything. He waited for her to do something. Her shoulders shook for a moment, and he heard a broken sob. Denton cried quietly for a while, the tears staining her already dirty face and dropping from her chin to her chest. Finally she leaned her head against his shoulder, and he could hear the sobs diminishing. In a couple of minutes, she was sound asleep.

Carefully he lifted her to the bed and tried to remove her pants, but then realized that he would have to take off her boots to manage it. That finished, he got her pants off and tossed them to the single metal chair in a corner. He was tempted to remove her bra, but it was under her T-shirt, and he figured she would not appreciate his removing it. He then took the dustcover from her bunk and spread it across her inert form, even though it was still fairly hot and the fan turning slowly on the ceiling did little to relieve the heat. He moved to the windows, which were covered by bare venetian blinds. Pulling two of the slats apart, he peered through them. He opened the window to catch the slight breeze from the sea. There were lights visible below, but nothing that was bright enough for him to identify the source. He let the blinds bang back against the plywood wall and window frame.

He walked across the room, stopped at the door for a second and looked at her. She was a very pretty woman who had had a lot to drink. She had red hair that was more auburn than red, a complexion that was tanned to a golden brown by time on the beach and eyes that were like liquid emeralds. He realized that, if the situation had been different, he would have been tempted to take her offer, but it had been the liquor talking.

Gerber felt an overwhelming sadness for the Louise Denton's of this world, for himself and for all those who found themselves in that place called Vietnam.

To himself, he said, "If you want, call me, Louise." He snapped off the light and closed the door.

As he left the quarters, he saw a couple of nurses playing cards in the dayroom at the far end of the hall. He walked toward it, the sound of his footsteps muffled by the dirty plywood of the floor. He leaned in and asked, "Any of you know Louise Denton?"

"Yeah. So?"

"She got some bad news tonight and drank quite a bit. Somebody might want to check on her. Make sure that she's all right."

"Okay, Captain. Sure will."

Gerber then went over to the Playboy Club where the Special Forces people drank when they came off duty. He ignored most of the men inside, not recognizing any of them. The Special Forces had expanded so much recently that it was no longer the elite bunch it had been where everyone knew everyone else. He bought a beer at the makeshift bar opposite the door and took it to a small table hidden in a corner where he could drink it alone. After he finished drinking the beer, he decided he didn't want another. He had had too much for one night, and he didn't want to get drunk. Finally he left, walking to the barracks reserved for transient military personnel where there was a room held for him. He took the bottle that he had saved from Denton's spree, poured himself a final drink and hoped that he wouldn't have to spend another day trying to tell someone that the person she loved had been killed in action. He didn't understand how the officers in the World could do it day after day.

6

SPECIAL FORCES
OPERATING BASE, NHA
TRANG, RVN

Unlike the mornings in the bush, Gerber awoke slowly. The sunlight, filtering through the screened window, woke him. He turned over, not wanting to leave the comfort of a real bed with real sheets on it. He didn't want to get up because that would mean returning to his responsibilities at Camp A-555. It would mean a morning of hassles with clerks who had momentary power over him with their manifests and flight rosters. It would mean standing in hot departure lounges waiting for aircraft that might not arrive because no one had printed schedules. Units were tasked to supply aircraft for the ash and trash flights, but mission requirements, not to mention enemy action, sometimes dictated the airplanes be diverted.

Gerber rolled to his back and opened his eyes. He could see a rough ceiling with two wires leading to a lone light bulb. To his left was a folding metal chair where he had put the uniform he had been wearing the night before. To the right was the single open window, the blinds locked to the top and a light, warm breeze blowing through. The walls, made of quarter-inch plywood, had been painted a revolting light green, and a woven bamboo mat rested on the floor. There was a shelf nailed to the wall opposite the window, with a bar under it to hang uniforms and civilian clothes. It was a stark, impersonal room that provided nothing except a convenient resting place for the men whose destination was Nha Trang.

He got out of bed, grabbed his shaving kit from his overnight bag and headed to the shower. Ten minutes later, feeling refreshed, he put on his clean uniform. Unlike those worn by the rear area progues, his uniform was not starched or freshly ironed. He checked out of his room and left the building.

Outside, he headed over to the PCOD lounge to see if he could find some breakfast. Failing there, he wandered toward the hospital, accidentally walked into a mess hall and was offered something to eat. Since they were serving fresh eggs, fresh fried potatoes and fresh fruit, Gerber decided not to argue and grabbed a metal tray, a metal cup and utensils that looked as if they had survived the Second World War. But since the food was better than anything he had at his camp, he was happy.

Two hours later Gerber was on a C-123 heading to Dau Tieng where he could hop on a chopper to take him to the Triple Nickel. He caught a ride about midafternoon and in less than an hour was standing alone on the helipad in a swirling cloud of red dust and debris, watching as a couple of the team members rushed over to see him.

"Colonel Bates is in the team house," Smith informed him before he had a chance to speak.

Gerber smiled at the sergeant and said, "Yes, Sully, I had a fine trip, and it's good to be back."

"Sorry, Captain. Thought you would want to know about the colonel."

"Yes, of course." He held out his overnight bag. "Get this to my hootch, and I'll trot over and see what the colonel wants."

"Orders," said Smith. "He brought our extension papers and orders for leave. Gave us about three days to clear out of town."

Gerber found Bates talking to Fetterman as the two men studied a map spread out on a table. As he entered, Fetterman looked up and said, "I was just showing Colonel Bates where we found that VC base camp."

"Go right ahead," said Gerber. "I'll grab a cup of coffee if any of you thought to leave some for me."

Without a word Fetterman turned back to the map, and as Gerber moved toward them, Bocker entered the team house. Grinning, he headed straight for Gerber. "Welcome back, Captain."

"You been talking to Sully?"

"Yes, sir. He said that you were in a bad mood and I should welcome you back before I said anything else to you."

"Well, I appreciate the thought even if the motives aren't all that swift," said Gerber, also grinning. He sipped the coffee he had poured. "Something I can do for you, Galvin?"

"Yes, sir. Got a lieutenant colonel on the line from some leg outfit. Claims that he has been detailed for a special mission and wants to coordinate with you. Wonders if tomorrow morning, about 0800 will be convenient."

Gerber shot a glance at Bates, who merely shrugged. To Bocker, Gerber said, "Where does he want to meet?"

"He'll fly in here, if that's all right."

"Tell him I'll be waiting for him."

As Bocker disappeared, Bates said, "Guess your little trip to Nha Trang did some good. I figured it would be a week before anyone moved on it."

LIEUTENANT COLONEL EDWARD THOMPSON looked the part of an Army officer as he stepped off his shiny helicopter at exactly 0800 the next morning. He was a short, barrel-chested man with stubby legs. Under the rim of his helmet, Gerber could see small, dark eyes and thin black eyebrows. The man had a large nose and a small mouth with thin lips. His cheeks looked as if they had been smeared with black shoe polish, but Gerber knew it was the stubble from a beard that he could not shave close enough to hide.

His fatigues were starched to within an inch of their lives, the creases knife sharp and his boots nearly radiating black. The camouflage cover of his steel pot had been washed recently, his flak jacket looked new and he didn't have an Army-issue weapon. He had a pearl-handled revolver in an Old West holster strapped to his hip. Gerber wondered if he could outdraw the VC.

Trying to suppress a smile, Gerber moved across the helipad to shake hands with the new arrival. When he was within speaking distance, Thompson shouted over the roar of the Huey turbine and the popping of the blades, "Don't you remember how to salute?"

Immediately Gerber knew that he was in trouble with this guy. Without saluting, he approached the colonel and said, "We try not to identify each other for the VC here. Saluting only tells Charlie who the officers are."

Thompson nodded once, "It's your base, Captain. Is there somewhere we can talk?"

"Thought we'd wait for your crew to get their aircraft shut down and then all go over to the team house."

"The crew will remain with the aircraft and do their jobs," the colonel said stiffly. "There is a war on, and we all have to make sacrifices. It won't hurt them to stand by here with their equipment." Thompson stepped away from the helipad, heading in the direction of the redoubt. "This the way to your team house?"

"Yes, sir." Gerber thought of a dozen things to say, a half-dozen pieces of advice about how to survive in the field, but decided to remain silent. He knew Thompson's type, the ones who never bent the rules, who went strictly by the book. Gerber knew it wasn't that kind of a war. Thompson would learn fast or be replaced after he was KIA.

In the team house Gerber introduced Thompson to Bates. Although Gerber hadn't been formally introduced to Thompson, he had read his name off the tag sewn to his flak vest. The two colonels shook hands solemnly. Then Gerber, with Fetterman's help, began the unofficial briefing.

After an hour Thompson nodded and said, "I have everything I need. I can begin airlifting my battalion in here this afternoon."

"Whoa, Colonel," said Gerber, waving his hands. "We don't have the facilities to support a battalion. We couldn't even accommodate a regular company."

"Don't worry about it, Captain. My boys are used to roughing it. They can see how well those shelter halves we issue to them work. We'll bring our own food, too. All you'll have to do is supply the ground for them to sleep on. Tomorrow we'll head out into the bush."

"Pardon me, Colonel," insisted Gerber, "but if you have the aviation assets, wouldn't it be easier to insert them closer to the target? Why make them walk fifteen klicks?"

"You let me run my battalion, Captain," said Thompson harshly, folding his map and sticking it into one of the large pockets in his fatigues.

"Glad to, Colonel," said Gerber. "But I don't want to see Charlie get away from the tunnels with all that equipment. There is too much hidden out there that could be used against us. A battalion-sized sweep through here is going to tip our hand and give the VC time to get the stuff out of there."

"From what your Sergeant Fetterman said, I doubt he could get all that much of it out."

"Unless he had a regiment in there and each one of them carries away two rifles. All we would find down there would be that damned antiaircraft artillery and the straw they use in some of the sleeping areas."

Bates, who had been listening to the argument with a great deal of amusement, entered the conversation. "Colonel Thompson, why not throw a company of infantry into the LZ closest to the village as a recon and blocking force? That should prevent the VC from evacuating their equipment."

"Because, Colonel, that would leave a company out in the open with no chance for immediate support if they got hit. Take us hours to march to their relief."

Gerber could contain himself no longer. "Oh, for crying out loud. You're airmobile. If they get hit, you can fly them reinforcements in a few minutes. Especially if you have the majority of your battalion here and the aircraft on standby."

"Don't you go taking that tone with me, Captain. I am fully cognizant of the capabilities of my unit and its aviation assets."

"Yes, sir," said Gerber. "Sorry."

"I'll tell you what, Captain. I will bring the battalion in here, and before we move out, I will dispatch a company as a recon and blocking force. I'll need one of your people to advise that company, and I would like another to guide the ground force."

"Ah, Colonel," interrupted Bates again, "Captain Gerber's team is scheduled for leave."

"All of them?" Thompson asked incredulously. "At once?"

"Yes. A special circumstance."

"Colonel Thompson," said Gerber, "I'll be happy to go with the recon company and delay my departure by a couple of days."

"Mack," said Bates, "the commercial flights are all arranged. You might not be able to get another one for a week or more."

"I'll take that chance."

"That leaves us one man short," said Thompson.

"Oh, no, sir," said Fetterman, speaking for the first time since the briefing had ended. "I'll go with your other force. I'm quite familiar with the terrain and the route."

"Tony?" said Gerber.

"If you can do it, Captain, so can I. That gets everyone else out on time. It's no big deal."

"What about Mrs. Fetterman and the kids?"

"Well, sir, someday I'll let you in on a little secret about Mrs. Fetterman and the kids, but for right now let's just say that they understand that my job sometimes requires a little overtime."

Then Gerber, with sudden insight, said, "Colonel Bates, would you like to accompany us on this operation? You don't get out into the war all that much."

"Why, thank you, Mack. I would be delighted."

THE NEXT MORNING Gerber had to admit that he was impressed. Thompson had gotten his battalion deployed from its staging area in Bien Hoa to the camp by sundown that same night. He saw to it that each of his companies had enough hot food to feed all the combat troops. Each man had some kind of shelter before the sun set. They were not much larger than the Second World War pup tents, made from the shelter halves issued to the men and staked to the ground. Each company had its own area, its own perimeter and its own guards. Thompson and his staff declined the offer of the team house and erected their tents in the center of the battalion. All in all, it was an amazing piece of logistical work.

At dawn Gerber and Bates climbed aboard a helicopter along with six other American soldiers from the 173rd Airborne Brigade. There were fifteen aircraft in the flight so that the force being lifted to an LZ some two klicks from the ville numbered almost a hundred and fifty.

The flight was short, and Gerber expected to be on the ground in minutes. What he hadn't expected was a burst of machine gun fire from the trees on one side of the LZ as the helicopters began the approach. Since it was only one weapon and the location was identified by the muzzle flashes, the flight continued, no one concerned about the single enemy soldier hiding there.

But then the situation changed as a dozen others opened fire, raking the right side of the flight. The gunship escorts rolled in, firing their 2.75-inch rockets into the trees in a futile attempt to suppress the enemy.

The door gunners, each manning an M-60 machine gun, began to fire, raking the trees with their concentrated 7.62 mm ammunition. Gerber, sitting beside an infantryman, yelled over the noise of the engine and the rotor blades and the hammering of the M-60s, "Why don't you fire back?"

"Pilots don't like the new boys shooting out the doors. Some of them tend to shoot holes in the rotors, and they frown on that."

Gerber shot a glance at Bates, who was also sitting beside him, clutching his M-14, knuckles turning white. But there was a grin on his face, and his eyes were sparkling as if he hadn't had so much fun in years.

The volume of fire from the ground seemed to increase, and Gerber could identify AK-47s, .30-caliber machine guns and a couple of 12.5 mm antiaircraft weapons. He watched part of the windshield disintegrate, but neither pilot seemed to notice as they fought to hold their position in the formation. One of the grunts grabbed at his shoulder and slumped to the deck of the helicopter, his blood splashing over the back of the pilot's armored seat.

Then they were on the ground with the crew chief shouting, "Unass the aircraft. Get the fuck off!" More enemy weapons joined in, filling the air with green-and-white tracers. Fountains of black dirt and filthy water geysered as mortars began falling around them.

Gerber leaped from the helicopter, took a single step and dived to the ground to find cover behind a bush. Behind him the choppers lifted as a unit and roared skyward rapidly, the door guns still firing into the trees in front of the grunts now on the ground.

Bates crawled to him and yelled unnecessarily, "Now what?"

"Let's see if the company commander knows what he's doing before we make any moves."

Before Gerber stopped talking, there was a series of pops, like fireworks being shot in sequence, and M-79 grenades began exploding at the edge of the tree line into tiny clouds of black smoke and silver shrapnel. At the same time the gunships, which had been escorting the Slicks off the LZ, returned, their rockets and machine guns strafing the trees where the heaviest of the enemy fire seemed to be located.

When that happened, there was a lull in the enemy firing, then the grunts were on their feet, running forward, some of them firing from their hips. Gerber and Bates joined the assault, and as they all reached the cover of the trees, the gunships broke contact, peeling away to the right and then standing off slightly as if waiting for the VC to try something else.

In the trees Gerber couldn't see much. Directly in front of him, there appeared to be a single enemy soldier sighting an AK. Gerber fired a quick burst, saw it hit the man high and spin him before he dropped to the ground, his weapon flying from his hand. Gerber sprinted forward, leaped a small bush and was crouching over the enemy corpse. One of the bullets had neatly removed the top of his head and another had severed the jugular.

Gerber picked up the enemy weapon, not as a souvenir but to deny it to the VC, and continued into the trees. Behind him he heard an M-14 fire twice and turned to see Bates disappear into the bush a few feet away. Before Gerber could move, a sound to his right caught his attention. He spun to see a VC leaping through the air, a knife clutched in his hand. Without thinking, Gerber moved to parry the attack. But the enemy crashed into him, slamming the flimsy rifle against his stomach. Gerber pulled the trigger once and let the momentum of the impact force them both to the ground.

Rolling clear, Gerber was on his feet, using his M-16 to cover the VC who had both arms clutching his stomach as blood leaked out his back in an ever-decreasing stream.

Gerber looked at the barrel of his rifle and saw that the force of the blow had bent it slightly. He didn't know how the weapon had fired without blowing up but was grateful that it hadn't. He pushed the barrel against a tree, bending it nearly double. He then ejected the magazine and put it in his pocket to keep the ammunition out of the hands of the VC. Throwing away the useless M-16, Gerber unslung the AK he had picked up. He made sure a round was chambered and then checked the two bodies for spare magazines.

Finally, with Bates, also holding an AK, in sight again, Gerber joined the sweep through the trees. There had been a momentary flurry of hand-to-hand combat as the Americans assaulted the enemy positions, surprising them with the ferocity and speed of the attack. But Charlie, realizing that he might not be outnumbered but was being out-soldiered, fled.

As Gerber reached the opposite edge of the tree line, he saw nearly a hundred VC and a dozen or so NVA fleeing across the rice fields, trying to reach safety on the other side where they would probably disappear into what they thought was the haven of their base camp.

Then to the right Gerber heard someone yell "Grenade!" He dropped to the ground and saw a grunt leap for the explosive. Rather than throwing himself on it as the Hollywood heroes often did, the soldier picked it up and threw it at the escaping VC. It detonated far short of the enemy but had been thrown fast enough that it inflicted no American casualties, either.

Getting to his knees, Gerber shouted at the man, "Well done."

Weapons fire from the Americans tapered off as the targets disappeared among the palms, teaks and mahogany trees of a finger of jungle across the paddies. Then the gunships, which had been waiting another turn, rolled in. For a moment Gerber knelt in the protection of the tree line and watched as the rockets, fired in ripples, whooshed overhead, and then miniguns, sounding like a gigantic buzz saw, raked the new enemy position. At first there was some sporadic return fire, but that quickly died as if the enemy had learned that shooting only brought a hostile response.

While the gunships were working out on the enemy, the grunt company commander crawled through the trees until he found both Gerber and Bates. When he was near them both, he asked, "What do you think?"

Without pointing and trying not to gesture, Gerber said, "We need to keep the VC off balance. They weren't really prepared for us, and those choppers are a little more than irritating, but I think Charlie is going to keep on the move. He's running now and won't stop until he's either in Cambodia or in that base we found."

"And we don't want him to get comfortable in that tunnel system," said Bates. "It would take us a month to dig him out of there. We have to keep the pressure on."

"But the colonel can't get here—"

"Captain," said Gerber, "I just saw fifteen choppers take off. He can have another company here in a few minutes. I would get on the horn and tell him to put a company into point X-ray Delta as soon as he can."

The grunt captain pulled his map from a pocket and looked at it. Gerber reached over his arm and pointed. "That's the clearing right there on the other side of the ville. If they sweep out of there, they should be able to hit the VC in less than thirty minutes. That keeps up the pressure Colonel Bates spoke of."

"And what do we do?"

"Should be obvious. We attack across the rice fields as quickly as we can."

As the grunt stood to go find his RTO, Gerber grabbed his sleeve. "I assume that your people are all fairly green. Tell them to step on the rice plants as we sweep through the paddies. It will keep their feet from sinking deep into the mud."

AT CAMP A-555 Fetterman watched as the rest of the team climbed aboard the Chinook CH-47 that would take them to Saigon so they could catch the Freedom Bird to the World. As Tyme started up the ramp, he stopped long enough to yell over the noise of the twin engines and popping blades, "You sure you don't need us?"

Fetterman leaned close to the other man's ear and shouted right back. "The captain and I can handle this little recon chore, and then we'll be joining you youngsters in the World."

"Then I have only one thing to say. FIIGMO. See you in a month or so."

"Right you are, Boom-Boom. Now get on this thing before I change my mind and go in your place."

Fetterman moved away from the aircraft as the rear ramp closed and the rotors began to pick up speed. Then the helicopter lifted off the ground, hung for a moment over the PSP of the pad, kicking up huge clouds of red dust, and turned to the north to begin its climb out. In only a minute it was a speck near the horizon. When it was out of sight, Fetterman turned toward the commo bunker where he could see a couple of the grunts waiting.

As he approached, Colonel Thompson came out, saw him and said, "Looks like your captain and my company stepped on their dicks. We're going to put in another airlift. You want to accompany me?"

"Be delighted, sir."

They entered the team house together, but Thompson stopped short. He saw Robin Morrow sitting at one of the tables, a can of beer in front of her as she worked a crossword puzzle.

"What is that civilian doing here?" demanded Thompson.

"That is Miss Morrow, a member of the press."

"Well, get her out of here."

Before Fetterman could move or speak, Morrow had picked up her puzzle and beer and said, "I think I will find somewhere else to sit." She swept by Thompson without so much as a glance in his direction, but as she neared the door, she mumbled, "Asshole."

When she was gone, Thompson spread his map out on the table. "Near as I can figure and from what the pilots have said, they ran into it near the LZ, which was right here."

Fetterman stared at where the colonel's finger tapped the map. The team sergeant nodded. It was the right LZ. He pointed and said, "The ville is here. Now on the other side of it, here, is an open area where we can put thirty helicopters if we have to. It's less than a klick to the village, and if the VC are retreating toward it, we should be able to make contact with them here. That would also take some of the pressure off the captain."

"You've been there, then, I take it."

"To that specific LZ, yes, sir. We passed through it once. There are no obstructions in it. There are bunkers surrounding it, but they were deserted when we swept through."

Outside, there was the sound of more than a dozen Huey helicopters as they approached for landing. Thompson turned to look but couldn't see anything through the side of the building. He grinned at Fetterman and said, "I believe our ride has arrived."

"I'll grab my weapon and meet you at the choppers, sir."

"Snap to it, sergeant," said Thompson unnecessarily.

7

EN ROUTE TO THE LZ
NEAR TRANG ME

Fetterman felt uncomfortable as the flight approached the LZ. Not because of the helicopter with its cloth troop seat or the steel pot on his head and the web gear hanging from his shoulders, but because he didn't know the men he was riding into combat with. He had never seen any of them in action, had no idea what kind of training they had had in the art of jungle fighting and didn't know if they were reliable when the shooting started.

All he could do was hope for the best and that was what had killed his great-great-great-grandfather, William J. Fetterman, who had hoped for the best when he rode out of Fort Phil Kearney with eighty cavalrymen and infantrymen to meet two thousand Sioux Indians led by Crazy Horse.

As the terrain under him changed from paddy fields reflecting the sun to sparse jungle that concealed the ground and possibly the enemy, Fetterman realized they were nearing the LZ. He chambered a round in his M-3 grease gun and fastened the chin strap of his helmet so he wouldn't lose it when he jumped from the helicopter. He noticed that the young men on the chopper with him let theirs dangle free just like John Wayne. It wasn't a good sign.

They began their descent, and Fetterman could see the hardwood teak and mahogany trees rising up until they towered over the chopper. Fetterman expected the shooting to start at any second, but there was none. As the skids of the aircraft touched the ground covered with short grass, Fetterman was out and moving toward the tree line, following the group of men who had been on the ship in front of him. Thompson was leading a charge at the innocuous-looking trees, running across the open ground, like a back on a broken field. Without a sound he entered the jungle and disappeared from sight, and Fetterman fully expected the ambush to spring at that second.

The helicopters lifted off safely and headed back toward the camp. Fetterman, still waiting for the ambush, entered the jungle and saw that the colonel and his men had stopped long enough to explore some of the abandoned bunkers. These were low affairs, a single log concealing the firing port, bushes and dirt spread on top for camouflage and a shallow hole in the back so that the VC could enter and retreat. Fetterman watched a lone man leap into the back of one, as he had probably been taught to do, and before Fetterman could shout a warning, there was a gigantic explosion that shook the ground and filled the air with a cloud of dirt and debris.

Immediately there was a second explosion, and he saw two more troopers fall. Over the noise and screaming, Fetterman ordered, "Don't move! Don't anyone else move!"

When he saw several heads turn toward him, he shouted, "Is there a medic here? Get a medic over here. And an RTO."

"Sergeant Fetterman," yelled Thompson, "we have to move out. There is a schedule to maintain."

"Yes, sir, there is. But let's take care of the wounded first." Fetterman pointed at two men who stood near the smoking remains of a bunker. "You two back up slowly, and try to put your feet into the prints you made moving forward." To the rest of them, he said, "It's probably only the bunkers that have been booby-trapped, but let's all take it easy."

For the next twenty minutes Fetterman directed the operation as the officers and top NCOs from the company stood by and watched, realizing that they were seeing something extraordinary. Fetterman got the men out of immediate danger, formed a defensive ring around the bunkers and then led the medics in to treat the wounded. Seven men had been severly injured in the explosions, and although Fetterman took a little longer than anyone liked, no one else tripped a booby trap. They had been about to question his methods when he found the trip wire that would have detonated a captured two-hundred-and-fifty-pound bomb, which could have killed an entire platoon.

A medevac chopper was called in. It circled, waiting for one of Thompson's men to throw a smoke grenade, and the wounded, along with four dead, were evaced out. That done, Thompson made his way to Fetterman and asked how he thought they should assault the village.

"I don't think we should assault anything, Colonel," Fetterman replied. "What we should do is simply take up a position on this side of it, fanning out in a modified U ambush, and wait for Captain Gerber and your people to push the VC into us."

"What about the tunnels?"

"They are probably already occupied, and our delaying will only show us the locations of some of the entrances if we can see the VC use them. It might also give us a clue as to the size of the force we're going to meet. Where are your X rays?"

For an instant Thompson was puzzled and then said, "Oh, the engineers. Still at your camp. Didn't think we would need them on the first lift."

"Probably right, sir. Once we get the enemy located, we'll need to blow some of the upper tunnels and the entrances to begin boxing in the VC. One thing, though. We'll never find them all, and we'll need to be extremely careful. We'll want to let Charlie know we're here and that we mean business. If he doesn't surrender, we have two choices. Dig him out, or seal him in, though I doubt we'll be able to seal him in. The system is too extensive. The choice will be up to you, as long as you don't let all that ordnance he has hidden down there get out."

"You're mighty concerned about all that, just like your captain."

"Yes, sir, and if they were going to be shooting it at you, you would be concerned too."

Thompson ran off to talk to his company commander on the scene. As Fetterman watched in growing horror, the men began to sweep through the jungle, hacking at the vines and bushes with machetes, chopping their way through the undergrowth, smashing the smaller trees to get them out of the way and shouting orders at one another. They had nearly no noise discipline; not one of them knew how to glide through the undergrowth without disturbing it. Then he noticed that Thompson's men only carried two canteens apiece. He sometimes carried as many as five because water was so much more important than food in a jungle environment. The heat of the sun seemed to drain the strength with a rapidity that was frightening.

They would learn, he decided, and it wasn't his place to try to teach them now. Crawling silently through the jungle would be of no advantage in this operation and maybe they sensed that. Perhaps next time they would know enough not to shout at each other or to hack at the jungle plants and to tape down the equipment that would rattle. When they returned to base, he could mention it to a couple of the older NCOs so that something could be done on the QT.

In twenty minutes they were in position. Fetterman was near the center of the line and watching the now deserted village. Even the water buffalo were gone. It was as if the inhabitants knew that something was going to happen and they had decided to vanish until the threat was over.

Thompson, his RTO close at hand, was mumbling into the handset, telling his company commander with Gerber that they were in position to block the enemy retreat. Fetterman wasn't sure he liked being that close to the RTO because Charlie, sometimes unsure who were officers, shot at everyone near the radio, figuring to get an officer or two that way. The antenna, sticking an extra two or three feet into the air, made the perfect aiming stake for enemy snipers.

As SOON AS WORD was passed that the other company was in position, Gerber told the captain with him to move out rapidly. The gunships had stopped hosing down the trees, and there was only sporadic sniping coming from the VC. The grunt captain had wanted to send squads out to deal with the snipers, but Gerber wouldn't let him. Instead, he told him to have the grenadiers lob grenades into the trees near where the snipers were hiding. They may not kill them that way, but they would surely stop the sniping. Besides, once they started the assault, they could deal with the snipers in an efficient manner.

On command from the captain, the whole company left the tree line and began a sweep across the rice fields. Immediately they were taken under fire, the round splashing in the water or kicking up dirt and mud from the dikes. A few of the grunts dropped to the ground, uninjured, but scrambled for protection behind the low dikes around the paddies.

"Keep moving," shouted Gerber as he fired a five-round burst from the hip. He was watching the tracers, using them to aim. "Get up and keep moving. Grenadiers, hit the trees. Let's move it."

"But they're shooting at us," someone mumbled.

Gerber didn't respond. He just reached down and grabbed one of the grunts by the shoulder straps of his pack and lifted him, pushing him forward toward the trees. Gerber was suddenly calm, watching for the telltale muzzle flashes in the shadows of the tree line. Since there were no mortars being fired and the shooting was so poorly directed, Gerber felt almost safe.

"There aren't that many of them. They're trying to hold us up to let their friends get away," Gerber told them.

In seconds they were in the next tree line and the shooting increased momentarily, but the VC could no longer see the Americans easily, and the muzzle flashes were now visible in the shade of the jungle. Each time a VC fired his weapon, a dozen Americans returned the fire, and it was quickly neutralized. Grenadiers were almost fighting one another to drop their rounds on the enemy. They were just getting into the rhythm of the movement when they heard firing in the distance and knew that the enemy had reached the village and the blocking force.

Gerber waved the men forward then, trying to get them to move rapidly through the trees, taking a couple of chances so that they would be in position if the VC tried to force their way back. Gerber figured that Charlie, not knowing the size of the blocking force, might decide to try to overrun his pursuers rather than tangle with the blocking force. Gerber wanted to be ready.

But the counterattack never came. The firing from the other side of the village died out gradually as Gerber and his people moved into position just inside the trees where they could see the mud hootches. When they were set, the company commander used his radio to get instructions from Thompson, and then both units slowly entered the village, leaving some of their men to establish security.

The two forces met near the hootch where they had found the first tunnel entrance. They didn't waste time standing around talking about it but found as much cover as possible near it. Men hid behind part of the fence of woven branches, near the corner of another hootch and among the coconut trees around them. One or two leaned their rifles against the trees and took long, deep drinks from the lukewarm water in their canteens. Others poured water on the go-to-hell rags wrapped around their necks.

"And now?" asked Thompson as he was joined by both Gerber and Fetterman.

"Obviously," said Gerber, shading his eyes and slowly searching the jungle in the distance, "we have Charlie on the run. He has faded into his tunnel system, figuring we have no idea that it's here. The fact that we haven't taken any sniper fire recently is significant. Charlie wants us to assume that he has left the area and is nowhere around. He wants us to move into the jungle chasing shadows and not search in this village. He doesn't know that we know."

"One thing," cautioned Fetterman, "these tunnels honeycomb the whole area so that he can pop up behind us. To lead us off, he may throw a couple of people to the wolves to draw us into the jungle. We don't want to lose anyone because of carelessness. We have to be alert outside the ville. That's where the problem will develop. You might want to get some patrols out, roaming at the edges of the perimeter. Deny Charlie the opportunity to get set."

Thompson turned to one of the company commanders, "You heard that, Jones? You get your people set and tell them to be ready for snipers. And get a couple of twelve-man patrols out there."

"Yes, sir." Jones started to salute, but his hand had frozen halfway and he stared at Thompson, a look of horror on his face. Thompson chose to ignore the mistake.

"I would also suggest," added Gerber, "that we spread this command party out. As the saying goes, 'One grenade can get us all.'"

Thompson pointed at a lieutenant and the other captain and then indicated the trees. Both officers took off into the jungle without acknowledging the order.

"Now?"

"We wait for the engineers," said Gerber.

"Unless we want to put some people into the tunnels to explore them," suggested Fetterman.

"Let's wait," decided Thompson. "I know I wouldn't want to go down there with the enemy hiding there. I couldn't order anyone else to do it."

"I think we should get charges set," said Gerber, "make a sapper attack into the upper levels, leave the explosives and then get out. The concussion of enough high explosives should pretty well scramble Charlie's brains, and then our people could go in and get him."

"If the tunnels don't collapse," offered Fetterman. "Or Charlie hasn't built in blast doors to direct the concussion."

"And if the tunnels collapse, we've got a bunch of VC buried a bit early," said Gerber.

"But we won't have an accurate body count," said Thompson. "We've got to get some kind of body count."

"Yeah," said Fetterman, "it would be a damned shame to kill a VC and not get a chance to count his body. Make everyone look real bad."

The engineers, looking as scared as a kid sitting in the principal's office, arrived fifteen minutes later carrying giant packs of explosives. A platoon of grunts, carrying more equipment, including detonators, det cord, rifles, grenades, flares and their normal packs, followed them into the village. Gerber quickly spread them out so that a clever VC couldn't kill all the engineers and destroy all the equipment with a well-placed bullet.

"Now that we have everything," said Gerber, "we sweep through here carefully, pinpointing as many tunnel entrances as we can. The security people can check their immediate areas because we know there are tunnels in the jungle. Once we have them spotted, we move into them in a coordinated effort, trying to set the explosives so they all go up at once."

Thompson nodded but said nothing.

"Then we check the tunnels themselves. We should put some people into them to try to assess the damage. We want to be sure that we seal the place off."

"How?" asked Thompson because he knew that it was an almost impossible task.

"We'll have to leave people here to watch. We must have patrols throughout this area for the next month so that each time a VC pops up, someone is there to see him and capture him. Failing that, they need to shoot him, but a prisoner can tell us more about the damage and show us tunnels we might have missed. A dead man is just so much cold meat."

"I don't like it," said Thompson.

"You have a better idea?" asked Gerber.

"No, Captain, I don't. That doesn't mean I have to like the plan. I don't like having my people in the field for too long."

"I understand," said Gerber. "But then, they're not that far from our camp and can be resupplied easily. You'll have the ville to use as a base. All you're doing is patrolling this area where you know the VC live."

"Oh, it's a good plan," agreed Thompson. "But I still don't like it."

Without further comment he walked over to one of his company commanders and began issuing instructions. In a few minutes the company stood on line, divided into platoons and given quadrants of the village to explore, with specific instructions about what they were to look for.

With Gerber and Fetterman to lead them, the grunts swept through the village, turning over everything in sight and digging into piles of manure, looking for hidden openings into the tunnel system. But they had little luck. They did find a dozen bunkers that were independent but only two or three tunnels that led deeper into the major system.

The troops positioned outside the ville, at the edge of the jungle, found another six tunnel entrances. And farther away, in the area where McMillan had been ambushed, they found another two. At that point they decided they had found enough.

Coordinating the activity, the engineers, led by grunts or, in the case of the main entrance that Fetterman had found a couple of days earlier, by Fetterman, entered the tunnels. Fetterman prepped his by dropping a grenade down it and then leaping to the tunnel floor before the dust had a chance to settle. But he could see nothing in the billowing cloud created by the grenade.

An engineer followed closely, communicating his nervousness to Fetterman by his rapid breathing and the hiccups he had caught as they entered the tunnel. Fetterman, pistol in hand, scrambled toward the ladder that led to a lower level. When he found it, he dropped another grenade and ducked back. As it detonated and the concussion carrying the dust washed over him like a wave on a beach, he whispered to the engineer, "Throw your satchel charge down there now with the delay fuse set for three minutes."

If the engineer was inclined to argue, he quickly forgot about it. He worked his way past Fetterman so that he could look down the ladder. He set the fusing of the satchel charge and tossed it into the dust that was still swirling in the tunnel. Before the engineer could speak, Fetterman had begun to rapidly crawl back the way he had come. In less than a minute he was out of the tunnel and running across the open ground to the cover of another hootch where Gerber waited. The engineer was right behind him.

As he leaped for cover, Fetterman said, "About a minute, Captain."

Then, almost as Fetterman stopped speaking, the ground began to shake, and there was a rumbling as the satchel charges placed by all the teams began to explode, the concussions reverberating through the underground channels, shaking the walls and floors of the tunnels. It was as if they had created a miniature earthquake that fed on itself, rocking the surface of the land, causing the hootches to sway like small boats on a choppy sea.

From nearly fifty locations dust and smoke came boiling out of the concealed entrances as more of the tunnels collapsed. For a moment it was quiet, and then, as if something underground had caught fire and exploded on its own, there was a violent rumble as the whole village lifted and then fell back, settling three feet lower than it had been.

"I think their arsenal went up then," commented Fetterman.

"Whatever it was," said Thompson, "I don't think we have to worry about anyone getting out of there."

Watching more of the dust pour out of the ground, Fetterman said, "It's too bad. I would have liked to have gotten that antiaircraft gun out of there. Would have made a real nice addition to the camp's weapons.

Gerber wanted to laugh. "Ah, Tony, you're never happy. What in the hell would we do with a 23 mm antiaircraft gun? Even if we could find ammo for it."

"I'm sure that Boom-Boom would have thought of something."

Thompson interrupted. "Well, as I said before, I don't think we have to worry about anyone getting out."

"No, sir," agreed Gerber, "but it wouldn't be a bad idea to leave some people in the area to make sure. And have some people check out the tunnels."

"I'll leave a platoon or two," said Thompson. "I'm going to whistle up the choppers now. I imagine you boys will want to catch a ride back so that you can begin your leave."

"Mrs. Fetterman and the kids appreciate it, sir," said Fetterman.

8

SPECIAL FORCES CAMP
A-555

It didn't take the helicopters long to pick up the teams. The flight back to camp seemed to be much shorter than the one that had brought them out. Gerber sat in the troop seat, leaning against the ripped gray soundproofing that failed to reduce the noise from the turbine, and thought about the nature of the Vietnam War. He had left his hootch early in the morning, spent the day in combat with the enemy, some of it hand-to-hand, and now he was on his way home. He could sit in his hootch, read the afternoon paper—the *Stars and Stripes*—listen to the radio, or even watch TV if he was so inclined. Not exactly the classic view of war, but more of a nine-to-five-type job.

In fact, with the huge influx of American troops in South Vietnam, there was a change in the culture. The Americans were bringing it with them. Instead of small bases in the boonies manned by a few American troops and a couple of hundred locals, the brass was building big base camps. Islands of American culture in the middle of Vietnam.

They were erecting steak houses, discos, television and radio stations, clubs for the enlisted men, NCOs and officers, tailor shops, souvenir shops, and bath houses employing young Vietnamese women. Thousands of troops were arriving, including the newly reorganized 1st Cavalry, which was now airmobile. And each of the troops in the field was supported by seven or eight in the camps. These troops consisted of clerks, cooks, maintenance men, supply men and people to brief news correspondents and design recreational programs. There was even talk of building a library.

It wasn't the way to fight a war, especially the Vietnam War, but the bureaucrats and congressmen—the chairborne commandos, Gerber thought wryly—wanted to be sure that the boys were comfortable while they were away from home. Gerber shook his head, wishing that President Johnson and Secretary of Defense McNamara would leave the fighting of the war to the officers who knew what they were doing. The whole thing was getting out of hand, and if they weren't careful, it wouldn't be fun anymore.

Gerber smiled at the thought: men in Washington with no concept of this war, or any war, were making policy that affected all aspects of the war. Of course, no one had asked his opinion, and maybe that was the problem. The policymakers hadn't bothered to learn what they needed to know to make intelligent decisions. They seemed to think money would solve a problem, and if that didn't work, the obvious answer was more money.

In the distance he could see the buildings of his camp twinkling in the late-afternoon sun, their tin roofs now rusted so that they seemed to glow gold. The camp was rectangular with a short runway on the western side. Just off the eastern edge of the runway was an oval redoubt, which was not more than seventy-five meters across. It was an earthen breastwork that was five feet tall and had only one tiny entrance on the east side, which was protected by .30-caliber machine guns. Six strands of concertina wire surrounded the camp. Scattered among the rows of wire were claymore antipersonnel mines, barrels of foogas, trip flares and booby traps. The nearest cover for an attacking force was a clump of trees almost five hundred meters away on the south side of the camp.

Smoke from one of the fires that was burning trash sent a cloud of black smoke into the sky from near the center of the Vietnamese hootches. Several rows of the small, eight-man hootches stood on the west side of the runway. Gerber made a mental note to tell Minh about it. Charlie could use the smoke as a spotting guide for his mortars, and he didn't think Minh would like it if the mortars kept falling among the strikers' hootches.

As the helicopter's skids touched the ground, Thompson leaped out to run over to the commo bunker so that he could make radio contact with his people still in the field. Bates, Fetterman and Gerber didn't see any need to follow him and, instead, walked toward the team house. Gerber knew that they should clean their weapons and even make a few notes for the after-action report that the brass hats in Saigon would want, but he was too tired to be worried about the bureaucratic trivia. Besides, he had a leave to get ready for.

As they approached the team house, Gerber said, "Come on, Alan, I'll buy you a beer."

"Just what I had in mind," said Bates. "How about Sergeant Fetterman?"

"He can buy his own. In fact, he has his own supply, and it's even cold. I can't offer you a cold one."

"Well, now, Captain," Fetterman said, "if your party with the colonel isn't private, I might be persuaded to supply the cold beer."

"Then by all means, join us," said Gerber magnanimously. He laughed and said, "And since when did you need an invitation?"

"Just trying to be polite in front of company." Fetterman unbuckled his pistol belt so that it hung open in the front supported by the shoulder harness. There were sweat stains where it had been locked around his waist.

Inside, they found Robin Morrow sitting at one of the tables, her feet propped up and four cans of beer in front of her. She was wearing shorts and a khaki shirt, which was unbuttoned halfway to her belly button and damp under the arms. She had her hair pulled back off a forehead beaded with perspiration. When she saw them, she said, "Welcome back, gentlemen. Would you care for a drink?"

Fetterman said, "No, but you can stay, anyway."

"I'll have one," said Bates.

Morrow let her feet drop to the floor and used her church key to open one of the cans. She pushed it across the table at Bates and said, "There you are, Colonel."

When they were all seated, Morrow asked, "So how did the mission go?"

Without looking at her, Gerber said, "The mission went fine. It was just fine. What do you want to know for?"

"I was assigned to do a story on the Special Forces, and the story isn't finished yet," she snapped. "You're welcome for the beer."

Fetterman leaped into the conversation by saying, "There are a couple of things we're going to have to do to get ready to take our leaves."

"I know," said Gerber. He looked at Bates. "I suppose you have some idea about who you want to send in for our replacements."

"I thought you said you were staying so that you wouldn't be replaced," said Morrow.

"Yes, but we'll be gone for thirty days, and there has to be someone in here to take over temporarily."

"Don't worry about it," said Bates, setting his beer on the table in front of him. "You've got almost a battalion here right now, and they won't be leaving for about a month. Also, I've got Captain Bromhead in Saigon organizing a new A-Team. There're quite a few unattached Special Forces troops running around, and it doesn't hurt to have an extra team. I'll bring him in here to hold things down. Once you've returned, I'll send him home for a month."

"That would work," said Gerber, nodding. "Johnny knows the area around here quite well. Be a real advantage for him to be working here. Should have thought of that myself. In fact, I should have thought about leaving him a couple of my NCOs to help him while he's getting his feet wet."

"I could stay an extra week, if that would help," said Fetterman.

"I don't think that's really necessary, Tony," said Gerber. "Hell, Johnny's been here a year and had some of the best training available. I guess he won't need the help."

"Besides all that," said Bates, "I plan to stay out here until we get him established. And there's Captain Minh, who will still be here."

"As far as I can see," said Gerber, "that leaves only one problem: what to do with Robin."

"Hey," she said, "I'm right here. Why not ask me if I have any plans before you go deciding?"

"Do you have any plans, Robin?"

"Thought I'd just stay here and see how the camp runs without you people. I might discover you're not the valuable asset that you claim to be."

Gerber looked to Bates again. "What do you think?"

"She can stay if she wants, though I don't see much point in it. Won't be anything happening. I'll be here to look after her until Captain Bromhead arrives."

"I don't need anyone to look after me."

"With all due respect," said Gerber, "I disagree. Hell, I would want someone out here with you even if you were a male journalist. It's not good policy to have Americans all alone in the field."

"That leaves only one question," said Bates. "What are you two going to do about leave?"

"Hadn't thought that much about it," interjected Fetterman before anyone could speak. "Leave seems to be an unnatural state for the soldier. Sort of like peace. Soldiers have to exist in peace because there is eventually going to be a war and then it's too late to train them, but they are out of place. It would be better if they could be frozen until they are needed."

"Lovely speech, Tony," said Gerber.

"Yeah, I kind of liked it. Anyway, the point is I haven't given it much thought."

"Well, while the master sergeant is trying to figure it out," said Gerber, "I thought I'd go to Hong Kong. Spend my time running from tailors to camera stores and researching the Oriental mind."

"That's a pretty bizarre plan," said Morrow. "Why go to Hong Kong?"

A hundred answers sprang to mind, most of them involving Robin's sister, Karen. Gerber wanted to say that he could go to Hong Kong and still be half a world away from her. He could go to Hong Kong and remain in a fairly alien environment where there wouldn't be constant reminders of Karen Morrow, where he wouldn't have to worry about running into people he knew who would ask complicated questions. It was a place to hide, and it seemed to be better than a dozen other choices that had crossed his mind.

Instead of any of that, he said, "It has an intrigue that attracts me. Besides, it's very close by air to a lot of other places I might want to see. It would be a good base to operate from. If I got tired of Hong Kong, I could go to Manila, Macau, Singapore, even Australia."

Fetterman sat across from Gerber and slowly nodded. "An interesting plan, Captain. I like that. Mind if I tag along?"

Gerber raised an eyebrow in question. "What about Mrs. Fetterman and the kids?"

"You know, Captain, you tend to worry about them more than I do. Mrs. Fetterman and the kids understand about the warrior. There will be no problem from that quarter."

"If you're sure, Tony, then by all means let's go to Hong Kong." Gerber turned his attention to Bates. "Colonel? How about you? You should be getting ready for some leave time. I know you've been here longer than a year."

Bates finished his beer, then set the can on the floor so that he could crush it under his boot. "While it's true that I've been here for about a year, it's also true that I have a leave coming up. I plan to use it to visit my wife and daughters." He smiled and nodded at Fetterman. "Mrs. Bates is not quite as understanding as Mrs. Fetterman seems to be. Cindi wants me to come home and end my career at some comfortable base on the West Coast. I told her I could get my eagle by extending here, so she has agreed. But as soon as I get things organized, I'm on my way home."

He uttered a cheerful laugh, as if at some private memory. "If it wasn't for that, I'd be on that plane with you. We could really tear up Hong Kong."

"I guess that pretty well settles it." Gerber got to his feet. "I'd better go pack if I'm leaving in the morning." He stopped talking and said, "Hey, how exactly does this work? I mean, we won't be screwing anyone up by just showing up to go to Hong Kong?"

"Just go to Tan Son Nhut and take a commercial flight out. Cost you some money, but that won't screw anyone up. If you don't mind sitting around Saigon for a day or two, you can check in with the military people down there and grab a space on an available flight. They don't fill those up until the people arrive and one or two, more or less, won't affect them. Might delay somebody by a couple of hours, but that would be it."

"Sounds like the ticket."

As both Bates and Morrow stood to go, Fetterman said, "Say, Captain, can I talk to you?"

Gerber waved a hand at Bates and Morrow and said, "Catch up with you in a minute." He sat back down and asked, "What's on your mind, Tony?"

"I think I might pass on that trip to Hong Kong, if you don't mind."

"Of course, I don't mind. Decide that maybe you ought to visit Mrs. Fetterman and the kids? Especially since you dumped Le Quan Kim on them?"

"I didn't dump him on them. I worked out all the details of the adoption beforehand. I even talked to our embassy and proved to the satisfaction of the Vietnamese government that Le Quan was an orphan. After his village was burned, the Vietnamese were very happy to get rid of him and Mrs. Fetterman was very happy to see him."

"Sorry. I didn't mean that quite the way it sounded. I just meant, did you decide they might want you to come home for a month?"

"No, sir. I want to stay here. On the camp."

"What in the hell for?"

"The reason we discussed before. The reason the whole team is going to come back. To get that Chinese bastard. We talked about this a couple of times, but since Ian got zapped, we haven't done much about it."

"No," said Gerber slowly, "we haven't. But then, we haven't had much of a chance. We've been busy, but I have a feeling he's going to be pretty busy himself for the next month. This is the first time we've had this many Americans on the camp. I don't think there is much he can do now. Not with Thompson's battalion running operations all over our AO. He's going to have to bide his time until a few of the people leave.''

"I know that, Captain, but—''

"But nothing, Tony. I'll bet our taking out that base camp has hurt him, too. That was something that took years to build and stock, and now it's gone. Granted, he can operate out of Cambodia, but it's not quite as convenient as having an arsenal in our backyard. It'll be a month or more before he can do anything here.''

"Yes, sir.''

"We deserve this leave. We should take it. Get some rest, and when we come back, we'll be more than ready to hit him. You know, you can overtrain.''

"There are things I could be doing during that month, sir.''

"Tony, no one said we *had* to stay away a month. We are *authorized* to stay away for a month.''

"Does that mean . . .''

"It means that if I get bored chasing women, drinking heavily and being a civilian, then I plan to come right back here and get into the swing of things. Besides, it's only thirty days.''

Fetterman rubbed his chin as he thought about it. "You know, it might be nice to be somewhere you could take a hot bath and not worry about someone dropping a mortar round in there with you.''

Now Gerber smiled. "It might be nice to be somewhere you could find a nice lady to wash your back for you.''

"I bet I could find you a volunteer around here,'' said Fetterman.

"Now what does that mean?'' asked Gerber, knowing full well what it meant.

"Are you really that blind?'' asked Fetterman. "Do you really think there are so many interesting things happening around here that a journalist would hang around waiting for the big story to break?''

Although Gerber knew what was coming, he said, "Maybe you better explain yourself, Master Sergeant.''

"I think I may have said more than I should have. Listen, Mack—'' he used Gerber's given name for the first time ''—it's none of my business and I know all about your trouble with Morrow's sister, but don't let what one bitch did color your thinking, no matter how closely related they are.''

Gerber got to his feet. "I think this discussion now borders on territory that you are forbidden to enter."

"Yes, sir. I understand. I just wanted to make sure that you aren't making a mistake by keeping your eyes closed. A terrible mistake."

"Master Sergeant!"

"I've said my piece, and that's all I'll say."

"Then I suggest we go pack so we can take the morning chopper out of here. I'll want to brief Minh about the operation today so he'll know what happened and will be prepared to help Colonel Thompson."

"If I was out of line, sir, I beg your pardon, but I wanted to make sure the situation was under control."

Gerber snorted. "I don't know what I might have said to make you think I had the situation under control. No, seriously, Tony, I appreciate what you've said, but I think you've read something into the situation that doesn't exist."

"Yes, sir. See you in the morning."

GERBER ATE BREAKFAST alone with a notepad beside his dish of cold powdered eggs and cold cereal covered with lukewarm milk that he had made earlier. He kept adding to the list of things he wanted to leave with Minh, wondering if he was overdoing it. He knew that Minh was as familiar with the camp as he was. In fact, the only thing Minh didn't know about yet was the operation run the day before and that was only because it had been an all-American mission.

Just as he finished eating, Minh wandered in, poured himself a glass of warm orange juice, ignoring the Vietnamese woman who was standing in the kitchen area washing dirty dishes in a large metal tub. Minh flopped into the chair opposite Gerber.

"I say, old boy," said Minh, "I hear you wanted to talk to me."

Gerber pushed his dirty plate aside, stood to make his way to the coffeepot to fill his cup and returned. He picked up his notepad.

"This is going to be redundant, I'm sure, but I want to make certain that we've covered all the bases."

"Go ahead, but you had better hurry because the mail chopper will be here soon."

Gerber moved to the bar that separated the kitchen from the rest of the team house. He told the woman she could go for now and finish the dishes later. When she was gone, Gerber moved back to the table and sat down.

For the next twenty minutes they discussed the operation of the camp, the locations where patrols would be the most useful and what to do in the event of a major attack against the facility.

Neither Gerber nor Minh believed such an operation would be mounted now that the VC base had been discovered and eliminated. Both believed that the enemy would spend six or seven weeks recovering from the loss of the base; Gerber and his whole team would be back long before anything happened. Besides, there was a whole new American battalion sitting around the camp so nothing could happen until that battalion redeployed to Bien Hoa.

There might be some mortar attacks or harassment raids, but nothing major. The VC had made a concentrated effort to take the camp when it was first built and had smashed the better part of a reinforced regiment against the camp's defenses. With a brandnew American battalion, five hundred men strong added to those defenses, the VC couldn't mount an attack.

Minh nodded through most of this and commented about some of it, taking it all in. To finish up, Gerber said, "Colonel Bates will be here most of the time, and you can count on him. He's a good soldier and will give you anything you need."

Fetterman entered then and dropped his two suitcases on the floor near the door. He was wearing new jungle fatigues so green they seemed to glow. There were no insignia on them, just metal master sergeant stripes pinned to the collar. His boots gleamed as usual, his hair was combed and he was freshly shaved. He looked as if he had just stepped out of an air-conditioned NCO barracks rather than coming from his own hot hootch. Gerber raised an eyebrow in question at the suitcases.

"Duffel bags are good for carrying equipment and jungle fatigues, but civilian clothes just don't travel well in them," Fetterman said. "Besides, I don't want to look like a soldier on leave because then you're a marked man. Everyone and his brother or sister will be out to separate me from my hard-earned money."

Gerber waved him over as Minh stood up. "I'll take my leave now," said Minh, draining the last of his warm orange juice.

"See you in a month, Dai uy," said Gerber as Minh disappeared through the door.

"As you can see," said Fetterman, pouring himself a cup of coffee, "I'm ready for this."

Before he could take a seat, Morrow appeared carrying a suitcase, which she placed next to Fetterman's. To Gerber, she said, "Do I have your guarantee that I can come back here if I take a couple of weeks off?"

Gerber rocked back in his chair and studied her. It was the first time that she had worn a dress since she had arrived on the camp. It was light yellow with a slightly dipped neckline and short puffed sleeves. The hem brushed her knees. She had washed her hair and trimmed it herself so that she had bangs.

"If I say no, will you go, anyway?"

"No. I'll sit here until I rot," she said with a smile on her lips.

"Well, then," responded Gerber, "I guess we'll let you come back, providing that Crinshaw and the boys in Saigon don't stop you."

Fetterman pulled a chair out and held it for her. "Where are you going, Robin?"

"I haven't decided yet," she said. "Just figured I'd ride into Saigon with you and then catch a flight out. Maybe go home for a visit."

Gerber felt his stomach turn over at that because he thought of Karen Morrow and her husband. He nodded and said, "Sounds like a good idea."

Fetterman eyed Gerber meaningfully but said, "Where are your bags, Captain?"

"In my hootch. As soon as I hear the chopper, I'll hotfoot it over there and pick them up."

"Robin," said Fetterman, "you look beautiful. You should spend more time dressed like this."

For an instant she was going to contradict him, to say that she was here to do a job and that she dressed to do it. Then she realized that Fetterman was not being condescending but trying to be nice.

"Thank you, Sergeant. I appreciate it."

Gerber stood and explained, "I should go find Colonel Bates before the chopper gets here."

From the door a voice said, "Don't bother, he has arrived."

"Tony and I are ready to go, Colonel," said Gerber. "Just as soon as the chopper arrives. Thought I should let you know and see if there was anything else I needed to do."

Bates made the ritualistic trip to the coffeepot and then to the table. He said, "I believe that, between Captain Minh and myself, we can handle anything." He turned his attention to Morrow. "Robin, you look exceptionally nice this morning. Is this a special occasion?"

"No, Colonel, I just decided to take a little vacation while the rest of the team is gone. Kirk promised me that I could come back here later."

"Kirk?" said Bates and Fetterman at the same time.

"My middle name," said Gerber, explaining the whole situation to them. "Sometimes I prefer it because it has no connection with the Army."

From outside came the sound of a helicopter approaching. Gerber said, "That'll be our ride."

Bates stood and held out his hand. "Good luck to you all on this. Have fun and try not to think of the rest of us here fighting to save the world from the evils of Communism."

"Don't worry," said Fetterman, laughing, "I won't."

Gerber took Bates's hand and shook it. "Thanks for everything, Alan. See you in about a month."

As they all approached the chopper, two of the crewmen leaped from the back and came forward to take the bags out of Morrow's and Gerber's hands. The helicopter sat on the pad, its blades stirring up a cloud of red dust. The rotor wash caught the hem of

Morrow's dress and flipped it about, revealing her thighs. She tried to hold it down as she ran toward the cargo compartment of the aircraft.

Gerber, relieved of his burden, stepped up so that he could shout into the cockpit window at the pilot. He looked in and smiled as he recognized the man.

"So, Randle, you fly us around again."

Randle nodded and moved the boom of his mike over so that Gerber could speak into it. That way Randle could hear what Gerber said on the intercom.

"Listen, you be careful on this one—we're going on leave so we don't want any trouble."

"Oh," shouted Randle over the noise of the Huey's turbine, "you mean you don't want to hear that we took fire on the way in."

Gerber almost shouted back and then saw the grin on Randle's face and realized that the pilot was kidding him. "Yeah, exactly like that."

"Well, hop in and we'll get you to Saigon in about forty minutes. Then I'll let you buy me lunch."

"You've got a deal."

With that, Gerber climbed into the cargo compartment of the helicopter. He noticed that both the crew chief and door gunner were helping Morrow get settled, and fastening her seat belt. Obviously enjoying it, she simply grinned at them and let them do it. She smiled at Randle when he turned in his seat to make sure that everyone was ready.

They lifted off, turned north and then back to the south as if Randle were circling the camp so that Gerber and Fetterman could take a look at it, but neither was interested in seeing it.

Gerber glanced to his left and saw that the wind whipping through the cargo compartment was toying with the hem of Morrow's skirt, trying to force it up. She sat with both hands holding it tightly around her knees.

The flight took forty-two minutes. They touched down at Hotel Three ten minutes before noon. Almost before the passengers could unbuckle their seat belts, Randle had the engine shut down and was standing outside the aircraft, stretching. He reached up with one hand to help Morrow down.

"I can make it myself, ah, Lieutenant," she snapped.

"Yes, I know you can, but I don't have many opportunities to try out the manners that Congress has graciously given to me. And I'm only a warrant officer."

"In that case, thank you. Can you tell me how to get over to the commercial terminal?"

"I would imagine you can catch a ride if you go over to the building with the tower on it," said Randle, pointing across the helipad. "They'll probably be more than happy to drive you over. I'll have the door gunner carry your luggage."

"That's not necessary."

"Of course it isn't, but he'll kill me if I don't order him to do it. That is, if you don't mind."

"In that case, I'll be delighted to have the help."

As Morrow and the door gunner started across the field, Randle leaned back against the side of the helicopter, his arms folded and said, "She seems to be a nice lady. I wonder why she hangs around with the grungy Green Beret types."

"She has no sense," growled Gerber. "You want food or not?"

"Say, Captain, your way with words amazes me. You ever thought of running for mayor?" Randle shot back.

"Okay, sorry. Let's go over to the O Club and I'll buy you a steak."

"And my Peter Pilot?"

"And your Peter Pilot."

BY THE MIDDLE OF THE AFTERNOON, Gerber and Fetterman had been manifested on a flight to Hong Kong that would leave the next morning. They had been assigned quarters for the night, both of them in a giant barrackslike building where senior NCOs and junior officers waited for flights. It resembled a warehouse in a bunk bed factory. There had to be two hundred bunks in the building, each of them with yards of gauze that served as mosquito netting. The walls climbed only halfway to the ceiling and the rest was enclosed in screen to let in the evening breezes. Sixty-watt light bulbs in funnel-like fixtures hung every twenty or thirty feet. Ceiling fans rotated above them but seemed to have little effect on the heat. Since everyone in the barracks was about to get out of Vietnam and because they were assigned bunks on the basis of which flight they were leaving on, no one was inclined to complain about the arrangement.

9

TAN SON NHUT INTERNATIONAL AIRPORT, SAIGON

The next morning Gerber and Fetterman presented themselves at the military counter in the airport. It took almost no time to check their baggage and verify authorization for leave outside of Vietnam. They showed their passports to the civilian customs officer, a Vietnamese man with long, straight black hair and oval brown eyes, who went through their baggage but didn't perform a body search. So he didn't find the .45 automatic that Fetterman had tucked away. Beside the customs man was an American sergeant with the black armband of the military police who wanted to see their orders. He inspected those and their other papers carefully, then handed them back with a bored smile and wished the two men a good trip.

With the customs requirements satisfied, they were led to a waiting room where a hundred other men, all dressed in civilian clothes, sat reading books and magazines or staring out the window, watching the jets take off and land. The room was furnished with mismatched furniture, tattered copies of magazines, mostly *Playboy* and other girlie glossies, newspapers and old paperback novels. The floor was littered with crushed cigarette butts and empty Coke cans. The air was hot and stale, and there was a low murmur from the men waiting for flights out of Vietnam.

After an hour they were led across the tarmac, which radiated heat in shimmering waves. The glare made it hard to see as they approached the ramp leading into a 707. Gerber shivered involuntarily as he entered the air-conditioned comfort of the plane. As he left the heat and humidity of tropical Vietnam, he thought it would be a while before he was that uncomfortable again. He forgot that Hong Kong was also close to the equator and near the ocean. It would be as hot and humid as Vietnam.

The flight took less than two hours. Gerber didn't have time to sample much of the booze stashed away on the aircraft. Since it was a commercial airliner, the stewardesses were allowed to serve limited quantities of alcohol, especially since it was such a short flight.

Fetterman kept his nose buried in a series of brochures about Hong Kong that he had found somewhere, mumbling occasionally that he had discovered something they should be sure to explore.

At those times Gerber merely nodded and said, "Well, put it down and we'll see about it."

Before Gerber could get used to the idea that he was leaving the war zone and that no one would be shooting at him for the next thirty days, the pilot announced their approach into Kai Tak Airport. He suggested that if window passengers looked below, they would be able to see the various islands of Hong Kong, the new territories and, with luck, some of Red China. Gerber didn't really care to see Red China, but Fetterman was interested if only because it was the birthplace of their biggest enemy.

They touched down and rolled to a stop, and just like in Vietnam, they were herded into the terminal where the Army had a small auditorium, which was filled with folding chairs facing a screen, so that the officials could explain the rules and regulations of Hong Kong and R and R. Those soldiers who were on R and R were informed which day they had to report back so they could catch their return flights to Vietnam. Those who were on leave would have to make their own travel arrangements but needed to make them at least three days prior to departure to ensure they got a seat. That done, and the various forms signed, they were told that, if they wanted to take the Army bus into the city proper, they needed to pick up their baggage and get outside.

As the others swarmed from the room, each fighting to be the first out the door, Fetterman said, "You aren't interested in the bus?"

"Thought it would be nice to get away from Army control as quickly as possible. Besides, did you really want to have the Army take us into Hong Kong? We'd end up doing it by the numbers, for Christ's sake."

Fetterman picked up his suitcases and gestured at the door. "Lead the way."

They left the Army's reception room and were back into the main terminal where hundreds of people hurried up and down the concourses looking for their departure gates. Following the signs that were in a dozen languages including English, Gerber and Fetterman found their way to the main exit of the terminal.

"Say, Tony," said Gerber, "I don't suppose you speak Chinese."

"No, sir. But since English is one of the two official languages of Hong Kong, I'll have a chance to practice my English."

"While we're here, how about knocking off that sir and captain shit. You know my name."

"Thought I did."

"Now what the hell does that mean?" asked Gerber.

"Nothing, Mack. Nothing at all."

Just as they reached the tinted glass doors, a voice yelled after them, "Hey, Kirk. Over here, Kirk."

Gerber thought nothing of it as the door swung open and the hot, humid air of Hong Kong rushed in to greet them.

"Hey, Kirk, wait up."

Fetterman said, "Somebody yelling at you?"

Then the voice came again, angry. "Hey, Mack. Will you wait for me?"

Gerber turned and saw Robin Morrow, still wearing her yellow dress, now wrinkled, running across the concourse. People were stopping and staring at her as she waved a hand to catch their attention.

"I think that is for you, Captain."

"Shut up, Master Sergeant. We've only been here for fifteen minutes and already you're a pain in the ass. Maybe that's why they don't want officers and NCOs to fraternize."

There wasn't much choice when Morrow caught them. She tried to grab one of Gerber's suitcases, and failing that, she took one of Fetterman's. Before they could say anything, Morrow began chattering away as she led them down a sidewalk, past the banks of parked taxis, most of which were old American-made automobiles. They hit a parking lot and walked between the cars. Gerber noticed that the day was not as hot as it would have been in Vietnam and wondered if the sea breezes blowing across the harbor were responsible for keeping the temperature in the low eighties.

"I've got a car," said Morrow, struggling with the suitcase she had taken from Fetterman. She set it down, grabbed it in both hands and started off again. "My boss paid for it. Gave me a suite downtown that you can share if you like. It has two bedrooms so there is no problem. I know that neither of you are overpaid, so sharing the room might help. My publisher is paying for it, too. Told him I might have to entertain some people, so he authorized it. I mean, I told him—"

"Stop," ordered Gerber. "Stop."

"Yes, Kirk. Mack?"

Gerber raised an eyebrow at Fetterman, who said, "It's your ball game, Mack-Kirk."

"Well, I don't know anything about this town," said Gerber, "so we'll let you take us to your hotel. Then we'll decide what to do from there."

They reached the car, a bright blue Mustang convertible, which had the top down. Morrow unlocked the trunk and then opened the driver's door so she could leap behind the wheel. "Pile in gentlemen and hang on. These people don't drive all that well, and I'm out of practice."

They filled the trunk with their suitcases, putting one in the backseat. Fetterman got into the back next to it, shaded his eyes with his hand and searched the skyline of Hong Kong, surprised at the number of tall buildings around him. Hong Kong was a large, modern city.

"This is terrific. I survived a year in Vietnam to die in a traffic accident in Hong Kong." Gerber climbed into the passenger's seat and reached for the seat belt.

After a short hair-raising ride through the city, they came to the hotel, a glass and steel high rise called the Regency. When Morrow saw the look on Gerber's face, she said, "I had to stay here. We have some kind of deal with the owners and get a good rate. Otherwise, I would have had to pay for it out of my own pocket."

Fetterman pushed on the back of Gerber's seat. "Come on, Captain. It won't hurt to look at the inside. We've come this far already."

Gerber started to open the door, but a uniformed man swooped out from under the canopied entrance to help him. The bellhop reached for the one bag in the back seat as soon as Fetterman was out of the way, then almost demanded that the trunk be opened so he could get the rest of the luggage.

"Do I let him have it?" asked Morrow.

"Why not?" said Gerber, shrugging.

Upstairs, as soon as the bellhop had been tipped, Gerber turned around. They were standing in the posh living room of the suite. There was a long, low, aqua couch along one wall and over it hung a seascape, which picked up the colors of the couch. End tables flanked the couch, and lamps with off-white shades and large bubblelike ceramic bases stood on them. Across from all that was a large, mahogany secretary that opened into a bar. It was well stocked with beer, Coke and a dozen bottles of Beam's Choice. In one corner of the room was a large TV console and sitting on it was another lamp, a smaller version of the ones on the end tables. In the other corner near the window was a round table surrounded by four armchairs. The window, hidden behind light, wispy sheers and heavier, darker drapes, stretched the length of the outside wall.

Morrow pointed across the room at a door near the couch. "You two can stay in there if you want."

Gerber went to the door and looked in. He was in a tiny foyer that separated the bedroom from the private bath. Between two double beds, covered with spreads of the same aqua color as the couch, was a small table that held a lamp and a bible. There was a massive dresser with nine long drawers against the wall. A chair stood in one corner with a floor lamp next to it. A walk-in closet filled one wall and a window the other. The curtains were open, and he could see Hong Kong Harbor.

His reflection in the giant mirror on the door of the bathroom startled him for a moment. He walked over to it and looked in. There was a huge bathtub inside. He looked back at Fetterman and Morrow and then at the tub. He hadn't had a bath in nearly a year. In fact, he hadn't had a hot shower in that year. There'd been cool or cold showers by the dozen and a couple of baths in the streams and rivers around the camp but not a long, hot bath with nothing to worry about except keeping the water warm.

Then he remembered another room in another hotel where he had found a bathtub. Except that it hadn't been the gleaming porcelain facing him now, but an old ceramic job with Victorian feet on it and rust stains where the water dripped. He put the scene out of his mind because it dredged up too many unpleasant memories of Karen Morrow.

To the others he said, "I think I'll take a bath, if no one has any objections."

"No objections," said Morrow, obviously relieved. "In fact, I was about to suggest the same thing."

"Tony, you can use the bathroom now if you like. Because I'll have it tied up for a while."

"No, sir. I thought I'd hit one of the tailor shops down the street. I'd like to get a new suit to wear in Hong Kong. I have the feeling that my collection of civilian garb is not sufficient for the task at hand."

"Well, don't let me stop you." With that Gerber closed the door, and moments later they could hear water running in the bathroom.

Morrow sat on one of the four chairs near the picture window in the living room. The curtains were closed so they couldn't see out into the city. She crossed her legs and took a deep breath.

"Tony? Can we talk?"

Fetterman studied her carefully and then moved to one of the other chairs. "What can I do for you, Miss Morrow?"

"Oh, for God's sake, call me Robin." She stopped and looked at the liquor cabinet, then rose from her chair to fix herself a drink. "I've noticed, Tony, that you don't miss much of anything. You have a finger on the pulse of everything that's going on around you."

"I thank you for the compliment."

"So," she said slowly and then blurted, "what am I doing wrong?"

Fetterman studied his hand intimately for a moment and then said, "I suppose you're referring to our captain."

Having finally begun the conversation, she decided to stay with it. "You probably figured that I came here because I knew you'd be here."

"And I take that to mean the captain would be here." He held up his hand before she could say anything more. "Sorry. I shouldn't do that. It's just a delaying tactic while I try to figure out what I should tell you and what the captain would like me not to say. It's a fine line that I'm now preparing to walk."

"I appreciate it." She sat down again but found she could not look him in the face.

"Let me say this," said Fetterman. "Mack Gerber is probably the finest officer I've ever met. He's the only expert on small unit tactics fighting the Vietnam War. I would never tell him that I recognize some of them from the Indian Wars, but that's where he got them. I say all this so that you'll know I'm a completely unbiased source." He grinned, but she missed it.

"All right. Your sister seemed to be the right woman for him. They got along well. Hell, they got along beautifully. They could have conversations and hardly exchange a word. They were so in tune with one another they didn't need to talk. It was an incredibly interesting thing to see. I think the captain had planned to ask her to marry him.

"Then suddenly it was over without a very good explanation. She just wanted nothing to do with him, and he couldn't understand it. Now we know the problem. She was preparing to go home to her husband, all of which you should know already."

"But men do it all the time. Have a girl in every port and leave them high and dry when they become a problem."

"Doesn't matter," said Fetterman. "Doesn't matter if a billion men have done it to a billion women. I mean, it doesn't make it right for her to have done it to him."

"That's a damned lousy attitude."

Now Fetterman was uncomfortable. "Let me rephrase that. Makes no difference if a billion men did it to a billion women or a billion women did it to a billion men. Didn't make it right for her to do it to the captain. He'd never do it to anyone."

"Sorry."

"The point of all this is that the captain is trying very hard not to let anyone get to him again. He just isn't in the right frame of mind to let it happen to him. I know he slips up now and then." Fetterman grinned as he watched the blush start at her neck and work its way up her face to her hairline. "And you have a second strike being Karen's sister."

"So what do I do?"

"If your feelings are real, then hang loose. If things are meant to work out, they will. Don't push it. The captain will realize what you mean to him in time, but you have to give him time, no matter what's happened in the past."

"You mean like coming to Hong Kong and then conning him up to the room?"

"Well, it's a bit late to worry about that, but I think in his frame of mind he won't really notice."

"Okay," she said and finished her drink in one hasty gulp. "Were you serious about buying a suit?"

"Of course. If I'm going to help you, I'll need some good clothes to escort you to the nicer places."

"Then by all means, let's go."

In the hotel lobby they decided to bypass the tailors in the same building and explore the streets nearby. There were signs proclaiming suits in less than twenty-four hours, but Fetterman wasn't sure the quality would be too high. He needed a custom-made suit, and he quickly learned that there were good off-the-rack selections available that could be fitted and altered in little more than an hour.

After searching several shops, Fetterman found a dark blue pin-striped, three-piece suit that he liked. The fit through the shoulders and the waist was good. The legs needed to be altered slightly.

They sat in a couple of old chairs arranged against one wall, each with a tiny table next to it, and faced four of the three-position mirrors, which allowed customers to see their new clothes from all angles. Fetterman noticed a smell in the shop that reminded him of cleaning fluid and laundries. The room itself was badly lighted with four spotlights over the four mirrors. There were plate-glass windows in the front, but the streets were narrow, preventing the sunlight from reaching the pavement. They could easily watch the bustling crowds from where they sat.

After a few minutes an old man approached them, smiled as he bowed and asked if they would like something to drink while they waited—no charge, of course. When the drinks arrived, Morrow and Fetterman sat back to observe the pedestrians jostling past the windows of the tailor shop.

Morrow wanted to talk about Gerber some more, to try to learn more about him, but didn't know how to bring up the subject again. And she was afraid that she had already told Fetterman more than she cared to have him know about herself and her feelings. Besides, she wasn't sure that she liked what Fetterman had told her. She cursed her sister under her breath, wishing that Karen had stayed in the World with her husband.

Fetterman sat relaxed, his drink in his left hand, and it seemed as though his eyes were closed, but his head moved occasionally as he watched someone pass the shop. Morrow had never seen anyone look so relaxed.

"I've spent years in the Army waiting," said Fetterman, as if reading her mind. "Waiting for clerks to type papers when they didn't want to, for officers to condescend to see me when they didn't want to, to get into the mess hall when I didn't want to. Waiting on everyone else to do a job that he didn't want to do because he had been drafted or lied to or was just in a bad mood. It does no good to worry about it, so I learned to use the time to rest and relax."

"Wish I could do that," she said.

"It's easy enough. Just remember there's nothing you can do about the waiting. If you appear agitated, then you've let the clerk win, but if you're enjoying yourself, he'll hurry to move you on and irritate you. Either way, you've won."

Morrow laughed. "I'll try to remember that."

"And to make this even nicer, I have the opportunity to spend the time with a very pretty lady."

"Why, thank you, Master Sergeant." She stopped talking for a moment and then asked, "Why do they call you 'master sergeant'?"

"You mean other than the fact that I am one?"

"Yes. They don't call Tyme 'sergeant first class', or Sully 'staff sergeant.' They're just called 'sergeant.'"

"The captain started it. I think it was because I was taking over from the last team sergeant who had been killed. He was trying to establish my authority by reinforcing the fact that I outranked them all. I think it's now come to mean that I'm a master of a lot of military trades. Or maybe master of all I see."

"I wouldn't think you'd need any help in establishing your authority," she said.

"That's the kind of man the captain is. He was taking no chances. Just trying to help the FNG."

The conversation had naturally evolved back to Gerber, and Morrow was wondering what she should say.

Fetterman, however, didn't give her a chance. He leaped to his feet, tried unsuccessfully to set his drink on the table and said, "I don't fucking believe it."

He dashed across the shop to the window and tried to look down the street. He looked back at Morrow and said, "You wait right here. I'll be back in a moment."

"What is it?" demanded Morrow, puzzlement written all over her face. "What's going on?"

But Fetterman had dashed to the door and raced into the street. In the distance he thought he could see the retreating back of a man he recognized. The sergeant pushed through the crowd, elbowing people out of his way, ignoring their shouts of protest in his hurry to close the gap. But the man's pace never slowed, and he never looked back. He seemed to know exactly where he was going, and Fetterman couldn't close the distance between them.

He could swear he saw the man turn a corner. But when Fetterman got there, he saw another crowded street with a dozen turns and a hundred shop entrances. There were a thousand places to hide if the man had wanted to hide, and Fetterman could no longer see him. For ten minutes he stood on the corner, searching the crowd, staring into hundreds of Oriental faces and thousands of tourist faces, but recognized none of them. Finally realizing that the man had eluded him, he returned to the tailor shop where Morrow stood waiting near the door, the puzzled look still on her face.

"What the hell was that all about?"

"You wouldn't believe me if I told you. I thought I saw someone I recognized, but before I could catch up, he was gone."

"Another American?" she asked, not really sure what she thought.

"No. A Chinese of my acquaintance. Well, we haven't really been formally introduced," said Fetterman idly. "Anyway, he got away."

10

THE STREETS OF
HONG KONG

Fetterman, having collected his new suit along with one for Gerber, left the shop and headed back down the street, looking for the man he had seen. With Morrow in tow, not sure what she was supposed to be doing, Fetterman nearly ran along, peering into windows like a shopper gone mad. No sooner did it seem they would stop than Fetterman took off again. He was up and down the side streets, narrow roads flanked by tall buildings and colored by a hundred neon signs, brushing by the hucksters and ignoring the kids trying to sell things.

Morrow, tired and hungry, didn't say a word. She followed, occasionally asking, "Just what are we looking for?"

"Nothing," said Fetterman, never doubting the identity of the man he thought he had seen. He would know the face anywhere, but the man had simply disappeared.

Finally realizing that it was getting late, Fetterman said, "He's probably gotten out of here by now. I won't find him until he's ready to be found. Let's head back."

"Is this all a secret," asked Morrow, "or would you like to explain what the hell you are talking about?"

"Later. I'll tell you it all later."

"I'll accept that," said Morrow.

"Now then," said Fetterman, trying to change the subject. "Do you have something special in mind for dinner? Should we dress for it?"

"I think—" Morrow nodded "—you should dress. I would like to be treated to a fancy restaurant, although I do have an expense account and probably should buy your dinner."

"I'm never one to turn down free food," said Fetterman.

Back at the hotel they rode up the elevator in silence. As Morrow stopped off at the door to her side of the suite, she said, "I'm gong to change. I'll be over when I'm ready."

Fetterman found Gerber sitting in a chair, spinning the dial of the television set. He stopped long enough to say, "Want to see Matt Dillon speaking Chinese?"

"Not really," said Fetterman. He dropped his packages onto the couch and said, "Robin said she wanted to be taken out to dinner and we should dress for it. She said her expense account would pay for it, but I think it'd be a nice gesture if we took her."

"Whatever you decide, Tony."

Fetterman disappeared into the bedroom to clean up. He came back briefly to pick up one of the packages and then went back to the bedroom. He returned after a few minutes. He went to the bar and poured himself a shot of Beam's and sat down. He noticed that Gerber had already poured himself a drink.

"Had a strange experience today, Captain," said Fetterman.

"What was that?"

"Saw the Chinese guy."

"What Chinese guy? There are millions of them out there."

"*The* Chinese guy. That bastard who has been giving us fits in Vietnam. Saw him outside the tailor shop."

Gerber moved to the bar and stood with his back to Fetterman, pouring another shot of Beam's into the crystal glass that had been set to one side of the cabinet. He was also pouring the Beam's over ice, something he had thought he would never do, but it had been so long since he had been able to get ice that he felt obliged to use it.

With the drink in his hand, he turned so that he could look out the window at the contrasting views of Hong Kong. High-rise buildings of glass and steel were surrounded by primitive structures of stone and wood, which had been there for decades, maybe centuries. In the distance Chinese junks sailed in the harbour as 707s flew over them.

Keeping his eyes on the scene outside, Gerber said, "Don't you think it's a little strange that we've been here only a couple of hours and you think you've seen the Chinese guy already?"

"No, sir, I don't."

Reluctantly Gerber took his eyes off the view of Hong Kong and looked at his team sergeant. Fetterman was decidedly out of place, too. The civilian clothes he had bought didn't to seem to fit right, although the tailor insisted that they couldn't be cut any better. Gerber figured it was because he was so used to seeing Fetterman in jungle fatigues, or even a ninja suit, that anything else looked bizarre. Or maybe it was Fetterman's military bearing that made him seem out of place in civilian clothes. Gerber had to admit that the suit was a fine one.

"That's a pretty big coincidence. We take leave in an area with the largest concentration of Chinese outside of China, and in less than a day you claim to have seen one specific man."

"Are you suggesting that I can't tell one Oriental from another? I thought we went through that at the trial."

"Take it easy, Tony. I just can't accept the fact that our man is here. It's too big of a coincidence."

Fetterman stood up and moved across the carpet slowly, as if he were afraid he would leave footprints in the deep pile. "I would agree," he said, "that as a coincidence it's too big. I suggest it's not a coincidence."

"What?" Gerber was thoughtful.

"Think about it logically. There is no way we could be in town for less than a day and run into a man we thought was still in Vietnam, unless he knew we were going to be in Hong Kong and came after us."

Gerber collapsed into one of the chairs. "Go on, Tony."

"I'm suggesting that McMillan was killed not because any American had been targeted. He was killed because he happened to be a member of our team and was out by himself."

"That would take an incredible intelligence system. Hell, they probably don't even know our names."

"But they do. You know, Captain, that there have been VC in the strike companies. That's how our cover was blown when we crossed the Cambodian border after the Chinese guy. I'm sure the embassy offices downtown are loaded with VC sympathizers. Our orders to Hong Kong had to be sent there, as well as circulated in a dozen military command structures, all of which could be riddled with VC."

"Okay, Tony," agreed Gerber. "Maybe they do know who we are and could get the information."

"Then it follows, sir, that the Chinese guy is going to know exactly who has spoiled all his plans. When we talked to the team about any Americans in our camp being the targets, I think we were wrong. The Chinese bastard is going to want to kill specific men and McMillan was the first."

Gerber drained his glass and sat down. "I can buy that the VC know who we are. I don't buy the fact that they would chase us to Hong Kong. Doesn't make sense."

"Makes the most sense of all. He's got us on foreign territory without the support of our team and without weapons." Fetterman smiled but didn't mention the .45 he had smuggled in. He wouldn't be surprised if Gerber knew about it, though. "He can move freely between here and China, bringing in weapons and men. He has another invisible line on the ground that will protect him. It's even better than the one between Cambodia and Vietnam because it's heavily guarded and there won't be any Occidentals crossing it without seventeen different types of identification and months of negotiation. We are helpless compared to him."

"No," said Gerber, shaking his head. "I just don't buy it. You found him too quickly."

"But that's the point, Captain. I didn't find him. He found us. There are only so many hotels in Hong Kong, and it wouldn't be all that hard to bribe a desk clerk to let him know when we checked in, or rather when Morrow let the desk know we were going to use half her suite."

"I don't buy," repeated Gerber slowly, as if he were considering the possibilities.

"If you want proof, I think you have it." Fetterman waved a hand around the room. "Robin managed to locate us pretty quickly, and all she knew was that we were coming to Hong Kong."

"But that's the point," snapped Gerber. "She knew."

"And I am saying that the Chinese bastard knew we were coming to Hong Kong. The information was lying around for the grabbing. Hell, we didn't try to keep it much of a secret around the camp, and there are still probably VC in the strike companies. The information was out there to be had, for anyone who wanted it. We just never thought the VC would want it."

Before Gerber could respond, there was a knock at the door. Gerber spun to face it, his right hand reaching for the pistol that he wasn't wearing. Fetterman chuckled. "I guess you do believe me. But I don't think he would knock. Blow the door in, riddle it with machine gun fire, but not knock."

Gerber laughed at his own paranoia. "You're right, of course, Tony. I would imagine it's our date."

"*Your* date, Captain. I'm just along for the ride, so to speak."

"If your attitude doesn't change quickly, you're going to be along for a quick trip out the window."

Since Gerber hadn't moved, Fetterman went to the door and opened it. Morrow stood there wearing a bright red silk dress, which looked as if it had been made just for her. It had long sleeves, a mandarin collar and was tight across the chest, stomach and hips. A slit up the side revealed her thigh each time she moved, and Gerber found it provocative even though he had seen her naked on a couple of occasions.

"Come in, Robin," said Fetterman, smiling broadly. "We were just talking about you." He stepped back out of the way and then said, "It's really your room. You didn't have to knock."

"I wanted to make sure that you both were dressed before I entered."

Gerber, still talking about the Chinese officer, whom Fetterman was convinced he had seen, asked, "What do you intend to do?"

Now Fetterman smiled. "I intend to offer Robin a drink and then find out where she wants to go for dinner."

"That's not what I meant."

"I know, but right now there's nothing to be done. All that has happened has been a recon. There will be no action until much later."

Morrow dropped onto the couch. "You guys come all the way from Vietnam so you can talk like you're still in the war?"

"No, of course not. Now," said Gerber, "where did you get that Suzie Wong dress?"

"You don't like it?"

"I think it's marvelous," said Gerber. "So what are we going to do for dinner?"

Fetterman suggested that since they were in Hong Kong, they should eat Chinese food the first night. But Gerber, having watched rice farmers fertilizing their fields, wasn't sure that he wanted to eat anywhere that served rice. Still, he deferred to Fetterman's idea. Morrow didn't care. She was happy to go out to dinner.

Then, they had to decide whether they wanted to take the car or walk. This time Gerber made the decision, saying that he would like the opportunity to see some of the sights without whizzing by them. Besides, he didn't want to ride with Morrow again right away. The experience had been too frightening.

The trio left the hotel and walked to Nathan Road, a wide avenue down the center of the Kowloon Peninsula. They headed north along Nathan, passing dozens of small shops that sold everything from jade and gold to silks and satins. After a while they turned onto a narrow road lined with bars that offered drinks and dancers, each advertised in glowing neons and flashing lights. Finally they found a small restaurant that wouldn't make them wait for dinner. Each of the three decided to order a variety of foods. The idea was to share them with one another so that they would have the chance to taste the different courses and the different sauces. Fetterman used chopsticks with an ability that suggested he had never seen a knife or fork. Morrow gamely tried to copy him but kept dropping her food. Eventually she gave up and decided to use her fork.

The mood was pleasant as they lingered over the meal, savoring every dish. Gerber was glad of the company. He tried not to let anything distract him. There was nothing pressing that any of them had to do the next day. They didn't have to worry about someone dropping a grenade in with them. Although the restaurant was small, it was air-conditioned, which made it as comfortable inside as it was in the hotel. The humidity and the heat were left on the street.

Fetterman summed it all up after they had finished eating. "This is how the rich do it. Spend their time eating big meals because there is nothing to do tomorrow."

"I doubt it's quite that easy," said Gerber, "because somebody has to keep track of the money."

"They hire people to do it. Meet them for lunch to talk about the money and then plan dinner."

Gerber was feeling the best he had in months. He had completely forgotten about Karen Morrow, even though her sister was sitting across the table from him. He was having fun talking with her and Fetterman, discussing things they had lived through during the past months.

Fetterman was particularly lively when telling about his adventures in France during the Second World War. It was great fun, and before the check arrived, Gerber suggested that they find somewhere to dance because the evening was young.

Morrow agreed immediately. Fetterman, sensing that Morrow would be happier if he found something else to do, said he wanted to go back to the hotel. Gerber wouldn't hear of it because it was their first night in town. Finally he agreed, too.

They left the restaurant, stepping into the blazing lights of nighttime Hong Kong. Gerber was surprised by the number of neon signs, the lights in shops and the almost holiday atmosphere of the streets. They followed the crowds for a while, dodging the kids trying to sell them small carvings and the men trying to sell them larger things, moving away from the center of the city where their hotel was located and into one of the more remote districts. They found themselves on the dock for the Star Ferry, saw that it was docked and decided to cross the harbour to Hong Kong Island.

They walked south on the Island and then turned to the east, following the crowds there. They turned down one street, heading more or less back toward the waterfront and moving into the area known as the Suzie Wong District.

They strolled along slowly, watching the people around them. The crowds thinned slightly, and the streets were less well lighted. Neither Gerber nor Fetterman thought a thing about it, but Morrow suggested that they should find somewhere else to walk.

Before either Gerber or Fetterman could respond, a fourth voice entered the conversation from slightly behind and to the right of them. It said in accented English, "The lady is right. This is not a safe place to be."

"Well, thank you," offered Fetterman, stopping and turning around.

A man materialized from a shadow near an alley. "You could be robbed. You could be injured."

"We'll watch our step," said Fetterman.

"To show your appreciation," said the man, who was definitely Chinese and looked to be in his twenties, "you should give me money." His voice had become slightly threatening.

Wordlessly both Gerber and Fetterman moved so that Morrow was protected between them. Fetterman was on the alley side and Gerber nearer the street and standing a little behind them.

"I think we'll pass on that," said Fetterman, "but still appreciate the advice."

"You do not understand. It was not a request. I will have your money."

Fetterman flexed his knees and took a small step forward with his left foot. "We don't want trouble but are prepared to give it. Now why don't you just fade away before you get hurt."

Three men emerged from the alley, standing side by side. The one in the middle reached behind him and pulled a knife, its blade gleaming in the little light thrown out by the streetlamps.

"Why don't you just give us all your money before you get hurt," said the one with the knife.

Fetterman shrugged his shoulders and slowly began to reach under his coat as if to find his wallet. His eyes never wavered from those of the guy with the knife. The sergeant, standing lightly on the balls of his feet, suddenly kicked outward and upward as if trying to punt a football. There was a high-pitched scream, and the man with the knife fell to the pavement.

Before his friend on the right could move, Fetterman spun, his foot slashing out again, connecting with the second guy's jaw. He staggered backward, as if trying to keep his balance, but hit the side of the building and slipped down into a sitting position.

The last punk had no chance to see any of it. As Fetterman was taking out the man with the knife, Gerber had leaped forward, his fist flashing. In rapid succession he hit the man in the chest and throat, then kicked his feet out from under him. He fell heavily to his side, landing on his arm with a sickening snap.

Fetterman shot a glance to his side where Gerber stood. He then leaned forward so that he could speak to the barely conscious man lying in front of him. "You just wouldn't listen, would you, asshole? I warned that you'd get hurt. Now if I was real irritated with you, I'd break both your knees. Just remember this next time you plan on ambushing some innocent tourists."

He straightened, looked at the second man and saw that he would be no problem. He turned and saw Gerber crouched over Morrow, who was sitting on the sidewalk with both arms wrapped around her stomach as if she had been punched.

"She okay?"

"Yeah," said Gerber. "Just a little scared."

Fetterman reached out to take one of her hands. "Spends months in Vietnam with us, weathers a dozen mortar attacks, even goes on patrol with us, and she's scared by three street thugs?"

With Gerber's help she got to her feet. She brushed off the back of her skirt, trying to look over her shoulder to see if there was any damage to her new clothes. "I just wasn't ready for this. I thought we were safe in Hong Kong."

"So did I," said Gerber, glancing at Fetterman. "So did I."

Back at the hotel, they all stopped in the main room of the suite to have a drink. Fetterman performed the bartending honors, making Morrow's drink extra strong because she seemed to be more upset by the mugging attempt than she was letting on. He noticed that both knees of her stockings were torn, as if she had fallen to them before landing on her backside.

As she took a deep drink, she exclaimed, "Hey! I got a question. Why didn't we report that to the police?"

"What for?" said Gerber. "They didn't steal a thing from us, and they were punished for trying. They came off a lot worse than we did."

"Robin," said Fetterman, "you look like you could use a long hot bath. Take some of the sting out of this."

Gerber, joking all the way, said, "And if you need someone to wash your back, I think we could find a volunteer." After he said it, he wondered if it had been a wise comment. He had spent the majority of the past few weeks trying to avoid just such a situation, but tonight, mellowed by the wine, it seemed like the thing to say.

She smiled at that and stood up. "I'll give you a shout. I may need a refill on this, too." She held up her glass.

"Just let us know," said Fetterman.

As soon as Morrow was out of the room, Fetterman spun on Gerber and demanded, "Now do you think I'm seeing things? That was no normal mugging. We were set up."

"Wasn't a very good attempt. You'd have thought they'd have guns."

"Captain, it's nearly impossible to get guns in Hong Kong. They send a couple of martial arts experts with knives at us and figure that they're going to take us. They overlooked the fact that we know the stuff too and can kick the shit out of almost anyone we meet."

Gerber took a sip of his drink before he spoke. "Not exactly the first team. And a stupid move because it alerts us."

"No. Not really. It appears to be a mugging. If they kill us, that's fine, but if they fail, they figure we think it was a mugging. No harm to them."

"I have to admit that I'm much more inclined to believe you now," said Gerber, rubbing his chin. "We haven't been out of Vietnam for twenty-four hours and we run into a street gang. We weren't exactly in the best part of Hong Kong, but still, the co-incidences are adding up too quickly."

"So what are we going to do?"

"Well, I don't plan to spend my whole leave hiding in a hotel room just so the Chinese bastard won't have a chance to kill me. I suppose we could always check out of here and go to Japan or Manila, or even home."

"Captain, let me remind you that we all volunteered to extend so we could kill the son of a bitch. Now that we know he's here, let's get him."

"Tony, I'm not going to start a war in the streets of Hong Kong."

"No one said a word about starting a war, but we do know he's here and he won't have all the protection of the VC around him. He's delivered himself into our hands."

Gerber sat on the couch and kicked off his shoes. He wiggled his feet, watching his toes. "I wouldn't go so far as to say he's delivered himself into our hands. We don't have him, and we don't know where he is. I would, however, guess that he can move back and forth across the Red Chinese border with ease. Something we can't do."

"So you're going to let this opportunity slip through your fingers because it might be a little bit difficult?"

"I might remind you, Master Sergeant, to whom you are speaking." Gerber grinned. "But I probably don't have to. Okay, let me say this. Right now we don't have enough information to work with. We need some more."

"And then?"

"The son of a bitch targeted us first. He's on my list. If we can manage it, we kill him."

11

HOTEL REGENCY,
HONG KONG

The breakfast dishes littered the table as Gerber sat sipping coffee and staring out the window at Victoria Harbour far below him. The junks still sailed next to modern hydrofoils on the deep blue water. Fetterman was finishing his eggs, toast and orange marmalade. As he took the last bite, he said, "How do we go about finding him?"

"I don't think we have to worry about it. He's going to be looking for us. All we have to do is make ourselves available and he's going to turn up."

"Okay, that makes sense." Fetterman pushed his plate away and picked up his coffee. "So we play Joe Tourist. Ride the bus, take the ferry, use the tram, just about anything a tourist would do. We let him come to us."

"Right."

"Then I have only one other question. We aren't normal tourists. Won't that look strange?"

"I wouldn't think so. Even though we're not regular tourists, we would normally do some things that tourists would. I mean, one of the first things you did was go buy a new suit. We went out last night to a Chinese restaurant. Tonight maybe we ought to head over to the Aberdeen area and have dinner on one of the floating restaurants. Those are things that would be expected of us. They are the things we should do."

Fetterman nodded and then added, "We've just come out of a year in Vietnam. Shouldn't we be looking for female companionship?"

"Tony, I'm surprised at you. First, we *have* some female companionship. But if you feel that we need more for protective coloration, then by all means we should try to obtain it."

"That brings up another question." Fetterman stood so that he could look out the window. "Shouldn't we tell Robin what's going on? She's as big a target as we are when she's with us."

Now it was Gerber's turn to be quiet. He continued to sip his coffee as he pondered the idea. Finally he said, "This is a very delicate area. We're playing fast and loose with a lot of international law and civilized ideals. We've moved the war from the Vietnam mainland into a different part of Asia, not to mention involving nationals from a couple of other countries."

"Yes, sir. Do we tell her?"

"It's a hell of a story."

"Yes, sir, and she has proved that she can hold back a story if it helps her friends."

"Tony, I think the last thing we need to do at this point is tell her. It's not that I don't trust her, I just don't think she needs to know right now. If the situation changes, we can tell her, but right now, I think we should hold our peace."

"So our plan for today is to run around Hong Kong as targets."

Gerber had to laugh. "Not much of a plan." At that moment, Morrow's door opened and she stood in the opening, her gaze moving back and forth between the two men.

"What's not much of a plan?"

Fetterman said, "The travel arrangements the captain made for us. I told him that it wasn't much of a plan, and he was repeating what I said."

"If that's the case," said Morrow, "I can come up with something better if you like."

"We're in your hands," said Gerber.

"Then if you're ready," she said, "let's get going." She ducked back into her bedroom long enough to grab her purse, then followed them into the hallway.

As they rode the elevator down, Morrow said, "If you don't mind, I'd prefer not to take the car. I mean, I have it parked now and I may never find another parking place for it. Nobody told me that you couldn't find parking places in Hong Kong. I thought the boss was doing me a favor by offering me the thing."

Gerber shrugged and said, "I guess it doesn't bother me." He turned to Fetterman. "Tony?"

"Can't see where it will make any difference," he said. "Might make things easier if we don't take it."

"Easier?" asked Morrow.

"Don't have the hassle with traffic and don't have to worry about a place to park. Besides, there's a lot of public transportation available."

Outside, they saw a green Rolls-Royce go by. Morrow pointed and said, "We should have stayed at the Peninsula. Those are the cars they use to haul their guests around. Better than the buses we're going to have to take."

They turned to the right, strolling along the sidewalk, looking into shop windows and trying to ignore the kids who were following everyone. They reached the gates for the Star Ferry and could see the green-and-white vessel as it sailed toward them. At first Gerber was going to suggest that they take a ferry to one of the other islands but then remembered they had been picked up by the muggers in the Suzie Wong district. Although he didn't want to make things too easy for the enemy, he could see no reason to make it too difficult, either. Without a word he steered Morrow toward the ferry.

As they boarded, watching the chairs being turned around for the return trip, she said, "We did this last night."

"But we didn't see much of Hong Kong Island. Besides, the ferry to Macau leaves from there, and we can gamble on Macau."

"If we do this right," said Fetterman, consulting the map he had found in the hotel, "we can get over to Aberdeen to have dinner in one of the floating restaurants."

Morrow looked from one man to the other and then outside as if she had never seen water before. She asked, "What is this fascination you have for the ocean? Ferries to Macau. Eating in floating restaurants. My God."

"Well," said Fetterman slowly as if considering the question carefully, "it limits the number of enemy approaches and greatly decreases the number of men needed for a successful defense."

"Thank you," she said. "I didn't know we were expecting an attack."

"Not a large one." Fetterman smiled.

After the ferry docked on Hong Kong Island, they spent an hour walking around, just watching the crowds and studying the architecture of the old buildings.

Much of the old British architecture of massive tan stone and giant windows with huge arches had given way to flimsy buildings with small windows and balconies that climbed the fronts. Mattresses, sheets, clothing and flags were draped over the railings of most balconies. A riot of sound, from radios tuned to Chinese stations, from televisions, people shouting and even bands playing, flooded the street.

There were cars, the drivers leaning impatiently on the horns although the snarled traffic was clearly going nowhere on the narrow, winding streets. Hucksters stood in front of small shops, demanding that pedestrians enter to purchase something, anything. Gerber and his two companions passed dozens of shops, theaters, banks, government buildings and hotels. They stopped in a few but bought nothing. Occasionally they separated, first Gerber and Morrow walking ahead, and then Fetterman and Morrow. At last Gerber suggested they take one of the buses to visit the other side of the island.

They found a red double-decker bus that would take them into Aberdeen. They were surprised that it was air-conditioned. They had been in the heat and humidity of the streets and found the sudden change in temperature slightly uncomfortable.

When Morrow seemed to be totally engrossed in sight-seeing, Fetterman leaned close to Gerber and said, "I think I've spotted him."

"Where?"

"Six seats back. I believe he's been with us for the past hour, but then there is a tourist couple that I've seen a few times this morning, too."

"I would opt for them," said Gerber, grinning. "Good protective coloration."

"Yes, sir. But I think it's the lone man. He's stuck to us tighter than they have, and it's not that unusual for a tourist to get on this bus at this time of the day."

"Keep an eye on him."

"What do you plan to do?"

"Let's see if we can get him alone somewhere and then question him. He's probably just hired help with no real knowledge, but he might be able to tell us something. Remember, the one thing we don't want to do is cause an incident. We have to be discreet."

"Yes, sir. Discreet."

They settled back to watch the scenery with the rest of the tourists, but as they passed the turnoff for Waterfall Bay, they noticed a car stalled across the road. Gerber shot a glance back at the lone man, but he seemed unconcerned.

Gerber felt a hand on his arm and looked at Fetterman, who sat with his other hand under his shirt as if reaching for a pistol.

Suddenly, two men dressed in three-piece suits, their coattails rippling in the breeze off Telegraph Bay, appeared at the side of the road holding AK-47s. Before the bus had time to come to a halt, they opened fire.

Gerber grabbed Morrow and shoved her to the floor, falling on her as he wrapped his arms around his head for protection. The glass in the windows disintegrated, showering the passengers.

The bus began rocking from side to side as the bullets drummed into it. Bits of metal flew as slugs ricocheted off the frame of the backrests. The relentless rounds chewed up the fabric and stuffing of the seats, creating a snowstorm of foam bits. There were loud bangs as the tires blew. Women and children screamed under the onsaught. One man lay on his side, blood staining his shirt, screaming over and over, "What the fuck?"

Fetterman rolled into the aisle and saw the lone man lying on the floor aiming a small pistol at him. Before the man could shoot, Fetterman drew his own hidden weapon and fired twice, putting one bullet in the man's right eye and the other through his throat. There was a spray of blood as he flipped onto his back, one hand clawing weakly at the wound in his neck. He shuddered briefly, then was still. As dead fingers released the weapon, Fetterman crawled toward him and claimed the gun.

"Mack. Hey, Mack," he called, and when Gerber looked up, he showed him the captured pistol. Gerber nodded once, and Fetterman tossed it to him.

The firing from the outside died, and there was a moment of unnatural quiet before a moan came from one of the wounded. That was answered by another, and there was a final burst of automatic weapons fire.

Fetterman then took cover behind a seat where he could get a good shot at the door if he needed it. He nodded to Gerber, who was on the other side of the bus, trying to protect Morrow and still cover the emergency exit, as well as providing backup for Fetterman.

Nothing happened right away. It was as if the men outside were waiting for word from their accomplice on the bus. When he failed to appear, one of the men came forward and kicked open the door, shattering the glass that remained in one of the bottom panels. He stepped up into the bus, his AK held loosely in both hands. He leaped to the center aisle, his feet spread wide, daring someone to do something.

Fetterman fired twice. The man spun to the right, throwing his weapon toward the driver's seat. The gunner collapsed to the floor as if his bones had suddenly turned to rubber. There was a splatter of blood on the window caused by one of Fetterman's bullets punching through the man's head.

That was answered by a burst from outside the bus, the sound of running feet and a car engine starting. Seconds later the sounds receded in the distance.

Gerber reached around to help Morrow up. "Are you all right?" he asked. "Were you hit? Are you all right?"

"I'm fine," she said shakily. "What in the hell was that all about?"

"I don't know," said Gerber. "Some kind of bus hijacking, I guess."

She turned her full attention on him, her eyes searching his. "You've been in Hong Kong little more than twenty-four hours, and already someone has tried to mug you and then hijack a bus with you on it. I'm not stupid. What the fuck is going on?"

Before Gerber could reply, Fetterman was kneeling near him. "We'd better get out of here."

"Get out?" asked Morrow, astonished. "What about the people who are hurt? We've got to do something for them."

"Yes, ma'am," he said. "The best thing we can do for them is get out of here and find help fast. There isn't much we can do without medical supplies."

Suddenly there was shouting all over the bus as if most of the passengers realized that the attack was over.

Fetterman got to his feet and leaped to the front where he made sure that the attacker there was dead. He grabbed the AK from the floor, stripped the magazine from it and ejected the round that was chambered. He put the weapon in the front seat but kept the magazine.

Cars were beginning to pull up, and the bus passengers were coming out of their shock. The vehicle rocked as people struggled to their feet and fought one another to get out. Others stopped to help the wounded who were lying on the floor or slumped in seats. A few were crying for help. Others were just crying hysterically.

Fetterman saw the bus driver. He had gotten out of his seat but had been shot three times in the chest and was crumpled behind his seat, nearly hidden. A woman was next to him, holding her leg in both hands and watching as the blood oozed from a wound in her thigh. She was grinning as if she had never seen anything funnier. Her face was turning waxy, and Gerber knew that she was in shock and dying from blood loss.

Gerber and Morrow, both on their feet, worked their way to the front door. Fetterman stepped to the ground to help them out. He then waited to assist the others as they straggled from the bus.

Gerber noticed that some of the occupants in the stopped cars and trucks were rubberneckers, while others seemed genuinely concerned, shouting in Chinese and English, trying to learn what had happened, asking if they could offer any assistance. In the distance there was the wail of a siren.

"Help is on the way," said Fetterman.

"Tony," said Gerber quietly. "You'd better get rid of that weapon."

"Why? I picked it up on the bus."

"Can you prove that?" asked Gerber, meaning he wanted to know if it could be traced to Fetterman.

"Can you prove I didn't?" replied Fetterman.

As the police approached, both Gerber and Fetterman dropped the pistols they held. Gerber didn't like doing that because he didn't know if the Hong Kong police could be trusted, but he had to take the chance. If they held on to the weapons, with so many dead and wounded around, the police might be inclined to shoot first.

"I'm afraid we're going to be busy the rest of the day, Robin," said Gerber. "I guess lunch is out."

"As soon as the police are through with us," she said, her voice low and steady, "you are going to tell me exactly what is happening, and I mean all of it."

"Yes," he said. "I suppose we owe you that much."

IT TOOK A LONG TIME for the threesome to free themselves from the clutches of the Hong Kong police, and even then they had help from the American Embassy, followed by a call from Morrow's paper before they were released. It was nearly dusk, and neither Fetterman nor Gerber wanted to be on the streets after nightfall a second time. They headed straight for the Star Ferry, with Morrow in tow, and returned to Kowloon Peninsula and the hotel.

As they entered the suite but before any of them could either pour a drink or call room service for dinner, Morrow demanded, "What the hell is going on?"

"Why don't you sit down," said Gerber reasonably, "and we'll tell you everything."

She stared at him for an instant, not moving. She then looked at her clothes, still splattered with the blood of the people killed or wounded during the attack, and felt her stomach turn over in her anger. She didn't understand how Gerber and Fetterman could stand there so calmly. But then, she had seen the same reaction from them after they had almost casually disposed of the three muggers the night before.

She paced along the couch, spun and headed back. She stopped and was going to shout something at them but thought better of it. She sat down and repeated, as calmly as she could, "What the hell is going on?"

Fetterman had stepped to the bar and had poured a large drink. He handed it to Gerber, who gave it to Morrow. He told her, "You'd better have some of this before we start."

Again she was going to shout at him but took a deep drink and breathed out the liquid fire of the Beam's as it nearly set her insides ablaze. "Stop stalling."

Gerber took another glass from Fetterman, swallowed nearly half the alcohol in it and said, "It started a long time ago, after we first built our camp."

For the next hour he explained about running into an enemy officer, who, it turned out, was Chinese. The man may have planned the first attacks on the camp, may have led the NVA while Gerber and the stripped-down team were working in North Vietnam.

Fetterman mentioned the times he had seen him during raids into Cambodia, or working in villages near the border. Gerber took over again, reminding her about the attempt to assassinate the Chinese officer, which was the case that she had helped them with. The story that she had withheld from publication to save Fetterman and Tyme from court-martial by General Crinshaw, who had pressed charges of murdering a foreign national in a neutral country. Gerber told her that he believed it was the same guy, and Fetterman nodded his agreement.

"And we think," said Gerber, "that it was this same officer who engineered the plan to capture us and then held Fetterman, Tyme and Washington in the POW camp. Since we beat him at that game, we think he is trying to kill us."

Morrow sat there quietly, staring at her feet, her breath coming in rapid gulps. She was remembering everything that she had seen in the past few months. She was remembering the deaths of Vietnamese strikers and Sergeant McMillan.

"How long have you known he is here?"

"We suspected it last night after the mugging. Tony and I discussed it. Finding us here wouldn't have been that hard since we didn't try to hide our plans. We just never assumed that the enemy would chase us into neutral territory. It was—"

"Why didn't you tell me? Don't you trust me yet?"

"Trust has nothing to do with it. We just didn't think it was time to tell you." Gerber shook his head. "We thought we might be followed during the day, but we didn't expect them to attack a busload of innocent people to get us."

"We have to tell the police," she said.

"Oh, no," said Fetterman from the other side of the room. "That's the last thing we have to do. We tell the police, and the Chinese bastard escapes across the border into Red China. No, we've got to keep him in Hong Kong where we can get at him."

Gerber waited for her horrified reaction, but it never came. She might have been thinking about all the death that had come about because of the Chinese officer, or she might have been thinking about fighting a war. In a war people died, and if you could keep those who died limited to the combatants, it made the war a little less horrible. Maybe she thought that by killing the Chinese guy in Hong Kong, they could limit the war in Vietnam slightly, and a smaller number of innocents would be killed.

When nothing was said for a while, Fetterman put his glass down. "Do we eat now?"

Morrow stood and smoothed down her wrinkled and dirty dress. "I think I'll just go to my room and take a bath. I'm not very hungry now."

"Would you like some company?" asked Gerber.

To his surprise, she said, "No. I would like to be alone for a while. I have a lot to think about." She moved to the connecting door and opened it. "I think I'll just spend the rest of the evening by myself."

"Sure," said Gerber. "If you need anything, let me know."

She left without another word.

As soon as the door was closed, Fetterman said, "From what you just said, Captain, I take it that we are going after the Chinese bastard."

"Of course."

"How are we going to accomplish this? We don't have any weapons, and we're alone here."

"Right. That's why, after we eat dinner, you're going to get on the phone and see how many members of the team you can find and convince to come to Hong Kong. I'm going to send a telegram to Bromhead and have him request leave. Then we go hunting."

12

HOTEL REGENCY,
HONG KONG

Fetterman glanced at his watch. He was sitting in a chair, staring at the phone as if willing it to ring. He said unnecessarily, "I make it about six in the morning in the World."

Gerber stood, unable to tolerate the quiet or the room any longer. He looked at the door that connected the room with Morrow's. "I think I'll go out and find a telegrapher's office and see if I can get word to Johnny."

"You can use the phone for that," said Fetterman.

"I know. I just need to get out for a while."

"You think that's wise, given all that's happened in the last couple of days?"

Gerber thought about that and said, "I was going to say I didn't think they'd try anything again so soon. And I didn't think they would attack if there were innocents in the way."

"That doesn't answer the question."

"No, Tony, it doesn't."

"So are you still going out?"

"Yeah. I can't stand it around here. I have to get out and do something."

Fetterman stole yet another glance at his watch and then put his feet up on the table as if he wanted to relax. He stretched and yawned. "You should learn how to relax, Captain. Sometimes you have to lie in wait for days before you have a chance to act, and if you expend all your energy trying to make something happen, you may find yourself short when the time comes."

"Thank you, Master Sergeant," said Gerber. "And no, you don't have to look at your watch again because only two minutes have passed since you looked at it the last time."

"Touché, Captain."

"I won't go far, Mom." Gerber smiled. "I just have to get out for a few minutes, even if it's only down to the lobby."

"I'll stay here and start the calls as soon as it's late enough in the World."

GERBER HAD BEEN GONE for more than an hour, but Fetterman wasn't worried about him. After all, Gerber was a Special Forces officer and was supposed to be able to take care of himself. Finally, when Fetterman figured it was about eight o'clock in the morning in Austin, Texax, where Tyme had said he was going to spend his leave, the sergeant picked up the phone and asked for the overseas operator. He gave Tyme's phone number, having memorized it before Tyme went on leave.

On the other side of the world, Fetterman heard the phone ring twice, three times, until someone finally answered it with a simple hello. He was a little surprised by that, used to having people answer with their rank, name and unit of assignment, but there was no mistaking the voice. Fetterman nearly shouted into the handset, "It's about time you answered."

There was a pause and then, "Sergeant Fetterman? Is that you?"

"It's me, Boom-Boom, calling you to find out what kind of trouble you've gotten yourself into without the old master sergeant around to keep you straight."

"You sound so far away. Are you in town?"

"Of course not. I'm in Hong Kong with the captain, trying to keep the world safe for democracy. Or maybe that's safe *from* democracy."

"Hong Kong? I'll be damned."

"Listen, Boom-Boom, this is costing me more than I care to think about. I've got a problem and I need some help. How soon can you get here?"

"Get there? To Hong Kong? Why?"

"Remember when we were in Bangkok and the captain told us that the wrong body had been shipped for burial? Well, the right one is here, only it's not a body yet."

There was a pause before Tyme spoke again. "You mean . . ."

"He's here. In Hong Kong."

"I don't know how fast I can get the arrangements made, Tony. I can probably get out to the West Coast this afternoon, but I don't know how soon I can get a flight west from there."

"Once you know that, send me a telegram, and we'll arrange transport for you from the airport." Fetterman went on to give him the name of the hotel and the room number. "I'll expect to see you in a few hours."

"Any special equipment you'd like me to bring? Anything that you might not have there?" asked Tyme.

"Just yourself. That's all we need."

"I'll let you know when I'll arrive. See you then."

As soon as Fetterman completed the call to Tyme, he asked the overseas operator to dial the number he had for Galvin Bocker. He went through the same ritual, trying to convince Bocker that they needed him in Hong Kong as soon as he could get there. Bocker, too, wanted to know if he should bring a weapon, and again Fetterman discouraged the idea. He told Bocker that they could find weapons in Hong Kong, that Special Forces NCOs were supposed to be resourceful and that they would have to make their weapons if they couldn't buy them.

Next Fetterman tried to locate Sam Anderson but had no luck. Instead, he spoke with Sam's father, who said he'd give the message to Sam that Fetterman had called. Then he asked the operator to connect him with Sully Smith. A woman answered the phone, and Fetterman asked for Sully. A moment later he came on the line, and Fetterman told him what he wanted. Sully said he would catch a plane as soon as he could.

Fetterman tried a couple of other team members after speaking with Sully. Either they weren't home, or no one wanted to answer the phone. T. J. Washington, the medic, had taken off on a car trip. No one was sure when he would be back or exactly where he had gone. Fetterman left his name and number in case Washington checked in soon.

It was the same with Derek Kepler. The Intelligence NCO could have been a real asset to them, but he was off doing something else and no one at his home knew exactly what it was. Fetterman mumbled something about stealing an aircraft carrier for the camp and then thanked Kepler's father.

JUSTIN TYME SLOWLY CRADLED the phone and turned to look at the blond woman who sat at the small, round kitchen table, which needed to be stained and was surrounded by three mismatched chairs. She was wearing a frayed, blue robe, which she hadn't bothered to fasten so it hung open. She wore nothing underneath. She was drinking orange juice and staring at him.

"What was that?" she asked.

"I have to go to Hong Kong."

Carefully, precisely, she set the glass on the table and said quietly, "Just like that? You get a phone call and have to go to Hong Kong. After I've waited nearly a year for you to come home, you calmly announce that you have to go to Hong Kong?"

Tyme sat down and picked up his fork. He was thinking about the call and what Fetterman had said. The Chinese officer was in Hong Kong. Out in the open where they could get at him. Slowly he became aware that the woman was talking to him.

"I'm sorry, Linda. I've got to go." He hadn't heard her and was trying to fill the gap in the conversation.

She stood, throwing her napkin onto the table. "Got to go. Just like that. No discussion. No explanations. You just have to go."

"Linda, you haven't given me a chance to explain. No chance at all."

But Linda wasn't interested in listening at that moment. She left the kitchen and ran to the bedroom to find her clothes. That did it, she decided. She wasn't going to spend another minute with him. She just couldn't believe that he was actually going to leave her after having been home for less than a week.

She heard footsteps near the doorway and looked up to see Justin watching her as she picked up the jeans she'd worn the day before. Wearing only panties and a bra, she turned to face him.

"How can you consider going back?"

"Linda, listen to me." He moved forward and sat on the edge of the bed. "I'm not going back right now. I'm only going to Hong Kong for a couple of days. If Sergeant Fetterman called, then there must be something wrong. He wouldn't have called otherwise."

"If you go, then we're finished. I've waited a year for you to come home. It hasn't been easy on me. A lot of people—men—have called, but I've tried to be loyal. And what for? So that you can run off the first time the phone rings. To make it even worse, you've volunteered to stay there killing innocent women and children for an extra six months. You didn't even have the courtesy to ask me about it."

Tyme pushed a hand through his hair. He reached out for her, but she pulled away. "Where the hell did you get that crap about killing women and children?"

"The news. I saw it on the news. A man burned himself to death in front of the Pentagon to prove that what we're doing in Vietnam is wrong. To let us know that we're killing innocent women and children."

Tyme's temper finally snapped. "Bullshit," he shouted. "There has been nothing on the news about us killing women and children. Maybe the VC, but not us. We haven't done anything like that."

"You drop bombs indiscriminately and that kills the—"

"What the hell are you talking about? I haven't dropped a bomb on anyone. I'm doing a necessary job that—"

"Supports a dictator who oppresses the innocent," she finished for him. "And they're using B-52s to drop the bombs. I saw pictures on the news. I saw it all."

Tyme jumped up and stormed to the door. He stopped and looked back, taking in the scene because he believed it would be the last time he would see it: Linda, still in her panties and bra, standing in front of the tiny closet with its sliding, wooden doors; the lavender bedspread that had mostly fallen on the floor; the little black-and-white TV on the nightstand; Linda's clothes on a chair.

"Where in the hell are you getting all this?" he asked again, his voice subdued now.

"I've been around. I've seen the reports. I've been to lectures on the campus."

"Oh!" he said. "Lectures on the campus. Impartial discussions of our imperialist advances on the oppressed people of South Vietnam. Pinkos who think that everything the VC does is all right and everything we do is wrong. Well, let me tell you about the lives we've saved with our medical assistance. Or the farmers who show us where all the enemy's booby traps are hidden so that we won't step on them. Does that sound like they don't want our help?"

Tyme turned to go, then stopped and looked back. "Can we talk about this seriously? I mean, what the politicians and the protestors say shouldn't come between us. You know me better than that."

She held up a blouse in front of herself as if suddenly embarrassed by her semi-nudity. "I know you can't sleep well at night."

Tyme felt he was gaining control again. "That's easy, Linda. Hell, one day I'm in Vietnam, where Charlie might drop a mortar round on me or begin an assault on the camp, and the next I'm in downtown Austin. Of course I can't sleep."

"It's more than that," she said quietly. "It's what you do and what I do and how I feel. Maybe it *would* be better if you just go."

"Maybe it would," he said. He turned and retraced his steps to the kitchen so that he could phone the airlines.

WHEN HE HUNG UP Galvin Bocker went back to the living room and sat down. His wife turned her attention from the new color TV that dominated one side of the tiny room in their quarters on the Army base. There were two chairs on either side of it and a couch, frayed from the kids jumping on it, faced the set. A worn, thin carpet of light gray covered the floor. She asked, "Who was that, dear?"

Bocker sat watching the TV for a moment. "One of the men from the team. Had some information for me."

"Oh, is he in town?"

Bocker looked at his wife and said, "No. He's in Hong Kong. He wants me to go there."

The woman looked from him to their two young daughters, who sat together on the floor coloring. They didn't like to color all that much and the weather outside was beautiful, but it had been so long since their father had been home that they just wanted to be near him, to reassure themselves that he was real, that he was home. They sensed the distress in their mother's voice but didn't understand it. Both turned to watch, the coloring books forgotten.

"When?" she asked quietly.

Now Bocker stood and said, "I'm sorry, Sara. As soon as I can. There is some kind of trouble, and they need my help."

There were tears in her eyes as she said, "But what if we need your help? We do need it. We need you." There was nothing in her voice that was accusing; there was only hurt because he would be leaving again so soon after arriving. A single phone call, and he had to go.

She had been the wife of a Special Forces NCO long enough to understand the unwanted calls. She knew her husband would have to respond to the call for help. She just didn't think it was fair because so many of the other service wives had husbands who didn't have to go. Other wives had husbands who worked regular hours in the motor pool or supply and who never had to go overseas.

"If you needed my help, I would stay," he told her. "I'll be back as soon as I can. I still have over three weeks left of my leave, and I can take some extra time if I want it. I have some extra leave time I can use."

"Let me help you pack." She moved over to him and reached out and took his hand. "The girls will be all right for a few minutes," she whispered.

Bocker smiled his understanding. "A few minutes?" he asked.

As they entered the bedroom, Sara closed the door and locked it behind her. She began to unbutton her blouse and said seductively, "Well, maybe more than a few minutes."

SAM ANDERSON SR. told his wife he had to go to the airport. She asked if there was something wrong. "I don't think so," he answered. "It didn't sound like it, but the sergeant who called said that he would appreciate it if I would tell Sam to call him."

The elder Anderson walked out to the garage and got into his car. He headed toward the airport, which was only ten minutes away. As he drove, he wondered if there was something more to the phone call, even though Fetterman had told him not to worry. Why would he call all the way from Hong Kong if there wasn't trouble?

At the small private airfield, Anderson Sr. pulled his car up next to his son's, which was parked in front of a light blue metal building. On the taxiway he could see a Cessna with the door on the passenger's side removed. As he watched, it took off and climbed, circling the field until it was a barely visible speck thousands of feet above him, weaving among the puffy white clouds.

Mr. Anderson turned off the engine and opened the door to let the early-morning breeze blow through. With his hand he shielded his eyes from the sun and watched as a tiny shape tumbled from the aircraft. It was followed by another and another until there was a string of six people falling.

As they plummeted to earth, Anderson Sr. wasn't worried. Then, as he could see shapes beginning to look vaguely human, he wondered if they weren't getting too close to the ground. He sat forward, waiting, silently praying for the chutes to open. He saw the deep colors of the jumpsuits and began to distinguish the arms and legs of the people.

"Where are the chutes?" he asked silently and then out loud again, "Where are the chutes?"

He started to get out of the car as the first chute blossomed, followed quickly by others until there was only one person freefalling. Anderson was sure he could recognize his son.

"Sammy," he yelled. "Pull your rip cord!"

And then he saw the parachute stream out of its pack, a tiny white blob trailing black cords and slowly, agonizingly slowly, open up, retarding the younger Anderson's descent.

Moments later all the sky divers were on the ground, gathering their chutes and then trotting across the airfield toward the buildings that housed the airport offices and training rooms.

Sam saw his father and waved once before disappearing into the building. A moment later he reappeared, escorting a tall, slender woman with long brown hair that hung to the middle of her back. She was dressed in a jumpsuit and had a baseball cap on her head. The skin of her oval face was nearly perfect, and when she smiled, she had deep dimples. The only flaw was a nose that was flattened slightly as if it had been broken sometime in the past.

"Hi, Dad," the demolitions expert said as he approached. "Do you know Brandi?"

"I don't think so," his father replied. "Hello, Brandi."

"Something you need, Dad? I'm sure you didn't come all the way out here just to watch me jump."

"No. Especially the way you do it. Scared me to death. Why do you have to wait so long before opening your chute? You were the last one."

"It wasn't all that long. I've made jumps where we couldn't open them until we were within five hundred feet of the ground. I popped it while at a thousand."

Anderson Sr. clapped both palms against his ears. "I don't want to hear it."

Grinning, Anderson Jr. took the woman's hand and said, "Okay, Dad. Won't tell you about it. Now what did you want?"

"You got a call from a Sergeant, ah, Fetterman? Yeah, Fetterman. Gave me a number and told me to have you call him when it was convenient."

"He tell you what he wanted?"

"No, just that he's in Hong Kong."

Anderson laughed. "Hong Kong. I wonder what he's doing there."

"Didn't say."

"Okay, Dad. Let me take care of my equipment and I'll be right home. Be about thirty minutes or so."

The elder Anderson smiled at the young woman. "Brandi, I'm sure that Mrs. Anderson would be delighted if you could join us this morning for a late breakfast, if you haven't eaten already. Or maybe I should say an early lunch."

The younger Anderson laughed and said, "Brandi, would you like some breakfast with my folks? My mom is an excellent cook."

"Hey, since I invited you," said Anderson Sr., "I figured I'd do the cooking."

"Okay, Dad," he said, turning to look at Brandi. "You want to eat at my house, even if my dad cooks?"

"Sure, Sam," she said. "Might be fun to eat with civilized people again. That is, if you promise to be on your best behavior."

"Thank you, Brandi. Make my Dad think I'm a slob."

"We'll see you in a little while, Sam. Brandi, it was nice meeting you." Mr. Anderson got into his car and started the engine.

SULLY SMITH REPLACED the receiver, then walked to the door and out to the garage where his 1957 two-tone Chevy was parked. The hood was up, there was a cloth over one of the red fenders and parts of the engine were scattered over the floor and a workbench. Rather than go back to work on the car, he opened the door on the driver's side and got in. He put his hands on the wheel as if he were going to back out of the garage. He just sat there.

Thirty minutes later his sister, a thin woman with long black hair, brown eyes and an olive complexion, entered the garage. She was wearing shorts and a blouse. For a moment she stood staring at her brother, wondering what had been said on the phone to upset him. Finally she asked, "Frank, what's wrong?"

He had been called Sully for so long that he momentarily forgot that his sister still called him Frank. He looked at the mess he had made of his car. "I won't be able to finish this."

"So?" she said. "You can leave it here. Tom won't mind."

"Right. He'll be thrilled to have your brother's car spread all over his garage with no prospect of getting it fixed in the next six months or a year."

"If he doesn't like it, he'll just have to put it back together himself."

Smith turned and looked at his sister carefully. "What does the family think of the war, sis? Or your friends?"

"What do you mean?"

"I mean, do they support us? Do they think we should get out? I see on the news that some people don't like what we're doing. I just wondered how everyone felt. Hell, I saw the antiwar rallies staged in Washington. I didn't know it was so widespread."

She pondered the question for a while, picking at a small scab on her bare knee. "I don't think they really give it much thought. They see it on the news, just like you did, but it's so far away, and if they don't really know anyone who is over there, they just sort of ignore it. They don't care. We stay in Vietnam or we leave it. This is the first time anyone has really protested the war. Ever since that guy burned himself to death in front of the Pentagon."

"Maybe they don't say anything because they know your brother is there."

"No, Frank. I think they just don't care. It doesn't affect them. Maybe there are some jobs at King Radio because of the war, but it doesn't affect them in any way they can touch. It's somebody else's problem. They don't think about it."

Smith got out of the car and let his eyes roam the inside of the garage. There were bikes that hadn't been used in a while. Boxes with labels telling him that they held old clothes or books or toys that the children had outgrown. There was a rack of garden tools and a red lawn mower in one corner. He could see outside, to the bright green lawn, which didn't seem to be as green as the vegetation in Vietnam, and the small garden, which didn't seem to be surviving the late fall too well. Middle-class America at its best. Things simple and easy. No hard choices and no chance to really live. Go to work, come home, then go to work again.

Suddenly Sully wished he could change places with his brother-in-law because, even if it wasn't an exciting life, it was one worth living. At the end of ten years, what would he have to show? Service stripes on the sleeve of his uniform, ribbons above the pocket showing bravery or service and tours of duty. Smith smiled. Or the memories of dozens, hundreds, of things that he had been allowed to blow up. Encouraged to blow up.

"I'm glad most of the people don't know about Vietnam," said Smith. Then, as an afterthought, he said, "I have to go to Hong Kong soon."

"We'll have your car here when you get back," she said.

He walked over to her and kissed her on the cheek. "I think that means more to me than anything you could have said."

IN THE HOTEL IN HONG KONG, Fetterman stood up and walked to the bar to pour himself a drink. He looked at his list and came to the conclusion that all in all he didn't have very good luck in finding the team. He wasn't sure exactly what Gerber had in mind but thought he might have gotten through to enough of them to complete the task. He wished he'd found T.J. because they might need the services of a medic. No matter.

He walked to the connecting door and put his ear against it, wondering what Morrow was doing. He could hear nothing on her side. She might still be in the tub, although she had left them a couple of hours earlier. She was probably in bed asleep, like a normal person.

Fetterman went back to the bar and topped off his drink again as he thought about Morrow. Her reactions during the shooting on the bus and its aftermath certainly hadn't been those of the average American female. She hadn't gotten hysterical; she had been thinking about survival and what had to be done. Maybe it was because she had seen so much blood and gore while in Vietnam, or maybe it was a result of some of the training she had taken prior to arriving in the war zone. Whatever the reason, her reactions had been very good. She was sensible, cool and quiet. She was an outstanding lady, intelligent, beautiful, and Fetterman decided he would be proud to have her on his team if it was allowed.

He went back to the chair, the one he had turned so that he could watch the lights of the city and the boats in the harbour. He reached over and turned off the lamp in order to see better and wondered what had happened to the captain.

Fetterman wasn't worried; it was just that the captain should have been back by now. As he had thought earlier, the captain was certainly able to take care of himself, but Fetterman didn't like the

way the forces had been divided. Team members scattered all over
the World, or world, he thought ironically, because Bromhead was
still in Vietnam, the captain out somewhere and Morrow apparently asleep behind a locked door. Fetterman didn't like it. Any of
it.

13

THE STREETS OF
HONG KONG

Gerber moved to one of the phones in the hotel lobby. He called a telegrapher's office to send the telegram. Then, feeling as if he hadn't spent enough time out of the room, he decided to take a walk around the block, at the very least. He exited the hotel, turned right and crossed the street so that he walked past the Peninsula Hotel as one of the green Rolls-Royces deposited a wealthy couple at the door. He looked at the woman carefully, his eyes focusing on the diamonds around her neck, figuring that she was wearing, at minimum, his whole year's salary.

He rounded the corner and looked back, but the couple was gone, waved inside by the uniformed doorman and aided by three bellhops. But, as he turned to continue his walk, he caught a flash as if someone was breaking for cover. Before he moved too far, he stopped again, wondering if he had picked up a tail already. Then up the street from him he saw a man in a soiled suit, sitting on the curb and holding his head in both hands. He was staring at the street dejectedly. Gerber walked rapidly over to him because he looked like an American.

Gerber approached and said, "Hey, you need a hand?"

The man looked up at him and tried to smile. "Sure."

The guy reeked of liquor, and it was only then Gerber realized that he was drunk. He had probably spent the last several hours in one of the better clubs, sucking down a lot of his military pay. That's what Gerber assumed because the man had short black hair and a very neat mustache. Both marked him as a military man. Not to mention the civilian suit that looked new.

"Name's Gerber. Want me to help you to your hotel?"

"Larko," said the man. "Dennis Larko. You American?"

"Uh-huh. Now would you like a hand finding your way back to your hotel?"

Larko smiled and then began to giggle. He rubbed a hand over his oval face, smearing the dirt that was on it. His dark eyes were a bit glazed. He looked like a tall, burly man, but it was hard to tell since he was sitting. "It's around here somewhere. I know it is. I just can't seem to find it."

Gerber helped Larko to his feet and stood back while the other man swayed back and forth, trying to maintain his balance. The captain asked for the third time, "Where's your hotel?"

Finally Larko said, "It sounds like an island or something. I forget the exact name."

"You mean the Peninsula?"

"Yeah! That's it. Air Force gave us TDY for the couple of days we're here so we thought we'd try the best."

"Well, it's not that far. Come on." Gerber half pushed, half guided Larko down the street until they arrived at the Peninsula. He kept his eyes open but didn't see a sign of the man he thought had been following him earlier. Maybe he had run off when Gerber stopped to help the drunk.

The doorman gave them a dirty look but didn't try to stop them as they entered the hotel. He even opened the door for them, but then stood away from them as if afraid he would be contaminated somehow. They made their way to a bank of elevators hidden away from the front desk and waited for one going up. Larko wasn't sure of the floor or the room number but gave one to Gerber anyway. Gerber suggested that they look at the key, but Larko claimed he'd lost it.

After two misses they found the right room. Another man opened the door and was surprised to see Larko accompanied by a stranger because he had left earlier with an Oriental woman. That could explain what had happened to his room key, Gerber thought.

He guided the man to the bed and tried to sit him down, but Larko collapsed on his side, drew his feet up, coughed once and then emitted a ragged snore.

The other man introduced himself as Loechner and thanked Gerber for helping his friend. Gerber noticed a couple of flight suits hanging behind the door. "You guys pilots?"

"No, flight crew. Have a C-130 parked out at the airport and we've got an RON here. Maybe be here a couple of days if we don't get a mechanical problem fixed."

"Well, have fun and don't get too drunk." Gerber left, thinking he had missed something but not sure what it was.

He returned to their suite at the Regency and found Fetterman sitting in the dark with his chair facing the window. He didn't turn on the lights and made his way to the bar. After pouring himself a drink, he asked, "You see anything more of Robin? She say anything to you?"

"Went to sleep a while ago. Never reappeared."

"How do you know she's asleep?" asked Gerber.

Although Gerber couldn't see it, Fetterman grinned at the window. "When you're a master sergeant, you have to know these things. Besides, I went in and checked on her."

"She didn't lock the door?"

"Of course she locked the door, but since when has a locked door stopped any of us? Don't worry, I relocked it on my way out so she won't know."

"Have any luck getting hold of the team?"

"Some of them." Fetterman stood and closed the curtains before turning on the light. "Probably begin arriving sometime late today or early tomorrow, depending on flight connections."

Gerber sat on the couch and said, "Got the telegram off to Johnny so he might be here soon."

"Okay, Captain, what's the plan now? We haven't really thought about that."

"Same thing, I imagine. He's going to be looking for us and knows where we are. We let him come to us. We'll just have to be ready."

"I don't suppose you have a weapon," said Fetterman. "I had to throw away the only one I had."

"Shit," said Gerber, slapping his knee. "That's what I forgot."

"Sir?"

"While I was out, I ran into a drunk airman. Helped him to his hotel and then didn't think to ask them if they could get us some weapons. They're a C-130 crew and might be able to do it."

"That could solve one problem."

"You have another?"

"I'm a little concerned about Robin," said Fetterman. "She's a very strong lady, but I don't think she responded to today's activities with enough emotion. She's got it bottled up in her, and I don't like that. She didn't rant at us for not telling her about the Chinese guy, and she didn't seem to be too upset by the number of innocent people killed or hurt today."

"It might be," said Gerber, "that she has seen enough death and destruction with us that she is slightly immune. She won't go to pieces at the first sight of blood."

"I thought of that," answered Fetterman, "but I decided that we are dealing with a woman who is basically a middle-class American and who has been shielded from some of the realities of the world. I'm afraid that we should get more emotion out of her, if only outrage at the way people treat other people."

"So what do you want to do about it, Tony?"

"I was thinking that maybe you should talk to her, Captain. Tomorrow, alone. Find out what she's thinking and feeling. I'm worried about her."

Gerber felt his chest go cold and his head spin as Fetterman made his suggestion. The last thing he wanted was to be thrown into a situation where he would be alone with her, talking about feelings and emotions. It was a minefield strewn with all sorts of extra booby traps.

"You think it's necessary?"

"Yes, sir, I do. The sooner the better."

"All right. Tomorrow, as soon as we finish breakfast, I'll have a talk with her." Gerber didn't relish the idea.

BEFORE GERBER HAD A CHANCE to talk to Morrow the next morning, they got a call from the Hong Kong police. There were a number of questions that needed to be answered again. The three of them left for the police station on Hong Kong Island just after nine o'clock. Gerber was studying Morrow, trying to see if there was something wrong with her, but after a good night's sleep she seemed to have shaken off the effects of the day before.

At the police station they were questioned individually. Gerber watched as Morrow was led away, two policemen flanking her and a female officer following. He stood there until they entered one of the interrogation rooms that lined the narrow hallway.

One of the two officers accompanying Gerber opened a door next to them and gestured to the American to go through it. There were two chairs, one on either side of a small, rectangular table shoved against a wall. A green glass ashtray rested in the middle of the table, and on the far wall there was a two-way mirror. Gerber sat in one of the chairs, wondering if they were going to play good cop-bad cop with him or if the interrogation technique would be less subtle.

One of the police officers took the other chair. He was a small man wearing a three-piece suit. He had straight black hair, large oval eyes, a small nose and very even white teeth. He grinned to show them and then stroked the pencil-line mustache over his wide mouth. For a moment he didn't say anything. He just smiled. Finally he pulled a pack of American Salem cigarettes from a side pocket and held them out, offering Gerber one.

Gerber smiled and shook his head. "No, thank you."

"Okay." The man had an English accent. "I am Detective Lo. We've invited you back because our interviews with the other surviving passengers suggest that you and your friend were armed. Would you care to explain that?"

"Well—" Gerber rubbed his chin "—actually, we were able to take the weapons away from the men who started shooting at us."

"Three or four heavily armed men and you were able to take their pistols away from them?" The detective rocked back in his chair and lit one of his cigarettes, blowing the smoke at Gerber.

"Of course, it wasn't quite that easy," said Gerber, "but that is correct. Sergeant Fetterman spotted one of them on the bus and was able to take his weapon."

"Sergeant Fetterman?" asked Lo, raising his eyebrows in surprise. "Sergeant of what?"

"Now don't be naive," said Gerber. "You know perfectly well that Sergeant Fetterman is in the United States Army. And so am I."

"Then you are familiar with weapons. You might say at home with them," said the police officer.

Gerber laughed out loud. "Listen, you're not going to get me to admit that I smuggled a pistol into Hong Kong. Do I have access to weapons? Yes. Hundreds of them, up to and including 81 mm mortars. If you'd like something larger, I think I could get it. Oh, and machine guns, too. But smuggle one into Hong Kong? No. I didn't do that. The weapons we used we took away from the men who attacked."

"Then you admit you shot them?"

Gerber took a deep breath and sighed. "I went over all this yesterday with your uniformed officers. They have the pistols. They have our statements."

"Yes, I read over those. Most interesting. I find there are questions I can't answer."

"Such as?"

The uniformed officer suddenly jumped so that he was standing next to the table. He pounded a fist on it, the sound ricocheting in the tiny room like a rifle shot. "Enough of this," he screamed. "Just enough. We know you're lying to us. Come clean and we'll forget about the smuggling. You did us a favor, but we don't like the way you lie to us."

Slowly Gerber turned to face the other police officer. He was dressed in a tailored uniform with a black Sam Browne belt. He held a high peaked cap under his arm. His eyes were wild, and his hair hung in his face. He had bad breath.

"I'm sorry," said Gerber, "but I'm sure you've checked my background by now. The American Embassy is sure to have helped you. You should know that I am an expert in unarmed combat. Sergeant Fetterman took the man by surprise. We used his own weapons on him. We used them on his friend."

The uniformed man began to chatter in rapid Chinese. His voice became louder as if he were losing his temper. He slapped the table twice and then stood erect, his hands on his hips.

The other man answered him slowly, calmly, smoking his cigarette. He crushed it out and lit a second one. He gestured with it and then knocked the ash into the tray.

The conversation continued like that until the plainclothesman put out his third cigarette. The uniform glared at him for a moment and then stormed out of the room, slamming the door behind him.

"He's not happy with me," said Lo. "He thinks you're lying and that we should get to the bottom of those lies."

"And you?" asked Gerber.

"I'm not sure. I'm not worried about it enough to pursue it. You did us a favor by breaking up the hijacking. I wish you could have done something about it sooner, but I'm glad you were there."

"Well, then, what's the problem?"

"The problem," said the detective, shaking another cigarette from his pack, "is that damned pistol. The big .45 that's standard U.S. Army issue. A punk like that shouldn't have had it."

"But we shouldn't have had it, either," responded Gerber.

"No," agreed Lo, "but you have a better chance of finding one." He hesitated and added, "Unless something new comes up about the weapons, I'm happy with your story. You won't be hearing from us again."

"Is there anything else? I'd like to get out of here."

"No, that's all for now," said Lo. "But please, if you find it necessary to leave Hong Kong, let the American Embassy know where you go in the event we need to speak with you again."

Gerber got to his feet and stepped to the door. "I'll be in town for another several days," he said.

The man escorted Gerber back to the entrance of the police station where Fetterman sat on a hard wooden bench waiting. He was sitting beside an Oriental woman who had one wrist handcuffed to the arm of the bench. The wall behind him was splattered with dried spit, vomit and blood. There was a large desk where the booking sergeant sat, elevated so he looked down on those brought in. There was constant traffic through the room, doors slamming and people screaming. Eyes closed, Fetterman looked as if he didn't have a care in the world or any idea where he was. Gerber stopped in front of Fetterman and asked, "Where's Robin?"

Fetterman opened his eyes. "Gone. Left about half an hour ago. Before I got out here."

"You didn't follow her?"

"I've only been out here about three minutes myself." Fetterman got up, smiled at the woman on the bench, then said to Gerber, "She said she'd meet us for lunch."

As they left the police station, Gerber said, "I don't like this. They separated us too easily, and now Robin has gone on without us."

"You think that might be a problem?"

They reached Jackson Road and began walking north toward the berth of the Star Ferry. As they passed the Hong Kong Club Building, a large, formidable structure, Gerber said, "Can't you see it as such? We haven't had control of anything since we got here. We've been letting the opposition have the initiative from the word go."

"We haven't had much choice."

"And we still don't, but we've got to keep everyone else from interfering with us. I should've told Robin to stay right there until we were finished, but I didn't expect things to break the way they did."

"You have a reason for feeling this way, Captain?" asked Fetterman. "Or are you just borrowing trouble?"

"Probably borrowing trouble. I'm just uneasy after all that's happened."

Back at the hotel they stopped at the front desk to see if there were any messages. They learned that Anderson thought he would be in about midnight. There was nothing from any of the other team members. They rode the elevator up and let themselves into the living room of the suite. Morrow was not there, and there was no evidence that she had been.

Gerber shrugged off his jacket and dropped it on the couch. He moved to the control knob of the air conditioner and turned it up, then wandered around the room, wondering if Robin had ordered lunch for them or if she had gone out shopping. He didn't think she would venture too far until they returned, but there was no telling. He went to the connecting door, knocked twice and called, "Robin! Robin? You in there?"

"I can open it, if you would like, Captain."

"Robin?" yelled Gerber, "we're coming in."

Fetterman moved to the door and took out a tiny kit, selecting two slender metal picks, one with a slight hook on the end. He slipped the hooked piece into the lock, twisted it and slowly inserted the second piece as he felt the tumblers fall. A second later he twisted the knob and pushed the door open.

Immediately Gerber was alert. The little of the other room that he could see was a shambles. Fetterman noticed it, too, and jumped back so that he was no longer in a line of fire from the other room.

They held their positions for a couple of minutes, but there were no movements or sounds in the room. Gerber glanced at Fetterman. He shrugged and pointed to the left, indicating he wanted to take that position. He would be going through the door at an angle, toward the bathroom. If anyone was hidden there, Fetterman would be in a position to see him.

Gerber nodded and pointed to the left, telling Fetterman that he would follow him but dive into the main part of the room. He held up one hand, counting down silently using his fingers.

When he reached zero, Fetterman leaped, rolled on his shoulder and came up facing the bathroom. He kicked the door open and let it slam against the wall, but there was no one hidden there or in the tiny closet opposite him.

When Fetterman moved, so did Gerber. He followed Fetterman but dived at the bed, rolled across the mattress and came to his feet with his back to the wall, facing the room. It, too, was empty.

"Clear here," said Gerber.

Fetterman appeared around the corner. "Nothing in there. Her clothes are in the closet and her other stuff still in the bathroom. None of it has been touched."

The sheets and blankets were off the bed. One of the chairs was overturned, the table lay on its side and two of the lamps were broken. Papers and books were scattered on the floor, and there was shattered glass everywhere. The phone had been ripped from the wall. Gerber was surprised that the hotel management hadn't been up to find out about the phone.

"I guess this means they have escalated the war," said Fetterman.

"She's still alive, though," said Gerber. "There's no blood anywhere, so they didn't shoot her or stab her. If they'd killed her, they would have left the body because there would be no reason to take it with them. Not to mention the problem of carrying it out."

"They would have had a similar problem taking her out alive."

"They could have walked her out," said Gerber. "Held a knife at her back and told her that, if she squawked, she would die, as would her rescuers. That would have kept her quiet."

Fetterman sat on the bed. "Okay. I think you're right about that. But why keep her alive?"

"Obviously because she allows them to control us. As long as she's alive, they know we'll obey their orders. They hold the trump card."

"Do they?"

"To a point, I suppose. We can't do anything reckless that would endanger her, but there'll be a point where that handle will break right off," said Gerber.

"And now?"

"Let's search through here carefully and see if we can find any clues. I doubt that it'll do us any good, but we can't afford to overlook anything."

"And if we don't find anything?"

"Then we order up some lunch," said Gerber somewhat callously, "and wait for them to make contact. They will."

14

HOTEL REGENCY,
HONG KONG

Although Gerber had talked about eating and not worrying, he was not eating and he was worrying. He sat with a large steak in front of him. He had cut into it once but only took the single bite. He drained his wine in one healthy gulp, then poured himself a cup of coffee. He just sat while the meal got cold.

The knock at the door came as no real surprise. They suspected that someone would be contacting them. They just didn't know what form the contact would take. Fetterman leaped to the door, waited until Gerber was in position, then whipped it open. No one was there, only an envelope that fell to the floor. Fetterman looked up and down the hallway, but it was empty except for an Oriental woman pushing a maid's cart slowly toward the elevator.

Without a word Fetterman picked up the envelope and handed it to Gerber, who thought about fingerprints and booby traps and then ripped it open. The talent being used was probably imported from Red China, and the fingerprints, if there were any, probably would be no good. No way to trace them. And they wouldn't booby-trap the envelope because it made no sense.

He held it up by the opposite end and shook out the contents. There was one piece of paper and one Polaroid-type photograph that landed facedown. Gerber ignored the photo, fearing the worst. Fearing it would be a picture of Morrow's body.

Gerber read the note.

The woman dies if you do anything to annoy us. We want to see you alone, tomorrow. Be ready. We will call. If you disobey, the woman dies.

Gerber reached down and picked up the photo. He turned it over and studied it slowly. There was no change in his expression. Fetterman had been watching closely. When Gerber didn't speak, he reached over and took the snapshot out of his captain's hand.

It showed Morrow, stripped of all her clothing, lying on her side, her hands bound behind her. She had been badly beaten. There were dark bruises on her stomach, chest, thighs and face. One of her eyes was nearly puffed closed, and there was blood on her chin and shoulder and splattered on her legs.

Fetterman turned the photo facedown on the table. "Captain?"

"Yes, Tony."

"What do we do?"

"Right now, we wait. There is nothing else we *can* do. Wait until the team gets here and hope they make it before we need them tomorrow."

"We can't meet them at the airport," said Fetterman. "The opposition will have someone there looking for us. Or in the lobby to follow us. If they find out the team is arriving, they'll kill her."

"Right, but if we're lucky, they won't know what they look like. We'll have someone else meet them and tell them to assemble here at the hotel."

"And then?"

"And then we see what happens. I'll call those Air Force guys and see if I can get them to help. Or maybe you can call the homes of the team members who are coming and find out what airline they're using. Maybe we can get a message to them that way."

"Yes, sir. Anything else?"

"Not right now." Gerber reached over, picked up the picture and looked at it one more time. He wondered what she must be thinking, how she must be feeling. He had promised himself to protect her and failed. She had followed them to Hong Kong, only to be kidnapped and beaten. He knew that the beating was done only to make him lose his temper. But the plan had backfired because it only made him stop and think. It had made him slow down and methodically think through each step. He knew what he would do. Still, he wondered about Morrow and her feelings.

MORROW TRIED TO OPEN HER EYES behind the blindfold but couldn't because it was tied so tight. Her mouth was filled by a gag, and she could feel saliva gathering and dripping out because she couldn't swallow easily. Her jaw ached from being held wide open by the gag.

Her body felt like one huge angry bruise from the beating. She tried to shift her position, but she was so tightly bound she could hardly breathe. She could only lie on her side, her knees drawn up and held in position by the ropes. She closed her eyes and tried to relax, hoping that Gerber would come to her rescue. She remembered the lengths to which he had gone to free his men from Crinshaw when the general had arrested them, and later from the POW camp when they had been captured. She was sure that he wouldn't forget about her.

In her mind she ran down the events after the police had questioned her. She had left the station after waiting for only ten minutes and being told that it would be an hour or more before the police finished with Gerber and Fetterman. There was nothing that she needed to worry about, they had told her, so she decided to meet them at the hotel. She asked the desk sergeant to tell them and left the station alone. She walked to the Star Ferry with no trouble, crossed the harbour and went to the hotel.

In her room she started to undress but changed her mind. Instead, she went into the living room and poured herself a drink. It was a bit early to be drinking, but she didn't think Gerber or Fetterman would care; besides, they weren't around.

A sharp knock sounded on the door to the suite, and she went to answer it. As she opened the door, it was shoved against her hand, and an Oriental man rushed in. Before she could say a word, the man hit her in the stomach. She felt the air flee her lungs, and she fell to her knees, her head spinning, as she rolled to her side. She tried to breathe, but it seemed as if her lungs were paralyzed.

A second Oriental, shorter than the first, entered the room and stepped over her, moving toward the window. The one who had hit her grabbed her by the arms and lifted her to her feet. She leaned against the wall, using it to support her as she struggled to catch her breath.

The men talked to one another in rapid Chinese. The first man pushed her through the doorway into her room, and she tripped, sprawling to the floor near the foot of the bed. Both men began laughing then, and one of them kicked her lightly on the bottom.

They both then began to search the room, throwing Robin's papers and books onto the floor. They jerked the blankets and sheets from the bed and knocked the phone onto the floor. It landed close to where she lay, and when they turned their backs to search through her suitcases and the dresser drawers, she grabbed the phone. She spun the dial, trying to get the operator, but one of the men saw her. He leaped toward her and jerked the wires from the wall.

They continued their search, ignoring her. They threw glasses at the walls, knocked one of the framed paintings onto the floor and kicked over one of the chairs. When they had done enough damage to the room, they jerked Morrow to her feet.

"We go now. You go with us. You make noise, we kill you. You understand?"

Morrow didn't want to talk to either of the men. She wanted them to leave her alone. She had hoped they were just there to rob her and prayed that they would leave when they had what they wanted. But they took nothing, and now they were telling her that she had to go with them.

One of them grabbed a handful of her hair, jerking her head back so that she was staring at the ceiling. The other demanded, "Do you understand?"

She tried to nod but couldn't with the man pulling on her hair. She gasped and said, "Yes. Yes! I understand."

She felt the pressure on her head relax slightly, then she was hit in the stomach again. She dropped to her knees and clutched her middle, trying to breathe, unable to move at all. There was a curtain of black descending over her eyes, but she finally gulped in a mouthful of air.

The man laughed and kicked her in the chest, sending pain through her. She felt as if she were going to throw up.

Again she was lifted to her feet, and one man pinned her arms behind her while the other stood in front of her and pretended he was going to hit her. Each time Robin flinched, they laughed uproariously, as if they had never seen anything funnier.

Then, before they left, he hit her a final time, aiming the blow at her crotch. She hadn't thought that a woman could be hurt like that but found out she was wrong. She wanted to reach down, to hold herself, but the man wouldn't let her. She tried to squeeze her legs together, but her knees were shaking, and she seemed to have no control over them.

She remembered little of the trip through the hotel lobby. No one seemed to pay any attention to her, although one of the men was helping her walk. She was dumped into the back seat of a car, and as they pulled away from the curb, she was pushed to the floor. When she tried to look up, the man shoved her head down. For a moment everything stayed like that. Then her captor grabbed her arms, forced her face to the floor and bound her hands behind her.

The trip seemed to last forever. The man wouldn't let her move at all. She had to stay on her knees, her nose pressed to the floor mat of the car. Each time she tried to turn her head, the man pulled her hair.

When the car finally stopped, she could smell the country air around her. The back door opened and she was dragged out. She had enough time to see that she was not in the city anymore before being pushed into a building. There were other Oriental men there waiting for her.

Everyone stood watching and then one of them moved forward, grabbed her blouse and tried to rip it from her shoulders. The cloth proved to be a little too tough, and someone handed him a knife. Carefully he cut all her clothes from her until she was standing in front of them completely nude.

Wordlessly they began beating her. Before they had been afraid to touch her face because she had to walk through the hotel lobby, but now they didn't care. Each time she fell down, they lifted her up and waited until she stopped swaying before hitting her again.

Finally she fell to her side, and they left her like that. They tied her more tightly, wrapping ropes around her knees and ankles, and then took a couple of pictures. That done, they gagged her, blindfolded her, and then left her where she was.

Now all she could do was wait. She knew what they were doing and knew that she wasn't in danger of dying soon. They wouldn't kill her because they still needed her, as a lure, to pull in Gerber and Fetterman. All she had to do was hang on until they came to rescue her. The beating, while painful, had really been only superficial. She could wait patiently, trying to remember what Fetterman had told her about patience.

GERBER SPENT THE REST of the day sitting in the hotel room, sipping Beam's Choice and trying to concentrate on the TV. There wasn't anything that he wanted to watch, but he tried to keep his mind occupied. He watched an English language broadcast of the news that announced the American First Air Cav had completed a sweep through the Ia Drang valley, claiming to have killed 1,771 VC and NVA. It was the first use of the airmobile concept and the first use of B-52s in the Vietnam War.

Occasionally he would glance away from the TV at the photo lying facedown on the table. He was tempted to reach over and look at it again but denied himself.

He wondered if he wasn't letting the enemy get to him with the psychological warfare they were waging but realized there was really nothing he could do at that moment. He couldn't go out to buy weapons because he was sure that he would be followed and the purchase reported. Anything he did would be reported—not that it mattered, if all he was doing was sight-seeing.

Fetterman had been strangely quiet. He sat in the corner, his chair positioned so that he could watch the harbour. He held a knife in his hand and was using a leather belt to strop the blade. Not that the blade was dull. It was just something to do while he waited for the captain to pull himself together. He knew it would happen sooner or later and that the captain had to do it himself.

Gerber finally got up and walked over to the TV and slammed a hand against the control knob to turn it off. He shot a glance at Fetterman. "No, Tony, I am not stewing in my own juices. I was just trying to get my mind set and decide what we need to do."

Putting down his knife, Fetterman asked, "And you've decided?"

"It strikes me that they'll have people watching all our movements. They may expect us to go to the police, though I doubt that. They may expect us to try to find weapons. To do that would let them know we don't have many. They may think we'll go to the various clubs and try to recruit American help. Or they may want us to stick to the room and brood about this."

"Yes, sir."

"So the last thing they will expect is for us to go sight-seeing."

Fetterman thought about it and then laughed. "It has possibilities."

"Sure it does. They think they hold all the cards, and in essence they do. What we have to do is something they don't expect. I would think that sight-seeing would be it. How in the hell can we go out and look at the sights without Morrow? Knowing that Morrow is being held captive? It's bound to shake them up."

"You don't think it might backfire, do you?"

"What do you mean?"

"They went to a lot of trouble to kidnap Robin. Now we have the picture and the demand that you meet them alone, but rather than sit around waiting for instructions, we take off for some sight-seeing. They might just kill her then."

Gerber rubbed his chin and said slowly, "No, I don't think so. They'll keep her alive until they've got us. If they kill her, they've played their trump card."

Fetterman clapped his hands together. "All right, then. Let's do it. Shake the bastards up."

"In just a minute. Let me see if I can get in touch with those Air Force boys once. They might be able to help us quite a bit."

"Give them a call while I change my clothes," said Fetterman.

As Fetterman left the room, Gerber picked up the phone and called the Peninsula Hotel, asking for Dennis Larko. He answered the phone on the second ring and said that he remembered Gerber.

"Got a favor to ask," said Gerber.

"Be glad if I can do it," he said.

"I know you're in Hong Kong for only a short time and the last thing you want to do is hang around the airport, but I've got some of my people coming in, and I won't be able to meet them. Wondered if you could do it?"

"Sure. What flight are they coming in on?"

Gerber switched the phone from his right ear to his left. "That's the problem. I don't know. And they won't be coming in together. I'll have to give you a description and let you try to find them."

"You mean I've got to stay out there and meet all the planes?"

"I would suspect that once you've found one of them, you can tell him to find the others. After all, he'd be able to recognize the men. Puts him one up on you."

"All right, I'll do it."

"Good. Thanks. Now the first flight should be arriving about midnight. That doesn't mean one of our guys will be on it, it only means that one could be."

Gerber went on to tell Larko how he wanted the guys to contact Gerber. That done, he thanked Larko for his help and told him that if he ever found himself in South Vietnam, he should look up Gerber, who would find some way to repay him.

As he hung up, Fetterman reappeared, dressed in a clean set of civilian clothes. "Let's go have some fun."

"Not fun, Tony," said Gerber, "but let's go throw out a smoke screen."

"Exactly what I meant."

15

KAI TAK AIRPORT,
HONG KONG

Larko sat outside the glassed-in customs area at the airport, studying the passengers as they disembarked from the planes that had just arrived from the World. He had the descriptions of four men dancing through his head, descriptions that Gerber had given him several times. When a big, blond American passed through Customs, Larko knew immediately that it had to be Sam Anderson.

Larko leaped to his feet, dodged two Asian stewardesses who were dragging their suitcases behind them, ran forward and yelled, "Hey, Sam. That you, Sam?"

The blond man halted in midstride and turned to look. He saw the dark-haired man running toward him waving, but didn't recognize him at all. "Are you talking to me?"

"You remember me, don't you?" asked Larko, seizing Anderson's hand and pumping it furiously. Under his breath he said, "For God's sake, pretend you know me. Call me Dennis."

Still bewildered, Anderson did as he was told. "Is it really you, Dennis? I didn't recognize you. Have you lost weight?"

Larko pulled Anderson to one side, near a bank of telephones and a group of coin lockers, away from the flow of traffic, and whispered, "Your man Gerber gave me a message for you. You're to wait here until Bocker, Tyme and, ah, one other, Smith, arrive.

Then you are to go separately to the Hotel Regency and check in under your own names. You are to call Gerber when you are settled."

"Anything else?"

"That's all I was told."

"Thanks for the message, Dennis."

"No problem. Gerber said to be careful because someone might be looking for you that you won't want to meet. See you in the funny papers."

GERBER AND FETTERMAN had crossed Victoria Harbour again and were walking through the Suzie Wong district, window-shopping and killing time. They kept the pace slow as they looked into dozens of shops that displayed jade, pearls or gold, or tailor shops filled with new suits and dresses or just bolts of cloth.

Although Hong Kong was noticeably cooler than Vietnam, the humidity was high, and they had begun to sweat within a block of the hotel. A welcome breeze from the harbour sprang up as they neared the berth of the Star Ferry. A fishy odor drifted toward them from the dock. They turned around then, walking back along Chater Road. At sunset they noticed more women on the street, dressed in short skirts and low-cut tops, walking alone or in pairs. As they were about to enter a restaurant, an Oriental woman with long, white hair boldly walked up to them.

"I go eat, too," she said. "I go eat with you."

Gerber's first reaction was to send her on her way, but Fetterman jumped right in. "Of course you will, my dear. What's your name?"

"You may call me Muffin. Everyone call me Muffin." She waited for Gerber to open the door for her and then led them into the restaurant as if she owned it. She nodded and smiled at the man behind a bar of dark wood and deep red, and ignored the hostess who wanted to seat them at a table that had a snowy cloth and red napkins. Instead, Muffin headed for a booth in the rear of the room.

"What can I say?" asked Fetterman. "I'm intrigued by her white hair. I want to know if it's real or just an imaginative dye job."

"There is only one surefire method I can think of to find out, Tony. What about Mrs. Fetterman and the kids?"

"I think they would like to know, too, Captain," he said with a smile. "You will have noticed that her eyebrows are also white. Besides, she has a cute figure."

"A little small for me," said Gerber, "but I'll admit she has pretty legs. Well, it's up to you, Master Sergeant."

"Thank you, sir. I shall try to live up to the standards set by the great Master Sergeant Protective Association."

They sat down and waited, and when a waitress arrived, they ordered drinks. Fetterman kept up a running conversation while Gerber tried to spot a tail. He was sure there had to be one. He had decided to stay out until fairly late, hoping that the tail would be with them and no one would be left to watch the hotel. It might mean that his team members could get in without anyone seeing them.

"So," said Fetterman after Muffin had ordered the most expensive entrée on the menu, "do you have a last name?"

"Yes. I am called after my father, who was an Englishman serving in Hong Kong. I am Muffin Hill."

"An interesting name," said Fetterman. He smiled again. "I understand that, when one of you finds a friend, you telephone all your friends and invite them for a party."

"I am alone."

"Yes. I see that." Fetterman was surprised when he noticed that she had green eyes. It was very strange to see an Oriental with anything but brown eyes, but then, they all had black hair, and Fetterman could see no sign of black roots. Either the dye job was so new that the hair hadn't grown out at all, or it was the natural color.

Gerber broke into the conversation. "You have your protective coloration. How do you know it's not a plant?"

Muffin looked from one man to the other but didn't understand what was being said.

"Does it make any difference?" answered Fetterman. "Either way, we are one up."

From that point they ate their dinner slowly. Sometimes, as he swallowed something that was particularly tasty or during one of the many outbursts of laughter, Gerber would remember the picture of Morrow bound and gagged. There would be a twinge in his gut, and he would find himself almost short of breath, but then he would force it from his mind, knowing that he was doing the only thing he could. He was fucking with the opposition in the only way he could.

From the restaurant they went dancing, with Fetterman and Gerber spending a great deal of money, buying expensive drinks in the clubs and discos that Muffin suggested. They were filled with young American men with short hair dancing with long-haired Oriental women. Strobe lights flashed in time to the beat of rock music sung in heavily accented English. In some of the clubs, seminude women danced alone in cages suspended from the ceiling or on the bar, while in others the women were naked and swayed in time to music that only they heard. Gerber gently but firmly rebuffed most of the overtures made by other women, sometimes dancing with them, sometimes buying them a drink, but always sending them away.

Muffin steered their course for them, taking them deeper into the Suzie Wong District but never mentioning money. They both assumed that she was getting a kickback from all the places they visited. Neither man cared. If the situation had been different, Gerber would have laughed about the probable reaction of the opposition. You don't grab someone's girlfriend and make death threats and expect the victim's friends to go out on the town, picking up prostitutes, dining and dancing.

Finally about two, having spotted no one following them, they decided to head back to the hotel. Fetterman was now holding hands with Muffin and talking to her as if she was his long-lost love. Gerber was amazed at the change in the man. He had seen the sergeant slit the throats of enemy soldiers, use a flamethrower to break up a human wave assault and fight in hand-to-hand death struggles. Fetterman was not someone who would be described as gentle, and yet he was treating Muffin with the greatest kindness. He was treating her as if she were the most important person in his life right at that moment, asking her questions about herself, about how she lived. But even the questions showed a gentleness because they weren't the typical "how-did-a-nice-girl-like-you" or "why-do-you-do-it" kind. They were about her family or her schooling or what she really liked.

Gerber sat back and watched the master, or rather, the master sergeant, at work. He was dancing with her, displaying a knowledge of the new steps that went with the driving rock music that surprised and amused Gerber. He wished he could do it himself.

As they walked back toward the Star Ferry, the evening having turned chilly under the bright stars overhead, it was assumed that Muffin would accompany them, although no one had said anything. At the gate Fetterman paid her penny fare and then carefully handed her enough money for the return trip. She smiled at him and then wrinkled her nose as the sea breeze brought the odor of dead fish to them.

They entered the hotel, and the bell captain nearly ran across the lobby toward them. He halted only a foot or so away and stared at Muffin with hate-filled eyes. He was trying to silently tell her to get out of his hotel because she didn't belong. She had not, or did not, pay him a kickback for his services.

Fetterman stepped forward. "Is there a problem here?"

"This woman . . ." he said. "This woman—"

"Is with us," said Fetterman. He patted the man on the shoulder and slipped a large bill to him. He winked at the bell captain and asked again, "Is there a problem?"

"No, sir. None at all." He stepped to the bank of elevators and pushed the Up button.

"Thank you," said Gerber.

Upstairs, as they entered the middle room of the suite, Gerber saw that the message light on the phone was blinking. He nodded toward it, and Fetterman indicated he understood. He held open the door to their bedroom and said to Muffin, "Would you care to freshen up?"

As soon as she was through the door, Gerber was on the phone for his message. He listened and held a thumb up to tell Fetterman it was good news. Into the receiver he said, "We're in room 802. You and Sully come on up. If there's anyone in the hallway, walk on by, you got that?"

He hung up and said to Fetterman, "That was Justin. He and Sully have made it. Saw Sam Anderson at the airport. We've got a couple of people here now."

"Good. Good."

Before anyone could say any more, the door to the other room opened to reveal Muffin. She had taken off her dress and had put on a garter and stockings. She had a light silk robe that hung to her hips wrapped around her shoulders. She moved directly to Fetterman and took his hand.

"Ah, Tony..." said Gerber.

"No. You misunderstand. We have a couple of visitors coming."

She grabbed the front of her robe and held it tightly clasped in front of her. "No way," she said. "I here for you, not for friends."

There was a knock at the door, and Gerber said, "Tony, take her into the other room, and tell her that we have to talk to our friends but that we have no big plans."

Twenty minutes later all the Green Berets that Fetterman had been able to phone were gathered in the room. They wore a variety of civilian clothes, from Tyme's navy-blue, three-piece suit to Sully's tan trousers and short-sleeved shirt. They looked like a convention of hit men. Anderson had arrived with Bocker after both Smith and Tyme had finished their first drink. At that point Fetterman joined them so that they could discuss the problem.

"I'm afraid," said Fetterman, "but I think Muffin believes we're all going to join her, one at a time, and she is going to get very rich. Right now she's enjoying the idea. At first she didn't like it, but when I didn't pursue the topic, she talked herself into it." He grinned at that.

"Okay, Captain," said Tyme, "why don't you let us in on what's going on." He waved a hand to indicate the others. "I think we all left some fairly pissed-off people in the World when we dropped everything to fly to Hong Kong. I know my girlfriend will probably never speak to me again."

"Justin, I'm sorry about that, I really am, but you know I wouldn't have let Tony call if it hadn't been important."

"Yes, sir, I know. If I didn't think it was, I would've stayed in the World. Besides, if she was that uptight about my coming here, I doubt things would have lasted much longer anyway. Especially with her attending the antiwar rallies in Austin."

Gerber nodded. "Any of the rest of you have a problem with leaving?"

There was a chorus of no's and not really's. Gerber said, "Fine. With luck we'll have this thing resolved in a day or two, and you all can head back home for the rest of your leave. If you want to take a couple of extra days, I'll make sure that it gets approved in Saigon."

Then he outlined everything that had happened right up until the time that Fetterman and he had walked back into the hotel. He told them everything in great detail. He told them that he wanted to try to find the Chinese man the next day and what he planned to do when they found him.

"You threw away your weapons?" asked Tyme sarcastically when Gerber finished the narration.

"I'm afraid so, Justin. Had no choice," Gerber told him.

"Even Tony?" he asked as if amazed that Fetterman would casually dispose of a weapon, even a .45.

"Yes, Boom-Boom," answered the master sergeant.

"Then you're lucky I came." Grinning, the team's light weapons specialist hauled a .45 from the inside of his shirt and laid it on the table. "I have a couple of others secreted in my suitcase. They're broken into small parts so that I could get them through Customs, but I can put them back together in an hour."

"Ammunition, Boom-Boom?" queried Fetterman.

"Probably not more than a hundred rounds. I have a false bottom in my case for extra mags and ammo. A very thin false bottom so that it's not obvious and holds very little."

"And you waltzed through Customs just like that?" asked Smith incredulously.

"The trick is to not look like you have anything you're not supposed to have. Besides, I figured that, as a member of the United States Army, if I got caught, they would tell me I was a very bad boy, confiscate the weapons and let me go. No big deal."

"The next item is to find a way to wire me up so you can all keep track of my whereabouts," said Gerber. "I respect everyone's tracking ability in the jungle, but this is the city, and I won't be leaving much in the way of footprints and broken branches and bent grass. I wondered if there was something we could get to make the task a little easier."

"How much time will we have, Captain?" asked Bocker.

"I don't really know. I figure they'll call sometime about noon."

"I'll have to wait until some of the electronics stores open, but I might be able to rig something up for us," said the common sergeant. "Be a little crude, but it should work."

Gerber clapped his hands and rocked back on the couch. He looked at the men in the room with him and nodded at them. For the first time since Morrow had been abducted, he felt really good. It was all going to come together. He was sure of that. Each of these men had a talent that would allow him to beat the Chinese bastard and get Morrow back. By nightfall the next day he was sure that the situation would be resolved. They might have to stay up all night working out the details, but he was positive they could be worked out.

He pulled out the orientation map that they had picked up in the hotel lobby and spread it out on the table. Looking at it, he realized that there was a lot more to Hong Kong than he thought. Lots of islands and lots of open country and still no clue about where to look. But that didn't matter because he had part of the team with him and they would be able to work their way through the problem quickly.

He had forgotten that on the other side of the door was a woman of Chinese and British descent who might not be the best friend of the Occidental men. He had forgotten that she could be standing with her ear to the door overhearing every word that was said.

16

HOTEL REGENCY,
HONG KONG

Tyme and Smith went into Morrow's room for some privacy while they assembled the weapons that Tyme had smuggled. Some of the mess in the room had been cleaned up by Fetterman while he waited for Gerber to come out of his trance during the afternoon. Tyme and Smith finished straightening it up, made the bed and then called the front desk to have the lamps replaced. Although he wasn't responsible for the breakage, Tyme assured the clerk that they would pay for the damage.

In the living room of the suite, Fetterman sat alone, staring into Victoria Harbour, fascinated by all that he could see out there. The buildings of Hong Kong Island seemed to grow out of the blackness of the harbour. The red, green and white lights shimmered on the water, reflecting back at him. And the lights of the buildings on the island, streaking in the water and shifting in the swells, flashed and flickered and melted like watercolors in the rain.

Bocker sat at the table, making a list of the components he would need to construct the radios early the next morning. He sketched a simple radio, looked at it and added a couple of things to it.

Gerber wandered around the room, as if he couldn't think of anything to do, while Anderson sat in front of the television, trying to find an English language program. The Hong Kong film industry seemed to be stuck in the feudal period with hundreds of men in bizarre costumes engaging in martial arts combat. There was no plot to any of the movies.

The sudden trill of the phone startled each of them. Only Fetterman seemed to remain relaxed. Gerber nearly leaped over a chair to get to it and snatched the receiver from the hook.

"Yeah," he demanded. "I mean, hello."

"Hello, Captain. This is Captain Bromhead."

"Johnny! Where the hell are you?" Gerber covered the mouthpiece with a hand and announced to everyone as if they hadn't heard, "It's Captain Bromhead." On the phone, he repeated, "Where the hell are you?"

"I'm here."

"In Hong Kong?"

"No, sir. Here in the hotel. I'm in the lobby and figured that I would come up, if you would be kind enough to give me the room number. Your return address on the telegram didn't have a room number."

Gerber told him and then cautioned him, "We think we might be watched. Come on up, but if you see anyone in the hallway, walk on by."

"See you in a few minutes." He hung up.

"Forgot about Johnny," said Gerber. "I guess I didn't really expect him to be able to shake himself loose from Crinshaw or the brass hats."

Anderson turned off the TV in disgust. "I'll hit the head, if there are no objections."

"You don't need to announce it, Sam," said Gerber. "You can just go."

Anderson opened the door, saw movement and jumped back. He looked in. "Hey, there's a lady in here."

"Oh, my God," said Fetterman, nearly exploding out of his chair. "I forgot all about her." He rushed to the door and reached in. "Muffin, I'm sorry. Please come out and join us. I just don't know what I was thinking."

Muffin had changed back to her street clothes, and there was no evidence that she had carried anything else with her. Her silk robe, garter and stockings were well concealed beneath her street clothes or in her tiny purse. She entered the room as if she were angry about being left alone for so long. She glanced significantly at the bar.

"Would you care for a drink?" asked Anderson.

"I take a banana daiquiri," she said.

"Fine, except that we have no bananas."

"Then I take whatever it is you have." She studied Anderson, impressed by his size.

While Anderson kept her occupied with the drink, Fetterman pulled Gerber to one side and said, "We can't let her go now. We don't know what she might have overheard."

"Damn, Tony, that was stupid."

"I know, Captain. I'm sorry about it. I thought the protective coloration would help us."

"I didn't mean to imply that it was your mistake. I should have remembered she was in there, too. Damned poor judgment on my part."

"Yes, sir."

"Okay, now we'll have to keep her with us at all times and not give her a chance to signal her friends, if she has any who would care."

"Let Anderson do it, sir," said Fetterman. "He seems to be getting along with her quite well."

"We'll see how things break in the morning and then decide who will have to remain behind. Damn, thought our force had been increased by one and now we've lost that again."

"Sir, if I might suggest . . ."

"Don't go getting formal on me all of a sudden, Tony. If you have an idea, let me have it. I haven't exactly been dazzling up to this point."

"Why don't you call your Air Force buddy again? I doubt he would be upset about having to baby-sit Muffin. All he has to do is make sure she doesn't have a chance to call anyone. If she is legit, then we pay for her time and she is happy. If she isn't, she can't squawk about it because we still hold her."

"I'll call him in the morning."

There was a knock on the door. Anderson, without waiting to be told, opened it and saw Bromhead standing there. "Captain Bromhead," he said.

"What happened to Johnny?" Bromhead asked.

"You're a captain now, sir, and I have to be polite to you. It's the code of the West and the law of the jungle and the way the cookie crumbles," he said with a grin.

"Fine. Then grab one of these suitcases and help me in with them. They weigh a ton apiece."

Gerber came forward to shake hands with his former executive officer. "How are things going at the Triple Nickel?"

Bromhead noticed the Oriental woman. With her white hair it was hard not to. He said, "I'll brief you in a moment."

"Well, get your ass in here, and let me buy you a drink," said Gerber. "Damn, I'm glad you made it."

An hour later, while Anderson and Muffin sat together in the other room discussing life histories, the rest of the team was in Morrow's bedroom with Tyme and Smith. Bromhead hauled his suitcases into the room, and when he saw Tyme and Smith working on the old .45s that they had stripped and cleaned, he smiled.

"I knew you incompetents wouldn't bring any real weapons." The new captain opened up one of his cases, unhooked a flap and started taking out pieces of metal. Then he looked up and saw the look on Gerber's face. "Oh, by the way, everything was under control at the camp before I left." He continued, "I went into the captured arms locker and found a couple of the better-looking AKs. I figured that if something was going on that was important enough for the captain to send me a telegram, then it was important enough for me to try to bring some real weapons." He shot a glance at Fetterman and added, "I couldn't get your flamethrower in here, Tony. The tanks are just too big to fit. Sorry."

Fetterman smiled. "That's all right, sir. The AKs are fine. Just fine."

"Jesus, sir!" said Tyme. "You sure took them apart."

"Didn't want them to look like anything resembling a weapon," he said. "They break into smaller parts than the M-14 or the M-

16. Afraid I had to leave the stocks behind because they looked just like stocks. Might have provided a clue for the customs guys."

"You bring any spare magazines?" asked Tyme.

"Of course. Took all the rounds out of them. Put about a dozen into my other suitcase. They really don't look much of anything else, except magazines for a weapon, but the customs guys just waved me through without really looking into the bags. Guess it was too late at night."

Tyme already had one nearly assembled. He said, "We'll just use them like grease guns. I suppose if we really need a stock, we can fashion one from some scrap lumber."

"You brought two?" asked Gerber.

"Sure did."

"Okay, with the weapons that Justin brought in, we're going to be fairly well armed. Coordination may be a problem, but we'll just have to work our way around that. First thing in the morning we'll go get the stuff that Galvin needs."

Fetterman spent most of the night sitting in his chair and staring at the lights of Victoria Harbour and Hong Kong Island. The lights began to fade slowly as the sun came up and the sky first paled, tinted to red and then started to brighten. As the outlines of the buildings and boats on the water seemed to materialize out of the gloom, Fetterman pushed himself out of his chair and found Gerber sleeping on the couch. He touched the captain's shoulder and told him it was time to get up.

Gerber, looking the worse for wear, his beard discoloring his face, rubbed his eyes and sat up. "Okay, let's get this show on the road."

"Yes, sir. Boom-Boom and Sully have the weapons ready. We don't have much in the way of ammo, so we can't go shooting indiscriminately, but we should have enough."

"Bocker?"

"Has his list and his plans and is going out in a couple of hours. He'll eat breakfast then. We don't want to order too much up here from room service, or the dining room might get suspicious, and that could tip our hand."

"We can order for four because there should be three of us and the bell captain knows about Muffin."

"Maybe we should only order three. That keeps the numbers right if someone wants to check. Besides, Boom-Boom and Sully have a room, so they can order all they want."

"You forgot about Morrow," said Gerber. "As far as anyone in the hotel knows, she's still up here."

"But the opposition knows that she's not, and if they start counting meals, they're going to get funny numbers."

"All right," said Gerber grumpily, "let's not get bogged down in trivia. Have the troops scatter, and we'll meet back here about ten. That'll give everyone a chance to do anything they need to and will probably give us some time before the call comes in."

"I'll have Sully come back as soon as he's eaten. He can help Galvin put the radios together."

"Anyone think about having Sully cook up some explosives for us?"

"I thought about that, but he said anything he makes would be fairly unstable, and it wouldn't be a good idea to blow up the room. Besides, he claimed it wouldn't give us that much of an advantage."

Gerber clapped his hands together a couple of times as if to rally a slumping ball team. "I'm tired of all this. Let's get going. We've been screwing around long enough. It's payday."

The morning slipped away quickly. Bocker went out and bought nearly a hundred dollars' worth of radio parts and rushed back to make his transmitters and receivers. He was proud of himself because he didn't think he had been followed. Still, he stopped two floors above Gerber's, then walked back down, figuring that any tails in the lobby would see that the elevator didn't stop on the right floor.

Tyme and Sully took Bromhead to their room and ordered a giant breakfast. Afterward, they all decided to catch a little sleep. When the phone rang, they all got up and took the stairs to the floor above them. There was no one in the hallway as they entered Gerber's room again.

As soon as it was late enough, Gerber called Larko and told him what he wanted. Larko was hesitant, pointing out that he had already returned the favor once and that he didn't have much time left in Hong Kong. It was only when Gerber mentioned that Larko would have to baby-sit a woman of questionable virtue for a couple of hours that Larko said he thought he could handle it.

At ten they were all back in the room, including Larko. Muffin was more than a little upset when she learned that Larko would be looking after her because she had thought she would have had an opportunity to earn some big money with all the Americans present. But so far only Anderson had touched her, and that had been on the knee as they sat together talking. She was also concerned because she hadn't had a chance to call the man who had asked her to count the number of Americans in the room.

Because they were waiting for the phone call, Gerber did not want to compromise the security of the mission, so he took the opportunity to get rid of Muffin and Larko. The look on Larko's face told Gerber that the flight engineer was only too happy to comply. Then Gerber carefully searched Morrow's room and found the keys to the rental car. He took the team members to the garage, telling them that he, Fetterman and Morrow hadn't used the car that much because there was no place to park in Hong Kong, but now, with two assault rifles, they could use the trunk. Since it had spent most of its time in the garage, Gerber doubted the enemy would know they had it.

Using the map once more, Gerber said, "I have to assume we'll end up in the New Territories because they are the closest to the Red Chinese border and there is a lot of empty space out there. Lots of hills and forests for them to lose themselves in. If we get on a boat for one of the other islands, we could be in trouble."

"We'll work around it somehow, Captain," said Fetterman.

Gerber rubbed his sweaty palms on his trousers. "Sorry. I'm more than a little nervous about this one. We're way out of our depth in the urban environment."

"Take it easy, Captain," said Tyme. "We all grew up in the city and know how to act. That's natural for us. Becoming jungle fighters was the unnatural act, and we've already accomplished that. So things might work out."

"I'm not sure I like that." Gerber smiled. He pointed at the equipment that Bocker had assembled on the table. "You want to show me this stuff?"

Quickly Bocker explained his radios. They were fixed frequency, and the one that Gerber carried would have a hot mike. It would transmit anything said near Gerber or by Gerber so that, if he was unable to press a button, he could still give clues as to his whereabouts. If that failed for whatever reason, they could always triangulate. That would get them into the right area.

With that, there really was nothing else for them to do. They were trained to react to the situation, and all the planning in the world wouldn't help now. Fetterman had even reminded them of the old military saying: "When the shooting starts, the plan goes out the window."

At ten minutes to twelve, the phone rang. Gerber leaped for it, stopped his hand inches from it and took a deep breath. It rang a second time and he said, "Here we go, gentlemen. Let's be cool." He then picked up the receiver and said, as casually as he could, "Hello."

"We have the woman. You come. Alone."

"Fine. Where?"

"We tell you. Now you go along Nathan Road to the park. You stop on the northeast corner outside the fence. You be told where to go then. We see anyone, we kill the woman." The phone went dead.

"That's it," said Gerber as he hung up. He quickly relayed to the team members the brief message he'd been given. "Time to move."

Before anyone could stand, Fetterman said, "Captain, I don't like this one little bit. If they wanted to assassinate us, they could do it anytime. This Mickey Mouse game they have designed makes no sense to me."

"It could be that they want to capture a Special Forces officer and take him into Red China for interrogation," said Tyme.

"Gentlemen, we don't know the motivations. Maybe the Chinese bastard wants to watch each of us die for some demented reason. Makes no difference now. Or maybe he threw this together because of the opportunity he found. Tony and me in Hong Kong, just a couple of miles from Red China. The cards have been dealt, and it's time to ante in. No choice in the matter, unless we want to let Morrow die."

"You didn't ask to speak to her," criticized Fetterman. "You should have asked to speak with her."

"Makes no difference now. She is either alive or she isn't, but now we get near the Chinese bastard."

17

NATHAN ROAD,
HONG KONG

Before Gerber could reach the door, Bromhead asked, "Shouldn't we try to rent another car or two?"

Gerber stopped with his hand on the knob, wondering if that was something he should have thought of, and then decided it wasn't. They had the one car, and Fetterman held the keys to it. Finally Gerber said, "Let's just play this one as it has been dealt now. We can sit here and try to think of everything, but when all is said and done, we could still be sitting here trying to think. We'd be like the team that trained so hard for the big game that we couldn't play when it happened."

"Still," said Bromhead, "we don't want to overlook something by rushing forward without thinking the whole thing through carefully."

"Everyone knows his assignment," said Gerber, ignoring that. "If you get separated, come on back here. We'll check in if we need to do anything." Gerber opened the door and stepped into the hallway. Before he moved, he checked his watch, and then began to walk toward the elevators.

When the door closed, Fetterman immediately said, "This is what the captain doesn't need to know. I'm not *that* interested in getting Miss Morrow back. That doesn't mean we should ignore the threats to her, but the major concern has got to be to protect the captain. He's going to be trying to protect her."

"Which means?" asked Tyme.

"Our priorities," said Fetterman. "First is to protect the captain whether he likes it or not. Second is to kill the Chinese son of a bitch because he deserves it. Third, we get Miss Morrow out of there. That is the way it has got to be."

"So what do we do?" asked Smith.

Fetterman glanced at Bromhead, who said, "This is your show, Master Sergeant. You've been in on it a lot longer than I have."

"Thank you, Captain. First, I want everyone to put on two or three extra shirts. As we move through the streets and rotate the tails, we can peel a shirt so that we don't become recognizable by our clothes.

"Second, I think the two guys in the car—" he looked at Tyme and Smith "—why don't you take it and proceed up Kowloon Park Drive to Austin Road, and then drive along it so that you'll pass the captain as he waits for his contact."

"And then?"

"We play it by ear just as the captain said, but I don't want him to be more than thirty seconds from help the moment he hits that corner of the park."

"Then we'd better get going," said Smith.

"We wait until he leaves the hotel," said Fetterman. "We know where he's going, and we have to assume that the bad guys have someone in the lobby watching for a big exodus of Americans. We have a few minutes."

Bromhead was going to take charge then, to give them some kind of a pep talk, but couldn't think of anything that needed to be said. Each of them knew what to do, and each would do it. All he had to do was let them do their jobs.

GERBER DIDN'T WANT to tip his hand so he didn't look back as he left the hotel lobby. He walked out the main entrance, stopped at the top of the steps and let the breeze from the sea wash over him. There was a faint odor of fish and salt in it, but he was becoming used to it. He put his hand to his eyes to shade them from the afternoon glare, then descended the steps, turned to his left and made his way to Nathan Road. Once there, he took a few seconds to look around, then headed north, almost as if he were window-shopping, but he kept his pace steady, figuring that anyone following would become suspicious if he moved too slowly.

The corner of the park where he was supposed to receive his next set of instructions was just under a klick from the hotel doors. He didn't like the way the meeting was set up, but he could do nothing about it.

As he walked past tailors, jewelry dealers, rug merchants and a multitude of bars, nightclubs and restaurants, he began to wonder about the whole setup because that was exactly what it was. A setup. One of the men, he forgot which one, had said it the night before. The whole thing made no sense. The Chinese bastard should have killed Morrow as soon as he got her picture taken. Keeping her alive made no difference one way or the other. She was a loose end that should be taken care of as soon as possible. In fact, she probably was already dead, and the whole exercise was ridiculous.

It was then that Gerber realized the only way he would not have begun the exercise was if her dead body had been found. At that point he would have packed up his marbles and gone home. The only way the Chinese officer could be sure that Gerber would come was to keep Morrow alive until he caught Gerber. If he balked at the meeting, the officer had to have some way to persuade him to come, and that was a living Morrow. Another picture or a phone call. They had to be sure he would be willing to risk his life.

At that moment Gerber felt Morrow was still alive. He didn't understand the rationale behind the plan, but he knew she would not die until he was safely in the hands of the enemy. For an instant he thought about turning around and letting one of the other team members walk the point. But he knew he couldn't do that. It was his job. His responsibility and he had to do it, although the other way was more logical.

Not far away he could see the corner of the park where he was supposed to wait. The area nearby was fairly open, making it hard for anyone to lie in ambush. There was a black wrought-iron fence around the park, a couple of broadleafed bushes with bright flowers on them a hundred meters from the street and several tall palm trees. But no real cover for anyone. Maybe that was the thought the opposition had. Keep it out in the open so no one could grab the messenger.

Over the transmitter, he said, "I'm about to enter the park. Johnny, don't grab the messenger. Let him go because he won't know anything anyway."

He had just set foot in the park when a young Chinese woman wearing a yellow silk dress accidentally bumped his arm. Gerber felt her try to slip him a piece of paper, and he grasped it without really looking at her. He took a couple of steps and mumbled, "I've got a note. Young woman gave it to me. Watch her, but don't touch her."

He stopped and unfolded the paper, then turned and looked but could not see any sign of the messenger. Over his radio, he said, "I'm going to the ferry pier just off Jordan Road. I'll take my time getting there. Johnny, get them positioned."

BROMHEAD, WHO WAS WALKING DOWN the street with Fetterman, looked at him and said, "We could grab a cab."

"I don't know. The driver will undoubtedly be Chinese."

"And the odds that he'll be working for our man are extremely remote. We're moving too slow as it is. . . ."

Fetterman stopped walking and crouched so that he could carefully examine his map, aware that the crowds around him were watching him closely. He could feel the comfortable weight of the .45 on his hip and touched it with his wrist as if to reassure himself that it was still there.

Finally figuring out what he wanted, he stood and told Bromhead where to place the others. "Have Tyme and Smith stationed on the north side. If this is the break, they'll be in the best position to follow."

GERBER PRETENDED that he was momentarily lost, killing nearly ten minutes getting himself back on the right track, although it was nearly a straight shot from the corner of the park to the pier. He stayed in the center of the sidewalk, avoiding the approach of hucksters and hookers. Finally he announced, "I'm going in. I hope you're ready."

Just as he said that, he spotted Bocker and Anderson arguing with a Chinese man who obviously thought he had made a sale. Gerber was on the side of the street opposite them, and neither looked up as he walked by. Then, from behind him, he heard the squealing of tires and turned in time to see a yellow car screech to a stop next to him.

"It's a yellow Volkswagen Beetle," he said quickly before he was grabbed by a small man. His abductor didn't speak, and Gerber's first reaction was to kick him in the crotch, but he resisted the temptation. Instead, he allowed himself to be forced into the back seat of the tiny car. Another guy sat there, making it a tight squeeze in the confines of the small German car.

As the door closed and they sped off, Gerber said, "Where are you taking me?"

There was no answer, and Gerber was about to say something to give his team directions, just in case, when he caught a flash of blue out of the corner of his eyes. He was sure it was the Mustang. He wanted to turn his head to look but was afraid of giving away the location of the chase car. Instead, he demanded once again to know where they were taking him.

In response, the man who had grabbed him reached over and began searching him for weapons. Gerber grasped the thug's hand as it touched him and held it in an ironlike grip so the man couldn't move. A click near his ear told Gerber that the second man had just cocked a pistol. The searcher grinned as Gerber relaxed the tension and let himself be frisked. All they found was a pocket knife with a razor-sharp blade, which Fetterman had insisted Gerber take as a cover. No one would believe he would leave the hotel without some kind of weapon, even one that was hardly lethal. They found his radio but didn't realize it because Bocker had disguised it in a cigarette package. They ignored it, tossing it to the floor of the car. Casually Gerber retrieved it and stuffed it into his pocket.

They rolled north out of the city, following the main road, picking up speed as the buildings and traffic began to thin. Gerber knew that, if he was being followed by his team, they would have to drop way back or be spotted. He stared out of the car windows, looking for some marker that he could alert his people to the moment he got the chance. They crossed some water and entered a smaller, built-up area that he thought was Tsuen Wan. He asked about it, but no one replied, as if they didn't speak any English, which Gerber didn't believe. Anyone brought in on this would speak English.

Before they left the city, they took the north fork of the road and began climbing into a mountainous region. Gerber remembered from the map that the road forked again, and although it eventually rejoined the main road, it would waste too much time if his boys went the wrong way. He took a chance and said, "I didn't know there were mountains in Hong Kong."

"You talk too much," said the man who had searched him.

Gerber grinned to himself. He now knew two things. He was right. They could speak English, and they didn't realize what he was doing. He relaxed, waiting for the turn that he would have to signal to his men.

IT WAS SMITH who spotted the yellow car as it flashed by. He pointed it out to Tyme. He floored the gas pedal, and they wove into the line of traffic, barely missing two other cars. Then Tyme slowed down until they were four or five vehicles behind the yellow VW. They could hear the static from the captain's radio and knew that it hadn't been found as they had left the city.

Tyme was afraid of the open area, but the traffic didn't drop off and they could maintain a loose tail without worrying about being seen. They felt sure they were right behind him when the captain asked if they were in Tsuen Wan.

Smith slapped the dash of the car with his hand and yelled over the noise of the wind, "That's right, Captain! Give us an itinerary. Fucking beautiful!"

In the city Tyme wanted to remain a safe enough distance away without getting too close. The traffic was heavy, and somehow the yellow car got farther ahead until they lost sight of it. Smith stood in the seat, trying to see over the vehicles just in front of them but had no luck. With one hand gripping the top of the windshield, he cupped the other at the side of his mouth and yelled, "I don't see him. I don't see him."

Tyme didn't even glance up. "We'll get them as soon as the traffic thins."

Then over the radio they heard Gerber say something about mountains, and Tyme knew immediately that he had taken the wrong turn. He slammed on the brakes, nearly pitching Smith over the top of the windshield. Behind him, there was a cacophony of car horns and squealing brakes as a dozen other cars swerved to avoid each other. A couple of cars grazed one another, but there was no major damage.

Tyme spun the wheel as he backed up rapidly, causing the Mustang to swing around abruptly. When they were facing the way they had come, he floored the accelerator and took off in a cloud of blue smoke as the tires fought to grip the pavement.

They came to the road that headed north, and Tyme took the corner without slowing, the car drifting to the other side. Tyme pulled in the direction of the skid until he corrected it, then hit the gas again. They flew forward, rocketing up the hill in pursuit of the yellow car. He didn't slow again until he caught a glimpse of it in the distance.

WHEN THEY TURNED onto a dirt side road, Gerber was tempted to say something, but there was no way to clue the rest of the team without alerting his captors. He rode on in silence, hoping that the Mustang had kept them in sight.

They kept going, eating up the distance, came to another side road and pulled into it. They stopped then, as if waiting to see if anyone were following them. Gerber held his breath, but the Mustang seemed to have lost them.

When they started moving again, Gerber asked, "Are we getting close?"

The man who had spoken earlier just grinned, displaying broken yellow teeth. He didn't answer the question and gave no indication that he had understood it.

Moments later they slowed for a gate, and a man appeared out of a bush to unlock it. His job was to guard the approach to the hideout and report anyone who came near. If the trespassers appeared too persistent, he would probably shoot them.

They continued down the road, went around a bend and stopped near an old frame house that showed obvious Victorian influences. The three-story house had lots of windows and two large, round spires. It couldn't have looked more out of place if it had been an Arab tent.

As they exited the car, Gerber could see a body of water nearby that appeared to be a reservoir. He had no idea what the name of it might be because he hadn't studied the map that closely. He hoped Tyme and Smith had been close enough to see which way the VW had turned because there was no way he could give that clue. But he could ask about the water.

"Is that a reservoir?" he asked innocently.

Feeling safe, the Oriental slapped Gerber and demanded that he shut up.

Gerber didn't respond to that. He rubbed his face as if the blow had been more painful than it was and said, "Sorry. Just asking. I guess this means we've arrived." He hoped his men would get the idea that they were no longer moving and he would have to ditch the radio. He prayed he wasn't premature with the decision.

As they moved to the house, Gerber worked the cigarette package containing the radio out of his pocket so that it lay concealed in his hand. When no one was looking, he dropped it and tried to kick it out of sight. The last thing he wanted was for the enemy to find it and know that his men could be closing in. Of course, they didn't know that he had any men other than Fetterman.

Gerber was escorted up the steps to the large, pillared porch. One of the men opened the door, and while they waited, he went inside. Then he was back and waved them all in.

The entrance foyer looked just as Gerber figured it would. A staircase led to the second floor, and doors concealed the rooms on either side. At the end of the hallway was another closed door.

Gerber was taken to the right after one of the men opened the double doors. The room there was a large, well-furnished library with a desk set near a bay window overlooking the lake. Bookshelves dominated three walls from floor to ceiling, and they contained hundreds of leather-bound volumes. Two wing chairs were positioned near a fireplace. Between them was a table that held a diorama depicting some ancient battle with hundreds of miniature figures locked in combat.

The men all filed out. The last one said, "You will wait right here. Do not try to escape because there are armed men all over the estate." The man had a pronounced British accent, which reminded Gerber of Minh. But then Hong Kong was a British possession.

"I have no plans for escape," said Gerber.

Left to his own, Gerber wandered around the room, trying to get a feel for it. The Orientals who left had seemed out of place. He decided that the house and the furnishings must have belonged to an Englishman who had been forced, persuaded or just plain wanted to sell it as it was. Everything about it, with the exception of the model battle, suggested the Occidental mind.

Gerber was studying the battle, trying to place it, although he didn't know that much about Chinese history, when the doors opened again. The two men standing there moved aside, and a third man entered.

Gerber had never gotten a good look at the man. Fetterman had seen him a couple of times, once through binoculars and once through the bars of a cage. Still, Gerber knew instantly who it was. The Chinese officer they had been chasing for almost a year. The one who had marked them for death more than once. The man who had failed every time he had run into Gerber's team.

He was shorter than Gerber had expected. In his mind the officer had taken on gigantic proportions. Looking at him now, Gerber thought he was smaller than Fetterman.

The man stepped into the room and pointed his pistol at Gerber's head. "If I had any sense at all, Captain," he said, "I would shoot you dead this minute."

18

THE STREETS OF
HONG KONG

Fetterman didn't like the enforced inactivity as he stood outside the car rental shop. When the men in the VW had grabbed the captain, his first reaction had been to run after them. Bromhead had jerked on his arm, dragging him in the opposite direction and shouting that they needed a car. Bromhead assured him that Tyme and Smith could keep up with the yellow car while they sought more transportation.

They had run back along Nathan Road until they found a car rental agency. While Fetterman stood outside watching the crowds, Bromhead hurried in to rent something.

Within minutes Bromhead reappeared driving a new green Chevy. He leaned out the window and said casually, "Care to join me for a ride?"

As Fetterman got into the car, Bromhead said, "Anything new? Still heading toward the north?"

"Yes, sir."

Bromhead spun the wheel and touched the gas pedal. The car responded as if he had floored the accelerator, and they shot back up Nathan Road, dodging the crowds, double-decker buses and rickshaws. Fetterman found a map in the glove box and used it to trace a path to Tsuen Wan. He looked at the street signs and discovered they were on the right path.

"Punch it, sir. We're doing fine."

They flashed up to Boundary Road, and Fetterman suddenly pointed. "There's Anderson."

Bromhead glanced through the windshield. There was no mistaking the hulking white man, but he couldn't see Bocker, who was supposed to be working with Anderson. The captain jerked the wheel to the right, crossed over the traffic coming from the other direction and swerved to the curb. He blew the horn twice, trying to get Anderson's attention.

Fetterman leaped out so that Anderson and Bocker, who materialized from the crowd, could climb into the tiny backseat. Almost before everyone could get into the car, Bromhead slammed the stick into Drive and shot forward again.

As they reached Tsuen Wan, they heard Smith's voice on the radio. "We think they have turned from the main road. We're going to drop back quite a ways so that we don't run up on them."

Seven minutes later Bromhead and his companions caught up with Tyme and Smith. They had pulled to the side of the highway and were standing there, looking along a dirt road. Bromhead turned in behind them, and everyone in the Chevy got out.

"I think they turned off here," said Tyme, pointing to the east along a dirt road. He spread the map he was holding out on the trunk. He laid an arm along one side of it to hold it down and pointed.

"The last thing we heard the captain say was something about a reservoir. There are two along this road, if the road goes through. There is the one here back the other way, but we should have seen it if that was the right one."

"You didn't follow?" asked Bromhead.

"No, sir. We were afraid they might turn off and wait to see if they were followed. We could get away with passing them on this road because it's a main one, but that dirt track would be a dead giveaway."

"Okay," said Fetterman, looking at Bromhead to see if he was going to object. "We have to press on. There is no way around it. I guess we take it slowly and stop at the top of each rise to explore the area around us before heading down."

"One other thing," said Tyme. "We haven't heard a word out of them since then."

"You lose the signal?" asked Bocker.

"No. We've got the carrier wave, but we haven't heard anything."

"We can't worry about that now," said Bromhead, studying the map. "We've got to find the captain."

"Let's split up," said Fetterman, noticing there were two roads that could lead them to the reservoir, if they had the right one spotted. "We don't have all day to debate this. Boom-Boom, you take Sully and Galvin and take the northern road. You find something, you give us a shout."

"All right."

Fetterman looked over his shoulder at Bromhead. "Sir, we follow the southern road and see if we can spot anything."

"Let's move it," said Bromhead.

FOR A MOMENT everything seemed to stand still. Gerber was almost afraid to move. He felt closer to death at that moment than he ever had before because he knew the Chinese officer was right. The quickest, smartest thing to do was shoot Gerber. If the situation was reversed, Gerber doubted he would hesitate.

Instead of shooting him, the officer walked toward the desk. He sat behind it, then placed his pistol on the top. Indicating the chairs opposite, he spoke again. "Sit down, Captain Gerber, and let us talk about Vietnam, the war and your death."

As Gerber started to speak, the Chinese man held up a hand to prevent it. He said, "You will not be helped. I know that your Sergeant Fetterman is still in your suite."

"How do you know that?" asked Gerber.

"I have my ways. I will say that a certain party would report to me if he had gone out."

Gerber took a deep breath and let his eyes roam around the room again. The two men still stood next to the door. He asked, "What is this all about?"

"I think you know, Captain. You have made me look bad many times. You have foiled plan after plan." His voice rose slightly, as if the memories were causing him to lose his temper. "You sent people out to kill me. You sent your men out to shoot me."

Gerber couldn't help himself. He smiled and said, "It was nothing personal."

The man stood and leaned his hands on the desk so that he had one on each side of the pistol. He glanced down at it, as if becoming aware of it for the first time, but he didn't touch it. He said, "You will not be laughing much longer." He nodded to the guards, and both of them disappeared.

"This is getting a little melodramatic," said Gerber. He was getting lost in the ridiculousness of the situation. It was only in the movies that people were kidnapped off the streets of Hong Kong and held prisoner. It all smacked of a poor movie plot, and he was having trouble taking any of it seriously. He was tempted to stand and walk out.

The doors reopened and Morrow, naked, her hands bound behind her, was pushed into the room. The blindfold still covered her eyes, and she tripped and tried to catch her balance. She fell heavily to her side with a grunt of pain, but she didn't move.

Gerber was on his feet. "Enough of this!" He started toward her, but someone grabbed him from behind. He felt a pistol pressed against the back of his neck and stopped moving.

Morrow turned her head as she heard his voice and nearly wailed, "Kirk? Is that you?"

"Gag her!" ordered the Chinese man.

Before Morrow could speak again, a rag was forced into her mouth and tied in place. All she could do was make sounds deep in her throat.

"Now," said the Chinese officer, "you will finally understand the error of your ways. You will see how the Oriental mind works. This is something that you, as a Western man, would never think of."

He gestured again, and Morrow was lifted to her feet. She stood there, afraid to move, while one of the other men brought an old wooden chair to the center of the room. She was forced to sit on it and then was bound to it.

In a calm voice, as if lecturing to a class of students about ancient civilizations, the Chinese man said, "You are going to have the pleasure of watching Miss Morrow tortured to death."

Gerber nearly jumped out of his chair, but several hands held him fast. When he stopped struggling and fell back, the man said, "If he moves like that again, shoot him in the knee." He pointed at Gerber. "And you will still have to watch, but it will no longer be too comfortable."

There were no more words spoken in the room for several minutes. Gerber stared at the Chinese man for a while, trying to see if he was bluffing in some kind of bizzare, sadistic game. Gerber then turned his attention to Morrow, who was sitting so rigid that her muscles stood out as if etched on her skin.

Gerber wanted to reach out and let her know that the situation was not nearly as bleak as it seemed. He couldn't tell her that their captor may have left men waiting for Fetterman to leave their hotel room, but the Oriental officer didn't know that Gerber had half a dozen men who should be out looking for them at that moment. Men who had a good idea of where Gerber was. He had faith in his men and knew they would arrive sometime. He hoped that Morrow would not have to suffer too much before they did.

She was sitting with her head erect, making sobbing noises deep in her throat. It was the only sound in the room except for the loud ticking of a clock.

IT WAS INCREDIBLY EASY to find the house, although they hadn't known they were looking for a house. Bromhead stopped on a hill. Fetterman took out a pair of Zeiss binoculars and scanned the countryside spread out in front of them. The yellow car sat partially concealed behind a large bush, but there was no mistaking it. As soon as they saw it, Anderson was on the radio, giving the details to the other team members, letting them know where the house was and which reservoir it was near.

While Anderson spoke on the radio, Bromhead pulled their car out of sight, then consulted his map. To Bromhead, he said, "I make it little more than a klick down there. Not a whole lot of good cover."

Unconfirmed Kill

"How many guards do you think they'll have?"

"Christ, sir, I can't guess."

They moved back to the crest and got down on their bellies so that they wouldn't be silhouetted against the skyline. Fetterman studied the valley below him. It wasn't much of a valley, more of a shallow depression in the terrain, like a huge saucer. The house sat at the bottom of the saucer but on a slight rise so that it was ten or twelve feet above the surrounding ground. A thin brown ribbon that was the access road wound its way along the depression floor, away from the reservoir and to the main road about three or four hundred yards away. Through the binoculars, Fetterman could see a metallic gate across the access road and the outline of a small guard hut hidden in a bush.

For five full minutes he studied the grounds around the house. When he looked up, he said, "To do this right will take nearly an hour. We have to approach all the guard positions carefully, several of them at the same time."

"How many guards?" asked Bromhead again.

"At least eight," answered Fetterman, "but I can see spots for another half dozen. We'll have to hit each of those because we can't assume they'll be unmanned."

He pointed across the dip in the terrain. "You see the giant tree near that finger of the reservoir? Well, if they put a guy there, he can watch four other positions. We'll have to take all five at once so that none of them will see us taking any of the others."

"Can we do that?" asked Anderson.

"We're going to have to. Now the guy at the gate we can ignore until the end because he can't really see any of the others. There are one or two other blind spots like that, and we'll hit them last."

"Okay," said Bromhead, taking over. "I see where you're going with this. We slip down the hillside from six different positions and hit six different guards at once. Then move on and take out some more, until we have the area cleared. One guy then goes for the gate guard while the rest of us slip into the house."

"Yes, sir. The coordination is going to have to be almost perfect for it to work."

They crawled back and retrieved the rest of their equipment from the car. Bromhead and Fetterman studied the maps, found the best place for the other car and radioed the position to Tyme, Smith and Bocker. Then Fetterman described the areas they should leave from, each man taking one of the positions that Fetterman was describing. As the last thing, he told them that he now had five minutes to one. At one o'clock they would jump off, and each of them would have to be in position no later than one-thirty. They couldn't afford to waste any more time than that. If they didn't hurry, they could assume that the captain would be killed, as would Miss Morrow. Bromhead nodded his approval of the plan, and Fetterman told them to begin.

As they reached the crest of the hill again, Bromhead said, "It wasn't much of a plan."

"No, sir. But we're stuck way out here without the benefit of artillery, air support or good prior recon. All we can do is try to approach the house without being seen, then enter it."

"I know," answered Bromhead, "but that doesn't mean I have to like it."

When they were in position, Bromhead took his pistol and stuck it in his pocket. He figured it would be hard to draw quickly, but he wasn't as likely to lose it as if he had it stuck in the waistband of his pants. Then he pulled his knife with its razor-sharp blade. He used some mud to dull the shine so that he wouldn't inadvertently alert the enemy. He noticed that Fetterman was ready, then looked far to the right. He could just see Anderson's back as the big man, hidden from the house by the hill, was running along, trying to get to his place nearly five hundred yards away.

When the second hand on his watch touched the twelve, letting him know that the five minutes had passed, Bromhead began to crawl down the hill, staying in the high grass, following the natural contour of the ground as it sloped downward. Occasionally he would look up over the grass, sighting his target. He wasn't hurrying but moving slowly, using the noise of the wind through the grass to mask the sounds of his movement. He stopped once to look at his watch, saw that he had plenty of time and slowed down. He didn't want to get too close to his man too soon. Although he didn't believe in ESP, he knew that the presence of another human could be detected on some subliminal level by some people. He couldn't see any reason to give his man a chance to play that game.

He was fifteen yards from the guard when he thought he heard a high-pitched scream from the house. It sounded like a woman's voice, and the sound was quickly cut off. The man in front of him snickered at the sound of pain.

Bromhead looked at his watch and realized that the laughing man now had less than five minutes to live.

As time began to run out for the guard, Bromhead started his slow, soundless crawl forward. The man was facing the house now, his attention drawn by the scream. It made Bromhead's job that much easier because the guard should have been studying the hillside around him. Any threat would come from the countryside, not from the house.

At that moment Bromhead heard something to his right and then, through the tall grass, saw it. Anderson had grabbed his man a little early, and in the struggle the two had stood. Bromhead's target heard the noise and turned to look, raising his AK-47 as he did. Bromhead leaped the last few feet, hitting the sentry in the back with his shoulder and sending him to the ground. Before he could recover, Bromhead plunged the knife into the guard's back to the hilt. There was a bubbling of blood around the wound as the knife pierced the man's lung. Bromhead twisted the blade, jerking it to the right as he held the man's face pressed to the soft earth.

Underneath him the lookout spasmed once, kicked his leg and then bucked as if trying to dislodge Bromhead. He kicked again and made a strange, gagging sound in his throat as he died. Bromhead jerked his knife clear, watching the blood drip from the blade.

Anderson, never realizing that he had been almost shot from behind, grabbed the guard he had stalked and stood him up. They faced each other for an instant, then Anderson seized the man's ears and twisted as sharply and quickly as he could. He snapped the man's neck easily and let the body drop to the ground. He went to one knee then, crouching near a tree and waited to see what the others were going to do. He couldn't see or hear anything. He just waited for the five minutes he was supposed to, then started off toward his second target.

Fetterman dispatched his mark quickly and professionally. He came up behind him quietly, slipped a hand over the nose and chin holding the mouth shut, and cut the man's throat with a clean swipe of his knife. With the guard dead, Fetterman laid the body down in the grass, checked it and found a ring of keys, a radio and, most important, a weapon with spare ammo. Fetterman was tempted to take the keys but was afraid they would jingle at the wrong moment so he left them. He made sure that the radio would not work again without major repair and then took the weapon and ammo. He checked the load and the spare magazines. That finished, he moved off toward the next guard.

Bromhead had no trouble with his second target. He could see evidence that a guard sometimes used that position but hadn't in the last few days. He crawled to the middle of it and stopped where he could watch the house. There were more screams coming from it, and although he couldn't really recognize the voice, he was sure it was Morrow's.

The drawn-out shriek seemed to hang in the air, then lose some of its human quality, and Bromhead wanted to rush forward, burst through the front door and save her. He knew it was a stupid plan and would result in them all dying, but the sound of the pain in the house was almost enough to make him forget rational thought. Under his breath he damned Fetterman and Gerber for getting Morrow into the trouble she was in even as he realized it wasn't their fault. It was her own. He just didn't want to think about what was happening to her.

Fetterman's luck with his second target was not as good as Bromhead's. But his man was not moving and was not looking around. He was sitting, a rifle across his knees. It looked as if he had gone to sleep in the warm sunlight of the lazy afternoon, but Fetterman didn't believe it. Slowly he got to his feet, keeping his head and shoulders low so that he couldn't be seen from the house. Taking a step toward the man, he measured the distance and then leaped. He jammed his knee into the man's back as he seized him by the chin, jerking his head up so that he could use the knife again.

The master sergeant sliced at the throat with such strength that he nearly severed the head from the body. He let the man slump to his side and began checking him for other weapons. Fetterman added a pistol to his collection and then broke open the rifle, taking the bolt and the trigger housing so that the weapon was useless.

Anderson made short work of the second sentry that he found. He came up behind the man who was urinating on a small bush. Without a word or a sound, Anderson kicked the man's feet from under him so that he fell to his back, and as he did, Anderson stomped on his throat, crushing it. The man's face went pale, then bright red and purple. He clawed at his neck, ripping the skin and leaving long, bloody gouges as his eyes bulged. The guard's feet began drumming on the ground as he slowly strangled.

To stop the noise, Anderson used his knife. He plunged it into the man's chest and drew it out. The wound was traumatic, and the shock killed the guard.

Like the other team members, Anderson searched him, picking up an extra weapon and ammo but leaving the radio alone. He then began moving toward the house as he had been instructed to do. He tried to come up on it slowly, carefully, so that anyone inside would not notice his approach.

He reached the rendezvous before everyone except Fetterman, who was crouched behind a large bush, watching the house. There were still screams coming from it, but they had lost some of the intensity. Fetterman suspected that the enemy in there, savoring their power, were giving their victim a chance to recover so that the show would be that much better for them. He knew from the screams that Morrow wasn't in danger of dying soon because she had too much energy. With luck they would have her and the captain freed in less than fifteen minutes.

When the rest of the team arrived, they took an inventory of the weapons and found that each now had two pistols, ammo for both and nearly everyone had either a rifle or an AK. Fetterman nodded, figuring they had more than enough to take the house and kill every enemy soldier in it. He had thought to kill only every Chinese in it but decided that the North Vietnamese might have supplied some of the men for the venture.

Quietly, almost without speaking, they made the final plans, mapping the doors and windows they would hit and how they would do it. Bocker was detailed to move a hundred yards down the road and ambush anyone who came up that way. Fetterman said he thought there should only be one man coming from that direction but wasn't certain. They didn't need a bunch of people showing up behind them. Bocker nodded his understanding.

Bromhead then looked at his watch, as if they were going to synchronize again, but said, "Everyone straight on what we're going to do?"

"We take any prisoners?" asked Anderson half seriously.

Bromhead looked at Fetterman, knowing how he felt about the Chinese officer. They had discussed it at length at the camp when they were both still in Vietnam, and he suspected that Fetterman would want to try.

But Fetterman, said, "You see him, you kill him. You don't give him a chance because if you do, he'll eat you alive. If he's standing in front of you with his hands up, he dies anyway. We take no more chances with that son of a bitch. He's too dangerous to live."

"Sarge—" Tyme started to say.

"Boom-Boom, kill him. Just remember that he is the one who planned the assassination of Ian. He was the one who planned our capture in Vietnam, and he is indirectly responsible for the deaths of every member of our team since we arrived in Vietnam. He knows the rules of the game and has elected to play."

Bromhead nodded at Bocker and said, "We'll go in three minutes. That's all the time you get."

"I'll be ready." He got to his feet, glanced at the house as if to check the position of the windows and began to move up the road using all the cover available, dodging from cars to bushes to trunks of trees.

When he was out of sight, Bromhead said, "Let's do it."

IN THE HOUSE, the Chinese officer started slowly, figuring he had all the time he wanted. At first he made sure that Morrow and

Gerber understood the nature of her helplessness. One of the others fondled her, watching her squirm as his hands rubbed her and pinched her. Each time Gerber so much as shifted his weight, one of his guards would point a weapon or cock a pistol until he relaxed.

Finally they tired of that because they were getting no real reactions from it. One of the men left the room and returned, carrying a small box with electrical cords on both ends. He set it on the desk in front of his superior and bowed his way back to his position.

"This," said the Chinese man, "is exactly what you think. A variation on the old field phone trick. I attach the electrical leads to sensitive portions of Miss Morrow's body, and with this rheostat, I can increase the voltage from a very mild, somewhat sexually arousing current to something that is quite painful. In fact, we can increase the power to such an extent that our victim will snap her own bones with her muscular contractions. Interesting, don't you think?"

Gerber couldn't think of anything that he found less interesting. But he wasn't concerned about that. He was more worried about the rest of the team because if they didn't arrive soon, it would be too late for them to be of any help. He wondered if they had somehow lost him and couldn't find him.

While he worried about that, the Chinese man watched as the electrodes were taped to Morrow's body. He then stood, walked to her and repositioned one of them so that it would be in a more sensitive location on her thigh. He checked the ropes to make sure she was securely fastened to the chair. That done, he smiled at her and patted her cheek.

"Now we shall see what you are made of, Captain," he told Gerber. "How much will you let her suffer before you have to try to stop it? Oh, you'll fail, but how long can you watch?"

He spun the rheostat, and Morrow's body contracted as the electricity coursed through it. With the gag in her mouth, she couldn't scream. When the pain stopped, she collapsed against the chair and felt the sweat bead on her body. She tried to cry out but didn't have the energy.

After several minutes of that, with Morrow becoming numb, the leader said, "I think that gag is inhibiting her. Please remove it." He then issued the order in Chinese so that there would be no mistake. "Now," he said, "let's see how long she can hold out."

He used the rheostat again and was very pleased with the piercing scream from Morrow. He nodded his approval. "I should have thought of that sooner. She didn't need the gag. It is much better this way." He looked at Gerber. "Don't you think so?"

IT TOOK THE TEAM only two minutes to get into attack position. After they had the house surrounded, they all moved to it so that each was standing beside the window or door he was supposed to use. Since they didn't want to give anyone a chance, they were all going to try to move at the same second. The first shot, however, would signal the assault if the time hadn't come yet.

As they all touched the house, there came a bloodcurdling shriek from inside, and that told Fetterman which room he wanted to hit.

Inside the house one of the men approached the Chinese man and whispered something to him. He gave the rheostat a sadistic twist that sent Morrow into a spasm of pain, then shut it off rapidly. He stepped across the room to where one of the guards stood at the door and said, "You say that the outside men have not reported in? Any of them?"

"None."

He assumed immediately that something had happened to the radio and started to the radio room to check it out. He didn't hear the Special Forces men step onto the porch or position themselves around the house.

It had taken them nearly three hours to get to that point from the time of the phone call. A lot had happened and more was about to. Fetterman studied the second hand of his watch as it crept around until it struck the zero minute. Without hesitation he turned and leaped through the window, shattering the glass and splintering the wood of the frame as he rolled into the house. He landed on his shoulder and came up with a pistol in each hand. He saw a flash of movement to his right and turned to meet it. He fired once, and the bullet took the man in the head, exploding out the back in a fountain of crimson. He died before he even knew that the house had been invaded.

Bromhead came through the other window and nearly landed on top of one of the Oriental guards. Both tumbled to the floor, but Bromhead had his pistols out. He pulled the triggers of the two he held. One bullet missed completely, burying itself in the floor, but the other went through his adversary's side, working its way into his leg and severing the femoral artery. He had a few seconds to realize that he had been killed before his blood jetted out of his body, staining the hardwood floor and the carpeting, pooling under him.

As the windows shattered, Gerber kicked out, striking the crotch of one of the men standing near him. The man went down with a high-pitched shriek. Gerber grabbed the man's hand, wrenching the gun from it. He turned it on the other guard and shot him four times in the chest. The slugs printed such a tight pattern it could have been covered by a quarter, and each would have been fatal. He spun then and kicked the screaming man in the head, trying to punt it into the lake outside the house.

With all the guards in the room either dead or out of commission and stripped of their weapons, Fetterman shouted, "Where is the son of a bitch?"

"Through there," gestured Gerber. "Just seconds in front of you."

Fetterman waved at Bromhead, and together they ran for the door. Bromhead wanted to stop to see how Morrow was, but Gerber was there, and he would have to take care of her. Bromhead needed to support Fetterman.

As the two of them ran from the room, Gerber went to Morrow, crouching in front of her. He untied the blindfold but held it in front of her eyes to protect them from the sudden light. He whispered to her, "I'm going to remove the blindfold."

When she nodded, he let the cloth drop away, and for the first time in a long time, he could see her whole face. He didn't like what he saw. There were pain lines etched among the bruises and dried blood. He looked deep into her emerald eyes and saw something dancing back there but wasn't sure if it was an accusation or relief.

From somewhere in the house, he could hear shooting. Single shots from pistols and maybe some from a rifle or two, but none from AKs. There were flurries of firing and then silence, followed by more as his men began to clear the house room by room.

Gerber was kneeling in front of Morrow, unsure of what to do next. He reached around her, felt the ropes that bound her wrists but couldn't get at the knots. They were pulled too tight. He glanced over her shoulder and saw that her hands were discolored, an ugly purple from where the rope bit into her flesh. He didn't want to move from in front of her but had to if he was going to free her from the ropes. A knife lay next to the dead man by the door. Gerber picked it up and slit the ropes. Morrow didn't react. Her arms swung forward and hung at her sides, devoid of muscular control.

Using the knife, Gerber cut away the rest of the ropes. Although free at last, Morrow didn't move. Gently Gerber reached out and lifted her. She staggered to her feet, trying to maintain her balance, like a child about to take its first steps. Then with some effort she lifted her arms, slipping them around his neck as if she were afraid that he would get away. Or maybe afraid that if she let go, she would discover that she was still being held captive and the rescue was just a dream.

Gerber's soldier instincts were to help his men, but he figured they could take care of the rest. He was needed right where he was. He carefully disengaged himself from Morrow so that he could look for some type of apparel for her. He almost didn't do it when he saw the look on her face, as if she thought he were deserting her.

In a hall closet he found a short silk robe. He took it from the hanger and draped it around Morrow's shoulders. She stood stiffly, as if afraid to move now that the blood was beginning to circulate freely in her hands and feet. She clenched her teeth as the pain, much more severe than the normal tingling from a limb that had gone to sleep, hit her. She moaned softly, and tears trickled down her cheeks as she struggled to keep from crying out.

Gerber took her in his arms and held her against his chest. She lapsed into a paroxysm of uncontrollable shivering, which seemed to match the chatter of automatic weapons fire echoing through the house.

19

THE VICTORIAN HOUSE,
THE NEW TERRITORIES,
HONG KONG

As soon as he saw that the captain was all right, Fetterman ran for the open door opposite where he was standing. He stopped for a moment next to the doorjamb, his back against the wall, listening for sounds beyond the opening. He glanced at Bromhead, who was on the other side of the entranceway, facing him. When he nodded, they burst through, but the hallway was empty except for the body of an Oriental. In the room across the hall, there were two more bodies but no sign of the other Americans who had broken through the windows there.

From upstairs Fetterman heard the sound of running feet, and he pointed upward. He leaped the first few steps, then started moving slowly toward the landing, keeping to the side, almost leaning on the dark, wooden rail so that there was less chance of the risers squeaking.

Bromhead followed a few feet behind him and on the opposite side of the staircase, keeping his back to the wall. He still held two pistols, one pointed upstairs and one down.

As they gained the landing, Fetterman halted because he was in a bad position. Bromhead could work his way across it, keeping his back against the wall and get a view of part of the second floor without having to expose himself too much.

When Bromhead was across and had a foot on the next step, he waved to Fetterman, who nearly leaped forward. Just as he did, Bromhead heard something above him, stepped up and saw the foot and shin of someone. He held up a hand to tell Fetterman to stop and then took careful aim. He pulled the trigger and was rewarded by a scream as a man fell to his side, grabbing at his shattered shin. As soon as he fell into view, Bromhead fired twice more. The bullets hit the man in the chest, rolling him to his back as he died.

Together they rushed up the stairs, figuring that anyone who had been in the upstairs hallway or watching would have ducked back into the rooms there. They would have a couple of seconds when no one would be watching.

Just as they thought, the hallway was empty, the hardwood floor bare. Now, below them, they heard a few shots and realized that one of the other team members had found something. Both men resisted the temptation to run back to see what was happening.

Instead, Fetterman turned to his right and kicked at the door there, hitting it near the knob. The wood splintered but did not give way. Rather than kick it again, Fetterman dived to the left as someone inside opened fire, putting four rounds through it.

Bromhead turned his back to that situation, watching the hallway. Someone poked a head out, and Bromhead snapped off a shot, smashing the doorframe near the face.

At that moment Fetterman kicked the door again, and as it swung open, he dived through it, landing on his stomach. He saw a shadow slide by him, rolled as someone fired, the bullets chewing up the floor where Fetterman had been.

Fetterman fired five times without aiming, tracking his weapon when he saw the shadow move. Two of the bullets struck the enemy in the shoulder, one in the chest and one in the stomach. The last one ripped through the man's pants, burning his leg but not doing any real damage. Not that it mattered. The man was dead as he hit the floor, his blood staining his clothes and the carpet.

Bromhead leaped through the door. "You all right?"

"No problem. This isn't the right guy, either."

"I think there's only one more guy up here. I took a shot at him but missed."

Fetterman got to his feet, checked the loads in his weapon and then picked up the pistol dropped by the enemy. He stuffed it into his back pocket. Then he moved to the door and peeked through it.

Quickly they went down the hall, peering into open doorways. There were places to hide but nothing obvious, and there was no good cover. Nothing that would really stop a bullet. But they had to hurry because they had yet to find the Chinese officer, and Fetterman was sure that the guy would have an escape hatch.

They took positions on either side of the only closed door left and waited for an instant. Fetterman nodded that he was ready. Bromhead's foot lashed out, impacting on the wood near the lock. The door crashed inward, slamming against the wall. Bromhead only had time to leap clear before someone opened fire with an AK-47 on full auto.

But the man was apparently watching Bromhead so intently that he never saw Fetterman, who jerked off a quick round. The bullet hit the enemy's weapon, cracking some of the wood, forcing the barrel away from Bromhead. The man pulled the trigger, stitching the floor with a short burst.

Fetterman fired again, and the man's head seemed to disintegrate into a cloud of crimson. He flopped backward, one shoulder landing against an antique table, knocking it over. A lamp crashed to the floor, shards of glass spraying across it.

From downstairs they heard a single shot, and Fetterman knew instinctively that it was the Chinese guy. He looked at Bromhead as if to confirm his belief and then ran from the room, racing downstairs.

IN THE LIBRARY, Gerber knelt near Morrow, who was now sitting in one of the wing chairs. Her eyes were closed, and her hands rested in her lap, the angry red welts from the ropes evident around them. Her breathing was slow and regular, almost as if she were asleep.

Gerber had kept his eye on the man he had kicked, and as he rolled over, trying to reach a weapon, Gerber had kicked him again, this time in the chin. The man lost consciousness then, and Gerber bound his wrists with the rope that he had cut from Morrow's body.

At the sounds of gunfire, Gerber would look at the wall or the ceiling, as if he could see through to the battle. There were sounds of bodies hitting the floor, and Gerber ached to run from the room, but he felt he had an obligation to Morrow. He felt somehow responsible for the ordeal she had had to face during the past few hours and it was his duty to stay with her.

As one battle erupted upstairs, Morrow opened her eyes and caught Gerber looking. She knew that the horror and trauma of the past few hours was so close that she was in a state of shock. But she knew that Gerber wanted to help his men.

She reached out, touched his shoulder and said simply, "Go on, Kirk. Do what you have to."

Gerber started at the sound of her voice and then reached up to pat her hand. "You're sure? You'll be okay?"

"Go. Please."

Gerber stepped to the door, stopped and looked out. He saw Fetterman running down the stairs followed by Bromhead. "Tony, what's the situation?"

"Think we've got the upstairs cleared. Going to check on the guys in the back now. Haven't found him yet."

"You got an extra pistol?"

Fetterman jerked the one in his rear pocket clear and handed it to Gerber, who immediately checked the clip. There were only five rounds in it, but he didn't think he would need more than that.

There was another shot, and the three of them ran toward the back of the house. There was a door leading into the kitchen, but they didn't hesitate at it. They all burst through, Gerber going one way, Bromhead the other and Fetterman straight ahead.

Tyme was sitting slumped on the floor, a pistol held in one hand. His fingers were stained with blood. He smiled up at them. "He missed me, almost. It was close, but it doesn't mean much."

"Where are the others?" asked Gerber.

"Downstairs. It's a whopping huge cellar down there."

Gerber frowned. Houses in Hong Kong didn't have cellars. Then he remembered the previous owner, probably some eccentric Englishman who needed to be reminded of home.

"Where are the stairs?"

Tyme nodded. "Through there. There's some kind of mud-room or pantry and a door to the left. Big window on the right. Stairs are in there."

There was a shout then, bubbling up through the floor, and they couldn't tell whether it was an American or Chinese. Then there were running steps on the wooden stairs as two shots were fired from below. Through the kitchen door they saw the cellar door fly open, and all three of them fired at once as a figure flashed by them and leaped headfirst toward the window.

Fetterman was the first to react because he had recognized the Chinese bastard. It was a brief glimpse, but he saw enough to know.

He crossed the floor in two giant jumps and reached the window. Outside, he could see the man fleeing across the grass, down the slope toward the reservoir. Fetterman dropped one of his pistols and used his other hand to steady his aim. For a moment everything that he knew about shooting came to mind, but his brain was moving too slowly so he forced the thoughts out and let his instincts take over. Carefully, cautiously, he squeezed the trigger, letting the weapon fire itself when it was ready.

It seemed to take the bullet forever to reach its target. He thought he had missed because the man kept running, but he staggered once, began running again and fell forward. Fetterman climbed through the window, keeping his eyes on the spot where his target had fallen, knowing instinctively that he wasn't dead.

It was like something from a horror movie. Just as everyone thought the monster was dead, it came back again, stronger than ever. The Chinese guy didn't just get to his feet, he exploded to them, running hard for the reservoir, as if there were some kind of sanctuary there.

Fetterman dropped to the ground and aimed again. His shot missed.

But the man seemed to be running slower, as if the life, the energy, was seeping from him. He stumbled slightly, regained his balance and then began a second sprint.

Fetterman took off after him, trying to reduce the range between the two of them. The master sergeant was stronger and seemed to be gaining strength as he moved. Fetterman felt he would catch the man soon before he got much farther away.

Suddenly the fugitive swerved to the right and ran out on a small pier that Fetterman had never seen. It looked as if he were walking on water.

Fetterman skidded to a halt, believing that there was no way he could catch the man if there was a boat hidden there. He had never considered the landlocked reservoir as an escape route, but if the man had a boat, he could lose the Special Forces men before they could find a way around the lake. He could lose himself in the New Territories and make his way back to Red China before any of them could get to a car and drive around the lake.

He raised his pistol, aimed and pulled the trigger. There was no reaction by the enemy. Fetterman fired again and again and kept firing until the slide locked back and the trigger jammed tight. He dropped his hand to his side and watched as the Chinese guy suddenly jerked upright, took one step forward and toppled into the water.

"Got you, you fucking bastard," said Fetterman. "Finally got you."

As he stood watching the shoreline, waiting for the man to reappear, he was joined by Bromhead and Gerber, neither sure what to say or if they should say anything at all.

"I'll check it out," said Fetterman. "I saw him go into the lake."

Bromhead started to speak, but Gerber stopped him. He said, "We'll go back up to the house and get ready to move out. Meet you there in twenty minutes or so."

They split up. Gerber and Bromhead found Smith and Anderson helping Tyme to his feet. He was laughing at them, trying to convince them that his wound was not very serious.

"Hell," he said, "I've hurt myself worse sliding into third base. This is nothing."

"You see anything or anyone else downstairs?" asked Gerber.

"No, sir. It's a maze down there—that's how he got behind us."

"Don't worry about it," said Gerber. "Let's just get everyone together and get the hell out. We don't need to find anyone else."

They hurried back through the house. Only Gerber entered the room where Morrow sat. She hadn't moved during the final action. Gerber had no idea how long it had taken. He moved to her and took her hand, squeezing it gently to let her know that he was there.

"We're getting out, Robin," he said.

She turned her head, staring at him, and said one word, "Good."

They all moved outside. Bromhead whistled once and then shouted, "Galvin! Let's get the fuck out of here."

Tyme pointed to the cars and said, "Anyone know how to hot wire those things?"

"Won't have to," said Smith. "There are keys in them."

Gerber said, "You guys go on without me. I'll wait for Fetterman. We'll all meet back at the hotel and then scatter. Back to the World or whatever. Oh, and tell Larko he can let Muffin go. She can't hurt us now. Thank him for his help."

They began to pile into the cars, all but Morrow. She stood her ground and said, "I'll wait with you."

"Robin, you really should get to a doctor. You've had a very rough time."

"I'll wait with you," she repeated dully.

Gerber looked to the others for help, but they offered none. Then Bromhead reached out and took her elbow. "Robin, let us take you to a doctor."

"No," she said quietly. "I'll wait here with Mack. I'm all right now. I want to stay."

Gerber finally said, "Okay. We'll catch up as soon as Fetterman gets here."

They both watched the others climb into two cars and take off. They didn't stop to open the gate but just smashed through it. None of them looked back.

Gerber opened a door of the car that was left there and helped Morrow in. He said, "You sure that you're all right? The last few days have been rough."

She tried to smile. "I ache all over and I think I have a broken rib. I've a couple of cuts on my face, but they'll only leave tiny scars. Those bastards didn't really do any permanent damage." She almost giggled. "They would have, but you showed up in time."

"Robin, I'm really sorry about all this. I—"

"Don't be sorry. It's not your fault. I'm the one who followed you. I'm the one who left you at the police station while I flitted back to the room, and I'm the one who opened the damned door when that bastard knocked on it. It's really my fault."

"Okay, you win. Listen, when we get back to the hotel, you want to make some arrangements?"

"Arrangements to do what?" she asked.

"Arrangements for us to go somewhere to rest and relax. Somewhere on the other side of the world. Maybe Hawaii or Bermuda or something." He held up a hand to ward off the protest that he expected and said all too fast, "I don't mean anything by that. I just thought that we might travel together as friends."

"Jesus," she said, "are all men as stupid as you? Yes, I'll take a trip with you. And I'm not worried about my virtue, especially now."

Before Gerber could respond, Fetterman reappeared. "I hit the guy," he said. "Twice. I know that. I saw him go into the water. I couldn't find the body."

Gerber looked at Morrow and smiled at her for some reason that he didn't fully understand. To Fetterman, he said, "Don't worry about it. It's over now. We can all go back to the hotel, then get out of Hong Kong. We more than made up for Ian's death."

"I couldn't find the body. Found blood on the dock," he said. "Found quite a lot of it, but I couldn't find the body."

Fetterman slid in beside Morrow, and Gerber walked around the front so that he could open the driver's door. "Don't worry about it," repeated Gerber as he started the engine. "You got him. I'm sure you did. He's not supernatural, he was just very good."

"I don't like it, Captain," said Fetterman. "I'm not going to be happy until I can touch his body and make sure there is no pulse."

"As I said, he is not supernatural. He eluded us in Vietnam only because he could use the border as a barrier to protect himself. He just let us catch him off guard here, away from the border. Hell, Tony, he was very good. You were better. That's all there is to it."

"Are you sure?" asked Fetterman, wanting to believe it.

"Of course. Now let's get out of here."

GLOSSARY

AC—Aircraft Commander; pilot in charge of the aircraft.

ACTUAL—Actual unit commander as opposed to the radio telephone operator (RTO) for that unit.

AFVN—Armed Forces radio and television network in Vietnam. Army PFC Pat Sajak was probably the most memorable of AFVN's DJs with his loud and long, "GOOOOOOOOOOOOOD MORNing! Vietnam." The Spinning Wheel of Fortune gives no clues about his whereabouts today.

AK-47—Soviet assault rifle normally used by the North Vietnamese and Vietcong.

AO—Area of Operations.

AO DAI—Long dresslike garment, split up the sides and worn over pants.

AP ROUNDS—Armor-piercing ammunition.

ARVN—Army of the Republic of Vietnam; a South Vietnamese soldier. Also known as Marvin Arvin.

ASH AND TRASH—Single ship flights by helicopters taking care of a variety of missions such as flying cargo, supplies, mail and people among the various small camps in Vietnam, for anyone who needed aviation support.

BAR—Browning Automatic Rifle.

BEAUCOUP—Many.

BISCUIT—C-rations; combat rations.

BLOWER—See *Horn*.

BODY COUNT—Number of enemy killed, wounded or captured during an operation. Used by Saigon and Washington as a means of measuring the progress of the war.

BOOM-BOOM—Term used by Vietnamese prostitutes to sell their product.

BOONDOGGLE—Any military operation that hasn't been completely thought out. An operation that is ridiculous.

BOONIE HATS—Soft cap worn by the grunts in the field when they were not wearing steel pots.

BUSHMASTER—Jungle warfare expert or soldier skilled in jungle navigation. Also a large deadly snake not common to Vietnam but mighty tasty.

C-123—Small cargo airplane; Caribou.

C-130—Medium cargo airplane; Hercules.

C AND C—Command and Control aircraft that circles overhead to direct the combined air and ground operations.

CARIBOU—Cargo transport plane; C-123.

CHINOOK—Army Aviation twin engine helicopter; CH-47; shit hook.

CHIEU HOI LEAFLETS—Propaganda leaflets telling the enemy that they would be well treated if they surrendered.

CHURCH KEY—Beer can opener used in the days before pop tops.

CLAYMORE—Antipersonnel mine that fires 750 steel balls with a lethal range of 50 meters.

CLOSE AIR SUPPORT—Use of airplanes and helicopters to fire on enemy units near friendlies.

CO CONG—Term referring to female Vietcong.

DAI UY—Vietnamese Army rank equivalent to Captain.

DCI—Director, Central Intelligence. The director of the Central Intelligence Agency.

DEROS—Date Estimated Return from Overseas.

DONG—A unit of North Vietnamese money about equal to an American penny.

FIIGMO—Fuck It, I've Got My Orders.

FIVE—Radio call sign for the Executive Officer of a unit.

FNG—Fucking New Guy.

FOOGAS—Jellied gas similar to napalm.

FREEDOM BIRD—Name given to any aircraft that took troops out of Vietnam. Usually referred to the commercial jet flights that took men back to the World.

FRENCH FORT—Distinctive, triangular-shaped structure built by the hundreds by the French.

FUBAR—Fucked Up Beyond All Recognition.

GARAND—M-1 rifle, which was replaced by the M-14. Issued to the Vietnamese early in the war.

GO-TO-HELL RAG—Towel or any large cloth worn around the neck by grunts.

GRUNT—Infantryman.

GUARD THE RADIO—Term meaning to stand by in the commo bunker listening for messages.

GUNSHIP—Armed helicopter or cargo plane that carries weapons instead of cargo.

HE—High-explosive ammunition.

HIT THE HEAD—Go to the bathroom. A navy term.

HOOTCH—Almost any shelter, from temporary to long-term.

HORN—Specific kind of radio operations that use satellites to rebroadcast messages.

HORSE—See *Biscuit*.

HOTEL THREE—Helicopter landing area at Saigon's Tan Son Nhut Air Force Base.

HUEY—Bell helicopter. Called a Huey because its original designation was HU, but later changed to UH. Called a Slick.

IN-COUNTRY—Term referring to American troops operating in South Vietnam. They were all in-country.

INTELLIGENCE—Any information about the enemy operations. It can include troop movements, weapons capabilities, biographies of enemy commanders and general information about terrain features. It is any information that would be useful in planning a mission.

KA BAR—Type of military combat knife.

KIA—Killed In Action. (Since the U.S. was not engaged in a declared war, the use of KIA was not authorized. KIA came to mean enemy dead. Americans were KHA or Killed in Hostile Action.)

KLICK—One thousand meters; a kilometer.

LBJ—Long Binh Jail.

LEGS—Derogatory term for regular infantry used by airborne qualified troops.

LIMA LIMA—Land line. Telephone communications between two points on the ground.

LLDB—Luc Luong Dac Biet; South Vietnamese Special Forces. Sometimes referred to as the Look Long, Duck Back.

LP—Listening Post. Position outside the perimeter manned by a couple of soldiers to warn of enemy activity.

LZ—Landing Zone.

M-14—Standard rifle of the U.S. Army, eventually replaced by the M-16. It fires the standard NATO 7.62 mm round.

M-16—Became the standard infantry weapon of the Vietnam War. It fires 5.56 mm ammunition.

M-79—Short-barreled, shoulder-fired weapon that fires a 40 mm grenade. These can be high explosive, white phosphorus or canister.

MACV—Military Assistance Command, Vietnam. Replaced MAAG in 1964.

MEDEVAC—Medical Evacuation; Dustoff. Helicopter used to take wounded to medical facilities.

MIA—Missing In Action.

NCO—Noncommissioned Officer; noncom; sergeant.

NEXT—The man who says he's the next to be rotated home. See *Short-Timer*.

NINETEEN—Average age of the combat soldier in Vietnam, in contrast to age twenty-six in the Second World War.

NOUC-MAM—Foul-smelling (to the Americans, at least) fermented fish sauce used by the Vietnamese as a condiment. GIs nicknamed it "armpit sauce."

NVA—North Vietnamese Army. Also used to designate a soldier from North Vietnam.

OD—Olive drab; standard military color.

OPERATION BOOTSTRAP—Program in the Army to help men on active duty complete their college education. Men in the program were still considered to be on active duty.

P-38—Military designation for the small, one-piece can opener supplied with C-rations.

PCOD—Personnel Coming Off Duty.

PETER PILOT—Co-pilot of a helicopter.

POW—Prisoner Of War.

PRC-10—Portable radio.

PRC-25—Standard infantry radio used in Vietnam. Sometimes called "Prick 25."

PROGUES—Derogatory term describing fat, lazy people who inhabited rear areas, taking all the best supplies for themselves and leaving the rest for the men in the field.

PSP—Perforated Steel Plate. Used instead of pavement for runways and roadways.

PULL PITCH—Term used by helicopter pilots that means they are going to take off.

PUNGI STAKE—Sharpened bamboo hidden to penetrate the foot, sometimes dipped in feces.

QT—Quick Time. It came to mean talking to someone quietly on the side rather than operating in official channels.

R AND R—Rest and Relaxation. The term came to mean a trip outside of Vietnam where the soldier could forget about the war.

RF STRIKERS—Local military forces recruited and employed inside a province. Known as Regional Forces.

RINGKNOCKER—A graduate of military academy. The term refers to the ring worn by all graduates.

RON—Remain Overnight.

RP—Rally Point.

RPD—7.62 mm Soviet light machine gun.

RTO—Radiotelephone Operator; radio man of a unit.

RULES OF ENGAGEMENT—Rules telling American troops when they could fire and when they couldn't. Full Supression meant that they could fire all the way in on a landing. Normal Rules meant that they could return fire for fire received. Negative Suppression meant that they weren't to shoot back.

SAPPER—Enemy soldier used in demolitions. Uses explosives during attacks.

SIX—Radio call sign for the unit commander.

SHIT HOOK—Name applied by troops to the Chinook helicopter because of all the "shit" stirred up by the massive rotors.

SHORT—Term used by a GI in Vietnam to tell all who would listen that his tour was almost over.

SHORT-TIMER—GI who had been in Vietnam for nearly a year and who would be rotated back to the World soon. When the DEROS (Date of Estimated Return from Overseas) was the shortest in the unit, the person was said to be "Next."

SKS—Simonov 7.62 mm semiautomatic carbine.

SFOB—Special Forces Operations Base.

SMG—Submachine gun.

SOI—Signal Operating Instructions. The booklet that contained the call signs and radio frequencies of the units in Vietnam.

SOP—Standard Operating Procedure.

STEEL POT—Standard U.S. Army helmet. The steel pot was the outer metal cover.

TAI—Vietnamese ethnic group living in the mountainous regions.

TDY—Temporary Duty.

THREE—Radio call sign of the Operations Officer.

THREE CORPS—Military area around Saigon. Vietnam was divided into four corps areas.

THE WORLD—The United States.

TOC—Tactical Operations Center.

TWO—Radio call sign for the Intelligence Officer.

VC—Vietcong. Also called Victor Charlie (phonetic alphabet) or Charlie.

VIETCONG—Contraction of Vietnam Cong San. A guerrilla member of the Vietnamese Communist movement.

VIETCONG SAN—Vietnamese communists. A term used since 1956.

VNAF—South Vietnamese Air Force.

WIA—Wounded In Action.

WILLIE PETE—WP; white phosphorus; smoke rounds. Also used as antipersonnel weapons.

XO—Executive Officer of a unit.

ZAP—To ding, pop caps or shoot. To kill.